CHERUB

MAXIMUM SECURITY

ALSO BY ROBERT MUCHAMORE

THE RECRUIT

THE DEALER

CHERUB

MISSION 3
MAXIMUM SECURITY

ROBERT MUCHAMORE

Simon Pulse
New York London Toronto Sydney New Delhi

This book is a work of fiction. Any references to historical events, real people, or real locales are used fictitiously. Other names, characters, places, and incidents are the product of the author's imagination, and any resemblance to actual events or locales or persons, living or dead, is entirely coincidental.

SIMON PULSE
An imprint of Simon & Schuster Children's Publishing Division
1230 Avenue of the Americas, New York, NY 10020
This Simon Pulse paperback edition April 2012

Originally published in Great Britain in 2005 by Hodder Children's Books
Published by arrangement with Hodder and Stoughton Limited

Also available in a Simon Pulse hardcover edition.
For information about special discounts for bulk purchases, please contact
Simon & Schuster Special Sales at 1-866-506-1949
or business@simonandschuster.com.
The Simon & Schuster Speakers Bureau can bring authors to your live event.
For more information or to book an event contact the Simon & Schuster
Speakers Bureau at 1-866-248-3049 or visit our website at www.simonspeakers.com.
Designed by Karina Granda
The text of this book was set in Apollo MT.
Manufactured in the United States of America
2 4 6 8 10 9 7 5 3
Library of Congress Control Number 2005928844
ISBN 978-1-4169-9942-3 (hc)
ISBN 978-1-4424-1362-7 (pbk)

WHAT IS CHERUB?

CHERUB is a branch of British Intelligence. Its agents are aged between ten and seventeen years. Cherubs are all orphans who have been taken out of care homes and trained to work undercover. They live on CHERUB campus, a secret facility hidden in the English countryside.

WHAT USE ARE KIDS?

Quite a lot. Nobody realizes kids do undercover missions, which means they can get away with all kinds of stuff that adults can't.

WHO ARE THEY?

About three hundred children live on CHERUB campus. JAMES ADAMS is our thirteen-year-old hero. He's a well-respected CHERUB agent, with two successful missions under his belt; although he does have an unfortunate habit of getting himself in trouble.

James's younger sister, LAUREN ADAMS, is now nearing the end of her CHERUB basic training. If she passes the course, she'll be qualified to work undercover. KERRY CHANG is a Hong Kong–born karate champion and James's girlfreind.

Amongst James's closest friends on campus are BRUCE NORRIS, GABRIELLE O'BRIEN, and the twins CALLUM and CONNOR REILLY. His best friend is KYLE BLUEMAN, who is fifteen.

AND THE T-SHIRTS?

Cherubs are ranked according to the color of the T-shirts they wear on campus. ORANGE is for visitors. RED is for kids who live at CHERUB campus, but are too young to qualify as agents. BLUE is for kids undergoing CHERUB's tough 100-day training regime. A GRAY T-shirt means you're qualified for missions. NAVY—the T-shirt James wears—is a reward for outstanding performance on a mission. If you do well, you'll end your CHERUB career wearing a BLACK T-shirt, the ultimate recognition for outstanding achievement. When you retire, you get the WHITE T-shirt, which is also worn by staff.

CHAPTER 1

COLD

Before you entered basic training, you probably heard stories from qualified CHERUB agents about the nature of this one-hundred-day course. Although every basic training course is designed to teach the same core abilities of physical fitness and extreme mental endurance, you can expect your training to differ from that of your predecessors in order to retain the element of surprise.

(*Excerpt from the* CHERUB Basic Training Manual)

It looked the same in every direction. The sunlight blazing off the field of snow made it impossible for the two ten-year-old girls to see more than twenty meters into the distance, despite the heavily tinted snow goggles over their eyes.

"How far to the checkpoint?" Lauren Adams shouted, breaking her stride to stare at the global positioning unit strapped around her best friend's wrist.

"Only two and a half kilometers," Bethany Parker shouted back. "If the ground stays flat, we should be at the shelter in forty minutes."

The girls had to shout for their voices to override the howling wind and the three layers of clothing protecting their ears.

"That's cutting it close to sundown," Lauren yelled. "We'd better get a move on."

They'd set off at dawn, dragging lightweight sleds that could be hooked over their shoulders and carried as backpacks on difficult terrain. The good news was, the two CHERUB trainees had the whole day to trek fifteen kilometers across the Alaskan snowfield to their next checkpoint. The bad news was that at this time in April, the daylight lasted just four hours and wading through half a meter of powdery snow put enormous strain on their thighs and ankles. Every step was painful.

Lauren heard a howling noise rising up in the distance. "It's gonna to be another big one," she shouted.

The girls crouched down, pulled their sleds in close and wrapped their arms tightly around each other's waists. Just as you can hear waves approaching a beach, out here in the Alaskan snowfields you could hear a strong gust stirring up in the distance.

They were both dressed for extreme cold. Lauren's normal underwear was covered with a long-sleeved thermal vest and long johns. The next layer was a zip-up suit made from polar fleece that covered her whole body, except for a slit around the eyes. The second fleece was designed to trap body heat. It looked like a baggy Easter bunny suit, minus the pom-pom tail and sticking up ears. Then came more gloves, another balaclava, snow goggles, and waterproof outer gloves that went all the way up to Lauren's elbows, ending in a tightly fitting elastic cuff. Finally, on the outside was a thickly padded snowsuit and snow boots with spiked bottoms.

The clothing was enough to keep them comfortable as they walked, despite the temperature being minus eighteen centigrade, but this dropped another fifteen degrees whenever a strong gust hit. The wind pushed the insulating layers of warm air between the girls' clothes into all the places where it wasn't needed, leaving nothing but a couple of centimeters of synthetic fiber between their skin and the ferociously cold air. Each blast ripped into their bodies, delivering searing pain to any exposed area.

Lauren and Bethany used their sleds as windbreaks when the gust hit. A spike of cold air punched through the tightly fitting rim of Lauren's goggles. She pushed her face against Bethany's suit and squeezed her eyes shut, as snow and ice pounded deafeningly against her hood.

When the gust passed and the snow had settled, Lauren brushed the dusting of powder off her suit and stumbled back to her feet.

"Everything OK?" Bethany shouted.

Lauren stuck up her thumbs. "Ninety-nine days down, one to go," she shouted.

Lauren and Bethany's home for the night was a metal container painted in a high visibility shade of orange. It was the kind of container you'd normally expect to pass on the motorway, mounted on the back of an articulated truck. There was a radio mast and a shattered flagpole lashed to the roof.

The girls had beaten the darkness. The sun's distant face was already touching the horizon and the light it sent through the mist of falling snow gave the whole landscape a powdery yellow hue. The girls were too exhausted to appreciate its beauty; all they cared about was getting warm.

It took a few minutes to dig out the snow from around the two metal doors that formed one end of the container. Once they were open, Lauren dragged the two sleds inside, while Bethany searched along a wooden shelf until she found a gas lamp. Lauren closed the metal doors, creating a boom that would have been deafening if the girls' ears hadn't been shielded by their outdoor clothes.

"We've got even less fuel tonight," Lauren shouted, as the lamp erupted in an unsteady blue glow. She looked at the single bottle of gas as she peeled off her goggles and outermost set of gloves. Her hands were freezing, but it was impossible to manipulate anything with three sets of gloves on.

On the first night of their week in the Alaskan wilderness, the girls had found two large bottles of gas in their shelter. They'd heated the room until it was toasty, cooked lavishly, and warmed up water to wash with. The fun ended abruptly when the gas ran out in the middle of the night and the indoor temperature rapidly dropped back below freezing. After this harsh lesson, the girls took pains to ration their energy supply.

Bethany fixed a hose from the gas bottle to a small heater and lit just one of its three chambers. This would slowly bring the temperature inside their container above freezing. Until it did, the girls would keep as many of their outdoor clothes on as the task at hand allowed.

They spent the next few minutes rummaging through the supplies that had been left for them. There were plenty of high-energy foods, such as tinned meats, flapjacks, instant noodles, chocolate bars, and glucose powder. They also found their mission briefings, clean underwear, fresh boot liners, and floor mats. Combined with the pots, utensils, and sleeping bags packed in their sleds, it would be enough to make the nineteen hours until the sun returned reasonably comfortable.

Once the girls had ensured that they had all the basics, Lauren couldn't help wondering what was under the tarpaulin at the back of the container.

"That's got to be something to do with our mission for tomorrow," Bethany said.

They stepped across and dragged the tarp off a giant cardboard box. It was over two meters long and almost up to Lauren's shoulders. Scraping at the layer of frost over the cardboard revealed a Yamaha logo and an outline drawing of a snowmobile.

"Cool," Bethany said. "I don't think my legs could handle another day trudging through that snow."

"Have you ever driven one?" Lauren asked.

"Nah," Bethany said, shaking her head excitedly. "But it can't be much different from the quad bikes we drove last summer at the hostel. . . . Let's open our briefings and work out what we've got to do tomorrow."

"We'd better take our temperatures and radio base camp first," Lauren said.

There was a radio set already linked up to the aerial on the roof. Its battery was cold and it took several seconds for the orange frequency display on the front panel to light up. While they waited, the girls took turns measuring their body temperatures with a small plastic strip that you tucked under your armpit.

The indicator lit up between the thirty-five and thirty-six degree marks on both of them. It meant the girls were running slightly below normal body temperature, which is exactly what you'd expect for two people who'd just spent several hours in extreme cold. Another hour would have been enough for them to develop early symptoms of hypothermia.

Lauren grabbed the microphone and keyed up. "This is unit three calling Instructor Large. Over."

"Instructor Large receiving . . . Greetings, my little sugar plums."

It was reassuring hearing a human voice other than Bethany's for the first time in twenty-four hours, even if it was that of Mr. Large, CHERUB's head training instructor. Large was a nasty piece of work. Pushing kids through tough training courses wasn't just part of his job; he actually enjoyed making them suffer.

"Just reporting in to say that everything is fine with me and unit four," Lauren said. "Over."

"Why aren't you using the coded frequency? Over," Mr. Large asked angrily.

Lauren realized her instructor was right and hurriedly flipped the scramble switch on the front of the receiver.

"Oh . . . Sorry. Over."

"You will be tomorrow morning when I get my hands on you," Large snapped. "Minus ten house points for Hufflepuff. Over and out."

"Over and out," Lauren said bitterly. She put down the microphone and kicked out at the side of the metal container. "God, I *really* hate that man's guts."

Bethany laughed a little. "Not as much as he hates you for knocking him head first into that muddy hole with a spade."

"True," Lauren said, allowing herself a grin as she recalled the event that had brought her first attempt at basic training to an abrupt end. "I suppose we'd better get cracking. You start translating the briefing. I'll go outside and bring in some snow to melt for drinking water."

Lauren found a bucket and grabbed the torch out of her sled. She pushed the metal door of the container and squeezed herself and the bucket through a small gap, so as not to let out too much heat.

The sun was gone and only the tiny shaft of light from inside the container enabled Lauren to notice the giant white outline in the snow. Half convinced that she was overtired and imagining things, Lauren flicked on her torch.

What Lauren saw left her in no doubt. She screamed as she scrambled back inside the container and swiftly pulled up the metal door.

"What's the matter?" Bethany asked, turning sharply from her mission briefing.

"Polar bear!" Lauren gasped. "Lying in the snow right outside the door. Luckily it seemed to be resting; another few steps and I would have trodden on it."

"It *can't* be," Bethany said.

Lauren waved the torch in her training partner's face. "Here, take this. Stick your head out and look for yourself."

It only took the briefest of glances to confirm it. The mat of white fur, with plumes of hot breath steaming out of its nostrils, lay less than five meters from the entrance to the container.

Once Lauren recovered from her near-death experience, the girls thought things through and decided that the situation wasn't too serious.

They could get all the drinking water they needed by leaning out of the metal doors and scooping up the snow around the entrance. Once they'd got enough snow, they decided to leave the giant bear in peace. It seemed unlikely the animal would leave itself exposed to the cold all night. Surely it would move away to find shelter before the sun came back up.

The inside of the container had now warmed up enough for the girls not to be able to see their breath curling in front of their faces. After their day in the cold, it seemed toasty. They stepped out of their boots and outer suits, hanging them on a line in the warm air above the gas heater, so that the moisture in them would evaporate overnight.

The metal floor of the container was cold to touch, so they put on trainers and laid out insulating foam mats retrieved from their sleds. They turned the heater up and lined icy tins of corned beef and fruit in front of it, as Bethany melted a saucepan of snow over a portable stove.

It took an hour to read the briefings for the final twenty-four hours of their course, under the flickering light of two gas lamps. The briefings only ran to five pages, but were written in languages with non-European alphabets that the girls had only started learning at the beginning of the course: Russian for Bethany and Greek for Lauren.

The gist of the briefings was simple. The girls had to unpack the snowmobile from its shipping crate and prepare it for first use: a task that involved screwing various bits together, lubricating the drive track and engine, and filling the tank with petrol. From sunup, they'd have two hours to make a thirty-five-kilometer journey by snowmobile to a checkpoint where they would liaise with the four other trainees for something the briefing ominously described as the "*Ultimate test of physical courage in an extreme weather environment*."

"Well," Lauren said, as she dug her spoon into a can of corned beef that was warm and greasy on the outside but rock hard in the centre, "at least the instructions for the snowmobile are in English."

CHAPTER 2

BOWLING

James Adams had been looking forward to spending Saturday night in town at the bowling alley, but now he was here he'd got himself in a mood. The four other CHERUB agents on the lane seemed to be having far more fun than he was.

Kyle was in great form, lording it over everyone, buying them hotdogs and Cokes with the small fortune he'd made burning pirate DVDs for half the kids on campus. Kyle always had some dodgy money-making scheme going on, but as far as James could work out this was the first one that had ever earned decent money.

The identical twins, Callum and Connor, were also enjoying themselves, despite their stupid bet with each other that one of them could get off with Gabrielle before the night was out. James had told the twins they were dreaming: They might be nice guys, but Gabrielle was thirteen and totally fit. If Gabrielle wanted a boyfriend—which as far as anyone could tell she didn't—she could do better than pick between two gangly twelve-year-olds with disheveled blond hair and a gap the size of a Mars bar between their crooked front teeth.

"*Strike . . .* ," Gabrielle shouted, as ten pins rattled off in different directions. She flailed her arms and jiggled her bum about, doing a kind of freaky war dance. "You're up, Kyle," she whooped.

Gabrielle turned away from the scene of her triumph to see Callum and Connor grinning at her from their plastic chairs, either side of where she'd been sitting before she bowled.

"Great shot," Callum beamed.

"Didn't I say you'd bowl better if you swung your arm back a little less?" Connor interrupted, as he shot an evil glance at his identical twin. "Your balance is much better now."

Gabrielle remembered the advice, but she hadn't bowled any differently from normal. The strike had been down to luck. She looked at her plastic seat and realized she couldn't handle another second of the two boys fawning over her. She reached under her chair and grabbed her bag.

"Where are you going?" Callum asked apprehensively. "What's the matter?"

"James looks a bit down in the dumps," Gabrielle

explained. "I'm gonna sit with him for a minute and see if I can cheer him up."

"Good idea," Connor grinned. "I'll come with you."

"No," Gabrielle said stiffly. "You two are gonna stay *right* there."

"But . . . ," Connor said, half standing up before sitting down again.

"Look," Gabrielle said. "I don't mean to be rude, but you two are acting seriously weird and it's getting on my nerves. Can't you let me have five minutes' peace?"

Gabrielle felt bad as she reached over and pulled her jacket off the back of her chair. Both twins had the exact same expression: like toddlers whose mother had punished them by confiscating their favorite toy.

James was in a daze, staring down at the floor between his legs. Gabrielle tapped him on the knee. "What's up, misery guts?" she asked, as she took the seat next to him. "Still thinking about Miami?" The previous summer, James had got into a bad situation and ended up shooting a man to save his own life. He still had nightmares about it.

"I guess," James shrugged. "And I kind of miss Kerry. I haven't heard from her in over a week."

"Neither have I," Gabrielle said. "But the last message I got said she'd arrived in Japan and was going deep undercover, so it's hardly surprising."

James nodded. "I spoke to her mission controller on the phone. He says everything's fine and hopefully Kerry will be home in a month or so."

"What about Lauren?" Gabrielle asked. "How's she getting on with basic training?"

"You know how it is," James said, "you only ever hear rumors, but I think she's doing OK."

Gabrielle started to laugh. "Remember when we were in training? Me and Kerry locked all you guys out on that hotel balcony and made you grovel to get back in?"

James allowed himself to smile a little. "Yeah, we never got you back for that."

Something cold touched the back of James's neck. He looked around and realized he and Gabrielle had been splashed with Coke and ice by the gang of sixteen- and seventeen-year-old boys who were playing the next lane. They were acting rowdy, rucking and throwing stuff around.

"Oi," Gabrielle stormed, as she scowled over her shoulder at a mass of acne in a Tottenham Hotspur shirt. "Do you mind?"

"Sorry," the kid said, grinning mischievously at the ice in the bottom of his cardboard cup. Gabrielle got the impression he wasn't sorry at all.

"James," Kyle shouted. "Your frame."

James got out of his seat and grabbed a bowling ball off the rack. He'd picked up a coupon and taken a couple of free bowling lessons, so when James was on form he looked the business: delivering the ball in a powerful arc and racking up respectable scores. But not tonight. In fact, James's mood had nothing to do with missing Kerry, or worrying if Lauren would pass basic training. James was feeling down because he couldn't aim a bowling ball to save his life.

He lined up, holding the heavy ball under his chin. He took a good smooth swing. The ball crashed nicely into the front three pins, and for a second James thought he'd scored his first strike in ages. But pin seven, at the back on the far left, merely wobbled and number ten on the extreme right didn't even have the decency to do that. James couldn't believe his rotten luck.

"Seven-ten split," Kyle shouted, slapping his thighs deliriously. "You're going *down* again, Adams."

James glanced up at the scoreboard. When they bowled in a group, James usually fought Kyle for first place and won more than he lost. But he'd already lost two matches tonight and was thirty points behind Kyle in this one, with four frames left to play. James thought Kyle rubbing in the misery was harsh, conveniently forgetting he would have acted exactly the same if it had been Kyle having a bad night.

James grabbed his ball as soon as it clattered onto the rack and stopped spinning. He lined up to take his second shot, glowering at the two pins standing on opposite sides of the lane.

To make a seven-ten split, you need to hit one pin so hard that it bounces against the wall behind, then spins out and knocks down the pin on the opposite side. The shot requires a hefty chunk of luck and even a world championship standard bowler wouldn't expect to make it often.

"You'll never hit both in a million years," Kyle goaded.

James turned back and smirked at Kyle, struggling to fake an air of confidence. "Sit your butt down and watch the master at work."

James swung the ball as hard as he could, but when you bowl fast you lose control. The ball did a little bobble as James let go. It had plenty of pace, but James knew straight away that it wasn't right.

"Turn back," James gasped desperately, as the ball edged closer to the gutter. "Come on*nnnnnn baby* . . ."

The ball thunked into the gutter a couple of meters shy of the pin. James put his hands over his eyes and cursed under his breath. He almost couldn't bear turning away, knowing he'd catch sight of Kyle's smug face.

"Eight points and a gutter ball," Kyle said happily. "Maybe you should wander down to the bumper lanes and ask the supervisor if you can play with the little red-shirt kids."

James huffed as he slumped back into his seat next to Gabrielle. "The way I'm going tonight, I reckon the little kids would beat me."

"You're doing better than Callum and Connor, though," Gabrielle said sympathetically, pointing up at the TV screen with the scores on it.

"Some consolation that is. Those two are hopeless."

Gabrielle smiled and brushed the back of her hand against James's leg. "Just not your night, I guess."

As she said it, both their backs got sprayed with more Coke. They turned quickly to see two beefy-looking guys in football shirts wrestling in a puddle on the floor. James waited until they broke apart before having a go at them.

"What are you two retards playing at?" James barked furiously. "I'm bloody soaked."

"My top's all marked," Gabrielle said, looking anxiously down her back and wondering if the stains would come out.

The two lads were giggling as they got to their feet. "We're just having a laugh," the one in the Tottenham shirt said.

The other lad looked less sympathetic. "There's loads of empty seats over there," he grunted. "Why don't you just move?"

"Because this is *our* lane," Gabrielle said. "I don't want to walk five miles every time I take my shot."

"Yeah," James agreed. "Why should we move, just because you want to roll around the floor with your boyfriend?"

The kid jabbed James in the back. "Are you calling me a queer?"

James and Gabrielle stood up and turned around to face the two lads, who towered over them.

"I didn't come here for a row," James said.

"Nor did I," the tough guy said. "But you're going the right way about getting into one; so why don't you just take your little *wog* girlfriend off and sit somewhere else?"

The tough guy had twenty-five centimeters and fifteen kilos on Gabrielle, so he never expected what happened next. Gabrielle, who was a second-dan karate black belt, launched a high kick over the row of plastic seats. Her bowling shoe slammed into the thug's kidney and by the time he'd got his breath back, he was pinned to the ground with a bloody nose and an orange painted thumbnail digging into his cheek.

"Call me that again," Gabrielle screamed, as she bunched up her fist. "Go on . . . I dare you."

Her voice echoed across the bowling alley's metal roof

as a hundred sets of stunned eyes turned towards her. The whole place went quiet, except for the sound of a couple of squealing toddlers and the blipping of arcade machines.

James quickly straddled over the rows of seats and rested his palm on Gabrielle's shoulder. "Come on, Gabrielle," he said soothingly. "Cool it. It's not worth getting upset over the likes of *him*."

Gabrielle released her hand from her victim's face and stood up. James thought he'd defused the situation, but then he realized four other lads were moving in to surround them. As he stepped forward to walk back to his lane, a clumsy punch glanced across the side of his head.

James instinctively swung back with his elbow to take out his assailant, catching him full in the face and deftly sweeping away his opponent's legs as he stumbled backwards. The other three lads didn't like this one bit. Two lunged at James, while the guy in the Tottenham shirt tried to take down Gabrielle by jumping on her back.

CHERUB had trained James to handle himself in a fight, but there's a limit to what you can do against three significantly larger opponents at close range. Luckily, the other cherubs were rushing to his defense.

Kyle, Connor, and Callum all piled over or around the seats and launched themselves at the thugs. James caught a second punch and his bowling shoe squealed as he lost his balance on the polished wooden floor.

He tried to get back on his feet, but found himself trapped on the ground, while a tangle of limbs waged war overhead. He caught sight of Kyle's knee hitting someone in the guts and Tottenham-shirt guy getting pulled into a painful arm-lock by the twins.

By the time a group of adults—including the two CHERUB supervisors looking after the younger kids in the bumper lane—charged in to break up the fight, there was no doubt about the result. The five yobs were crawling around on the floor in varying degrees of pain, with a ring of steely faced CHERUB agents surrounding them, defying them to make another move.

James rolled onto his back and took a big gasp of air. He got a little rush from being on the winning side, even though his main contribution had been getting thumped in the head and falling over. He reckoned the older kids deserved what they'd got; the way they'd started on Gabrielle was totally out of order.

But James's mood darkened as he levered himself up onto the plastic seats. His head hurt, his clothes were filthy, and there were going to be consequences when they got back to campus.

Dr. Terence McAfferty, usually known as Mac, stared at the five kids lined up in front of his big oak desk, wondering exactly how many times he'd faced similar line-ups of worried faces in the thirteen years since he'd been appointed chairman of CHERUB. He was sure the number ran into thousands.

"So," Mac said wearily, "what caused the fight at the bowling alley earlier this evening?"

"This guy on the next lane had a go at Gabrielle," Kyle explained, stepping forward and taking the lead role because he was the oldest. "They were chucking their drinks around and acting like idiots. We all kind of lost our temper and piled into them."

"You all *simultaneously* decided to pile in," Mac said, clearly not finding this explanation likely. "And I suppose none of you is any more to blame than anyone else?"

"That's right," Kyle lied.

The rest of the line-up nodded. They'd huddled together and sorted out their cover story on the mini-bus ride back to campus. Gabrielle had started the punch-up, of course, but she'd been racially abused and none of the other kids thought she deserved to cop all the blame.

"I understand," Mac said reluctantly. "If that's the way you want me to deal with this, so be it. But I spoke to the staff members who were at the scene and I think I have a pretty accurate idea of what *really* happened."

As he said this, Mac cast deliberate glances at Gabrielle and James.

"I shouldn't have to tell you how serious this incident could have been," Mac continued. "It's been drilled into you all time and again. What is the number one priority for groups of CHERUB agents when they're off campus?"

The line-up droned the answer, at different speeds and with varying degrees of gusto: "Keep a low profile."

"A *low* profile," Mac nodded. "CHERUB is a secret organization. The safety of your colleagues who are currently away on undercover missions depends upon the fact that nobody knows we exist. When you're off campus, I expect you to behave in a manner that doesn't attract undue attention. I expect you to avoid trouble at all costs, even under extreme provocation. Is that clearly understood?"

"Yes sir," everyone nodded somberly.

"A whole bunch of people saw your little display of fighting skills at the bowling alley this evening. Don't you think they're going to be extremely curious about who you are and how a group of youngsters might come by advanced martial arts skills like that? Can you imagine the fuss that would have been caused if one of the boys you assaulted had been seriously injured? I know you're all trained in unarmed combat and had the good sense to use minimal force, but freak accidents can still happen.

"On top of that, you can count yourselves extremely lucky that I have connections at the local police station. I had to use all my leverage to ensure that the five of you aren't sitting in a police cell at this very moment facing criminal charges. So, your punishments."

It was midnight. The kids had been tired and fidgety while they listened to the lecture, but they snapped to attention at the mention of punishments, anxious to know what they were going to get.

"First of all, you're all banned from going into town for the next four months," Mac announced. "Second, we're always short of pupils at CHERUB and right now we're getting desperate for new blood. . . ."

Mac reached into his desk drawer and pulled out a pad of pre-printed mission briefings. James let out a little groan as he realized he was about to be sent off to some strange children's home to recruit a new CHERUB agent. James had never been on a recruitment mission before, but everyone he knew who had said they were a complete nightmare.

CHAPTER 9

WILDLIFE

It was near midnight when Lauren and Bethany finished readying the snowmobile for its journey the next morning. The vehicle was designed to be taken from its packing crate and assembled, lubricated, and fuelled by anyone who could follow basic instructions.

The girls zipped their sleeping bags together and snuggled up. If you believed the cold weather survival manual, sleeping in individual bags was warmer. But textbooks don't take into account the comfort factor of falling asleep beside your best friend, even when the fleece-covered arm she wraps around your back stinks of petrol.

• • •

A few streaks of light penetrated the container when the first sun crept over the horizon, despite the bits of cardboard the girls had pushed into the gaps around the metal doors to keep out the draught.

Lauren and Bethany were sleeping heavily when their wristwatch alarms began bleeping, just a few seconds apart. The girls were taking no chances. They'd set two alarms in case one of them made a mistake, or one of the watches went wrong. Any kind of error could lead to them missing the final checkpoint and their ninety-nine days of suffering would all be for nothing. They tried keeping thoughts of failure out of their minds, but it was like being trapped in a burning building and trying not to think about the flames creeping towards you.

Lauren pulled back the zip and slid out of her sleeping bag, then stood up and lit one of the gas lamps. The floor of the container was freezing cold on her socked feet. Bethany was always a slow starter and like every other day since training began, it took a nudge from Lauren to get her moving.

"Come on, lazy head," Lauren said. "You start packing up our equipment, I'll make the porridge. It'll be safest if we get going the second it's light enough."

As she said this, Lauren squatted over a metal bucket in the middle of the floor and began the undignified process of peeling off the outer fleece suit and thermal underwear she'd slept in.

"Why couldn't I have been a boy?" Lauren asked rhetorically, as Bethany sat up on the sleeping bag and pushed the detachable linings into her boots. "A penis would make this lark *so* much easier."

"Imagine what our brothers are doing right now," Bethany said. "With the time difference, it's bedtime over there. I bet they're sitting in front of their TVs, with hot drinks and chocolate biscuits."

Lauren laughed. "Knowing James, he's out on the athletics track running punishment laps."

"Probably alongside Jake," Bethany grinned. "My brother's almost as bad as yours."

"You want to use the bucket before I sling this lot outside?" Lauren asked, as she adjusted her underwear and pulled up the zip on her fleece suit.

"Yeah. Hand it over, I'm busting," Bethany said. "I hope that bear's gone."

Lauren smiled. "If not, he's about to get woken up by having a bucket of pee chucked over his head."

After Bethany had peed, Lauren cautiously pushed the metal door open with her shoulder. It was hard to shift because half a meter of snow had blown against it during the night. The cold air stung her uncovered hands and face. She slung out the contents of the steaming bucket and glanced through the sleet.

"Dammit," Lauren said anxiously. "It's still out there."

The sleeping bear was now blanketed in the overnight snowfall, except for a patch around its snout that had been melted by the breath rising out of its nose.

"Look at the size of him," Lauren said. "I bet he could kill us both in one swipe. It's going to be too dangerous dragging the snowmobile out before he's gone. We'll have to shoo him off."

"We should do it now," Bethany said, as she crept up to the crack in the container door beside Lauren. "That way he'll be long gone by the time we have to leave."

Lauren nodded in agreement. "Those TV shows always say that even big animals are easily scared, so it shouldn't be that hard."

She pushed the metal bucket through the doors and whacked it as hard as she could against the container door. The girls had to bury their ears in their hands to dull the eardrum-shattering clang. The bear, on the other hand, didn't move a millimeter.

"Stupid creature," Lauren snapped.

"Maybe we should lob something at it," Bethany suggested.

The open door was letting out the heat and the girls were underdressed. They retreated inside to put on gloves and balaclavas. Bethany rummaged around for a good throwing object, while Lauren poured porridge oats, powdered milk, and water into a tin and set it over the camping stove so that their breakfast was warming while they dealt with the wildlife problem.

Bethany approached the doors holding two saucepans, the only items amongst their lightweight camping equipment that seemed sufficiently hefty to rouse a polar bear.

"I'll have to get close to make sure I don't miss," Bethany said. "But it might charge at me, so you hold the door and be ready to pull it shut the second I come back through."

Bethany's heart drummed as she crept to within three meters of the bear, holding a saucepan in each hand. She hurled both saucepans, before spinning around and charging back to the container in a flurry of white powder.

Lauren slammed the doors of their metal cage. Bethany's momentum carried her forward over Lauren's sled, and she ended up sprawled out on the floor beyond it.

"Are you OK?" Lauren asked.

"I'll live," Bethany gasped, as she rolled onto her back. "Did it work?"

Lauren's main concern had been Bethany's safety. She hadn't seen the bear's reaction through the clouds of snow. She pushed the door back open a couple of centimeters and took a peek.

"I do *not* believe it," Lauren gasped.

Bethany poked her head through the gap between the doors and didn't believe it either. The bear still hadn't moved. All that had changed was that there was now a saucepan on the ground in front of its snout and another buried in the snow over its midsection, swelling up and down with each breath.

"It had to happen this morning, didn't it?" Lauren said, sounding stressed out. "We should have eaten breakfast, packed up, and dragged the snowmobile outside by now."

"Think, girl!" Bethany said, pounding her gloved hand against her thigh. "There *must* be a way to make it move."

"Maybe it's deaf or something," Lauren said.

"Think, think, think . . . ," Bethany repeated. "What if we loaded everything on the snowmobile and pushed it outside quietly? It wouldn't catch up with us once we're moving."

"Too risky," Lauren said. "What if we disturbed it at the wrong moment and it went after one of us? We wouldn't stand a chance."

"True," Bethany said. "But looking at that dozy lump, I'd say you'd have to shove a firework up its butt for it to budge."

"That's *it*," Lauren gasped. "Bethany, you're a genius."

"What?" Bethany asked. "We don't have a firework. We do have our distress flare, but if we set that off the rescue helicopter will come for us and we'll fail training."

"Not a firework," Lauren explained. "But we can make fire. Animals are scared of fire."

Feeling that she couldn't spare time to explain, Lauren plunged into the wreckage of the snowmobile packaging at the back of the container. She grabbed one of the long pieces of cardboard and tore off a ragged section, thirty centimeters wide and three meters long. Then she rolled it into a tube.

"Tie this off with some of that tape," Lauren ordered.

Bethany picked up the strong plastic binding strip they'd cut off the outside of the snowmobile box before opening it. She wound it around the tube, tying knots as she went.

"Are we gonna poke it with this?" Bethany asked.

"Uh-huh," Lauren nodded, as she gathered up the bits of oily rag they'd used when they were working on the snowmobile and stuffed them into one end of the tube.

"The oil on these rags will burn easily," Lauren explained. "It won't stick around long enough to feel any more than a quick lick of flame."

"Good thinking," Bethany said admiringly.

Bethany found some waterproof matches in her sled, as Lauren moved up to the door with the long cardboard tube.

"Be ready to pull up the door after me," Lauren said. "He's not going to like this one bit."

Bethany went up on tiptoes with a match in her hand. The oiled rags instantly erupted in blue flames. Lauren pushed the burning tube through the doorway, hoping that the freezing wind wouldn't snuff out the flame.

The fire turned orange as Lauren tilted the tube forward and the cardboard caught light. Her second crunching step through the snow took the flaming end to within half a meter of the bear's head. When the flame was almost touching its nose, Lauren lowered the tube onto the snow and rolled it towards the bear's face. Certain that the bear would rear up the instant the flame touched it, she scrambled desperately back towards the container and Bethany clanged the door shut behind her.

The girls caught their breath for a moment, before cracking the door back open. They were expecting to find a four-hundred-kilogram bear with a burned snout on the rampage, but what they saw was more shocking: The bear's head was in flames, and its eye socket had sunk down through its skull into its head.

"We killed it," Bethany shrieked. "The poor thing must have been old, or sick."

But Lauren wasn't buying it. She'd noticed the gray wisps of smoke venting out the back of the mound in the snow. Lauren didn't know much about the anatomy of polar bears, but she was certain their insides weren't hollow.

“It’s fake,” Lauren announced.

Lauren plunged into the snow towards the smouldering bear and leaned over it. Although it was smoky, she got a reasonable view inside the cavity where the head had melted. The bear was made of nylon fur, stretched over a frame shaped out of chicken wire. Inside, she could see the plastic bellows, rubber tubing, car battery, and electric pump that had made it breathe.

‘We should have known,” Bethany stormed, angrily kicking up a flurry of snow. “After all the tricks the instructors have played on us.”

Lauren looked at her watch. “I reckon we’ve lost fifteen minutes of daylight. Let’s get breakfast down our necks and get out of here.”

The porridge was bubbling over the side of its tin when they got back inside the container. Lauren laced the porridge with a heavy dose of glucose powder and a slow-release energy supplement designed for long-distance runners. The girls’ bodies would need every calorie of this high-energy food to keep warm on their thirty-five-kilometer snowmobile journey. When it was all mixed in, the porridge had a gritty texture and the gray pallor of cement, but the girls barely considered this as they half spooned and half drank the soggy mixture.

“I hope there’s no more tricks,” Lauren said, as she wiped a dribble of porridge from the corner of her mouth.

Bethany spoke with her mouth full. “If we can just keep our heads together for four more hours . . .”

CHAPTER 4

SUNDAY

Kids who live on CHERUB campus miss a lot of school when they're away on missions. One of the ways they catch up is by having lessons on Saturday mornings. James thought this was cruel, because it left Sunday as the only time when he got a chance to lie in.

It was nearly eleven when he decided to untangle himself from his duvet. Dressed only in boxers and a grubby CHERUB T-shirt, he glanced through the slats in his blind and saw that it was a typical April morning, with a light frost on the grass and a drizzle of rain. A football match was being played on the pitches beyond the tennis courts. The players were a bunch of muddy eight- and nine-year-olds, mostly boys.

James wandered across to his laptop, flipped up the screen, and tapped on the navigation pad to check his e-mail. He was hoping for a message from Kerry, but all he had was spam from a company offering him a *Free online personality test that could change your WHOLE life!!!* and a schedule notification from the mission controller Zara Asker:

> James,
> Please ensure you attend the mission preparation building, room 31, at 1530 this afternoon, where you will be briefed on your upcoming recruitment mission.
> Zara Asker
> (Mission Controller)

James thought about sending an e-mail to Kerry, but he'd sent her three since she'd last replied, and the only news he had was about the fight at the bowling alley, which he didn't feel like going into.

He felt too lazy to go down to the canteen, so James flicked on Sky Sports News, poured himself a bowl of cereal, and got milk and orange juice from his miniature fridge. There was a knock on the door while he ate.

"Not locked," James munched.

Kyle and Bruce came in, both dressed in shorts and trainers, and holding carrier bags with a towel and a change of clothes in them.

"Aren't you ready?" Kyle asked.

James looked at the clock on his bedside table. "Sorry," he said, "I never realized it was time."

James went to the fitness training session with Kyle and Bruce every Sunday morning. Most boys preferred playing football or rugby, but after thirteen years of missing open goals, tripping in the mud, and getting smacked in the face by balls that came out of nowhere, he'd reluctantly accepted that ball games were not his forte.

"I'll get some clothes on," James said, as he sat on the edge of his bed and grabbed one of the crusty sports socks scattered over his floor.

"Way to go at the bowling alley last night, James," Bruce sneered.

"You would have been involved if you hadn't *already* been on punishment detail in the kitchens," James sneered back.

"Yeah well," Bruce smiled, "better spending a couple of hours down on my knees cleaning out the ovens, than a month stuck in some god-awful children's home. Mind you, it's always a shame to miss a punch-up, whatever the consequences."

"You know what?" James said, as he pulled on a white sock that didn't match the first one. "I don't see what all this fuss is about recruitment missions. It can't be *that* bad being sent off to some children's home to try and get another kid to join CHERUB."

Kyle, who'd been on five recruitment missions for his many sins, nodded. "They're not awful. They're just really boring and a lot of the kids you meet in those places are complete scumbags; nicking your stuff and that. One time I got sent to this place in Newcastle. I had guys starting on me every five minutes. I was there for three weeks and I must have been in a row every day."

"Did you recruit anyone?"

Kyle nodded. "Those two blond twins with the Geordie accents. Remember I pointed them out to you? They were only seven at the time, but they had more brains than all the other kids in that dump combined."

There were three gymnasiums on CHERUB campus. Fitness training was taught in the oldest of them, which was still known as the Boys' Gym, from the days when physical education was a single-sex affair. James had a soft spot for this dilapidated building, with its mahogany wall clock permanently stuck at a quarter to five, dim light bulbs suspended from long wires, and shrunken floorboards that creaked underfoot. His favorite feature was the hand-painted sign hanging over the entrance:

ANY BOY BRINGING IN MUD OR DIRT ON
HIS PLIMSOLLS WILL BE THRASHED.
P.T. BIVOTT (SPORTS MASTER)

Today's teacher was Meryl Spencer, a retired Olympic sprinter who could think of a couple of kids she wouldn't have minded thrashing if corporal punishment at CHERUB hadn't been banned more than twenty years earlier.

The gym had been laid out with forty stations. Some were as simple as a foam mat with a laminated card on it saying PUSH UPS. Others were more complex: traffic cones set out for shuttle runs, a chest-press machine, a chin-up bar.

The thirty kids in the class picked a station to start at. They worked it for two minutes, after which Meryl would blast her whistle and the kids would run to the next. The whole circuit took eighty minutes and the only relief from exhaustion came at the two rest stops along the way. Anyone who looked slack found Meryl or her assistant yelling in their face, calling them soft and threatening them with *a good boot up the backside*.

Eight boys piled into the showers when the session ended. James toweled off and put on clean jeans, then flexed his chest muscles and biceps in front of the steamed-up mirror. He'd sprouted eight centimeters in the last three months and packed on muscle since starting regular strength training.

Bruce flicked James's back with his towel. "You little poser," Bruce grinned. "Stop poncing about."

James turned away and grinned as he rolled deodorant under his arms. "You're just jealous because I'm looking so beefy these days," he said. "It's hardly surprising that half the girls on campus are chasing after me."

"You reckon, do you?" Bruce huffed.

Kyle spotted a golden opportunity for one of his trademark wind-ups. "I think you're right, actually," he said, stepping forward and putting his hand on James's bum. "I think you're hot stuff."

James leapt half a meter in the air and screamed. "Cut that gay shit out, Kyle."

After a great deal of persuasion from Kerry and a few others, James had eventually decided that there was nothing wrong with his friend Kyle being gay. Sometimes it still gave him the creeps though. He spun around and furiously shoved Kyle away, his face burning with rage as Bruce and the other boys started laughing. James realized the only way to save face was to outdo Kyle at his own game. He quickly balled up all the saliva he could muster, grabbed Kyle around the back of the neck, and planted a massive soggy kiss on his cheek. Kyle recoiled in horror, with a glistening trail of James's spit rolling down his face.

"You filthy *little . . .* ," Kyle shouted, as he scoured his wet face on his towel.

"What's the matter?" James asked sweetly. "Come on, baby. Won't you give us a snog?"

Bruce and the others were killing themselves laughing, as Kyle bundled up his clothes and scrambled to the opposite end of the changing room.

Sunday lunch was an occasion on campus. It was the only meal of the week when the individual tables in the dining room were pushed together. Table cloths were laid and places set with the good cutlery. The traditional Sunday roast with all the trimmings was James's favorite meal of the week, but the atmosphere at his table was miserable, because everyone except Bruce was being briefed for their recruitment missions later that afternoon. Even the banter riding back and forth about James and Kyle fancying each other didn't do much to lighten the mood.

Kyle, James, and Gabrielle shared the first appointment with Zara. They strolled through the drizzle without speaking, their bloated stomachs deadening their progress.

The brand-new mission preparation building was a kilometer away from the main building, where they'd eaten lunch. The banana-shaped construction looked impressive as you approached: a hundred meters of reflective glass, bristling with satellite dishes and aerials. Impressions took a turn for the worse when you got close and realized that the paths up to the building comprised wooden boards laid over mud. There were still wheelbarrows, cement mixers, and building materials everywhere, and the high-tech entry system that was supposed to identify you by scanning the lattice of blood vessels in the back of your eye had a soggy Out of Order notice drooped over it.

The three kids passed along a corridor that smelled of new carpet tiles. The offices all had the names of CHERUB mission controllers printed on the locked doors.

Zara Asker was one of the most senior mission controllers. She had a big office at the end of the corridor, with a semi-circle of floor-to-ceiling windows and some rather swish-looking furniture with lots of curving wood and flashy chrome trim. She struggled out of her seat as the kids walked through her open door, revealing a set of baggy dungarees stretched over an almost nine-months-pregnant belly.

"Well, well, well," Zara grinned, nodding at James and Kyle. "Dr. McAfferty told me it wouldn't take long to find a few bodies to send on recruitment missions. I can't say I'm surprised to see you two hooligans here. . . . And you must be Gabrielle, I don't believe we've had the pleasure."

As Gabrielle and Zara shook hands, James couldn't help smiling guiltily. Zara had been one of the controllers on his last mission and he'd got on well with her.

"How's Joshua these days?" James asked.

Zara broke into a smile. "He's grown a lot since you last saw him. His back teeth are pushing through and he's driving me and Ewart crazy. As a matter of fact, any time you fancy coming over to the staff quarters to baby-sit . . ."

James laughed. "I'll give that offer a miss, thanks."

"OK," Zara said, returning to business. "I take it you all know what a recruitment mission entails? We've put together a background scenario and false identity for each of you and you can expect to be sent off to a children's home within the next week. As with any other CHERUB mission, you have an absolute right to refuse to undertake it. However, if you refuse in this instance, I expect Dr. McAfferty will issue you with an alternative punishment, which you can expect to be a lot less pleasant than a few weeks in local authority care.

"When you arrive at the children's home, your job is to check everyone out. You're looking for a potential CHERUB recruit, which means a smart, physically fit kid. Family ties are a big no-no. Foreign language skills and identical twins will be looked upon very favorably. It's all in the mission briefing."

Zara leaned across her desk and handed James, Kyle, and Gabrielle a photocopy of the standard briefing for recruitment missions.

"Good candidates can get shipped off to foster homes in no time," Zara continued. "So if you spot someone who looks the business, get on to me or one of the assistant mission controllers straight away and we'll arrange to have the kid drugged and brought here to undertake the recruitment tests. . . ."

There was a gentle knock on Zara's open door.

"John," Zara said, breaking into a smile. "Good to see I'm not the only mission controller who comes in on Sunday afternoons."

James turned around and instantly recognized the silver-rimmed glasses and pale, bald head of John Jones. John had only just taken a job as a CHERUB mission controller, but James had worked with John the year before when he was still employed by MI5, the adult branch of British intelligence.

"I thought I spotted James in here," John said awkwardly. "You're not sending him out are you?"

"He got himself in *another* spot of bother," Zara explained. "Mac wants him to go on a recruitment mission, but I'm sure he'll yield if you've got James penciled in for something important."

James's heart leapt at the prospect of escape.

John Jones nodded. "Perhaps I could have a quick word, in confidence?"

Zara looked at the kids. "Sorry," she said. "Would you step out into the corridor for a jiffy?"

As soon as James shut Zara's office door, Kyle glowered at him.

"I can't believe you're gonna weasel your way out of this, James," he said indignantly.

James folded his arms and broke into a smug grin.

It was ten minutes before Zara pulled her door open and the three kids filed back in. "Well, James," Zara said. "I just rang Dr. McAfferty and you're off the hook, provided you accept the mission John is going to offer you at a briefing later this evening."

"*So* jammy," Kyle whispered under his breath.

James couldn't help smiling.

"I wouldn't look so satisfied if I was you," John Jones said. "You might decide you'd prefer the recruitment mission when you see what I've got lined up for you."

CHAPTER 5

ROPE

Eleven kids had started basic training three months earlier. Lauren stood to attention in the snow with the five others who'd made it to the final checkpoint on their snowmobiles. Mr. Large, the head instructor, was eyeballing her.

"Can anybody here tell this young lady what polar bears do in the winter?" he shouted.

A couple of kids grumbled a response: "Hibernate."

"That's right, Miss Thicko," Large grinned. "They dig a big hole under the ice and they drift off to snoozy land until the daffodils pop up in springtime. If you'd *bothered* to study the training manual, you'd also have seen that bears eat fish and live on the ice floes near the coast. Not out here, over a hundred kilometers inland. Is that understood?"

"Yes, sir," Lauren said meekly.

"And the radio. Why did you forget to switch on the encryption device?"

"I was cold and tired, and . . ." Lauren saw Mr. Large's eyes bulge out behind his snow goggles and realized she was giving the wrong answer. "Sorry, sir . . . No excuse, sir," she said sharply.

Mr. Large shoved Lauren to the ground and plunged his size-fifteen boots into the snow on either side of her head.

"When I woke up this morning, Lauren *Adams*," Large spat, "my back hurt. It hurt the same way it's hurt every *single* morning since a nasty little girl hit me with a spade five months back. Can you remind me who it was that did that?"

"Me, sir?" Lauren inquired innocently.

"If I'd had my way, you would have been permanently excluded from CHERUB."

Lauren had been surprised that Mr. Large hadn't made training harder for her from day one. Now she had the horrible realization that he'd saved up his revenge for the very end.

"And *so*," Mr. Large said, "to the ultimate test of courage that was mentioned in all of your mission briefings. There's been a slight change of plan. The briefing should now read, *Ultimate test of* Lauren's *courage*."

Lauren felt a tear welling up behind her snow goggles as the icy ground chilled her back. She didn't reckon she could face a third attempt at basic training. Failure now would be the end of her CHERUB career.

Mr. Large crushed Lauren's knuckles as he tugged her back to her feet.

"Who's the best swimmer out of you six trainees?" Mr. Large asked, eyeballing Lauren again.

"Me, I suppose," Lauren said.

"That's *riiiiight*, isn't it?" Mr. Large said cockily. "Quite the little mermaid, I recall . . . So if one of you had to swim across a fast-flowing river, grab six lovely gray CHERUB T-shirts, and then swim back again, you'd be the ideal candidate. Wouldn't you?"

"Yes, sir," Lauren barked, trying desperately not to show Mr. Large how upset she was. He absolutely loved it when he made a trainee cry.

Mr. Large took a step back and addressed the whole lineup. "I'd suggest that all of you do what you can to help Lauren out; because if she doesn't come back with the T-shirts, I'll make each of you swim across individually and fetch your own. The river is four hundred meters away, over the brow of the next hill. I'd suggest you get moving if you want to be indoors by sundown."

Lauren led the row of kids scrambling uphill through the deep snow, dragging their equipment sleds behind them. Mr. Large and the two assistant training instructors, Mr. Speaks and Miss Smoke, followed them.

The rushing water made a roar that overpowered all but the most persistent howls of wind. The river would have been over a hundred meters wide in the summer, but the banks were iced up, cutting Lauren's swim to less than sixty.

Miss Smoke, a woman who was butch even by the standards of retired kickboxing champions, pointed her muscular arm at the opposite embankment. "Your gray T-shirts are in a waterproof backpack behind that traffic cone," she rumbled.

The six trainees huddled up and pulled their balaclavas away from their mouths, so they could hear each other speak. As their steaming breath mingled, nobody could look Lauren in the eye. They felt sorry for her, but at the same time it was a relief not to be suffering alongside her.

"It could have been worse," Lauren said, trying to sound cheerful and break the silence. "I'll have to go in naked. If I'm wearing clothes, they'll freeze solid the second I step out of the water and I'll never get them off."

A twelve-year-old Kurdish boy called Aram replied. "We've all got Vaseline in our first-aid packs. It will act as insulation if Lauren smears it on."

"That'll help keep me warm," Lauren nodded.

"What if we tie our rescue ropes together and knot them under Lauren's arms?" Bethany suggested. "It should be long enough to reach across the river and we can haul her in if she gets in trouble."

"Good idea," Lauren grinned. "I'll still have to swim out, but you guys can pull me back with the rope."

"Do you think you can make it over?" Aram asked.

"It's gonna be cold and the current looks vicious," Lauren said. "But the distance is only a bit more than one length of a swimming pool."

The six trainees tied their rescue ropes together. Lauren double-checked all the knots, then the kids burrowed inside their sleds and grabbed their tubs of Vaseline.

Bethany led the way out to the riverbank and began

helping Lauren unzip her outer layers of clothing. The kids knew from their survival manuals that any water flowing in these parts would be a couple of degrees above freezing. You wouldn't swim in it out of choice, but it was survivable. Lauren's real problem was the air outside the water, which was more than fifteen degrees *below* freezing. A few minutes' exposure to temperatures this low would blister Lauren's bare skin, as surely as if she'd jumped into a bath of boiling water.

Two of the boys laid a foam-insulating mat on the snow and weighted down the ends with sleds to stop it blowing away.

"OK," Lauren said. "Does everyone know what their job is? I don't want any holdups."

After a line of nods had satisfied Lauren, she sat on the foam mat and two of the boys started tugging at her snow boots. Once they were off, Lauren stood up, and stepped out of her snowsuit and outer fleece layer in a single frenzied movement. Next, she peeled away the tightly fitting inner fleece, followed by her socks and underwear. Bethany gathered up the inner layers of clothing as they were cast off and pushed them inside her snowsuit so they didn't freeze up.

As soon as Lauren had hurled her knickers away, she dived on to the foam mat and the boys threw a couple of sleeping bags on top of her.

Bethany leaned in and yelled, "Are you OK?" forgetting that Lauren no longer had three hats covering her ears.

Lauren shuddered as she poked her head from under the sleeping bags and nodded. "Give me the grease."

Aram and his younger brother, Milar, began passing Lauren the tubs of Vaseline. She sunk her numb fingers into each tub and smeared it thickly over her body, trying not to wriggle too much because she didn't want any grease wasted by rubbing off on to the sleeping bags.

When Lauren was well slathered, Bethany pushed one end of the nylon climbing rope under the sleeping bags. Lauren wound the rope under her arms and tied it into a bowknot, like a shoelace. That way she could pull on the bow and release herself easily if the rope became snagged.

"All ready?" Aram asked.

"As ready as I'll ever be."

Bethany and Aram each grabbed a corner of the insulated mat and dragged it on to the ice at the edge of the river, with Lauren curled up under the sleeping bags. They stopped a couple of meters shy of the water's edge where the ice looked dangerously thin.

Miss Smoke was waiting for them. She pulled back the sleeping bags and tested the knot in the rope under Lauren's arms.

'Remember, the air is much colder than the water," Smoke said gruffly. "Keep your head under, except when you have to breathe, and don't hang around when you get to the other side."

With no sleeping bags over her top half, Lauren was shivering too badly to speak, but she managed a nod.

"OK," Smoke said. "Get going."

Bethany whipped the sleeping bags away from Lauren's legs. As Lauren sprang up, Aram gave her a quick inspection, before moving in with a Vaseline-smeared glove and patching up a few areas where the coating looked thin.

Lauren had too much on her mind to give a damn about everyone seeing her naked. She took three quick tiptoe leaps over the thin ice and took a huge breath as she speared into the water. Because Lauren had acclimatized to a temperature nineteen degrees colder than the water, a sense of calm passed over her as she began to swim. It almost felt warm.

She set off in a powerful front crawl, turning her head to breathe whenever the choppy water allowed her to. After two minutes' swimming flat out, Lauren thought she must have almost reached the opposite bank. She raised her head out of the water to get a look. A blast of sleet pounded her face, but she managed to keep her eyes open long enough to see that she was barely halfway across.

Lauren felt crushed as she dived back under, swimming at a diagonal into the fierce current; pushing as hard as her aching body would allow. She now had serious doubts about her ability to make it across. The next minutes were the most agonizing of Lauren's life. Her skin felt numb and she was fighting a stitch down her left side.

Finally, more than four shattering minutes after setting off, Lauren spotted the orange cone less than five meters from her face. Touching the ice sheet on the embankment was a relief, but getting out of the water was another challenge.

Lauren's fingers were numb and the ice gave her nothing to grip on to. Her first three goes at climbing out of the water failed and she started getting desperate. At the fourth attempt, a wave pushed her at exactly the right moment and she managed to lift a knee on to the ice.

The danger now was of her bare skin freezing to the ice beneath the snow. The only way to prevent this was not to let any part of her body touch the ground for more than a fraction of a second.

Shivering so violently that she could barely control her movements, Lauren quickly smeared the soles of her feet through some extra thick grease on her ankles. By the time she'd done this, a few dozen drips of water that hadn't been repelled by the Vaseline had frozen to the skin on her back. Every bead felt like a nail drilling her flesh.

Lauren stood up to an eruption of encouraging screams from the opposite embankment. She took four quick leaps towards the orange cone and plucked the small backpack out of the snow behind it. When she'd hooked it over her shoulders, Lauren allowed herself a moment of triumph, turning to the other trainees and raising a thumb in the air.

The first step back towards the water made Lauren scream out, as a layer of skin tore from the ball of her foot. The grease had rubbed away and her damp sole had taken less than two seconds to freeze to the ground. She glanced back at the trail of blood in the snow, then took three painful steps and dived into the water.

As soon as Lauren hit the water, she felt the rope dig into the joints under her arms as the other trainees began hauling it. She thought about trying to swim, but she was being dragged through the water too fast for it to make any difference. In fact, Lauren thought the five kids standing on the embankment were overdoing it. The rope felt like it was tearing her arms out of their sockets and it was a struggle getting her head above the water for long enough to take a proper breath.

At least the return journey was fast. Within sixty seconds, Lauren found herself being lifted out of the water and on to a sleeping bag by the two Kurdish boys. Once they'd dragged her away from the thin ice, they grabbed the soggy backpack off Lauren's shoulders, while the other three trainees descended on her with towels. They rubbed off as much water as they could, before rolling Lauren's gasping body on to the foam sleeping mat and throwing all their sleeping bags on top of her.

Lauren felt her vision go out of focus as Bethany waved a thermal vest under her nose.

"Snap out of it," Bethany shouted. "You've got to get your clothes back on before . . ."

When Lauren came around, she got a sniff of the grease still smeared over her body and shots of pain from the dressing over her foot and the rope burns under her arms.

"Hey," Bethany said gently. "Welcome back, partner."

Lauren realized she was on the floor, at the base camp where they'd set off on their Alaskan trek five days earlier. The building was fantastically warm, with electric light and proper central heating. The other trainees were scattered around the carpet on giant floor cushions, dressed in shorts and gray CHERUB T-shirts. Their hair was wet and mussed, like they'd toweled off after a shower. Most of them held steaming mugs.

"How long . . . ?" Lauren asked, erupting into a coughing fit before she could finish her sentence.

Bethany looked at her watch. "You've been out for about forty minutes. Miss Smoke says you're suffering from mild hypothermia and exhaustion. She reckons you'll be fine after a few hours' rest and some hot food and drink. And you'll be pleased to know that you making it across that river put Mr. Large in a stinking mood."

"Where's my gray T-shirt?" Lauren asked drowsily.

Bethany smirked. "You're holding it in your hand. I didn't take it out of its packet in case you got grease over it."

Lauren's fingers still felt numb, but now she realized the T-shirt was in her hand, she pulled the polythene-wrapped square up to her face and stared at the gray fabric with the CHERUB logo on it.

"No more training," Lauren grinned.

"Yeah," Bethany smiled. "Undercover missions here we come."

CHAPTER 6

MISSILES

John Jones showed James into his office. It wasn't as nice as Zara's, but it was a decent size with three computers, a giant LCD television hanging on the wall, and a long suede-covered sofa. It was dark outside and the floor-to-ceiling window overlooked moonlit trees.

A sixteen-year-old wearing a black CHERUB T-shirt was sprawled over the sofa. James got excited when he realized it was Dave Moss. Dave was a legend. He'd earned his navy CHERUB T-shirt at eleven and his black T-shirt at thirteen, on a mission that brought down half the Ukrainian mafia. He spoke five languages and had won every CHERUB karate and judo tournament he'd ever entered.

There were lots of talented kids at CHERUB, but Dave was one of the ones who managed to pull it off without everyone thinking he was a swot. His looks helped. Dave was tall and muscular: handsome in a grungy sort of way, with bright green eyes and long blond hair. His girlfriends were always the hottest on campus and there was even a rumour he'd got one of them pregnant. James had pretended to be appalled when Kerry told him; but as far as all the guys were concerned, the whiff of sex made Dave seem even cooler than he was already.

"Do you know David Moss?" John Jones asked.

"No, I don't," James said nervously, as he reached out and shook Dave's hand. "Pleased to meet you, David."

"Call me Dave," Dave smiled.

James felt like a tit. Who introduced themselves to someone like Dave Moss by saying 'Pleased to meet you'? It was the kind of thing you'd say to an old granny at a funeral.

"David is highly regarded amongst the mission preparation staff," John Jones explained, "and we're looking for two good agents to work alongside him on one of the most important missions CHERUB has ever undertaken."

James couldn't stop himself from grinning. "I knew it was big," he stuttered. "I mean . . . everyone knows Dave's reputation. You're not going to send him on some piddly little mission."

"You've not done badly yourself, James," Dave said reassuringly. "I've read your personnel file. You've only been on two missions, but what you lack in quantity you more than make up for in quality."

"Cheers," James grinned. The compliment made him

feel a little more relaxed in the company of the campus hero. "So what's this mission about?"

Dave looked at John Jones. "Can I show him now, boss?"

John nodded. "I'll just make it clear to James before you do: Whether or not you choose to accept this mission, everything you hear from now on *must* stay within these walls."

James nodded. "Of course, same as always."

Dave reached down the arm of the sofa and picked up a fat aluminium tube with a shoulder stock and trigger hanging underneath it.

"Do you know what one of these is?"

"It looks like a missile," James said.

"Got it in one," Dave said. "You rest it on your shoulder and aim it at a tank, helicopter, whatever. You get one shot, then you throw the launch module away. This one is the latest model. The missile has a solid-fuel rocket engine with a ten-kilometer range and more brainpower than a roomful of nerds."

John went into detail. "Around the time you were born, James, the Americans used Tomahawk cruise missiles in the first Gulf War. Until then, everyone dropped unguided bombs out of airplanes five kilometers up in the sky and crossed their fingers. You'd count yourself lucky if one bomb out of twenty hit the spot, and unlucky if you happened to live anywhere near a target. Then the Tomahawk missile came along. Suddenly, you could sit in a control room five hundred kilometers from a war zone and send off a missile accurate enough to smack the target on the nose ninety-nine times out of a hundred. This kind of accuracy gave the Americans a big tactical advantage, but it didn't come cheap: every Tomahawk cost half a million dollars. They were spending two billion dollars on missiles every day the Gulf War lasted and even the Yanks don't have that sort of cash to throw around."

Dave passed the missile across to James for a look.

"So," John continued, "the big challenge for the boffins wasn't to make precision-guided missiles bigger, or to give them longer range, or more accuracy. The challenge was to make them cheap. The weapon you're holding in your hand is the result of fifteen years' development. Its official acronym is PGSLM: Precision Guided Shoulder Launched Missile, but everyone calls it a Buddy missile. It's built using off-the-shelf components, like those you might find inside computers, or in-car navigation systems. You can program in targeting data using any laptop computer or handheld device capable of running an internet browser, or you can download live data on a moving target such as a car or ship, via a satellite link. Then, all you have to do is move within ten kilometers of your target, either on the ground or from a helicopter. You point the dangerous end at the sky, press the trigger, and the missile weaves its merry way to the target."

James admiringly turned the metal tube over in his hands. "So how much does this cost?" he asked.

"That one's a mock-up," John said. "But the real deal comes in at under fifteen thousand dollars a shot. Of course, the Americans will only sell this kind of technology to their closest allies."

"Safe," James said, as he pulled on the trigger and made a *ka-pow* noise. "I'll start saving up."

John smiled. "As a matter of fact, James, we're hoping you'll be able to get your hands on some real ones."

"I thought the Americans were our allies. Won't they sell them to us?"

John smiled uneasily. "The manufacturers gave the British army thirty-five preproduction samples for field trials. A little under three weeks ago, we sent a Royal Air Force freighter aircraft to pick them up from a military base in Nevada. The truck carrying the missiles never showed up."

"You mean somebody nicked them?" James gasped.

"Precisely," John nodded. "The only consolation is that we think we know who took them."

"Terrorists?" James asked.

"No; at least not directly. U.S. intelligence thinks they were stolen on behalf of an illegal weapons dealer called Jane Oxford. These missiles are worth millions to the right buyer. We think she'll be holding on to them until some terrorist group or tin-pot dictatorship is able to raise a very significant sum of money to buy them. Assuming we're right about this, Jane Oxford's greed will buy us time."

"How much damage could one of these missiles do?" James asked.

"They're not big enough to pack an enormous explosive punch," John explained. "But you don't need it with a weapon this accurate. Imagine a terrorist pointing a Buddy missile out of a bedroom window in a London suburb and blasting Her Majesty out of bed at Buckingham Palace. That's the kind of capability we're talking about here."

"Is there anything you can do to defend against the missile once it's fired?"

"Not a lot," John said. "The Americans are looking at protecting their president by fitting a rapid-firing anti-missile Phalanx gun onto a flatbed truck. But you're talking about a weapon designed for use on ships, that rips off a thousand twenty-millimeter shells every minute. It's not the kind of thing you want going off accidentally in the middle of a presidential motorcade."

"Definitely not," James grinned. "So where does CHERUB fit into getting these missiles back?"

"A decision was taken at cabinet level on both sides of the Atlantic not to release any information to the public about the stolen missiles, because of the panic it was likely to cause," John said.

Dave interrupted. "*And* because it would make a lot of politicians who claim to be winning the war on terrorism look dumb."

"The trouble is," John continued, "law enforcement and intelligence agencies on both sides of the Atlantic have been trying to track down Jane Oxford and other members of her organization since the early 1980s. They've got no more reason to believe they can catch her now than at any other time in the last thirty years. However, the Americans have one highly unusual lead. Only someone your age would be able to pursue it."

"Don't the Americans have their own version of CHERUB?" James asked.

John shook his head as he pulled a mission briefing out of his desk drawer and threw it into James's lap. "You'd better read this."

CHAPTER 7

BRIEFING

CLASSIFIED
MISSION BRIEFING FOR JAMES ADAMS
THIS DOCUMENT IS PROTECTED WITH
A RADIO FREQUENCY IDENTIFICATION TAG.
ANY ATTEMPT TO REMOVE IT FROM THE
MISSION PREPARATION BUILDING
WILL SET OFF AN ALARM.
DO NOT PHOTOCOPY OR MAKE NOTES

JANE OXFORD
(FORMERLY JANE HAMMOND)
—EARLY YEARS

Jane Hammond was born on a United States Army base in Hampshire, England, in 1950. She was the daughter of Captain

Marcus Hammond, a U.S. Army logistics specialist and his wife, Frances, a British citizen he'd met and married while based in the United Kingdom.

Jane spent her early years living at various military installations around the world. She was a bright girl with a rebellious streak. At fifteen, while living in Germany, Jane ran away with a nineteen-year-old private in the U.S. Marines. They surrendered themselves to the Parisian police three weeks later, when they ran out of money.

By this time Jane's father, Marcus Hammond, had risen to the rank of general and was close to retirement. He requested a final military posting near to his birthplace in California, believing that a return to the United States would help Jane settle down and gain qualifications to attend college.

General Hammond was posted to Oakland naval base in California. He was put in charge of the supply chain, shipping troops and equipment across the Pacific to the escalating war in Vietnam.

Jane, meanwhile, did not buckle down to her education as her father had hoped. She began to skip school regularly and hang out with a group of hippies.

Photographs from this era show a grubby-looking girl with long braided hair, strings of beads around her neck, and flared jeans with holes over the knees.

Jane became interested in anti-Vietnam War issues through a boyfriend called Fowler Wood. Twenty-year-old Fowler was a dropout from the nearby University of California and the chairman of a radical anti-Vietnam War protest group.

Fowler became fascinated with General Hammond's job. He'd been searching for a nonviolent way to blunt the American war effort and came up with the idea of sabotaging weapons passing through Oakland docks. Jane began digging into the papers her father brought home each night. She even broke into his office and took blank security passes for the wharves where the goods were being loaded onto ships.

Jane learned about a regular shipment of assault rifles. Fowler and his antiwar movement colleagues hatched a plan. It involved using stolen security passes to bring a truckload of caustic lime into the docks. The protestors planned to break open the weapon crates and shovel powdered lime over the guns. By the time the guns arrived in Vietnam, the lime would have corroded the metal, making them useless.

Two nights before the raid was set to take place, Fowler's peace group took a vote and decided that the guerrilla action was too risky. Or as Jane put it, "The little wimps chickened out." She immediately broke up with Fowler. She stole his car and her mother's checkbook and headed south, paying her way towards Mexico with bad checks.

JANE HAMMOND MEETS KURT OXFORD

Jane got as far as San Diego, which borders the Mexican town of Tijuana. She found a room in a cheap motel and began scouring the local bars, looking for someone who could sell her the fake passport and driver's licence she needed to cross the border. Instead, she found Kurt Oxford.

Kurt was a mountainous twenty-eight-year-old outlaw biker, complete with beard, tattoos, and a prison record for violent behavior and armed robbery. He'd cofounded a motorcycle club called the Brigands. At the time it was the second largest motorcycle gang in California and a bitter rival of the internationally famous Hell's Angels. Jane took up the offer of a room in Kurt's house, which also served as a clubhouse for the Brigands.

The Brigands were suspected of paying for their lifestyle by smuggling drugs across the border from Mexico, and Kurt's house was under twenty-four-hour police surveillance. Archived photographs show Jane making a rapid transformation from hippy to leather- and denim-clad biker. Police didn't bother enquiring as to who Jane was or where she had come from, because of the notoriously low status of women within the biker subculture (according to the rule book of the Brigand Motorcycle Club, women were not allowed to join the gang as full members, ride motorcycles except as pillion passengers, engage in any criminal activity, or speak at official club meetings except to offer food or drink to the men).

Kurt became excited when he heard Jane's story about the stolen security passes and the cases of guns at Oakland navy base, but he was no peace protestor. His plan was to steal two truckloads of guns and sell them on the black market to a drug dealing acquaintance in Mexico, who would in turn sell the weapons to rebel and terrorist groups in Africa and South America.

Jane had attended dozens of antiwar demonstrations while living in Oakland. Despite this, she readily agreed to Kurt's gun-smuggling plan. Criminal psychologists have described Jane's behavior as a textbook example of an extreme thrill seeker: a person with few moral scruples who finds everyday life boring and constantly craves dangerous relationships and activities.

THE RISE AND FALL
OF KURT & JANE OXFORD

Kurt Oxford and Jane Hammond robbed the docks at Oakland navy base on three separate occasions, earning themselves over $25,000 (equivalent to $145,000 at today's prices). Jane did some research and realized that every military supply depot in the United States used identical, easy-to-fake, security paperwork. Over the next two years, Kurt and Jane staged over eighty robberies on United States military facilities.

Jane had stolen reference books from her father that showed where different kinds of military supplies were stored. She would place an order over the phone, pretending to be the assistant of a senior officer in the logistics corps. The next day, a clean-shaven Kurt would arrive at the supply depot in an army surplus truck, wearing a uniform and carrying a set of authentic-looking paperwork that Jane had typed up in her motel room the night before. The truck would be loaded up and Kurt would drive out laden with weapons. The Mexican arms dealer would then ship the load to South America.

The beauty of this scheme was that the robberies went unnoticed; at least to begin with. With a quarter of a million troops on duty in Vietnam, thousands of U.S. military trucks were moving weapons and ammunition around the country. The paper-based stock control system made keeping an up-to-date tally on every movement impossible. Even when someone checked the paperwork and noticed that a truckload of guns had vanished, it would be several months after the event and everyone would assume it was a clerical error rather than a robbery.

By 1968, Kurt and Jane were earning over $20,000 (2005 equivalent – $110,000) a month from their illegal weapons business. With over half a million dollars stashed in overseas bank accounts, they had started flying first class and staying in five-star hotels.

They also stopped doing robberies themselves and began relying on members of the Brigands motorcycle gang to do their dirty work.

On 26 December 1968, Kurt Oxford and Jane Hammond landed in Las Vegas and booked a suite at the Desert Inn resort and casino. Kurt purchased a two-carat diamond ring and the next morning, he took his eighteen-year-old girlfriend on a limousine ride to a wedding chapel. After the ceremony, Kurt and Jane changed into swimwear, got drunk at the poolside, and began losing heavily at a floating blackjack table.

Kurt took offence when another blackjack player called him a fool. Kurt punched the man out and ended up being hauled into a back room by casino security. He was taken to the local police station, where the Las Vegas police ran a routine check. They found that Kurt had skipped bail on a Nevada assault charge five years earlier, following a fight between rival motorcycle gangs in Reno.

Less than six hours after getting married, Kurt was locked up in Las Vegas county jail, facing a three- to five-year sentence. Jane pledged to stand by her husband, but was then shocked to discover that her husband had violated his

California parole and that police there wanted to question him about an unsolved murder.

Kurt Oxford was extradited to California. On 24 January 1969, five days before his trial for murder was due to begin, Kurt became involved in a fight in the prison exercise yard. A guard fired a warning shot, but the fight continued and Kurt received a shotgun blast in his chest. He died of his wounds in the prison hospital eleven days later.

JANE OXFORD
—INTERNATIONAL ARMS DEALER

By the time she turned nineteen, Jane Oxford had run away from her family, amassed a half-million-dollar fortune (equivalent to $2.6 million today), got married, and seen her husband die in prison. Jane had no police record, apart from a missing persons report filed by her father in Oakland. Fearing a public scandal, General Hammond had honored the bad checks and compensated Fowler Wood for his stolen car.

Some people might have quit while they were ahead, but Jane Oxford spent the 1970s transforming herself from a thief into a big-time black-market weapons dealer. The business of stealing from the U.S. military thrived. When the army launched an investigation into the large amount of missing equipment and tightened up security, Jane developed more sophisticated techniques for relieving the U.S. military of its weapons. Every American base had its share of bored, broke, and homesick servicemen who were willing to turn a blind eye, or drive a truck off-base in return for a car, or enough cash to put down a deposit on a home.

The next step in developing the business was for Jane to bypass her Mexican connection and deal directly with people who wanted to buy the stolen weapons. She traveled the world using a variety of aliases and disguises, making contacts with terrorist groups, drug tsars, local warlords, and dictators. Jane brokered deals to sell weapons from all over the world, but most of her profits continued to stem from her unique web of corrupt contacts within the U.S. military.

THE GHOST

In 1982 a retired member of the Brigands bike gang called Michael Smith was arrested at the gates of an army base in Kentucky after attempting to pass a security check with a truckload of mortars. Smith had lost the paperwork given to him by an associate of Jane Oxford and stupidly tried to carry out the robbery using crudely altered paperwork from a previous raid.

Smith had been involved in dozens of military supply thefts over the preceding decade. He offered to give the U.S. military police information on Jane Oxford and her organization in return for a light prison sentence. Smith was stunned by the answer the U.S. military police gave him: Not only was nobody looking for Jane Oxford, they'd never even heard of her.

Following Michael Smith's tip-off, Jane Oxford went from being an unknown to a spot on the FBI's most wanted list. The FBI, CIA, and U.S. military police set up a two-hundred-person task force to bring Jane Oxford to justice. The trouble was, almost nothing was known about her.

After fourteen years of successfully stealing American weapons, Jane had put distance between herself and the day-to-day operation of her organization. Nobody knew who her deputies were, what country she lived in, if she'd married again or had children. Jane had made no contact with her parents since leaving home sixteen years earlier, and the nearest thing to an up-to-date picture was the photograph found in the uncollected personal effects of the late Kurt Oxford. It had been taken in the Las Vegas wedding chapel in 1969 and to this day it remains the most recent photograph of Jane Oxford on FBI records. After numerous stings, surveillance operations, attempts at infiltration, and twenty million hours of police work, Jane Oxford is still at large. The FBI task force chasing after Jane call her The Ghost.

CURRENT STATUS OF JANE OXFORD'S ORGANIZATION

The world is now awash with cheap, illegal weapons produced in former communist countries. Consequently, it is impossible to turn a profit stealing everyday weapons from the American military. Nowadays, it is America's high-tech weapons that are of interest to black-market weapons dealers.

Since 1998, it is believed Jane Oxford has orchestrated more than twenty carefully planned thefts of high-tech equipment from the U.S. military. Stolen items have included night-vision sights for sniper rifles, unmanned miniature surveillance aircraft, radar-jamming equipment, plasma-injecting anti-tank shells, and surface-to-air missiles. These relatively compact loads are easily smuggled across the U.S./ Mexican border and each one is worth millions of dollars to the right customer.

The latest and most serious act was the theft of thirty-five PGSLM Buddy missiles, which were crossing the Nevada desert en route to a British military cargo aircraft. After this theft Jane Oxford was promoted to second place on the FBI's list of most wanted criminals.

AN UNEXPECTED BREAKTHROUGH

In May 2004 a troubled fourteen-year-old boy named Curtis Key escaped the night curfew at an Arizona military boarding school and ploughed through a set of locked gates in his commandant's car. He parked up at a nearby liquor store, picked up a bottle of Coke, and asked the clerk for vodka from behind the counter. When the clerk asked for proof of age, Curtis Key produced a handgun and shot the clerk through the heart. He calmly emptied half the bottle of Coke onto the floor, topped up the bottle with vodka, and took a long drink. CCTV cameras inside the store filmed the entire event.

On the way out Curtis spotted a man getting out of a Jaguar. After shooting the driver and his girlfriend dead, Curtis took the Jaguar and drove more than twenty miles at high speed, slugging the mixture of vodka and Coke the whole time. When he heard the sirens of three chasing police cars, Curtis—by now paralytically drunk—pulled up at the roadside. He picked his gun off the passenger seat, pushed the muzzle against his head, and pulled the trigger. The bullet jammed in the chamber.

Under Arizona state law, anyone aged fourteen or over charged with a serious offence such as murder can be tried and sentenced to the same prison term as an adult. In October 2004 Curtis Key was deemed mentally fit and given life without parole. This sentence means Curtis will spend the rest of his life in prison. He is currently one of the 270 offenders serving time in the specially built young offenders unit at Arizona Maximum Security Prison, known by its staff and inmates as Arizona Max.

Bizarrely, Curtis's parents did not come forward after his arrest. The home address registered at the military school turned out not to exist and Curtis's school fees had been paid from an untraceable bank account in the Seychelles. Curtis claimed that he had lost his memory and remembered nothing about his mother and father.

Arizona police suspected Curtis was protecting a parent or parents who were wanted criminals and sent his DNA profile to the FBI. The profile showed there was a 99 percent chance that Curtis was a descendant of General Marcus Hammond, who had agreed to give a DNA sample to the FBI team trying to locate his daughter.

There was only one possible explanation: Curtis Key was the son of Jane Oxford.

WHAT USE IS CURTIS OXFORD?

The FBI was delighted. The unearthing of Curtis Key was the biggest breakthrough in the twenty-two-year hunt for Jane Oxford. The FBI didn't let on that they'd uncovered Curtis's true lineage and mounted close surveillance on him. They sent an officer into Arizona Max to work as a guard on Curtis's young offender unit and carefully monitored all his communications, both with other prisoners and with the outside world in the form of letters and telephone calls.

Jane Oxford was clearly working behind the scenes. Her

connections within the biker community put out word inside Arizona Max that Curtis was untouchable. Anyone trying to bully, extort money, or otherwise harm Curtis could expect both themselves and their families on the outside to face savage retribution. Two prison officers on Curtis's unit also reported to their superiors that they had been approached by a mysterious biker, offering them $1,500 a month if they agreed to look out for Curtis and occasionally smuggle items into his cell.

While Jane Oxford was doing all she could to look after her son, the FBI's hopes that she would stick her neck out and try to visit Curtis were never realized. Apart from his lawyer, the only people on Curtis Key's list of approved telephone contacts and visitors were two men from Las Vegas who claimed to be Curtis's uncles. Covert DNA tests carried out on the men showed that they were not blood relatives of Curtis. Despite this, the men were put on the approved contacts list and the conversations that took place during their visits were bugged.

Curtis seemed to know his visitors well and they clearly had contacts with his mother. The men are still under FBI surveillance. Unfortunately, this surveillance has yet to yield any useful information on the activities or whereabouts of Jane Oxford.

As Curtis's first months in prison passed by, the FBI became convinced that their big breakthrough had turned into a damp squib. To minimize the already slight chance that anyone would dare to harm Curtis, his visitors informed the prison authorities that his real name was Curtis Oxford, and told Curtis to reveal his true identity to fellow inmates. Once this secret was out, the FBI realized that the chances of Jane ever visiting her son had shrunk to zero.

ESCAPE & INFILTRATE

If Jane Oxford wasn't planning to visit her son in prison, the next best thing would be if Curtis got out and someone could follow him back to his mother. The FBI studied a number of options for getting Curtis out of prison. They looked for legal loopholes that would get Curtis off the hook and considered a scheme where the Arizona police miraculously discovered new evidence that would make Curtis look innocent.

The problem was, clear video

footage showed Curtis shooting the clerk in the liquor store; he had pleaded guilty in court, and the feelings of the families of his three victims also had to be taken into consideration. Besides, Jane Oxford has spent the last thirty years sniffing out FBI stings. If her son was miraculously released from prison, she would undoubtedly smell a giant rat.

The FBI realized that Jane would be less suspicious if her son escaped from prison. They devised an elaborate plan that they called "Escape and Infiltrate." It involved sending undercover agents into Arizona Max as prisoners. The agents would win Curtis's trust and then announce that they had found an escape route. They would offer Curtis a chance of escape; in return, they would ask Curtis to get Jane Oxford to protect them and set them up with false identities in another country.

Jane Oxford might be suspicious, but the FBI reckoned that if every detail of Curtis's escape was made to look absolutely real, including the faked murder of a prison guard and a full police alert to recapture the escapees, she might just buy it.

If the agents managed to pull off their escape and hold Jane and Curtis up to their end of the bargain, they would gain unprecedented access to Jane Oxford's organization and perhaps even make contact with Oxford herself.

The FBI agreed that it was a risky plan. They rated the chances of success at less than one half, and the undercover agents would be at serious risk of death or injury at the hands of other law enforcement agencies that would be out trying to recapture them. But the biggest stumbling block was that under Arizona law, juveniles may be tried as adults and held inside adult prisons, but they cannot be held "within sight or sound" of adult prisoners. If the FBI wants to get undercover agents to befriend Curtis Oxford, they will have to wait until he turns eighteen and is moved into the adult population of Arizona Max. This is not due to happen until 2009.

THE ROLE OF BRITISH INTELLIGENCE & CHERUB

Although Jane Oxford was known to British intelligence, she had never stolen British military equipment and was regarded as an American problem until the theft of the thirty-five Buddy missiles in March 2005. The British began an investigation to see if anyone on their side of the Atlantic had leaked details about the movement of the Royal Air Force cargo aircraft sent across the Atlantic to collect the missiles. They also sent a senior British intelligence officer to America to work alongside the FBI team investigating the theft.

The MI5 officer sent a top-secret briefing back to Britain. It included details of the FBI's long-term plan to send undercover agents into Arizona Max and escape with Curtis Oxford. When the chairman of CHERUB read this briefing, he realized that the FBI's ambitious "Escape and Infiltrate" plan could be carried out immediately if underage CHERUB agents were sent into the juvenile unit at Arizona Max. An escape carried out by people too young to be employed by law enforcement agencies would also make it easier to convince Jane Oxford that the escape is genuine.

John Jones has been selected as Mission Controller and has begun working out exact details of a plan that will send two CHERUB agents into Arizona Max, with a third CHERUB agent aiding the escape on the outside.

NOTE: THE CHERUB ETHICS COMMITTEE PASSED THIS MISSION BRIEFING ON CONDITION THAT ALL AGENTS UNDERSTAND THE FOLLOWING:

This mission has been classified HIGH RISK. All agents are reminded of their right to refuse to undertake this mission and to withdraw from it at any time. The mission will involve incarceration in a dangerous prison environment and pursuit by armed prison guards and police. For security reasons, only a tiny number of senior law enforcement officials will be aware that CHERUB and the FBI have set up the escape.

While every possible step will be taken to ensure your safety, the agents deployed on this mission are urged to consider the dangers carefully before accepting their role.

"Wow," James said, when he put the briefing down on John Jones's desk. "That whole breaking-out-of-prison deal sounds *berserk*."

"I'm not asking for an instant decision," John said. "But this is our only half-decent shot at getting hold of Jane Oxford and the Buddy missiles. How about you think it through and come and see me in the morning?"

James shook his head. "I'm not *scared*," he said firmly. "I'll do it."

John smiled. "I'd be much happier if you slept on it

before making a final decision. I'll even allow you to discuss it with Meryl Spencer if you want."

"Whatever," James said dismissively. "I take it me and Dave are the two people going into Arizona Max?"

John nodded. "You're only a few months younger than Curtis Oxford and roughly the same physical size. You're a perfect candidate to make friends with him. For the purposes of the mission, Dave will be your older brother. We need a big guy like him to protect you on the inside and to dress up as a guard during the escape. He's also got lots of high-speed driving experience."

"So who's the third person on the mission?" James asked. "The one who's going to help our escape from outside the prison."

"We want someone who would pass as a sibling or cousin to you and Dave," John explained. "But we're having a tricky time finding the right person."

"What about my sister, Lauren?" James asked. "Today's her last day of basic training. If she gets through she'd be eligible to come."

John smiled. "Lauren's a good kid, James. But I'm really looking for someone more experienced."

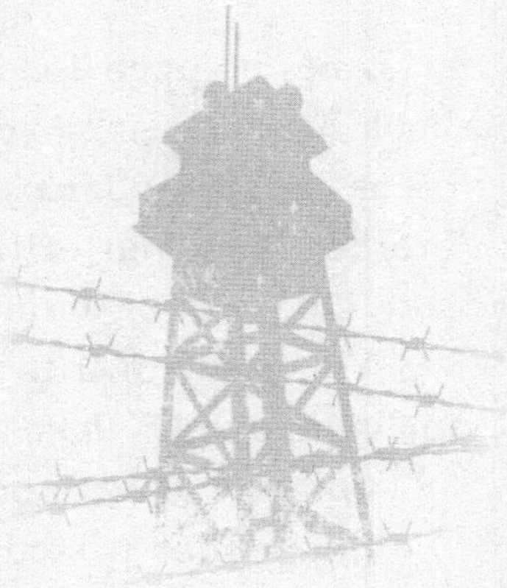

CHAPTER 8

WARMER

James caught a glimpse as the minibus driven by Mr. Large passed the window of his classroom. He leapt noisily out of his chair, making his maths teacher turn away from the whiteboard in mid-sentence.

"They're back from training," James explained excitedly, grabbing the olive-colored combat coat off the back of his chair. "Can I go meet my sister?"

Luckily, maths was James's best subject and he was on good terms with Mrs. Brennan. She handed James his homework assignment, which he stuffed inside his backpack as he jogged down the corridor between the classrooms and out through a set of double doors into the cold.

James stopped for a moment to zip up his coat and hook his backpack over both shoulders so it didn't slide off as he ran. As James did this, Bethany's eight-year-old brother burst out of the doors behind him. Jake was a cute kid, with big brown eyes and spiky hair.

"You going over to meet them as they leave the training compound?" Jake asked.

"Course," James nodded.

"I hope they passed training," Jake said.

"Didn't Bethany call you or anything?" James asked, surprised. "I was out at a mission briefing, but there was a voice mail on my mobile when I got back. Lauren was in the terminal at Toronto airport, waiting for a flight to London. She said she'd hurt her foot, but everyone had made it through."

"Safe," Jake grinned. "I'll race you."

Jake belted off across the grass with his backpack rattling up and down. James jogged after him at a steady pace. There was no reason to run flat out; Mr. Large would make the trainees pack up all their stuff and tidy the training compound before he let them go.

When Jake got a hundred meters ahead, he stopped running and turned back towards James with a wounded look. "Are you racing or not?" he shouted.

James was looking forward to seeing his sister and Jake's enthusiasm was contagious. "I'm just giving you a start," he jeered, as he broke into a full sprint. "You'll need it."

Jake squealed and started running again. It took James a couple of hundred meters to close the gap, by which time the two boys were running across a couple of muddy football pitches. The wire fence around the training compound was visible in the distance.

Instead of sprinting past, James decided it would be funny if he ran up behind Jake and gave him a friendly shove in the back. Jake stumbled forwards and ploughed into the soft ground.

"Enjoy the mud, El-Squirto," James hooted.

He started to think he'd overdone it when Jake made no attempt to get back up. He stopped running and walked back towards the little ball rolled up on the grass.

James leaned over nervously. "Are you OK?"

"I think you broke my arm," Jake whimpered.

James felt a queasy sensation rise up from his guts. There'd be no easy way to talk himself out of hurting an eight-year-old, even though it was an accident. Jake might end up in the hospital, he'd be in trouble, and it would ruin Lauren and Bethany's return from training.

"I'm sorry," James said, gently rubbing Jake's shoulder. "Can you move your arm at all? Do you really think it's broken?"

Jake's expression changed to a grin as his muddy hand tightened around James's wrist. The eight-year-old yanked James's arm forward, while simultaneously hooking his foot around James's ankle and sweeping his boot from under him.

James overbalanced, ending up sprawled out on the soggy ground alongside Jake. The younger boy quickly scooped up a clod of mud, splatted it against James's cheeks and then combed his mucky fingers upwards through James's blond hair.

While James lay on the floor, stunned by the icy

brown water trickling down his neck, Jake exuberantly sprang to his feet.

"I'm in *so* much pain," Jake sneered. *"Suck-ahhh."*

Jake jogged the last stretch towards the gates of the training compound, flailing his arms in the air and bowing to an imaginary crowd. James staggered to his feet and did the best he could to wipe the water out of his ear with a crinkled-up tissue.

"Cheating little git," James shouted bitterly, as it occurred to him that he should have known better: every kid at CHERUB did karate and judo training and even little guys like Jake knew some smart moves.

James saw the funny side once the shock wore off. When he got up to the gate of the training compound, joining siblings and close friends of the other trainees, he pulled out the chocolate bar he'd been saving for morning break and gave Jake two squares to make it clear there were no hard feelings.

"I'll have to get you back for that," James said.

"Can try if you like," Jake shrugged confidently, as he crammed the rectangle of chocolate into his mouth with his grubby fingers.

James got excited as soon as he saw the trainees in their gray T-shirts. The first four jogged down the concrete path from the compound, but Lauren was limping slightly. She had her bandaged foot in an unlaced trainer and Bethany loyally at her side.

James didn't like Bethany much. He was happy that Lauren had found a close friend, but when the two girls were together they drove him mad with their girlie talk and half-hour giggling fits over the lamest jokes.

Jake got scooped into his big sister's arms, as James wrapped Lauren in a tight hug and kissed her cheek. Lauren looked taller and her shoulders seemed more muscular than before. James felt a twinge of sadness at the passing of the chubby-faced little sister he'd had when their mum died eighteen months earlier.

"You look so grown up," James sniffled happily. "Congratulations . . . I'm so proud of you."

"I missed you," Lauren sniffed back.

Lauren's mood evaporated when she saw the dirty brown marks James had smeared over her uniform.

"For *God's* sake," she gasped, as she backed away. "Where have you been? What happened to your hair?"

"Me and Jake had a race on the way over here," James explained. "It got a bit out of hand."

"And *I* won," Jake interrupted.

"Rolling in the mud with an eight-year-old," Lauren sneered, as she smudged a tear off her cheek. "That sounds about your level. . . . We had to wait five hours when we changed planes at Toronto airport. I got you a present in the gift shop."

Lauren pulled a brown paper bag out of her jacket and handed it to James. He opened it up, revealing a fleece hat with yellow and blue tassels dangling off either end.

"Cheers," James grinned, as he stretched it over his muddy hair. "It's in Arsenal away colors."

Bethany had bought an identical hat for Jake and the two boys headed back towards the main building, hats on, listening to their sisters rabbiting about stuff that had happened during training.

• • •

James wasn't sure if his teachers would let him off the rest of the day's lessons to hang out with Lauren. He got around this thorny issue by not bothering to ask. He decided if he got pulled up, he'd act emotional about Lauren's return and get off with a few punishment laps at worst.

Lauren had been allocated one of the newly converted rooms on the eighth floor, where the old mission preparation suites had been. She wouldn't let James cross the threshold until he'd washed his hair and put on clean uniform.

The layout was the same as the room James had two floors below. There was a double bed, ensuite bathroom, laptop, mini fridge, microwave, and a little lounge area by the door with a two-seat sofa, where you could watch TV or play video games.

James was a bit jealous: he'd inherited his room from another kid, whereas everything in Lauren's room was spanking new. The rooms at the front of the building also had sliding glass doors and balconies that overlooked gardens, rather than the windows overlooking the muddy football pitches you got at the back.

It took three round trips in an electric golf buggy to bring Lauren's stuff over from her old room in the junior building, followed by a dozen rides carrying boxes up to the eighth floor in the lift. It was lunchtime by the time James and Lauren were through.

Lauren hobbled down to the storeroom on the fourth floor and got a ton of junk food to stock up her fridge: drinks, snacks, and chocolate. She also grabbed two Snickers ice creams and two microwave burritos out of the freezer for their lunch.

The microwave meals were supposed to be for kids who'd arrived back from a mission, or training, after the canteen closed in the evening. James would have preferred the proper food being served downstairs, but Lauren wanted to zap something in her new microwave.

When they'd finished the burritos, James and Lauren opened the balcony doors to let out the stink and sprawled out next to each other on the double bed, too stuffed to bother getting on with the unpacking.

"Man," Lauren said, rubbing her tummy and doing a little burp. "At least I've got a week off before I have to restart lessons. I'm so whacked after training, I'm gonna sleep till noon every day, then steam in the bath all afternoon, reading books and stuffing my face."

"Sounds good to me," James smirked. "I'm only gonna be around for a couple more days. I'm off on some mission in America. I tried to get you on it, but John Jones didn't sound keen. He thinks you're too inexperienced."

"What's the mission all about?" Lauren asked.

Before James got to answer, he had a mental jolt. "Oh shit . . . ," he gasped. "John's gonna kill me."

Lauren sat up anxiously. "Why? What have you done?"

"It's like, a *massive*, important mission and I was supposed to give him my final decision about going on it this morning."

James dived off Lauren's bed, grabbed her telephone and dialed John Jones's extension. It got picked up straight away.

"James," John said tersely. "Where have you been? I've been to your room, I've been round all your teachers,

I've been asking all your friends if they've seen you, and I've even left messages on your mobile."

"I'm *really* sorry," James groveled. "My mobile's flat and the mission totally went out of my head when Lauren got out of training this morning. I started helping her unpack and—"

"Are you with us on this mission or not?" John interrupted.

"Sure," James said. "You knew there was never any doubt in my mind."

"I'd like to speak with Lauren too," John said.

"You said she was too young."

"I've thought it through," John said. "Time is tight, and we don't have a lot of suitable candidates for the third spot. If we tweak things slightly, the cute little girl factor might even work in our favor when you're on the run."

"I don't know if she's up to it, John. She's got a bad foot and she's wiped out from training."

Lauren realized she was being talked about. She scrambled excitedly across the bed and whispered in her brother's ear, "I'm not *that* tired."

James moved the earpiece away from Lauren, so he could hear what John was saying:

"Her part of the mission wouldn't start until after you escape from Arizona Max, so she'll have a few days to relax."

"She seems quite keen," James said, as his sister nodded frantically.

"Good," John replied. "Now, stop whatever you're doing and get over here sharpish."

"One day out of training and I've already got my first mission," Lauren squealed, as James put the phone down.

"*Bloody* hell," James moaned, as he pulled his ringing head away from his sister. "Did you have to shout that right down my ear?"

"Sorry," Lauren giggled. "I'm just excited. Bethany's gonna be *hell* jealous."

CHAPTER 9

BACKGROUND

John Jones was concerned by Lauren's eagerness to go on the mission before she'd even read the briefing. He sent James and Dave Moss out of his office and sat on a corner of his desk, telling Lauren about the dangers she might face and trying to satisfy himself that a ten-year-old would be able to handle them.

John had spent the previous eighteen years working for the adult branch of the intelligence service. He'd been in charge of undercover missions in all parts of the world and had seen operatives killed, imprisoned, and badly injured. John could get his head around boys like James and Dave going undercover—they were teenagers and their unarmed combat training meant they could handle themselves against most adults—but Lauren made him uncomfortable.

Part of John's problem was that his own daughter was a few months older than Lauren. He worried about her crossing two main roads on her way to school, and whether she was being properly looked after when she went off on camping trips with her youth group. John's gut instinct told him something was deeply wrong about sitting with a girl of the same age, discussing jail breaks and the best thing to do when the cops start shooting at you.

But Lauren was well trained. Her answers to John's questions showed she was intelligent enough to understand the risks she was being asked to take and the reasons why they were worth taking. After an hour going through every detail of the mission, John had stopped worrying about Lauren and started asking himself what his own daughter might be capable of if she'd been pushed through CHERUB training, instead of spending her days being chauffeured between piano lessons, drama club, and friends' houses in his ex-wife's car.

A CIA officer based at the American embassy in London worked into the early hours of Tuesday morning, creating identification documents in the names of James Rose, Lauren Rose, and David Rose. Lauren's and Dave's dates of birth were their real ones, but James's had been put back exactly one year to make him fourteen: old enough to be sentenced to Arizona Max.

A motorcycle messenger drove through the night. He arrived at CHERUB campus at 6 a.m. with a sealed pouch containing three American passports and four sets of diplomatic paperwork. This paperwork gave John Jones and the three young agents immunity from American laws for the duration of the mission.

It was dark outside, but James was already up. He'd showered, packed his bag, and received a call from Lauren, who sounded like she'd worked herself into a state.

"I don't know what to pack," Lauren said, when James got upstairs to her room. "And I can't find half the stuff I do want."

James put it down to first-mission jitters. Once he'd calmed Lauren down, he helped her go through all the unpacked boxes and find the clothes and equipment she needed for the mission.

"You usually get a list of what to pack," James explained, as he rummaged through a cardboard box, searching for the spare battery and charger for Lauren's digital camera. "But this has all been put together at the last minute. I guess John didn't have time."

When Lauren was satisfied that everything she needed was packed, both kids put their in-flight packs over their backs and wheeled their suitcases along the corridor to the lift.

Downstairs in the canteen, John and Dave were at a table together. They had their luggage standing beside their chairs and their cooked breakfasts were already half eaten.

John glanced at his watch. "Cutting it a bit fine, aren't we?"

"My fault," James said. "Alarm didn't go off."

Lauren gave James a smile as they grabbed plates at the breakfast buffet. "Thanks for taking the blame."

According to the background story John had devised for the mission in conjunction with the FBI, James and Dave were presently being held in a Nebraska prison, awaiting transfer back to Arizona, where they were about to be tried for murder. This ruled out flying into Arizona aboard a commercial jet, in case one of the four hundred other passengers had links with Arizona law enforcement or prisons.

They were flying from a Royal Air Force base fifteen minutes drive from campus. The CHERUB driver pulled up the minibus on a taxiway beside the wingtip of a small passenger jet. The RAF pilot and copilot loaded the luggage into the cargo hold, while a customs official shook John Jones's hand and took a cursory glance at the four American passports.

John and the kids went up six metal steps. Everyone except Lauren had to duck as they passed through the door into the aircraft. The cabin was cramped but luxuriously fitted with deep pile carpet, a spray of fresh cut flowers, walnut trim, and four leather armchairs down each side that faced each other so you could hold a meeting.

By the time James had done up his seatbelt and kicked off his trainers, the copilot had pulled the steps in and was shutting the cabin door. Thirty seconds later, the aircraft began taxiing towards the runway.

"Cool," James said to Lauren, who was sitting opposite. "Beats arriving at the airport three hours before check-in."

The copilot stood in the middle of the cabin with his neck stooped to avoid the ceiling. "Welcome aboard the Royal Air Force's high-speed taxi service," he grinned. "Make sure your seatbelts are on for takeoff. We're going to be flying higher and faster than the commercial jets you might be used to, so we should make it to Arizona in around seven and a half hours, including our refueling stop. The toilet is in the back and there's a fridge stocked with sandwiches and things. There's also a microwave and hot-drinks machine up there, so feel free to tuck in whenever you get the munchies."

The copilot stumbled through the juddering aircraft to his seat in the cockpit and belted himself in as the plane stopped moving at the end of the runway. James noticed Lauren's fingernails digging into the arms of her leather chair.

"Still not keen on flying?" James grinned.

"Shut your face," Lauren said stiffly.

The engines opened up and the pilot's voice came over the intercom. "All passengers, prepare for takeoff."

"These little planes crash all the time," James shouted, as his body was pushed against the arm of his seat by the rapid acceleration. "They're really dangerous."

Lauren booted James in the shin as the nose-wheel lifted off the runway.

Once the plane leveled off, John Jones got everyone hot drinks and biscuits, including the two pilots. When they'd finished drinking, he closed the cockpit door so the pilots couldn't overhear.

"How are you all getting on with memorizing your

mission details and background stories for your characters?" he asked.

"I'm getting there," Lauren said.

James and Dave didn't look so confident.

"So let's test you out," John said. "Lauren, first, what accent are you going to speak in?"

"My normal English accent."

John nodded. "Good. Why is that?"

"Because it's impossible to keep up a false accent over a long mission, particularly when you're under stress."

"No, no," John said. "I wasn't asking why we try and avoid using accents generally. I mean how do you explain your English accent if someone asks why you speak that way during the mission?"

"Right, sorry," Lauren said. "Our father was Robert Rose, a businessman who worked in London. We grew up there, but moved back to live with our uncle in Arizona three years ago, after our father died of throat cancer."

"Excellent," John said. "James's turn. What was your first criminal offence?"

"I got picked up by Arizona police after Dave and me ram-raided a branch of PC Planet. We stole fifteen thousand dollars' worth of digital cameras and made a clean getaway, but we got busted a month later when we tried to sell them on eBay."

"What sentence did you receive?"

"Twelve months' suspended prison sentence and two hundred hours' community service."

"*Fifty* hours," John said tersely. "You need to know your background story like it's your own life, James.

Tell me how you got the alarm codes to break into the car dealership?"

"Dave and I were pretty lonely. We didn't have any friends in Arizona, so we started getting into computer hacking. Dave drove around Phoenix, while I sat in the passenger seat using a laptop computer and sniffer software to find unsecured wireless networks. We were hoping to get someone's credit card number, or details of company bank accounts. When we hacked into the network at a secondhand-car dealership, we found a document on the hard drive that had all the staff burglar-alarm codes.

"I hid in the boot of a BMW on the car lot, climbed out after closing time, and turned off the alarms. We stole eight thousand dollars in cash and drove away from the scene in an almost new Lexus RX300. During our get-away the car veered up onto the sidewalk and killed a homeless woman who was sleeping there. This robbery and the death of the homeless woman were reported in local newspapers at the time, so we're covered if Jane Oxford wants to check our story out."

"What if they find the people who really robbed the car dealership?" Lauren asked.

"The FBI frequently sends officers into prisons to work undercover, either to wheedle information out of suspects or uncover drug trafficking and gang activities," John explained. "A realistic background story is essential for the officers' safety inside prison, so the FBI creates so-called *ghost crimes*. Ghost crimes are set up by FBI officers and reported to local police and media as if they're for real."

"But what about the homeless woman?" Lauren asked.

John shrugged. "I expect they found a homeless woman who died of a heart attack and changed the details on her death certificate so that it looked like she'd been hit by a car. The FBI likes to have a few unsolved ghost crimes in every state so that they can rapidly infiltrate any prison in the country."

Lauren nodded. "That's clever."

"So, Dave," John said, "what happened after you ran the old lady over?"

Dave cleared his throat before he spoke. "James and I got out of the car to see what I'd hit. When I realized it was a person, we panicked and drove home. We grabbed our money and stuff, left a note for Lauren and our uncle John and headed north. We spent two days on the run in the Lexus, before we got into another traffic accident in Nebraska. I got some head injuries that match up with a real scar I got in a skiing accident last year. James escaped unhurt and got caught by police after a brief chase on foot."

"OK," John said. "James, take the story from there."

"The police busted us and put us in a remand home. We got taken to Omaha juvenile court and sentenced to six months."

"Why didn't any other prisoners see you when you were in Nebraska?"

James looked blank. Lauren stuck her finger in the air and started rocking from side to side. "I know," she said excitably.

"This is *not* good, James," John said, shaking his head. "You should have remembered basic details like this by now. If necessary, we're going to spend this entire flight going over this story, until all three of you can recite it backwards, forwards, and inside out. . . . Go on, Lauren; tell your brother why no other prisoners saw James and Dave during their six months in Nebraska."

"Because they nearly escaped," Lauren said. "Dave managed to pocket some handcuff keys in the Nebraska courthouse. James and Dave released each other and got as far as the lawn in front of the courthouse before a police officer spotted their orange prison uniforms and pulled a gun on them. Because they were an escape risk, James and Dave were locked up in single cells with no privileges and no contact with the rest of the prison population."

John explained. "The idea behind having this escape in your back story is that it will make your plan to get out of Arizona Max seem much more credible when you're trying to make Curtis Oxford believe that he has a realistic chance of escaping with you."

CHAPTER 10
ARIZONA

They cleared customs at a United States Air Force base in Wisconsin. The opportunity to stretch their legs at the side of the runway while the jet was refuelled turned into a snowball fight. By the time they touched down at another USAF base in Arizona three hours later, John and the kids were sick of being cooped up and desperate for some hot food.

The change in time zones meant it was 7:45 a.m., just twenty minutes after they'd set off from England. As they stepped off the plane, the sun was breaking and the air felt dry on what looked like becoming a typical sunny day in the Arizona desert.

An Air Force man in a jumpsuit, mirrored sunglasses,

and ear protectors brusquely ordered them to follow the yellow line painted on the tarmac to the terminal—though terminal was a grand description for a metal hut with a chipboard floor, five seats, and a coffee machine. The only person inside was a stocky black man wearing a powder-blue suit and cowboy hat. He stood up and shook John's hand.

"Marvin Teller, FBI special ops."

"Good finally to meet you in the flesh," John replied. "And these three must be the undercover team."

Marvin crushed Dave's and James's hands as he shook them. James realized it was a test of character and didn't wince. When Marvin got to Lauren, he pulled his hand away and broke into a smile.

"How old is this little lady?" Marvin asked. "Doesn't look like she's been out of diapers more than a couple of months."

"I'm ten," Lauren said defensively. "What's a diaper?"

James smirked. "It's what the Yanks call nappies."

"So, you all hungry?" Marvin asked. "I know a diner a few miles down the way that'll fill you up with a gut-busting breakfast at four bucks a head."

After stuffing themselves with steaks, hash brown, eggs, and toast, Marvin took John and the kids on a sixty-mile journey along the interstate in a black saloon car. Everyone craned their necks around when they passed the exit marked ARIZONA MAXIMUM SECURITY PENITENTIARY, but the prison was set in a desert basin two miles from the turnoff, so there was nothing to see except the Arizona state flag and a few hundred meters of sand-swept tarmac.

They finished up at a lonely wooden house at the end of a secluded dirt track, twenty miles from the prison. The sun had cracked the paint off the wooden slats covering the outside, while the inside suggested that the previous inhabitants had been elderly. There were extra handrails on the stairs and two high-backed chairs in the living room, pointing towards an ancient TV that made you get off your butt and twiddle a knob to change the channel.

"We've found ourselves a friendly judge who'll hear James and Dave's guilty plea early on Thursday morning," Marvin explained. "That gives you the rest of today and all of tomorrow to settle in and rest up. There's food in the fridge and two cars in the garage, both with blacked-out windows like you asked for."

"Was that a problem?" John asked.

Marvin shook his head. "A lot of people have the windows darkened out here in the desert. It keeps the sun off."

"I want to get these kids some driving experience on American roads," John explained. "They'll need it during the escape, and we don't want anyone seeing James or Lauren behind the wheel."

"I've got errands to run at my office over in Phoenix," Marvin said. "I'll be coming back to drive you to the courthouse Thursday morning. I'll also be sending our undercover officer inside Arizona Max up here to give the boys some pointers on keeping out of trouble on the inside."

By noon, the temperature was around 35 degrees Celsius and the antiquated air conditioning in the house seemed to be expending all its effort on making noise, rather than actually cooling anything down.

John was permanently on the phone, either to CHERUB campus or the FBI office in Phoenix, so James and Dave took it upon themselves to sweep out the bottom of the small outdoor swimming pool and try filling it up. They found pool chemicals in the garage, but the filter was blocked and all they got for their efforts was a little brown puddle and mucky fingers.

Lauren sat beside the pool on a plastic lounger, reading background material for the mission and watching the sweat patches on the boys' shirts growing bigger. She'd have liked a swim herself, but the campus doctor had told her to keep her foot dry until the wound on her sole healed up.

The boys eventually gave up and went inside to shower and change clothes. When they re-emerged, they stood on either side of Lauren's sun lounger with mischievous expressions on their faces.

"What?" Lauren asked suspiciously.

"Nothing," James grinned. "It's just, the escape plan recommends that you get some elementary driving experience, in case you end up behind the wheel when we're on the run from the cops. John wants us to give you your first driving lesson."

Dave jangled a set of car keys. It wasn't true that John had wanted the boys to take her driving. They'd begged John and he'd reluctantly agreed, because he was having trouble concentrating on the mission preparations with three bored, jet-lagged kids lurking around the house.

They got into a beat-up Toyota station wagon with blacked-out windows. Dave took it out of the garage, before switching seats with Lauren. She had to prop herself on a cushion, and even then the only way she could see over the dashboard and put her feet on the pedals at the same time was by sitting at the edge of the seat and practically hugging the steering wheel.

James adopted a crash position in the back and started giggling. "We're all gonna die."

Once Dave had explained the controls, he let Lauren take off the handbrake and slide the automatic gearbox into drive. She rolled forward a few meters before stamping clumsily on the brake and sending James sprawling out of his seat in the back.

Dave looked around at him. "Put your seatbelt on, dummy."

Driving an automatic car when there's no other traffic around is pretty easy. Once Lauren had mastered the driveway and made some easy three-point turns to get used to steering and reversing, Dave let her out on the dirt road leading up to the interstate.

Half an hour in, Lauren started complaining that her foot was hurting. James hadn't driven a car in three months and after sitting in the back watching Lauren, he was busting to give the car a thrashing on the dirt road. After he switched places with Lauren and belted up, he turned around to Dave.

"You got any American dollars on you?"

Dave nodded. "Why?"

"Remember that donut place we passed on the interstate? How about I drive out there and pick a box up?"

Dave checked out the money in his shorts. "I've got enough. Have you driven in America before?"

"Heaps," James lied. "I was on a mission in Miami last year."

James had only managed one brief high-speed getaway in Miami, but the CHERUB intermediate driving course he'd been on a few months earlier covered skills for fast roads as well as a few high-speed maneuvers, so he was a reasonably competent driver.

He floored the gas pedal, setting the rear wheels into a spin. As he got faster, the car started rocking and pebbles were clattering against the bottom of the car.

"Slow down," Dave said firmly.

James ignored him and kept his foot on the gas as the car approached the crest of a small hill. Dave put his hand on James's shoulder and spoke louder.

"Cut it out *now*, James. You're going way too fast."

James broke into a smile. "Who stuck a rod up your arse, Dave? I thought you were cool."

The front wheels lifted up as the car skimmed the top of the hillock. James spotted a pickup coming through the glare in the opposite direction, less than a hundred meters away. The road was wide enough for the vehicles to pass, but James hadn't anticipated any other traffic and was driving near the middle.

He felt a shot of adrenalin as he swung hard to the right and stamped the brake pedal. He avoided the pickup, which had swerved the other way, but now James was heading for the drainage ditch at the roadside. He desperately twirled the steering back to the left.

The nose turned in, but the violent maneuver made the back end swing out and the rear wheels dropped into the ditch.

The steering wheel juddered violently as airbags exploded in James and Dave's faces. The car lurched on crabwise, with two wheels up off the ground and half a mind to roll over.

When it stopped moving and crashed down on to the baked ground, James was too stunned to move. All he could do was breathe petrol fumes and grit, while staring dumbly at the half inflated airbag. His hands were shaking out of control.

Dave stumbled out of the passenger door, before opening up the rear and helping Lauren step out over the ditch. She was breathing hard, but didn't seem hurt.

James finally got his head together enough to realize there was a risk of leaking fuel causing a fire. He undid his seatbelt and stepped out into a cloud of dust. A figure emerged from the glaring sunlight and bundled him against the car.

"I *told* you," Dave shouted furiously. "You could have got us *killed*, you stupid little prick."

James realized that Dave was about to slap him, but he got pulled off by the driver of the pickup.

"Calm it down there," the driver shouted.

James's legs felt like jelly as he staggered away from the car. Lauren was standing a few meters away, but the thunderbolts coming out of her eyes made it clear she was in no mood to help out.

When the pickup driver had calmed Dave down, he stepped back and let out a wry laugh. The blond-haired man was wearing black trousers and a shirt with a crest and the initials ADOP embroidered on the sleeve. James realized it stood for "Arizona Department of Prisons."

"Name's Scott Warren," the man said. "I just finished my shift, and I headed down here to see three British kids and a man named John Jones. It's not exactly what I had in mind, but I guess I've found them. . . ."

CHAPTER 11

REGRET

James knew he was an idiot. He felt like running off into the desert and never coming back as he sulked in a stiff-backed armchair. The skin was peeling off the back of his neck where Dave had shoved him against the baking hot roof of the car.

John had dished out a twenty-minute lecture: how totally irresponsible he was, how he could have ruined the mission before it had started, how a two-hundred-horsepower car is not a toy, and how he was going to spend all the time between now and his court appearance grounded at the house studying the background materials for the mission.

James kept seeing the crash in his head, imagining

what might have happened if the car had rolled, or Lauren hadn't put her seatbelt on. He'd never have been able to live with himself if she'd been hurt.

While James sat with the curtains drawn feeling seriously sorry for himself, the others were cleaning up his mess. Dave found a tow rope and Scott Warren used his undamaged pickup to pull the back end of the Toyota out of the ditch and tow it back to the house.

The sideways slide had torn off the exhaust, buckled the front suspension, and damaged the chassis on the driver's side. The car didn't look a wreck, but Scott said it wouldn't be economical to do much repair work on an elderly car that was only worth a few thousand dollars.

Meanwhile, John drove out to a restaurant on the interstate and picked up fried chicken. When he got back, he told James to wash his face and come to the dining table.

James dragged his chair up to the big Formica table in the kitchen. Lauren and Dave both looked pissed at him. He considered saying sorry, but an apology didn't seem to properly reflect the gravity of what he'd done. He avoided eye contact as he grabbed a box of fries and a couple of drumsticks.

John put a bottle of Coke on the table and handed Scott a cold beer, before sitting down.

"I've spoken to James and he's been punished," John said firmly, addressing everyone at the table. "We're all aware of how lucky it was that nobody got hurt. Now, whatever your personal feelings are, we have to draw a line under what happened and get on with preparing for our mission as a team. This mission is too dangerous for us to have people holding grudges and not speaking to one another. Is that understood?"

Dave and Lauren nodded unenthusiastically.

"Good," John said. "James, shake Dave's and Lauren's hands."

James reached across the table. Shaking hands seemed like the kind of thing you'd ask a couple of six-year-olds to do, but he understood the point John was trying to get across.

"I'm really sorry," James said, as he let go of Lauren.

"You should be," she replied tersely.

"I shouldn't have shoved you," Dave said, as James grasped his chicken-grease-smeared hand. "I just freaked out after the crash."

James smiled uneasily. "Maybe you scared a bit of sense into me."

"Anyway," John said, "as you know, Scott is an FBI special agent. He's spent the last three months working undercover as a correctional officer inside the boys' wing at Arizona Max. He's just finished a twelve-hour shift and I expect he's tired, so I want you to listen carefully and we'll try not to waste any more of his time."

Scott had to chew up a mouthful of fries before he began speaking.

"Nothing I say or do can totally prepare you boys for what you're gonna face inside Arizona Max, but I'll give it my best shot. I guess the best way to start is by trying to give you an impression of the kind of kids who end up there.

"Pick up any newspaper, or switch on the TV news, and you'll see items about crimes that turn your stomach. You're going to be sharing that cell with the kind of people who committed those crimes. I'm talking about the meanest, nastiest kids on the face of the earth. Don't underestimate what they're capable of. Most of them have already killed someone, and in a prison environment, violence and ruthless bullying only enhances their status."

"Don't they get punished?" Dave interrupted.

"Like how?" Scott said, shaking his head. "These guys have zero chance of *ever* being released from prison, and there's no threat of the death sentence because the Supreme Court says you can't execute anyone under the age of eighteen. So, even if one of them kills you, the most we can do is move them into solitary confinement for a few months.

"This hard-core of thugs makes up about a quarter of the population, and they make life thoroughly miserable for the remainder. The weaker inmates are mostly kids who went off the rails one time and got themselves in deep trouble: guys who stuck up convenience stores so they had money to splash out on their girlfriends, middle-class kids who thought they could make some easy cash dealing drugs, or who snapped and murdered relatives who beat them up. A lot of these guys didn't get many breaks in life and they're usually a bit underpowered in the brains department. To be honest, I feel sorry for them."

"So what's the prison itself like?" James asked.

"Inexpensive," Scott answered abruptly.

The three kids all looked baffled, until Scott began to explain:

"Twenty or thirty years ago, a maximum-security prison was made up of cells, with bars along the front and a sliding door, exactly like you see in the movies. Most of the time you'd be locked up alone, perhaps with one other cellmate. But the prison population in America is exploding and cells are expensive: Everyone needs their own walls and doors; their own locks, and washbasins, and toilets, etcetera, etcetera. Once you've built all those expensive cells, you need lots of guards to make sure there's nothing naughty going on inside them.

"To get around this, modern facilities like Arizona Max have dormitory cells. The cell you'll be living in has two rows of eighteen single beds along the walls. Between each bed there's a waist-height partition, a small locker, and just about enough room to swing out your legs. At one end of the cell there's a bathroom with two toilets, three urinals, and two shower stalls. A few meters above your heads is a metal gantry, from where hacks like me can look down and keep an eye on you.

"The good thing about this arrangement is that it gives you twenty-four-hour access to Curtis Oxford. The bad news is that if one of your cellmates takes a dislike to you, he'll have twenty-four-hour access to *you*."

"How much violence is there?" Dave asked.

"In the three months I've been on that cellblock, I've only seen two stabbings, but there are regular fistfights and the weaker inmates get badly bullied. Young offenders' units are often nicknamed *gladiator schools*, because you've got no option but to learn to fight. Teenage boys are the most impulsive and dangerous section of the prison population."

John interrupted. "This is why we want you guys in and out of Arizona Max within two weeks."

"Don't the guards do anything to stop the violence?" Lauren asked.

Scott shook his head. "The guards—or hacks as everyone on the inside calls them—aren't going to do you any favors. The prison is twenty percent understaffed and pay isn't far above minimum wage, so don't expect them to risk their necks on your behalf.

"In the daytime there's about one hack for every forty inmates, at night it drops to one for every hundred. Those kind of staffing levels mean you're on your own. If things get brutal, we might fire a couple of baton rounds down from the gantry to break up a fight and we'll drag someone off to the prison hospital if there's a lot of blood sloshing around. Apart from that, you've got to fend for yourself."

"So what's the best way to deal with the violence?" James asked.

"You can't show any weakness," Scott said. "The second you walk into that cell, there are gonna be thirty guys sizing you up. The bad guys will want to know if they can get their hands on your money and belongings. The weaker inmates need to know if you're going to be trying to get your hands on their stuff, or if you're one of the real psychopaths who'll beat them up just for the fun of it.

"Statistics show that you have a seventy percent chance of being in a physical confrontation within your first two days inside an American prison. Where you're going inside Arizona Max, I'd put the chances at closer to ninety-nine percent. Dave is going to be a physical match for anyone in there, but James is going to be one of the smallest. Dave will have to protect him."

"I've done self-defense training," James said. "I'm a second-dan karate black belt."

"It's good that you can handle yourself," Scott said. "But nobody knows that when you walk through the cell door. All they'll see is that you're young and small, which makes you a target for the bullies. If someone starts on you, go in hard and try to make a good account of yourself. That way you'll earn respect and find that other inmates want you on their side."

"What about Curtis?" Dave asked. "Who looks after him?"

"Curtis has a couple of seventeen-year-old skinheads called Elwood and Kirch who make sure he doesn't get damaged. There's also word out that anyone who touches Curtis will be stabbed to death by a biker."

"Are there any bikers in that cell?" James asked.

Scott shook his head. "No, bikers are mostly men in their twenties and thirties, but all the kids in your cell are doing long sentences. They'll get transferred to the adult section of the prison when they turn eighteen and there will be a whole bunch of bikers ready to stab someone for Jane Oxford."

"How come?" James asked.

John answered the question. "One of the ways Jane has kept her organization strong is by looking after anyone who gets sent to prison. That means quality legal representation, financial support for families, and physical protection inside prison. She's very loyal to people who stay on her side. That's also one of the reasons we're optimistic that Jane will be happy to help you guys out if you successfully bust Curtis out of prison."

"Of course, it's a double-edged sword," Scott added. "People have tried to cut deals with the FBI and give information on Jane Oxford in return for immunity, or a shorter prison sentence. Most of them either met a nasty end inside prison, or withdrew their evidence when members of their family were threatened. One guy even got taken out by a sniper when he was supposed to be under protective custody."

James threw down a chicken bone and pushed away the last of his fries. Kyle, Gabrielle, and the others had probably started their recruitment missions by now. Scott's description of the brutality inside Arizona Max made him wonder if he wasn't really the one who'd drawn the short straw.

CHAPTER 12

sentence

James kept his head down on Wednesday morning, staying in his bedroom reading background documents for the mission and feeling bad about the accident he'd caused the day before.

His reading material included the inmate rulebook for Arizona Max, the personnel files of the officers who worked in the young offender block, and criminal records of the twenty-nine inmates who currently shared the dormitory cell with Curtis Oxford.

John managed to clean the gunge out of the pool filter and fill it up. They ate lunch in the sunshine at the poolside, while John re-tested the kids on their background stories and ran through the details of the escape plan.

When he was satisfied that everyone understood their job, he went inside to make phone calls.

James and Dave sat next to each other in the shallow end of the pool. Lauren was a few meters behind on a sun lounger. She resented the dressing over her foot, as she stared at the cool water and lazily fanned herself with a frond she'd snapped off one of the poolside palms.

Dave looked at James. "You don't seem like yourself. Are you scared?"

"A bit," James admitted. "Gladiator school sounds brutal."

Dave smiled. "I always get the jitters the day before a mission. You ever been on a roller coaster?"

"A few."

"Missions are like roller coasters. You know the bit when you first get on and you're going clunk-clunk-clunk up the lift hill? And you're thinking to yourself, *Why the hell am I putting myself through this?* Then after the ride, you get off and you're buzzing. You want to run straight around to the back of the queue to have another go."

James nodded. "When I got back from my last mission, they told me I had to spend a few months catching up with schoolwork. I was *so* gutted."

"I couldn't imagine leaving CHERUB and going back to being normal," Dave said. "It must be so boring having nothing in your life except school, homework, and a few mates."

"Sorry I didn't slow the car down when you told me to. I was being a tit."

Dave shrugged. "I guess we all make mistakes. I've certainly made my share."

"What's the dumbest thing you've ever done on a mission?"

"*Good* question," Dave laughed. "There's been a few. You know I nearly got kicked out of CHERUB after that mission with Janet Byrne?"

"Why's that?"

Dave made a bulge over his stomach using his hand. James kicked his feet out of the water and burst out laughing.

"Oh *that,*" James giggled. "Janet's totally hot. I can't *believe* you got her pregnant."

The idea of Dave having a kid was funny, but James mostly laughed out of relief that Dave didn't seem to be holding a grudge over the car wreck.

"It's not a joke, you know," Lauren said bitterly, suddenly looming over the side of the pool. "Janet's my Spanish tutor. She cried in her room for days worrying about what to do."

James couldn't control his giggling, so Lauren whipped him across the back with the dried-out palm stalk.

"That hurt," James whined, as he scrambled out of range towards the deep end of the pool.

"Good," Lauren yelled, as she hurled the palm away and stormed towards the house. "You're both sexist pigs."

James made sure Lauren wasn't coming back out before settling down beside Dave again.

"In a few years' time, some poor guy is gonna get a crush on your little sister, and you can't help but feel sorry for him."

"Yeah," James nodded, as he rubbed the red mark across his back. "All girls are nuts."

• • •

Lauren came into James's room at 5 a.m. on Thursday morning. Already dressed, she flicked her brother's ear to wake him up.

"John says you'd better get your worthless butt moving."

James scratched his head as he sat up. Lauren had barely spoken to him since the crash, so he was pleased when she leaned in and wrapped her arms around his sweaty back.

"What's that in aid of?" James grinned.

"Try not to do anything too stupid on the mission, eh? You might be an idiot, but you're the only brother I've got."

James laughed. Lauren felt a twinge of guilt as her index finger ran over the scratch where she'd whacked him the afternoon before. "I'm making a nice cooked breakfast for everyone," she said softly.

James was shocked when he got out of the shower and walked through to the kitchen. Lauren looked composed as she slid a trio of perfectly browned pancakes onto a plate, while bacon and scrambled eggs sizzled over the gas hob.

"I remember you cooking when Mum was alive," James gasped. "Burned bits stuck to the pan and mess over the cabinets. When did you get so good at it?"

"I did a few cookery classes on campus."

"You're getting so mature," James said. "You're always surprising me, and you never seem to ask me for help and advice like you used to."

Lauren started to laugh.

"What?" James asked.

"Nothing," Lauren sniggered. "It's just . . . ," She paused to let out a snorting noise. "The thought of asking *you* for advice. You're not exactly Mr. Maturity, are you?"

James was wounded. "I'm mature," he said defensively.

"If you say so, bro'," Lauren snickered.

James didn't get a chance to push the argument, because there was a white car pulling up on the driveway.

The Arizona police car sprang up like it was letting out a sigh, as Marvin Teller hoisted himself out of the driver's door and sited his cowboy hat on his head. Today's suit was custard yellow, with white leather boots.

Marvin walked around to the trunk and reached inside. James felt a nasty pang of reality when Marvin lifted out two sets of bright orange overalls and swung a body chain over each shoulder.

Everyone gathered around the table to eat breakfast. Dave, John, and Marvin raved about Lauren's cooking and tucked away seconds; but James could only manage a few bites.

His stomach was turning somersaults. He ran upstairs to the toilet and retched a couple of times, but didn't bring anything up. All the stuff James had learned about the dangers inside prison was really getting to him. He splashed cold water on his face and took slow, deep breaths to try and get hold of himself.

When he got back down to the kitchen, John looked concerned. "What's up?"

"Nervous," James confessed.

"You know the rules," John said. "You can pull

out of this mission at any time and you won't be punished."

It was true that James wouldn't be punished. It was also true that if he bailed on a critical mission at this stage and ruined it, nobody would ever offer him a spot on another one. He'd spend the rest of his time at CHERUB doing routine surveillance, break-ins, and security checks. James wasn't prepared to throw away all the effort he'd put into training and missions, because he'd woken up with a touch of nerves.

"Don't sweat it," James said, trying to sound cool. "Once the mission starts, I won't have time to worry."

Marvin took the boys through to the living room, while John and Lauren stacked the dishwasher. Marvin told them to strip everything off, including watches and jewelery. They replaced their socks, T-shirts, and underpants with prison issue. The underwear smelled of disinfectant, but the stains and rips were an uncomfortable reminder of previous occupants.

The baggy orange overalls they wore on the outside were designed for high visibility, so that a prisoner who escaped in transit could be easily seen. Two suits with OMAHA STATE PRISON printed on them had been shipped in especially for the occasion. In addition, James and Dave had to pull on fluorescent yellow bibs, like the ones kids wear in football training. They had DANGER: ESCAPE RISK printed on them in huge letters. The only normal clothes the boys were allowed were their trainers.

"You won't get any toilet breaks once these are on," Marvin explained, jangling the chains.

James and Dave both dashed upstairs and took a piss.

When they got down, Marvin had the two sets of shackles laid out on the carpet.

He put James's on first. James winced as Marvin clamped the bracelets around his ankles.

"Does it have to be so tight?"

"It's supposed to bite the skin so the bracelet can't move," Marvin explained. "Someone would ask questions if I fitted them on loose. . . . Hands front."

Marvin squeezed cold metal cuffs onto James's wrists. A length of chain linked the ankle bracelets to the handcuffs, preventing James from raising his hands any higher than his waist.

"Take a stroll around the room while I fix up Dave," Marvin said. "Moving around in those things takes some getting used to."

The individual holding cells at the Phoenix courthouse were barely one pace wide by three long. The only facilities were a drinking fountain and a filthy steel toilet bowl. James had passed more than a dozen of these sweltering little cages on the way to his own and, judging by the shouts and screams passing in all directions, there were hundreds more.

James and Dave were supposed to have gone into court first thing that morning, but something caused a holdup and James had lost track of time. Inmates weren't allowed watches and there were no windows. James guessed it was between twelve and one when a clingfilm-wrapped sandwich and bottle of no-brand cola got passed through the bars, but that had been several hours ago.

"Rose, James," a woman's voice shouted.

The stocky female guard stood by the bars outside the tiny cell holding a clipboard. She had a red face and a torrent of sweat drizzling out of her hair. James scrambled up from the floor. He still had the ankle bracelets on, but his handcuffs had been released on arrival.

"Cuffs," the hack said sharply.

James picked the handcuffs attached to his ankle chains off the floor and put them on a small metal shelf in the barred door.

"Come on," she said crossly, "wrists."

James realized he was supposed to post his hands through the slot so the hack could fix the cuffs on. She squeezed them a notch further than Marvin Teller had done: tight enough that the tendons in his wrist hurt every time he moved his fingers.

"What's the dirty look in aid of, kid?"

They walked past two rows of the tiny cells and up six flights of stairs to the second floor of the courthouse. This level was air-conditioned and James was pleased to catch sight of Dave waiting outside the courtroom.

"What was the holdup?" James asked.

Dave shrugged. "Like they'd tell us."

The hack knocked on the courtroom door and waited a few seconds, before the boys were ushered in. James had expected a grand setting, with loads of people in the room and wood paneling, like you see in the movies. He got a windowless office with frayed carpet, barely bigger than his room on campus.

The gray-haired judge sat behind a cluttered desk in her stockinged feet, sipping out of a Starbucks cup. Her shoes and handbag rested on the floor beneath an

American flag mounted on a pole. There was a stenographer sitting at a smaller desk off to one side, a guard armed with a shotgun, and two lawyers, one of whom James and Dave had met briefly that morning before being taken down to the cells.

The lawyer had explained that when an Arizona defendant pleads guilty, the case is dealt with using a system called *plea bargaining*. The charges and prison sentence are haggled over in advance between the judge and the two opposing lawyers. The court hearing was a formality.

James and Dave stood in the back third of the room behind a red line. A sign on the wall guaranteed a ninety-day sentence to any prisoner who dared step over it.

"OK," the judge said, taking a quick glance at her watch. "It's late, let's roll this along. James and David Rose versus the state of Arizona, case number six-zero-one-nine-nine. Minors charged as adults, with one count of robbery and one count of murder. The defense council has offered to plead guilty to charges of robbery and second-degree murder, with an attached term of eighteen years. Does the prosecution formally accept this bargain?"

"Yes, ma'am," the prosecution lawyer nodded.

The judge looked up at James and Dave. "Has your lawyer explained to you that by pleading guilty to these charges and accepting the bargain, you lose any right of appeal?"

James and Dave both nodded. "Yes, ma'am."

"Very well," the judge said solemnly. "Let the record show that a sentence of eighteen years has been passed on James and David Rose."

The two lawyers leaned forward and took turns shaking the judge's hand. James looked at the clock on the wall and realized that he'd spent the whole day sweltering in a cell, waiting for a hearing that had lasted less than three minutes.

CHAPTER 19

INDUCTION

The bus to Arizona Max had a metal cage blocking off the exits and bars over the windows. Two hacks with pump-action shotguns sat up front, facing towards a dozen prisoners riding a bus with room for more than fifty.

James and Dave sat near the back. A couple of women had been placed in the middle, and the men were at the front. Pride of place went to a giant with a long red beard who'd been put on board last and clamped into his seat with a tubular metal bar.

James looked back to Dave in the row behind. "What the hell did he do?"

The only other kid on the bus leaned across the aisle and answered. He was a skinny fellow called Abe, who was no taller than James. The tuft of bristles on Abe's chin was the only hint that he was nearly seventeen.

"That's Chaz Wallerstein," Abe said, as if this should mean something.

James and Dave both looked blank.

"You know," Abe said. "Bank robber, turned into a hostage deal. He shot up fifteen people, killed eleven of them. It was all over the TV news. Where have you two been, Mars?"

James straightened up his overalls so you could read the word OMAHA. "They had us in solitary up there."

Abe smiled. "Mars, Nebraska, same kind of thing I guess. . . . You know you're gonna cop trouble when the hacks see those escape-risk bibs?"

Arizona Max was opened in 2002 to deal with the state's rapidly expanding prison population. It was a multi-role prison, capable of holding 6,500 inmates inside fourteen H-shaped cellblocks. Nine blocks held maximum-security adult male prisoners, two held female prisoners, and two were super-maximum-security (supermax) units containing Death Row, along with the most dangerous inmates in the state. The final unit held close to 300 boys under the age of eighteen.

The vast prison compound stretched over thousands of acres and was surrounded by three electrified fences and two stacks of barbed wire coils more than ten meters high. All vehicles or persons entering the prison had to pass through a single entry point.

The bus carrying James and Dave drove through the first set of gates and into a small holding pen surrounded by twenty-meter-high walls. These outer gates were operated from a control building beyond the prison perimeter, while the inner set operated from the main control room inside the prison. This dual-control security system, known as a *sally port*, means that inmates can't escape, even if they manage to overpower every guard inside the prison.

Only when the gates behind the bus were locked could the second set of gates leading into the prison be opened. Once they'd passed into the compound, James pressed his face to the window and looked out at the concrete cellblocks radiating across the desert.

He watched the inmates in the wire-fenced exercise yards around each unit. There were armed guards on the roof of the buildings, ready to take a shot if trouble broke out, and tiny specks of men standing inside the air-conditioned watch towers dotted along the perimeter, several hundred meters away in every direction.

Hacks received the prisoners as the bus drew up outside each cellblock. The men got dropped off first, then the women, then Chaz Wallerstein was left outside the supermax block and his single cell on Death Row. The young offender unit was the final stop, a quarter mile further along the road, past a stretch of bare ground set aside for building more cellblocks.

The ankle chain was kept short to stop a prisoner from moving fast. It also meant the only way off the bus was a two-footed jump off the step. Abe, who didn't seem the most athletic type, managed to lose his balance. One of the hacks grabbed him out of the dust and bounced him furiously against the wire fence.

"Better keep upright if you don't want your ass kicked."

The two hacks shoved the kids through a wire gate and towards the cellblock. The twin-level building was made out of prefabricated concrete sections with a flat metal roof and every window deliberately narrower than a human body. They passed through a steel door, into a spartan reception area, with a long plywood counter down the middle and showers off to the side. A black inmate, who looked about fifteen, stood behind the counter.

One hack removed James's chains and told him to strip off and run to the shower stall at the end of the room. The other one shook green disinfectant powder over James's head and handed him a chewed-up bar of soap.

James felt sorry for Abe as he twirled in the shower next to him. There was no muscle anywhere on Abe's body and his arms and legs were like sticks. James reckoned Lauren could have taken him in a fight. He wouldn't even make a light snack for the prison bullies.

"Ain't got all day," the guard shouted, as he dragged James from under the water and handed him a towel. James put the towel to his face and realized it was damp and musty, like it had been used plenty of times before.

By the time James threw his towel down, the guard had pulled a thin flashlight out of his shirt pocket and stretched a set of disposable gloves over his fingers.

"Face the wall."

The hack began his search at the bottom, making James lift each foot in turn, to inspect his soles and in-between his toes. Next he made James bend forward and pull apart his butt cheeks, before shining the torch under James's armpits, in and behind his ears, and vigorously rubbing his fingers against James's scalp to make sure nothing was hidden in his hair.

"Face front."

The hack shone the light in James's eyes, up his nose, and inside of his mouth, including under his tongue and around his gums, assisted by a finger that tasted of rubber. He crouched down and flashed the light into James's belly button, before making him lift up his penis and balls and finally roll back his foreskin in case he'd stashed anything naughty up there. When the hack was done, he gently smacked James on the arse.

"OK, get dressed."

The black kid behind the counter had laid out three sets of prison uniform. The clothes they'd arrived in were gone. The other guard was holding the two yellow ESCAPE RISK bibs in the air and James instantly knew there was going to be trouble.

"Do you know how many people have ever escaped from this prison, James Rose?" asked the tubby little superintendent, whose name was Frey.

James didn't want to act smart, so he lied. "No, sir."

"Nobody has *ever* escaped from Arizona Max," Frey said, stepping forward and grinding the heel of his boot against James's foot. "Got that?"

"Yes sir," James said, determined not to let the pain show on his face.

Frey took his boot away, leaving James with a red horseshoe across the top of his foot.

James pulled on grimy prison boxers and T-shirt. The

outer clothing was gray cotton shorts and a baggy orange polo shirt with ESCAPE RISK printed on it.

"If you're classified as an escape risk, you've got to wear the orange shirt whenever you're out of the cell," the inmate explained. "If they catch you without it, they'll stick you in the hole and just as likely stomp on you as well."

After pulling on the shirt, James looked under the counter and saw that his Nikes had been replaced by a pair of flimsy cotton slippers.

"Prison issue only," the inmate explained. "No possessions from the outside, except your legal paperwork and two family photographs. Anything else you want *must* be purchased from the prison commissary."

The commissary was a kind of prison shop. James had read about it in the rulebook the day before.

He picked his meager possessions off the bench: identity card with his picture and inmate number, a prison rule book, a threadbare towel, bedding, one spare pair of boxers, one T-shirt, a plastic cup, toothbrush, toothpaste, a bar of soap, and a roll of toilet paper.

CHAPTER 14

CELL

The thirty-strong population of Cell T4 stopped what they were doing and stared at the three new inmates in the doorway. There were murmurs about James and Dave's orange *escape risk* T-shirts, including a shout:

"When you going over the wall, man?"

Dave smiled. "A week next Tuesday. Wanna tag along?"

The noise inside the cell was intense. Prisoners were allowed to buy radios and tiny black and white TVs. Each one was tuned to a different station, with the volume up high.

The smell was even more in your face. There were fans near the ceiling at either end of the cell, but the sun had been cooking the metal roof all day, pushing the temperature into the forties. It was like living under the armpit of someone who never washed.

There were six empty beds in the middle of the room. James and Dave knew the names of their cellmates, what crimes they'd committed, and how long they had to serve, but a few seconds looking around gave them more essential knowledge than all the background reading.

Curtis Oxford had a bed next to the entrance, surrounded by the beds of the toughest white inmates, who were all skinheads. The areas around these guys' lockers were overflowing with personal possessions. Their prison-issue clothes looked pristine and were accessorized with brand-name trainers and tracksuit tops, in clear breach of the prison rules. As you got to the middle of the cell, the inmates looked steadily weaker until you got down to fragile looking kids who possessed nothing, except nervous dispositions and the prison-issue clothes they stood up in.

The empty beds at the center of the cell marked a racial divide. The radio stations and chatter beyond this point were mostly Spanish. The inmates were all Latino, and the beds at the bottom of the cell were an olive-skinned mirror of the beds near the door, with the biggest and meanest of the Latinos strutting in crisp underclothes and designer accessories.

Short of turfing someone off their bunk, James and Dave's only immediate option was to take two beds next to each other in the center of the room, while Abe grabbed one across the aisle. James spread his sheet and blanket over his skimpy plastic mattress, then crouched down and put everything else in his locker before crashing out on the bed.

It took a couple of hours for the loud conversations and competing radios and TVs to really start drilling into James's skull. It was seven at night and the closest thing to excitement came when an inmate passed through the cell with a food trolley. Everyone got a paper bag containing sandwiches, a quart of government-surplus milk, and two chocolate cookies.

According to Mark—a kid with a black eye who had the bed next to James—lunch was the only hot meal of the day. To save the expense of a large canteen and seating area, inmates got served in twenty-minute shifts between 11 a.m. and 4 p.m., in a small building on the exercise yard.

Like most teenage boys, James was always hungry. He now wished he'd had the stomach for Lauren's pancakes at breakfast. He'd flushed most of the revolting sandwich at the courthouse and the Arizona Max offering was worse: perspiring cheese, brown lettuce, and mayonnaise that had soaked through the bread.

"Not eating that?" Dave asked, as he snatched James's clingfilm package off the partition between the beds.

"Mayo makes me spew."

As Dave crammed the sandwich down his neck, James stared miserably into his paper bag and bit the corner off his last cookie.

"Can I have one of your cookies, for the sandwich?" James asked.

"Can't," Dave said, as the tip of his tongue lapped up an oily streak dribbling down his chin.

"Come *on*," James begged. "That's a good trade, one cookie for a whole sandwich."

"Already eaten them, though," Dave said.

James fumed as he slumped down on his mattress. The only things he'd eaten all day were two cookies and a few forced mouthfuls of sandwich. He was getting serious hunger pangs and knew they'd get worse through the night.

"Did you get your commissary form?" Dave asked. "It's in the food bag."

James found his folded sheet of paper and a stubby—too short to stab someone with—pencil. His inmate number was scrawled at the top of the form and he started reading the commissary rules printed on the back.

To discourage bullying, gambling, and drug dealing, inmates weren't allowed cash. Every prisoner got a commissary account and up to $50 per week could be paid in by a friend or relative on the outside. Prisoners got a commissary form every week and you put a tick next to whatever items you wanted to order, up to your spending limit. The hundreds of items ranged from miniature TVs at $99, down to phone cards, Marlboro cigarettes, hair mousse, strawberry Pop-Tarts, and Reese's peanut butter cups.

According to James's form, the balance of his account was $103.17, which included $20 given to all young inmates by a prisoners' welfare charity and $83.17 that had supposedly been transferred from a commissary account in Nebraska.

Abe came over to the foot of James's bed, holding a cookie and his commissary form.

"I'm not hungry," Abe said, smiling like he wanted a favor.

"Cheers," James said, snapping the cookie in half and downing it in two bites.

"I don't get this," Abe said, waving the form.

James took the form and started explaining how the commissary worked. All Abe had in his account was $20 from the charity.

"You'll need to speak with your mum, or whoever, and try to get them to pay money in every week," James explained. "You should buy a ten-dollar phone card first, so you can call her."

"And these?" Abe asked, running his finger down the list of items.

"You tick the box for whatever you want, hand in the form, and collect your parcel a few days later."

"Can you help me choose? I don't read so good."

James grabbed Abe's form and ticked the box next to where it said phone card. He looked up and realized there were two guys closing in. The absence of cash was supposed to discourage extortion and bullying amongst the inmates, but all it really did was turn the commissary forms themselves into a kind of currency.

To Raymond and Stanley Duff, the sight of two new prisoners with commissary forms had the same effect as a shark sniffing blood in the water. The red-headed brothers weren't quite among the cell's elite, but they were hard enough to hold a place near the top of the pecking order. They were fifteen and sixteen, heavyset, with flabby stomachs sagging over the waistbands of their shorts.

The Duff brothers were serving life without parole for kidnapping and murdering an eight-year-old girl. Nearly all of James's cellmates were killers, but this was the crime that got under his skin when he read about it. The dimple-cheeked victim pictured in the newspaper clipping had been born two days after Lauren and even looked a little like her.

"We'll help Skinny with his commissary," Raymond, the younger of the brothers, grinned as he reached out to snatch the form off James.

"Rob him blind, more like," James said, scurrying backwards across his bed to keep the form out of reach.

"You don't want to give *us* trouble," Raymond said, tutting and shaking his head.

Dave stood up and faced off the two redheads.

"Lay one finger on my brother, I dare you."

Anyone could have worked out that Dave packed muscle where Stanley had flab, but brainpower didn't seem to be the Duff brothers' forte.

Stanley swung his thick arm. The punch might have hurt, but Dave could have sat on his bed and clipped his toenails in the time it would have taken to connect. After easily intercepting the fist, Dave plunged an elbow into Stanley's guts before sweeping his feet from under him as he doubled over in pain.

James remembered what Scott said about going in hard. He sprung up and charged at Raymond. His chunky opponent stumbled backwards across the aisle under a blitz of well-aimed punches, ending up spread-eagled on Abe's bed with a bloody nose and split lip.

James jumped on top and pinned Raymond's arms to his side. James could see the dimple-cheeked face of the little girl Raymond had killed. Bristling with rage, he used one hand to clamp Raymond's neck to the mattress and pulled back his arm, intending to smash Raymond's jaw.

"That's enough," Dave shouted.

James realized he'd overdone it and let Dave pull him away. They had to step over Stanley, who was sprawled out on the floor in a daze.

"Sorry," James gasped.

One of the Latinos shouted a warning. "On the rail."

James looked up to see a hack stepping onto the metal gantry that ran the length of the cell above the beds on Abe's side of the room.

"Stan*ding* count," the guard shouted.

James and Dave didn't know what this meant, but the others all scrambled. They switched off their TVs and radios and stood at the foot of their beds, ready to be counted. Once they twigged, James and Dave did the same.

Stanley Duff managed to drag himself into position, but Raymond remained on Abe's bed, holding his hands over his face and sobbing in pain. The hack leaned over the balcony, inspecting Raymond's face.

"All *keep* still," the hack shouted. "Anyone who moves or opens their smart mouth gets two nights in the hole."

The hack moved briskly to the end of the rail and

grabbed a telephone. If the threat of the tiny pitch-black cell known as the hole wasn't enough to keep the inmates in line, there was a rack at the end of the metal gantry containing stun grenades and guns that could fire tear-gas cartridges or plastic baton rounds.

The boys stood to attention for a quarter of an hour, waiting for two trustee inmates from the prison hospital. When they'd rolled Raymond onto a stretcher and taken him away, the hack gave the order to stand down.

People started moving around and the radios and TVs got switched back on. James looked at the smears of blood on his hands, then at Dave, expecting some kind of rebuke.

"Well," Dave said, as he raised a single eyebrow. "I guess everyone knows we've arrived."

CHAPTER 15

TACTICS

Going to the bathroom meant taking a trip into Latino territory. James and Dave walked down the aisle between the beds, stepping over a dice game and respectfully asking people to move aside.

A scrawny fourteen-year-old Latino boy kept the bathroom spotless. Everyone called him BAM, which was short for *bucket and mop*. In return for his cleaning duties, BAM got looked after by the toughest Latinos, who slept close to the bathroom entrance and didn't want to be troubled by nasty smells.

After James had used the urinal and washed his hands, face and arms, he realized he ought to clean the blood off his T-shirt as well. He tugged it over his head, while BAM fussed over a few splashes on the floor around the urinals. James didn't have his bar of soap, so all he could do was give the shirt a soaking and rub out as much blood as he could, before quickly wringing out the water and heading for the exit.

"We like our toilet clean," one of the Latinos said.

Cesar was a big shot, dressed in a black Fila tracksuit with a gold chain around his neck. He had his hairy palm against the wall, blocking the exit of the bathroom.

"You respect our toilet, yeah?" Cesar said. "Then we'll respect *you*."

Dave nodded. "We've got no problem with that."

"And you," Cesar said, putting his hand on James's bare shoulder and giving it a friendly squeeze, "you messed up that baby killer. Good for you. Give your shirt to BAM and he'll wash it properly. We have soap powder. He puts it up near the fans and makes it dry for you by morning."

James handed his soggy T-shirt to BAM and nodded his appreciation to Cesar, who took his hand off the wall to allow them out of the bathroom.

Cesar looked at one of his lieutenants. "Have we still got the lemon soft?"

The lieutenant reached under his bed and produced two plump yellow rolls of toilet tissue for James and Dave.

"Thank you, Cesar," Dave said.

"The prison issue is *brutal*," Cesar grinned. "You need anything else?"

Dave shook his head. "We're cool."

"You're two tough guys," Cesar said. "As long as you leave my people alone, you and I have no problems."

"You haven't got any food going, have you?" James interrupted. "I'll replace it when I get my commissary order."

Dave gave James a stern look, as if to say *don't push your luck*; but Cesar laughed noisily and grabbed a melted Snickers bar and a small can of sour-cream Pringles out of his locker.

"Beauty," James grinned.

James ripped the lid off the Pringles can as he led Dave back to their beds.

"Seems a cool guy," James said, crashing onto his bed with a mouthful of chips.

"Don't you believe it," Dave smiled. "Cesar just wants to needle the skinheads."

"What do you mean?" James asked.

"Sit here."

James stepped over the partition and sat up close to Dave, so they could talk in confidence.

"There's a pissing contest going on between the Latinos at that end and the whites at this end."

"Obviously," James nodded. "It's not exactly an advert for racial harmony in here, is it?"

Dave grinned. "Elwood and Kirch are the top dogs on the white side, and we pose a threat to them. They'll see BAM washing your T-shirt, they'll see our baby-soft toilet tissue and you filling your chops with Latino munchies. If Elwood and Kirch think we're getting support from Cesar, they're going to start worrying about us undermining their whole power base in this cell."

"Couldn't we just go up to Elwood and Kirch, shake hands and say hello?"

"If we go over there now, we might look scared," Dave explained, shaking his head sharply. "Before we can convince Curtis to escape with us, we've got to earn his respect. We'll only manage that if Elwood and Kirch respect us too."

"So, what then?" James asked.

"Well," Dave said slyly, "it doesn't take a tactical genius to work that out. Does it?"

James looked irritated. "So I'm not a tactical genius; just *tell* me."

"You put Stanley Duff's little brother in the prison hospital. You can guarantee that a meathead like Stanley will try to get us back. I doubt Elwood and Kirch will show their hand until they see how well we deal with that."

"Got you," James grinned. "So we've got to take out Stanley Duff."

"*No*. Elwood and Kirch might get worried if we're too aggressive. We'll wait for Stanley to come after us. He knows we can do him, so he'll try a surprise attack, probably with a knife."

"You reckon he can get hold of a knife?"

Dave nodded. "I don't think he'll find it hard. You've seen how much contraband there is floating around in here."

"When do you think he'll move on us?" James asked.

"Tonight most likely, when he thinks we're both asleep. We'll have to take turns staying awake. If we take out Stanley tonight, then tomorrow we can straighten things out with Elwood and Kirch in the exercise yard. We'll make it clear that we're not in bed with the Latinos and we just want a fair share of the action. Once that's sorted, you can start chumming up with Curtis."

"Always assuming Stanley doesn't stick a knife in our guts before we get a chance," James said, smiling uneasily as he held the Pringles can up in the air and drained the crumbs into his mouth.

"Just in case," Dave said, "rub the end of your toothbrush against the concrete floor to sharpen the end. Then sleep with it in your hand."

CHAPTER 16

SLEEPERS

A standing count at 10:30 p.m. was followed by lights-out. The guards needed to be sure that the inmates weren't digging a tunnel or killing each other, so a line of tubes down the middle of the cell stayed on. It was enough light to read by and most of the TVs and radios kept going too, along with the bragging matches and rowdy dice games.

The noise died back after midnight, but James still felt like he was in hell. He sat on his bed with his back to the wall, studying the beads of sweat rolling down his chest. There always seemed to be at least one winged black speck wandering over his skin, while hundreds of larger insects had decided to spend the night clanking their heads against the fluorescent lights near the ceiling.

James wrestled with his sheet, but it was soggy and hopelessly tangled around his legs, so he threw it away in frustration. He studied the white marks covering the shiny plastic over his mattress. He hadn't been able to work them out earlier, but now he disgusted himself by solving the riddle: It was crusted salt from the previous occupant's dried-up sweat.

James looked over the partition. Dave had put a towel over his eyes to shield the light and been asleep by 10:45. James remembered how his mum used to call people like Dave sleepers. Lauren was another sleeper: Stick her in the back of a car or on a couch in some strange house, and she'd be out in no time. Unless he was exhausted, or sick, James could never do it. He needed a decent bed, with pillows and the duvet tucked under his chin exactly how he liked it.

"Dave," James said, nudging him awake.

Dave sat up drearily, with a string of drool stretched between his face and his pillow.

"Keep lookout a minute. I need a slash."

James tucked the sharpened toothbrush handle into the waistband of his shorts, grabbed his empty cup, and wandered towards the bathroom, while Dave rubbed his eyes. It was a clear walk up the aisle, though a few kids were still lying awake with their tiny TV screens flickering in the half-light. They either ran on headphones or were turned down to a whisper.

It took James's eyes a while to adjust to the brightly lit bathroom. One of the younger Latinos stood by the middle sink, pushing down the tap head and splashing water over his chest. James thought he heard the kid sob while he stood at the urinal. When he moved to wash his hands, the kid sobbed again.

"You OK?" James asked.

James reeled when the kid turned to face him. He had a burn on his chest, surrounded by a black scorch mark in the exact shape of the plastic mug in James's hand. The skin was all blistered and weeping pus.

"My baby brother got toothache," the kid explained tearfully. "Grandma paid the dentist instead of my commissary, which meant Cesar didn't get what I owed him."

James felt scared when he realized this horror had happened tonight, while he'd been only a few meters away. With all the noise, you could be screaming in agony and nobody would notice.

"How?" James asked.

"Cesar's trademark: He makes a hole in the bottom of a cup and fills it up with matches. Then he press it against your skin and sets them alight."

"Jesus."

James remembered that he was deep in Latino territory. If one of Cesar's guys came in, he'd want to know why James was sticking his nose where it didn't belong. James pressed on the tap, splashed water all over his body to cool off, and then gulped some down before refilling his mug to take back to bed.

"I'm sorry," James said uneasily, as he backed away.

The kid edged a smile. "Not as sorry as me."

James shuddered, thinking how excruciating the burn must feel, as he walked back to his bed. Something thumped into him. Thick arms wrapped around his stomach as he hit the concrete floor between two empty beds with Stanley Duff on top of him.

"For my brother," Stanley announced theatrically, as he reached into the waistband of his shorts and pulled out a twenty-centimeter blade made from a strip of sharpened metal.

"Help," James yelled desperately, realizing that Dave must have dropped his guard and fallen back to sleep.

The blade would have plunged through James's neck if he hadn't found the strength to move at the last second. He got hold of Stanley's wrist and started trying to twist the weapon out of his grip.

"*Dave*. For God's sake, help me. . . ."

James spotted Abe's skinny legs cutting across the aisle to Dave's bed. Stanley was far heavier than James and he was gradually winning the battle to free his wrist and take a second stab. The blade nicked James's palm as Stanley snatched it free.

Stanley broke into a big grin. James reached to pull out his toothbrush handle, but as Stanley raised the blade into the air, James spotted the kind of opening you dreamed about every time you got thrown to the mat in combat class. He thrust his hand forward, smashing his palm into the base of Stanley's chin. Stanley's head whipped back and made a sharp crack as the vertebrae in his neck impacted.

Dave was out of bed and committed to a charging movement. He crashed into Stanley, knocking him off James, as the rows of lights over the beds started flickering. This was followed by a popping noise, like the loudest cork bursting out of the biggest champagne bottle you've ever seen. It echoed around the cell, as Dave somersaulted onto the bed beside him and screamed out in pain.

A shout came from one of the two guards who'd run onto the gantry. "Break it up."

James caught a glance of the hack holding the huge baton-round gun, as it recoiled from the second plastic shot. It hit Stanley in the arse, making him buck forward and smack head-first into the cell wall. The plastic round deflected off the bed frame and tore into James's thigh.

"Stand apart, *now*."

Scared that he was going to be the next target, James dragged himself up and stumbled out into the aisle, fighting a dead thigh muscle.

"Standing count," a female guard shouted. "Standing count."

The whole cell had been woken by the shots and everyone started moving to the end of their beds; except Dave and Stanley, who'd each taken a baton round and were in no state to go anywhere. James looked up at the gantry, unsure if he was supposed to move.

The hack with the gun rocked his head and tracked James the four paces back to his bed. James knew a third, excruciatingly painful plastic round would come his way if he stepped a millimeter out of line.

James was expecting the medical team, like earlier, but the guards had pressed the emergency alarm, which brought out the Prison Emergency Response Team, commonly known as PERT. The six-strong team rolled back the cell door and burst through at a run. They looked fearsome, dressed head to toe in black body armor, with gloves, crash helmets, and their leader yelling his lungs out:

"Beds and *heads*."

James copied his cellmates, as they jumped onto their beds and sat with backs to the wall and hands on heads. Kirch, who was nearest the door, didn't have time to move. He was smacked into the aisle with a riot shield and got his ankle crunched under a running boot.

The first to reach Dave and Stanley threw down his shield and ripped a can of incapacitating pepper spray off his belt. Dave screamed out and rolled in a ball, as the PERT leader blasted him with the gooey liquid.

James breathed a hint of the concentrated pepper that had drifted into the air and immediately felt tears in his eyes. It must have been a million times worse for Dave.

Each member of the PERT team had a specific role. While the leader moved in on Stanley with the pepper spray, the second through fifth members dragged Dave into the aisle and grabbed one limb each. When Dave was spread out in an X-position, the final member of the team laid a plastic harness over his back. Strings of pepper spray dangled out of Dave's long hair as he panicked for breath.

The two men holding Dave's arms bent them into the harness and pulled them tight under a heavy nylon strap. Once they were secure, Dave's legs were twisted until his heels almost touched his bum, then strapped into this excruciating position.

The PERT team moved their attention to Stanley, dragging him out into the aisle by his ankles. But the leader screamed out.

"Break it *off*. . . . Look at the head."

Stanley was now unconscious and you only had to look at the way his head was twisted unnaturally backwards to see that something was badly wrong. The smallest on the PERT team, who James now realized was a woman, took off her gloves and helmet and crouched down over Stanley. She flinched as she got a whiff of the pepper spray, then looked up at her team leader.

"It might be a broken neck. He's definitely a hospital job."

The leader looked up at the two guards on the rail. "Get us a medical team." Then he pointed at Dave. "Take *that* to the hole."

Two of the PERT team put their hands under Dave's armpits and picked him up. His eyes and nose were streaming and he had a huge red welt on his ribs where he'd been hit by the plastic bullet.

James trembled as he watched Dave get dragged out of the cell with his bare knees grazing along the concrete floor. James knew it could as easily have been him who'd ended up being hauled away in agony. Or even worse: What if Stanley had got the knife in?

CHAPTER 17

YARD

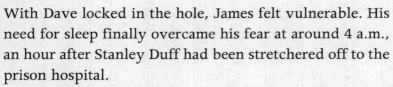

With Dave locked in the hole, James felt vulnerable. His need for sleep finally overcame his fear at around 4 a.m., an hour after Stanley Duff had been stretchered off to the prison hospital.

The cell door and the gates onto the exercise yard opened at nine, but most kids were still asleep as James limped towards the bathroom with his bar of soap and toilet roll. He had the sharpened toothbrush handle tucked into his waistband, just in case.

BAM hovered with his mop, while James took a dump. The steel bowls were mounted on the wall without doors or partitions, so you got zero privacy. The shower was even worse. The water only ran while you held the button down and the lukewarm dribble meant you couldn't get soap out of your hair.

James dried off quickly, desperate to get out of the rank cell and breathe fresh air. A corridor led past three other cells and up a short ramp. To get to the exercise yard, you stood in line to get padded down by a hack before passing through a metal detector.

As James's canvas slipper took its first step into the sand, another inmate passed him a white paper bag containing his breakfast. James got called back before he had a chance to see what he'd got.

"Rose."

Superintendent Bob Frey was the potbellied, yellow-toothed man who'd crushed James's foot in the reception room the previous afternoon. Frey took James under a veranda and made him stand with his back pinned to the cellblock wall.

"Been in *my* cellblock less than fifteen hours, haven't you?"

"About that, sir."

"I got two brothers in the hospital. One of 'em's just a busted nose and concussion, but the other fella's got neck damage that's gonna cost this prison tens of thousands in medical bills."

James shifted awkwardly, not knowing how to answer.

"Then I got your brother in the hole," Frey grinned. "You ever been in the hole, boy?"

"No sir."

"You got no light, no ventilation, not a strip of clothes, and no toilet. We hose it out once a day, like an animal cage. Any more trouble and that's where I'll have you. Understood?"

"Yes sir," James nodded. "How long's Dave in there for?"

"Long enough," Frey grinned. "Now get out of my sight."

James opened up his breakfast bag as he walked onto the sun-bleached yard. The milk was warm, the three pieces of fruit were past their best, and the muffin was on the dry side, but it was edible and James was starving. His last decent meal had been the fried chicken two nights earlier.

The yard was oval-shaped and the size of three football pitches. It was scooped out of the desert basin around the back half of the cellblock. The facilities were basic: shelters to keep off the sun, a few basketball hoops and chin-up bars, and the small prefabricated building where lunches were served. Beside the perimeter fence was a five-meter stretch of concrete behind a red line, which was known as the shooting gallery. No inmate was allowed on the shooting gallery and to make it clear, the notices dotted along the fence had a little stick man standing inside a gun sight with LETHAL FORCE AUTHORIZED written beneath him.

"Hey," Abe said, jogging up behind James with a banana in his hand.

James smiled. "You did me a big favor last night. Dave was *supposed* to be watching my back. . . . I just gotta hope Stanley doesn't have any pals popping out of the woodwork."

"The two big white guys were in the shower when I went for a piss. They asked if I'd seen you."

"Which guys?" James asked anxiously.

"Elwood, and the one with the German name."

"Kirch. What did they want?"

"They just asked where you were."

"Did they sound angry?"

Abe shrugged. "All they said was one sentence. 'Have you seen the little psychopath?' I told them I thought you were already out on the yard."

"They called me a psychopath?" James said, unsure if this was a bad sign or a mark of respect.

"I think you broke that guy's neck."

"It was me or him: He *was* about to slit my throat."

James threw away the core of his apple and took a slug from his bottle of milk. He was frightened. If Dave had been around, Elwood and Kirch would have been manageable. But with Dave in the hole, he'd be outgunned if things turned heavy.

"I'll wait for them to come on the yard," James said. "At least there's space to run away out here."

James and Abe found a spot under a shelter with a view over the whole yard and sat together in the dirt.

Kirch came through the metal detector first. He was a seventeen-year-old skinhead, two meters tall, with massive pectoral muscles inside a sweat-stained vest. Elwood was taller and thinner, shaved bald. A swastika with MOM written underneath it was tattooed on his neck. Curtis came next. He was an average build and the same height as James, but he looked undernourished standing between his massive bodyguards.

The three boys joined up with a bunch of similarly fierce looking skinheads from another cell who were standing around a set of chin-up bars taking it in turns to do sets. The gang was bigger and meaner than James had expected. He realized they were going to have no problem hurting him if they wanted to.

A couple of minutes later, while Kirch was on the chin-up bar, Elwood spotted a little guy passing by. He tucked the kid's head under his arm and squeezed until it turned red. After a while he let go and knocked him down with a savage right hook. The kid was fighting tears and holding onto his face as he walked off.

"I gotta split," Abe said, shocked by what he'd just witnessed.

James knew Abe wasn't going to be any help in a fight against the Elwoods and Kirches of the world, but he appreciated having a friendly face to talk to.

"What's your problem?" James asked.

"They already asked me where you are. If they find me with you, they're not gonna like it."

"I guess I'll have to face them some time today," James said pensively. "So go and earn yourself some merit points by telling them I'm right here."

After what had happened to the last passerby, Abe didn't sound keen. "Why don't *you* go over to them?"

James pointed a finger at the armed hack standing on the roof of the cellblock less than ten meters away. "I feel safer here."

Abe reluctantly set off across the dirt towards Elwood and the others. His steps seemed to slow down as he got closer. At one point Abe changed direction so much, James thought he was going to chicken out and walk straight by.

Abe got off with a nod of thanks for his trouble. Elwood immediately set off towards James, backed up by an entourage that included Kirch and three younger skinheads, with Curtis dragging up the rear.

James looked up for comfort, only to discover that the hack on the roof had disappeared.

"You look pale, Rose," Elwood said, when he got up close.

"I figure six against one is never good," James said, trying to keep the fear out of his voice.

"True," Elwood grinned, looking back at his crew.

"What is it you want?"

"I liked the way you dealt with Stanley Duff."

"Those two started it," James said. "I didn't go looking for trouble."

"I've got no beef over that pair of walnut brains," Elwood said. "But you gotta understand my concern when guys like you and your brother arrive in my cell and start turning people over."

James nodded.

"I've either got to cut you to pieces, or cut you a deal; unless you've already got one with the Latinos."

"My brother said Cesar was trying to stir up trouble between us," James said, feeling a glimmer of confidence, as he sensed that he might get through the meeting unscathed. "But Cesar only cares about the other Latinos."

Elwood nodded. "Your bro' sounds smart."

"When he stays awake," James said bitterly.

"So why'd you accept gifts from Cesar?"

"Because I was hungry."

Elwood roared out with a false laugh, which set off all his cronies. "I guess free food is free food, wherever it comes from. . . . So what about your bro'? You got word?"

James shook his head. "That hack, Frey, pulled me over. He wouldn't tell me when they're letting him out of the hole."

Elwood laughed again. "I've been in that hole *enough* times, but the max is forty-eight hours if you're under eighteen. After that they either put you in a single cell, or back in the dorm."

"Right," James said, relieved that Dave would probably be back soon.

"So, to business," Elwood said. "Me and Kirch run our cell. That means *everyone* kicks up to us, including you."

James nodded, not that he was in any position to negotiate.

"I want you and your brother to give me ten bucks of commissary each, every week. In return, I'll give you Abe."

"Abe?" James said, confused.

"Abe's your personal property. Rip off his commissary, beat his brains in; do what you like. I don't want you touching any of the others, they belong to Kirch and me. I'll also set you up with decent prison-issue clothes and blankets, and I'll make it known that I'm on your side when the Duff brothers come back."

"Sounds fair," James nodded, as they shook on the deal.

"Did you lose anything good when you came in through reception?" Elwood asked.

"Only my trainers."

"For ten dollars of commissary, I can get them back if you want them."

"Course," James said, looking at his canvas slip-ons. "These things are rubbish."

"You better stick with us until your brother comes back," Elwood said, scratching at the swastika on his neck. "Not everyone around here is a sweetie-pie like me."

CHAPTER 18

BEASTS

James loved animals when he was tiny: the furry toys on his bed, the singing characters in animated movies, and the overweight cat that wandered into his nan's garden, knowing it would get a saucer of milk just for bothering to turn up.

Aged seven, James did his first school project on lions. His mum taped a show off the Discovery Channel that was on after bedtime. He watched the female lions licking their cubs and lazing under a tree in the sun. Then the animals went hunting.

The lionesses chased into a herd of antelope. They dragged down a straggler and began tearing it apart. Ripping off its legs, clawing open the stomach, and then dipping their snouts inside the twitching carcass; tearing out hunks of flesh and running their long tongues through the blood on their faces. Until that moment, James had no idea nature could be so brutal.

He got as far as the living room door, intending to find his mum and start bawling, but something changed his mind. He went back to the couch, tentatively rewound the video and watched it again. He watched it over and over, appalled, but utterly fascinated by what the lions were doing.

The in-your-face nastiness of the young skinheads in the Arizona Max exercise yard reminded James of the video for the first time in years. They brought out the same mixture of feelings: power and viciousness combining into a perverse kind of glamor.

James showed off, working up a sweat on the chin-up bar before lying back in the dirt next to Elwood and listening to him talk about things the gang of skinheads had done. Elwood pointed out scared kids who handed their commissary form to him each week in return for not getting beaten up too badly. He reveled in stories about people he'd tortured, stabbed, poured boiling water over, and bullied to the point where they'd tried to kill themselves.

The history of violence wasn't all one way. Elwood proudly showed off scars on his leg, chest, and back from three different knife attacks. He said you could never judge who would snap and come at you with a knife. It was as likely to be the puny little bookworm as the brooding psychopath with arms like joists.

James was appalled, but he listened intently and

laughed when he was expected to. It was mostly out of relief. The last forty-eight hours had been amongst the most traumatic of his life, but with the skinheads offering some protection, the tight ball in his stomach had eased off. He finally felt he was getting to grips with the mission. The next step was to chum up with Curtis.

Lauren didn't have much to do back at the house; her part of the mission would only begin once James and Dave escaped. She welcomed the chance to catch up on sleep and relax after basic training, though it would have been more fun if there'd been someone like Bethany to hang out with.

John took her to a shopping mall and even let her drive part of the way, so she could get used to handling the car in traffic. Unfortunately, the pair had radically different ideas on shopping.

Lauren would have happily cruised the mall all day: nosing around, maybe buying clothes and some things for her new room on campus before stopping off at the food court for lunch. John's idea of shopping was to write a list and take the place by storm: finding the quickest route between shops you had to visit on the map by the entrance and then charging from one to the next. When Lauren suggested that they *have a look around* before leaving, John scowled at her like she was a three-headed alien and steamed towards the car park.

The latex swimming sock was the one good thing to come out of the trip. Lauren could pull it over the small dressing on her foot and it would keep dry while she was in the pool. It was the hottest part of the day when they got back to the house and she put it to immediate use. She swam a few gentle lengths, but mostly just floated on a blow-up lounger and laughed at the rude bits in a teen magazine she'd got at the mall.

John had threatened lunch, but after an hour Lauren dripped into the kitchen, only to find him yelling at a telephone.

"As far as I'm concerned . . . Well . . . I don't know if he can do it. . . . Sure James has his head screwed on. But we *are* talking about a thirteen-year-old boy. . . . So what does Scott Warren say? . . . OK, OK. . . . If he can get me in I'll drive up there straight away."

"Was that Marvin?" Lauren asked. "Are the boys OK?"

John had been so involved in the call he hadn't noticed Lauren standing behind him.

"James is fine," John said. "But there was a fight and Dave ended up in the hole. He's had a bad night in there and . . . Listen, everything's up in the air and I don't know all the details myself. Can I leave you here on your own for a couple of hours? Don't spend any more time in the pool, you've got fair skin and it's not used to that kind of sun."

"What if anyone calls?"

"I'm on my mobile," John said, snatching his keys and a false FBI badge off the kitchen cabinet. "Don't wander off from the house. I'll pick up something for dinner on the way back."

James's hot lunch was watery mash, peas, and a rectangular slab of mincemeat that everyone, including the servers, referred to as baked turd. Dessert was a comparatively edible fruit sponge, washed down with the inevitable government-surplus milk.

"Not bad, compared to the filth you get in Omaha," James said. "Practically gourmet."

"You want another dessert?" Kirch asked.

"Mmm, sure," James said. "Can I go up to the counter and get one?"

The five skinheads around the table laughed.

"Just tax one," Curtis said.

James looked over his shoulder at the table behind him. He realized he'd look weak in front of his new friends if he didn't rip off someone's pudding, but fate had twisted the knife: Out of the four kids at the next table, Abe was the only one who hadn't started eating his sponge.

James stood up. "Abe man," he said awkwardly, "you eating that pudding? Only . . ."

"I'm eating it," Abe said guardedly.

The skinheads roared with outrage.

"You cannot say that, man," Elwood gasped, shaking his head and pounding on the table. "*Serious* disrespect."

Abe realized the error of his ways and pushed the plastic bowl towards James. But it wasn't fast enough for Kirch, who reached over and dragged Abe off his chair by the scruff of his shirt.

"You got no manners, boy," Kirch shouted.

He banged his fist against Abe's mouth, then dropped him to the floor, before spitting a mouthful of milk and chewed-up food in his hair. James looked anxiously at the hack standing behind the serving counter, but it was exactly like Scott Warren said: Hacks didn't interfere as long as nobody was getting killed.

"You'd better start learning," Kirch growled.

Elwood and the others were laughing as Abe crawled back to his seat with milk streaking down his face. James joined the laughter as he took Abe's pudding and sat back down, but he really felt terrible. Abe had saved his life by waking Dave up a few hours earlier. Now he had to sacrifice their friendship for the good of the mission.

It was the middle of the day when they trawled back out onto the exercise yard. With the temperature touching the forties, Kirch led the gang to the cell. With no air conditioning, it was no cooler indoors than out, but at least you were shielded from the blinding sunlight.

James's status as an associate of Elwood and Kirch meant a bed nearer the door. Kirch took five seconds to bust open the combination locker on the bed opposite his own. He threw out Stanley Duff's belongings, while James collected his things from his old bed in the middle.

Stanley had some decent stuff. James grabbed his deodorant and shampoo, as well as a bunch of snack foods, and a radio. What James didn't want got thrown out for the weaker guys to fight over. Abe grudgingly accepted first pick of an electric razor, some rice crackers, and a half used toilet roll.

"That was messed up in the canteen," James whispered guiltily.

Abe had a fat lip from the punch. "A guy like you and a guy like me were never gonna move with the same crew for long," he said casually.

James found Abe's acceptance of his low status depressing. Abe was doing twenty years, and it looked like he'd be spending most of it getting slapped around and bullied. James wanted to think up some desperately clever scheme that would make everything fair, but he knew the world didn't work that way; least of all inside a place like Arizona Max.

James's new bunk was comfortable. The bed had three thin mattresses laid on top of one another. Extras were only supposed to be issued to inmates with bad backs, but inevitably it was the bullies who gained the extra comfort.

Elwood's connection in the prison laundry had already delivered James a spare set of sheets and an extra pillow, plus a towel and some underwear. It looked years newer than the rags he'd received in reception and his black Nikes were supposed to be on their way.

James laid back on his bed reading a book about the Mafia that had belonged to Raymond Duff. It wasn't as exciting as the cover suggested, but it was all James had to take his mind off the heat, until a hack leaned over the gantry above his head and shouted his name.

"Rose, you got an EA."

"A what?"

"Educational Assessment," Curtis explained, shouting over the bed between them. "They must have sharpened their act up, it usually takes weeks to sort out the new inmates. I'll show you the way if you like. I can ask if my books have arrived."

CHAPTER 19

CURTIS

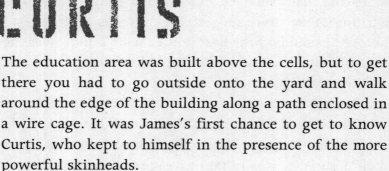

The education area was built above the cells, but to get there you had to go outside onto the yard and walk around the edge of the building along a path enclosed in a wire cage. It was James's first chance to get to know Curtis, who kept to himself in the presence of the more powerful skinheads.

"What courses do you do?" James asked, as they walked side by side.

"Everyone's supposed to get three hours' education a day," Curtis explained. "But there's not enough teachers for normal classes, so they just give you textbooks to read. I only go because you're allowed to buy extra books. It's supposed to be related to what you're learning, but the censor only stops a book if it tells you how to make explosives, or if it's porno or something."

"Do they force us to go to class?"

Curtis laughed. "It's compulsory; but imagine you're a teacher and you've got twenty guys like Elwood in your class. How hard would you try to make them turn up?"

"See your point," James grinned.

"I'd like to do an art course," Curtis said. "All I ever did when I was a kid was paint or draw, but all they'll let you have here are the stubby pencils like you get with your commissary forms. I did get a box of coloring pencils smuggled in, but the hacks wouldn't stand for any big stuff."

James tried to gently move the conversation towards the idea of escaping as they rounded a corner.

"So, you ever getting out?" James asked.

"Doesn't look like it," Curtis said. "You?"

"Eighteen years," James said.

"Not bad," Curtis said. "You'll be in your thirties. You've got a shot at living some kind of life."

"I'm getting out *way* before eighteen years," James grinned.

"Nobody escapes from here, James. This place is new-built, state of the art."

"Me and Dave worked out a plan when we were in Nebraska. If they'd ever let us out of solitary, we'd have pulled it too. But here's the *weirdest* coincidence: Omaha State and this joint are exactly alike. They must have been built by the same people."

James knew that Omaha State and Arizona Max were twins: designed by the same architect, built by the same construction company, and opened within six months of one another. It was an essential detail in the background story that explained how James and Dave could know how to escape from Arizona Max within days of arriving.

"The *exact* same?" Curtis said.

"More or less. Same security systems, same kind of cellblocks, even the same fixtures and fittings. When me and Dave were in solitary, we had this hack on our landing who used to talk to us all the time. He'd come over to my cell door for a chat. I think he felt sorry for me because I was young, but he was one of those guys who loved his own voice. He moaned non-stop. I mean, I'm the one locked in solitary twenty-three hours a day, but he'd be whinging about *his* life. His wife, his kids, his house, and about the superintendent busting his balls and keeping him on night shift.

"Whenever he moaned about work, I started asking subtle questions. Like, how many staff there were on duty at night and what kind of security passes they used. Dave's cell wasn't far away and he started doing the same. By the time we'd been in solitary for a few weeks, this big-mouth had told us *way* more than he should have."

"You really believe you could escape?"

"I reckon I'd make it out the gate. The tricky part is what to do after that. You need money and connections to pay for a false identity and set up a new life. There's no point going on the run for a few weeks, getting caught, and ending up buried in solitary with ten years added to your sentence. You've got to find a way of avoiding the cops for the whole rest of your life."

"How would you break out?" Curtis asked. "You've got to get out of a locked cell for starters."

"No offense," James said, "but the only people who'll ever know that are the ones going out with me."

Curtis seemed to understand the need for secrecy and they were nearly at the metal door of the education unit anyway. A hack padded the boys down before they passed through another metal detector. It was two flights of stairs up, then past three small classrooms to a door with EDUCATION OFFICER written on it.

"You mind if I go in quickly first?" Curtis asked. "I want to ask Mr. Haines if my books have arrived."

Curtis knocked on the door and got hailed in by a voice James recognized as Scott Warren.

"Isn't Haines here?" Curtis asked, looking surprised as he pushed the door open.

Scott, who was sitting at a desk, shook his head. "I'm covering for him today."

James spotted John Jones standing behind the desk.

Curtis pointed at James. "I came to show him the way and see if my books were in."

"Yeah . . . umm, sorry," Scott stuttered. "What's your name, son?"

"Curtis Oxford."

"Curtis . . . it's probably best if you wait until the education officer is back . . . tomorrow. I'm not familiar with the procedure for handing out books."

Curtis backed out of the office, looking at James. "Do you know the way back on your own?"

James nodded. "I'll see you out there."

He stepped into the office and shut the door behind

Curtis. John and Scott were both in a state of shock. They stared at a black-and-white CCTV monitor until it showed Curtis reaching the end of the corridor and starting down the stairs.

"Sheesh!" Scott said, putting both hands over his heart. "That gave me a fright. . . . I never expected our target to come wandering into the room with you."

"You might have guessed what was going on," John said tersely.

"You only said we might have to meet in the *visitors'* room," James snapped back.

"Well, whatever . . . ," John huffed.

James felt his temper rise up as he ran his hand through his sweaty hair. "You know what?" he said angrily. "I'm boiling hot, I've not slept or had a decent shower, I've eaten nothing but crap food, I've seen people get beaten up, pepper-sprayed, and have their skin burned off . . . I've even had some psycho come at me with a knife and try to kill me. If you don't like the job I'm doing here, you can take this mission and shove it *right* up your arse."

John looked startled by the outburst.

"We appreciate that you're working under a lot of stress," Scott said gently, trying to calm James down.

"James," John said, sounding extra sincere, "I apologize. I didn't mean to have a go at you. It was just a shock when Curtis came in here and saw all of us together. . . . We called this emergency meeting because there's a serious situation with Dave."

"Why don't you sit down?" Scott said, as he reached over to a water dispenser. "How about a cold drink?"

James sat down, as Scott filled a paper cup from the water cooler.

"They pulled Dave out of the hole for a doctor's examination earlier this morning," John explained. "The baton round fractured three of his ribs. One of them broke badly. A bone fragment has snapped off and punctured the surrounding tissue, causing internal bleeding."

"How serious is that?" James asked.

"If Dave had been x-rayed and treated immediately, it wouldn't have been bad," John said. "But by the time they dragged him out of the hole this morning, a blood clot had formed on his chest wall. He's having difficulty breathing and he'll be hospitalized for at least two weeks. After that, he'll be on medication to break up the clot. He won't be back to full fitness for a couple of months, at least."

"So that's it," James sighed. "You're gonna pull me out of here?"

"As soon as practicable," John nodded. "We're as sorry as you are that this didn't work out, James. I've been in the intelligence game for twenty years and I'm afraid complicated plans like this have a habit of going awry."

James drained his paper cup and nodded when Scott offered a refill. Part of James was relieved at the prospect of getting back to campus unscathed, but a much bigger part was bitter at having gone through so much stress for nothing.

"Is there no way I could carry on without Dave?" James asked.

"I can't see how," John said. "You need protection."

"Not any more I don't. You saw me come in with Curtis, and Elwood spent half the morning telling me his life story. Nobody's gonna give me hassle when we're best buds."

This was news to Scott and John, who exchanged a long glance.

"Hmm," Scott said, drumming his finger thoughtfully against his cheek. "Sounds like you've put in some valuable work there. It might put a different complexion on things. . . ."

"But how would James handle the escape without Dave?" John asked. "Dave was the advanced driver and the only one big enough to wear your uniform during the escape."

"I'm a good driver," James said. "Lauren can navigate and the roads over here are nice and straight."

"Your driving didn't seem so great to me the other afternoon," Scott said bluntly.

"I've been able to drive for nearly a year and that's the only accident I've ever had. Well . . . except, right at the beginning when I nearly killed some woman's dog."

"Actually," John nodded, "despite James's idiotic little adventure the other afternoon, he did score top marks on his intermediate driving course. But there's *still* no way he can get out of here disguised as a hack."

Scott rested an elbow on the desk and waggled his finger at James. "Stand up a minute, James. How tall are you?"

"A hundred and sixty-two centimeters," James said, as he climbed out of his chair.

Scott looked baffled. "What's that in American money?"

John smiled. "About five feet two inches. Have you got any men that small?"

"Not men, I haven't. But we're an equal opportunity employer and there's a young lady on our cellblock who's about James's size."

John broke into a smile. "Could you alter the staff rota so that she's on duty the night of the escape?"

Scott nodded. "That shouldn't be too tough. We might have to make a few adjustments to the plan, but this is definitely doable."

"So we're back in business?" John asked.

"I can't see why not," Scott said. "As long as James is sure he's up to it."

CHAPTER 20

TIME

Of course I'm up to it. The words glided out easily enough. The mission was saved, and James felt like a hero as Scott grasped his hand and shook it robustly.

Reality dawned as James passed down the stairs and out of the education block. The sun was brutal and the mountains of barbed wire lining the prison compound shimmered in the heat. The same light caught the powerful torsos of the predators scouring the yard and the guns cradled by the hacks on the cellblock roof.

James felt smaller than one of the grains of sand under his canvas shoe as he looked around and realized what he'd got himself into: a thirteen-year-old boy alone against a black-hearted machine built to contain the nastiest people on the planet. For an instant, he considered running back to the office and telling John he'd changed his mind. He stopped walking, took a deep breath, and ran his tongue around his dry mouth.

James thought about the moment he'd pulled the trigger on the guy in Miami, scared out of his mind. It had been a terrible experience, but he could draw strength from it now.

He thought back to his training, all the seemingly impossible things he'd achieved when the instructors pushed him through the pain barrier. Whenever a trainee was on the point of giving up, Mr. Speaks used to scream in their ear: "This is tough, but cherubs are tougher." James had got so sick of the phrase he thought he'd never want to hear it again, but now the words felt like a comfort.

He whispered it under his breath as he started walking again. "This is tough, but cherubs are tougher."

The exercise yard was at its most comfortable in the hour before the inmates were locked down for the night. The sun was low and a gentle breeze made the heat almost tolerable. James sat with Curtis near the chin-up bars, while Elwood and the others prowled for some unfortunate who'd failed to deliver his commissary package to Kirch's bunk earlier in the day.

The two boys had been talking for an hour, sitting in the sand, trading stories, and getting friendly with each other.

"So, you shot three people dead and tried to blow your own brains out," James said, giving Curtis a shocked look, as if this was news to him. "If I'd met you in the street, I'd never have booked you for anything other than a totally straight kid."

Curtis smiled, clearly pleased to have somebody brighter than Elwood and Kirch to talk to. "We were always moving around when I was growing up. Canada, Mexico, even South Africa for a while. It was cool, just me and my mom together, but we had some close scrapes with the law. I started getting stressed out, worrying about what would happen if Mom got busted. Sometimes I got so depressed. The blackest feeling, like the whole world was closing in on me."

"Did you see a doctor, or anything?" James asked.

Curtis nodded. "I've had every kind of pill going. In a lot of the places we lived, my mom would take me to see a psychiatrist. Every one of them acted like they knew what they were talking about, but they all came up with different answers. If you ask me, psychiatrists are a bunch of phoneys.

"Two years ago, it started getting real bad. I'd go to bed and stay under the covers all day. My mom took me to this shrink in Philadelphia—some hotshot she'd read about in a magazine article. He reckoned my problems were down to a lack of structure in my life: moving from place to place and not having proper schooling or relationships with other kids my own age. So he puts this bright idea in my mom's head to send me to a military school. I begged her not to send me, but I was a mess and Mom had tried everything else, so she went along with it.

"The place was a toilet. They had me up every morning running laps. Making beds, polishing boots, and that whole playing at being soldiers gig. One night the commandant ripped into me for not knotting my tie properly. He gives me this little nailbrush and tells me to start scrubbing out this whole massive shower room. I did it for about ten minutes, then I ran off, busted into the weapons locker, and stole the commandant's car keys. Two hours later, there's three dead bodies and I've got half the Arizona police department pointing guns at me."

"That's what you call chucking a wobbler," James grinned, making a mental note to mention Curtis's visit to the famous child psychiatrist in Philadelphia to John or Scott as soon as he saw them. "Do you still get depressed?"

"Not so much," Curtis said. "Though it gets really boring in here sometimes."

James spent the evening watching Curtis's miniature TV and eating Stanley Duff's snacks. Stanley's battered brother was back from the hospital. Raymond looked like he was going to cry when he saw that Kirch had stripped everything he owned from his locker. He didn't even have a change of underwear or a pillow.

When James woke up with his neck clamped to his bed and a cut-throat razor glinting in front of his eyes, he guessed it was Raymond Duff, but he was wrong.

"You one of us?"

James got a whiff of BO, a flash of grinning teeth, and the rush of sheer terror that you get when you think you're about to feel serious pain.

"Are you one of us?" Elwood growled again.

Curtis and the other skinheads were standing around James's bed, laughing.

"I am," James said, though the hand crushing his windpipe made it come out as a croak.

Kirch's arm reached over from the next bed and dabbed James's cheek with a wet brush.

"You look too hairy to me, Rose."

Elwood pressed the razor against James's skin, close to the point of making a cut.

"What is this?" James gasped. "Come on guys . . ."

"If you're one of us," Elwood grinned, "you gotta get rid of that faggot haircut."

Kirch waggled a wet shaving brush in his face.

"Cut my hair," James nodded, as Elwood let go and allowed him to sit up. "But can't you use the battery razor I gave to Abe?"

Kirch, Curtis, and the three others who'd got out of bed for the occasion laughed.

"Where's the fun in an electric razor?" Elwood giggled. "You're not scared, are you?"

"Why would I be scared of you?" James asked, trying to act as though being woken at 3 a.m. with a psycho waving a razor under his nose was the kind of thing that didn't bother him in the slightest.

Kirch moved in with the shaving brush and sploshed warm, soapy water into James's hair. After a couple of strokes, he got fed up and drained the whole mug of sloppy mixture over James's head. James screwed up his face in pain as it streamed into his eyes.

"Better keep still," Elwood giggled.

He placed the razor against James's forehead and

swept it upwards. A soapy blond clump dropped into James's lap. Elwood hacked off hair from here and there, until James's head was a shocking mixture of bald spots, crazy tufts, and the occasional bloody nick from the blade.

"Perfecto," Elwood said, backing away like an artist admiring a painting.

The skinheads were cracking up as they sauntered back to their beds. When the others were lying down, Curtis came back with a set of battery-powered clippers.

"You want me to sort that mess out?"

James and Curtis walked to the bathroom. After James had wetted a towel and mopped the soap and blood off his head, he knelt on the tiled floor, while Curtis leaned over and finished shaving him bald.

"So your brother's definitely not coming back?" Curtis asked, as he rinsed the clipper attachment under a tap.

"With his escape record and Stanley getting his neck broken, that hack Warren told me he's put in a request for Dave to be re-categorized as a high-risk inmate. He'll be put in a single cell over on the supermax block."

"So the escape is off?"

"It's hard without Dave," James whispered, "but my uncle beats the shit out of my little sister and I really want to get her out of there. The thing is, Dave could have got a job or something, but I don't see how someone our age can survive on the outside without help."

"You know what I said about my mom? Hiding out, living under false names and stuff?"

James nodded.

"I don't know where she is right now," Curtis said. "But I know people who can contact her. If we busted out together, she'd be able to set you up with a new life."

"So now *you* want to escape," James said, trying to sound cynical, while containing the ten-meter-wide smile that wanted to break out across his face.

"I got nothing to lose," Curtis said. "They can't add one day to life without parole. And so what if they shoot my ass? What's worth living for in Arizona Max?"

"If I *did* let you break out with me, it's just you, me, and my kid sister," James said firmly. "It's my show and I don't want Elwood, or any of those other lunatics muscling in."

Curtis nodded. "But if I can keep my mouth shut, you'll take me?"

"You can't get out of here without me and I can't make it on the outside without you," James smiled. "Funny how life works. It must be fate . . . or something."

CHAPTER 21

WEDNESDAY

FIVE DAYS LATER

James got hold of a spare bed sheet. When everyone at his end of the cell seemed to be asleep, he began cutting it into meter-long strips, using the sharpened end of his toothbrush. He ripped the cloth quietly, stopping now and then to make sure there wasn't a hack spying down from the metal gantry above his head. After he'd turned the sheet into strips, he took three pieces at a time and plaited them together for strength.

When James had finished, he put the lengths of rope in his locker and noticed that sunlight was flickering behind the blades of the ventilation fans in the cell wall. He was dreading another sweat-soaked day inside Arizona Max. But if things went to plan, this would be the last one.

James asked Curtis to hang back when the rest of the skinheads went onto the yard. The cell never emptied out entirely, but no one was paying attention as James pulled a strip of cardboard out of his shorts.

"It's my visit today," James explained. "If I can get Lauren on her own for a few seconds, without my uncle, I'll tell her to pack a bag and expect us at the house at three tomorrow morning."

Curtis nodded. "What's with the cardboard?"

"That's how we're getting out of here."

"*Cardboard,*" Curtis said, looking at James like he was insane.

James stepped across to the emergency door in the middle of the cell. There were two of these sliding doors along the cell wall in between beds. They were designed to allow the PERT team to enter if the prisoners rioted and barricaded the main door, or as emergency exits in a fire.

"How *exactly* do you plan to get a solid steel door open with a piece from a Kleenex box?"

James grinned confidently. "Watch and learn."

He checked the gantry to make sure there wasn't a hack around, then walked to the door and went up on tiptoes. He slotted the card through the gap between the top of the door and its frame, and jiggled it in and out before tucking it back into his pocket.

"Now we wait," James said, as he moved away and sat on the end of a bed.

"This is your great plan?" Curtis asked indignantly.

Thirty seconds later, a hack walked purposefully onto the rail. He disappeared down a flight of spiral stairs behind the door. The door slid open thirty centimeters and the hack pushed his head through the gap. He inspected the inside for signs of tampering before shutting it again.

"*What* . . . ?" Curtis gasped, as the guard walked back up the steps. "What happened?"

"Remember I told you about that big-mouthed hack in Omaha?"

"Yeah."

"He always moaned about the faulty doors. Every door inside Omaha State had an anti-tamper device. If someone starts fiddling, an alarm goes off on the console in the cellblock control room. They have to send a hack out to check both sides of the door and reset the alarm, but they're very sensitive. All it takes is a gust of wind, or someone hitting the door to set it off. The hack said he spent half his life wandering around canceling false alarms."

"And the doors here are the same?"

James nodded. "*Exactly* the same. And the thing is, the guards get so sick of the alarms, they assume every one is false."

Curtis nodded. "That hack didn't even look over the rail to see if someone was waiting on the other side."

"Within a minute of taking out the guard, we can be up on the rail and tooled up with stun grenades and pepper spray."

"And from there?"

"You've seen how few staff there are on duty at night," James said. "If we rip off the hacks' security passes and put on their uniforms, I reckon we can bluff our way out of the front gate before the alarm goes off."

"Definitely tonight?"

James nodded. "As long as I get a chance to speak with my sister. Let's hit the yard."

There'd been a knife fight between two rival gangs the previous morning. Everyone had been sent back to their cells and locked down for the rest of the day. As James and Curtis lined up to pass through the metal detector, all the other inmates seemed tense, like something bad could flare up at any second.

As they closed on their regular spot by the chin-up bars, James spotted a kid balled up on the ground sniffling. Elwood had just slapped him around in front of a dozen laughing skinheads.

"James," Elwood said, pointing down at the ball. "Wanna finish him off?"

"I'm good," James said, waving his hand in front of his face.

The victim was Mark, the friendly kid with the black eye who'd slept next to James on the first night. Mark had no relatives on the outside to pay in commissary money. This ruled out extortion but didn't stop Elwood beating him up for fun.

"Boot him," Elwood snarled. "You're such a pussy, James."

James spun quickly and kicked Mark up the arse. He knew this would amuse the crowd without hurting his victim too badly. The skinheads roared as Mark rolled over in the dirt. James pulled down the front of his shorts.

"Now get out of here before I piss over you," he snarled.

Mark scowled back at James, as he scrambled to his feet and limped off.

"Why'd you let him go?" Elwood asked angrily.

James shrugged. He kept trying to find ways to minimize the daily violence without appearing soft, but he knew that the more time he spent with psychos like Elwood, the more chance there was he'd end up involved in an incident where someone got badly beaten, or stabbed.

"So," James said, desperate to change the subject. "Is there a riot going down, or not?"

The prospect had been hotly debated in the cell overnight. Whenever there was serious violence, the hacks closed the yard and locked everyone in the cells. But locking inmates down for long stretches only fermented the anger.

"I *love* riots," Kirch said, making a rare excursion into the world of speech.

"Yeah," Elwood said. "You should have seen the last one, James. There were baton rounds whizzing across this yard from every direction. *Poom, poom, poom.* I was one of the last to make it back to the cell and dudes were laid up everywhere: either stabbed, or shot up."

Kirch looked at the sky with a smile across his face. "Happy days," he nodded. "Easily worth a month of lockdown."

James sat down in the dirt. After a week of Kirch and

Elwood's bullying and bragging, he could happily have laid them out in return for five minutes' peace.

"The riot was the scariest hour of my life," Curtis whispered, leaning into James's ear. "I thought I was gonna die. Elwood hid under one of the shelters. He was as scared as I was."

James smiled. "What about Kirch?"

"Kirch really *is* a psycho. I think he loved every minute."

"We've gotta get out of here," James said, shaking his head. "This place is doing my brain in."

If the cellblock was put back in lockdown, visitation would be canceled. James wouldn't get to see Lauren and the escape would be off. As the morning wore on, James got increasingly nervous. There was a fight inside the canteen when the first batch of lunches was being served. It was shut down while the mess was cleared up inside and a rumor flashed around the yard that it wouldn't reopen. A sullen crowd, most of whom had missed their main meal because of the lockdown the day before, gathered around the prefabricated building looking for trouble.

Superintendent Frey prowled on the roof, watching the commotion through binoculars. James anxiously studied his body language for any sign that the cellblock was going back into lockdown, but the canteen reopened and the backlog of prisoners gradually got served.

When it was time, James enthusiastically walked to the reception room at the front of the cellblock. Before entering the visitors' area, he had to strip naked and put his clothes in a cardboard box. After a body search, he buttoned on a pocketless yellow overall that nobody had ever thought to wash.

The visiting room had tables for six inmates, but Lauren and a wiry FBI agent James had never seen before were the only ones in the room. James walked barefoot across the tacky floor and sat opposite them. Lauren leaned forward and gave her brother a hug.

"What happened to your head?" Lauren gasped, looking at the five-day growth of stubble.

"You hang with skinheads, you gotta look like one," James grinned. "If I don't get out of here soon, I might end up with a tattoo."

"Prison tattoos are very dangerous," the FBI man said stiffly, in the poshest American accent James had ever heard. "The needle penetrating the skin is unlikely to be sterile. You'd risk being contaminated with any number of infectious diseases including hepatitis and AIDS."

"I read my briefings," James whispered. "I take it you're my new uncle John."

"Theodore Monroe," the stick man nodded as he shook James's hand, "but everyone calls me Theo. I'm afraid John Jones was compromised when Curtis saw him in the education block. Scott Warren already works here and Marvin . . . well, it would obviously be inappropriate to send an African American undercover pretending to be your uncle."

James smiled. "So are we expecting company in here?"

"Scott organized the visiting roster so that it only contained inmates who never get visitors," Theo explained.

"Are we being bugged?"

Theo shook his head. "There is recording equipment in this room, but they need permission from a judge to switch it on. We have to get it every time Curtis's supposed uncles turn up."

"You know that note you passed to Scott Warren about the psychiatrist in Philadelphia?" Lauren asked excitedly. "The FBI followed up your lead and found a picture of Jane Oxford."

"At least we think it's her," Theo interrupted, reaching inside his impeccably tailored suit and pulling out a blurry color photo.

James stared at the face of an ordinary looking middle-aged woman, wearing large rectangular glasses. The boy standing at her side was clearly Curtis.

"It's a video surveillance picture from the first class check-in counter at Philadelphia International Airport, a couple of weeks before Curtis was sent to the military school. Interestingly enough, the psychiatrist Curtis visited turned out to be on the board of directors at the military school."

James laughed. "Curtis *said* psychiatrists are a bunch of crooks. I bet he earned a nice bonus for every poor kid he sent there."

"The FBI has also traced multiple transactions on the credit cards Jane Oxford used to book the flights. All in all, it's a commendable piece of intelligence work. John Jones and Marvin Teller told me to pass on their heartiest congratulations."

James couldn't imagine the phrase *heartiest congratulations* ever passing the lips of John Jones or Marvin Teller, but he got the point.

"So, does any of this actually get us anywhere?" James asked.

"Perhaps," the FBI man said, as he swept invisible crumbs from his jacket with his spindly fingers. "Even if your escape attempt fails, this photograph represents a significant breakthrough."

"What about the escape?" James asked. "We'd better still be on for tonight. I can't handle it here much longer. I was scared about what might happen to me at first. Now I'm more worried about what I might be forced into doing to someone else. Things are on a short fuse out on the yard right now."

"There's no holdup at our end," Theo nodded. "There will be three staff on duty in your cellblock tonight. Scott Warren, of course, the female guard Amanda Voss and lastly a man named Golding, who will be working at the cellblock control console. You have to be exceedingly cautious around the control room. Golding will be within reach of an emergency alarm that can instantly deactivate every door in the prison, even for those with swipe cards.

"When you get out of the cellblock and reach the staff lounge, you're unlikely to bump into a member of staff. I'm led to believe that the conditions are rather insalubrious. It's not the kind of place where you'd want to spend time hanging around after your shift.

"Apart from Warren, the only other person who will be on duty inside the prison and who knows about the escape attempt is a man named Shorter. He works inside the central prison control room and operates the staff exit door. As you know, Dave has certain physical similarities to Scott Warren and the original plan was for him to show his face to the security camera when you passed through the main gate. Unfortunately, neither yourself nor Curtis are big enough to easily pass as an adult male, so we've brought in Shorter as an insurance policy. He's been an employee of the Arizona Prison Department for nearly forty years, and we expect the inquiry into your escape to make him the scapegoat. Shorter understands this, but the FBI has agreed to offer to pay for his early retirement, in return for cooperation."

"So that should get us out of the front door," James said. "What next?"

"You meet up with Lauren, as per the plan. It is of considerable importance that you move quickly. Arizona is sparsely populated and there are not many roads in and out of the state. You can expect police roadblocks to be set up on all the major roads near to the prison within half an hour of the escape being detected."

"I've already tuned the car radio to a local news station," Lauren said. "So we'll know as soon as the alert goes out."

"Assuming you make it away from the prison, we're then relying on Curtis to find the way back to his mother," Theo explained. "We recorded the conversation during Curtis's visit on Saturday and he made no mention of the escape. Do you have any idea where you'll be going?"

"I told Curtis we should go into a heavily populated area to minimize our chances of being recaptured," James said. "Curtis says he knows people who used to work for his mum in Los Angeles, so that's where we're heading.

He didn't mention the escape to his visitors because he knows this room is bugged. Don't forget, Curtis has spent his whole life on the run. He might only be fourteen, but he probably knows more about police and FBI operations than most major criminals."

"That's a valid point," Theo nodded. "So is his plan clear? Has Curtis mentioned where any of these connections live, or how they came to do business with his mother?"

"I get the impression they're bikers," James said. "Or ex-bikers. The idea is that we get out of Arizona as fast as we can. When we reach L.A., we find a phone booth and start making calls."

They spoke for a few more minutes about the finer points of the escape plan before the FBI man wished James luck and headed for the door. James gave Lauren another hug.

"Play it safe," Lauren said. "Don't go getting yourself killed tonight."

CHAPTER 22

DOORS

Scott Warren took the 2:30 a.m. count. Unlike a standing count, when inmates stood to attention at the end of their beds, this one only required Scott to lean over the gantry and count heads. He'd only wake the inmates up if he couldn't see someone.

When he was done, Scott clanked along the metal gantry to the control room. If things went as planned, the escape wouldn't be noticed until the next count was due in four hours.

Scott reached the control room at the center of the H-shaped cellblock and tore a form off his clipboard. He handed it to the chunky figure of Golding, who sat at a three-meter-long console covered in switches, surveillance monitors, and lights.

Golding stared at the sheet as Amanda Voss came towards him and handed him another.

"No escapes, boss," the petite twenty-three-year-old grinned.

Golding picked up a telephone and called the central control room. "Hey Keith, this is cellblock T for trouble. I'm calling in a count of two-fifty-seven inmates at two-thirty-seven in the a.m. Situation here is all normal."

Warren rolled his chair back so he could put his feet up on the console and picked up a newspaper. As he did this, a buzzer sounded, accompanied by a flashing red light.

Golding angrily flung down his newspaper. "Those *freakin'* doors . . . Cell T4, side entrance B. One of you go and shut that thing up."

"I gotta take a dump," Scott said guiltily, looking towards the toilet. "Can you deal with it, Amanda?"

Good people sometimes get hurt when you're trying to catch bad ones. When the door began to slide, James's conscience tripped over the idea of laying out a girl; but the mission depended on him holding his nerve.

His fist smacked Amanda in the temple, with enough force to knock the opposite side of her head against the edge of the metal door. There's no such thing as a good head injury, but a clean shot to the thinnest part of the skull was unlikely to leave Amanda with anything more than a mild concussion and a two-day headache.

James dragged Amanda's unconscious body backwards and lowered her to the floor at the bottom of the spiral staircase.

"Come on," James whispered anxiously to Curtis. He wanted the door closed before any other inmates spotted the opening and decided to come with them.

Curtis stepped through and slid the door shut, as James put on Amanda's ADOP baseball cap, then unbuttoned her black shirt and pulled it on. Combined with his black trainers and a pair of Curtis's black tracksuit bottoms, James could pass as a prison officer provided nobody looked too hard.

"Tie her up before she comes to," James ordered. "Ankles and mouth gag, then tie her hands around the stair rail. Use the constrictor knot, like I showed you."

Curtis had a couple of James's plaited ropes slung over his shoulder. While he tied up Amanda, James swiftly ran up the spiral stairs and crept across the rail to the weapons rack. He grabbed a can of pepper spray and tucked a stun grenade into his pocket as Scott came through the door. James looked behind to make sure Curtis was still out of earshot.

"You OK?" James asked.

Scott nodded. "Go for my nose and make it look real bloody. Be careful around Golding, he was a football player at high school. Use the handcuffs in the blue storage cupboard behind the console."

James stepped back into a fighting stance and thrust his palm at the base of Scott's nose. Blood trickled over Scott's lips as he laid himself down on the metal floor. James ripped the safety pin from a can of pepper spray. He shot a quick blast into Scott's hair and face, then quickly crammed a piece of balled-up rag into his mouth.

"Sorry, mate," James whispered, as he rolled Scott on to his chest and began tying his wrists.

Curtis was coming up the spiral stairs a little too noisily for James's taste. Scott went limp, as though James had knocked him out.

"Ssssshh," James said. "Is she well tied?"

Curtis nodded. "Just how you showed me."

"Did you get her ID badge and swipe card?"

"Course," Curtis whispered, grinning as he looked down over the rail. "I never thought I'd see the view from up here."

James unhooked an electric shock device from Scott's belt and stripped everything out of his pockets, including his keys and wallet, before shuffling down to tie his ankles. He threw Curtis the bunch of keys.

"One of those works the gun locker," James explained.

Curtis opened the clear plastic front of the cabinet, while James bent Scott's legs up and began tying the bindings on his wrists to the bindings on his ankles.

Curtis took one of the large baton-round guns. "Looks complicated," he said.

"Help me move him, then I'll show you."

They pushed Scott's body to the inside of the gantry, so that the inmates below couldn't see him. James grabbed a small cylinder of compressed gas from the locker and snatched the gun from Curtis.

"I watched the hacks do this the other day," James explained. "Screw the gas cylinder on the top of the gun, like so. Turn the valve, then you break her open and . . . Give us a baton round."

Curtis handed James one of the fat plastic slugs. James slid it into the barrel, closed the gun, and handed it to Curtis.

"Only fire if we have to," James said. "You know how noisy they are."

Curtis shoved more pepper spray, stun grenades, and rounds for the baton guns into his pockets while James armed another gun for himself.

James opened the door at the end of the gantry. The short corridor led to the control room. James kept his back to the wall as they crept forward with their guns poised.

When James reached the end, he poked his head into the control room and eyeballed Golding, who sat with his feet on the console reading the sports page. It was eerily silent, apart from the hum of the air conditioning.

"We've got to distract him from the console or he'll hit the alarm," James whispered.

Curtis nodded, as James crouched down and pulled out one of Scott's coins. He rolled the coin out into the room. Golding heard it drop in the middle of the floor and looked over the top of his newspaper.

"You've dropped a quarter down here, Scott," Golding said. He stared for a few seconds, before shrugging and going back to his newspaper.

James looked at Curtis, shaking his head with frustration. He rolled another coin. This time Golding looked put out. Too lazy to stand up, he slapped his newspaper down and wheeled his chair backwards towards the coins.

"What's going on there, Scottie? You got a hole in your pocket or something?"

As Golding spun his chair around to look down the corridor, James and Curtis both fired. The rounds hit Golding in the chest and stomach. His chair shot backwards, before tipping over. The fat man roared as he blasted the chair out of his way with a powerful kick and rolled over, struggling to stand up.

James's ears were whistling from the gun blast as he ran towards Golding and drenched his face in pepper spray.

"See what we do when we catch you," Golding gasped, as he slumped blindly back to the floor, trying to rub the spray out of his eyes. "Scott . . . Amanda . . . Where the hell are you?"

"They won't be along any time soon," Curtis gloated.

"When we get you two in the hole, I'm gonna come in after you and bust every bone in your bodies."

Golding had plenty of fight in him and James didn't fancy a tussle with somebody so heavy. He pushed another plastic round into the gun and held it menacingly in Golding's face. Although classed as a nonlethal weapon, the baton round was deadly if fired into a vulnerable area from close range.

"Hands in the air, fat boy," James shouted ferociously.

When the muzzle touched his face, Golding put his arms up and allowed Curtis to knot them together. After this, he let Curtis stuff a piece of cloth in his mouth and tie a gag over it. Meanwhile, James located the rack of handcuffs Scott had told him about.

It took both boys to drag Golding a few meters across

the polished floor towards the staircase leading down to the reception room. James cuffed Golding's hands around the top stair rail. Curtis cruelly stepped on the bracelet, so it closed down a couple of extra notches.

"Remember when you put them on me?" Curtis snarled. "You like them nice and tight, don't you, Golding?"

Golding screamed curses into his gag as the boys ran back to grab their guns. James noticed Golding's backpack under the console. He tossed out a baseball magazine and sandwich box and stuffed the pack with baton rounds, pepper spray, and stun grenades before slinging it over his back.

Curtis found a lightweight black jacket with the Arizona Prisons Department logo on, which had belonged to Amanda Voss. He zipped it over his black T-shirt and found that it fitted OK.

The boys sprinted downstairs, emerging through an unsecured door into the reception room on the ground floor. James jogged towards the exit door and swiped Amanda's card through the lock. He smiled with relief when it clicked.

"Keep calm," James said, as they stepped out into fresh air. "Remember, it looks suspicious if we run."

James swiped the card again and they passed through a wire gate into the main prison compound. The tarmac road went arrow-straight, all the way down to the exit. The only light came from a few lamps around the wire fences of the cellblocks and the glowing watchtowers around the distant perimeter.

A passing refuse cart and a wave from a hack taking a cigarette break was the only excitement during the eight-minute walk towards the sally port, but James tortured himself with images of sirens, gunfire, and the savage beating he'd undoubtedly take if the hacks recaptured him.

A hundred meters shy of the vehicle gates, there was a giant signpost ordering everyone to follow a color-coded line painted on the asphalt: red for inmates under transportation, yellow for visitors, and green for staff. The area beyond the sign was floodlit and CCTV cameras were perched every place you looked.

Curtis's voice was quaking. "We're never gonna pass through this."

"Act normal," James whispered. "We're dressed like staff, we have swipe cards. Unless the emergency siren goes off, there's no reason for anyone to look at us too hard."

The green line ended at the door of a small metal shed marked Staff Only. James peeked through a window into a small room with a line of vending machines. A miserable looking hack sat on a plastic chair drinking from a tiny cup. James swiped his card in the entrance door, went up two steps, and cautiously poked his head into a narrow corridor that smelled of floor polish.

"Looks sweet," James said.

They stepped inside, passing by the frosted glass entrance of the room with the vending machines, then dashing along the corridor towards the staff exit.

James swiped Amanda's card through the lock on the door. A man's voice came out of a loudspeaker. James hoped it was the friendly Mr. Shorter in the central control room, but he had no way of telling.

"Look up at the camera, state your name and staff ID."

"Voss, Amanda, Y465," James said, trying his best to sound like a girl.

"Who's your buddy?" the loudspeaker asked.

Curtis looked uncertainly up at the camera. "Warren, Scott, KT318."

"Hey Scottie, you don't sound so good tonight. You got flu or something?"

"Yeah," Curtis said uncertainly.

"Sorry to hear that, man. You go home and catch yourself a good rest."

The door buzzed to indicate that it had been unlocked. James and Curtis passed through and walked along a wire-enclosed path. They stood behind a red Wait sign, while a chunky door built into the armor-plated wall of the sally port rumbled backwards. Once it was fully open, the boys stepped into a tunnel.

When the door at their backs closed fully, a green bulb began pulsing above the door at the opposite end. James realized there was a slot for a swipe card. He couldn't remember if he was supposed to get interviewed a second time and was relieved when the metal door began rumbling.

As they stepped out of the secure compound, James spotted the sign pointing towards the staff car park and headed off briskly. Curtis was so shocked that he could barely open his mouth.

"Unbelievable," Curtis mumbled. "Unb*eeeee*lievable. You're a genius, James."

"Don't count your chickens," James said, as they strode along a paved path through the night air. "This is only the beginning."

CHAPTER 29

CARS

James couldn't risk hanging out in the car park too long, but there were more than fifty parked vehicles and he couldn't walk straight up to Scott's without Curtis wondering how he knew which one it was. James aimed the plipper at every car until he got a blip and a set of flashing lights from a Honda Civic in the next row across.

As they cut between two cars, a battered pickup rolled over a speed bump into the car park. The boys instinctively ducked as the truck pulled in a few spaces along from the Civic. The driver swung out his legs and paused on the edge of his seat to light a cigarette. James recognized the face as it glimmered in the match light.

"Frey," Curtis whispered anxiously.

James had read Superintendent Frey's personnel file. It said he was a hard worker who thought of cellblock T as his personal property, but nobody had expected him to turn up three hours before a shift. This was bad news. James had to think fast.

Frey was wearing a football shirt and jeans, but even allowing time for him to change into uniform, maybe drink a coffee in the staff lounge, and walk up to block T, he'd still be discovering the tied-up hacks and raising the alarm within half an hour.

Taking Frey out was the obvious option, but the boys were on open ground and there were CCTV cameras everywhere. James decided to let Frey go unmolested. He was far from certain it was the right decision, but he remembered how the PERT team had treated Dave and he didn't want Golding's prediction of them ending up in a dark cell getting a beating to come true. The farther away from the prison they were if they got caught, the greater the chance that John Jones and the FBI team would be able to pull James out before the hacks got hold of him.

Once Frey had locked his truck and headed off down the cactus-lined path towards the staff entrance, they ran across to the little Civic and jumped inside. It was a flash model: racing seats, ten-spoke alloys, and a beefy engine. James pulled a red seatbelt across his waist and hit the start button. He remembered what had happened the last time he'd driven a car, but there was too much adrenalin flowing for him get hung up over it. He had to get on with the job.

James kept the speed down on the road leading out of the prison, but once he hit the interstate he couldn't hang about. The sporty little car had a firm suspension and the steering felt sharp. James got a sense of invincibility as he dodged between the three lanes of traffic.

The twelve-mile ride to the dirt road turnoff took less than ten minutes. A Ford Explorer with bull bars on the front was parked up, with its headlamps switched on, a few hundred meters past the junction.

"Grab the weapons," James said to Curtis, as he pulled the Honda up alongside the Ford and flung open his door.

Lauren had left the engine of the four-wheel-drive Ford running and was already belted into the front passenger seat. James climbed into the driver's seat and hit the gas as soon as Curtis slammed the door behind him.

"You got the car up here OK?" James asked Lauren, as he pulled on to the dirt road.

"Uncle John didn't wake up," Lauren nodded. "I got his road maps and worked out the route to Los Angeles." She looked behind. "And you must be Curtis."

"Hey," Curtis smiled. "Good to meet you, Lauren. Where'd you learn how to drive?"

"Me and Dave taught her," James explained. "We took her with us a couple of times when we were out on the rampage."

"I'm a bit short to reach the pedals," Lauren added. "But there's hardly any traffic on the road up from our house."

"What you got in the backpack over there?" Curtis asked.

"Clothes, money, toiletries," Lauren explained. "I even managed to sneak into the bedroom and get John's forty-four."

"We've got a proper gun?" Curtis asked. "Where is it?"

Curtis didn't need an answer; he spotted the huge revolver on the armrest between the two front seats.

The 4x4 seemed like it was on sleeping pills after driving the nippy little Honda. James pressed the gas pedal as they hit the interstate and it felt like nothing happened at all.

"Forty-four magnum," Curtis grinned as he picked up the gun. "Dirty Harry special. You can blow a guy in half with one of these."

Lauren looked out the window as the donut place whizzed by. "James, you *tit*, we're going the wrong way."

"What?" James gasped.

"You turned the wrong way when we pulled on to the interstate."

"Arse."

There was a metal barrier between the lanes. James started looking for a junction where he could pull off and turn around.

"Didn't you tune that radio?" James asked.

"Oh, yeah," Lauren said, reaching forward and flicking it on.

"We saw the superintendent of our cellblock in the prison car park," James explained. "We're not going to get anything like the four hours we'd hoped for. We'll be lucky if we get another twenty minutes before the police are on our tail."

James spotted a break in the barrier and swung the tall car into a wide arc, across a strip of scrub in the middle of the road, and into the opposite lane. A sedan car blasted its horn, as the driver slammed her brakes to avoid shunting them up the back.

"Whoops," James said, as he floored the gas pedal and began slowly picking up speed. "So how far is it to the border with California?"

"Just under sixty miles," Lauren said. "Los Angeles is two hundred miles farther than that. It's a five-hour journey if we don't stop."

"We'll have to stop at least once, for gas."

Traffic was light and the unlit road almost straight. When James checked the speedometer he was doing eighty miles an hour, which was over the limit, but in line with what most of the other traffic was doing at this time of night. If he drove any faster, he'd look conspicuous.

The radio station was holding a phone-in and the topics were "Are there alien beings walking among us?" and "Who is the greatest popular musician of all time?" As far as James could work out, most of the people who rang in believed that the answer to both questions was Elvis Presley.

The digital clock on the dashboard said 03:43 when the DJ cut off a caller and got seriously excited.

". . . We're picking up breaking news of an escape from Arizona Max. Two male escapees, both aged fourteen. That's one four, folks, not four zero. . . . One prison officer is believed to have died during the escape. Arizona police are setting up roadblocks at strategic locations. The escapees are described as white skinheads, going by the names of James Rose and Curtis Oxford. Both are convicted murderers and police say that you should treat the boys with the

same degree of caution as you would if you spotted a dangerous adult offender. . . . That's red-hot news, listeners, stay tuned, because were gonna be keeping you up to date on this all night long. . . ."

"You *killed* someone," Lauren gasped.

Scott Warren's faked death had always been part of the plan, but they had to act surprised in front of Curtis.

"We didn't kill nobody," Curtis said.

"One of the hacks must have had a heart attack or something," James said.

"This is *so* bad," Curtis said. "If you kill a hack, you're done for. They stick you in solitary and the hacks make your life hell: spitting in your food, playing loud music right outside your cell until it drives you nuts . . ."

"Then we'd better not get caught," James said.

"Oh God," Curtis said, shaking his head and sobbing.

"What do you want me to do," James shouted bitterly. "Go back and kiss him better?"

"What if there's a roadblock?" Curtis asked. "We've only got one proper gun and they'll shoot us to pieces if we try to ram through."

"Just stay cool and give me a chance to think," James said. "Lauren, how far are we from the California border?"

Lauren looked at the map spread out across her legs. "Thirty-five miles or so."

"They can have roadblocks in California too, you know," Curtis said.

"Of course," James said. "But there can't be many cops out here in the desert and they don't know what way we're going. The farther out you get, the more roads they'd need to block, so if we hit a roadblock I'd bet on it being sooner rather than later."

James watched the lines of cat's eyes whiz by for a few more minutes. A woman called the radio phone-in and said that the escapees should get the death penalty, even though they were only fourteen. The follow-up callers all agreed.

". . . OK folks. A little more news on the jailbreak. Police are now looking for a silver Honda Civic IS. Apparently that's a distinctive Jap box with fancy wheels and a little wing over the back window. . . ."

James smiled. "We're one step ahead of 'em."

"The cops will check out your uncle's house pretty soon," Curtis said. "They'll find this car is missing."

"But it buys us some time," James said.

"Up ahead," Lauren squealed.

Sitting on the right gave Lauren half a second's advantage in spotting the flashing blue lights blocking the road.

Roadblocks are usually positioned after bends, so that approaching traffic doesn't get a chance to pull off, although they have to leave stopping room or cars would smash into them. There was a queue of about a dozen cars, passing through a single lane that had been created by parking two cop cars with their lights flashing across the other two lanes of the interstate. Every car was being stopped while an officer inspected the passengers inside with a flashlight.

James pulled into the side of the road and slammed to a halt. He looked back over his shoulder. All four tires screeched as he did a backwards U-turn through the traffic. If the cops hadn't seen this maneuver, they certainly heard the horns of two approaching cars blasting as they swung out of his way. One car sideswiped the metal barrier in the center of the road, making a shower of orange sparks as it juddered to a halt.

"Dammit," James shouted, as he pushed the stick back into drive and rammed the gas pedal, heading into the oncoming traffic.

The police cars in the roadblock sounded their sirens and began moving towards them, as James noticed a break in the metal barrier and ploughed across the central reservation on to the correct side of the road.

"Lauren," James said anxiously. "Where's that backpack I brought with me?"

"Down by my feet," Lauren said.

"Take it, it's full of weapons. They're not looking for you, so soon as we stop I want you to jump out."

Lauren nodded. "I'll see what I can do."

"You can't *stop*," Curtis screamed. "We've gotta get out of here. If they catch us now that hack's dead, our lives won't be worth shit."

"I got you this far," James shouted back angrily. "Just *calm* down."

"Screw you," Curtis hissed, furiously grabbing the magnum off the armrest as the car pulled up in the sand at the side of the road.

Lauren dived out with the backpack and rolled down a modest slope into some scrub. Both cop cars pulled up, one in front and one behind the 4x4. A cop jumped out of each car with their gun pulled: one male, one female.

"There's no way I'm going back to prison," Curtis yelled.

The man stood behind in a covering position, while the lady cop jogged through the headlight beams towards the big Ford with her handgun pointing.

"Turn off the engine and put your hands on the steering wheel," the lady cop shouted.

James did as he was told, but he heard Curtis cocking the gun. The cop didn't see Curtis until she got in close because of the tinted windows.

"There's no need for that," the cop said.

James assumed Curtis had the magnum pointing at the cop, but he glanced in the driver's mirror and realized Curtis was pointing it at himself.

"Curtis, *don't*," James shouted.

James heard the gun click.

A white light and a deafening blast flashed as a stun grenade exploded in the wheel hub of the front police car, ripping apart the tire. Four more grenades exploded along the roadside, followed by a final blast that took out a tire on the cop car at the rear.

James, Curtis, and the two cops were temporarily deafened and blinded by the pulses. A few passing drivers had wobbly moments, but the traffic was mercifully light and the only harm done was a couple of tire squeals and a car almost swerving off into the desert.

Lauren had buried her face in the sand after laying the last grenade. She counted the explosions with her fingers plugged tightly in her ears. After the sixth blast, she jumped up and ran towards the male cop. Before he regained his sight, Lauren gave him a 90,000-volt nip with Scott's electric stun gun.

He collapsed in a shuddering heap, where he would remain paralyzed for the next couple of minutes. Lauren snatched the gun from the cop's limp hand and fired it harmlessly into the air above the Ford. The lady cop had regained enough hearing to duck, as Lauren closed her down and zapped her with the stun gun.

Lauren dropped the ammunition clips out of the police pistols and hurled the guns into the desert, then opened the driver's door next to her brother.

"James," Lauren shouted.

James could barely hear Lauren's voice over the high-pitched whistling in his ears, but the white smears in front of his eyes were starting to clear.

"How many stun grenades was that?" James asked.

"All of them," Lauren grinned, as she clambered over her brother's legs and back into the passenger seat. "Can you see to drive?"

"It's getting better," James said, as he reached forward and turned the key in the steering column to restart the engine.

James rubbed his eyes, while Lauren looked back at Curtis. He was lying across the back seat with a tear running down his face.

"What the hell just happened?" Curtis asked, staring at the end of the gun.

"I'm not keen on guns," Lauren explained. "I didn't load the magnum because I didn't want anyone getting shot. It's for fright value only."

"You're nuts," Curtis screamed. "The cops keep bullets in *their* guns you know, little girl."

"Only so idiots like you can shoot themselves," Lauren screamed back.

"I wish I was *dead*," Curtis whined.

"Will you two *shut* up," James said anxiously. "I'm trying to concentrate."

He waited for a gap in the traffic, before maneuvring out between the two disabled police cars and pulling through the gap in the metal barrier onto the side of the road that headed towards California.

As James put his foot on the gas, the steering wheel shuddered violently out of his hands. He nudged the pedal more gently and the car picked up a little speed.

"What's wrong?" Lauren asked.

"No idea," James said, as he fought to keep the car going straight. "But I did hear something go crunch the last time we passed over the barrier."

They were doing less than thirty miles an hour and a truck was closing up behind at double that speed. The driver blasted his horn as he swung into the middle lane to overtake. James tried giving the accelerator another dab. The steering wheel almost ripped his arm off as the car veered dangerously towards the side of the passing truck.

"It's OK when it's slow, but I can't put any power down."

"What are we gonna do?" Lauren asked.

"God knows," James said, shaking his head. "We're certainly not gonna get anywhere near Los Angeles in this box of bolts."

CHAPTER 24

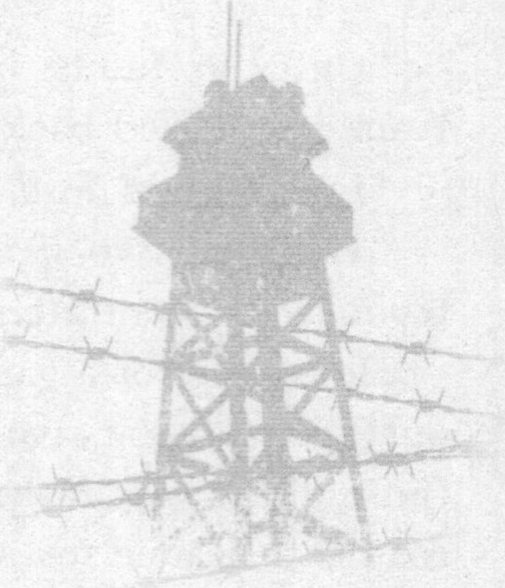

TRUNK

The interstate ran through open desert where their abandoned car would rapidly be spotted, but every few miles there was a cluster of outlets: drug stores, diners, fast-food joints; and at this time of the morning they were all closed. James pulled off at the first batch he came to, arms aching from his battle with the steering wheel.

He flipped off the headlamps, put the car in neutral and coasted into the empty parking lot of an ice-cream store, navigating by the light from a giant pink sundae dangling over the highway. He pulled around to the back of the store, stopped beside a row of Dumpsters, and flipped on the vanity light above his head.

James glanced back at Curtis. He kept pulling the

trigger of the empty revolver and laughing, but at the same time he had tears pouring down his face.

"You think one day I might get a gun that works when I try and blow my brains out?"

James was shocked by the way Curtis had turned into an emotional wreck. It looked pathetic, but was actually scary. For the first time, James truly felt the presence of a personality that could murder three complete strangers after a minor bust-up with a teacher.

"So where are we exactly?" James asked, leaning over Lauren's lap.

"If I've followed the map right, the interstate goes on for a couple more miles before it passes by a small town called Nix."

"So, that's where we'll go," James said. "The cops don't know we've had car trouble. As long as nobody discovers this car, we should have an hour or two before anybody comes looking."

"What's the plan when we get there?" Lauren asked.

James shrugged. "Either we find some place where we can hole up until they take down the roadblocks, or we steal a car and try to make it through. We'll have to play it by ear based on what we find."

Lauren folded the map, while James walked around to the trunk and took out the backpack containing their money and essentials. Curtis was still slumped over the rear seat. James opened up the door beside him.

"Come on," James said stiffly.

"What's the point?" Curtis sobbed. "I never should have listened to you. I was being looked after inside."

James had to get Curtis in shape and there wasn't

time for persuasion. He reached in and grabbed Curtis out of the car by the scruff of his jacket. Although the two boys were about the same size, James was fitter and much stronger.

"You listen," James snarled, as he thumped Curtis's back against the outside of a car. "You *asked* to come with me and you knew it would be dangerous. It's too late to change your mind now."

Curtis stared into space as though James wasn't even there.

"We're gonna walk into town and get our hands on another car. Then we're gonna get to L.A. and you're going to contact your mum, exactly like we planned."

Curtis didn't reply until James bunched a fist. "OK," Curtis sniffed reluctantly.

"We got this far," James said, changing his voice from mean to friendly. "We all need each other and we can still pull this off if we keep our heads."

Curtis looked like he wanted to believe James but didn't. It was the look you get off a scared kid when you're trying to convince them that there aren't monsters under the bed.

Lauren had the pack with the weapons over her back, ready to move off. She caught a glimpse of herself in the window of the car and was surprised by the tangled hair and sandy clothes looking back. She could hardly believe she'd just taken out two cops. It had been the wildest night of her life, but she felt oddly calm, as though her brain couldn't believe that all this was for real.

She got a shock as she snapped back to reality and

looked up at the boys. "You better lose the clothes," she said sharply.

James realized he was still wearing Amanda Voss's black prison-issue shirt. As he unbuttoned it, he was relieved to see Curtis removing his jacket without any prompting. Hopefully he was settling down.

James hooked the backpack of clothes and stuff over his shoulder and started walking briskly towards the interstate, with Lauren at his side.

"Do you think we've still got a chance?" Lauren whispered quickly, before Curtis overheard.

James shrugged. "The plan was based on us being in California before the alert went up. We're probably screwed, but I'm not giving up until we're forced to. . . . Whatever you do, don't let suicide boy get his hands on another gun."

Curtis jogged up beside them. "What are you two whispering about?"

"You," James said bluntly. "Are you back in the human race now?"

"I'm really sorry," Curtis said. "But there's no way I'm going back to prison."

"Think positive," James said. "This time tomorrow, you could be back with your mum."

A police car flashed by as they walked. A minute later they dived into the scrub when a whole row sped past. The three kids had done less than a third of the walk to Nix when they reached a line of broken wire and wooden posts that might have been considered a fence about a decade earlier.

"Trailer trash," Curtis spat, as they stared into a gloomy

field of the outsized aluminium caravans Americans call trailer homes.

Lauren looked at James. "Reckon we can pinch a car from here?"

"Do you know how to steal cars?" Curtis asked.

"I can hotwire the old ones," James explained. "But every recent car has a security chip in the ignition key. You need special tools to get those going."

"You don't find many rich people in trailer homes," Curtis said. "So this is where it's at if you're looking for scrap metal."

"We want something that'll make it to Los Angles, though," Lauren reminded them.

They cut along the wire fence, heading away from the interstate, and ducked through one of the gaps. There were a few trailers in a cluster near the entrance, but there was too much risk of being spotted around there. Lauren took the lead, crunching her way towards a lonely trailer at the rear of the park, with only a burned-out shell a couple of berths along for company.

There was a lamp on inside the trailer and a hum from the air conditioning unit on the roof. James crept up to a Dodge sedan parked alongside and peered through the driver's side window. Although the car was shabby, it had an airbag in the steering wheel and a CD player: Both indications that it was too modern to be started by short-circuiting the ignition.

"No chance," James whispered, as he looked back over his shoulder. "They're probably asleep in there. I suppose I could try sneaking inside and grabbing the key."

As James said this, he heard the aluminium door of the trailer crash open, followed by the unmistakable sound of a double-barrelled shotgun being pumped. He spun around in time to find the end waving under his nose.

"So *you're* the brats that keep messing with my car," the woman shouted. "Where you from? I've never seen you round here."

She looked only about twenty, with long brown hair, wearing mules and a nightshirt.

"I don't want trouble," James shouted, raising his hands in the air. "We're out of here, don't worry."

"Oh, you think you're just walking away, do you?" the woman asked. "It cost me two hundred bucks when you slashed my tires. You're coming inside and I'm callin' the cops."

"We've never been here before," James said. "We're—"

The woman tutted. "Don't feed me your lies, kid. . . . You're lucky it's me that caught you. Some of the guys in the trailers down the front are so sick of you kids busting up our cars, they'd have busted *you* up rather than calling the law."

Lauren crept forward and sobbed theatrically. "Please don't shoot my brother."

The woman looked confused as Lauren moved another step closer. She backed up to the door of the trailer.

"Don't you come no closer, girl."

"Pleeeeeease," Lauren sobbed.

"*Listen,*" the woman said, anxiously shifting her gun towards Lauren.

James could tell from the woman's expression that she didn't have the heart to shoot anyone, least of all a ten-year-old girl. He ducked under the gun and grabbed the muzzle, while Lauren scrambled to safety behind the car. James forced the gun around so that it was parallel with the woman's chest and used it to pin her back against the side of the trailer.

"Let it go," James said, grabbing the woman's skinny wrist and peeling her hand off the stock.

The woman sobbed as James took control of the gun. "Please don't hurt my baby."

"Get inside," James snarled.

The woman walked up two metal steps and into the trailer.

"Is there anyone else in here?" James asked, as he flipped a light switch.

"Just my daughter."

Lauren and Curtis followed them inside and quickly pulled up the door.

"Lauren," James said. "Find a radio and tune it to that station: We need to know what the cops are doing."

The inside of the trailer was well worn, but clean, with little kids' toys scattered everywhere. There was a sofa on one side, a row of kitchen cabinets opposite, and a three-year-old asleep on a small mattress by the window.

"Sit on the sofa," James ordered.

Lauren found a radio and switched it on. James realized that the gun was terrifying the poor woman. He broke the barrel open and tipped the cartridges out on to the carpet.

"I'm not gonna hurt you, but we do need your help," James said. "What's your name?"

"Paula."

"Paula," James said, "the three of us are in a spot. We're on the run and our car died on us."

"On the run?"

"From the cops. Me and Curtis here just busted out of Arizona Max."

Paula buried her head in her hands and took a deep breath as the radio confirmed James's story:

". . . Two police officers were seriously assaulted at a roadblock six miles outside the town of Nix. Police say the two teenage killers are now heading for California along Route Sixty-three. They are believed to be traveling in a blue Ford Explorer SUV and armed with guns and explosives.

"One of the escapees, James Rose, has at least one previous escape attempt under his belt and the police are warning everyone to be ultra-cautious around these individuals. . . . I sure hope we don't lose any more law-enforcement officers out there tonight, folks. Remember to keep them in your prayers and stay tuned to Western Arizona's number one station for news and talk. . . ."

Lauren went to the fridge and passed out cans of soft drinks.

"Are we staying or going?" Curtis asked, as he sat on a kitchen chair drinking from his can.

"Give me a minute to think," James said.

He was feeling the pressure. On James's previous missions, he'd always had mission controllers or older agents close by. This time it was down to him to outsmart the entire Arizona police department.

James had an idea. He looked at Paula. "How big's the trunk of your car?"

"I don't know," Paula said. "It's a normal trunk. . . ."

"Could you fit someone in it?"

"I guess. It's pretty roomy when you take all my junk out."

"What are you thinking?" Lauren asked.

"I don't think we can stick around here," James said.

Lauren nodded. "When the cops find that car, this trailer park is the first place they'll come knocking, but there are bound to be roadblocks in our way somewhere between here and California."

"That's why either me or Curtis has to go in the trunk," James said. "Paula can drive, with one of us in the front and one in the back next to the baby."

"That's not a bad plan, bro'," Lauren nodded, as she realized it made sense. "We'd look like a family outing. The cops might just fall for it."

"Or they might look in the trunk and bust us," Curtis said.

Paula looked completely stressed out. "You want *me* to drive you past the police roadblocks?"

"And on to Los Angeles."

Paula rubbed her eye. "Assisting an escape, you know that's serious jail time?"

"Please, Paula," Lauren groveled. "If my brother gets caught, he'll go back to prison for the rest of his life."

"And what if the cops start shooting at us? What if my daughter gets hurt?"

"Why are we asking her permission?" Curtis said. "Stick the bloody shotgun in her back and make her do what she's told."

"Because . . . ," James said, wrestling with the uncomfortable fact that Curtis had suggested the course of action that most desperate fugitives really would have taken.

"What else *can* we do?" Curtis asked. "If we leave her here we've got to tie her and the brat up so they don't snitch."

James hadn't planned for any strangers to get tangled up in the escape, especially not taken hostage. He had three options and none of them were nice: tie Paula up and steal her car, make Paula drive them, or restrain Curtis and call John Jones to say that he'd decided to abandon the mission.

"Listen," James said, looking at Paula. "I don't want to go sticking a gun in your back, but if the cops get hold of Curtis and me, we're dead meat. Once we get to L.A., you can go to the cops and say we forced you to drive us. You won't get punished. . . . Hell, you'll probably make a few bucks selling your story to the newspapers."

"Either that or you tie us up?" Paula said, nervously rocking her legs up and down.

James noticed a gaudy pink and white dress hanging on the door by the toilet.

"You work in that ice-cream place down the road?" James asked, deliberately ignoring Paula's question. "How much does that pay?"

"Six bucks an hour."

"Lauren," James said. "You grabbed John's savings, didn't you? What have we got?"

Lauren nodded. "There's about four thousand bucks in the large backpack."

"I'll give you half our money if you drive us," James

said. "Think of all the ice cream you'd have to shovel to earn two thousand buckaroos. A thousand stays here in the trailer. You'll get the other half in L.A."

Curtis was shaking his head. "Why are we doing this?" he sneered. "Elwood kept saying you were a pussy."

James angrily stepped up to Curtis and faced him off. "What use is Paula if she freaks out the second a cop shines a flashlight in her face? If I'd listened to you, we'd have already ended up getting shot to pieces after some stupid car chase."

Lauren sat beside Paula on the couch and did a big sniffle. "Could you please help us?" she begged. "My uncle beats me up so bad. . . . *Please* don't make me go back to him."

Paula's expression altered completely when she heard this. She looked towards Lauren and smiled gently. "My step-dad knocked me into the hospital when I was about your age."

"You know how it feels then," Lauren sniffed, troweling on the waterworks and feeling guilty about the way she was manipulating Paula.

Paula reluctantly looked up at James, who was standing over her. "I got problems, and two thousand bucks can fix most of 'em."

CHAPTER 25

LUCK

Curtis volunteered to ride in the trunk. James couldn't predict his mood: One minute Curtis was bright and cooperative, the next he was suicidal. Kids who haven't been through CHERUB-style training usually have difficulty handling dangerous situations, but Curtis didn't seem up to any kind of stress and James was getting worried. If they made it to Los Angeles, they'd be relying on him to keep his head together and make contact with associates of his mother.

It was 4:30 a.m. when they hit a big roadblock, a mile shy of the border with California. Five police cars blocked the left-hand lanes and a long snake of rear lights merged slowly into the single remaining lane.

More police cars were parked on the opposite side of the road, with pursuit drivers ready to give chase and a helicopter circling overhead. James knew the chopper would pack a heat-sensitive camera, able to detect anyone who tried to bail out of a car and cut through the desert.

Considering what they were putting her through, Paula was keeping her head together. Lauren sat next to her in the front, pretending to sleep. James was in the back with a hoodie pulled over his skinhead and Paula's three-year-old daughter, Holly, was dead to the world in the child seat next to him.

It took a quarter of an hour to crawl to the front of the queue. Every car got a cursory glance, as cops shone a torch inside and fired a couple of quick questions at the driver. Most cars were waved on, but any that looked suspicious were told to pull into a second line for a detailed inspection. This roadside check involved everyone getting out of the car and having their ID run through the police computer, while the inside of the car was thoroughly searched.

James knew it would all be over if they got picked for inspection. With Paula behind the wheel and thirty well-armed cops in the vicinity, any attempt to escape would be short and bloody.

Paula opened her window as she rolled up alongside a cop.

"Licence, registration, ma'am."

The cop glanced at the documents, while another walked around the car shining a flashlight inside.

"Are these your children?"

"The little girl in the back is my daughter. These two are my brother and sister."

The other cop knocked on the window beside James's head. "Let's have a look at you, son."

James rolled down the window and got a blast of the flashlight in his face.

"How old are you?" the cop asked.

"Thirteen," James said.

"Would you pull that hood down for me?"

James's heart banged as he slid the hoodie down, revealing the half centimeter of bristles on his head.

The cop looked at his colleague. "Got a blond skinhead here; about the right age too."

The other cop leaned in beside Paula. "I'm sorry, miss, but I'm gonna have to ask you to join that queue over to your left for an inspection."

James silently mouthed a string of curses. He just hoped John found a way to pull him out before he got hauled back to Arizona Max. Paula rolled forward a single car-length to join the tail of the inspection line. Lauren glanced over her shoulder at James with a resigned look.

"We gave it our best shot," James shrugged. "I'm sorry we put you through this for nothing, Paula. Tell the cops we threatened to hurt Holly if you didn't help us."

"How much extra time will they give you for escaping?" Paula asked, sounding as if she genuinely cared.

"Enough," James said. "Five, ten years, maybe."

"You don't seem like no criminal," Paula said sympathetically. "At least, I've known a few and you seem far too nice a guy to have gotten yourself in so much trouble."

All their heads snapped around as a cop thumped on the metal roof above them. The next car in line had been ordered to pull over, but the inspection queue hadn't moved up and there wasn't room for it to join without blocking the traffic that was being waved through.

Paula reopened her window as the cop crouched down beside the car. "We got too many cars backed up here," he explained. "I'm gonna let you guys pass through. You seem pretty harmless to me."

"I've never been called harmless before," Paula grinned sweetly, "but I'll settle for it if it gets me to L.A. before the little lady in the back wakes up."

"You have a safe journey, now," the cop smiled, as Paula backed up, making enough space to pull out of the queue.

With the traffic being filtered through one car at a time, the three lanes heading towards California were deserted.

Lauren looked back at James and gasped. "That was *too* close."

James grinned. "*Way* too close."

They pulled up at a McDonald's fifty miles into California. Lauren went inside and bought some breakfast. James checked no one was around, before letting Curtis out of the trunk. Once he'd walked the cramp out of his legs, Curtis faced the sunrise over the desert and stretched out his arms.

"Beautiful," he said, turning around and slapping James on the back as he pulled him into a hug. "You were *so* cool, man. I'm sorry I messed up last night. . . . When my head goes dark like that, I act like a total dick."

"Glad Lauren didn't put bullets in the magnum now?"

Curtis smirked. "Your sister must be my guardian angel, or something."

Lauren came around the side of the restaurant holding a cardboard tray of drinks and two brown paper bags stuffed with food. Curtis snatched one of the bags and took out a muffin.

"Double sausage and egg," Curtis said, tearing out a massive bite. "I love these, man. It's been a year since I had one of these. *Mmm* . . . This is *sooooooo* good."

James left Curtis to eulogize over his McMuffin and leaned in the back of the car to speak with Paula. Holly had woken up grumpy and Paula sat next to her daughter, trying to persuade her to eat something.

"You did us a big favor back there," James said. "I owe you one."

"You *owe* me a thousand," Paula said, only half joking.

James nodded. "As soon as we get to L.A.; you've got my word on that."

"I don't think I've ever had a thousand dollars in one go," Paula said. "When I was a little girl, I always wanted to go to Disneyland and stay in a real hotel, but we were as poor as dirt. When I drop you guys off, I'm gonna drive Holly up there. It's only thirty miles."

"Sounds fun," James smiled, "but it's better if you call the cops first. You don't want to get in trouble for helping us and they'll hardly believe your story if you head off to Disneyland."

Paula looked a little crushed. "I guess you're right."

"You don't have to tell the cops about the money, though," James said. "Drive out there in a week's time, or something."

With Paula and Curtis both happy, James felt more at ease than he'd done for ages. He was miffed when Lauren broke the mood.

"We better get moving," she said. "We might have got past one roadblock, but that doesn't mean the cops have stopped searching for us."

They caught the morning rush hour when they reached the outskirts of Los Angeles, ending up in fourteen lanes of solid traffic, crawling along at walking pace. When they hit a downward slope, there was a vista of tens of thousands of cars packed in close formation, with sunlight reflecting off the windscreens. After fighting their way out of the sparsely populated desert, it was a relief to be sitting in one anonymous car amidst thousands.

They had to find a place to split from Paula. Lauren picked out a route to Hollywood on the map, because it was the only place in town that she'd heard of. They wound up at a gray mall on Hollywood Boulevard called Showbiz Stores. It was 10 a.m. and James couldn't help getting a little buzz when he spotted the famous Hollywood sign on a hill in the distance.

They parked in an underground lot beneath the mall. James walked around to the back of the car and counted a thousand dollars out of the backpack before slinging it over his shoulder. Paula grabbed Holly and they took an elevator up to the food court on the top level. James got everyone drinks and an ice cream for Holly.

He passed the thousand dollars under the table to Paula as he spoke. "We passed a taxi rank on the way inside. You sit here and finish your drink. Give us twenty minutes or so to get away, then cover yourself by calling the cops before you do anything else. OK?"

Paula nodded as she took the money.

"Can I trust you?" James asked.

Paula smiled. "If it works out, you can send me a postcard."

"Remember," James said, "if the cops hear about the money, they'll take it off you. But they're trained to sniff out lies, so you've got to tell the truth about everything else."

"OK."

James drained his mug of hot chocolate and tousled Holly's hair as he pushed back his chair.

Curtis smiled at Paula. "Sorry about last night."

Lauren, Curtis, and James scrambled quickly down two escalators to the ground floor. They strode through a corridor of upmarket shops and stepped outdoors near the head of the taxi rank.

James looked at Curtis. "You've lived in L.A.: Where's a good place to go? Somewhere three kids won't stand out and you can make your phone calls?"

"Santa Monica beach," Curtis said, without a millisecond's thought.

The cab journey was a fifteen-mile ride down Sunset Boulevard, passing through Beverly Hills on the way to the beachfront. James and Lauren stepped out to a scene that reminded them of their mum taking them on a day trip to Brighton five years earlier: There was an old-fashioned pier with a funfair at the end and wooden decking along the seafront. The palm trees, restaurants, and lavish beachfront hotels gave off a glimmer of serious money.

"This is the kind of place where I'll live when I'm a millionaire," Lauren said.

James smiled. "How are you planning on becoming a millionaire?"

"Pop star, successful businesswoman . . . possibly both."

Once the cab pulled away, they stood in a line looking out at the waves crashing in the distance.

"My mom had a beachfront house down the road in Venice," Curtis explained. "My first elementary school was a few miles up that hill over there. Even after we left, we'd come back here for a few weeks most summers."

"It looks nice," James said. "But we can't hang around; you've got calls to make."

"Call," Curtis said. "Just one."

James looked surprised. "You said you had to find some numbers. I thought it was going to take a while."

"No offense, James," Curtis said, "but I had to feed you a line. I couldn't totally trust you until I knew this escape was for real. When I was living with my mom, there was always a chance something would go wrong while I was out at school or something. Wherever we stayed, there was always a backup plan."

"So who are you planning to call?" James asked.

"When Paula goes to the police, they'll track that cab

down and ask the driver where he took us, so I couldn't go direct to my dad over in Pasadena. This little diversion to Santa Monica should throw the pigs off the scent."

"Your *dad*," James gasped.

According to the background information James and Lauren had read before the mission, Curtis claimed to have no idea who his father was and neither did the FBI.

Curtis nodded. "I've only met him a few times, but he's the one guy in town who'll definitely know how to get in touch with my mom."

CHAPTER 26

TECHNOLOGY

The FBI team was following the kids' movements by tracking the signal from a cell phone in Lauren's shorts. While Curtis made his call, Lauren pretended that she needed to use one of the beachfront toilets. She locked herself in a stall, grabbed the tiny flip-phone, and speed-dialed the FBI office in Phoenix. She told Theo their exact location and about Curtis's revelation that his father lived somewhere nearby.

John Jones and Marvin Teller had landed in L.A. a couple of hours earlier and were at the airport awaiting developments. A second FBI team was using the cell phone signal to shadow James and Lauren's movements, at a distance of around half a mile.

While Curtis and Lauren were making their phone calls, James popped fifty cents into a newspaper rack and took out an *LA Gazette*. The pictures of Curtis on the front page looked fine, but someone on Marvin Teller's team must have got inside James's criminal file and doctored the picture taken at Phoenix courthouse, because it barely looked like him.

James read the accompanying story:

4 A.M. NEWS—OFFICER KILLED AS BOYS, 14, ESCAPE ARIZONA MAX

(Maricopa county, AZ) A correctional officer, Scott Warren, died after a daring prison breakout by two boys. The fourteen-year-olds, James Rose and Curtis Oxford, are believed to be the first minors ever to escape from a maximum-security institution.

Oxford is the son of internationally renowned arms dealer Jane Oxford, who is currently in the number-two slot on the FBI's Most Wanted list. Rose was recently transferred from Omaha State prison, where he had been held in solitary confinement after the failure of a previous escape attempt.

Following the escape, two police officers were overpowered at a roadblock heading westbound along I63, using grenades and a stun gun stolen from the prison armory. Despite this setback, a spokesman for the Arizona State Police said that officers were confident of recapturing the two young killers.

The high-tech, 6,500-inmate, Arizona Maximum Security prison has been plagued by operational difficulties since it was opened in 2002. These include critical glitches in the software that controls security systems and low wages that have resulted in up to 30 percent of job vacancies at the prison remaining unfilled.

Prison staff and friends have paid tribute to Scott Warren, the 32-year-old officer who died during the escape. Warren, a New Yorker with no known family, was attacked with pepper spray and then gagged and bound by the youths. He was known to suffer from respiratory illness and police suspect that the officer died following an asthma attack brought on by the spray. A female officer was also taken to the hospital with a concussion and required a number of stitches to a cut in her head, while the two police officers attacked at the roadblock were treated for minor cuts and bruises.

The three kids sat on a bench at the edge of the beach reading the newspaper until a limousine Curtis had ordered on his father's account stopped at the curb. It took them on an hour-long freeway ride to a business park in Pasadena, on the eastern outskirts of the city.

The black Mercedes pulled up in the parking lot outside a cube-shaped office building clad in reflective black glass. The corporate logo over the automatic door was a fighter plane with ETIENNE DEFENSE CONSULTANCY written above it. The security guard sitting behind his plinth looked rather surprised by the three grubby kids walking towards reception. He was powerfully built, more like a nightclub bouncer than the middle-aged men who usually sit in the entrances of office buildings.

Curtis rested his elbows on the high counter. "Call extension five-five-three and tell Mr. Etienne that Curtis is on his way to see him."

Curtis stepped towards the elevator, but the guard called him back.

"Don't move *one* more step, boy," the guard said firmly. He picked up the phone behind his desk and dialed five-five-three.

The guard had a brief conversation.

"Looks like you're wanted," the guard said, beckoning the kids towards the elevator doors with his beefy hand.

The guard swiped a security pass through the elevator control panel and hopped out of the car before the door closed. They went directly to the fifth floor, exiting into a large reception area, where they were greeted by a middle-aged lady in a gray business suit.

Curtis smiled as the woman swept him into her arms. "Hey, Margaret."

"You've grown," Margaret said. "You must have been nine or ten the last time I saw you. . . . I'm afraid your father is away at a conference in Boston, but he saw the reports on the television news and sent a message to say there was a chance you'd end up here."

James looked around at the fancy halogen lighting and the abstract paintings on the walls. He didn't have a clue what a defense consultancy did, but if its owner was Curtis's dad, it surely had some connection with Jane Oxford.

"It will take me some time to organize your documentation and arrange air transportation to somewhere safe. In the meantime, the three of you can use Mr. Etienne's shower and put on clean clothes. I'll arrange for lunch to be delivered if you're hungry."

Mr. Etienne could have lived in his office if he'd wanted to. As well as the workspace, with a massive desk and a row of Bloomberg financial information screens on the wall, there was a bathroom, a lounge area with massive sofas, and even a room off to the side containing a bed and a wardrobe full of suits.

After the kids had taken turns showering, Margaret brought in a selection of delivery menus from nearby restaurants. They settled on an upmarket hamburger joint.

James tucked away a steak sandwich with a side of onion rings, followed by a chocolate dessert for two, which he managed by himself after Lauren said she was full. CHERUB kept James on a tight fitness regime so he usually avoided pigging out, but after a week of prison food he reckoned he deserved a treat.

Curtis turned on the TV in the lounge and they switched to a local news channel. There was only a tiny bit about the escape at the end of each half-hourly bulletin. Lauren snuggled up beside James in her clean T-shirt and shorts and was soon fast asleep.

James had been too stressed to feel tired while he'd been on the run, but now his belly was full and he'd calmed down, he realized he'd barely slept in the last fifty hours. He closed his eyes and drifted off.

CHAPTER 27

COUNTRY

By the time the kids woke up, Margaret had driven out to a local mall and bought each of them a new set of clothes for their onward journey. It was a sensible precaution, because the cops investigating the escape would have made attempts to identify the clothing that the kids had taken with them.

James and Curtis both got tracksuits and trainers, but Lauren got a white dress, pink canvas deck shoes, and a sparkly silver headband. Her scowl could have melted a steel bar. The last time Lauren had worn a dress, she'd been a seven-year-old bridesmaid and she'd deliberately trailed it through mud to get out of wearing it.

"You'll look so *pretty,*" James said, howling with laughter as soon as Margaret and Curtis were out of earshot.

"One more word," Lauren said angrily, wagging her finger in his face. "One more word and I'll deck you."

"*Quite* the little princess."

"Wait a minute," Lauren gasped, anxiously looking around at the carpet. "Where are my dirty shorts?"

James shrugged. "Looks like Margaret took them away while we were asleep."

"Crap," Lauren scowled. "The phone was in the pocket. I should have stuffed it down the sofa cushion, or something."

James looked around the floor, in case it had dropped out of the pocket. "If it's gone it's gone," James said. "You can act innocent and ask Margaret for it back, but I get the impression that she's a lot more than Etienne's secretary. She knows it might be used to track us and I bet she won't let you have it."

John Jones and Marvin Teller spent the afternoon sitting around in the FBI station at Los Angeles airport. Theo Monroe and Scott Warren—now going by his real name of Warren Reise and sporting cropped hair—had just arrived on a scheduled flight from Phoenix.

John stood up and shook Warren's hand, as he walked into the drab office. "Back from the dead, my friend. Your nose looks a mess. Is it broken?"

Warren nodded. "James might only be thirteen, but that's one of the hardest whacks I ever took."

"That's how we train 'em," John grinned. "When I went to my job interview at CHERUB, I was shown the martial arts training area. You wouldn't believe these eight- and nine-year-olds with their black belts, pulling off the most frightening moves. . . . I tell you, I wouldn't want to tangle with *any* of them."

Marvin nodded. "It certainly produces impressive results. When I was with Lauren the other day, I had to keep reminding myself that I was talking to a ten-year-old girl."

"Kids' brains are like sponges," John explained. "They're capable of way more than most adults give them credit for. When I worked for MI5, we sent agents on six-month courses to learn foreign languages. CHERUB can train a bright eleven-year-old to the same standard in two. . . . Did you check in on Dave before you left Arizona?"

Theo nodded, as he hung his jacket over a hook on the wall. "I purchased books for Dave to read in the hospital. He is fine physically, but still rather depressed about not being involved in the escape. Arizona State Police came in to interview him early this morning. He set them off on a few false lines of inquiry, as we discussed."

"And that doctor won't declare Dave fit to return to Arizona Max?" John asked.

"Under any circumstances," Theo nodded. "The doctor knows the score and the hospital doesn't much care as long as the bed is being paid for."

"I'd like to send Dave back to Britain," John said. "But Oxford has proved so good at sniffing out undercover operations over the years, we can't pull him out of the Arizona prison system in case she finds out and smells a rat."

"How are the other two getting along?" Warren asked.

"They spent the afternoon at the headquarters of Etienne Defense Consultancy," Marvin explained. "We had two local agents outside the building all afternoon. The kids were picked up half an hour ago in a limousine. The limo company uses uncoded radio and according to their signals, the car is taking them to Orange County airport as we speak."

"Is Etienne on the radar?" Theo asked.

"No," Marvin said. "The FBI has no file on either Jean Etienne or his company. There are hundreds of small, high-tech companies like EDC in Pasadena: The California Institute of Technology acts as a magnet for them. Etienne specializes in developing military hardware. They've done consultancy work for most of the big weapons manufacturers. Cutting-edge stuff: unmanned aircraft, reactive body armor, electromagnetic pulse weapons."

"So is it a front for Jane Oxford?"

"Too early to be sure, Theo. We can't start any kind of investigation into Etienne right now without creating suspicion and endangering James and Lauren. But we will eventually and if I were a betting man, I'd have my dollars on Oxford and Etienne being in cahoots."

Theo smiled. "This is the best lead we've had since I joined this team three years ago."

"EDC is a nice juicy fish," Marvin nodded. "But that company won't be going anywhere. Right now, we've got to stay focused on our little cherubs out in the field, trying to reel in the whale herself."

Warren picked up a ringing phone and took a short call.

"That was FBI Orange County," he explained. "She says there are seventeen flights out of Orange this evening. Three are aircraft for hire, which are the ones I think we need to be looking at. One has filed a flight plan for Chicago, one for Philadelphia, and one for Twin Elks, Idaho."

"What about regular passenger flights?" John asked.

Warren shook his head. "There's a seven o'clock curfew on large jets out of Orange. Check-in closed on the final flight fifteen minutes ago."

"Has Lauren called in on her mobile?" Theo asked. "I diverted the Phoenix number through to here."

John shook his head. "The last call we got was an adult female, probably pressing the last number redial to see what she got."

"Was she suspicious?" Theo asked.

"I don't think so. I pretended I was Lauren's uncle. When the kids left, the cop said Lauren was wearing a white dress. I've lived with her for the last couple of weeks and it's not her style."

"The change of clothes makes sense," Theo nodded. "It looks like they're being looked after by someone who knows how to play the game."

"OK," Marvin said, clapping his hands together. "We can't afford to lose these kids. I'm gonna call downstairs and have an FBI jet fueled up and put on standby. As soon as we know which airplane the kids are getting on, we'll set off after them."

"Can we hold them up?" John asked.

Marvin nodded. "Sure, I'll get air traffic control at Orange to delay their takeoff clearance, so we arrive before them."

• • •

The flight to Idaho in the north-west of the United States took three and a half hours. The small turboprop aircraft had seen better days, with the logo of a previous owner clumsily painted over and the six passenger seats ripped up. The foam inside crumbled to dust when you brushed against it. The three youngsters were alone, apart from the pilot's cigarette smoke creeping through the top of the cockpit door.

It was dark when they landed at Twin Elks aerodrome, a tiny facility used primarily by amateur pilots. James and Curtis ignored the freezing air and sprinted to the side of the runway to pee in the grass. Lauren looked around forlornly, until she spotted a grubby toilet block beside the control tower. Halfway through peeing, she heard a muffled ring from a telephone in the next stall.

It rang three times before stopping. Lauren stood up and poked her head into the next stall, noticing that a flip-phone had been abandoned on the plastic cistern lid. She picked it up and looked at the display:

1 MISSED CALL
RING BACK?

Lauren leaned outside to make sure nobody was around before hitting the redial key.

"Hello?" It was John Jones's voice.

"You got here quick," Lauren said.

"Our jet was faster than your turboprop. The only trouble was, with so few flight movements out here in the wilderness, we thought it best to go to another airport. We had to hire a car and race over here."

"How did you know I'd come over to the toilet?"

John laughed. "Three hours on a plane without facilities, it was a fair guess. I'm in the trees about thirty meters away from you. Now listen up, we've only got a minute. It's too risky tracking you by cell phone. It would be suspicious after they confiscated the other one and I doubt you'll get a reliable cell phone signal out here in the back of beyond anyway. I've taped a packet of short-range tracking devices under the cistern lid. They go on your body, like a sticking plaster. Put one on whenever you're about to move and press down hard for about three seconds to activate it. It'll send a tracking signal every thirty seconds until the battery runs out—look out, someone's heading towards you."

Lauren quickly bolted the stall door. A strange man's voice boomed out.

"Lauren honey, we're waitin' in the car. We need to get out of here as fast as we can. The local sheriff likes to come and poke around if someone lands out here at this time of night."

"Oh, um . . . I'm doing number twos," Lauren said, turning red with embarrassment. "Just a minute."

She waited until she heard the man step back outside, then prised the lid off the toilet cistern. She peeled away a small plastic bag and tucked it into her jacket. After quickly washing her hands, Lauren stepped outside and was greeted by a bearded man dressed in jeans and a plaid shirt.

"Name's Vaughn Little," the man explained as they

jogged towards a black Toyota four-wheel drive that already had James and Curtis sitting in the back.

It was an hour's drive through dense forest, winding up hillsides, past huge trees silhouetted against the moonlight. James kept the window beside his head open and found the blast of cool air a thrill, after all the sweat-glazed hours inside Arizona Max.

"You boys are back on CNN," Vaughn said, in a honeyed voice that gave the impression of a man about to break into a song about his lonesome cattle. "Seems your cellblock tilted off the edge when they heard you bunked out. Half a million dollars' worth of damage. Took the riot squad six hours to get the inmates back under control."

"Hope they busted up some hacks," Curtis grinned.

"Anybody injured?" James asked.

"A few got hurt bad," Vaughn said. "But nobody dead."

James could see how the news of the escape would have played on the minds of the other inmates and turned the already tense situation into a full-scale riot. He hoped that guys like Abe and Mark had come out OK. On the upside, he couldn't help feeling the riot was another detail that would make the escape more believable to Jane Oxford.

"Have you heard from my mom?" Curtis asked.

Vaughn nodded slowly. "You're gonna be staying up in the mountains with us for a few weeks. She's out of the country and she wants the heat to die down before meeting up with you."

"What did she say about James and Lauren?"

"Says she'll fix them up with a good family. Get false ID. Cross the border into Canada, maybe."

"Good," Curtis smiled. "You ever been to Canada, James?"

"Nah."

"It's nice," Curtis nodded. "Clean, safe, you'll like it. . . . Can I call Mom tonight?"

Vaughn shook his head. "You know what she's like. Won't even say hello unless she has the call scrambled and bounced off five different satellites."

The car pulled onto a track and Vaughn sent Curtis out to open a metal gate. Two women emerged in a shaft of light on the doorstep of a large timber-framed house, as the car slipped around on a muddy path, heading towards them. One was Vaughn's wife, Lisa; the other his fourteen-year-old daughter, Becky. When they piled out of the car, Lisa stepped barefoot onto the cold gravel and squeezed Curtis into a hug.

"Good to see *youuuuuu*," Lisa said, as she pushed a handful of hair away from her face. "You remember Becky, don't you? When we lived at the old place down the hill, you two used to act so cute together. I've got stacks of pictures of you in the albums."

"I remember," Curtis said vaguely, sounding like he wished he didn't.

James stepped up to the house and glanced at the cute teenager standing on the doorstep in her socks. She wore jeans and a plaid shirt, like a clone of her parents.

"Hey," Becky said sweetly. "You must be James."

Becky led James and Lauren to the kitchen, where something smelled good.

"You want hot soup?" Becky asked, reaching into the cupboard and pulling out a stack of bowls. "It's homemade and we got coffee in the jug if you want a warm-up."

The smell of vegetable soup made James and Lauren realize they were hungry. They pulled out chairs and sat at the dining table.

CHAPTER 28

HOBBIES

TWO WEEKS LATER

Crime wasn't supposed to pay, but Lisa and Vaughn Little seemed to have done well enough out of it. Vaughn had been a heavy-duty weapons smuggler in the 1970s. He'd served six years in a New Mexico prison. When his parole was up, he moved north to Idaho, bought a small ranch, and spawned four daughters. Only Becky, the youngest, still lived at home.

Lisa bred Arabian horses and Vaughn earned money customizing and restoring motorcycles, but these businesses were more like hobbies. The Little family's comfortable lifestyle was mostly funded by the well-invested proceeds of thirty-year-old weapons deals.

Everyone fell into a daily routine. Lauren hung out with Lisa and learned to ride and groom the horses. She'd never shown any interest in riding before, but took a shine to the animals and a bigger one to Lisa.

Most days, Curtis disappeared off on long walks into the woods with a sketchbook. Sometimes he'd come back with a drawing of a leaf or rusted-up car, others a whole landscape sketched in impossibly tiny pencil strokes. He was more than a kid who was good at drawing; his work could easily have passed as that of a professional artist. When it rained too hard to go out, Curtis lay on a rug in front of the Discovery Channel and sulked.

James hung out with Vaughn each day and it was like the two of them had been missing each other their whole lives. Vaughn had always wanted a son and James would have settled for a dad just like him. Vaughn had a million stories and a way of telling them that always made James smile. Everything from punching out his high school principal, his wild exploits as a member of the Brigands bike gang, shady weapons deals, and stories from his time in prison.

Vaughn took James out on little jobs around the ranch, mending broken fences and old guttering. They'd usually spend a couple of hours in the afternoon working on the motorbikes and Vaughn was patient, explaining to James the way a bike worked and how the different parts fitted together.

Usually when adults ask a kid to help, the kid ends up standing around holding a spanner like a gherkin for three hours, but Vaughn kept James busy and actually trusted him to do stuff. He even let James blast around the muddy ranch tracks on a little Kawasaki dirt bike, though his pleas to have a go on one of the Harley Davidsons got short shrift.

James and Lauren slept in the guest room, which had a double bed. They acted as if sharing a bed was some kind of hellish punishment, while both secretly quite liked it. Lauren had been asleep for an hour and had managed to wind most of the king-sized duvet around herself.

James undressed quietly and brushed his teeth in the en suite bathroom, then pulled the cover back and tried to slip under without waking his sister. He enjoyed the first few moments of warmth, looking at Lauren's long hair spread out over the pillow and listening to her breathe.

Before his mum died, James had never given a moment's thought to how much he loved his little sister. But ever since, he had tortured himself with the idea that something unexpected could happen to her as well. Lauren could get run over, or get cancer, or get hurt on a mission, or. . . . A couple of times James made himself cry just thinking about it, although he'd never admitted that to anyone, even the counselor he occasionally saw on campus.

James closed his eyes and started thinking about a cool Japanese bike he'd read about in one of Vaughn's magazines. All the time he'd spent hanging around the workshop listening to Vaughn's biker stories had convinced James that he wanted his own motorcycle more than anything in the world.

James wasn't sure how old you had to be to ride a

motorbike in Britain, but if it was seventeen like a car, he realized he'd be able to get one in three and a half years. He could use some of the money his mum left him when she died, maybe get some kind of job to pay for insurance and petrol. . . .

James was doing a hundred miles an hour down the motorway, with a fit girl hugging his waist, when Lauren jabbed him in the ribs.

"You awake?" she asked acidly.

"Just about," James said, opening his eyes and letting out a big yawn.

"How's *Becky*?" Lauren asked.

"Fine. Why?"

"I put my head around her bedroom door to say good night."

"Oh," James said anxiously. "We just started talking and one thing led to another. . . . You know. Besides, there's no law against snogging. I'm nearly fourteen, I know guys my age who get up to a lot worse."

"But what's Kerry gonna say when she finds out you cheated on her?"

"She's ten thousand miles away," James said.

"Was that the first time you snogged her?"

"Yes," James lied, knowing that eighth or ninth was probably nearer to the truth. "And one snog is hardly cheating."

"I doubt Kerry would see it that way," Lauren snapped. "Swear you'll break it off with Becky and I won't say anything, but I'm not gonna sit back and let you cheat on Kerry. She's my friend too."

"OK, I swear," James said, trying to sound extra sincere.

"On our mum's grave," Lauren added.

"On our . . . *No,*" James gasped. "Can't you just stay out of this? You're ten. You're too young to understand."

"I might not be into boys yet, but I still know Kerry would be really upset."

"Why don't you keep your voice *down* and your snout out of my business?"

Lauren turned away and buried her face in the duvet. "You're a total pig, James. *Good night*."

CHAPTER 29

OINK

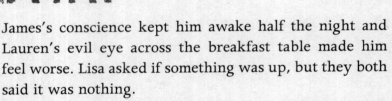

James's conscience kept him awake half the night and Lauren's evil eye across the breakfast table made him feel worse. Lisa asked if something was up, but they both said it was nothing.

James knew cheating on Kerry was shitty, but he hadn't seen her for months and he fancied Becky like mad. He couldn't see what harm a little fling would do, but Lauren finding out made everything more complicated.

James rushed up to Becky's room when she got home from school.

"Lauren knows," he said. "She saw us last night."

Becky shrugged. "So?"

James could hardly tell Becky he was a secret agent

with a girl back home. He'd spent half the day thinking up a way to explain why Lauren shouldn't find out.

"Lauren's been through a lot," he said. "First our dad dying. Then my uncle giving her a hard time and me and Dave getting sent to prison. It's not surprising she wants me to herself for a while."

"So, you're *never* gonna have a girlfriend in case your sister gets jealous?" Becky asked, as she combed ink-stained fingers through her short brown hair. "She'll just have to grow up a bit."

"I just think we should stop all this," James said. "I'm moving on to Canada, or wherever, in a few days and—"

"James, you're a cute guy. I know this isn't gonna last forever, but it's more fun than sitting downstairs every night."

James didn't appreciate being regarded as nothing more than an alternative to TV, but Becky healed his wounded look by stepping closer and kissing his cheek.

"You know what your trouble is, James?" Becky grinned. "You think too much."

James tried not to imagine the grievous injuries Kerry would inflict on him if she found out about this, as he leaned forward and returned Becky's kiss.

Lisa made spaghetti and meatballs for their evening meal. The Littles always ate as a family at the dining table, then moved to the living room for dessert in front of the TV.

James stacked the dishwasher, while Vaughn and Becky got the wood-burning fire going. They were set for walnut cake and the second part of a mini-series when the phone rang in the hallway.

"Curtis," Vaughn shouted.

Everyone looked around anxiously, knowing there was only one person who'd be calling for Curtis.

"Mom?" Curtis grinned, as he snatched the receiver. "What's going on? . . . Can't you tell me where I'm flying to? . . . OK, but we'll meet up at the other end? . . . Great, so I'll see you tomorrow. . . . Yeah, James is right here, I'll call him over. . . . James, my mom wants to speak to you."

James could hear his heart thumping, almost as loud as the faint voice in his ear. "Mrs. Oxford, hi."

"Hey there," Jane said. "My son tells me good things about you, James. I expect this is the only time you and me are ever gonna be safe to talk, but I had to thank you in person for what you did."

James couldn't help smiling. "That's OK. What's gonna happen to me and Lauren?"

"I got you new identities. There's a hotel in Boise sorted for tonight and you're on an early flight to Canada in the morning. I've got you and your sister set up with a real good family up there. I've sorted it financially, so there's money behind you. You'll be safe, as long as you keep yourself on the right side of the law."

"Sounds brilliant," James said. "Thanks."

"That's my four minutes up. Tell Vaughn it's the Comfort Lodge."

The phone clicked abruptly. James hooked the receiver over the wall-mounted phone and wiped a sweaty palm against his leg.

"She's not one for good-byes," Vaughn explained. "The shorter the call, the less chance the FBI has of tracking her down."

"How far is Boise?" James asked, still startled by his brief conversation with one of the world's most wanted.

"Three hours by road."

"When are we leaving?"

"'Bout as soon as you've got your things packed."

Lauren looked solemnly at Lisa. "Can I say good-bye to the horses?"

"I can pack her stuff if you want," James said. "We've only got a few clothes and bits."

Lisa tapped Lauren on the back. "Quickly then," she said. "Go and put your coat on."

James tried to think as he took the stairs two at a time. With him and Lauren flying to Canada, and Curtis off to meet his mother in some unknown destination, it looked like his prospects of a face-to-face meeting with Jane Oxford had shrunk to zero. All he could do was try and find out where Curtis was going, so that the FBI had a team waiting to intercept him when he met his mother.

James stepped inside his room and began stuffing everything into a backpack. Becky came up behind him.

"I guess this is it then," James said, feeling a mixture of sadness and relief that he couldn't get a handle on.

A pistol and a couple of large ammunition clips bounced onto the bed in front of him.

"You might need those," Becky said.

James was shocked. "Is that your dad's gun? You'll get in trouble."

"Don't trust Jane Oxford. I've heard talk about things she's done over the years and believe me, you might want that by your side."

"She said she's found me and Lauren a family," James said, staring indecisively at the gun on the bed.

Becky picked up the lightweight gun and shoved an ammunition clip into the base. "What was your bargain with Curtis? You break him out, Jane sets you up with a new life."

James nodded.

"Well, you already broke Curtis out. So what are you to Jane Oxford now, except trouble and expense?"

This thought had occurred to James on a number of occasions, though the mission briefing described Jane as loyal to anyone who helped her out.

Becky held the gun in front of James's face. "Pull back the stock to load the first bullet, like this. . . . The safety is this little lever here. It's a Glock machine pistol. Each magazine holds twenty-five shots and it's fully automatic, like a machine gun. Just flip the switch to auto."

"You really don't think we can trust her?"

Becky shrugged as she pulled the elastic of James's tracksuit pants and tucked in the gun. "I don't know. Better safe than sorry's all I'm saying."

The last time James had got into a bad situation with a gun, he'd ended up killing someone. He didn't want to get into that situation again and it was the only thing on his mind as Becky's parting kiss brushed his cheek.

"I'll leave you to it, James Rose," Becky said sadly. "Pull your hoodie on, so no one can see the gun, and look after yourself."

James smiled a little. "I'll do my best."

Lauren looked torn up as she passed Becky in the doorway.

"That didn't take long," James said.

"I couldn't face them," Lauren sniffed. "I ran back to the house."

James was surprised at how attached Lauren had become to the horses. He gave her a quick squeeze.

"Here, put this on," James said, handing his sister one of the tracking patches. "We might get separated."

Lauren unbuttoned her jeans and stuck the transmitter, which looked exactly like a sticking plaster, to the top of her thigh where nobody would see it. At the same moment, a crashing sound erupted from Curtis's bedroom.

James shot down the hallway and into a sea of torn paper. Curtis had shredded his dozens of sketches and drawings, then ripped his wardrobe door off its hinges, before burrowing into a narrow space between his bed and the wall.

"What's the matter?" James gasped.

"I like it here," Curtis sobbed. "My mom's gonna go mad at me for killing them people. Then we'll be on the run again. She likes the danger, but I get scared and it does my head in. I just want to stay in one place and draw my pictures and go to school. . . ."

James couldn't think what to say as Vaughn stepped into the room behind him.

"Are you two fighting?" Vaughn asked angrily. "Look at the state of this room."

"He's messed up," James said, uncertainly. "He needs help."

James looked at Curtis, sobbing pitifully into the wall and wished there was something he could do.

"I don't want to go back to prison," Curtis howled. "I don't want to go back on the run. I wish I was dead, but I'm too useless even to kill myself. . . ."

James sat on the end of the bed and touched Curtis's hand.

"You know these moods always pass," James said. "Once you're back with your mum, you can have a proper talk with her and sort yourself out. I bet it'll be OK."

"She never listens," Curtis sobbed.

"I need the pair of you downstairs and ready to roll in five minutes," Vaughn said firmly. "James, get Curtis a cloth to wipe his face. We've got a long drive ahead. He'll have to get a grip on himself."

CHAPTER 90

CALLS

John Jones and the three-man FBI team had been unable to contact James and Lauren during the two weeks they'd spent on the isolated ranch. To compensate for the lack of access, they'd watched any comings and goings from a safe distance and set up laser microphones in the trees. The invisible beams of light detected vibrations in the windows and converted them into muffled speech using a laptop computer.

Theo was starting a six-hour shift, sitting in the trees fifty meters from the front gate of the ranch, when he heard the kids were on the move. He pulled off a skiing glove and grabbed a radio to call Marvin.

John, Warren, and Marvin were fifteen miles away,

having a meal in a pizza place near their motel. As Marvin was talking to Theo on his walkie-talkie, he extracted a ringing cell phone from his jacket and handed it to Warren. The call was confirmation from the FBI phone-monitoring unit, who had overheard both ends of Jane Oxford's telephone conversation.

"OK," Marvin said, taking a final bite of pizza as he stood up. "I'll make some calls to see what kind of manpower we can rustle up around Boise. I'll try and get someone to stake out the Comfort Lodge, then I'll drive on ahead. There's so little traffic around here, they'll spot us in three seconds flat if we tail them. John, I want you and Warren to take the second car and try to follow the tracking signal from the kids, but keep your distance. Theo will have to sit tight until they leave the ranch and catch us up."

Vaughn's big Toyota had three rows of seats. Lauren sprawled out with a row to herself as they drove towards Boise in the darkness. She closed her eyes and tried not to get upset again.

Making and breaking close relationships was the part of CHERUB missions that newly qualified agents often found toughest to deal with. Lauren knew James would tease her about blubbing over a bunch of horses, but she couldn't help feeling sad every time she thought about them. She remembered the first morning at the ranch, when Lisa had lifted her into the saddle and led her around the small paddock on a rein. Lauren had been terrified of falling off, but time had turned it into a fond memory.

Curtis was a wreck, slumped down without his seatbelt on. The wet streaks on his face caught in the headlight beams of the cars going in the other direction. Before the mission, all James knew about Curtis came from reports about the killings and Warren's observations from inside Arizona Max. Now James had got to know him, he couldn't help wondering if such a sensitive soul would have turned into a killer if he'd grown up in a normal home, instead of on the run with his thrill-addicted mother.

James sat up front, alongside Vaughn. The drive was boring, but he felt too edgy to do anything other than stare at the road ahead, with the handle of the Glock digging into his belly. Shortly after a sign reading BOISE 15 MILES, Vaughn handed James a cell phone.

"Dial information and get the number of the Comfort Lodge."

James held the phone to his ear with his shoulder, as he scrawled the number on the corner of a road map. He dialed and waited to hear ringing before handing the phone back to Vaughn.

"That the Comfort Lodge?" Vaughn said into the handset. "My name is Hermann. I got a reservation with you for tonight, but I'm supposed to be meeting a pal of mine first. I believe he's left me a message in the lobby to say where I'm supposed to meet him for dinner. Would you be kind enough to read it to me?"

Vaughn held the phone silently, while the woman on the other end retrieved a folded slip of paper from a cubby behind her head and read it out.

"So that's the Star Plaza," Vaughn nodded. "You

wouldn't happen to know where that is, would you? . . . Don't worry yourself, sweetheart. I'll get my buddy here to look it up on the map."

Vaughn ended the call and chucked the phone on the dashboard.

"Who are we meeting?" James asked, as he unraveled a map of Boise city center.

"Nobody. It's a precaution, in case Jane's phone was being bugged. She tells you to go to one hotel, then leaves a message there under a false name. The message gives you the name of some hotel on the other side of town, which is where you'll really be staying."

James had hoped that the FBI would have the room at the Comfort Lodge staked out by the time they arrived. Now he was relying on the patches stuck to his and Lauren's skin, and these tiny devices were notoriously unreliable.

"You don't really think the FBI could have tracked us all the way up here, do you?" James asked.

Vaughn shrugged. "I doubt it, but Curtis's ma has to be real careful. The feds pull out the stops once they put you on that most wanted list. See that cell phone?"

James nodded.

"Came to me in a Fed Ex package two days ago with instructions not to even switch it on until we were on the move. Maybe Jane is over-cautious, but there are prisons full of people who weren't cautious enough."

The Star Plaza was a bog-standard business hotel a few minutes' drive from Boise airport, with the usual marble and faux-antique furnishings in the lobby. Vaughn looked nervous as he strolled past reception with the three kids in tow. He approached two old-timers, sitting in armchairs around an occasional table. They wore cheap looking suits and their long white beards suggested the men had been bikers in their younger days.

"Bill, Eugene," Vaughn said, nodding guardedly. "Didn't expect to find you two in this neck of the woods."

"Well you did," Bill said grumpily, furrowing his brow as though he resented the fact Vaughn existed.

Vaughn gestured with his hand. "This is James, Curtis, and Lauren."

"You don't say?" the old geezer croaked. "The lady says you'll get your money transfer in a few days. We'll take 'em up to the rooms. No need for *you* to stick around."

James got a whiff of pomade, as Bill hauled himself out of his chair. He noticed that Eugene, the other old man, wore a hearing aid.

"So, I'd best be going," Vaughn said, as he looked fondly at James. "I can see you out there in Canada, cruising on your Harley in a few years' time."

"Yeah," James smiled, "I hope so."

"But at least my daughter's safe from you now."

James missed a beat, as Vaughn burst out laughing. "You think Lisa and me didn't realize you were carrying on?"

"Yeah um . . . well . . . ," James babbled nervously, as he caught an extremely frosty look off Lauren.

"When my eldest got her first boyfriend, I wanted to kill him. By the time you get to the fourth one, you know better than to put up a fight."

James grinned, as Vaughn gave him a hug and slapped him on the back. Lauren and Curtis got the same treatment.

"For Christ's sake," Bill grouched, as he took a step towards the elevator. "We got everyone in the world eyeballing us here."

James felt a touch of sadness as he snatched a final glance at Vaughn, heading into the darkness through a revolving door. He might have been a gun smuggler, but Vaughn Little was one of the nicest guys James had ever met.

They had two connecting rooms on the fifth floor of the hotel, each with a pair of double beds. Eugene and Bill already had their old-man stuff spread out in one room: bottles of pills, hip flasks, Y-fronts, and the most unfashionable trainers known to man with gray socks balled up inside them. The connecting door was wedged open and Eugene turned the TV up loud enough that you could have heard it on Mars.

The kids had checked out the room and were chilling on their beds for a while when Bill wandered through.

"Can we go and use the pool?" James asked, desperate to get out of the room and contact the FBI, in case they hadn't picked up on the change of lodgings.

"Nah," Bill said, scratching his armpit and revealing a glimpse of the holster under his jacket. "It's gone ten o'clock. You boys have been all over the news, so you're better off staying out of sight. Order food from room service if you're hungry, then shift yourselves to bed. Eugene's taking a nap. If he wakes up, tell him I'm down at the bar having a nightcap."

Within thirty seconds of Bill heading out the door, Curtis dived off the bed and grabbed a can of beer and a bunch of miniature spirit bottles from the fridge.

"Minibar time," Curtis grinned, hurling James a little Jack Daniels bottle as he drained his own into his mouth.

James was wary: The last time Curtis got drunk he ended up getting a life sentence. On the other hand, with Eugene asleep, Bill at the bar, and Curtis hitting the bottle, he had a golden opportunity to contact Marvin. It was too risky using the phone in the room, because the call would get itemized on the bill, but he'd seen pay phones in the lobby downstairs.

"I know," Lauren said excitedly, "why don't we try and find out where we're all going tomorrow?"

"Good idea," James said, impressed by how smart his sister could be at times. He'd been so focused on making sure the FBI team knew where they were, he'd forgotten that their main objective was to find out where Curtis was going to meet his mother.

"Where are you gonna look?" Curtis asked.

James shrugged, but Lauren dived purposefully into the next room, where Eugene was sleeping soundly, and grabbed a snazzy leather document wallet she'd eyed up earlier.

"Bet it's in here," Lauren said.

James understood her logic: The smart item was out of style with the elderly men's other possessions. Someone else had clearly handed it to them.

Lauren unzipped the case on the bed. It contained a brown envelope stashed with a mix of U.S. and Canadian dollars and three fake passports. The first was Brazilian, containing a picture of Curtis under the name Eduardo Santos. There was a computer printout inside, detailing flights from Boise to Dallas and a connecting flight to Rio de Janeiro.

"Eduardo Santos," Curtis said, in a rubbish attempt at a Spanish accent. "Sounds good, hombres?"

He gulped a small bottle of gin as Lauren pulled out the two Canadian passports.

"Go easy on the booze, eh?" James said, still holding the unopened Jack Daniels in his hand. "So where are we going?"

Lauren and James looked set to become Scott and Ellen Parks, of Toronto. James was no expert on forged documents, but the passports looked good to him. Fake identification of this quality would have cost thousands of dollars.

"OK," James said. "Put the case where you found it, before Bill gets back."

Curtis crashed on his bed and ripped open a packet of dry-roasted cashews. James and Lauren walked into the other room together. They made sure Eugene was still asleep before exchanging hurried whispers over the noise from the TV.

"Keep Curtis busy," James said. "Start a pillow fight or something. I'll run out and try to make a quick call."

"What if Curtis asks were you are? Or Bill comes back?"

"We're kids," James shrugged, "people expect us to muck about. Just say I'm getting ice, or whatever."

James opened the door, while Lauren wandered back to join Curtis. He peeked along the corridor, finding nothing except a couple of uncollected room-service trolleys. Their room was at the end of a long corridor near a fire escape. James walked through the fire door and down a single flight of concrete steps to the fourth floor, where there would be no chance of bumping into Bill.

James was planning to use the phones in the lobby, but he spotted an old-fashioned phone with a dial hanging on the wall near the entrance to a cleaner's closet. It was designed for internal use by hotel staff, but James knew most switchboards are programmed to allow any phone to dial out to an emergency number. He picked up the receiver and dialed 911.

"Emergency, which service please?"

James smiled with relief. "FBI, I have a station number. It's three-two-four-six and the application code is T."

Within a second of the operator patching the call through to the FBI, it diverted via an office in Phoenix and on to Marvin Teller's cell phone.

"We're sorry, the mobile number you are dialing is currently busy. Please try again later or leave a message after the beep."

James cursed under his breath. "Marvin, it's me. I'm at the Star Plaza, room five-three-four. Curtis is on a zero-nine-thirty flight to Dallas on American Airlines. He's flying on to Rio using a passport in the name of Eduardo Santos. . . ."

CHAPTER 31

BRAZIL

James got back to the room without Bill, Eugene, or Curtis even noticing that he'd gone. He was almost certain Marvin would have listened to the cell phone message, but it played on James's mind as he lay in the dark room, with Lauren and Curtis asleep and Eugene's snores rumbling through the connecting door.

James was half awake at 5:30 a.m. when Bill crept up to Curtis's bed and shook him awake. The teenager seemed to be suffering the aftereffects of his attack on the minibar as he sat up in bed.

"I thought the flight was later," Curtis moaned, picking at a gluey eye.

"Keep it down," Bill whispered. "I just made a

scheduled call to your mother. She's nervous about this whole show. There's been another change of plan and we don't want the two brats over there knowing about it."

"Mom's whole life has been a change of plan," Curtis sighed. "Can't I say good-bye to James and Lauren?"

"Let 'em sleep. You know how this works better than anyone: The less they know about when you got out of here and where you went, the better."

James had a crick in his neck, but didn't dare move in case the old man realized he was awake.

Curtis swung off his bed, dashed to the bathroom, and bolted the door. James heard him pee, followed by a retching sound as he spewed up in the toilet bowl. James stifled a laugh as Bill wandered over and rapped gently on the locked door.

"You OK in there, boy?"

There was an array of noises from the bathroom, as Curtis cleaned himself up and gargled mouthwash.

"Man," Curtis gasped, as he exited. "Must have been something I ate. I hope I'm not sick again on the plane."

"Something you drank, more like," Bill grumbled. "I can smell it comin' out your pores."

Curtis stumbled meekly across the floor and started picking up his belongings.

"Forget that junk," Bill said. "Put your pants and sneakers on, then we're shipping out."

James racked his brain, wondering if he should follow Bill and Curtis. If Marvin hadn't got the message, or if they were expecting Curtis to be getting a later flight and were still in bed, they'd permanently lose the trail to

Jane Oxford. On the other hand, James would blow his cover if he was caught sneaking around after them.

"Ready?" Bill asked, as Curtis wriggled his foot into his trainer and stood up.

"I guess," Curtis said, uncertainly. He stepped across the room towards the other bed and looked at James. "Have a nice life, buddy," he whispered softly.

Curtis followed Bill through the connecting door and they exited via the other room. James sprang up as soon as the door clunked. He leaned in the next room to make sure Eugene was asleep before scrambling into tracksuit bottoms and trainers and grabbing a room entry card from the table beside his bed.

He poked his head into the corridor, as Bill and Curtis's backs disappeared around a corner, heading for the elevators. James raced down the back stairs, planning to catch up with them in the lobby. Unfortunately, there were no guest rooms on the ground floor. James found himself at the back of a conference suite, staring at a blank gray fire door that only opened from the other side.

Anxious not to lose Curtis for good, James broke open the fire door and found himself standing in the hotel car park. The sun was peeking over the horizon and his T-shirt did nothing to ward off the bitter wind sweeping across the open tarmac.

James quickly glanced around, making sure there was nobody in sight, before jogging between the lanes of parked cars towards the hotel entrance. When he got close, he noticed a queue of people stepping onto a small bus with STAR PLAZA—AIRPORT SHUTTLE written down the side. Curtis and Bill were in the line.

James ducked between two cars. He was desperate to go into the lobby and call the FBI team to make sure they knew what was going on, but he was pinned to the spot until the bus left.

Finally, the last passenger boarded and the hydraulic door hissed shut. As the bus began rolling away, a man thumped desperately against the side. The driver hit the brake sharply to let on a final passenger. He was huge black man, wearing a cowboy hat and a suit the color of red wine. James smiled with relief. He needn't have worried: Marvin Teller had got the message.

Lauren woke with a fright. She caught half a second's glance inside the old man's toothless mouth before her whole world turned black. Eugene smeared a pillow over her face and squeezed down so hard she could feel the mattress springs digging into the back of her head. Lauren arched her back and tried to wriggle free, but Eugene swung his knee across the bed and used it to pin down her thighs.

There was no air in Lauren's lungs to scream. She tried to pull some in, but the pillow driving into her face made it impossible, like trying to suck wet concrete through a drinking straw. She knew the numbers from when she'd learned to scuba dive: five minutes to suffocate, but only three for the lack of oxygen to cause permanent brain damage.

Where was James?

Lauren wondered if her brother was already dead, as she realized her right arm was free to move. She felt a glimmer of hope as she fumbled blindly over the top of the bedside cabinet, hunting for some kind of weapon. She recalled the Biro with the *Star Plaza* logo on it as soon as she touched it. She gripped it tight and flipped off the lid with her thumb. It wasn't much, but it was all she had.

Lauren's concentration drifted for a second: the first sign of losing consciousness. She bit her tongue to help focus her mind and blindly thrust with the pen. It hit Eugene in the shoulder, causing only mild discomfort and a blue trail down the sleeve of his shirt. Irritated by the prospect of having to wash out a stain, Eugene shifted his weight as he tried to grab the pen with his free hand.

The pressure moved off Lauren's thighs as Eugene leaned forward. She used all her strength to thrust her knees up into the man's behind. Eugene's grip on the pillow loosened as he jerked upwards, enabling Lauren to twist her head to one side and haul in a lungful of air. Eugene immediately shifted his entire bodyweight back on to Lauren, inflicting extra pain by digging his kneecap into her belly.

Lauren refused to let the excruciating pain deter her desperate escape attempt. She glanced a shaft of light between the sheet and pillow, then spotted one of Eugene's fingertips, as he attempted to straighten her head and reposition the pillow over her face.

"Quite the little fighter, ain't you," Eugene said, clearly not regarding the ten-year-old's struggle as anything more than a minor setback.

Lauren wriggled her head forward a few centimeters. When she felt the base of Eugene's fingernail pressing against her lips, she bit down hard. The knee slipped off her stomach as the bite sent the old man into a spasm.

Temporarily abandoning his murder attempt to concentrate on his finger, Eugene snatched the pillow away. With the finger still clamped between her teeth, Lauren inhaled through her nose and, now she could see what she was doing, aimed the pointed end of the Biro into the soft tissue at the side of Eugene's throat. The pen sounded like a sink plunger, as the metal point speared his wrinkled flesh.

Lauren let the finger out of her mouth as Eugene slumped across the bed, wailing in agony. Lauren pulled her legs from under him and knocked him cold with a two-footed karate kick to the side of the head.

Shaking with fear and clutching her painful stomach, Lauren rolled off the bed and lifted the corner of the mattress to retrieve the Glock handgun she'd seen James stash there the night before. She flipped the safety off and quickly checked the bathroom and the floor beside the other bed, terrified she was about to discover her brother's suffocated body.

She held the gun two-handed as she crept into the connecting room, again checking between the beds. The bathroom gave Lauren a shock: Eugene had carefully set out knives and polythene sheeting to dispose of her body.

Lauren was still no closer to knowing what had happened to James. Maybe Eugene had knocked him out while he was sleeping and dragged him off to be suffocated in another room, or maybe he'd been invited downstairs for an early breakfast with Bill and Curtis.

You might as well let Lauren sleep in if she's tired. Eugene will look after her. . . .

With Eugene unconscious and James's fate a mystery, Lauren knew she had no option but to call Marvin. As she picked up the receiver, she heard someone enter the next room.

Realizing she had surprise on her side, Lauren crept towards the connecting door, but managed to stub her bare toe on the leg of a table. Her tiny gasp was enough to send the figure in the next room diving into the shadows behind one of the beds before she'd got a proper look at him.

"I've got a gun," Lauren shouted as she leaned into the doorway, squeezing the trigger to fire a warning shot.

Lauren didn't realize the Glock was capable of repeat fire, or that she'd inadvertently flipped it to automatic when she took off the safety. She felt like there was a high-pressure hose in her hands, as the recoil from half a dozen bullets shoved her backwards. The shots plunged into the wall, smashed the mirrored front of a wardrobe, and knocked clumps of plaster out of the ceiling. Lauren ended up sprawled backwards over one of the beds.

A stunned shout came out through the dust clouds and broken glass in the next room. "It's *me*," James coughed, as he stood up with his hands in the air.

"Where the *hell* did you disappear to without bothering to wake me up? I nearly got killed."

James stepped through the dust and snatched the gun from his sister. "Mental gun, eh?" he said. "It's what the SAS use. You're supposed to stand with one leg behind the other so it doesn't push you backwards."

"So where's Curtis?"

"On his way to the—"

Before James finished speaking, the locks in both room doors clicked simultaneously. James spun around, ready to spray more bullets.

"FBI," Warren shouted, aiming a gun into the room.

"All safe," James and Lauren shouted back frantically.

John and Theo had rushed into the other room and ended up staring at James through the connecting door.

"We heard the gunfire. What happened?" John asked.

"The unconscious guy with the Biro sticking out of his neck just tried to smother me," Lauren explained matter-of-factly.

"That doesn't make sense," James said. "What about the Canadian passports we saw last night?"

"Look for yourself if you don't believe me," Lauren said, pointing indignantly towards the bathroom. "I don't go round sticking people with Biros for the fun of it you know."

James, John, Warren, and Theo peeked at the equipment laid out in the bathroom. James felt queasy when he imagined what had nearly happened.

"Wasn't Jane Oxford supposed to be loyal to people who help her out?" James asked bitterly.

"We clearly overestimated the extent of that loyalty," Theo said. "But the passports are a classic Jane Oxford ruse. She always makes three or four different plans and only tells people which one she's going to use at the very last moment. It's possible that Bill was given the passports and believes that you two were going to be sent to Canada, while Eugene was under instructions to kill you."

"It's a clever tactic," Warren added. "We've had it a few times where we've broken down one of Oxford's operations and made arrests, only to find that there's a mass of evidence pointing in different directions. When it gets to court, the defense lawyers use the contradictions to pull you apart: *If Jane Oxford intended to kill James and Lauren Rose, why did she spend ten thousand dollars buying them false identities, booking airline tickets, and arranging for them to stay with Mr. and Mrs. La-de-da in Toronto*. And so on."

"But why would she try to kill us?" Lauren asked. "We never did anything to hurt *her*."

"I suppose she thought you might have talked if you were ever recaptured," Theo said. "You knew about Etienne and the Little family. She clearly wanted you dead the second Curtis wasn't around to see it happen."

"Heartless bitch," James said, shaking his head. "We helped her own son escape and her only thanks was to try and kill us."

"It figures though," Warren said. "Oxford hasn't evaded the law for twenty years by being sentimental."

"We can speculate all we like once this is over," John said tersely. "Right now, I suggest we put our heads together and concentrate on working out where we go from here."

"I think we'd better call an ambulance for Eugene first," Theo said. "Things are starting to look a little gooey over there."

"Apart from that, all we can do is make sure we don't lose track of Curtis," Warren said. "We've got agents on standby at Dallas airport and in Brazil. Hopefully Jane will show her face wherever Curtis ends up. Trouble is, she'll run a mile if she finds out that everything here just went pear-shaped."

Theo's cell phone rang. He grabbed it out of his jacket and had a brief conversation with Marvin.

"You're not going to believe this," Theo groaned. "Bill got a phone call while he was on the airport bus. When they arrived, Marvin got off and hung back to follow Bill and Curtis, but Bill told the bus driver he'd left something back at the hotel and they're staying on for the ride back."

"Is Marvin still with them?" John asked.

Theo shook his head. "It would have been too suspicious if he'd re-boarded the bus. Curtis and Bill should be back at reception any minute now."

CHAPTER 32

motel

The shuttle bus only took fifteen minutes to ride between the hotel and the airport.

"So here's what happened," John said, thinking as he spoke. "Eugene tried to kill James and Lauren, but got his comeuppance. Once they realized Jane Oxford wanted them dead, James and Lauren grabbed the money and valuables and left the hotel in a big hurry."

Warren pointed at Eugene, who was still unconscious on the bed. "What about him? He needs an ambulance."

John shrugged. "He was about to kill the kids, so forgive me if I haven't got a lot of sympathy for him."

Theo leaned over the bed and inspected Eugene's injury. "It's behind the windpipe and he's not losing much blood. With the Biro still bunging up the hole, I believe he'll be good for a few hours, at least."

"OK, let's grab the valuables and clear out of here sharpish," John said.

Theo pocketed Eugene's wallet, while Lauren grabbed the briefcase with the money and passports. They were almost out of the door when the phone rang.

John made a split-second decision. "James, you answer that."

"Hello," James said, as he frantically grasped the receiver and stumbled onto the bed.

"Eugene? Is that you?" Bill asked.

"It's James."

"Oh," Bill said, sounding exceptionally surprised. "I didn't expect you to still be around. Is Eugene there?"

"He's been locked in the toilet for ages," James said, trying to sound cool. "I don't know what he's playing around at in there."

John gave James a smile and thumbs-up for his quick thinking.

Bill sounded angry. "You tell Eugene to get his sorry old ass moving. Tell him I've checked Curtis in for his flight, but I'm on my way back here to find a certain car and I'll meet him at the motor lodge this evening."

"OK, I'll pass that on," James said. "Thanks very much for helping us out, by the way."

Bill sounded stunned. "Um . . . that's OK, James, it was a pleasure."

The call went dead.

"What did he say?" John asked.

"Something about being on his way to find a car, but he said he'd dropped Curtis off at the airport."

John shrugged. "I guess he said that for your benefit."

"It's classic Jane Oxford, again," Theo said. "She has Bill set up with a passport and an airline ticket. Then she pulls the plan at the last minute and sends him off on a car journey."

"But why wait until he gets to the airport, then send him back here?" Lauren asked. "Wouldn't it have been better to send him to pick up the car somewhere else?"

"I guess Bill was running early," Theo said. "Jane probably thought he was still here."

"Judging by that phone call, Bill and Curtis won't be coming back to this room, which makes our lives easier," John said. "We've got to get downstairs and make sure we don't lose them when they get off the airport shuttle and try to find this car."

"Someone will have to stay here and deal with Eugene," Theo said. "We can't leave him for the poor maid to find."

"OK, Theo," John said. "You stay here and deal with that, but don't call for an ambulance until after you see us leave. Warren and I will go down to the car park, see what car Bill and Curtis get into, and chase after them."

"What about me and Lauren?" James asked.

John thought for a second before digging out his car keys. "You can navigate and operate the radios. It's a black Chrysler, parked in row F. Get in, start the engine so that the car's ready to pull away as soon as I get there, then belt yourself into the passenger seat."

Warren dangled his keys in front of Lauren. "Blue

Volvo, parked next to John's. Make sure you keep down if you see Bill or Curtis."

James and Lauren raced five floors down the back stairs, out through the fire doors, and into the car park. They found row F and were climbing into the cars as the Airport Shuttle stopped in front of the lobby. A rumble of static burst out of the police radio in the dashboard, as James started the engine and climbed over to the passenger seat.

Curtis and Bill both disappeared inside the lobby. James looked across at Lauren in the next car and shrugged, hoping that they weren't changing plans again.

Warren's voice erupted from the loudspeaker. "I'm in the lobby and I think we're OK. They've both gone into the bathroom. Curtis looks a little green around the gills."

James spotted them emerging through the revolving doors a couple of minutes later. Both kids dropped down in their seats, so they were out of sight, as Bill led the way out into the rows of cars. He stopped when he reached a shabby yellow Nissan that looked like a retired taxi. He stepped back to read the registration plate, then fumbled around under the front wheel arch until he located an ignition key.

James was feeling tense. He jumped out of his skin as John opened the driver's door beside him.

"Look in the glove box," John said, as he slammed the door and pulled his seatbelt across his chest. "Get the best map you can find. Try to keep track of where we are and remember the names of shops and landmarks as you pass them. In any pursuit, you must be able to accurately relay your position to other cars."

James nodded, as he rummaged through the glove box for a map. As John pulled away, he passed Warren walking briskly towards the other car.

Theo's voice broke out over the radio. "I'm looking out of the hotel window. I see a yellow Nissan pulling right. Over."

John pointed at the microphone. "You work the radio, James."

James picked up the plastic microphone and looked unsure what to say.

"Just tell him we're on it," John said.

By the time Marvin had sprinted across Boise airport to the taxi rank and arrived back at the Star Plaza, an ambulance crew was on the scene to deal with Eugene. Marvin hurled money at the cab driver, and rushed off without getting change. As he pulled his car out of its spot, Marvin asked for a fix on Bill and Curtis over the radio.

"This is car F. We're eight miles ahead, on route sixteen, heading southwest," James replied.

Bill clearly didn't want to risk getting pulled over for speeding and kept the yellow Nissan dead on the limit, enabling Marvin to catch up with John and Warren.

Marvin and Warren had been trained in pursuit driving on the opposite side of the Atlantic to John, but the basic technique is the same wherever you learn. The lead car kept the yellow Nissan in sight. The second car held back between a quarter and half a mile, ready to continue the chase if the suspect made a sudden maneuver and fooled the driver of the first car. The third car followed another mile behind that. To minimize suspicion, the cars switched positions every fifteen to twenty minutes.

An hour and a half after leaving Boise, they'd passed into the state of Oregon and were traveling northwest on a busy section of interstate towards Baker City.

Lauren's voice broke across the radio from the lead car. James was dead impressed by how professional she sounded. "Yellow Nissan is off at Rouge Court Motor Inn. That's Rouge Court Motor Inn. We have passed the exit, but can come around if needed."

"Negative," Marvin answered. "Pull up somewhere a few miles ahead and keep the engine running. We might need you later. I'm gonna pull in after them. John, I need backup. I want you to pull up short and try to cover me from the side."

A mile and a half sounds a long way to hang back, but at seventy miles an hour it took John only a minute to reach the Rouge Court. The motel formed part of a strip, along with a burger joint, diner, and gas station. John rolled up in front of the diner. They jumped out of the car and crouched behind some bushes overlooking the Rouge Court parking lot. James had nothing but a T-shirt covering his top half, so he tucked his hands under his armpits to ward off the cold.

"Have you still got the Glock?" John asked.

James nodded, as he pulled it from the elastic of his tracksuit pants. John swapped it for his revolver. "I might need the extra firepower."

Bill stood in front of a locked glass door, ringing a buzzer to try and get into the motel reception. Marvin couldn't get out of his car, in case Bill recognized him from the airport shuttle ride. Curtis sat in the front seat of the yellow Nissan, with his elbow resting on the ledge of the open window.

James heard the door of one of the motel rooms clunk shut. The woman who emerged was dressed in a pink T-shirt, with big glasses and a towel around her hair, like she'd just washed it. Her mules scraped along the damp pavement with every step she took.

She was almost level with the yellow Nissan, when James recognized the glasses from the photograph he'd seen in the visitors' room at Arizona Max.

"It's her," James whispered, nudging John excitedly. "Jane Oxford."

"I don't think so," John said, shaking his head.

By the time John had finished denying it, Curtis had jumped out of the car and wrapped his arms around her.

"Holy *cow*," John stuttered, grabbing his walkie-talkie out of his jacket. "Warren, Marvin, I'm eyeballing Jane Oxford *right* now. Get over here."

A shout came at James and John from behind. "Hey, what you hidin' down there for?"

It was the cook from the diner, a greasy man dressed in an even greasier apron. Curtis and Jane both turned towards the shout. It left John with no option but to move immediately.

"Cover the door of her motel room," John said urgently. "She might have backup in there."

James clicked the safety off the revolver. John leapt out of the bushes and fired a shot into the back of the yellow Nissan to make it clear he meant business.

"FBI, *freeze*."

John closed Jane and Curtis down, looking nervously from side to side, with the gun held in a two-handed grip.

Marvin and Bill both heard. Bill pulled his gun from its holster and headed around the corner to Jane's rescue, not realizing that an FBI agent was emerging from a car behind him. Marvin had never struck James as the kind of man who stood any nonsense and he proved it by pulling his gun and shooting Bill twice in the back, without even bothering to shout a warning.

Marvin snatched Bill's gun, as he stepped over the bleeding man and rounded the corner to the yellow Nissan.

"This is turning into a real good morning's work," Marvin grinned, unhooking the set of handcuffs on his belt as he closed in on Jane.

James kept one nervous eye on the door of Jane's motel room, and the other on Curtis, trying to read his face. No sane person would make a run for it with two guns pointing at them from close range, but that didn't take account of Curtis's suicidal tendencies.

While John covered him with the Glock, Marvin made Jane Oxford take her hands off her head and fixed a set of cuffs over her wrists.

"Look at that," Marvin said smugly, as he squeezed them on. "Perfect fit."

Jane lashed her head around and spat down the lapel of Marvin's suit. Marvin furiously lifted Jane into the air and thumped her down on the hood of the Nissan. While pinning Jane with one hand, he unhooked a can of pepper spray from his belt and held it in her face.

"Don't make me use this," Marvin said firmly.

Angered by what was happening to his mother, Curtis made a sudden lunge towards John. James's heart jumped, knowing John only had to pull on the trigger to tear Curtis apart. But John had no intention of using a gun on an unarmed fourteen-year-old. Instead, he wrapped an arm around Curtis's waist and bundled him backwards onto the damp tarmac. The boy thrashed around, letting out a giant moan, as John zipped a set of disposable plastic cuffs over his wrists.

By the time Warren rolled onto the forecourt, Jane and Curtis were cuffed up in the back of Marvin's car. While Warren leaned over Bill and used his cell phone to call an ambulance, James crept around the bushes and climbed in the back of the Volvo behind his sister.

Lauren glanced over her shoulder. "It looks like Jane's crying."

"Good," James said sourly. "She wanted us dead. I hope she burns in hell."

"I feel sorry for Curtis though."

"Poor sod's not all there, is he?" James said. "Those drawings he ripped up were fantastic."

Lauren clambered over the armrest between the two front seats and crashed next to James in the back. She rested her head against James's shoulder as he put an arm around her back.

After all James and Lauren had been through, the scene they overlooked was an anti-climax: a quiet car park, three cops, two suspects cuffed in the back of a car, and a man lying unconscious on the ground. When the manager of the motel emerged from reception, he had the resigned look of someone who'd seen it all before.

"Are you OK?" James asked, pulling his rather sad-looking sister a little tighter.

"My tummy still hurts, from earlier," Lauren said. "It's all a bit of a letdown really."

James looked confused. "We caught Jane Oxford, what more do you want?"

"I don't know. . . . I guess I was expecting a big shoot-out, or something."

"Fancied some blood and guts, eh?" James smiled. "Helicopters chasing us down the road firing machine guns, and cigar-chomping mercenaries with strings of ammo around their necks."

"Yeah," Lauren giggled. "And it all ends up at Jane Oxford's mountain lair, where we find the stolen weapons and blow them all up. Diving out of the way seconds before a ball of flame erupts from the mouth of a cave."

James nodded. "And I get to rescue a whole bunch of hottie cheerleaders, who Jane was holding hostage. The two best looking ones give me their cell phone numbers. . . ."

"Trust *you*," Lauren tutted. "Of course, my hair would remain perfect throughout."

"If only we lived in the movies," James sighed, straightening up his grin. "Seriously though, the only thing that matters is that we captured Jane without any good guys getting hurt."

Lauren nodded. "Do you think they'll find the missiles, now they've caught her?"

"Hopefully," James shrugged. "We've done our bit.

I'm just looking forward to going home and chilling out. Kerry should be back by now."

"Will you tell her about Becky?"

"Not if I can help it. You know what her temper's like, she'd break my legs."

"Oh," Lauren said.

James sounded anxious. "You're not gonna spoil everything by grassing on me are you?"

"I suppose not," Lauren sighed, "seeing as you're my brother. But I still think you're a dirtbag. You don't deserve someone as nice as Kerry for a girlfriend."

CHAPTER 33

CAMPUS

After twenty hours of cars, airplanes, airport terminals, a train into town, and a minibus ride to campus, James was a wreck. His joints ached, like every drop of liquid had been sucked out of his body and replaced with chewing gum and he was so desperate for sleep his eyes felt like lead balls.

Lauren made the journey worse. She pulled off her usual trick of sleeping effortlessly, while James twisted in his economy-class seat, suffering through two dreadful romantic comedies.

It was past noon when they arrived back at campus. James ignored Lauren's exuberant pleas to help her unpack the boxes that had been piled up in her new quarters for nearly a month. He went to his room, stripped to his boxers, buried himself under his duvet, and fell asleep inside two minutes.

James woke four hours later with muddy fingertips sweeping across his cheek.

"I thought I'd better wake you up," Kerry said softly, as she sat down on the edge of James's bed. "If you sleep for too long now, you won't be tired tonight and you'll still be jet-lagged tomorrow."

James yawned, as he sat up in his bed. "What time is it?"

"Quarter to five. I just finished football practice."

James rubbed his eyes and couldn't help smiling as he took his first proper look at his girlfriend in three months. Kerry had done some growing up, and even with shin pads and streaks of mud on her legs, James thought she looked beautiful. He leaned forward and they exchanged a long kiss.

"I smell all sweaty," Kerry said, when she eventually pushed James away.

"I don't care," James said, moving in for another kiss. "I like your smell."

"Well, I don't much like yours," Kerry said, with a tiny hint of sharpness. "You smell like that horrible air freshener they spray on airplanes."

"Do I?" James asked, raising his arm and sniffing his pit. "That's pretty nasty, actually."

"You're a class act, James," Kerry grinned as she stood up. "Oh . . . you didn't notice," she added, pulling her T-shirt down over her football shorts.

James stared at Kerry's breasts bulging out of the T-shirt. "Of course I noticed, they're miles bigger than they were before."

Kerry stepped forward and whacked him across the shoulder. "*God,* is that all you boys ever think about?"

James grinned guiltily. "Pretty much."

"What about my T-shirt?" Kerry said indignantly. "The *color* of my T-shirt?"

"Oh," James gasped. "You got the navy T-shirt, congratulations!"

"Thank you," Kerry grinned sweetly as she headed for the door. "I'm gonna have a shower, then I'll see you downstairs for dinner."

The dining hall was packed when James got downstairs. He passed Lauren and Bethany, who were sitting amongst a group of the youngest gray-shirt kids, making a racket. James queued up and picked spaghetti Bolognese, salad, and chocolate trifle before heading across to the tables where his friends always sat.

Gabrielle and Kerry were the only ones there. James sat opposite them.

"Where is everyone?"

"Callum, Connor, and Shakeel are still away on their recruitment missions," Gabrielle explained. "Bruce is on a mission in Norfolk and Kyle's over at the back of campus, up to his waist in slurry."

"And *I've* got a bone to pick with you," Kerry said, folding her arms seriously.

James grinned as he crammed in a fork-load of spaghetti. "Oh, that *does* make a change."

"I hear you've been cheating on me while I was away."

James inhaled two hundred strands of spaghetti as he gasped. He couldn't believe that this had happened after Lauren had promised not to tell.

"Listen . . . ," James coughed. "Whatever she told you, it's not true."

Kerry shook her head slowly, as James hacked chewed-up pasta into a serviette.

"Don't lie to me, James. Bruce and half a dozen other guys saw everything that happened."

Now James was seriously confused. *"Bruce?"*

"I'm OK with it," Kerry said. "You know, if you ever feel that you want to explore your gay side . . ."

"My what?" James gasped, shaking his head. "What are you on about?"

"Look," Kerry giggled, "I just wanted you to know that if you ever feel the urge to snog Kyle again, I won't be holding any grudges."

James felt like a five-billion-ton weight had lifted off his chest as the pieces fitted together. This had nothing to do with Becky. Kerry was winding him up about the time he'd kissed Kyle as a joke after fitness training.

"Yeah, me and Kyle," James groaned, as he desperately tried to recap everything he'd said to make sure he hadn't accidentally given the game away. He realized the pasta had probably saved him. He dreaded to think what he might have blurted if he hadn't been choking. "Real funny . . . Did I hear you say Kyle's on punishment cleaning out ditches again?"

Gabrielle nodded. "That boy is *so* dumb."

"Why?" James grinned. "What's he done this time?"

"You remember the little DVD production line he was running?"

James nodded, his mouth too full to speak.

"I think the staff was prepared to turn a blind eye while he was running off the odd movie for his mates," Gabrielle explained. "But he started getting greedy."

"How come?" James asked.

"Kyle started getting more orders than he could handle by himself, so he employed Jake Parker to help burn the DVDs and put the labels on."

James nodded. "I know Jake, he's Bethany's little brother."

"Jake thought it would be funny to mix up the labels."

James broke into a smile. "That's *not* good."

"No it wasn't," Gabrielle said. "Especially not when a bunch of six-year-olds ended up at a sleepover with a copy of *The Texas Chainsaw Massacre* instead of *Harry Potter*."

"Classic," James yelled, banging on the tabletop and howling with laughter.

Kerry kicked him under the table. "It's not funny, James. One poor kid peed her nightie."

"I guess it's not really funny," James said, before erupting into a fresh round of hysterics.

Kerry was struggling to keep a straight face herself. She leaned across the table and stared into James's eyes. He wiped the Bolognese from his mouth and kissed Kerry on the lips. It was good to have her back.

EPILOGUE

JANE OXFORD did not cooperate with the FBI. She refused to answer any questions, except to acknowledge her name. She faces charges for murder, racketeering, and weapons smuggling and can expect to spend the rest of her life in prison. The complexity of the charges against her mean that a trial is unlikely to take place for several years. In the meantime, she remains on remand at the federal supermax prison in Florence, Colorado.

After Jane's arrest, the FBI used information in her possession at the time to uncover homes and assets she controlled around the world. As more secrets were unveiled, it became clear that Jane Oxford had changed the focus of her operations from stealing weapons, to stealing the technology underlying them. She then used front companies, such as Etienne Defense Consultancy, to sell this knowledge to other weapons manufacturers.

With the global armaments industry turning over half a trillion dollars a year, Jane found this business far more lucrative than selling arms to terrorist groups and poverty-stricken third-world governments. The FBI has already uncovered assets belonging to Jane Oxford worth more than $1.4 billion. Not only is this figure well in excess of what the FBI had expected to find, it is more than Jane's relatively modest lifestyle would ever have required. It seems that, true to her psychological profile, Jane Oxford carried on her criminal activities purely for the thrill of it.

So far, no specific information has been found about the PGSLM Buddy missiles. The FBI now suspects the missiles were stolen to order on behalf of a rival weapons manufacturer. However, until concrete evidence is found, there is no way to be certain of this. The possibility remains that the weapons have fallen into the hands of terrorists or even that Jane Oxford did not steal them at all.

CURTIS OXFORD was reclassified as an escape risk and returned to a single cell inside Arizona Max, after forty-eight hours in the hole.

A few months later, Curtis's Las Vegas based "uncles" discovered that the psychiatrist who recommended he be sent to the Arizona-based military school was being investigated for accepting money in return for recommending his patients to the school. They instructed a lawyer to appeal Curtis's case, on the grounds that the murders he committed were a result of the inappropriate advice given by the corrupt psychiatrist.

On appeal, the judge accepted the arguments of Curtis's lawyers, stating that: "Curtis Oxford has a long history of mental health problems. While Curtis must clearly still accept some responsibility for these very grave actions, this new evidence shows that it was inappropriate to try and sentence him as an adult."

Curtis's original convictions for first-degree murder were quashed. Charges relating to the death of Scott Warren and the subsequent escape were also dropped. Three weeks later, Curtis pleaded guilty to four counts of the lesser charge of manslaughter in an Arizona youth court. Following a detailed psychiatric evaluation, he received a sentence of seven years, to be served in a medium-security young offenders institution. The families of the three people Curtis shot appeared on a local TV station saying that they were appalled by this decision.

It has also emerged that Jane Oxford had set up a trust fund for her son, thought to be worth more than $30 million. This money has been thoroughly laundered through the international banking system and FBI sources believe it will be impossible to prove that it is the proceeds of criminal activity. When he is released from prison in 2012, Curtis Oxford will be an extremely wealthy young man.

Among the other prisoners, ELWOOD and KIRCH both turned eighteen and were moved into the adult section of Arizona Max shortly after the escape. The brothers

STANLEY and RAYMOND DUFF fully recovered from their injuries and returned to cell T4 once the riot damage had been repaired.

The Arizona Department of Prisons has a long-standing policy of naming cellblocks after officers who died in the line of duty. The SCOTT WARREN memorial cellblock is due to open soon in a new prison complex east of Phoenix. The inquiry into the escape made several recommendations for tightening up security inside Arizona Max. These included replacing the oversensitive doors and issuing all correctional officers with personal attack alarms that activate automatically when an officer is knocked down. A lack of money means these recommendations are unlikely to be implemented.

WARREN REISE (aka Scott Warren) quit his job as an FBI special agent so that he could spend more time with his wife and three young children. THEODORE MONROE and MARVIN TELLER remain on the FBI team investigating the legacy of Jane Oxford's criminal activities.

PAULA PARTRIDGE was questioned by police in California and Arizona. They saw no reason to doubt her story about being held hostage. She later received an undisclosed compensation payment from the Arizona Department of Prisons and $7,000 from a news agency for an interview about her "Terrifying ordeal at the hands of ruthless teenage killers." The article appeared in more than one hundred newspapers and magazines across the United States and around the world. The money enabled Paula to move out of the trailer park and make the down payment on a small house. She also took her daughter, HOLLY PARTRIDGE, for an overnight stay at Disneyland.

VAUGHN LITTLE's ranch was searched by the FBI and a significant cache of illegal weapons was found. These included Glock machine pistols, mortar rounds, and sniper rifles. Vaughn and his wife LISA LITTLE were charged with harboring a fugitive and possession of unlicensed firearms with intent to sell. Vaughn was sentenced to eight years in prison while Lisa received a term of four years. The ranch and Arabian horses had to be sold to pay legal costs and REBECCA LITTLE (Becky) moved to live with her eldest sister in California.

EUGENE DRISCOLL recovered fully after the Biro was removed from his neck. WILLIAM BENTLEY (Bill) similarly recovered from the gunshot wounds inflicted by Marvin Teller. Police checks indicated that the two men had been working together as contract killers for more than forty years. They were wanted for thirty murders in eleven U.S. states and two Canadian provinces.

After the two men had recovered, the FBI transported them to Texas. Following a three-week trial, they were found guilty of six counts of murder and sentenced to death by lethal injection. The lengthy appeals process means it will be several years before their death sentences are carried out.

DAVE MOSS was quietly removed from his guarded room in the Arizona hospital and arrived back at

CHERUB campus a few days after James and Lauren. He resumed light physical training shortly after returning and was declared fully fit two months later, when ultrasound scans showed that the blood clot on his chest had dissolved.

A detailed report is written on every CHERUB mission. The report on the prison break congratulated all participants for the overall success of the mission. However, JAMES ADAMS was severely criticized for his reckless crashing of the Toyota and Dave Moss for falling asleep and almost allowing James to be stabbed by Stanley Duff.

Only LAUREN ADAMS escaped without rebuke. The report described her as "Courageous, clear thinking, cooperative," and as a "young agent with massive future potential." After reading the report, Dr. McAfferty decided that her role in the mission justified giving her the navy T-shirt, making her one of the youngest ever to wear it.

While the staff at CHERUB had some reservations about the performance of their young agents, over in America the CIA and FBI were delighted with the capture of Jane Oxford. Four weeks after James returned to campus, Dr. McAfferty received a package from CIA headquarters. It contained three boxes made of highly polished piano wood, one each for James, Dave, and Lauren.

James wondered what was in the box when he came up to his room after lessons and spotted it resting on his pillow. He pulled open the tightly sprung hinge and stared at the gold disc, with the head of an American eagle at the center of a five-pointed star, before reading the inscription beneath it:

The Intelligence Star is a medal awarded by the United States for a voluntary act, or acts, of courage performed under hazardous conditions, or for outstanding achievements or services rendered with distinction under conditions of grave risk.

James couldn't help grinning as he turned the medal over and read his name engraved on the back.

CHERUB: A HISTORY (1941–1996)

1941 In the middle of the Second World War, Charles Henderson, a British agent working in occupied France, sent a report to his headquarters in London. It was full of praise for the way the French Resistance used children to sneak past Nazi checkpoints and wangle information out of German soldiers.

1942 Henderson formed a small undercover detachment of children, under the command of British Military Intelligence. Henderson's Boys were all thirteen or fourteen years old, mostly French refugees. They were given basic espionage training before being parachuted into occupied France. The boys gathered vital intelligence in the run-up to the D-Day invasions of 1944.

1946 Henderson's Boys disbanded at the end of the war. Most of them returned to France. Their existence has never been officially acknowledged.

Charles Henderson believed that children would make effective intelligence agents during peacetime. In May 1946, he was given permission to create CHERUB in a disused village school. The first twenty CHERUB recruits, all boys, lived in wooden huts at the back of the playground.

1951 For its first five years, CHERUB struggled along with limited resources. Its fortunes changed following its first major success: Two agents uncovered a ring of Russian spies who were stealing information on the British nuclear weapons program.

The government of the day was delighted. CHERUB was given funding to expand. Better facilities were built and the number of agents was increased from twenty to sixty.

1954 Two CHERUB agents, Jason Lennox and Johan Urminski, were killed while operating undercover in East Germany. Nobody knows how the boys died. The government considered shutting CHERUB down, but there were now over seventy active CHERUB agents performing vital missions around the world.

An inquiry into the boys' deaths led to the introduction of new safeguards:

(1) The creation of the ethics panel. From now on, every mission had to be approved by a three-person committee.

(2) Jason Lennox was only nine years old. A minimum mission age of ten years and four months was introduced.

(3) A more rigorous approach to training was brought in. A version of the 100-day basic training program began.

1956 Although many believed that girls would be unsuitable for intelligence work, CHERUB admitted five girls as an experiment. They were a huge success. The number of girls in CHERUB was upped to twenty the following year. Within ten years, the number of girls and boys was equal.

1957 CHERUB introduced its system of colored T-shirts.

1960 Following several successes, CHERUB was allowed to expand again, this time to 130 students. The farmland surrounding headquarters was purchased and fenced off, about a third of the area that is now known as CHERUB campus.

1967 Katherine Field became the third CHERUB agent to die on an operation. She was bitten by a snake on a mission in India. She reached hospital within half an hour, but tragically the snake species was wrongly identified and Katherine was given the wrong antivenom.

1973 Over the years, CHERUB had become a hotchpotch of small buildings. Construction began on a new nine-story headquarters.

1977 All CHERUBs are either orphans, or children who have been abandoned by their family. Max Weaver was one of the first CHERUB agents. He made a fortune building office blocks in London and New York. When he died in 1977, aged just forty-one, without a wife or children, Max Weaver left his fortune for the benefit of the children at CHERUB.

The Max Weaver Trust Fund has paid for many of the buildings on CHERUB campus. These include the indoor athletics facilities and library. The trust fund now holds assets worth over £1 billion.

1982 Thomas Webb was killed by a landmine on the Falkland Islands, becoming the fourth CHERUB to die on a mission. He was one of nine agents used in various roles during the Falklands conflict.

1986 The government gave CHERUB permission to expand up to four hundred pupils. Despite this, numbers have stalled some way below this. CHERUB requires intelligent, physically robust agents who have no family ties. Children who meet all these admission criteria are extremely hard to find.

1990 CHERUB purchased additional land, expanding both the size and security of campus. Campus is marked on all British maps as an army firing range. Surrounding roads are routed so that there is only one road onto campus. The perimeter walls cannot be seen from nearby roads. Helicopters are banned from the area and airplanes must stay above ten thousand meters. Anyone breaching the CHERUB perimeter faces life imprisonment under the State Secrets Act.

1996 CHERUB celebrated its fiftieth anniversary with the opening of a diving pool and an indoor shooting range.

Every retired member of CHERUB was invited to the celebration. No guests were allowed. Over nine hundred people made it, flying from all over the world. Among the retired agents were a former prime minister and a rock guitarist who had sold 80 million albums.

After a firework display, the guests pitched tents and slept on campus. Before leaving the following morning, everyone gathered outside the chapel and remembered the four children who had given CHERUB their lives.

Don't miss Mission 4:

THE KILLING

Before you entered basic training, you probably heard stories from qualified CHERUB agents about the nature of this one-hundred-day course. Although every basic training course is designed to teach the same core abilities of physical fitness and extreme mental endurance, you can expect your training to differ from that of your predecessors in order to retain the element of surprise.

(Excerpt from the CHERUB Basic Training Manual)

AUGUST 2004

The two thirteen-year-olds wore nylon shorts, sleeveless tops, and flip-flops. Jane leaned against the concrete wall of the housing block where she lived, peeling away strands of hair stuck to her sweaty face. Hannah was sprawled over the paved steps a couple of meters in front of her.

"I dunno," Jane huffed.

The words were meaningless, but Hannah understood. It was the middle of the summer holidays and the hottest day of the year so far. The two best friends were broke, irritated by the heat, and weary of each other's company.

"Makes me sweat just looking at 'em," Hannah said, staring at the preteen boys kicking a football around a tarmac pitch less than twenty meters away.

"We used to run around like that," Jane said. "Not football. I mean, racing our bikes and stuff."

Hannah allowed herself to smile as her brain drifted into the past. "Barbie bike grand prix." She nodded, remembering herself on a little pink bike, the white spokes blurring as she juddered over the gaps between paving slabs. Jane's nan always sat out in a deck chair keeping an eye on them.

"You and me had to have everything the exact same." Jane nodded as she curled her toes, making her sandal clap against her foot.

The voyage down memory lane was rudely interrupted by a football. It skimmed Hannah's hair and stung the wall behind her, missing Jane by centimeters. "Jeeeeeesus," Hannah gasped.

She dived forward, wrapping her body over the ball as it bobbled down the steps alongside her. A boy ran up to the bottom of the staircase. Nine years old, with a Chelsea shirt tied around his waist, he displayed a rack of skinny ribs every time he breathed out.

"Give us," the kid panted, putting out his hands to catch.

"You nearly whacked me in the face," Jane yelled furiously. "You might at least say sorry."

"We didn't mean it."

The other lads who'd been playing football were closing in, irritated by the break in play. Hannah appreciated that the kick was an accident and she'd been set to give the ball back until one of the kids gave her lip. He was the biggest lad there, ten years old with cropped red hair.

"Come on, you fat cow, get us our ball."

Hannah barged between a couple of sweaty torsos and

faced the redhead, squeezing the football between her palms. "You wanna repeat that, Ginger?"

Hannah was three years older than the kid she was facing off, with height and weight on her side. All Ginger could do was stare dumbly at his Nikes, while his mates waited for him to come out with something clever.

"Cat got your tongue?" Hannah glowered, enjoying the way Ginger was squirming.

"I just want our ball," he said weakly.

"Go fetch it then."

Hannah let the ball drop and booted it before it hit the ground. It would have been OK in trainers, but as the ball soared towards the goalpost on the opposite side of the pitch, her sandal flew after it.

Ginger quickly backed up and picked the sandal out of the air. Enjoying his newfound power, he smirked as he held the sandal up to his nose and took a sniff.

"Your feet stink, girl. Don't you wash?"

Hannah made a grab for her sandal as the young footballers jeered. Ginger ducked out of the way before throwing the shoe underarm to one of his mates. Lumps of gravel dug into Hannah's sole as she stepped unevenly toward her new tormentor. She felt like a total wally for letting this gang of runts get one over on her.

"Give us that shoe or I'm gonna batter you," she snarled.

The shoe changed hands again as Jane stepped into the fray to help her mate. "Give it back," she steamed.

The angrier the girls got, the harder the boys laughed. They were spreading out, anticipating an extended game of piggy in the middle, when Jane noticed changing expressions on the young faces.

Hannah sensed something was wrong too. She turned sharply, catching a fast-moving object out of the corner of her eye a second before it smashed into the ground. It hit the staircase in the exact spot where she'd been sitting a minute earlier.

Hannah froze in shock as the metal banister crumpled. By the time her brain got up to speed, the terrified young footballers had abandoned her sandal and were shooting off in all directions. She found her eyes focused on the well-worn tread of a boy's trainer. His denim-clad bum poked out of the crumpled metal and dust. The adrenalin hit hard as Hannah recognized the mangled body and screamed out.

"Will . . . No, for God's sake . . ."

He looked dead, but this couldn't be for real. She covered her face with her hands and screamed so hard, she felt her tonsils dance in the back of her throat. She tried to tell herself it was all a dream. Stuff like this didn't happen in real life. She'd wake up in a minute and everything would be back to normal. . . .

UNIFORM

For the past three years George Stein has worked as an economics teacher at the exclusive Trinity Day School near Cambridge. Recently, information has come to light suggesting that Stein may have links with the environmental terrorist group Help Earth. (Excerpt from CHERUB mission briefing for Callum Reilly and Shakeel "Shak" Dajani.)

JUNE 2005

It was a fine day and this part of Cambridge had the whiff of serious money. The immaculate lawns were coiffured by professional gardeners, and James drooled over the expensive lumps of German metal parked on the driveways. He was walking with Shakeel, and both boys felt self-conscious in the summer uniform of

Trinity School. It consisted of a white shirt, a tie, gray trousers with orange piping, an orange and gray blazer, and matching felt cap.

"I'm telling you," James moaned, "even if you sat down and tried *really* hard, I don't think you could come up with a way to make this uniform look any dumber."

"I dunno, James. Maybe we could have partridge feathers sticking out of the hats or something."

"And these trousers were meant for Callum's skinny butt. They're killing my balls."

Shak couldn't help seeing the funny side of James's discomfort. "You can't blame Callum for pulling out of the mission at the last minute. It's that stomach bug that's going around campus."

James nodded. "I had it last week. I was barely off the bog for two whole days."

Shak looked at his watch for the millionth time. "We need to up the pace."

"What's the big deal?" James asked.

"This isn't some London comprehensive full up with scummy little Arsenal fans like you," Shak explained. "Trinity is one of the top fee-paying schools in the country, and the pupils aren't allowed to wander around the corridors whenever it suits them. Our arrival's got to coincide with the changeover between third and fourth periods, when there's hundreds of other kids moving around."

James nodded. "Gotcha."

Shak looked at his watch for the millionth and first time as they cut into a cobbled alleyway that was barely wide enough for a single car.

"Come *on*, James."

"I'm trying," James said. "But I'm seriously gonna rip the arse out of these trousers if I'm not careful."

Once they'd cut between two large houses, the alleyway opened out into a run-down park with knee-high grass and a set of tangled swings. To the boys' left stood a chain-link fence topped with barbed wire, behind which lay the grounds of Trinity Day. The main gates were carefully monitored during school hours, so this was their only way in.

Shak wandered through the long grass next to the fence, placing his shoe carefully to avoid turds and litter, as he searched for an entry point made by an MI5 operative the previous night. He found the flap cut in the wire behind the trunk of a large tree. Shak lifted it, doffed his cap, and attempted a snooty accent. "After you, James, my good man."

James fed his backpack and hat through the gap before sliding under. He stood with his back against the tree and brushed dirt off his uniform while Shak followed.

"All set?" James asked as he slung his backpack over his shoulder. It weighed a ton and the equipment inside clattered around.

"Cap," Shak reminded him.

James let out a little gasp as he leaned forward and picked the cap out of the grass. A claxon sounded inside the school building a couple of hundred meters away, indicating a lesson change.

"OK, let's shift," Shak said.

The boys broke out from behind the tree and began

jogging across a rugby pitch towards the school building. As they did, they noticed a groundskeeper striding purposefully towards them from the opposite end of the field.

"You two," he bellowed.

Because James had been pulled onto the mission at the last minute to replace Callum, he'd only had time to skim through the mission briefing. He looked uneasily at Shak for guidance.

"Don't sweat it," Shak whispered. "I've got it covered."

The groundskeeper intercepted the boys near a set of rugby posts. He was a fit looking fellow with thinning gray hair, dressed in workman's boots and a grubby overall.

"Exactly *what* do you think you're doing out here?" he demanded pompously.

"I was reading under the tree at lunchtime," Shak explained, pointing backwards with his thumb. "I left my cap behind."

"You know the rules of the school, don't you?"

Shak and James both looked confused.

"Don't try playing the fool with me, you *know* as well as I do. If you're not attending a lesson, a match, or an official practice, you do not set foot on the games pitches because it causes unnecessary wear and tear."

"Yes," Shak nodded. "Sorry, sir. I was in a hurry to get to my lesson, that's all."

"Sorry," James added. "But it's not like the pitches are muddy or anything. We're not really tearing them up."

The groundskeeper took James's comment as a threat to his authority. He swooped down and showered James with spit as he spoke. "I make the rules here, young man. *You* don't decide when you can and can't set foot on *my* pitches. Got that?"

"Yes, sir," James said.

"What's your name and house?"

"Joseph Mail, King Henry House," James lied, recalling one of the few elements of his background story he'd managed to remember from the mission briefing.

"Faisal Asmal, same house," Shak said.

"Right," the groundskeeper said, bouncing smugly on the balls of his feet. "I'll be reporting both of you to your housemaster, and I expect your cheek will have earned you both a detention. Now, you'd better get yourselves to your next lesson."

"Why'd you answer back?" Shak asked irritably as the boys walked towards the back entrance of the school.

"I know I shouldn't have," James said, raising his palms defensively. "But he was *so* full of himself."

They passed through a set of double doors into the main school building, then up a short flight of steps and into the busy thoroughfare that ran the length of the ground floor. There was plenty of noise, but the Trinity boys walked purposefully, nodding politely to the teachers standing in the doorways as they entered their classrooms.

"What a bunch of geeks," James whispered. "I bet these dudes don't even fart."

Shak explained the situation as they headed up the stairs to the second floor. "Every kid has to pass special exams and an interview to get into Trinity. There's always a humungous waiting list, so they can afford to boot out anyone who doesn't toe the line."

"Bet I wouldn't last long." James grinned.

By the time they reached the second floor, most kids had found their way to lessons and the classroom doors had been pulled shut. Shak pulled a lock gun from the pocket of his blazer as they passed by a couple of classroom doors. He stopped at the door of an office with a nameplate on it: *Dr. George Stein BSc, PhD, Head of Economics and Politics*.

Shak pushed the tip of the lock gun into the keyhole. James stood close by, blocking the view of a bunch of kids waiting outside a classroom fifteen meters away.

The lock had a simple single-lever mechanism, meaning Shak only had to give the lock gun a brief wiggle and pull on the trigger to open the door. The pair hurriedly stepped into the office and put the latch down so that nobody could burst in on them, even with a key.

"Stein should be teaching two floors up," Shak said. "We've got until the next lesson change in thirty-six minutes; let's get to work."

ABOUT THE AUTHOR

Robert Muchamore was born in London in 1972 and used to work as a private investigator. CHERUB is his first series and is published in more than twenty countries.

CHERUB

THE DEALER

ALSO BY
ROBERT MUCHAMORE

THE RECRUIT

CHERUB

MISSION 2
THE DEALER

ROBERT MUCHAMORE

Simon Pulse
New York London Toronto Sydney

This book is a work of fiction. Any references to historical events, real people, or real locales are used fictitiously. Other names, characters, places, and incidents are the product of the author's imagination, and any resemblance to actual events or locales or persons, living or dead, is entirely coincidental.

SIMON PULSE
An imprint of Simon & Schuster Children's Publishing Division
1230 Avenue of the Americas, New York, NY 10020
This Simon Pulse paperback edition August 2011

Originally published in Great Britain in 2004 by Hodder Children's Books as *Class A*
Published by arrangement with Hodder and Stoughton Limited

Also available in a Simon Pulse hardcover edition.
For information about special discounts for bulk purchases, please contact
Simon & Schuster Special Sales at 1-866-506-1949
or business@simonandschuster.com.
The Simon & Schuster Speakers Bureau can bring authors to your live event.
For more information or to book an event contact the Simon & Schuster
Speakers Bureau at 1-866-248-3049 or visit our website at www.simonspeakers.com.
Designed by Mike Rosamilia
The text of this book was set in Apollo MT.
Manufactured in the United States of America
4 6 8 10 9 7 5
Library of Congress Control Number 2004118122
ISBN 978-1-4169-9941-6 (hc)
ISBN 978-1-4424-1361-0 (pbk)

CHERUB

THE DEALER

WHAT IS CHERUB?

CHERUB is a branch of British Intelligence. Its agents are aged between ten and seventeen years. Cherubs are all orphans who have been taken out of care homes and trained to work undercover. They live on CHERUB campus, a secret facility hidden in the English countryside.

WHAT USE ARE KIDS?

Quite a lot. Nobody realizes kids do undercover missions, which means they can get away with all kinds of stuff that adults can't.

WHO ARE THEY?

About three hundred children live on CHERUB campus. JAMES ADAMS is our twelve-year-old hero. He's basically a good kid, but he has a habit of getting himself in trouble. There's also his younger sister, LAUREN. KERRY CHANG is a Hong Kong–born karate champion. GABRIELLE O'BRIEN is Kerry's best friend. BRUCE NORRIS, another karate champion, likes to think of himself as a hard man but still sleeps with a blue teddy under his chin. KYLE BLUEMAN is a more experienced CHERUB agent. He's two years older than James, but still a good mate.

AND THE T-SHIRTS?

Cherubs are ranked according to the colour of the T-shirts they wear on campus. ORANGE is for visitors. RED is for kids who live at CHERUB campus, but are too young to qualify as agents. BLUE is for kids undergoing CHERUB's tough 100-day training regime. A GRAY T-shirt means you're qualified for missions. NAVY is a reward for outstanding performance on a mission. If you do well, you'll end your CHERUB career wearing a BLACK T-shirt, the ultimate recognition for outstanding achievement. When you retire, you get the WHITE T-shirt, which is also worn by staff.

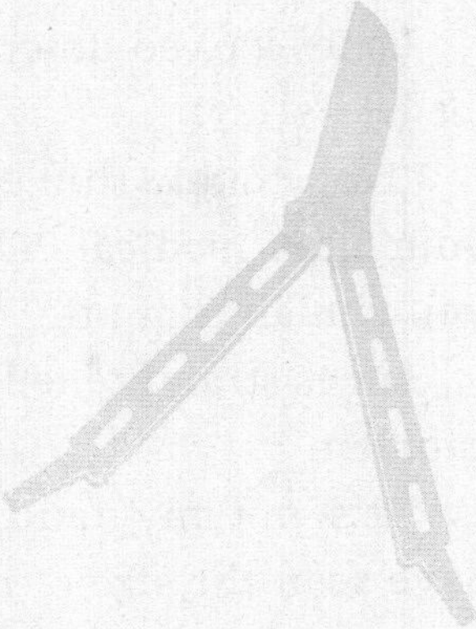

CHAPTER 1

HEAT

Billions of insects fizzed about in the sunset. James and Bruce had given up trying to swat them off. The boys had jogged ten kilometers along a twisted gravel path. It was uphill, heading towards a villa where two eight-year-olds were being held hostage.

"Better give us a minute," James huffed, leaning forward and resting his palms against his knees. "I'm wiped."

If James had wrung out his T-shirt, he could have filled a mug with sweat.

"I'm a year younger than you," Bruce said impatiently. "You should be the one pushing me. It's that gut you're carrying."

James looked down at himself. "Give over, I'm hardly fat."

"Not exactly thin either. You're gonna get crucified at your next medical. They'll put you on a diet and make you run all that off."

James straightened up and drank some water from his canteen.

"It's not my fault, Bruce. It's genetic. You should have seen the size of my mum before she died."

Bruce laughed. "There were three Toffee Crisp and one Snickers wrapper in our bin last night. That's not genetic, that's being a pig."

"We can't all have little stick-insect bodies like you," James said, bitterly. "Are you ready?"

"We might as well check the map now we've stopped," Bruce said. "See how far it is to the villa."

James got a map out of his pack. Bruce had a GPS clipped on his shorts. The tiny unit told you your exact position anywhere on the planet to within a couple of meters. Bruce transposed the coordinates on to the map and used his finger to trace the winding gravel path towards the villa.

"Time to go off road," Bruce said. "It's less than half a kilometer away."

"It's really steep," James said, "and the ground crumbles around here. It's gonna be a nightmare."

"Well," Bruce said, "unless your plan is to walk up to the front gate of the villa, ring the doorbell, and say, 'Excuse me love, can we have our hostages back?' I think we'd better cut into the bushes."

Bruce had a point. James gave up trying to fold the

map properly and stuffed it in his pack. Bruce led the way into the scrub, the tinder-dry plants crunching under his trainers. It hadn't rained on the island for two months. There'd been bush fires in the east. When the sky was clear, you could see the plumes of smoke.

James's damp skin soon had a coating of grit. He grabbed on to plants, using them to pull his way up the steep slope. You had to be careful: some plants had barbs, others erupted from the dry ground as soon as you pulled on them, leaving you holding a clump of roots, clutching desperately for something sturdier before you tumbled backwards.

When they reached the wire fence around the villa, they backed up a few meters and lay flat on the ground, collecting their thoughts. Bruce was moaning something about his hand.

"What are you whinging about?" James asked.

Bruce showed James his palm. Even in the half-light, James could see the blood trickling down Bruce's arm.

"How'd you do that?"

Bruce shrugged. "Somewhere coming up the hill. I didn't realize until we stopped."

"I'd better clean it up for you."

James tipped some water out of his canteen, washing away most of the blood. He got a first aid kit out of his pack; then lit a small torch and clamped it between his teeth, so he could see what he was doing while keeping both hands free. A thorn bulged under the webbing between Bruce's middle fingers.

"Nasty," James said. "Does it hurt?"

"What kind of stupid question is that?" Bruce snapped. "Of course it does."

"Am I supposed to pull it out?" James asked.

"Yes," Bruce said wearily. "Do you ever listen in class? Always remove splinters, unless there is severe and profuse bleeding, or you suspect you've punctured a vein or artery. Then apply disinfectant and a clean dressing or sticking plaster."

"You sound like you swallowed the textbook," James said.

"I was on the same first aid course as you, James. Only I didn't spend the entire three days trying to get off with Susan Kaplan."

"It's a pity she had a boyfriend."

"Susan doesn't have a boyfriend," Bruce said. "She was just trying to get rid of you."

"Oh," James said, crushed. "I thought she liked me."

Bruce didn't answer. He was biting down on the strap of his backpack. He didn't want anyone in the villa to hear if the pain made him scream out.

James lined up his tweezers. "Ready?"

Bruce nodded.

The thorn slid out easily enough. Bruce moaned as a fresh dribble of blood trickled down his hand. James mopped it up, rubbed on antiseptic cream, and wound a bandage tightly between Bruce's fingers.

"All done," James said. "Are you all right to carry on?"

"We can't turn back after going this far."

"You rest for a minute," James said. "I'll sneak up to the fence and check out the security."

"Watch out for video cameras," Bruce said. "They'll be expecting us."

When James switched off the torch, there was only

moonlight left. He shuffled to the fence on his belly. The villa looked impressive: two storys, four-car garage, and a kidney-shaped pool out front. The lawn sprinklers chugged gently, the spouts of water illuminated by the porch lights. There was no sign of any cameras or hi-tech security stuff; just the yellow siren box from a cheapo burglar alarm, which would be switched off while anyone was in the house. James turned back towards Bruce.

"Get up here. It doesn't look too serious."

James got out his wire cutters and snipped links in the fence until there was a slot big enough to squeeze through. He followed Bruce over the lawn, crawling swiftly towards the house. James felt something squish against his leg.

"Oh . . . man," James said, sounding totally revolted. "Jesus."

Bruce hushed him up. "Quiet, for God's sake. What's the matter?"

"I just dragged my knee through a colossal pile of dog crap."

Bruce couldn't help smiling. James looked set to puke.

"This is bad," Bruce said.

"Tell me about it. I've had it on my shoe before, but this is on my bare skin."

"You know what a massive pile of dog mess means?"

"Yeah," James said. "It means I'm extremely pissed off."

"It also means there's a massive dog around here."

The thought focused James's mind and got him crawling again. They stopped when they got to the wall of the villa, adjacent to a row of French doors. Bruce sat against the wall and checked out the room inside. The light was on. There were leather sofas and a snooker table inside. They tried sliding the French doors, but every one was locked. The keyholes were on the inside, so there was nothing to use their lock guns on.

WOOF.

The boys snapped their necks around. The mother of all rottweilers stood five meters away. The huge beast had muscles swelling through its shiny black coat and strings of drool hanging off its jaw.

"Nice doggy," Bruce said, trying to keep calm.

The growling dog moved closer, its black eyes staring them down.

"Who's a nice doggy-woggy?" Bruce asked.

"Bruce, I don't think it's gonna roll over and let you tickle its tummy."

"Well, what's *your* plan?"

"Don't show it any fear," James quaked. "We'll stare it down. It's probably as scared of us as we are of it."

"Yeah," Bruce said. "You can tell. The poor thing's cacking itself."

James began creeping backwards. The dog let out more volcanic barks. A metal hose reel clattered as James backed into it. He considered the reel for a second, before leaning over and unrolling a few meters of plastic hose. The dog was only a couple of steps away.

"Bruce, you run off and try to open a door," James gasped. "I'll try fending it off with this pipe."

James half hoped the dog would go after Bruce, but it

kept its eyes fixed, pacing closer to James until he could feel its damp breath on his legs.

"Nice doggy," James said.

The rottweiler reared up on its back legs, trying to knock James over. James spun away and the paws squealed down the glass door. James lashed out with the hosepipe. It cracked against the dog's rib cage. The beast made a high-pitched yelp and backed up slightly. James cracked the pipe against the patio tiles, hoping the noise would scare the dog away, but if anything the whipping seemed to have made it crazier.

James felt like his guts were going to drop out, imagining how easily the huge animal could rip into his flesh. James had nearly drowned once. He'd thought nothing could ever be scarier, but this had the edge.

A bolt clicked behind James's head and the French door glided open.

"Would Sir care to step inside?" Bruce asked.

James threw down the hose and leapt through the opening. Bruce rammed the door shut before the rottweiler made a move.

"What took you so long?" James said anxiously, trying to stop his hands from shaking. "Where is everyone?"

"No sign," Bruce said. "Which is definitely weird. They'd have to be deaf not to hear that psycho mutt barking at us."

James grabbed one of the curtains and used it to wipe the dog crap off his leg.

"That's so gross," Bruce said. "At least it's not on your clothes."

"Have you checked all the rooms out?"

Bruce shook his head. "I thought I'd make sure you weren't being eaten first, even if it meant we got caught."

"Fair play," James said.

They worked their way across the ground floor, creeping up to each door and checking out the rooms. The villa looked lived-in. There were cigarette butts in ashtrays and dirty mugs. There was a Mercedes in the garage. Bruce pocketed the keys.

"There's our getaway vehicle," he said.

There was no sign of life on the ground floor, which made the staircase likely to be some sort of trap. They stepped up gingerly, expecting someone to burst onto the landing pointing a gun at them.

There were three bedrooms and a bathroom on the second floor. The two hostages were in the master bedroom. The eight-year-olds, Jake and Laura, were tied to a bedpost, with gags over their mouths. They wore grubby T-shirts and shorts.

James and Bruce pulled the hunting knives off their belts and cut the kids loose. There was no time for greetings.

"Laura," James barked. "When did you last see the bad guys? Have you got any idea where they might be?"

Laura was red-faced and seemed listless.

"I dunno," she shrugged. "But I'm busting to pee."

Laura and Jake knew nothing about anything. Bruce and James had been expecting a battle to get at them. This was far too easy.

"We're taking you to the car," James said.

Laura started limping towards the bathroom. Her ankle was strapped up.

"We don't have time for toilet breaks," James gasped. "They've got guns and we haven't."

"I'm gonna wet my knickers in a minute," Laura said, bolting herself inside the en-suite bathroom.

James was furious. "Well, make it snappy."

"I need to go too," Jake said.

Bruce shook his head. "I don't want you disappearing. You can pee in the corner of the garage while I start the car."

He led Jake downstairs. James waited half a minute before thumping on the bathroom door.

"Laura, come on. What the hell is taking you so long?"

"I'm washing my hands," Laura said. "I couldn't find any soap."

James couldn't believe it.

"For the love of God," he shouted, hammering his fist on the bolted door. "We've *got* to get out of here."

Laura eventually hobbled out of the bathroom. James scooped her over his shoulder and sprinted downstairs to the garage. Bruce sat at the steering wheel inside the car. Laura slid onto the backseat next to Jake.

"It's kaput," Bruce shouted, getting out of the car and kicking the front wing. "The key goes in but it won't turn. It's showing a full tank of petrol. I don't know what's wrong with it."

"It's been sabotaged," James yelled back. "I bet you any money this is a trap."

Bruce looked awkward as the realization dawned. "You're right. Let's get out of here."

James leaned inside the Mercedes.

"Sorry you two," he said, looking at Jake and Laura. "Looks like we've got to make a run for it."

But it was too late. James heard the noise, but only turned around in time to see the gun pointing at him. Bruce screamed out, as James felt two rounds smash into his chest. The pain knocked the air out of his lungs. He stumbled backwards, watching bright red streaks dribbling down his T-shirt.

CHAPTER 2

STINGING

Fired from close range, the next paintball knocked James backwards on to the concrete floor. Kerry Chang kept the gun on him as she closed in. James had his hands in the air.

"I surrender."

"Pardon?" Kerry said, blasting a fourth paintball into James's thigh.

It wasn't going to do permanent damage but, fired from close range, the paintballs had left him in a heap on the ground.

"Kerry, please, not again," James gasped. "That *really* hurts."

"Pardon?" Kerry said. "Can't hear what you're saying."

She stood astride James, pointing the muzzle of the paintball gun at him. On the other side of the car, Bruce screamed as Gabrielle shot him a couple more times.

Kerry fired into James stomach from less than a meter away, doubling him over.

"You mad *cow,*" James howled. "You could have my eye out doing that. You're supposed to stop shooting as soon as I surrender."

"Did you surrender?" Kerry grinned. "I misheard. I thought you said, 'Please shoot me again.'"

The girls rested their guns on the roof of the car.

"Did we whip your little pink butts?" Gabrielle whooped in her thick Jamaican accent. "Or did we whip your little pink butts?"

James struggled to sit up, clasping his hands over his stomach. The pain was bad, but losing to the girls on a stupid training exercise hurt a hundred times more.

The powered garage door started rolling upwards. A huge man stood silhouetted against the moonlight. It was Norman Large, CHERUB's head training instructor. He had the rottweiler on a leash at his side.

"Well done, ladies," Mr. Large shouted. "You've distinguished those pretty little heads on this one."

Kerry and Gabrielle smiled. Mr. Large stopped walking when his size fifteen boots were almost touching James's leg. James put his hand over his face, shielding his nose from the growling dog's rank breath.

"That thing's not gonna bite me, is it?" James asked.

Mr. Large laughed. "Luckily for you and Bruce, Thatcher has been trained to pin a man to the ground and never bite. Her brother, Saddam, now that's a different question. He's trained to sink his teeth in. We'd have been picking chunks of flesh off the lawn if you'd been up against Saddam. Unfortunately, the chairman banned me from using him. . . . Anyway, James, get on your feet. Gabrielle, help that other little idiot to stand up."

Bruce limped around the car, using the bonnet for support. The yellow paint from Gabrielle's gun trickled down his legs. Both boys stood with their backs against the car. Mr. Large hollered right in their faces.

"Tell me everything you did wrong."

"I'm . . . not sure, really," James shrugged.

Bruce looked down at the floor.

"Let's start at the beginning," Mr. Large bawled. "Why did it take you so long to reach the villa?"

"We jogged all the way," James said.

"Jogged?" Mr. Large shouted. "If I'm being held hostage at gunpoint, I at least expect my rescuers to have the decency to *run* to my rescue."

"It's boiling hot out there," James said.

"I could have run," Bruce said, "but James was knackered after ten minutes."

James gave Bruce a fierce look. Teams were supposed to stick together, not drop one another in it at the first opportunity.

"Can't manage a little ten-kilometer run, eh, James?" Mr. Large said, breaking into an evil grin. "Looks like you've let yourself get out of shape holidaying out here in the sunshine."

"I'm fit," James said. "It's just the heat."

"So, because you took so long to arrive, it was dark when you got to the villa, making it much more difficult to survey. Not that it matters, because you didn't do a proper survey anyway."

"I had a good look through the fence," James said, defensively.

Large banged his fist on the roof of the car.

"That's a survey, is it? What have you two been taught?"

"Before entering hostile premises, always do a thorough survey, investigating the building from all sides," Bruce said mechanically. "If possible, climb a tree or go to higher ground and get a look at the layout of the building from above."

"If you remember what it says in the training manual, Bruce, why did you decide that a glance through the fence was sufficient?"

Bruce and James both looked sheepish. Kerry and Gabrielle loved watching the boys squirm.

"If you'd done proper survey, maybe you would have seen the dog kennel. Maybe you could have planned a proper entry and exit strategy, instead of crawling up to the house and hoping for the best. Then, once you'd recovered the hostages, you decided to escape using the car. Didn't it occur to you that the car was the most obvious way to escape and was almost certainly booby-trapped? Or were you blinded by the prospect of lighting up the tires and taking it for a spin?"

"It did occur that it was obvious," James said.

"So why did you try to escape that way?" Large screamed.

"I mean . . . But . . . I only realized right before I got shot."

"This has got to be the worst performance on a training exercise I have *ever* seen," Mr. Large shouted. "You two have ignored every piece of training you've been given. If this was a real operation, you would have been killed ten times over. You're both getting grade F and James, I'm putting you on an emergency fitness plan. Ten kilometers running a day and, as you're so worried about the heat, I'll let you start when it's nice and cool. How does five in the morning sound?"

James knew better than to answer back, it only earned you push-ups. Mr. Large stepped back and took deep breaths. His head looked like a redcurrant after all the shouting.

"What grade did me and Gabrielle get?" Kerry asked, using her crawliest voice.

"B, I suppose," Mr. Large said. "You did a bang-up job, but I can't give you an A because you were up against such feeble opposition."

Gabrielle and Kerry smiled at each other. James wanted to knock their stupid smug heads together.

"Right, time to head back to the hostel," Large said. "Bruce, I need the car key."

Bruce chucked it over.

"That won't work," Gabrielle said. "That's for the front door of the villa. I put it on a Mercedes key ring so it looked like the car key. You want this one."

Mr. Large caught the real car key and loaded Thatcher the dog on to the front seat. Gabrielle and Kerry got in the back, squashed up with the two eight-year-olds.

"Oh no," Mr. Large grinned, as his massive body sank into the driver's seat. "Not enough room in the car. It looks like James and Bruce will have to find their own way home."

"But we drove in the van for ages before they dropped us off," James gasped. "I've got no idea how to get back to the hostel from here."

"How *awfully* sad," Mr. Large said, sarcastically. "I tell you what, if you manage to make it home before midnight, I'll put your grade up to a D and you won't have to repeat the exercise."

Mr. Large turned the key in the ignition and the car started rolling forward. Thatcher poked her head out of the window and barked as the car crunched down the gravel driveway. James and Bruce looked despondently at each other.

"I don't think that it's that hard," Bruce said. "It's three hours until midnight and it's all downhill."

James looked totally miserable. "My legs feel like blocks of wood."

"Well," Bruce said, "I'm gonna start walking. You can go through this again if you want to, but I'm not going to."

"What I can't believe," James said, "is that everyone told me to get my act together and I never listened."

CHAPTER 9

SUN

Unless they're away on a mission, every kid at CHERUB spends five weeks in the summer on the Mediterranean island of C—. It's mostly a holiday: a chance to muck about on the beach, play sport, ride quad bikes over the sand dunes, and have a shot at being normal kids. But cherubs aren't normal kids: they could be sent on an undercover mission at any time. Even on holiday, they are expected to stay fit and do the odd training exercise.

Like loads of cherubs before him, James found it easy to slack off when there was a beach on the doorstep and tons of other kids to muck around with. For the last four weeks, he'd skipped fitness training. He'd spent his days messing about on the beach and his nights watching

DVD marathons while stuffing his face with popcorn and chocolate. When James got his training assignment, he ignored Kerry's advice to study it thoroughly and went out on a Jet Ski instead.

James considered his folly as he sauntered through the sticky night air toward the CHERUB hostel. The physical training instructors were going to make his life a misery. Once you gave them a reason, they didn't let you off until you were back in top shape. James couldn't make any excuses: Amy, Kyle, and loads of teachers had warned him to exercise and take the training seriously, but he'd lost all sense of responsibility the second he hit the beach.

Even after getting lost a couple of times, James and Bruce beat the midnight deadline for getting back. James had a grazed elbow where he'd tripped in a pothole in the dark and they were both gasping for a drink.

A bunch of older kids were having a moonlit barbecue in the gardens at the front of the hostel. Amy Collins came running over the lawn when she noticed James. She was beautiful, sixteen years old, with long blond hair. She wore denim shorts and a flowery top that stopped above the gold ring through her navel.

"Nice paint job, boys," she giggled. "Gabrielle and Kerry said they scrubbed the floor with the pair of you."

"You're drunk," James said.

Drinking alcohol wasn't allowed, but CHERUB staff turned a blind eye with the older kids, as long as they didn't go mad.

"Just a teensy drop," Amy said. "We went out on a boat and caught fish."

Amy spread her arms out to the size of a big fish, almost lost her balance and doubled over in drunken hysterics.

"You want barbecued fish?" she spluttered. "And there's fresh bread from the village."

"It's late," James said, shaking his head. "We'd better clean up."

"We emptied the whole ocean," Amy giggled. "Anyway, I'm busting to pee. I'll see you two scumbags in the morning."

As Amy staggered away, she thought of something and turned back.

"Oh, James."

"What?"

"I told you so."

James gave her the finger and wandered towards the main entrance of the hostel with Bruce in tow. The less contact they had with other kids, the less they would get flamed for mucking up the training exercise. They ducked down as they passed the recreation room, where about thirty kids were watching a horror movie on a projector screen. A couple of little red-shirt kids snickered at their paint-spattered clothes as the boys walked upstairs to the second-floor bedroom they shared with Gabrielle and Kerry.

The room was an L-shape, with the girls' beds at one end and the boys' around the corner at the other. It was basic compared to their individual rooms back at campus: ceiling fans, tile floor, wicker chairs and a tiny TV. It hardly mattered because the kids were always busy and only used the rooms to wash and crash out.

Kerry and Gabrielle had been back a couple of hours. The TV was showing an episode of *The Simpsons* in Spanish, which both girls could understand. They kept quiet, not even commenting on the stench of sweat.

"Well?" James said.

Kerry gave an innocent smile. "Well, what?"

"I know you're gonna start on us," James said, sitting on his bed and pulling off his trainers. "So go on, get it over with. Rub our noses in it."

"We'd never do that," Gabrielle said. "We're nice girls."

"My arse," Bruce said.

Kerry sat up on her bed. She was pink and shriveled, like she'd just finished a long bath. James dumped his filthy polo shirt on the floor.

"You better take that stuff down to the laundry when you've had your showers," Kerry said. "It'll stink the whole room out."

"If *you* don't like my stink," Bruce said, kicking off his trainers, "*you* take it down there."

He balled up his crusty sock and lobbed it on to Kerry's duvet. She flicked it away with the end of a biro.

"So, how come it took you so long to get back here?" Kerry asked, trying not to grin.

As soon as she said that, Gabrielle started cracking up.

"What are you laughing for?" James asked. "It's fourteen kilometers between here and the villa. I'd like to see you two do it any quicker."

"They're *so* thick," Gabrielle howled. "I can't believe it."

"What?" James asked. "What's thick?"

"Didn't you bother checking out the house?" Kerry grinned.

"We couldn't hang around," Bruce explained. "We had to be back here by midnight."

"There was money all over the kitchen cabinet," Kerry said.

"What good could that do us?" Bruce asked.

"And there was a working telephone," Kerry continued. "And a telephone directory."

James was getting impatient. "So what?"

"This isn't Outer Mongolia," Gabrielle said, making a telephone receiver out of her hand and putting it to her ear. "Why didn't you pick up the phone and call a taxi?"

"Eh?" James gasped, turning around and giving Bruce a blank stare.

"Taxi," Kerry snorted, hardly able to get the words out over her giggles. "T-A-X-I, they're a normal car, with a man to drive you and a little orange lamp on the roof."

"Oh . . ." James said bitterly, looking at Bruce. "Why didn't we get a cab?"

"Don't have a go at me," Bruce said. "You never thought of it either."

Gabrielle was rolled up in a ball, laughing so hard the frame of her bed was shaking.

"You two dickheads walked fourteen kilometers when you could have called a taxi and been home in an hour," Kerry said, pedaling her feet in the air with delight.

James's socks were bloody where they'd chafed on the long walk. His back and shoulders hurt from carrying the pack, his elbow was agony and his leg still stank of dog mess, even though he'd washed it. One day, he would be able to laugh about this, but right now he was ready to explode.

"This is *bull,*" James screamed, hurling his trainers against the wall.

He kicked out at his wardrobe, but he was tired and lost his balance. He ended up in a heap on the floor, making the girls laugh even harder. Bruce looked just as mad, but he concentrated his energy into ripping off his clothes and heading towards the shower.

"Give us two minutes before you go in there," Kerry said, wiping tears of joy from her eyes. "I want to go to bed in a minute. Can I quickly brush my teeth?"

Bruce tutted. "Go on then, but don't take all night."

Kerry padded barefoot into the bathroom and squeezed out a ball of toothpaste. Bruce and James waited by the open doorway in their boxers while she brushed. Kerry tried to control her laughing, but she couldn't resist having another dig.

"Fourteen kilometers," she shrieked, spluttering white toothpaste foam all over the bathroom mirror.

Bruce couldn't take any more abuse.

"Let's see how you like being laughed at," he shouted.

As Kerry bent over the tap to rinse her mouth, Bruce dunked her head. He only meant to nudge her so she got water over her face, but he did it too hard. Kerry's front tooth hit the tap and she sprung up furiously.

"You idiot," Kerry stormed, nervously feeling inside her mouth. "I think you've chipped my tooth."

Bruce realized he'd overdone it, but he wasn't about to go apologizing to someone who'd spent the last ten minutes taking the mickey out of him.

"Good," he snapped. "Serves you right."

Kerry grabbed a glass off the sink and threw it at Bruce's head. He ducked and the glass shattered against the wall.

"Cool it," James said. "This isn't worth fighting over."

"Do you think I'm gonna grow a new tooth?" Kerry screamed.

She stepped forward and gave Bruce an almighty shove. Bruce adopted a fighting stance.

"You want a piece of me?" he shouted.

Kerry looked ferocious as she wiped her lips on to the sleeve of her nightshirt.

"If you want to get your arse kicked by a girl for the second time today," she snarled, "that's fine by me."

James wedged himself between Kerry and Bruce. He was taller and stockier than the two kids he was trying to keep apart.

"Get out of the way, James," Bruce said.

"I'm going for Bruce whether you like it or not," Kerry said, drilling James with her eyes. "If you're in my way, you'll get damaged."

James could beat either Kerry or Bruce for strength, say in an arm-wrestle, but fighting was more about skill. Kerry and Bruce had done combat training at CHERUB for five years, whereas James had come to CHERUB less than a year earlier. He'd be out of his depth in a stand-up fight against either of them.

"You're not fighting," James said unconvincingly, hoping Kerry was bluffing. "I'm staying right here."

Kerry stepped forward, swept James's ankle away, and jammed two fingers into his ribs. It was an elementary technique for knocking someone over without seriously hurting them. James crawled towards his bed as violence exploded over his head.

Kerry was off balance after knocking James out of the way. Bruce used this to his advantage, putting Kerry out of action with one blow. Kerry staggered forward, gasping for breath as the end music for *The Simpsons* came on TV.

Bruce thought the fight was as good as won. He moved to put Kerry in a headlock, but she'd played Bruce for a sucker. She quickly regained her balance, spun out of the way, hooked a foot around Bruce's ankles, and swept his legs away.

James clambered on to his mattress; half horrified, half curious to see who would win. There was no way for him or Gabrielle to get help: the fight was blocking the doorway.

Within seconds of hitting the floor, years of self-defense training collapsed to the level of two drunks grappling on pavement. Bruce had a clump of Kerry's hair wound around his wrist and Kerry was dragging her nails down Bruce's cheek. They thrashed about, cursing one another and eventually rolling into the TV table. The first couple of knocks rocked the TV close to the edge. The third made the TV topple, face first, into the floor. The glass screen cracked and orange sparks spewed across the floor. Some of them hit Bruce's and Kerry's bare legs, then the lights went out and the ceiling fans went silent.

James looked out of the window. All the lights outside had gone too. The exploding TV had fused the electricity for the whole hostel. The fight kept going, but all James could discern were shadows and grunts.

Now Bruce and Kerry were over by the TV, James had an opportunity to get help. He sprang off his bed and grabbed the door handle. Gabrielle thought the same thing at the same moment and they nearly collided in the dark.

The corridor was tinged with green emergency escape lighting. Kids had their heads sticking out of their rooms, all asking each other why the electricity had gone off. James could hear Arif, a seventeen-year-old kid who was over six feet tall. He was exactly what was needed to break up the fight.

"Help us," James shouted. "Bruce and Kerry are killing each other."

That exact moment, someone reset the fuse and the lights came back on. Arif ran towards James's room, along with twenty other kids who wanted to get a look at the action. Arif was first into the room, followed by James and Gabrielle.

Bruce was nowhere. Kerry was in the middle of the floor. Her face was twisted with pain and she had her hands wrapped over her knee.

"Oh God," she sobbed. "Help me."

Kerry had shattered her kneecap in training a couple of years earlier. It had been repaired with titanium pins, but it was still weak. Arif scooped her off the floor and sprinted downstairs to the first aid room.

"Where the hell is Bruce?" Gabrielle asked angrily.

James shooed the onlookers out and slammed the door. He leaned into the bathroom.

"God knows. He's not in there."

Then he heard a sob under Bruce's duvet. Bruce was a skinny thing, so when he pulled the covers up over his head it was easy to assume he wasn't there at all.

"Bruce?" James asked.

"I didn't mean to hurt her knee," Bruce sobbed. "I'm sorry."

"If you start a fight, people get hurt," Gabrielle said severely. "That's how it works."

James had more sympathy. He sat on the edge of Bruce's bed.

"Leave me alone, James. I'm not coming out."

"Bruce, come downstairs with me," James said. "Everyone loses their temper sometimes. I'm sure the staff will understand—and speaking from personal experience—it's always best if you get your own side of the story in first."

"No," Bruce sobbed. "Go away."

Meryl Spencer, a retired Olympic sprinter who was James's handler, burst into the room. She'd been in bed and was wearing a nightshirt and unlaced trainers.

"What's happened here?" Meryl shouted.

"They got in a fight," James explained. "Bruce is under his duvet and won't come out."

Meryl smiled. "Won't he now?"

She leaned over the bed.

"Bruce," she shouted. "You're gonna have to face the music for hurting Kerry. Stop acting like a baby and get out of there."

"Go away," Bruce said, tightening the duvet around his head. "You can't make me come out."

"You've got three seconds," Meryl shouted. "Or I'm gonna seriously lose my temper."

Bruce didn't move a muscle.

"One," Meryl said. "Two . . . Three."

On three, Meryl grabbed the tubular frame of Bruce's bed and tipped it on to its side. Bruce thumped onto the floor and Meryl whipped the duvet off him.

"Stand up," she shouted. "You're eleven years of age, not five."

Bruce jumped to his feet. His face was a teary mess. Meryl grabbed his shoulder and shoved him up against the wall.

"I want all three of you in my office. You're in serious trouble. This kind of behavior is not acceptable."

"Me and Gabrielle didn't do anything," James pleaded. "We tried to break it up."

"We'll discuss it in my office," Meryl said. She took a deep breath and realized that James and Bruce still stank.

"You two have ten minutes to shower, put clean clothes on, and get downstairs. And if anyone starts up this hiding under the duvet nonsense again, I'll have them running laps until they puke, every day for the rest of their miserable lives."

CHAPTER 4

GRASS

"What did you do this time?" Lauren asked. "When did you get back to campus? How come they sent you home early?"

James was half asleep in bed and he wasn't in the mood for his nine-year-old sister. Lauren had knocked on his bedroom door three times. When James ignored her, she picked the lock. The most irritating things about living at CHERUB was that every kid knew how to pick locks. James was planning to buy a bolt next time he went into town. There's no way to pick a bolt.

"Come *on*," Lauren said, sitting herself on the swivel chair at James's desk. "Spill the beans. Everyone saw the ambulance take Kerry to the medical unit."

Lauren was James's only family since their mum had died the year before. James loved his sister, but he still spent a lot of his life wishing she'd go some place and stick her head in a bucket. She could be a total pain.

"Tell us," Lauren said sharply. "You know I'll just sit here bugging you until you do."

James threw back his duvet and sat up, picking at a gluey eye.

"Why are you up so early?" he asked. "It's pitch black outside."

"It's half past ten," Lauren said, turning slowly around on the chair. "But it's raining."

James swung out of bed and peered through the blind. Rain trickled down his window. The sky was gray and the outdoor tennis courts were under water.

"Great," James said. "There's nothing like British summer to cheer you up."

"You've got a good tan," Lauren said. "Mine's almost gone and I've only been back from the hostel three weeks."

"Best holiday I've ever had." James grinned. "We'll have to try and fix it so we go at the same time next year. Me, Kerry, and about six other kids had this massive race on the quad bikes."

"Racing's not allowed," Lauren said.

"Isn't it?" James smiled, guiltily. "Anyway, there was a humongous crash. Me and Shakeel. You should have seen the state the bikes were in. Front tires ripped off, petrol gushing everywhere. It was mad."

"Did you get hurt?"

"Shakeel twisted his ankle, that's all. I can't wait for next year."

Lauren smiled. "We dared Bethany's brother to drive one of the quad bikes through the dining room. It was so funny when he got busted. . . . Anyway, are you gonna tell us why they kicked your butts home early, or not?"

James slumped miserably back on his bed, realizing he was now about as far as you get from racing over sand dunes.

"I got totally stitched up," he said.

"Give over, James, you always say that."

"Yeah, but this time it's true. Bruce and Kerry had a punch-up. They trashed our room and Kerry busted her knee, but Meryl sent me and Gabrielle home early as well. We've got to go see the chairman this afternoon."

"You must have done *something,*" Lauren said.

"Lauren, all me and Gabrielle did was try to break the fight up. It was a total miscarriage of justice. Meryl wouldn't let me get one word in."

"Makes up for all the things you haven't been caught for," Lauren grinned. "How's Kerry?"

"She's in loads of pain. They had to do a medivac: flew her home on a special plane because she can't bend her leg."

"Poor Kerry," Lauren said.

"I'll go and see how she is when I've got my uniform on. You coming?"

"I've got karate class in a minute," Lauren said, shaking her head. "I want to be in top form when my basic training starts."

"Oh yeah," James grinned. "Only a month to go now. I'm gonna have such a laugh hearing about all the ways the instructors make you suffer."

Lauren folded her arms and scowled at her brother. "You're not scaring me, you know."

The medical unit was a ten-minute walk from the main building. When James got to Kerry's room, Gabrielle was already there.

"Look what *your* friend did to her," Gabrielle said, as if it was somehow James's fault.

Kerry was propped up on pillows beneath a NIL BY MOUTH sign. MTV blared from the portable TV hanging over her bed. She was on painkillers, but still had wet eyes and looked like she hadn't slept.

James put Kerry's MP3 player on her bedside table.

"Thought some tunes might help take your mind off it," he said. "Hope you don't mind me going in your room."

"No problem," Kerry said. "Cheers."

"Has the doctor seen you?" James asked.

Kerry nodded, pointing to a light box on the wall.

"Show James the thing," she said.

There was already an X-ray mounted on the light box. Gabrielle walked up and switched on the lamp.

"That's Kerry's kneecap," Gabrielle explained, pointing to a round gray area on the X-ray. "See the four black bars?"

James nodded.

"Those are the metal pins put in when Kerry broke her kneecap two years ago. When Bruce twisted Kerry's leg, that pin there shifted. So now Kerry's got a piece of metal sticking out the back of her kneecap. Every time she moves, the metal cuts into the tendons underneath."

"Yuk," James said. "What can they do about that?"

"They're taking her to hospital," Gabrielle said. "They're operating this afternoon. Kerry can't eat or drink before the anaesthetic. They're going under her kneecap and cutting out the bent metal. The broken bone has grown back together, so the metal isn't doing anything now anyway."

James felt queasy imagining surgical instruments poking around inside his leg.

"OOOOOOOOHHH God!" Kerry screamed.

"What?" James asked, rushing over to the bed. "Are you OK?"

"It's nothing," Kerry said. "I just moved my foot. This is actually more painful than when I broke my knee."

She let out a low groan. James sat beside the bed and stroked her hand.

"Has Bruce been to see you?" he asked.

"No," Gabrielle huffed. "Like that little jerk would have enough class to come and apologize."

"James," Kerry said, "will you do us a favor?"

"Course," James said. "Name it."

"Go and see Bruce. Tell him I'm not making a big deal out of this."

"You call this no big deal?" James laughed. "You're joking."

"I'm not," Kerry said. "I don't want this turning into some massive feud. Remember I told you I broke Bruce's leg when we were red shirts?"

"Sure," James said.

"It was in karate practice. Bruce fell awkwardly. I came down on him full force and crunched his leg.

I never should have done something like that in practice. Bruce was cool about it. He shrugged it off like it was nothing. Everyone does stupid stuff sometimes. Remember that one, James?"

Kerry held out the palm of her right hand. It had a long scar where James had stomped it during training. "You can't hold grudges against people for every mistake they make," she said.

"Point taken," James said. "I'll speak to him."

James hated the row of plastic seats outside the chairman's office. If you had to see him for something good, Dr. McAfferty—usually known as Mac—let you straight in. When you were in trouble, he kept you hanging outside in suspense. James sat between Gabrielle and Bruce. He was combed and deodorized, in his neatest set of CHERUB uniform: polished boots, army-green trousers, and a navy T-shirt with the CHERUB logo embroidered on the front. The other two wore the same, except they were only entitled to wear gray T-shirts. Bruce had four red lines down his face where Kerry had clawed him.

Kerry might have forgiven Bruce, but Gabrielle wasn't talking to him. James felt like he was on a tightrope. Every time he said something to one of them, the other one huffed as if he was siding against them. James realized it was easiest if he kept quiet.

They waited a good half hour before Mac finally leaned out of his doorway. He was in his sixties, with a neat gray beard and a Scottish accent.

"Come on then," Mac said wearily. "Let's sort you three out."

James led the way towards Mac's mahogany desk.

"No, no, come and look at this," Mac said, heading towards an architectural model standing on a table by the window.

The kids stepped up to the model of a crescent-shaped building. It was a meter long, made entirely out of white plastic, with polystyrene trees and tiny white figures walking along paths outside.

"What is it?" James asked.

"It's our new mission preparation building," Mac said enthusiastically. "We're turning those shabby offices on the eighth floor into extra living space and building this beauty to replace them. Over five thousand square meters of office space. Every big mission will have its own office, with new computers and equipment. We'll have encrypted satellite links to our mission controllers all over the world, as well as to British Intelligence headquarters and the CIA and FBI in America. This model just arrived from the architect's office. Isn't it fantastic?"

The kids nodded. Even if they'd hated it, they wouldn't have wanted to get on Mac's bad side by saying so. Mac treated CHERUB campus like his own personal LEGO set. He was always having something built or knocked down.

"It's an eco-building," Mac enthused, lifting the plastic roof off so the kids could see the offices filled with miniature furniture inside. "Special glass retains the heat, so it stays warm in the winter. Solar panels on the roof power fans and heat the water."

"When's it being built?" Bruce asked.

"It's already being made in prefabricated sections in a

factory in Australia," Mac said. "That way we can minimize the number of construction workers we have to let loose on campus. Once the concrete base is poured, the whole lot is bolted together in a few weeks. Fitting out the interior should be completed early in the new year. You wouldn't believe the amount of arm twisting I've had to do to secure the funding."

"It's really cool," James said, hoping his enthusiasm would translate into a lighter punishment.

"Anyway, I suppose I have to sort you three hooligans out," Mac said. He clearly would have preferred to go on about his new building all afternoon. "Plant your bums at my desk."

The three kids sat in the leather chairs opposite Mac. Mac leaned over his desk, interlocked his fingers and stared at them.

"I've already spoken to Kerry," he said. "So what have you lot got to say for yourselves?"

"It's well unfair that me and Gabrielle got sent home," James said. "We were the ones who tried to break the fight up."

He noticed Lauren and her best friend, Bethany, with their noses squished against the outside of the window behind Mac's desk.

"As I understand Meryl Spencer," Mac said, "the four of you came back from a training exercise, went into your room, and began taunting one another and bickering. Is that true?"

The kids gave a mix of shrugs and nods. Outside, Lauren and Bethany were sticking their tongues out and mouthing rude words.

"As far as I'm concerned, that makes all four of you responsible for what happened," Mac said. "Gentle ribbing leads to teasing, which leads to nastiness and, as in this instance, it sometimes leads to violence and an eight-thousand-pound bill for an air ambulance. While each of you is serving your punishment, I want you to reflect that you'd all be enjoying another two weeks of holiday if you'd had the sense to behave decently towards one another instead of winding each other up. Is that understood?"

The three kids nodded. James hated how Mac's way of twisting the facts around made him feel partly responsible for Kerry getting hurt. What made him even more annoyed was Lauren sticking a sheet of paper up to the window that said JAMES SUCKS in giant black letters. Gabrielle couldn't stop herself smirking.

"By way of punishments, I want the three of you to report to the head gardener after you finish lessons every afternoon. We don't have enough staff to give the lawns the attention they deserve in the summer, but you guys putting in two hours' mowing a day for the next month will certainly help."

James groaned to himself. With extra fitness training in the mornings and mowing in the evenings, the next month was turning into a nightmare.

"Any questions?" Mac asked.

The kids shook their heads and stood up to leave.

"And James," Mac said.

James turned back. "What?"

Mac raised a picture frame off his desk and turned it towards James. It showed Mac standing with his wife, his six grown-up children, and an ocean of little grand-kids.

"James, would you kindly inform your sister that the glass in this picture frame gives me a very good reflection of everything that's going on outside my window. I want to see Lauren and Bethany in this office and you can tell them that they'll be joining you on gardening duty for the rest of the week."

CHAPTER 5

SLEEP

TWO WEEKS LATER

James got up at 5:30 a.m., despite his whole body begging him to stay under the duvet. He put on his running clothes and headed to the athletics track as the sun rose over campus. It took him an hour to run twenty-five laps: a distance of ten kilometers. He showered, then traded some homework with Shakeel over breakfast. Lessons went from 8:30 until 2:00, with half an hour for lunch. After lessons, there was karate practice topped off with forty-five minutes' circuit training. Boiling hot, James downed half a liter of orange juice and collected one of the ride-on mowers from the gardeners' storeroom. It wasn't hard driving the mower, but the sun was on him the whole time and the grass pollen made his eyes itch.

It was 6:15 p.m. by the time James got his first chance to relax. Dinner was a social event, with everyone mucking about and catching up on gossip. Most cherubs had done their homework before dinner and had the evening to themselves, but the mowing meant James hadn't even got started. Homework was supposed to be two hours a day. Some teachers were decent. Other piled on so much work it took heaps longer.

When James got back to his room it was gone 7:00. He sat at his desk, spread out his textbooks, and opened his homework diary. In the two weeks he'd been back on campus, James had acquired a backlog of homework that sucked up every second of his free time.

It was a warm evening, so James left his window open. A breeze clattered into the plastic slats of his blind. James's eyes were gluey and the words in his textbook drifted out of shape. His head slumped on the desk and he dozed off before he'd written a word.

Kyle lived across the hall. He was nearly fifteen, but he wasn't much bigger than James.

"Wakey, wakey," Kyle said, flicking James's ear.

James's head shot up from his desk. He opened his eyes, inhaled deeply, and looked at his watch. It was gone ten o'clock.

"OHHHHHH crap," James said, startled. "If I don't get this history report done by tomorrow, I'm dead meat. It's a two-thousand-word essay and I haven't even read the chapters in the textbook."

"Get a deferral," Kyle said.

"I've had a deferral, Kyle. And I've had a deferral of the deferral. I've got extra laps to run before school and mowing after. There aren't enough hours in the day. I spent all day Sunday doing homework and I still keep getting further behind."

"You should speak to your handler."

"I tried," James said. "You know what Meryl said?"

"What?"

"She said, if I was so snowed under with work, how come I had time to spend sitting in her office whinging?"

Kyle laughed.

"I swear, they're trying to kill me," James moaned.

"No," Kyle said. "They're trying to instil a sense of discipline in you. After a month of being worked like a dog, maybe you'll think twice about ignoring the rules next time. It's your own stupid fault. All you had to do on holiday was keep in half reasonable shape and study the briefing for the hostage training. Everybody warned you. Me, Kerry, Meryl, Amy. But you always reckon you know better."

James angrily swept his arm across his desk, shooting his books and pens on to the floor.

"Good idea," Kyle grinned. "That'll solve your problems."

"Spare me another lecture," James shouted. "I'm so knackered I can hardly keep my eyes open and I'm sick of everyone saying I told you so."

"What's that report you're doing?" Kyle asked.

"Two thousand words on the foundation of the British Intelligence Service and its role in the First World War."

"Interesting stuff," Kyle said.

"I'd rather eat a bowl of snot," James said.

"I might just be able to help you out, kiddo. I did that course two years ago. I've got my old notes and an essay in my room."

"Cheers, Kyle," James grinned. "You're a lifesaver."

"Ten quid," Kyle said.

"*What?*" James gasped. "Some friend you are, trying to make money out of me when I'm at my lowest ebb."

"This essay is a beauty, James. Grade A material. The girl I mucked it off is now studying history at Harvard University in the States."

"Fiver," James said. He reckoned the essay was easily worth a fiver. He'd have to swap bits around and rewrite in his own handwriting, but that would take about an hour, whereas doing the essay from scratch was a whole night's work.

"You're bleeding me dry," Kyle said, twisting his mouth as if he couldn't make up his mind. "But I'm a little low on funds. You can have it for a fiver, if you give us the money right now."

James went to his desk and got a fiver out of his cash box. Kyle stuffed it in his pocket.

"This better be a good essay," James said.

"Anyway," Kyle said, "I didn't come here to help with your homework. I'm the senior agent on a big mission that's coming up. We need three other kids. Me and Ewart Asker discussed it and you're on the team if you want the gig."

James wasn't that enthusiastic.

"I don't want to work with Ewart as my mission controller again. He's a psychopath."

"Ewart raves about you," Kyle said. "He thinks you did a great job on that antiterrorist mission. Plus, this is a big team. Ewart's wife will be there as well. She keeps him under her thumb."

"Who else is going?" James asked.

"Me, of course," Kyle said. "And Kerry. She's walking with a stick, but they reckon she'll be healed up before blast-off. There's a vacancy for another girl. It was going to be Gabrielle, but she's being held back for something in South Africa."

"Nicole Eddison," James said.

"Who?" Kyle asked.

"You know her," James said. "She was on my basic training and quit after one day. She got her gray shirt at the second attempt. I think she's done a couple of missions, but nothing major."

"I think I know who you mean," Kyle said. "Is it that girl with the huge chest you're always going on about?"

"She is *so* stacked," James grinned.

"James," Kyle said, indignantly, "you can't pick a girl for a mission because she has big breasts."

"Why not?"

"Well, for starters, it's unbelievably sexist."

"Come on, Kyle. Nicole's a really good laugh. She's in my Russian class and she's always getting chucked out for messing around. And as long as Kerry doesn't find out and kick my butt, who cares if it's sexist or not?"

"I'll ask Ewart to put her name on the list of candidates," Kyle said, reluctantly. "But he'll only pick her based on merit. The first mission briefing is tomorrow. There's tons of background studying to do."

"Oh, great," James said. "When am I gonna get time to do that?"

"Didn't I mention?" Kyle said innocently. "It's been arranged with Meryl. You still have to do morning laps, but we've cut out some of your lessons and Mac has agreed to knock the mowing on the head."

"Cool," James grinned. "Another two weeks of that workload was gonna send me under. What lessons have I been dropped from?"

"Art, Russian, religion, and history," Kyle said.

"Superb," James said, deliriously drumming his hands on his desktop. Then the penny dropped. "Did you say *history*?"

"Uh-huh," Kyle nodded.

"I just paid you five quid for a history essay."

"A good price for a good essay."

James leapt furiously out of his chair. "I don't care if it's written on gold parchment by that bloke who does the history shows on channel four," he spluttered. "I don't need the essay if I don't have to go back to history class."

"It goes to prove the old saying," Kyle giggled.

"What saying?"

"Cheaters never prosper."

"I tell you who'll never prosper," James stormed, grabbing one of the pens off his carpet. "You. And you know why? Because you're gonna have an extremely hard time prospering after I've rammed this biro up your nose. Give us my fiver back."

"What fiver?" Kyle asked. "I don't recall any fiver. Did you get a receipt?"

James gave Kyle a shove.

"You're a bandit, Kyle. Normal people don't go around conning their mates."

Kyle backed up, with a giant grin and his hands out in front of himself.

"I tell you what," he said, "I'm seriously short of cash. So, even though it goes against my sacred ethical code, I'll do you a deal."

"What deal?"

"If you let me keep the fiver, I'll get Nicole on to the mission."

"That's worth five quid," James smiled. "What's this mission about anyway?"

"Drugs," Kyle said.

CHAPTER 6

BRIEF

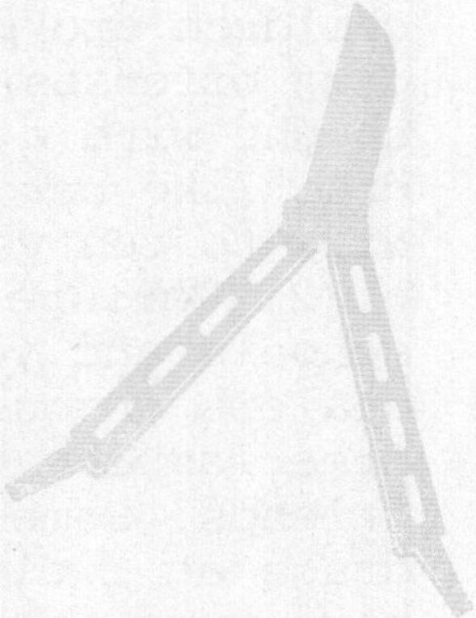

CLASSIFIED
MISSION BRIEFING:
FOR JAMES ADAMS, KYLE BLUEMAN,
KERRY CHANG, AND NICOLE EDDISON
DO NOT REMOVE FROM ROOM 812
DO NOT COPY OR MAKE NOTES

CHILDREN IN THE DRUG BUSINESS

Children are used by drug dealers throughout the world, to sell, smuggle, and deliver illegal drugs. There are a number of reasons why children are used:

(1) Kids selling or using drugs are usually viewed as victims rather than criminals. In most countries

children are punished lightly for drug offenses, whereas an adult caught with a large quantity of a drug like heroin or cocaine faces five to ten years in prison.

(2) Children have access to schools and young people. Drug dealers encourage children to give free samples of drugs to their friends. Someone who starts dealing drugs at twelve or thirteen can have hundreds of customers by the time they reach adulthood.

(3) Children have few sources of income and plenty of spare time. Many will do a drug dealer a favor, such as making a delivery for just a few pounds, or even for nothing, because they think it makes them look cool.

WHAT IS COCAINE?

Cocaine is an illegal drug extracted from the leaves of the coca plant (not to be confused with the cocoa plant, which is used to make chocolate). Coca grows at high altitude in the mountainous regions of South America. The leaves are refined into a crystalline white powder. Before reaching users, the powder is diluted with cheaper substances, such as lactose or borax, or it is mixed with other drugs such as methamphetamine (commonly called speed).

The powder is snorted up the

nose. It can also be injected, or mixed with other chemicals to form a smokable version of the drug called crack. Users of cocaine feel a sense of confidence and well-being that lasts fifteen to thirty minutes. Cocaine also causes numbness and was once used as an anaesthetic by surgeons and dentists. More effective anaesthetics are now available.

Unlike heroin or cigarettes, cocaine is not addictive. Despite this, many who try the drug enjoy its effects so much they use it to excess. Whereas a heroin or cigarette addict needs a regular fix, cocaine users often go days without using before going on a binge. Cocaine use risks serious side effects, including heart attacks, liver failure, brain seizures, strokes, and damage to the lining of the nose and mouth.

COCAINE IN BRITAIN

Cocaine was once the champagne of the drug world: a luxury only the rich could afford. A moderate user might get through a gram of powdered cocaine in an evening. In 1984, a gram of cocaine cost £200-£250. Twenty years later, the street price of cocaine has dropped to less than £50 a gram. In some areas of Britain, a gram of low quality cocaine can cost as little as £25.

The United States pays South American governments to hunt and destroy coca plants in the highlands where they grow. Despite this, the street price of cocaine has continued to drop, suggesting that supplies are still plentiful.

Most cocaine brought into Britain arrives via the Caribbean. There are thousands of smugglers in British prisons. Tough sentences have done little to stop the trade. Cocaine dealers continue to find people willing to act as drug couriers, often in return for less than a thousand pounds and an airline ticket.

It is impossible to catch every smuggler entering Britain. The police must aim higher and capture the people in control of the drug gangs. Close to one third of the cocaine entering Britain passed through an organization commonly referred to as KMG. The initials stand for Keith Moore's Gang.

KEITH MOORE AND KMG: BIOGRAPHY

1964 Keith Moore was born in the newly built Thornton housing area on the outskirts of Luton in Bedfordshire.

1977 After being caught selling cannabis in his school library, Keith was arrested by police and excluded from school. He became a chronic truant, suspected of many car thefts and burglaries.

1978 Keith began training as a boxer at the JT Martin Youth Center. JT Martin was a retired boxer and armed robber who controlled the underworld in Bedfordshire from the early 1960s until 1985. JT used his boxing club as a recruiting ground for young criminals.

1980 Keith was spotted in police surveillance photographs of JT Martin. In the pictures, Keith is a slightly built sixteen-year-old who looks out of place amongst JT's crew of boxers and nightclub bouncers.

1981 Keith became JT Martin's chauffeur when a previous driver was banned for speeding. Moving around with JT gave the seventeen-year-old an insight into all aspects of the drug business.

1983 After eleven amateur fights, with a record of one win, two draws, and eight defeats, Keith retired from boxing. Shortly afterwards, he married Julie Robertson, a girl he had known since infant school.

1985 Police captured JT Martin and a number of associates selling drugs. JT was sentenced to twelve years in prison. Keith Moore had been JT's driver for four years, but the rest of JT's crew regarded him as a wimpish hanger-on.

1986 With JT in prison, a power struggle erupted amongst

his former employees. Keith kept away from the violent struggles and developed an interest in JT's cocaine business. Cocaine was a tiny proportion of the criminal empire, which made most of its money selling heroin and cannabis. JT also owned nightclubs, pubs, and casinos, as well as dozens of small businesses such as laundrettes and hairdressing salons.

1987 The price of cocaine kept falling and supply was growing. Keith Moore was one of the first people in Britain to realize that the cocaine business was about to explode.

While his colleagues battled over heroin and nightclub profits, Keith traveled to South America and met with members of a powerful Peruvian drug cartel known as Lambayeke. He agreed to buy regular bulk shipments of cocaine at a discounted price. To sell this increased supply of cocaine, Keith launched a telephone delivery service, based on similar services that were thriving in the United States. It took advantage of two new technologies: mobile telephones and message pagers. Instead of having to go searching for a drug dealer, rich clients dialed a number and Keith had someone deliver drugs to their doorstep, usually within an hour.

1988 The cocaine business was earning Keith over £10,000 per week. This cash enabled him—at just 23 years of age—to take effective control of JT Martin's criminal empire. Keith avoided violence whenever possible. He manipulated jealous rivals, setting them against one another. When manipulation failed, he bought rivals off by handing them parts of the business that did not interest him.

Keith's next ambition was to build his profitable cocaine business into the biggest in the country. The only part of JT's empire Keith held on to was the youth center/boxing club in the neighborhood where he grew up.

1989 Keith's first son, Ringo, was born (now aged 15).

1990 Keith's business grew tenfold in three years.
Cocaine delivery expanded into Hertfordshire and London. He also began selling wholesale quantities of cocaine to other dealers all over Britain and mainland Europe.

1992 Julie Moore gave birth to twins, April and Keith Jr. (now aged 12).

1993 Keith's youngest child, Erin, was born (now aged 11).

1998 Drug dealing is often a short career. Anyone who is successful attracts attention from police and customs. They usually end up behind bars.

After investigations failed to gather enough evidence, police tried to get undercover officers into Keith's inner circle. Dozens of people working for KMG have been prosecuted. Even when they have agreed to cooperate, police have never been able to produce clear evidence linking Keith Moore with his drug business. At the core of KMG, an expensive legal team and fiercely loyal deputies have so far succeeded in keeping Keith Moore out of prison.

2000 As the cocaine business continued to thrive, Keith Moore's personal fortune was estimated at £25 million. After being arrested for non-payment of tax, he pleaded guilty to a minor charge and paid a £50,000 fine.

2001 Julie Moore left Keith after eighteen years of marriage. Keith kept custody of the children and the family home. Julie moved into a house across the street and remains on good terms with her ex-husband.

2003 Police launched Operation Snort, the largest taskforce of drugs officers ever assembled in Britain. The official aim was to stop the cocaine business. Unofficially, everyone knew Operation Snort was gunning for Keith Moore and KMG.

The operation descended into chaos when it uncovered corruption within police forces all over the country. Forty officers were found to have taken bribes from KMG. Eight of these were working on Operation Snort and included the chief superintendent who was in command of the whole operation.

Although Operation Snort is still running, its effectiveness has been blunted by infighting over the bribery allegations.

One national newspaper reporting on Operation Snort said, "If all the corruption allegations are true, it would appear that Keith Moore has more police officers protecting him than the queen and the prime minister combined."

2004 (Present Day) Despite a personal fortune now estimated at between £35 and £50 million, Keith Moore has shunned the trappings of the super rich. He lives with his children in a large detached house less than twenty minutes' drive from the housing area where he was born. His four children attend the local comprehensive school. He works from an office at home and socializes with family members and friends he has known since boyhood. His only extravagances are a collection of Porsche sports cars and a beachfront house in Miami, Florida.

MISSION REQUEST

In early 2004, frustrated by the lack of success in bringing down KMG and outraged by police corruption, the government asked the intelligence service to find a way of infiltrating KMG at the highest level. MI5, the adult branch of British Intelligence, could see no reason why it would have any more success at this than the police. CHERUB was suggested as a method of last resort.

Keith Moore is close to his four children. Appropriately placed CHERUB agents may be able to befriend them and gather vital information.

MISSION PLAN
Husband and wife mission controllers, Ewart and Zara Asker, will move into a house in the Thornton housing area with their baby son and four CHERUB agents. For the purposes of the mission, the agents will be adopted children of Zara and Ewart. The family surname will be Beckett. To minimize confusion, everyone will use their normal first names.

PRIMARY OBJECTIVE
Each agent has been selected to befriend one of Keith's children, as follows:

James Adams – Junior Moore (Keith Junior)
Kyle Blueman – Ringo Moore
Kerry Chang – Erin Moore
Nicole Eddison – April Moore

If the cherubs succeed in making friends, they must attempt to socialize out of school and try to get inside Keith's home, gathering information wherever possible. Each cherub will be placed in the same tutor group as the child they are supposed to befriend.

SECONDARY OBJECTIVE
Many children in the Thornton area run errands and deliver drugs for KMG associates. Each cherub should identify children who are working for KMG and try to get involved themselves. Children usually work for small-time dealers, delivering drugs to individual clients using mobile phones and pushbikes.

Evidence suggests that children who attend Keith Moore's boxing club and make reliable couriers are promoted rapidly and given responsibility for moving wholesale quantities of drugs. If these children can be identified, they may provide information that will enable police to prosecute senior figures inside KMG.

NOTE: ON THE 13TH DAY OF AUGUST 2004 THIS MISSION PLAN WAS PASSED BY THE CHERUB ETHICS COMMITTEE BY A 2:1 VOTE, ON CONDITION THAT ALL AGENTS UNDERSTAND THE FOLLOWING:

This mission has been classified HIGH RISK. All agents are reminded of their right to refuse to

```
undertake this mission and to
withdraw from it at any time.
Agents will be at risk of violence
and exposure to illegal drugs.
Agents are reminded that they
will be excluded from CHERUB
immediately if they willingly use
cocaine or any other class A drug.
```

It was breaking all sorts of rules, but Zara Asker let them take the mission briefings outside and read them in the sun. She'd made a picnic, spreading a tablecloth over the grass and covering it with sandwiches and snacks. It was a chance for baby Joshua to get used to Kyle, Kerry, Nicole, and James. The eight-month-old sat under a sunshade, wearing nothing but a nappy. Kerry and Nicole leaned over him with giant grins.

"Look at his tiny fingers, James," Kerry beamed. "He's so cute you could gobble him up."

James lay back in the grass with sunglasses on, thinking he looked cool and wondering how Kyle had managed to get Nicole on the mission.

"It's a baby, Kerry," he said, "I've seen one before, they all look exactly the same."

Kerry tickled Joshua's belly.

"That's James," she said. "Isn't he Mr. Grumpy today?"

"Ooogy woogy woo," Nicole added.

Ewart was striding across the grass towards them, carrying an icebox and some bottles of soft drinks. He was a big muscular guy, with bleached hair and half a dozen earrings. He wore a Carhartt T-shirt and old jeans with the legs ripped off.

Zara was older than her husband. She looked like a typical harassed mum, with scraggy hair and puked-up milk on her T-shirt. Like most CHERUB staff, she was a former pupil. She'd gone to university and worked for the United Nations before returning to CHERUB as a mission controller. Kyle had worked with Zara a couple of times before. He said she was one of the best mission controllers to get. Everyone agreed. Ewart was the toughest.

"Hey, Nicole," Kyle said, swatting a fly away from his paper plate. "You should have seen how happy James was when he found out you got on this mission."

James sat up, surprised by Kyle's outburst. Nicole turned away from the baby.

"Was he?" she said, breaking into a smile. "Is that right, James?"

James was flustered. Kerry would kill him if she found out he'd paid Kyle to get Nicole on the mission.

"That's right," James spluttered. "I've never got a chance to know you, but the few times I've spoken to you, you've always seemed . . . nice."

"Thank you, James," Nicole smiled. "I was worried I'd be the odd one out because you three are already close."

Kyle grinned. "And James fancies you."

"Piss off, Kyle," James said.

Kyle was one of James's best mates, but he was always trying to con you or wind you up. Sometimes it got annoying. Zara cuffed Kyle around the back of the head.

"I'm only telling the truth," Kyle said.

"Kyle, *behave*," Zara said sharply. "And James, you watch your language in front of the baby."

James could feel his face burning with a mix of anger and embarrassment.

"I know James doesn't fancy me," Nicole said. "Everyone knows James and Kerry have a thing going."

"Says who?" Kerry gasped.

"Yeah," James said defensively. "Me and Kerry did basic training together and we're good mates. It doesn't mean we fancy each other."

Kyle laughed. "If you say so, lovebirds."

"At least I've *had* a girlfriend," James said, looking at Kyle. "You're nearly fifteen and I've never seen you anywhere near a girl."

Kyle looked offended. "I've had girlfriends."

James grinned, sensing he'd put Kyle on the back foot.

"Girls in dreams don't count, dickhead."

A second later, James found himself dangling in the air with Ewart eyeballing him.

"Fifty laps," Ewart barked.

"What?" James gasped.

"You shut that filthy mouth in front of my son."

"He's a baby," James said. "He can't understand a word."

"But he'll learn," Ewart snarled. "Get over to the running track, now."

Fifty laps of the track took two hours and left you for dead when you stiffened up the next morning. Zara intervened before James boiled over and told Ewart where to shove his laps.

"Ewart, darling," Zara said gently. "James needs to be here while we discuss the mission. I'm sure an apology will be sufficient."

James, still suspended in mid-air, didn't think anyone deserved an apology, but it was better than running laps.

"OK," James said. "I'm sorry."

"For what?" Zara asked.

"I shouldn't have sworn in front of the baby."

"Apology accepted, James," Zara said. "And Kyle, quit being smart. You're the senior agent on this mission. I expect you to help the less experienced agents, not keep stirring up trouble."

After Ewart had put him down, James straightened his clothes, sat on the grass, and started piling chicken drumsticks and sandwiches on to a paper plate. Nicole shuffled up beside him and pinched a couple of his crisps.

Zara began reading notes from a long list.

"OK, as you all know, we're leaving first thing the day after tomorrow. Pack light. There are seven of us and it's a small house. State school starts Tuesday, giving us nearly a week to settle in before term starts. I've prepared a hundred-and-sixty-page dossier on Keith Moore, his associates, and his family, I want all of you to read it and memorize as much as you can. . . ."

CHAPTER 7

MOVING

It was pandemonium. They had a big moving van and a people carrier. The van was already stuffed, mostly with baby stuff like pushchairs and walkers. Kerry had five bags of clothes and junk, which James had to hump downstairs because her knee was still weak. Kyle, who was always ridiculously neat, wanted to take his clothes rail, eight pairs of shoes, and his own ironing board. Ewart was going beserk, using language that would have earned James thousands of laps.

"I'm only making one trip," Ewart shouted. "So you lot better sort yourselves out."

James was the only one who'd followed instructions to pack light. He had a backpack, with toiletries, spare trainers, a jacket, and a few changes of clothes. His PlayStation and TV had gone ahead the day before with the furniture.

Lauren came tearing around the corner towards them. She was in uniform and she was crying. It was the last thing James expected.

"What's the matter?" he asked, bundling his sister into his arms.

Her T-shirt was sweaty and the sobs made her whole body shudder.

"Just . . ." Lauren sniffed.

James pulled her tighter and rubbed her back.

"Is someone bullying you, or something?"

"I'm ten in two weeks," she explained. "It's doing my head in thinking about basic training."

Lauren acted tough most of the time, but she couldn't always keep the nine-year-old girl inside herself under control. Whenever there was a chink in her armor, she came to James for comfort.

"Lauren, *I* passed training," James said, feeling a bit emotional himself. "I'd never done karate and I could barely swim. With all the fitness and combat exercises you've done, you're a million times better prepared than I was."

Lauren dragged her wrist over her eyes. Kerry got Lauren a tissue.

"Come on, kids," Zara shouted, as she climbed into the people carrier. "I want most of this drive out of the way before Joshua wakes up and starts screaming."

"I wish you weren't going away," Lauren said.

"Bethany's going into training with you," James

said. "She'll probably be your partner. You two will do great."

Lauren stepped back from James. Kerry gave her a quick squeeze.

"Just think, Lauren," Kerry said. "In four months, basic training will be a memory and you'll be able to go on missions. I'll bet you, any money you like."

Lauren smiled a bit. "Yeah. I hope so."

"If you want," James said, "I can probably arrange for you to visit us in Luton on your birthday. We can have a laugh."

Lauren looked surprised. "Will they let me?"

"They won't mind. It'll be good experience for you: getting a taste of what it's like being out on a mission and stuff."

"You better go then," Lauren sniffled, dabbing her eyes with the tissue. "I don't know what made me start crying. It just . . . Sorry . . . I feel really dumb now."

James pecked his sister on the cheek, before saying good-bye and climbing in the back of the people carrier.

Kyle leaned out of the side window. "You'll make it through training, Lauren," he shouted. "Don't go losing any sleep."

James pulled up the door and buckled his seatbelt.

"Sorry I shouted, James," Zara said, from the driver's seat. "I didn't realize Lauren was upset. Is she OK?"

"I think so," James nodded.

Lauren waved as they drove away. James's eyes were a bit damp, but he wasn't worried. Lauren had a good brain and she was fit. A serious injury was the only thing likely to stop her getting through basic training.

• • •

Ewart and Nicole traveled in the moving van with the luggage. Zara drove the people carrier, with Kyle next to her in the front. James and Kerry sandwiched Joshua's baby seat in the back. The baby woke up an hour before they arrived. Kerry had a go at feeding him, but he screamed his head off. She passed him over to James while she hunted round her feet for a bottle Joshua had batted on to the floor.

Joshua stopped screaming as soon as James took him. When Kerry tried to take Joshua back, he went nuts again. Kerry gave James the bottle and Joshua began drinking calmly.

"Looks like we've found James's job for this mission," Zara said, grinning. "He likes you for some reason."

Kyle laughed. "Kerry probably traumatized him with the funny faces she was pulling the other afternoon."

James wasn't used to babies. He was terrified he might do something wrong and either hurt Joshua or get puked over. It turned out OK, apart from a few dribbles of milk. After feeding, Joshua lay quietly in James's lap playing with the laces on his shorts. Once James got used to it, he thought having the warm little body wriggling on his lap was quite cool.

A third of the houses in the Thornton area were boarded up. The detached homes looked decent enough, but nobody wanted to live in them because of the airport a kilometer south. Every few minutes, a couple of hundred people thundered overhead, shaking the ground and filling the air with the sickly smell of jet fuel.

You only ended up living in Thornton if you didn't

have a choice. The residents were a mix of refugees, students, ex-convicts, and families who'd been chucked out of better places for not paying the rent.

A gang of lads had to stop their football match to let Zara drive through. Ewart and Nicole had arrived minutes earlier. Nicole had unpacked the mugs and started making tea.

The windows in the house were triple glazed to keep out the aircraft noise, but that didn't stop everything vibrating. Besides, it was too warm to leave every window closed.

There were three bedrooms between seven people. Kyle and James got a box room with bunk beds, a chest of drawers, and a tiny wardrobe.

"Just like old times," James said, remembering when he and Kyle shared a room in a council home before he joined CHERUB.

"There's nowhere to hang my clothes," Kyle said miserably. "They'll get creased."

"You can have the whole wardrobe," James said. "I'll just dump my stuff in the bag or under the bed."

"If there's anything that stinks in this room, I'm chucking it out," Kyle said. "I don't care if it's a sock or a seventy-quid pair of trainers—if it smells like you, it's going in the bin."

James laughed. "I'd forgotten what a complete tart you are."

Zara made dinner for everyone: fish fingers and oven chips, with frozen peas.

"Sorry," she said, handing plates to the line of kids in

front of the TV. "You better get used to my cooking. It's not exactly gourmet."

Something crashed outside the living room window. All the kids downed cutlery and bundled towards the window. There was rubbish all over the front lawn and a metal dustbin rolling towards the gutter. A couple of boys were sprinting off down the pavement. Ewart burst out of the front door, but they'd disappeared up an alleyway.

As James mopped his last chip through his ketchup, Ewart strode in and switched off the TV.

"I always watch *Neighbours,*" Kerry gasped.

"Not today you don't," Ewart said. "You kids have a job to do."

"Go outside and start making friends," Zara said. "There's bound to be some dodgy characters in an area like this, so stick together. I want you back here as soon as it gets dark."

"And James," Ewart said, "you better pick all that rubbish off the front lawn before you go."

"Why's it my job?" James said bitterly.

Ewart broke into a smile. "Because I said so."

James thought about starting a row, but you never win against someone like Ewart.

It was easy starting conversations. The summer holidays had dragged on for weeks and the local kids were bored. James and Kyle played street football until they got knackered. Kerry and Nicole stood by the curb, nattering with a bunch of girls. When it started getting late, the four of them got invited to a kiddies' playground.

There was nothing special about it: a burned-out park keeper's shed sprayed with graffiti, a busted roundabout, a climbing frame, and a slide. But once the sun started to go down, it came alive. Kids aged between ten and sixteen gathered in fours and fives; smoking, arguing, and being loud. There was a tense atmosphere. Flash kids dressed like Nike commercials ripped into refugees dressed out of the charity box. Boys were trying to get off with girls and there was a rumor going around about a gang from another neighborhood turning up and starting a fight.

Apparently, a kid had been stabbed in the playground a couple of months earlier. He'd ended up with between eight and two hundred stitches, depending on what version of the story you believed.

"This is boring," Kerry said, after half an hour of standing around without anything happening except a lot of talk. "We better go home."

"You go if you want," James said. "I'm staying to see if a fight breaks out. It might be good."

"It might also be dangerous," Kerry said. "I've seen a couple of kids with knives and Zara told us to be home before . . ."

James interrupted, mocking Kerry's voice. "Zara told us da-de-da-da. . . . Chill out, Kerry, what's the point of having a curfew unless you're going to break it?"

Kerry looked at Nicole for moral support. "Are you coming?"

"No way," Nicole said. "I want to see some action."

They all waited another twenty minutes. A guy aged about fifteen came over and started chatting up Nicole.

Then someone's mobile rang and a rumor shot around. There was a car coming.

"So what?" Kerry asked.

"Stolen car," one of the local kids explained. "Joy-riders. They usually put on a good show."

Fifty-odd kids piled out of the playground and hurried to a deserted car park a few hundred meters down the road. A cheer when up when everyone spotted the headlights. It was a Subaru Impreza turbo, metallic silver with a giant wing on the back. The driver did a couple of handbrake turns, spinning the car and stinking up the air with tire smoke. Then he overdid it and smacked into a bollard, leaving a massive graze down one side of the car. The audience whooped and cheered, even though he'd nearly splattered a couple of girls standing astride their bikes.

"These guys are nutters," James giggled. "I'd love to have a go at that."

Kerry gave him a filthy look. "It's so stupid. They could kill themselves, or an innocent bystander."

"Loosen up, Kerry," James said. "You sound like an old fart."

The Subaru squealed to a halt a few meters away. As the cloud of tire smoke cleared, the driver and his mate opened the doors and ran around the car to switch seats. They both looked about fifteen.

"Where are our babes?" the new driver shouted.

A couple of tarty-looking girls jogged to the car and clambered in the back. When they were inside, the driver lit up the rear tires and started driving circuits around the neighborhood. He skidded on every corner, nearly losing the back end a couple of times on sharp turns. When the car was out of sight, you could still hear the engine and squealing tires. The joyriders kept coming back to the car park for more adulation from their audience.

The excitement level went into overload when a police siren went off. James was hoping to see a chase, but the joyriders didn't fancy their chances. They slammed on the brakes, jumped out, and merged into the crowd of kids as three police cars turned into the car park.

Everyone started running. One of the guys they'd been playing football with tugged James by his T-shirt.

"Don't stand there gawping," he said urgently. "The pigs will bust you if they get hold of you."

Kerry, Kyle and Nicole were already gone. James sprinted off, but the whole of Thornton looked identical in the dark and he couldn't remember the way home. He ended up in the center of the neighborhood, in a large paved square with lanes of identical houses branching off in six different directions.

"You know which way?" a voice asked breathlessly.

James spun around. It was a massive relief to see Kyle. Kerry and Nicole were with him.

"We can ask one of the policemen," Kerry said.

"Are you totally brain dead?" James asked, tapping his head. "The police are looking for two boys and two girls. They'll nick us."

Kerry looked perplexed. "But we didn't steal the car."

"Kerry," Kyle said, laughing, "how naïve are you? In an area like this, cops and kids are like oil and water: They don't mix."

"Well," Kerry said indignantly, "none of this would

have happened if we'd gone home when I said."

"Oh, shut your smug hole," James said.

"So, which way?" Nicole asked.

They were all out of breath when they burst through the front door. It was pure luck finding the right street at the second attempt, without bumping into any cops. Zara leaned out of the kitchen into the hallway.

"Ahh . . . Here they are. My little monsters," Zara grinned. "Late as usual."

The kids were expecting a roasting, but they got off because there was an old couple sitting at the table in the kitchen, drinking tea with Zara and Ewart.

"This is the adopted family," Ewart explained. "Kids, meet Ron and Georgina. They live next door and they brought us homemade biscuits to welcome us to the neighborhood."

"You kids dip in," the old girl said. "My biscuits have won prizes."

They stuck their hands in the tin and grabbed one. They tasted like they'd been baked in 1937, but they could hardly start gobbing them out in front of the old lady.

"Delicious," James said, gagging for some water to get the stale taste out of his mouth.

"Would you like another one?" the old dear asked.

Zara clamped the lid on the biscuit tin.

"They're off to their rooms now," Zara said. "They're not really allowed sweet stuff this late. It's bad for their teeth."

They were all thankful that Zara had saved them from

another biscuit. James led the scramble upstairs to the bathroom.

"SHUSSSHH, you lot," Zara whispered after them. "Joshua's asleep."

The four of them queued at the bathroom tap to get a drink; then they slugged mouthwash to get the taste out of their mouths.

"It's like a single bite sucks every bit of saliva out of your mouth," Kerry said.

"I bet she knows how disgusting they are," Kyle said. "Probably gets a kick out of watching everyone suffer."

"Hope the old bag dies," Nicole said.

James started laughing. "I think that's a *tiny* bit extreme, Nicole."

"I can't stand old people," Nicole said. "Wait till they're sixty, then give all of 'em both barrels of a shotgun."

"My nan was great," James said. "I got a Kit Kat or Wagon Wheel every time I saw her . . . I was her favorite. She never liked Lauren much."

Kerry grunted. "No accounting for taste, I suppose. When did she die?"

"When I was ten."

"Is Lauren OK now?" Kyle asked.

"I haven't spoken to her since this morning," James said. "Suppose I'd better ring her before I go to bed."

After he undressed, James climbed into his bunk and gave Lauren a call on his mobile. She was embarrassed about crying earlier and didn't want to talk about it.

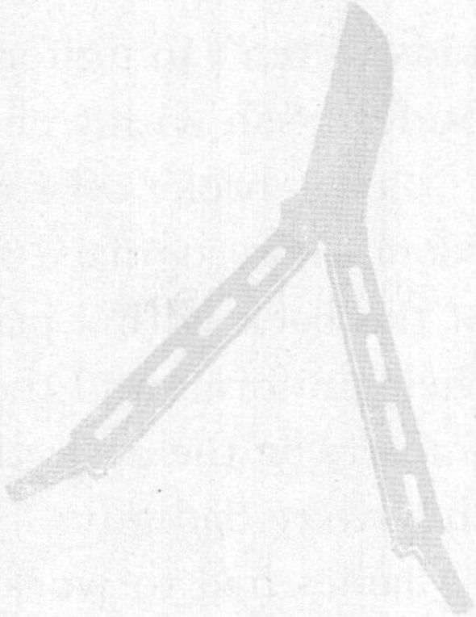

CHAPTER 8

CONTACT

It was the first day of a new school year. The lines of miserable kids had short haircuts and new uniforms to grow into. Kyle offered to run the iron over James's stuff to "make it nice and crisp," as he put it. James had forgotten how annoying it was to wear a tie and blazer all day. The only good thing was, Nicole looked fit in her white blouse, with her tie loose around the collar. She'd altered her skirt so it was half the length of Kerry's.

James had been to a few different schools since his mum died. Grey Park looked like it was the bottom of the pile. The smell was a mixture of toilets and floor polish. The curtains and walls in the entrance hall were stuck up with thousands of bits of chewing gum, half the kids weren't in uniform, and there was an aquarium full of dead fish with a chair floating in it.

James broke off from the others and found his classroom. He recognized Junior Moore straight away, sitting at the back with a mate. You could tell, by the state of their uniforms and the way they were sitting with their trainers on the desk, that they wanted everyone to think they were bad guys.

James had to work his way in with them gradually. If you went straight up and introduced yourself to kids like that, they'd treat you like a joke. James's plan was to act cool and win them over with bad behavior.

The teacher came in. He was a titchy little donut in a beige suit called Mr. Shawn. He seemed full of himself; the kind of teacher who gave you an urge to muck about, just so you got the pleasure of seeing him flip out.

"O-KAYYYYYY!" Mr. Shawn shouted, slamming a book on his desk to get everyone's attention. "Summer is over, welcome to Year Eight. . . . Find your seats and settle down."

James sat at an empty desk in the middle. This seriously weird kid sat next to him. He was tall, but stick thin. His uniform was too small and his walk was bizarre, like he was trying to move in twenty directions at once.

"You're new," the weirdo said. "I'm Charles."

James didn't want to be nasty, but a geeky pal was the last thing he needed if he was going to make friends with Junior.

"I can show you around if you want," Charles said.

"It's OK," James replied awkwardly. "I'll manage, but cheers for the offer."

Charles didn't carry a backpack like the other kids; he had a brown leather briefcase. Judging by the noise when he put it down, he kept a couple of bricks inside. Charles stooped over the desk and began frantically scratching at the back of his hand. A snowstorm of skin flakes drifted on to the table in front of him.

"I've got eczema," Charles explained noisily. "It gets worse in the summer when I sweat."

Mr. Shawn started handing out timetables and burbling on about the fabulous opportunities presented by the after-school chess and drama clubs. Ten minutes into school, James already wanted to burst out of the front gate and run for the hills. He'd always found school boring, but after being at CHERUB, where the classes were small and the teachers pushed you, normal school made him feel like his life was running in slow motion.

Charles was bored as well. He got an apple out of his briefcase and crunched into it. Mr. Shawn stopped talking and glowered at him.

"Charles, what on earth are you doing?"

"Eating an apple," Charles said, as if he'd been asked the world's stupidest question.

"We don't eat in class, do we?" Mr. Shawn said.

Everyone started laughing. If a cool kid had bitten the apple, they would have laughed at how funny it was. But they all had Charles down as class loser, so everyone was shaking their heads and there were a few murmurs of "spastic" and "retard."

"Put it in the bin, Charles."

Charles took a final bite of the apple, before hurling it at the metal bin behind Mr. Shawn's desk. He missed, so he lumbered over and picked it off the floor. The back of his trousers looked set to rip open when he bent down and you could see his bright green Y-fronts.

"Nice knickers, Charles," one of the girls shouted.

"Yeah," someone else shouted. "But they were white when he put them on."

The kids went into another round of laughs.

Charles missed the bin a second time, even though he was dropping the apple from less than a meter. He lost his temper and kicked out. The bin smashed against the wall and the metal got bent out of shape.

"Charles, calm *down,*" Mr. Shawn shouted.

"I hate bins," Charles steamed, booting it again.

"Into your seat now, Charles, unless you want a detention tonight."

Charles stumbled back to his seat.

Their maths teacher was a fruitcake. She had the key for the wrong classroom. Everyone stood around in the corridor while she went looking for the caretaker. Junior and his pal wandered up to Charles. James was standing next to him.

"Did you miss us this summer?" Junior asked.

Charles kept quiet. Junior grabbed his wrist and bent back his thumb.

"Did you bring us any presents from your holidays?" Junior asked, tightening his grip until Charles's face twisted up in pain.

"No," Charles gasped.

"That's not nice. I think you deserve a slap."

Junior let Charles's thumb go and clocked him around

the face. It wasn't hard. It was mainly done for humiliation.

"And who's your new friend?" Junior asked.

"James," Charles stuttered.

Junior faced James off. He was a fair bit shorter than James, but he had beefy arms and shoulders, as well as a mate to back him up. He gave James a little shove.

James felt edgy. CHERUB training had taught him that your first encounter with someone sets the tone for everything that follows. If James appeared weak, Junior would never consider him an equal and they'd be unlikely to make friends. But if James lashed out, they might become enemies and that would be even worse. He had to get the right balance between the two.

"Try pushing me around if you want to," James said casually. "But I wouldn't recommend it."

Junior turned to his mate and smiled.

"What's this, Del?" he laughed. "Looks like the new boy thinks he's a hard man."

Junior tried to grab James's wrist. James dodged out the way and jabbed two fingers into Junior's belly, sending him into a spasm.

"Too slow," James said, shaking his head in contempt.

Junior lunged again. His fist hit James in the guts, knocking the wind out of him. The force behind it surprised James. In a flash of anger, he hooked his foot around Junior's ankle and shoved him over. All the other kids backed up, expecting a fight.

James stood over Junior with his fists bunched, defying him to get up. Junior didn't look too confident. After a couple of tense moments, James smiled and reached out his hand.

"If you want a row, there's plenty of easier targets than me," he said.

Junior looked pissed off, but grudgingly let James help him up.

"Where'd you learn to do that?" Junior asked, brushing off his uniform.

"From Zara, my stepmum," James said. "She's a karate instructor."

"Cool," Junior said. "What belt are you?"

"Black, of course," James said. "What about you? Who taught you to throw a punch?"

"Boxing club," Junior said. "I'm undefeated. Eight fights, eight victories."

By the time the teacher got the classroom door open, the lesson was half finished. There was a spare seat next to Junior.

"Mind if I sit here?" James asked.

"Free country," Junior shrugged. "This is Del and I'm Keith; but that's my dad's name, so everyone calls me Junior."

"I'm James. Thanks for rescuing me from sitting with freak-boy over there."

James was pleased with himself. It had only taken an hour to break the ice. He sealed the deal by blowing a massive raspberry when the teacher asked him to be quiet. Junior and Del cracked up laughing.

Junior slapped James on the back as they walked out to morning break.

"You've got bottle, James," he said. "What lesson's next?"

Del got a timetable out of his pocket.

"History," he said.

"Balls to that," Junior said. "What about this afternoon?"

"Maths and French."

"Don't fancy that," Junior said. "You coming, Del?"

Del looked anxious. "I dunno. I don't think we should bunk off first day. My dad's gonna kill me if we get suspended again."

"Well," Junior said, "it's sunny outside. There's no way I'm sitting cooped up in some classroom. You wanna tag along, James?"

"Where you going?"

"God knows. We can get burgers or something, hang around the shopping center."

"Whatever," James said. "Anything beats lessons."

One of the coolest things about missions was being able to break all the rules without getting into trouble.

The two boys crawled under the back gate and ran a couple of hundred meters away from the school. Junior did a strip. He had a Puma T-shirt and shorts under his uniform.

"If you're gonna bunk off," Junior explained, "it's best to get rid of the uniform. Otherwise you get some old bat spotting the badge on your blazer and ringing up your school to complain."

"Smart," James nodded. "But all I've got under here is bare skin, so unless you want me to walk around in my boxers, I'm stuck with it."

"You want to go to the Reeve Center?" Junior asked.

"What's that?"

"Big shopping place. You're seriously telling me you've never been there?"

"We only moved here a week ago," James explained.

"Why's that?"

"We were in London," James lied, repeating the cover story they'd all had to memorize. "My stepdad got a job at the airport, so we moved up here."

"If you've never been to the Reeve Center, we should definitely go. It's half an hour on the bus. There's sports shops, games shops, and a big food court."

"Sounds cool," James said. "But I've only got the three quid Zara gave me to buy lunch."

"I can lend you a fiver, James. But I'll send my geezers round to smash your legs if you don't pay me back."

James laughed. "Cheers."

CHAPTER 9

THEFT

They wandered round the Reeve Center for an hour, looking at trainers and computer games that they didn't have any money to buy. It wasn't as boring as school, but it wasn't exactly exciting either. When they got hungry, they got stuff off a Mexican stand in the food court.

"My dad's loaded," Junior said, taking a chunk out of his burrito. "But he's so tight. He says he doesn't want me turning into a spoiled brat. I'm telling you, half the poor scum living down in Thornton get more cool stuff than I do."

"That's where I live," James said.

"Sorry," Junior smiled. "No offense."

"None taken."

"Actually, it's quite a laugh hanging out in Thornton. I was down there in the holidays and some kids started chucking bricks at the police."

James laughed. "Excellent."

"It was brilliant. One cop car got the windscreen smashed and everything. I go to boxing club down there as well. Have you been round there?"

"No."

"My dad sponsors it, actually. You should come along, everyone who goes boxing is a nutter. It's a good crowd."

"Maybe I'll try it," James said. "Does boxing hurt?"

"Only when you get punched," Junior said, grinning. "So that's something you should definitely try to avoid."

"So how come your dad's loaded?" James asked. "What does he do?"

James knew what Keith Moore did, of course, but he wondered what Junior would say.

"Oh, he's a businessman. Import and export. He's a millionaire actually."

James acted impressed. "Seriously?"

"No kidding. That's why I get so pissed off he won't give me decent pocket money. There are six PlayStation games I want really bad. I'll get a couple of them for my birthday, but that's not till November."

"Steal 'em," James said.

Junior laughed. "Yeah, but knowing my luck I'd get busted."

"I know a few things about shoplifting," James said. "My mum was into it, before she died."

"Did she get nicked much?"

"Never," James said. "Shoplifting is a snip, as long as you use forward planning and kitchen foil."*

"How many times have you done it?" Junior asked.

"Hundreds," James lied.

In fact, the only time James had tried shoplifting was when he was in care shortly after his mum died. He'd ended up in a police cell.

"So what's the tinfoil for?" Junior asked.

"I'll show you, if you want to go for it."

"I'm in if you reckon it's safe."

James gurgled up the last of his Coke. "There's no guarantee, but I've never been caught before."

He reckoned shoplifting was a good way to cement his friendship with Junior. If they got away with it, he'd be a hero and he could invite himself round to Keith Moore's house to play the games. It would be trickier if they got caught, but the experience of getting in trouble together would probably bring them closer.

James wouldn't get in real trouble with the police, because they would arrest and charge James Beckett, a boy who didn't really exist. As soon as the mission ended, CHERUB would pull James Beckett's criminal file and have it destroyed, so no fingerprint or DNA evidence would ever be linked back to James's real identity.

---

* The author of this book would like to point out that the shoplifting technique described here only works with certain outdated security systems. I've got no intention of telling you which ones they are because I don't want angry dads turning up on my doorstep and kicking my head in because their little darling just got busted trying to nick something from a shop.

James bought a roll of tinfoil in one of those everything for a pound shops. They locked themselves in a disabled toilet. James gave Junior the stuff out of his backpack and lined it with a double layer of the shiny aluminum.

"What does it do?" Junior asked.

"You know those alarms that go off when you take something out of a shop?"

Junior nodded.

"They're metal detectors," James explained. "They put those sticky metal tag thingies on everything, and the alarm goes off when it detects them."

"So, won't the metal foil make it go off?"

"It only goes off when it detects the right-sized piece of metal. Otherwise, it would ring for every umbrella and belt buckle. So, as long as you wrap the security tags inside something made of metal, the alarm thinks it's something different and doesn't go off."

"Genius," Junior said, breaking into a grin.

"All we need is a shop where they keep the PlayStation disks in the boxes, not behind the counter."

"Gameworld does," Junior said.

"We'll have to go in separately. I'll go up and stick the games in my pack. Your job is to distract the security guard, or any staff that comes near me."

"How?"

"Anything to take their attention off me. Just walk up and ask where something is."

"You're sure this isn't going to go wrong?" Junior asked excitedly. "If we get caught, my dad will crucify me."

"Trust me," James said. "Besides, you're only a look-out. I'm the one taking the big risk."

James felt confident as Junior led him through the shopping center towards Gameworld.

The security guard stood in the entrance. James went straight up the back to the PlayStation games. His foil-lined backpack was already unzipped. He found four of the games Junior wanted, then realized he might as well grab a few for himself while he was taking the risk. It was dead easy: The security guard was picking his nose and the guy at the checkout was texting on his mobile.

James zipped the pack up and slung it over his back. Junior stood in the doorway, with the security guard pointing out the DVDs to him. James headed towards the exit as nonchalantly as he could, but his heart was thumping. As he passed through the detector, an alarm went berserk and a mechanical voice boomed out:

"We're sorry, an inventory tag has been left on your item. Please return to the store. We're sorry, an inventory . . ."

The guard took hold of James and tried to drag him into the shop. Junior could have kept his head down and nobody would have been able to prove he was involved, so James was impressed when he charged towards the security guard and punched him in the side of the head. James kneed the guard in the stomach and started running, with Junior a few paces behind.

The security guard in the store opposite had seen the whole show and came after them. When James glanced back over his shoulder, the guard was shouting into his walkie-talkie, requesting back-up.

"You tit," Junior shouted, as shoppers dived out of their way. "What a great plan."

James couldn't work out what he'd done wrong. Two security guards came out of a department store up ahead, blocking their path and forcing them to cut into a women's clothing store. A woman with a buggy went flying into a display of leggings as James crashed into her. The store was crammed with rails of clothing that brushed against James as he ran. Junior stumbled. One of the security guards got a hand on him, but he spun away and recovered his balance.

James burst out of the fire exit at the back of the shop, setting off another alarm. He'd hoped the door would lead out on to the street, but he'd emerged into the central concourse of the shopping centre. There was big fountain and a stand where they did temporary exhibitions. The yellow banner hanging over the exhibition stand sent James into shock:

BEDFORDSHIRE POLICE THEFT PREVENTION SQUAD.
FIND OUT HOW TO PROTECT YOUR
HOME AND CAR FROM CRIME.

There was a long fold-out table, with three policemen behind it handing out crime prevention leaflets.

"Holy shit," Junior gasped, stopping in his tracks.

With the police up ahead and security guards behind, their chances looked about nil. James considered surrendering, but Junior noticed a door with a toilet sign a few meters away and barged it open. He led James down a narrow corridor, with six pairs of men's shoes clattering after them. They passed the entrance to the ladies' toilet and crashed through a fire door, into the dim confines of a multistory car park.

They sped towards the lift, but there was no time to wait for it. Instead, they scrambled on to the staircase and ran down, leaping three steps at a time, fueled by adrenalin. James twisted his ankle, but he didn't have time to think about the pain, or the fact that if he tumbled he'd smash his head open on bare concrete.

The policemen were more cautious on the stairs and the boys had gained ground by the time they booted open a set of doors that led into a sunlit alley. There were massive steel bins and boxes of rubbish piled around them. They clambered over everything, reaching the front of the shopping center as the police emerged through the doors at the bottom of the stairs. The security guards had given up.

There was a pedestrian crossing, with two lanes of waiting traffic. James saw the green man flashing and they made a dash for it. They ran into the outdoor car park, crouching low and jogging between the bumpers of two lines of parked cars.

The police got stranded on the other side of the road, waiting for the lights to change. One cop tried to stop the traffic with a hand signal and nearly got splattered by a motorbike. By the time the cops had halted the traffic and made it across, James and Junior were crouching behind a car a hundred meters away.

The three cops stood on the pavement by the car park, staring hopelessly at row after row of parked cars. The boys kept low until they came to the far side of the car park. They pushed themselves through shrubs, emerging on to the narrow pavement beside a fast-moving dual carriageway. Junior started to run.

"WHOA," James said. "Keep cool."

Junior turned around. "What?"

"Walk," James said. "It looks less dodgy if we're spotted."

They walked nervously for twenty minutes, looking back over their shoulders and having miniature heart attacks every time they spotted a white car. When they noticed a bus coming, they sprinted to the stop and hopped on. They went upstairs and sat at the back, well away from the other passengers. James finally felt safe.

"Sorry about that," he said breathlessly. "You're not pissed off with me, are you?"

Junior burst out laughing. "That was *mental*. The look on those cops' faces when we lost 'em. Oh man . . ."

"I'm an idiot," James said. "You know what I did? When I put the games in, I must have pushed the foil down the bag so it wasn't covering them over."

"Who cares now?" Junior grinned. "Gimme, gimme, gimme."

James unzipped his pack and pulled out nine PlayStation games. Junior read out the price stickers.

"Forty, forty, twenty-five, thirty-five. How much is that?"

"A hundred and forty."

"Thirty-eight, twenty-four, and three at thirty- five."

"Three hundred and seven quid," James said.

"You add fast," Junior said. "Over three hundred quid's worth of games. That's so cool, we've got to do it again some time."

"I dunno," James said. "I'm not sure if my underwear can take the strain."

• • •

"You're late, James," Zara said. "Dinner's nearly ready."

Kerry and Kyle were sitting at the kitchen table while Zara did frozen lasagna in the oven.

"Sorry," James said.

"You could have rung us," Zara said. "We were all worried."

Kerry looked up. "Where were you? I didn't see you at lunchtime."

"I was around," James said, defensively.

"So, how was school?" Zara asked.

"Oh, you know," James shrugged. "Same old, same old. Boring as hell."

Zara wouldn't have minded that he'd bunked off with Junior, but James didn't want her to find out about the shoplifting and the chase. If cherubs steal something, or make money while they're on a mission, they're supposed either to return the goods or donate them to charity. James had no plans to give away five top PlayStation games after going through so much exertion stealing them.

"How did you get along with Junior?" Zara asked.

"Really good," James said. "He's my sort of person. I reckon we would have ended up mates even if I hadn't tried. Where's Nicole?"

"Doing homework with April Moore and a bunch of other girls," Kyle said.

"Wow," James smiled. "She's a fast worker. How did you two get on with your targets?"

"Erin Moore and her weird friends chucked paper at me and started calling me 'peg-leg' because of my limp," Kerry said miserably.

"Ringo's a swot," Kyle said. "Nice kid, taking his GCSEs very seriously. The thing is, I reckon he's too straight to be involved in his dad's drug business."

"James," Kerry said, "why's there tinfoil sticking out of your backpack?"

"What?" James gasped.

Kerry leaned towards the pack. James whipped it away before she got a chance to see inside.

"You've been up to something," Kerry grinned. "What's in there?"

"Nothing," James said, jumping up from the table. "I better go and um . . . I'll give Lauren a call before dinner's ready."

Kyle and Kerry exchanged looks as James thumped upstairs to his room.

"Tinfoil?" Kerry whispered, not wanting Zara to hear.

"Don't ask me," Kyle shrugged. "But he's been up to something, that's for sure."

CHAPTER 10

PUNCH

It was Friday, after school. James, Kyle, Kerry, and Nicole sat on the living room couches in their school uniforms, drinking cans of Coke. The TV was on but nobody was watching.

James looked at Kyle. "I'm going boxing tonight with Junior. You wanna come?"

"You in a boxing ring," Kerry giggled. "That's something I'd pay money to see."

James clucked. "It's training, stupid. They don't make you fight on the first night."

"I'll pass on getting punched in the head," Kyle said. "I got invited to a party."

"Oh," James said. "Thanks for inviting me."

"It's Ringo Moore and his mates," Kyle said. "Year Ten and Eleven kids. They won't want the likes of you biting their ankles."

"I'm meeting April at the youth club," Nicole said. "The boxing gym is upstairs."

"So, Kerry," James said, breaking into a grin. "I'm going out with Junior Moore tonight. Kyle's partying with Ringo Moore and Nicole's at the youth club with April Moore. What are you and Erin Moore doing?"

"Ha-ha, very funny," Kerry said miserably. "Erin is the biggest geek. There's this student Spanish teacher."

"Miss Perez," James said. "I've got her as well."

"That's her," Kerry said. "Erin and her little friends wound her up so much, they made her run out of the classroom in tears. I felt really sorry for her."

"Yeah," James giggled. "Perez is always crying. My class had her bawling three times on one lesson. It was *soooo* funny."

Kerry looked mad. "James, that's horrible. How must that poor woman feel?"

James shrugged. "Who cares? She's only a teacher."

"You know what, James?" Kerry snapped. "Teachers have feelings the same as anyone else."

"Whatever," James said. "I know you're only angry because you can't get on with Erin and you'll probably get your botty kicked off this mission."

"Oh, shut up, James," Kerry shouted, putting her palm in front of her face. "I spend all day stuck in a class with a bunch of stupid, noisy morons. I don't want to come home and deal with another."

"Touchy, touchy." James giggled.

Kyle gave James a nudge. "Leave it out, eh?"

James realized he'd overdone it. He was getting a filthy look off Nicole as well.

"Sorry, Kerry," James said. "But you were taking the mickey out of me going boxing just a second ago."

Kerry didn't answer. She just scowled into the bottom of her empty Coke can.

"You don't have to sit here all night watching telly, Kerry," Nicole said. "You can come to the youth center with me if you want."

"I don't want your pity, Nicole," Kerry said tersely. "Our mission briefing says if you can't get on with your target, you should try and get involved in KMG through another kid. So, for your information, I won't be sitting in front of the TV. I'll be at the youth center with someone tonight, the same as Nicole and Mohammed Ali over there."

Kerry got off the sofa and stomped up to her room. Kyle reached over and punched James's shoulder.

"What the hell was that for?" James asked, furiously.

"Being an insensitive pig," Kyle said. "You know what a big deal Kerry makes about being the best at everything."

"Jesus," James said, rubbing his arm. "I was only having a laugh. It's not my fault she's so touchy."

"Go up and apologize," Kyle said.

"I better not," James said. "She probably wants to be on her own."

James noticed the look he was getting off Nicole.

"OK then," James huffed, standing up. "I'll go and say sorry."

James went upstairs. Kerry and Nicole's room was at the end of the corridor. As James got closer, he started to bottle it. Kerry had a violent temper and he didn't want to get on the wrong end of it. For the first time ever, James was happy to hear Joshua crying. He leaned into Ewart and Zara's room, making sure they weren't in there, then walked over to the cot and picked the baby up. Joshua rested his head on James's shoulder and changed his bawling to a gentler sucking kind of noise.

"Come on," James said, rocking Joshua gently. "Let's find Mummy."

He went down to the kitchen. Ewart was at the table.

"Cheers for picking him up, James," Ewart said. "Zara's just gone down the shop for some bread."

"Get his bottle warmed up," James said. "I'll take him into the living room. He likes watching the telly."

Ewart smiled at James. "Joshua still won't let Kyle or the girls go near him. You know why I think he likes you?"

James shrugged. "Why?"

"You've got blond hair, the same as me and Zara."

"Maybe," James said.

He carried Joshua through and sat next to Nicole on the sofa.

"Look who's here," Nicole said, grinning and wiggling Joshua's big toe.

Since he'd been on the mission, James had learned something about girls: if you want them to like you, don't worry about buying them gifts, or saying the right thing, or where you take them. What you need to do is grab the nearest brat and stick it on your lap. Nicole, who'd been furious at James a few minutes earlier, shuffled up close to him on the couch.

"You know, James," Nicole beamed, "someday you're gonna make a really good dad."

The stairs leading up to the boxing club had signed photos and newspaper cuttings of boxers James had never heard of on the walls. The door at the top of the stairs creaked and James got a nose full of thirty-degree heat and old sweat. About twenty guys were working out. Dark patches on their clothes, lifting weights, punching bags. James felt awkward, imagining they were all sizing him up, estimating how many milliseconds it would take to punch him out.

A massive guy stopped a set of crunches and started mopping his bald head with a towel.

"New fish?" he asked, looking at James.

James nodded. "I um . . ."

The guy pointed his thumb. "You want the back room, with the other kids. Try not to tread on anyone."

James had to step over gym mats and barbells to get through. The back room was bigger, with twenty-odd boys aged between nine and fourteen working out. Two young coaches stood in a ring up the back, mucking about and taking punches off some little kids. James recognized Junior, Del, and a couple of guys he'd seen around Thornton and at school.

"You Junior's new pal?" a voice asked from behind.

James turned. The guy sat in a plastic chair. He wore tracksuit bottoms and a stained vest. His shoulders were a mat of wiry gray hair. Even though the guy was thirty years past his prime, he still didn't look like a man you wanted to mess with.

"I'm Ken," the guy growled. "If you're here for the night, it's fifty pence."

"Junior said it's cheaper if I get a monthly ticket," James said.

"Fifty pence for tonight," Ken said. "I don't want to rob you. This is too much like hard work for most kids. They don't come through that door more than once or twice. If you're one of the ones who sticks it, I'll take what you've already paid off the monthly pass."

James nodded and dug some coins out of his shorts.

"Go see your friend Junior and try to follow what he does," Ken said. "You're here to train. That means you don't stand around talking. You don't mess around and you don't make jokes. Any kid starts a fight without my say so and I'll give the nod to someone who'll make them sorry. You got that?"

James nodded. "Don't I get coaching or something?"

Ken laughed. "I sit here with my eyes open. Give it a week or so. Follow what the others do. When I think you're ready, I'll get one of the trainees to start you off with a little sparring."

James wandered over to Junior.

"Enjoy the lecture?" Junior asked, grinning.

Junior, Del, and a couple of other guys trained in a group. Everything was a competition: how many push-ups or crunches, how fast you could skip, how many times you could punch the hanging ball in thirty seconds. CHERUB training had made James fit. He could hold his own at everything except skipping, which he'd only ever tried in PE lessons years earlier. Everyone except James got a turn in the ring, either sparring with each other or getting coached by Kelvin and Marcus, the two brutal-looking seventeen-year-olds the club employed as apprentice coaches.

When they were all half-dead, the group piled into the locker room, showered off the sweat, and put on fresh clothes. On their way out, Ken blocked James's way with his leg.

"You coming back?" Ken asked.

"I'd like to," James nodded, still out of breath. "If that's OK."

"You've done some kind of martial arts training, haven't you?"

"Yeah, karate and judo. How could you tell?"

"You're in good shape and you can punch," Ken said, "but a boxer needs fast feet as well. You want to be able to skip a hundred and fifty times a minute. Take this home and practice half an hour a day."

James took the end of a frayed skipping rope. He stuck it in his carrier bag, on top of his damp clothes.

Junior slapped him on the back as they went down the staircase.

"He must think you've got talent, James. I kept coming here for three weeks before he said a word and my dad practically owns the joint."

James couldn't help smiling, though it was hardly surprising he showed promise after all the combat training he'd done at CHERUB.

"You coming down the youth club with me and Del?" Junior asked. "It's packed out with girls, Friday night."

The youth club was on the ground floor, under the gym. It was supposed to be a disco, but the music wasn't very loud and nobody was dancing. James sat with Junior and Del on some slashed-up seats in a dark corner. There were plenty of boys and plenty of girls, but everyone sat in single-sex groups.

"So," Junior said, "which babes are us three studs gonna snap up tonight?"

Del looked at his watch. "None. I'm off to work once I've drunk this."

Del always had money and James thought it probably came from delivering drugs. He straightened up in his seat, sensing an opportunity to get information, but trying not to make it obvious he was prying.

"Work?" he asked. "At this time of night?"

Junior burst out laughing. "Ah . . . The voice of innocence."

"I work for KMG," Del said.

"KM what?" James said.

"Keith Moore's Gang," Del explained. "I deliver coke for Junior's daddy."

"Who wants Coke at this time on a Friday?"

"Not Coca-Cola, you wazzock," Junior said. "Cocaine."

James acted like he was surprised. "Cocaine? Isn't that seriously illegal? You told me your dad was in import export."

"He is," Junior said. "Imports drugs, exports cash."

"Hell." James grinned. "No wonder he's so loaded."

Del went into his backpack. He pulled out a small polythene bag filled with white powder.

"Cocaine," he explained.

James grinned as he took the packet and inspected it.

"Don't let everyone see it, you moron," Del gasped, knocking James's hand out of the air.

"Sorry," James said. "So how much is this?"

"One gram in every bag. They give me ten grams at a time, then they ring me on my mobile and tell me where and when to deliver it."

"How much do you make?"

"Fifteen per cent," Del said. "This is sixty a gram, so I get nine quid. If I work Friday and Saturday evenings, I can easily make a hundred quid. Sometimes though, like at Christmas, you get people loading up for office parties and stuff. I had this one guy who lived two streets away from me. He was buying ten grams at a time. Ninety quid for a ten-minute bike ride. It was beautiful."

"Do you blow all the money?"

Del shook his head. "I used to, but you end up wasting it on junk. Now I only spend twenty pounds a week. I stick the rest in my savings account and when I'm eighteen, I'm gonna buy a ticket and go off backpacking."

James looked at Junior. "So how come you're always broke?"

Del burst out laughing. "This baby's not allowed to go anywhere near drugs."

Junior explained miserably. "My dad's paranoid that he'll get arrested. If I get caught with drugs, it gives the police an excuse to question Dad and search our house."

"That's a shame," James said.

"Tell me about it," Junior said bitterly. "My dad's

a millionaire and half my mates are making a packet selling coke. What have I got? Holes in my jeans and supermarket-brand football boots."

"Can't you do it on the sly?" James asked.

"Won't happen," Junior said. "The word is out. Anyone who gets me or Ringo involved in the drug business will be in serious trouble if my dad cops them."

"So you're stuffed," James laughed. "You reckon there's any chance I can get in on this delivery lark?"

Del shrugged. "I'll go upstairs and have a word with Kelvin if you like. I don't know if he needs anyone right now, but I can try and get him to set you up with a few bags of coke and your own phone."

"I've already got a mobile," James said.

Del shook his head. "You have to use the phone they give you, so the police can't trace it."

"But there's definitely a chance?"

"I haven't got a clue," Del said. "All I can do is put a word in."

"Thanks," James said.

Del stood up. "Anyway, I've got a nine o'clock delivery, so I better dive home and pick up my bike. I'll see you two hard-up losers at school on Monday."

James smiled. "Yeah, see you."

"I'll be thinking about you sweating away on your bike in a couple of hours," Junior said. "When I've got my hand up some girl's shirt."

"In your dreams, Junior," Del shouted as he walked towards the exit.

James shook his head, grinning in false disbelief. "I can't believe your dad is a drug dealer."

"Who cares?" Junior said. "Do you want to try and get off with someone?"

They both glanced around.

"Look at that bird sitting by the Coke machine," Junior gasped. "I've not seen her here before."

James turned around. He'd guessed it was Nicole before he even saw her.

"She's reserved for me," he said. "That's my stepsister."

"You can't get off with your sister, you pervert."

"*Step*sister," James said. "We're not blood relatives. Why don't you go for the one sitting next to her? She looks like a right dog."

"That's my twin, you cheeky git," Junior said. "And you better not call April a dog again, unless you want a slap."

April had her hair done differently from the surveillance photos. James hadn't recognized her.

"I tell you who else is good looking," Junior said. "Pity she's already with someone."

"Who?" James asked.

"At the table behind our sisters. That Chinese-looking girl, with long black hair. She's well tasty."

James peered over. All he could see was the back of the girl's head. Then she turned and he saw her in profile.

"That's my other stepsister," James gasped. "That's Kerry. Who's that she's with?"

"Dinesh Singh. He lives up my road. His dad runs a firm that makes those microwave meals for supermarkets. So, you want to go over?" Junior asked. "I'll go for Nicole and you can have a run at April. She's not too picky, to be honest with you, so even you might stand a chance."

"Jesus," James said, feeling like his head was going to burst with jealousy. "Dinesh just put his arm around her."

"What's the problem? Do you fancy all your sisters, or something?"

"It's just, Kerry's really young."

"How old is she?" Junior asked.

"Twelve."

Junior burst out laughing. "We're twelve."

"Yeah," James said. "But we're in Year Eight, she's only a Year Seven."

"If you ask me," Junior said, "it's none of your business what your stepsister is up to. But if it makes you feel better, Dinesh is a weed. Just go over there and slap him one."

"I've a good mind to," James said.

This was a total lie. Kerry would break him into fifty million pieces if he even thought about it.

"Anyway," Junior said, "I'm not sitting here all night. Are you gonna ask April out or not?"

"You go," James shrugged. "I'm not in the mood."

April Moore was OK-looking and being friendly with her would be good for the mission, but James couldn't get Kerry out of his head.

Junior pulled up a chair next to Nicole and started chatting her up. James sat by himself and kept glancing over to see what Kerry was up to with Dinesh. He realized he couldn't sit on his own all night being jealous of Dinesh and decided to go across to April, but company arrived before he got a chance.

It was Kelvin and Marcus, the two coaches he'd seen at boxing club. They were both over six feet tall and solid muscle. They sat either side of James, squashing him even though there was plenty of room.

"I'm Kelvin," the black one said. He pulled a mobile phone out of his pocket and stuck it on the table. "Del tells me you're interested in doing deliveries."

James nodded. "I could do with the cash."

"Del said you're a solid kid," Kelvin continued. "What you gonna say if the cops pick you up for holding drugs?"

"Nothing, of course."

Kelvin nodded. "That's right. You don't know us, you ain't never seen us. Tell 'em you found the drugs in a bush and stick to that story no matter how they try to mess with you. You know what happens if you grass us up?"

"I get beaten up?"

"Cut up, more likely," Kelvin said. "And that's just for starters. They'll send people round your house and start on your family. Smash the furniture, batter your mum and dad. Del said you have two sisters, they won't look so pretty after we finish with them. So you better understand, James, even if there's some massive cop threatening to lock you up and throw away the key, you better keep your trap shut."

"Don't worry," James said. "I'm no grass."

"You got a good bike?"

"It's pretty crap actually."

"Good," Kelvin said. "You don't want nothing fancy or you'll get mugged. How cool are your parents about you being out late?"

"It's OK until about half-ten."

"Marcus, set the kid up with three bags. I think we'll give him a trial run."

Marcus got three bags of cocaine out of his tracksuit.

"I want you on call school nights," Kelvin said. "Monday through Thursday. That means you keep your phone switched on and you're always ready to go. We don't want to hear that you're grounded, or you're busy doing something. Whenever they call, you jump to it."

"Can't I do weekends?" James asked. "Del reckons that's when you make the real money."

"Everyone starts at the bottom with weekday deliveries and no regular customers. The powers that be will see how you do. If you're reliable and you deliver fast, you get moved on to better paid work. Questions?"

"I've only got three bags of coke, how do I get more?" James asked.

"There's people at your school. We'll arrange for you to meet up with them when you need to."

"What if someone tries to rob me or something?" James asked.

"If you lose the stuff or get mugged, that's your problem and you owe us for what you lost. If the customer tries any funny business, don't sweat it. Give the customer what they want and some of our muscle will show them the error of their ways."

Kelvin and his silent pal got up from the table.

"One last thing," Kelvin said. "If you're out late, you'll get hassled sooner or later. Never carry more coke than you need to. A lot of kids carry knives, but if you ask me, you're safer throwing the stuff on the ground and legging it."

CHAPTER 11

KITCHEN

James ended up walking home from the youth club with Nicole. He didn't feel too good: a mix of nerves about his delivery job and seeing Kerry with Dinesh. They ended up in the kitchen, drinking glasses of milk. Zara and Ewart were already in bed.

"Did Kerry say anything to you about this Indian guy?" James asked.

Nicole grinned. "Jealous, are we, James?"

"No. It's just we're good friends and I like to look out for her."

"Can you smell something?" Nicole asked.

"No," James said, looking at the bottom of his trainers.

"I can," Nicole sniffed. "You know what it is?"

"What?"

"Bullshit."

"Very funny, Nicole."

"James, you *totally* fancy Kerry," Nicole said. "Why don't you just admit it and ask her out?"

"Give us a break, we're just friends. How did you get on with Junior?"

"He's not bad-looking," Nicole said. "But the kid could seriously use some mouthwash."

James laughed.

"So," Nicole said, "if you're not as keen on Kerry as everyone says, what do you think of me?"

James looked uneasy. "You're a nice person, Nicole."

"That wasn't what I asked."

"Well . . ." James squirmed. "Actually, yeah . . . You've got a nice body and that."

"You're not so bad yourself," Nicole said, leaning against the kitchen cabinet. "Come over here."

"Why?" James asked.

"Kiss us."

James laughed. He leaned in and pecked Nicole on the cheek.

"Is that all you've got?" Nicole asked.

The second time James moved in, Nicole wrapped her arms around his back and they started snogging.

The door clicked open and they burst apart. James crashed into the kitchen table as Kerry stepped into the room.

"Hello, hello," Kerry grinned. "Did I break something up?"

"No," James gasped. "It's nothing. We're just drinking some milk before we go up to bed. You want some?"

"Cheers," Kerry said.

James got a glass off the draining board and poured out some milk.

"Anyway," he said, stretching into a yawn. "It's gone eleven. I might as well go up to bed."

Kerry called him back.

"What?" he asked.

"You better wash the lipstick off your face," she said. "Unless you want it all over your pillowcase."

James walked up the stairs in a confused state. He fancied Nicole, but he didn't like Kerry knowing about it.

Kyle was in the top bunk when James got to their room.

"Some party animal you are," James said. "Home before eleven."

"Put the light on if you want," Kyle said, sitting up in bed. "I'm not tired. It was a decent party, but one of the neighbors complained and the cops came and broke it up. How was boxing?"

James explained about everything that had happened. He tried to make it sound matter of fact, but the Kerry and Dinesh thing was getting to him and he blurted out something he'd never admitted to anyone.

"Kerry kind of . . . Sometimes I lie awake at night thinking about her. She's really, I mean . . . She's not stunning . . . Not the sexiest girl in the world or anything, but there's something about her that goes through me like a big warm whoosh."

"You've *got* to ask her out," Kyle said.

"But I want her to carry on being my mate. What if we end up rowing and hating each other?"

"You've got to risk it," Kyle said.

"What if she doesn't even want to go out with me?"

"Look," Kyle said firmly. "You just got off with Nicole, so you should be excited about that; but all you're talking about is Kerry, Kerry, Kerry."

"What do I say to her?"

"Try the truth," Kyle said. "Tell Kerry how much you like her and then it's up to her."

"Maybe you're right," James said. "I'll say something to her first chance I get. I mean, you never know, it might even work out between us."

"That's right," Kyle said.

James clicked out the light and climbed under his duvet.

"Kyle, what I don't get is: How come I'm taking all this advice off you when I've never seen you with a girl?"

"I've never had a girlfriend," Kyle said.

James was surprised by the honesty. He'd expected Kyle to be defensive.

"Seriously?" James asked.

"Yep," Kyle said.

"But there's loads of girls at campus. I'm sure I could fix you up with one."

"I don't want a girlfriend," Kyle said.

"What?" James asked. "Did a girl hurt you really badly or something? Is it like one of those romantic films my mum used to watch?"

"No, James. I don't like girls."

"What, you mean you only like old birds? Like, in their twenties or something?"

Kyle laughed. "No. I like boys."

James shot up off his mattress. "Piss off you do."

"James, I'm gay."

"No bloody way," James said. "This is another Kyle wind-up."

"I'd appreciate it if you didn't go shouting it off to the whole world, but you were honest with me about Kerry, so there you go. It's the truth, whether you want to believe it or not."

"Wow," James said. "Do you swear that you're gay, on your life?"

"Yes," Kyle said.

"Wow," James said.

He felt like his head was going to explode. He already had too much going on in there, with Kerry and Nicole and the drug dealing.

"Who else knows?"

"I've told a few people," Kyle said.

"I can't believe it," James gasped. "You don't seem anything like a poof."

"Actually, I'd prefer it if you didn't call me that."

"Oh, right . . . Sorry."

James lay awake the whole night, listening to the airplanes rumbling over the house. He got up with the sun, had a shower, got a bowl of Shreddies and made himself tea. When the newspaper dropped through the letterbox, he read the sports page at the kitchen table, but it was like the words were going through his eyes and bouncing straight off his brain. All he could think about was Kerry with Dinesh and Kyle being gay.

Kerry and Nicole came downstairs. James didn't like that they were together; it made his paranoid side imagine that the two of them were working together and scheming against him.

"I'm making bacon sarnies," Nicole said. "You want one, James?"

"Mmm," James said. "Cheers."

Kerry sat on the opposite side of the table and poured orange juice. Kyle had asked him not to tell people he was gay, but James was practically bursting. He had to tell someone. It felt too big to keep locked up.

"I spoke to Kyle last night," James said.

Kerry looked up from the color supplement. "And?"

"He told me something. It's totally mind-blowing, but you can't spread it around."

"Whatever," Kerry said. "Spill the beans."

"Kyle told me he's gay."

Kerry smiled a bit. "Well duh. Of course Kyle's gay."

Nicole looked away from the spattering bacon. "It took you *this* long to work out Kyle's gay?" she said.

"He said he'd only ever told a couple of people."

Kerry smiled. "You must have at least suspected."

"No. Why would anyone suspect Kyle's gay?"

"Well, dingus," Kerry said. "He's always clean and neatly dressed. Unlike most of you guys, his room isn't covered in disgusting pictures of half-naked women and nobody has ever seen him within five kilometers of a girl. I mean, short of walking around with a plaque on his forehead saying 'Gay Boy,' how obvious do you want it to be?"

"But I share a room with him," James gasped. "He sees me naked."

"So what?" Kerry said. "I've seen you naked."

"Well, he's gay."

"You think he fancies you?" Kerry giggled. "I wouldn't flatter yourself."

Nicole turned away from the frying pan with a big smile on her face. "Come to think of it, I've seen him eyeing you up, James."

"Shut up," James said. "It's not funny. It's disgusting."

"You think being gay is disgusting?" Kerry tutted. "I thought Kyle was your friend."

"He is," James said. "But . . . I'm not comfortable with the whole gay thing."

"Do us some bread, Kerry," Nicole said. "Bacon doesn't take long."

Kerry got the loaf off the cabinet and started buttering.

"You know, James," she said, "it must have been hard for Kyle to admit something like that to you. Especially when you're always calling people faggots and queers."

Nicole moved the pan off the heat and helped Kerry make up the sandwiches.

"I heard that one person in ten is gay," Nicole said. "So it's not that unusual. If you think about it, every football team probably has one gay player on it."

Kerry giggled. "I wonder who the gay one at Arsenal is? Actually, the big clubs have loads of players and reserve teams. There's probably at least four or five."

James stood up from the table and boiled over. "That's not funny," he shouted. "There's no such thing as a gay Arsenal player."

Kerry slammed James's plate on the table in front of him. "Sit down and eat that," she said angrily. "Kyle's your friend, so you better be supportive. If you say anything that upsets him, I'll show you the meaning of uncomfortable."

CHAPTER 12

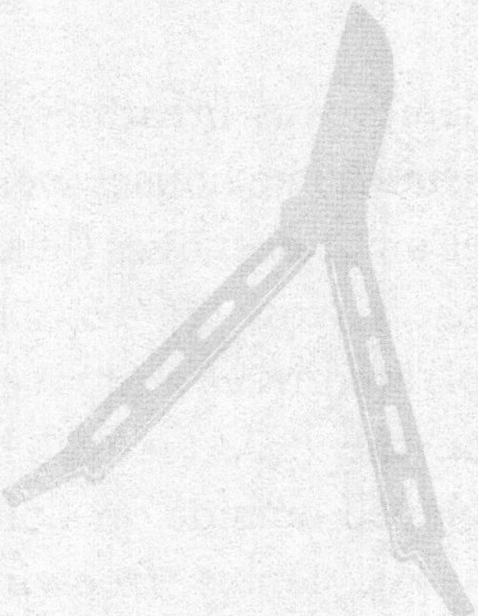

SUBURBAN

It was Wednesday evening, and James was on his third night making deliveries. His phone went off a couple of times a night; always the same calm female voice on the other end. James had no idea who or where she was, only that she seemed motherly, was happy to give directions, and always signed off with the same words: "You be careful out there, young man."

The deliveries were never more than a few kilometers' ride. The job would be nasty in the winter, but on sunny early autumn evenings it was no hardship. James had imagined his customers would be scraggy-haired women in night clothes holding screaming babies, or wild-eyed men with beards and motorbikes, but it was nothing like that.

• • •

James was breathless by the time he found the housing estate. The houses were brand new. There was a developer's signpost over the entrance: LAST FEW HOMES REMAINING—PRICES FROM £245,000. The houses were neat, with newly planted trees and recent-plate Fords and Toyotas parked on the driveways. There was no traffic and little kids played outside on skateboards and microscooters.

As James freewheeled down a gentle slope, he noticed the streets were named after musical instruments: Trumpet Close, Cornet Avenue, Bassoon Road.

He turned into Trombone Villas, the most exclusive street in the development. The gray tarmac became red and the cars on the driveways changed to Range Rovers and Mercedes. He was looking for Stonehaus, and like millions of delivery people before him, James had learned to hate house names. With numbers, you knew that 56 was after 48, and 21 was on the other side of the road. Stonehaus could be anywhere. He found it after a search, the signpost hidden behind a BMWX5 and a Grand Voyager. He wheeled up the driveway and pressed the bell, which sounded off in a tinny version of "When the Saints Go Marching In."

A boy ran down the hallway and opened the door. He was eight or nine, wearing the long gray socks and fancy uniform of a fee-paying school. At this time of day, the kid was in a state, with his bare chest showing under his unbuttoned gray shirt.

"Daddy!" the kid shouted.

A man holding a whiskey tumbler hurried down the stairs, while the kid ran back to the TV.

"HEYYYYY there," the man said, trying to sound cooler than the fat balding man he really was. "Four grams, wasn't it?"

James nodded. "Two hundred and forty quid." He went into his backpack and got the four bags of cocaine. The man peeled five fifties off a roll of notes.

"I don't have change," James said.

Del had taught James to pretend never to have change. If the customer kicked up a fuss, you miraculously remembered you had money from a previous delivery in your backpack; but you were hoping the average middle-class coke snorter didn't want to keep a drug dealer hanging about on his doorstep and simply said:

"No worries, son, keep the change for yourself."

James smiled and tucked the money in his pocket. "Thanks, mate," he said. "Enjoy yourself."

The man closed the door. James couldn't help smiling. He'd just earned thirty-six pounds commission, plus a ten-pound tip, for a half-hour bike ride.

It was gone nine when James got home. Everyone was waiting for him in the living room. Two weeks into the mission, Ewart and Zara wanted a conference to see what everyone was doing and to work out the best way forward.

"Sorry I kept you waiting," James said. "But I've got to deliver when I get a call."

Zara had rearranged the sofas in the living room and brought in kitchen chairs, so everyone could sit facing each other. James squeezed on to a sofa between Kyle and Nicole.

"OK," Ewart said. "I want each of you to say what you think you've achieved so far. Keep it short, you've all got to get up for school tomorrow."

"Nicole," Zara said, "why don't you start?"

Nicole cleared her throat. "You pretty much know. I've been getting on OK with April. She knows what her dad does for a living, but keeps out of it. I've been to Keith Moore's house a few times doing homework and stuff and I've met him; just exchanging hellos and that."

"That's a good start," Ewart nodded. "Do you think you can carry on getting regular access to the house?"

"Sure," Nicole said. "April likes having the girls round and showing off her giant bedroom. She likes to think of herself as the leader of our group. I'm going to a sleepover there this Saturday."

"Have you had much chance to nose around the house?" Zara asked.

"I thought I'd play it safe to start with," Nicole said. "You've got all the notes and stuff I copied from the cork board in the kitchen."

"Do you think you could place minicameras and listening devices around the house?"

"Easily," Nicole nodded. "The house is big, so if anyone asks what I'm doing, I can pretend I got lost and wandered into the wrong room."

"Excellent," Ewart said. "Could you get a nose inside Keith's office?"

"I doubt it, he's usually in there. The one time he was out, I tried and the door was locked. I suppose I could take my lock gun."

"No way," Ewart said. "If someone sees you with a lock gun, it will put you in serious danger and blow this whole operation."

"The next best target would be Keith's bedroom," Zara said. "He's the kind of guy who gets phone calls at all hours, so you can be sure he takes important calls in bed. Have a good snoop and put in a listening device."

"Why can't you tap the phones from out in the street?" James asked.

"They've been tapped for years and Keith knows it," Ewart said. "A serious villain like Keith Moore uses mobiles or face-to-face meetings. He'll pick up a pay-as-you-go mobile and use it for a day or two, then switch to another one before we know he's got it. He also speaks using code words, and uses something to disguise the sound of his voice, so you could never go into court and prove it was him saying what he said. Our only chance of getting useful information is to have a microphone in the actual room where Keith is talking."

"So, Nicole," Zara said. "That's your target. Get a microphone in Keith's bedroom and maybe a few others around the house. The risks are low, because nobody is going to suspect that a twelve-year-old girl is planting a microphone, but you should still be careful."

"OK," Ewart said. "Good work, Nicole, keep it up. Do you want to go next, James?"

James nodded. "Me and Junior are top mates, bunking off and going to boxing and stuff."

"How much do you think Junior knows about his dad's business?"

"He comes out with stuff," James said. "He's curious

about what his dad does. If any one of Keith's kids knows anything worth knowing, I'd bet on Junior."

"And the deliveries," Zara said. "How are they going?"

"Good," James said. "It's mostly nice houses and offices I'm going to. I was worried at first, but it's like having a newspaper round, only with decent wages."

Ewart spoke. "The mission briefing mentioned that kids around here aren't just delivering small amounts of drugs to individuals, but are getting deeper into the organization and delivering in bulk to dealers from other parts of the country. Have you seen any sign of that?"

James shrugged. "Some kids are making serious money, so it wouldn't surprise me."

"Your number one job is to find out how they're making that money," Zara said. "Make friends, ask questions, and keep pestering until you get an answer. Remember to keep safe when you're out on deliveries. If you think a situation is dangerous, pull out and we'll clean up the mess afterwards. We'd rather abandon the whole mission than risk one of you guys getting hurt."

"Kyle," Ewart said. "Your turn."

"Ring's a bust if you ask me," Kyle said. "He's a straight-up guy, though he smokes a fair bit of cannabis. I'm getting in with his crowd. There are drug dealers at their parties and plenty of kids using all kinds of drugs. I might get some information from one of them, but I'm not hopeful."

Ewart and Zara looked at each other.

"Just keep trying, Kyle," Zara said. "That's all you can do until we think of something else."

"So," Ewart said. "Last but not least, Kerry."

"Me and Erin can't stand each other," Kerry said. "She's weird and immature and her friends sit in a group and don't talk to anyone else."

"What did you do to try and get in with them?" Ewart asked.

"We're just so different," Kerry explained. "I don't think we'll ever get on."

"The thing is, Kerry," Ewart said, "you've been trained to work out what type of person your target is and then act in a way that makes them your friend. If Erin mucks about and upsets teachers, then that's what you should do, even if you think it's silly and immature. If Erin swears and bunks off, you should do that too. I know you can't guarantee forming a friendship with a target, but I don't ever expect to hear a cherub say they're too different from someone to get along."

Kerry looked angry. "You'd need a world-class psychiatrist to work out Erin. She's part of a weird little clique and they shut everyone else out."

Zara spoke. "If you haven't hit it off with Erin by now, I doubt it's ever going to happen. I can't see much reason for you to stay on this mission. We can send you back to campus and say you've moved back to live with your real parents, or something."

Kerry looked close to crying. "I don't want to be sent back. I'm trying to get involved with someone else, like it says in the briefing."

"I can't see much point," Ewart said. "If you were a boy, you might be recruited as a courier, but that's all done through the boxing club, which is boys only."

Zara nodded, agreeing with her husband. "I'm sorry this mission didn't work out, Kerry, but don't be disappointed. Think of it as a learning experience."

"Let me stay," Kerry begged. "There's a boy in my class called Dinesh. I'm getting friendly with him and I think he knows something."

James put his wrist up to his lips and made a loud smooching noise.

"Grow up, James," Zara said wearily. "Kerry, what is it you think Dinesh might know?"

"His dad runs a company that makes microwave meals for supermarkets. When I was talking to him about Erin, he mentioned that his father has dealings with Keith Moore."

Zara didn't look too impressed. "Keith is a wealthy man, Kerry. He has business dealings with lots of people."

"But it's the way Dinesh said it," Kerry explained. "It's like Dinesh had a bad taste in his mouth. It might be nothing, but I'd like a chance to dig deeper."

Ewart and Zara looked at each other.

"*Please* don't send me back to campus," Kerry groveled. "Just give me a few more days."

"You're fond of this boy Dinesh, aren't you?" Zara said. "Is that the real reason you're so keen to stay?"

"I'm a professional," Kerry stormed. "It's not because I've fallen for some boy. I've got a hunch and I'm asking you guys to show faith in me."

"OK, Kerry," Zara said gently. "There's no need to get upset. Ewart and I will postpone our decision on sending you back to campus until next week. How does that sound?"

Kerry nodded. "Thank you."

"Anything else, before we all go off to bed?" Ewart asked.

"Yeah," James said. "It's Lauren's birthday this weekend, is it still OK if she visits?"

"No problem," Zara said. "If she meets up with any of the local kids, you'll have to tell them she's your cousin. It'll seem weird if you suddenly have a sister popping out of nowhere."

"If that's everything," Ewart said, "let's all get some shut-eye."

With only one bathroom, there was a scrum over the toothbrushes. Kerry stayed on the couch sulking and James thought he'd give the others a few minutes to fight it out.

"You're really good at this," Kerry said, looking at James.

"What?" he asked.

"Missions. You go into a room and everyone likes you. Good old James, even the baby likes you. I study hard and I get some of the best marks on campus, but I'm rubbish out on missions where it really counts."

"Come on, Kerry," James said. "You're being way too hard on yourself. This is your first important mission. Nobody expects you to be brilliant."

"And it'll be my last big mission, after this disaster," Kerry said. "I'll probably spend the rest of my CHERUB career doing mundane security tests and recruitment work."

James moved across to the other couch, next to Kerry. "I've been meaning to talk to you," he said.

"Talk about what?"

"We haven't been getting on that well since this mission started," James said. "But you still like me, don't you?"

"Of course I like you," Kerry said, breaking into a smile. "You're one of my best friends."

James decided to be bold and put his arm around Kerry's back. She smiled and rested her head against his shoulder.

"You've done all you can on this mission," he said. "And there's no way they're not gonna give you another shot at a big mission. With your fighting skills and the five billion languages you speak, who'll be able to turn you down?"

Kerry smiled. "For someone who acts like a moron half the time, you can be a really nice guy sometimes."

"Thanks," James grinned.

He thought about starting the speech he had prepared in his head, telling Kerry how kissing Nicole was a one-off and how he liked her a hundred times more than any other girl and wanted to be her boyfriend. But Kerry still looked upset. It wasn't the right moment.

CHAPTER 19

VISIT

One of the CHERUB staff dropped Lauren off on Saturday morning. James was barely out of bed when he heard the doorbell.

"Happy birthday," he said, giving his sister a hug. "You made double figures, the big one zero."

Lauren smiled. "I missed you, James . . . for some strange reason."

They walked inside. Everyone was wandering between the kitchen and living room, munching on triangles of toast. Joshua was shuffling down the hallway on his bum. Lauren had never seen him before.

"OOOH," she said. "Aren't you cute? What's your name?"

Joshua gave Lauren an odd look, as if to say, "Oh God, not another kid," and started bawling for Zara.

"Hey, Ewart," James shouted, "there goes your theory that Joshua likes anyone with blond hair."

Lauren wandered into the living room, threw off her bomber jacket, and sat on the couch. Kerry and Kyle wished her happy birthday.

"So," Lauren asked, "where's all my prezzies?"

"Actually," James said, "I haven't got you one yet."

"Typical," Lauren huffed.

"Now I'm a bona fide drug delivery boy, I thought you might like to spend my ill-gotten gains." James burrowed down his jeans, pulled out a fistful of scrunched-up bank notes and dumped them in Lauren's lap.

Lauren grinned. "How much is this?" She straightened out the notes and started counting. "Twenty, forty, sixty, eighty, a hundred, and ten, fifteen. Wow . . . How long did it take you to make a hundred and fifteen pounds?"

"Four nights," James said. "The only thing is, if you want me to take you shopping you'll have to pay my bus fare. I've only got sixty pence left."

"Is there a Gap near here?" Lauren asked eagerly. "I want some new jeans. And a Claire's Accessories? If there is, I can get those cool black hair scrunchies like Bethany's got."

"Can't you just use an elastic band?" James asked.

Lauren ignored her brother and glanced at her watch. "What time do the shops open?"

"Calm down, you idiot," James said. "The money's still gonna be there in a couple of hours. Why don't you go in the kitchen, get some toast and say hello to Zara and the others."

"Whatever," Lauren said. "But let's go early. The shops get really busy on Saturday."

Zara dropped the kids at the Reeve Center. James hoped none of the security guards remembered him.

"Why are you wearing those sunglasses?" Lauren asked.

James shrugged. "Am I? I forgot to take them off."

"You look a right twit," Kerry said.

"It doesn't have anything to do with the five PlayStation games you've got stuffed under your bed, does it?" Kyle asked.

"What were you doing spying under my bed?" James asked indignantly.

"Remember Monday, before school?" Kyle asked.

"No."

Kyle mocked James's voice: "I can't find my PE shirt, Kyle. Will you help us look for it?"

"Oh yeah," James said, "that."

"So let me guess," Kyle said. "You don't want to go anywhere too near Gameworld either."

"But if he stole them as part of a mission, he's allowed, isn't he?" Lauren asked.

"He's supposed to give the proceeds of any crime to charity," Kerry explained.

"Well he should give them to charity then," Lauren said. "You're not on this mission to make a profit, James."

"Does that include the birthday money in your pocket?" James asked.

"Oh," Lauren gasped.

"Yeah," James giggled. "That shut you up, didn't it?"

Normally, going around the girly shops would have driven James mad, but being the big brother treating his sister felt good. Lauren, who wouldn't be seen dead in a skirt, got two hooded sweatshirts in the Gap, a pair of faded jeans, and some silver stud earrings. She treated everyone to lunch in the food court and even got James a pair of novelty socks as a thank-you. He was never going to wear the ghastly things, but it was a nice moment when she gave them to him.

After lunch, Kerry went off to meet Dinesh. She told James to give Zara a message that she wouldn't be back until after dinner. Kerry being with Dinesh pissed James off, but he didn't want to spoil Lauren's birthday, so he tried not to think about it.

When they got home, Zara had ordered a fancy cake. The icing was camouflage green and there was a miniature assault course built out of marzipan, with a climbing tower, a water jump, and toy soldiers running around. The iced message around the edge said HAPPY BIRTHDAY LAUREN & GOOD LUCK IN TRAINING.

Joshua thought the cake was a toy and kept lunging out of Ewart's lap towards it. After Lauren had blown out her candles, everyone sat around the table, cracking up at the huge mess Joshua made with his tiny piece of cake.

Lauren was tired out by half-nine and James decided to go up to bed with her. She started off with a sleeping bag on the floor, but she decided it was uncomfortable and climbed in with James. She'd always gotten into his bed when they were little, but they'd grown since those days.

"This is ridiculous," James said, wriggling up to the wall so she had more room.

"I'm still scared about training," Lauren said quietly. "I don't even see the point of it."

"You'll understand after you've done it," James said. "Training's horrible, so when something tough happens on a mission, instead of being scared, you remember that you've been through worse and you can handle it."

"Sometimes," Lauren said, "just thinking about it make me feel like puking."

"The fear is worse before training starts," James said. "Once you're there, you're too worn out to think."

There was a knock on the door.

"Yeah," James shouted. "We're awake."

Zara pushed the door open and stuck her head in.

"James, when Kerry left you earlier, did she say if she was going anywhere after she left Dinesh's?"

"No," James said.

"I rang their house," Zara said. "Dinesh said Kerry left before eight. She ought to be home by now."

"Did you try her mobile?" James asked.

"That's the first thing I did. I even sent a text."

"Maybe we should go out looking," Lauren said.

"I wouldn't panic yet," Zara said. "She'll probably turn up. You two get some sleep and try not to worry."

A mobile woke James up. He'd forgotten Lauren was asleep next to him and bumped into her as he sat up.

"That's your tasteless ring tone," he said, giving her a kick. "I bet it's that idiot Bethany."

Lauren got out of bed, flicked on the light and found her phone inside her jacket. James looked at his clock. It was gone midnight.

"Hello?" Lauren answered. "Kerry, *wow*. Everyone's looking for you. . . . Hang on, yeah, James is here."

James snatched the Nokia off Lauren.

"Kerry?"

"Oh, thank God," Kerry said. "Why did you switch your phone off?"

"It's probably gone flat," James said.

"I couldn't get an answer from Kyle, or Nicole either. I tried Lauren as a last resort."

"Where the hell are you?" James asked. "Zara's going frantic. She's sitting downstairs waiting for you to get in."

"I'm outside Thunderfoods. I need a huge favor."

"What's Thunderfoods?" James asked.

"Dinesh's dad's company," Kerry explained. "I think I'm on to something, but I need you and one of the others to ride out here and give me a hand breaking in."

"Why don't you explain everything to Ewart or Zara?" James said. "They'll know what to do."

"Because if I'm wrong, I'll look like an idiot and they'll boot me back to campus."

James couldn't refuse. After all, he spent half his life telling Kerry to be more relaxed about rules.

"OK," he said. "What is it you want?"

"I'd like Nicole or Kyle to come as well," Kerry said.

"Nicole's at her sleepover. Kyle's out partying."

"But I'm here," Lauren said, sounding excited.

James looked at his sister. "No way, you're not trained."

"It's better if there's three of us to search," Kerry said. "But two is OK. I need you to bring some stuff: torches, your lock gun, your digital camera, and some beer."

"Where the hell can I get beer at this time of night? Even if there *was* some somewhere, I'm too young to buy it."

"There's a few cans in the bottom of our fridge," Kerry said. "Sneak one out."

"What do you need beer for, anyway?" James asked.

"James," Kerry snapped, "I don't have time for two hundred questions. Get the stuff, get on a bike and ride your butt out here."

James took down directions and ended the call.

"What's happening?" Lauren asked.

"God knows why," James said, "but Kerry wants to break into some food factory. She doesn't want Ewart or Zara to know what she's doing in case she's wrong about whatever it is she thinks is going on."

He stepped into some tracksuit bottoms and trainers.

"I'll go get the beer for you," Lauren said.

"Thanks."

Lauren crept down to the kitchen, while James churned through the mess under his bed and got his lock gun and camera. He grabbed Kyle's camera in case they needed two and took Lauren's phone because his was flat.

Lauren came back with the cold beer.

"Thanks," James said. "It's gonna be well hard, sneaking my bike out of the garage without Ewart or Zara noticing."

Lauren started putting on clothes.

"What do you think you're doing?" James asked. "You're not coming. No way."

"Kerry asked for a third person."

"You're not trained."

"I'll ride along," Lauren said. "If Kerry doesn't want me, I'll look after the bikes."

James knew how stubborn Lauren could be. He didn't have the time or energy to argue.

"Fine," he said. "But don't think I'm taking the rap for you if we get in trouble."

"I'm ten years old," Lauren said proudly. "I can make my own decisions."

CHAPTER 14

CURRY

There wasn't much traffic, but what there was drove dangerously fast. It took twenty minutes to ride across to the industrial park. Thunderfoods had a full car park and lights on everywhere. The factory worked 24/7, sending out truckloads of chilled pastas and curries to supermarkets.

Kerry led them to an alleyway between two warehouses.

"Are you sure you want to do this, Lauren?" she asked. "We could get in serious trouble if we're caught."

"If you want me to help, I'm up for it," Lauren said.

"So what's this about?" James asked.

"I got more information from Dinesh," Kerry explained.

"It's amazing what you can wheedle out of a boy if he think you're up for a snog."

"Did you snog him?" Lauren asked.

Kerry laughed. "No chance."

James was relieved. It was worth being dragged out of bed at midnight just to hear that.

"Anyway," Kerry said, "Dinesh doesn't get on with his dad. He reckons Mr. Singh is a hypocrite when he tells him to behave and do his homework, when he's a crook himself. So I go: 'How is your dad a crook?' And Dinesh started explaining how his dad nearly went bankrupt and KMG bailed him out. I said I didn't believe him. Dinesh tells me there's a storage building at the back of Thunderfoods' production plant. He says he's been inside and seen bags of cocaine. Security seems pretty lax: I've already sneaked right up to the warehouse door, but I can't get inside without my lock gun."

"What if there's a security system?" James asked.

"There is," Kerry said smugly. "You need a swipe card."

She pulled a plastic card out of her shorts. "I nicked this one off Mr. Singh."

"And what about the beer?" Lauren asked.

"We need a cover story," Kerry explained. "If we get caught, we act like kids who got drunk and decided to cause some mischief."

Kerry took the beer off Lauren. She pulled the tab and swallowed a few mouthfuls, then dribbled some down her T-shirt.

"It's more believable if we've got the smell of drink on our clothes and breath."

James took the can off Kerry and did the same. Lauren hated the taste and spat hers in the gravel. "I don't want to get beer on my new top," she said.

"Give us," James said.

He snatched the can off Lauren, poured most of it on the floor and splashed the dregs over her hair.

"OK," Kerry said. "Don't forget to act drunk."

They staggered through the Thunderfoods car park, keeping behind the cars. Then it was over a stretch of lawn to the side door of the warehouse. James handed Kerry his lock gun.

"You're quicker than me," he said.

Kerry fiddled with the lock, while James and Lauren sat in the grass yawning. It was an eight-lever deadbolt, one of the trickiest kinds to pick.

"You want me to try?" James asked.

Kerry sounded edge. "You won't do it. It needs a different attachment."

She unscrewed the back of James's lock gun. There were nine different-shaped picks inside and it was tough to tell them apart in the dark.

"This one or bust," Kerry said, clicking a different pick on to the gun.

She rattled about for another half minute.

"Finally," she sighed, pushing the door open.

The alarm pipped until she swiped the security card. They couldn't turn the light on in case someone saw it through the windows. It felt spooky, shining their torch beams around the cavernous black space. The racks of metal shelving were filled with sacks and tins of ingredients for the factory next door.

"Maybe that's how they get the cocaine into the country," James whispered. "Disguised as curry powder or something."

"No," Kerry said. "Dinesh described clear bags filled with white powder. And he said KMG people came and did something with it upstairs."

"Kerry," James said, "I hate to say this, but maybe your little boyfriend is just trying to impress you. This building doesn't even have an upstairs."

"We should split up," Kerry said, deliberately ignoring James. "There's a lot of shelving to cover."

They each took a row of shelves and started working along, searching for the white powder. The shelves went up ten meters. You'd need a forklift to access the higher bays.

Lauren whispered to Kerry between the rows of shelves. "Come look at this."

Kerry dashed over. Lauren's torch shone on a few clear polythene sacks filled with white powder.

"Borax," Lauren said. "It's what you mix with pure cocaine to make the weaker stuff they sell on the street."

"How do *you* know that, Miss Smarty-Pants?" James asked.

"I read your mission briefing," Lauren said casually.

James tutted. "Lauren, do you know how much trouble you could have got in if you'd been caught reading someone else's mission briefing?"

Lauren laughed. "Less than the amount you'd have been in for leaving a secret briefing lying on your bathroom floor."

"James," Kerry gasped, "you're not even supposed

to take briefings out of the mission preparation rooms."

"I know," James said, shrugging. "But I usually smuggle a few bits to read while I'm on the toilet."

Kerry took photos of the borax.

"So, Keith Moore stores his borax here," James said. "There's nothing illegal about borax. Mr. Singh will just say they use it as disinfectant."

"There must be more to it," Kerry said. "Keith wouldn't bail out a company this size in return for shelf space. Dinesh said about upstairs."

"I hate to keep saying it," James said, "but there *is* no upstairs."

"Yes, there is," Lauren said. "This building has a pointed roof, but the ceiling in here is flat."

"Good thinking, Lauren," Kerry said. "You obviously got all the brains in your family. There must a loft up there."

The three of them pointed their torches at the ceiling. The beams got dim over such a distance, but they eventually spotted a hatch that had to lead into the loft.

"How can we get up there?" Kerry asked.

"Easy," James said. "It's like a computer game. If you look, the shelves in some bays are closer together. You can use them like a ladder."

"And we thought all those hours on the PlayStation were wasted," Kerry said, smiling. "Lauren, you stay down here and keep lookout. Me and James will climb up."

Lauren nodded. James doubted she'd have been so agreeable if he'd been giving the orders. They clambered up the closely spaced shelves, feeling their way with their hands. They walked along the shelves, stepping over sacks and tins until they came to the next easy-to-climb section. Lauren shone her torch on them, lighting their path as best she could.

The top level was fifteen meters above ground, but the shelves were three meters deep, so if felt safe. There was a wooden pole with a hook on the end for undoing the loft hatch. Kerry pulled it open. James shone his torch into the hole while she pulled out the ladder. It clattered down, banging against the metal sheet on which they stood. The hundreds of fluorescent tubes in the ceiling a few centimeters from their heads started plinking to life. James and Kerry stared down and shielded their faces while their eyes adjusted to the light.

"What the hell did that?" James whispered.

"Someone must have come in," Kerry said. "They'll never see us up here, but where's Lauren?"

They crawled to the edge of the shelves on their bellies. James leaned over one side, Kerry over the other.

"I can't see her," Kerry said. "It looks like she's had the sense to get out of sight."

There were two sets of footsteps, accompanied by women's voices. James caught a glance of them. They were both fat, wearing hairnets and dark blue overalls.

"Bay forty-six," one woman said.

They walked slowly, reading the numbers printed on the shelves.

"Potassium carbonate," the woman said, leaning into the bay. "This is it, in the blue drums."

Something whumped against the floor, echoing around the warehouse. James peeked over the side. A sack of orange powder had exploded on the ground, almost directly below them. Lauren must have knocked it off a shelf.

The two women started walking towards the spill.

"I better see if Lauren's OK," James said.

Kerry nodded. "Be careful. Keep out of sight."

But when he turned around, Lauren was crawling along the metal towards them.

"Why didn't you hide behind something?" James whispered angrily.

"Sorry," Lauren said, looking ashamed of herself. "I wanted to be with you guys."

Even though it was tense, James couldn't help smiling. "Now you know why you need training: so you don't get scared so easily."

"I wasn't scared," Lauren said defensively. "Just . . ."

Kerry anxiously shushed the pair of them. "You're making too much noise."

Down at ground level, the two women were standing by the burst sack, hands on hips, staring up at the ceiling.

"We must have a ghost," one woman grinned.

The other one laughed. "I'm not sticking around to see if he chucks another one at us and it's not gonna be muggins here who cleans that mess up, either."

The women picked up their boxes and switched out the lights as they left. The three kids kept still, making sure the women were gone and letting their eyes readjust to blackness. Kerry lit her torch and shone it up the metal ladder.

"Bet you a pound there's nothing up there," James said.

Kerry didn't find him funny. "There better be after all this messing about."

She went up the ladder first. There were no windows in the loft, so it was safe to switch on the lights. Even before James got up the ladder, he could tell they'd found something good from the grin on Kerry's face.

Kyle woke up at 3:30 a.m., in a smoky room snarled up with sleeping bodies. He didn't know if he'd passed out or fallen asleep, or what the stain on his trousers was, but he remembered it was the wildest party of his young life. The host would be grounded for years when her parents got back from the Lake District.

Kyle had hammered himself with alcohol and thumping music. Now he was suffering. Anyone else would have crashed back to sleep, but Kyle wanted to get home, have a shower, and put his clothes to soak. He'd always been neat. One of his earliest memories was of chucking a tantrum over going on to a beach with a load of other kids because he didn't like getting sand in his clothes.

It took Kyle a while to find the room where he'd dumped his sweatshirt. He got abused when he trod on some naked guy's ankle in the dark. He stepped over more kids crashed out on the front lawn as he went out of the front gate towards the bus stop. He waited forty minutes for the night bus, which dropped him on the wrong side of Thornton at half-four in the morning. Everything looked wrong as he stumbled towards the house: All the lights were on and there was a gray Toyota he didn't recognize parked on the drive.

Nicole wasn't home, but everyone else was in the living room. Lauren had dropped to sleep on the couch.

Ewart had his laptop computer on the coffee table. A balding man in a suit and tie sat next to him.

"What's going on?" Kyle asked. "Did I miss something good?"

"Yeah," James grinned. "It turns out bringing Kerry on this mission wasn't a dumb waste of time after all."

Kerry gave James a look, but she was too full of herself to get offended.

Zara introduced Kyle to the stranger. "This is John Jones. He's in charge of the MI5 taskforce that's targeting KMG, so we called him over to look at the pictures."

John Jones reached over and shook Kyle's hand before speaking. "You kids are amazing," he grinned. "When Dr. McAfferty offered me a CHERUB unit, I thought it was some kind of joke."

James looked surprised. "You must have heard about missions where cherubs have done a good job."

John shook his head. "I'd been an MI5 agent for eighteen years without ever hearing of CHERUB."

Zara explained. "Thousands of people work for MI5, but only the most senior ones know about CHERUB. People like John only find out if they have to work with us."

"Even then," John said, "there are forty-three MI5 agents working on Operation Snort and I'm the only one who knows about you kids."

"So what's happened?" Kyle croaked, his throat raw from the smoke at the party.

"Come and look at the pictures James and Kerry took," Zara said.

Kyle leaned over the laptop screen while John Jones explained what had been photographed.

"KMG smuggles in cocaine at a very high purity, ninety percent or more. The stuff that gets sold on the street is between thirty and fifty percent pure. What you see in these pictures is a production plant. The pure cocaine gets mixed with borax and some other stuff in those aluminum vats. Then . . ."

John Jones clicked on the mouse, changing to a different picture.

"The machine in this picture is a real beauty. It must have cost over fifty thousand pounds. It's designed to package seasonings, like soy sauce or pepper. You turn it on, load up a roll of polyurethane bags, and tip your powder or liquid in the top. This one has been set up to package one-gram bags of cocaine."

"So did you find much coke?" Kyle asked.

"None at all," Kerry said.

"There could be drugs hidden in the warehouse," John said. "Or somewhere else on the Thunderfoods site, but I doubt it. Most probably, a couple of guys turn up with a few kilos of cocaine, spend a few hours mixing and bagging it, and then take it away with them when they leave."

"So," Kyle asked, "are you gonna bust this place up?"

"No," John said. "We're going to put it under surveillance. We'll get an undercover team to rig the loft up with video cameras and microphones. We'll watch who comes and goes and where they're coming from and going to. Hopefully, we can track the drugs that are processed at Thunderfoods back to wherever they're being smuggled in."

"So it's really only the beginning," James said.

"You kids have got our foot in the door," John said.

"That's not the same as bringing down KMG, but it's going to be a lot easier now we know where their cocaine is being processed."

John shook everyone's hand before he left. The sun was on its way up and Lauren was the only one who'd managed any sleep.

It was three in the afternoon when James surfaced from under his duvet. He was busting for a pee, but Kerry was in the shower, merrily singing her head off. Lauren had left a note on the kitchen table.

James
U looked peaceful! Didn't want 2 wake U up. CU soon.
Lauren
XXX

James was miffed. He'd wanted to say a proper good-bye and wish Lauren luck in training. He sprinted back upstairs as soon as he heard Kerry unlock the bathroom.

"What took you so long?" James gasped, lifting the toilet seat and starting to pee without bothering to close the door behind him.

"Sorry," Kerry said, toweling her hair. "Have you seen Ewart or Zara?"

"Not yet. They're at the supermarket."

"They want a word with us later on," Kerry said.

"You think we're in trouble for not asking before we broke in?" James asked.

"Lauren got a blasting from Ewart before she left."

"Was she upset or anything?"

Kerry shook her head. "She seemed to handle it OK."

"So, what do you reckon they'll do to us?"

"Kyle overheard Ewart and Zara talking," Kerry said. "Apparently we've landed ourselves washing-up duty for the rest of the mission."

James shrugged. "We could have got worse, I suppose."

CHAPTER 15

CONTENDER

Not much happened in the three weeks after they broke into Thunderfoods. That's how undercover mission usually work: You find a few things out quickly, then it starts getting tougher. You have to be patient, slowly winning the confidence of your targets and working your way deeper in to the organization.

Meryl Spencer sent James an e-mail to say Lauren had completed her first week of training and was coping well.

Nicole had put listening devices and miniature cameras around Keith Moore's house. James still liked Nicole, but he hadn't kissed her after the first time because he was more interested in Kerry.

Kerry had wired Mr. Singh's house with microphones and was spending a lot of time with Dinesh, trying to squeeze out more information. James still hadn't found the right moment to tell Kerry how he felt about her. At least, that's what he told Kyle. There had been loads of opportunities, but James always chickened out.

Kyle had given up targeting Ringo Moore and was helping a couple of Year Ten kids make deliveries for KMG on weekends. James still couldn't get his head around Kyle being gay, but it hadn't changed anything in their day-to-day lives.

Some days, James almost forgot he was on a mission. It was like being a normal kid: getting up and playing with Joshua, going to school, sitting through boring lessons or bunking off, coming home, and eating whatever frozen delight Zara had warmed in the oven, then going out making deliveries.

It wasn't a bad life. There was a hundred a week in drug money to spend. James had got new jeans and tracksuit tops, video games, and the dearest Nike trainers he could find. School was a doss and Junior and James always messed around and had a laugh. The two boys had loads on common: They both supported Arsenal, hated school, liked PlayStation, and had similar tastes in music and girls.

James hadn't been in a proper three-round fight yet, but he'd done some sparring and loved the buzz you got in the boxing ring. As soon as you get punched, the chemicals in your body rise up and make you mad, like somebody plugged you into the electricity. Your bad side takes over and you're not scared of anything.

James couldn't manage Ken's target of a hundred and fifty skips a minute, but he'd got well past the stage where the other boys pissed themselves laughing every time he picked up a rope. He stopped skipping and mopped the sweat off his face when Kelvin called him to ringside.

"One round sparring with Del," Kelvin said.

Del had a longer reach and seven fights under his belt, but James wasn't worried as he stepped through the ropes wearing gloves and a head guard. James was built for boxing: solid arms, big shoulders, and strong enough to take a punch.

"Touch gloves," Kelvin said, stepping back from the two fighters.

James charged forward on the bell. Del landed the first hit, a glancing blow on the side of James's head guard. James hit Del's head harder, sunk another punch in Del's guts, and then covered his face, blocking Del's jabs while spying for an opening through the crack between his gloves. When it came, James pounced forward and landed his glove in Del's face. The next punch caught Del off balance, sprawling him out over the canvas.

James wanted Del to get up so he could thump him again, but Del waved his gloves in front of his face and crawled to the ropes. James was disgusted. He spat out his mouth guard before tugging off his glove and hurling it at Del's back.

"Call that a fight?" he shouted. "Come back for some more, you little wimp."

Kelvin grabbed James by his shoulders and pulled him backwards. "Cool it, tiger," he grinned. "Try and remember this is amateur boxing. You win on the number of clean punches you land, not on how hard you punch or even how many times you knock the other guy down."

"I wanna fight somebody really good next time."

Kelvin laughed. "You're a strong lad, James, but you need to work on your speed, so don't start getting cocky."

James unbuckled his head guard and jumped out of the ring. Junior was walking towards him.

"You almost look good enough to fight me," Junior said, smiling.

"I'd fight you now if they'd let me."

Del had staggered around from the other side of the ring. His hair was soaked in sweat where it had been trapped under his head guard.

"You're too strong for me," Del gasped.

"Sorry I called you a wimp," James said. "I got carried away."

Del and James gave each other a sweaty hug. It was always the same: in the ring you wanted to kill someone, but once you got out you were mates again. As James walked over to his training pals, Kelvin called him back.

"I hear you've been a reliable delivery boy since you started," Kelvin said. "Don't think it's gone unnoticed."

"Cheers," James said, his mind still fixed inside the ring.

"You fancy a little train ride tomorrow evening?"

"How far?" James asked.

"We need a package delivered down St. Albans way. You up for it?"

"Sure."

"There's twelve kilos of coke split into four bricks. Get someone you can rely on to help you carry it. You'll earn forty pounds each."

"Sounds fair," James said. "Where do I pick the stuff up?"

"You know Costas?"

James nodded. "I've seen him around."

"He'll meet you in the Thornton playground at about six o'clock. Bring your mate so we can check him out."

Kyle was on another delivery, so James offered the job to Kerry.

"It's fifteen minutes' ride on the train," James said, "and we'll be earning twenty pounds each."

Kerry shrugged. "I was gonna do homework with Dinesh after school, but I'm not getting anything new out of him."

It was a drizzly night, so nobody else was in the playground. Costas was a burly sixteen-year-old who'd dropped out of school the year before. His face was a mass of zits and he didn't like the look of Kerry.

"Are you kidding me?" he asked. "You weren't supposed to bring your girlfriend. You need someone with a bit of presence in case there's trouble."

"This was arranged at short notice," James said. "Kerry's all I could get and she's well up to the job."

Costas looked at Kerry. "No offense, babe, but we don't use little girls."

Unless you were a very large person, preferably armed with a baseball bat, calling Kerry "babe" was a seriously bad idea.

"I'm not your babe," Kerry sniffed. "And I'm quite capable of defending myself."

"I'm sure you are, sweetie," Costas sniggered. "Sorry, James, but this is not gonna happen. Bringing a chick on a delivery, man . . . What are you thinking?"

"Give us those drugs," Kerry said furiously. "Or you're in deep trouble."

James smiled at her. "Kerry, calm down. I'll make a couple of phone calls and smooth this out."

"No," Kerry said. "I'm not letting this bag of pus talk to me like that."

Costas snorted noisily.

"What you gonna do, baby cakes, pull my hair?"

Kerry lunged forward, slamming a karate chop into the front of Costas's neck and sweeping his legs away as he stumbled backwards. Costas was on the ground with Kerry's knee crushing his windpipe before he even realized the fight had started.

"Baby cakes?" Kerry shouted, pressing her knee in harder as Costas gasped for breath. "Nobody calls me baby cakes."

"OK," Costas gurgled. "I'm sorry. You can go with James."

Kerry stood up and let Costas sit while his face returned to its normal color.

"You surprised me," Costas said angrily, as he got to his feet. "But you better not try anything like that again or I'll seriously hurt you."

Kerry couldn't help grinning. "I'll try to keep that in mind."

Costas made sure nobody was around before unzipping his backpack. Kerry and James each grabbed two plastic-wrapped bricks of white powder and tucked them in their backpacks. James started walking away.

"Hang on," Costas said. "Unless you want me to keep the eighty quid."

Kerry snatched the money out of Costas's hand.

"Pleasure doing business," she said.

She started jogging after James.

"Eighty quid, James?" Kerry said angrily. "I can't believe you tried to rip me off when you've got a roll of twenties in your pocket and I'm only getting pocket money."

"It was a mistake," James lied. "You can have half, of course."

"I'm keeping the lot," Kerry said, tucking the money into her jeans. "Unless you want to fight me for it."

CHAPTER 16

LOST

James and Kerry stepped off the train on to the platform at St. Albans.

"It's a shame we couldn't have got here earlier in the day," Kerry said. "St. Albans is really historic. There's Roman ruins and mosaics and stuff."

"Tragic," James said sarcastically. "Nothing gets my pulse racing like a good mosaic. We're not going into town anyway. We've got to get out to some housing area."

Taxis were lined up outside the station. The driver wanted to see James's money before he'd take them anywhere. The ride took them past farms and some seriously expensive houses, then from nowhere they found themselves surrounded by graffiti and concrete. It was like an alien spaceship had sucked a neighborhood out of the middle of London, then decided it didn't like the look of it and dumped it in the middle of nowhere.

The cab pulled up outside a shopping arcade. Everything was boarded up, except a pub that had been converted into a snooker club. It had a reinforced metal door and bars over the slits of glass that passed for windows.

Kerry looked around nervously as the cab pulled away. It was already turning dark.

"It must be the pits living in a place like this," James said. "Thornton may be a dump, but at least it's near to town. Out here you've got nothing."

It turned out the shops were the high point of the area. Beyond them were eight low-rise housing blocks. Three were boarded up, with CONDEMNED BUILDING notices and signs warning people not to go inside without masks to protect them from the asbestos dust. There was a pack of dogs roaming around, druggies in dark corners, and the only normal-looking people you saw walked fast, like they were afraid of being mugged.

James got the directions out of his pocket.

"Twenty-two, third floor, Mullion House."

They found Mullion House, then walked up a foul-smelling staircase and along the third-floor balcony. The door numbers ended at twenty. James rang the bell and an Eastern European–sounding woman shouted out of the letterbox in bad English.

"What is you like?"

"Do you know where number twenty-two is?" James asked.

"What?" she shoutd.

"Number twenty-two."

"Wait. I fetch my son."

The kid who came to the letterbox was about ten. His English was perfect.

"There's no number twenty-two," he explained. "I think all the floors are the same. It only goes up to twenty."

"Cheers," James said miserably, turning away from the letterbox. "Sorry to bother you."

"What do we do now?" Kerry asked.

"There's obviously a mistake with the address," James said. "I'll call the lady who rings my deliveries through. She'll sort it out."

James pulled the mobile out of his tracksuit and dialed. The phone made a bleep and a message flashed on the display: NO SIGNAL. Kerry tried hers and got the same.

"Crap," James said. "You really know you're in the middle of nowhere when you can't get a mobile signal."

Kerry looked down off the balcony towards the shops.

"There's a phone box by the bus stop," she said.

James looked down. "I'd put the odds of it working at something like a million to one."

They didn't have any other choice, so they went to take a look. The phone wasn't so much vandalized as annihilated. There was no glass, no handset, and no buttons; just a burned-up mess.

"This place is giving me the creeps," Kerry said. "Do you think they'd let us phone from inside the snooker club?"

"I wouldn't chance it," James said. "It looks like the kind of place where you'd get your throat cut."

"So what then?" Kerry asked.

"Let's get the hell out of here. There's no way to call another cab, so we'll wait for the bus. Our phones will work once we get to town. I'll make some calls and sort this shambles out."

They wandered across to the bus stop. Kerry glanced at the timetable.

"There's only one bus an hour," she said. "I think we just missed one."

There was hardly any traffic about. They sat on the pavement near the bus stop with their feet in the gutter. Kerry picked a dandelion from a crack in the tarmac and twirled it between her fingers.

"Do you think you'll get in trouble with KMG for this?" she asked.

"I've got the bit of paper with the address written in Kelvin's writing, so they can hardly blame me."

"It's pretty incredible," Kerry said.

James nodded. "Especially when you think what these drugs are worth."

"How much?" Kerry asked.

"There's twelve kilos. I sell coke for sixty a gram and there's a thousand grams in a kilo. So each kilo is worth sixty thousand pounds. That's . . . seven hundred and twenty thousand altogether."

"*Wow,*" Kerry gasped. "That makes our eight-pound delivery fee look a lot less generous."

"Course, that's the street price and this is being sold wholesale, but I'd still bet KMG isn't shifting this lot for any less than three hundred grand."

"You could buy a nice house with that sort of money."

James giggled. "Maybe we could do a runner."

"You know, it's cool the way you can do those sums in your head."

"I've been able to do it since nursery," James said. "Before my mum died, she ran this huge shoplifting gang and she got me to work out her sums; like, who owed how much and who was due what wages."

"Did she ever get busted?" Kerry asked.

James shook his head. "Nope. But when I was little, I used to have nightmares where the police came and took Mum and Lauren away. Junior made some comment the other day about his dad ending up in prison. He acted like it was a joke, but I could tell it worries him. I remembered how I used to be, and it made me feel really shitty about us using him to help put his dad in jail."

"I suppose every bad guy has someone who loves them," Kerry said.

They watched the sunset as the minutes dragged by. When the streetlights flicked on, James looked at his watch.

"The bus shouldn't be long now," Kerry said.

Three lads came out of the snooker club and started walking towards them. One was a big guy in his twenties, with a beard and curly brown hair down his back. The other two were skinheads in their late teens. Probably brothers, with ghostly complexions and spindly limbs. They weren't the first people who'd passed by, but something about them put Kerry and James on edge.

The taller skinhead stopped by Kerry.

"Waiting for a bus?" he asked.

"Yes," Kerry said, standing up. "That's what people usually do at bus stops."

"I thought you might be waiting for a hunk like me to come by and sweep you off your feet."

The shorter one gave James a shove. "You her boyfriend, blondie?"

"Piss off," James said, shoving him back.

"Got any money?" Shorty said, eyeballing James. "Not for very long you won't have."

Both skinheads pulled knives out of their pockets. CHERUB training teaches you to make an instant decision when you see a knife: either grab the assailant's wrist before the blade is in a threatening position, or back away if you don't have time. James and Kerry went for the first option, grabbing the two skinny wrists and yanking their arms behind their backs. Kerry twisted the tall one's thumb until his knife dropped on to the pavement, then smacked his head against the concrete bus stop. After freeing the other knife, James punched Shorty in the back of the head, before ducking down and picking both blades off the floor. He handed one to Kerry.

"We don't want trouble," Kerry said, waving the knife. "We're just waiting for the bus."

The two skinheads didn't back off, but they didn't look confident either. The guy with the long hair had waited in the background the whole time. He moved up between the skinheads and smiled.

"You two seem to know some pretty fancy moves," he said, breaking into a grin. "You got any that will stop one of these?"

He slid a sawn-off shotgun out of his jacket and pointed it at them. James looked at Kerry, hoping she had some smart move up her sleeve, but she looked as scared as he felt.

"This is a twelve gauge," the guy with the big hair explained. "One shot will blow the pair of you to smithereens. So, if you want to live beyond the next few minutes, you're going to do exactly what I say. OK?"

James and Kerry both nodded.

"First of all, pass the knives back to their owners, handles first."

The skinheads took the knives.

"Now put your hands on your heads."

Once their hands were on their heads, the skinheads rummaged through James's and Kerry's pockets, taking their money, keys, train tickets, and phones. Then they stripped off their watches.

"Now, lose the backpacks."

"You know you'll be in serious trouble if you take those packs?" James said. "You've no idea what's in them."

"I know exactly what's in them," the hairball laughed. "And you can tell Keith Moore that if he sends any more grubby little brats down here, we'll give them a lot worse than the beating we're about to give you."

Shorty looked at the gunman. "Can I have his trainers before we batter them?"

"Eh?"

Shorty pointed at James's trainers. "You said we could keep whatever we knicked off them. Those trainers are a hundred and nineteen ninety-nine. My little brother would love 'em."

The gunman shook his head in disbelief. "Go on, then."

James looked mortified as he surrendered his almost-new Air Max.

"Now," the gunman said, smiling sweetly, "after we go, you're gonna walk or crawl the hell out of here. If I ever see you again, I'll be the last thing you ever see. And I wouldn't bother waiting for the bus. Kids kept chucking bricks through the windscreen, so they stopped running them after dark."

The gunman made James and Kerry lie flat on the ground with their hands behind their heads, then he told the skinheads to give them a good going-over.

CHAPTER 17

CRAZY

Kerry and James crawled out of the road and lay in the grass verge behind the bus stop, catching their breath. As kickings go, it hadn't been bad, but they'd have plenty of bruises in the morning.

"I guess they wanted us fit enough to walk home and give Keith his message," Kerry said.

"How's your knee?" James asked.

"I'm OK. Your lip's bleeding."

"You feel up to walking, or do you want to rest for a minute?"

"I can walk," Kerry said. "What are we gonna do?"

"Exactly what the man with the gun told us to do," James said. "It'll take at least an hour to get into town.

Or if we pass a phone box that works, we can call home and reverse the charges."

"This will ruin the mission," Kerry said.

"Nah. I'll just explain what happened to Kelvin. It's obvious we've been set up."

"What if they think you were in on it?" Kerry asked. "There's plenty of delivery boys. If there's any doubt, KMG will just dump you and use someone else."

James realized she was right. "They're not exactly gonna be happy about me losing three hundred grand's worth of coke, are they?"

"They'll check all of us out," Kerry said. "Not just you and me. Kyle, Nicole, Ewart, and Zara will be under the spotlight as well. The whole mission will be down the toilet."

"I don't see how we can get the drugs back," James said. "That guy had a gun. I don't even have trainers."

"He was small-time," Kerry said.

"What makes you say that?"

"You heard what the skinhead said when he took your trainers. That hairball was paying them by letting them keep our stuff. That's hardly the modus of a big shot."

"OK," James said. "He's small-time, but he's still got a gun."

"He won't kill us in a million years," Kerry said. "He's been paid a few hundred quid to scare us, grab the drugs, and send a message to Keith Moore. There's a huge difference between that and murdering two kids."

"Supposing you're right," James said. "How do we find this guy?"

"I think there's only one road in and out of this chunk of paradise, and we haven't seen him leave. We're looking for a tall, fat drug dealer with tons of curly hair and a beard. I bet one of the scumbags hanging around here will be able to put a name to a description like that."

"And we just walk up and they'll tell us?"

Kerry shrugged. "We'll make some excuse why we need to find him."

"The thing is," James said, "if you've just ripped off KMG for three hundred grand, you won't be hanging around here for long."

"I know," Kerry said. "But he doesn't think KMG will know what's happened until we get into town. He'll be off his guard the next hour or so."

"You're serious, aren't you?" James smiled. "I'm really gonna go chasing after some gun-toting drug dealer in my socks?"

"I think it's worth the risk, but I'm not forcing you. If you're not up for it, we'll head home."

James thought for a second as he dabbed his bloody lip on the bottom of his T-shirt. He didn't fancy their chances. If it had been anyone but Kerry, he would have said no.

"Let's go and get shot," he said, climbing to his feet and taking his first painful steps since the beating.

They cut around the back of the shops, dodging the snooker club in case anyone inside spotted them. They found a couple of skinny women at the bottom of a staircase and got blank stares when they described the hairball. They got lucky on their second attempt, when Kerry described him to a group of teenagers.

"Was it some kind of heavy metal T-shirt?"

"Yeah," Kerry said. "Do you know where we could find him? He dropped his keys outside the snooker club and we picked them up."

"Sounds like Crazy Joe," one kid said. "He lives in Alhambra House. You want to be careful, he's a serious lunatic and he's drugged-up half the time."

"You know where exactly?" James asked.

"What do I look like?" the kid laughed. "Directory enquiries? Try the second or third floor."

"Cheers," James said.

"Nice socks," the kid replied.

Alhambra House was the furthermost block. There were twenty flats on each floor, but finding the right one was easier than they expected. Loads were boarded up and most of the others didn't look the part: old-person-style wallpaper in the hallways, or ethnic names written under the doorbells. Joe's flat turned out to be a give-away: the front door was painted black with a devil's-head knocker and underneath the word "Joe's" was written in Tippex. They peered through the glass. There was an Aerosmith poster pinned to the kitchen wall and all the lights were on.

James and Kerry didn't have their lock guns or anything with them. They couldn't get in, so they had to lure Crazy Joe out.

"Check he's at home first," Kerry said. "Ring the bell and run."

James pressed the buzzer and they sprinted to the end of the balcony and hid in the stairwell. Crazy Joe waddled on to his doorstep in his T-shirt and boxers and looked down the balcony. He swore about "bloody kids" and went back inside.

"So now what?" James said. "If he's half undressed, he's probably home alone."

"There might be a girlfriend in there as well."

"I don't reckon any woman lives in that house," James said.

"Based on what?" Kerry asked.

"Did you see the filthy sink and cutlery piled up on the draining board?" James asked. "That's a single man's kitchen if ever I saw one."

"There's something messed-up about this," Kerry said. "You'd think he'd be running or driving some place in a hurry, not sitting around in his underwear."

"None of this makes any sense," James said. "We need to take him down quickly and without making any noise."

Five minutes later, Crazy Joe emerged from his flat a second time to find James grinning at him.

"I warned you," Joe sneered.

As Joe lunged for James, Kerry landed her hardest punch into the side of his head. It hit the sweet spot above the eye socket where the skull is thinnest, giving Joe's brain a good rattling. All his muscles went limp and James had to dodge out of the way as he slumped across the balcony.

"Get moving," Kerry said anxiously, looking at James. "He'll start coming around in no time and I don't want to have to knock him out twice."

James stepped over Joe and ran into the flat, checking inside every room to make sure nobody else was home.

There were pizza boxes and rubbish everywhere. The smell of stale cigarette smoke made his eyes water. Once he knew the flat was empty, he helped Kerry drag the semiconscious Joe through to the living room.

"Find something to tie him up with," Kerry shouted.

James ripped the electric cables out of the back of the video and satellite box. Joe struggled a bit, but they managed to knot the flex tightly around his wrists and ankles.

"Where's our drugs, Joe?" Kerry asked, bunching her fist in the air above him.

"How old are you guys?" Joe grinned. "Thirteen, fourteen?"

"Nearly thirteen," James said.

"I've seen it all now," Joe said. "You guys were supposed to get scared and run home to Mummy."

"Shut it," Kerry said in a firm voice. "From now on, you talk when I say so and you better make sure I like the answer. So, for the second time, Joe, where are our drugs?"

"Found 'em," James said, spotting the two backpacks beside the couch.

He unzipped them, making sure the stuff was still inside.

"Look for the gun, and anything else you don't want him coming after us with," Kerry said. She kept Joe under control while James searched the flat. The shotgun was inside Joe's leather jacket, hanging up by the front door. James found a pistol and more drugs under the bed. It was cocaine in one-gram bags, identical to what James delivered most nights.

He'd been trained where to look for hidden stuff and an uneven piece of skirting board was a dead giveaway. James pulled it off and found two supermarket carrier bags stuffed with more cocaine, and a few thousand pounds in scrunched-up cash. James stuffed the drugs into the carrier bags on top of the money and carried the lot into the living room.

"Shall we take all this?" James asked.

"Why not?" Kerry said, smiling. "He made us suffer."

"We better not hang around here," James said.

"You kids are in way over your heads," Joe gasped.

Kerry bunched up her fist. "Did I ask for your opinion?"

She grabbed a wad of serviettes out of a greasy pizza box and forced them in Joe's mouth.

"Are we gonna call a cab, or what?" James asked.

Kerry pointed at a picture on the wall. "Is that parked around here somewhere?"

James looked over his shoulder at a framed photo of a slimmer, younger Joe, standing in front of an American car. It was a fancy two-seater, with mad-looking air scoops on the bonnet and a two-tone orange paint job. James read the little gold plaque stuck on the frame: 1971 FORD MUSTANG MACH I. TUNED TO 496 HORSEPOWER.

"They look like car keys on the coffee table," Kerry said.

Joe wriggled his arms and furiously tried to shout something through the serviettes plugging his mouth.

James grinned as he picked up the keys. "Sure beats hanging around for a minicab to turn up. Where's it parked?"

"You wouldn't leave that on the street around here. It

must be in one of the garages out the back." Kerry pulled the soggy wad of tissue out of Joe's mouth. "What's your garage number?"

"If you *touch* my car," Joe gasped, spitting bits of white fluff off his tongue, "you're both dead."

Kerry smashed her trainer into Joe's guts.

"Next time it'll be your balls. . . ." Kerry shouted, as Joe groaned in agony. "What's your garage number?"

"No way," Joe grunted.

"James," Kerry said sweetly, "hand me the gun, please."

James passed it across. Kerry pulled down on the stock to load it and pointed the sawn-off barrel at Joe's knees.

"The next word out of your mouth had better be the garage number," Kerry snarled. "Or it's gonna take a miracle to get the bloodstain out of this carpet."

James knew Kerry wouldn't pull the trigger, but she put on a good act and Joe wasn't so confident.

"Forty-two," Joe said.

"How hard was that?" Kerry said. "And if you're lying, I'll come back here in a minute and blow off your foot before I ask again."

"OK, OK," Joe gasped. "I lied. . . . It's in number eighteen. Why don't you call a cab? It's a very powerful car. Do you kids even know how to drive?"

"Don't you worry yourself about that," James said.

All CHERUB agents are taught to drive. It's essential to be able to escape on wheels if things turn nasty.

"Why don't you take a pair of Joe's trainers?" Kerry asked.

"Too big," James said. "They'd be like clown shoes on me."

"We better rip the phones out," Kerry said. "We don't want him calling his pals before we're well on our way."

She pulled the phone out and kicked the socket off the wall with her heel. James pocketed Joe's mobile and demolished the extension in the bedroom.

Kerry grabbed both packs.

"Ready to go?" she asked.

James got the carrier bags with the money, pistol, and Joe's drugs. They went out of the front door and walked briskly along the balcony, down the stairs, and around to the garages at the back. Kerry's head was spinning so fast, she never noticed that she still had the shotgun in her hand.

The padlock sprang open and James noisily rolled up the metal door of garage number eighteen. The Mustang looked better than the day it had come out of the showroom, thirty-five years earlier. Crazy Joe had spent serious money on it.

"Bags I'm driving," James said, unlocking the driver's door and lowering himself into the leather seat. Kerry didn't care, she wasn't into cars.

James moved the seat as far forward as it would go so he could reach the pedals. He'd learned on the private roads around campus in a little car with an engine the size of a thimble. He wasn't prepared for the thunderstorm when the tuned V-8 blasted to life, juddering through the pedals into his socked feet.

"Hooooooly mother!" James grinned, searching for the headlight control.

The road ahead lit up and the dials on the dashboard turned electric blue. James put the automatic gearbox in drive and rolled the gargling beast out of its pen.

The first couple of kilometers were dodgy. The car had big acceleration, but the brakes had much less bite than on a modern car. It caught James out when he nearly went into the back of someone at the first set of traffic lights. Once they were a few kilometers clear, he parked. Kerry found a road atlas under her seat and worked out the route home. By the time they got on to the motorway, James was feeling confident. When the road ahead was clear, he couldn't resist slamming the accelerator and taking it up to 110 mph.

The trim inside the car started to shake and Kerry started going bananas.

"Really sensible, James," she shouted. "Two kids in a stolen car carrying guns and drugs. I tell you what: Why don't we attract lots of attention by slaughtering the speed limit?"

After seeing the way she dealt with Joe, James decided it might be best if he slowed down.

They parked the stolen Mustang at the back of a DIY store about a kilometer from Thornton. It was gone eleven o'clock and, now the adrenalin rush had worn off, James and Kerry felt like they could sleep for twenty hours.

"We could leave the keys in the door and someone will nick it," James said.

"It's got our fingerprints all over," Kerry said. "Joyriders usually burn cars out. If we don't want it to look suspicious, that's what we'll have to do."

James gave the car an admiring glance. "Seems a shame to kill it."

Kerry leaned inside and flipped open the glove box.

She found Joe's cigarettes and lighter, then tore pages out of the road atlas and screwed them up into loose balls. When there was a mound of paper on the passenger seat, she flicked the lighter and set the edges alight. The left the passenger door open so the fire could breathe, then ducked into some trees and waited until they were sure the flames had taken hold.

The front seats were quickly ablaze. Once the roof lining caught, the flames flashed into the back. The whole interior glowed orange and smoke started curling out from under the hood.

"Better run," James said. "There's bound to be a security guard round here somewhere."

They'd only gone a hundred meters when the heat blew out one of the back tires. A few seconds later, the fuel caught and the back end of the car went up in a fireball.

It was less than a kilometer home, but they were feeling their injuries and the walk seemed to take forever. James had a pounding headache. When they staggered through to the kitchen, Ewart jumped up from the table, surprised by the state they were in. He made them both hot drinks and sandwiches while Zara and Nicole cleaned up their cuts and bruises.

"Shower and go to bed," Zara said, after they'd explained what had happened. "Don't bother getting up for school in the morning. You both need a good day's rest."

"I better ring Kelvin first," James said.

"OK," Ewart said. "Do that while Kerry's in the shower, then go straight to bed."

CHAPTER 18

RISKS

James was out as soon as he hit the pillow and the next thing he knew it was 10 a.m. the following morning. He had six huge bruises, a couple of grazes, and a giant scab on his bottom lip. When he stood up, his thigh muscle felt tight and he could only manage short steps.

Down in the kitchen, Joshua was on the floor playing with some magnets he'd pulled off the fridge door and Kerry was at the table in her nightshirt. She looked shell-shocked.

"Sleep OK?" James asked.

"Not bad," Kerry said. "Zara just made a pot of tea if you want some."

James poured a mug and got a bowl of cereal.

"I can't believe all we went through last night," Kerry grinned. "If I didn't hurt in ten places, I might believe it was all a dream."

"Same here," James smiled. "You were so tough on Crazy Joe when you had him tied up. I know you've got a temper, but I've never seen you juiced-up like that before."

"I was so angry," Kerry said. "I mean, what kind of scuzzball pays skinheads to beat up kids?"

"At least Kelvin seemed cool when I explained how we got the drugs back; and we saved the mission."

Zara stepped in from the garden and threw an empty laundry basket down beside the washing machine. She'd heard James's last line.

"You know," she said, "sometimes a mission isn't worth saving."

"What?" James gasped.

Kerry looked surprised as well.

"I respect what you two did last night," Zara said. "You made a decision under tricky circumstances and it came off. But Ewart and I both feel you should have come home. It was an unacceptable risk going up against a man with a gun."

James and Kerry both looked wounded.

"There's no need for those faces," Zara said.

She picked Joshua up off the floor and sat him on her lap at the table.

"CHERUB is one of the most secret organizations in the world," Zara explained. "Only two people in the British government know it exists: the Intelligence Minister and the Prime Minister. When politicians first find out about CHERUB, they're usually queasy about putting kids in danger. Then Mac explains about all the useful work cherubs do and the lengths we go to make you guys safe.

"Imagine if you two had been hurt, or even killed, last night. Mac would have had to go to London to explain the facts: two kids got mugged and went chasing after an armed drug dealer. At the least, Mac and the senior people within CHERUB would be sacked for letting something so irresponsible happen. The politicians might even decide they can't stomach what CHERUB does and shut the whole show down."

Kerry nodded. "When you put it like that, I can see it wasn't worth it."

"Sorry," James said.

"You've got nothing to be sorry for," Zara smiled. "Just try to be less gung ho from now on."

Kelvin rang James's mobile around midday.

"I've been making calls about what happened," he said. "Can you meet us down here at the boxing club and bring everything you got off Crazy Joe with you?"

"I'm not in shit, am I?" James asked.

"No, no way," Kelvin said. "I just want you to fetch the stuff down and we'll see you right. And that bird you had with you."

"Kerry," James said.

"Yeah, bring her as well."

Kerry had never been up to the boxing club. The gym was quiet at this time of day, just a few of the more serious boxers putting themselves through punishing workouts. Ken, as always, sat in his chair holding a mug of tea and watching everything that happened.

"They're using my office," he said. "Knock before you go in."

A gigantic man in a suit and tie stood guard at the door of the dingy office. James did a double take when he got inside. Crazy Joe was leaning against a back wall; he had a bloodstained dressing over a cut on his forehead. Kelvin sat on a cabinet off to one side and the big cheese himself was in the cracked leather chair at the desk.

"Take a seat," Keith Moore said.

He didn't look like anyone special. A smallish man, with cropped brown hair. He wore Levis and a white polo shirt. The only conspicuous sign of wealth was a chunky gold ring.

"I haven't had the pleasure before," Keith said, reaching over and shaking James's and Kerry's hands. "Have you brought everything you took off Joe?"

James rattled the carrier bags between his legs.

"It's all in there."

"I take it you know who I am?" Keith asked.

"Yeah," James said. "I've seen you at your house. I was on the PlayStation with Junior."

"My business runs itself these days," Keith said. "People go off to South America to buy stock, stock arrives, stock gets distributed."

James noticed that he never referred to drugs or cocaine, in case the room was bugged.

Keith continued, "Sometimes I go for weeks hearing the same message: 'All the usual problems, boss, but nothing we can't handle.' Then, just when you think nothing is ever going to excite you, something turns up like what you two did last night."

"It was a test, wasn't it?" Kerry asked.

"That's right," Keith smiled. "You won't last long in business without loyal people. The best way to find what they're made of is to give them some fake merchandise and put them in a situation like we put you two in last night. Some people get scared and turn hysterical. Those are the ones who'll cause problems if they get busted. We have to kick them out. Some people are sorry for losing the merchandise, but they tough it out and beg for another chance. That's what we're hoping for: guts and determination. Until last night, though, nobody ever showed enough guts to hunt down and get revenge on the guys we paid to rob them. What you two did was very impressive."

James and Kerry both smiled.

"This is all nice and cozy," Crazy Joe said bitterly. "But what about my stuff?"

"Yes," Keith said. "You'll have to return what you took from Joe."

"What about us?" James said. "I've lost my best trainers. We both lost our watches and mobiles and stuff."

"Joe can return them," Keith said.

Joe cleared his throat. "Actually, I said the two guys who duffed them up could keep what they took."

"OK," Keith said. "Take five hundred quid out of Joe's money, that'll cover it."

"That's a bit steep," Joe said tersely. "It's not my fault the brat was wearing expensive trainers."

Keith repeated himself. "Take five hundred quid out of Joe's money, that'll cover it."

He didn't change his tone or anything, but Joe knew his place and didn't push the argument. James took five hundred pounds and split it with Kerry. After that, he slid the carrier bags over to Joe.

"Is that everything you took?" Keith asked.

James nodded. "Everything."

"Where's my Mustang parked?" Joe asked.

James and Kerry looked awkwardly at each other.

"We were scared you'd report it stolen and our fingerprints were all over the inside," James said.

"You didn't clean them off with white spirit, did you?" Joe asked. "White spirit dries out the leather."

"No, we didn't," James said. "We, erm . . ."

He didn't have the bottle to say it.

"We burned the car out," Kerry blurted.

"You did *what*?" Crazy Joe shouted, lunging over the desk and grabbing James by his T-shirt.

"Let him go," Keith said, firmly.

"I'll kill these little pricks," Joe shouted, dragging James across the desk and trying to get his hands around his throat. James thrashed about, trying to push Joe off.

Joe had ignored Keith's order, so Keith gave Kelvin the nod. Joe was no match for the powerfully built boxer; Kelvin picked up the fat man like he weighed nothing, banged him against the wall, and slapped him around the face. Joe let out a high-pitched yowl that could have come from an eight-year-old girl.

"That car was my baby," he sobbed. "I spent months working on her."

Kelvin backed off with a stunned look on his face. Joe dabbed up tears with the end of his beard.

"Wasn't it insured?" Keith asked.

"That's not the point," Joe sniffled. "I invested love in that car. You'll never get that back."

Keith was killing himself laughing. "Joe, it's only a car. Get a grip on yourself."

"Those kids should pay damages, or something. They shouldn't get away with it."

"Joe," Keith said, looking a little angry. "It's not my fault you let yourself get outwitted by two twelve-year-olds. I've done what you wanted, now get out of here before I ask my minder to step inside and knock your head through the wall."

Joe grabbed his carrier bags and stumbled out of the office. He looked such a shambles James almost felt sorry for him. Keith got up from behind the desk, shaking his head.

"You know," Keith said, as Kelvin helped him into his overcoat, "if you two kids stay loyal and work hard, you're gonna make a lot of money."

James and Kerry both grinned. The bruises were worth it if they'd earned Keith Moore's respect.

"Actually," Kerry said, "I came along as a favor to James. All your deliveries are done by boys."

"I thought girls were soft until I met you," Keith said.

"I can set her up, if you like," Kelvin said.

"These two are really special," Keith said, grinning. "They've got brains and balls. Keep them busy and make sure they're properly rewarded."

"Thanks," Kerry said.

"And James," Keith said. "If you're over my house with Junior any time, be sure to stick your snout into my office and say hello."

Keith left with his minder like he was in a hurry. James looked at Kelvin, who was shaking his head in disbelief.

"I'm gonna have to treat you two right," Kelvin said. "With Keith singing your praises, I might just end up calling one of you boss someday."

CHAPTER THIRTEEN

Friday before school, Kerry knocked on the boys' bedroom door.

"Are you decent in there?"

"I'm still in bed," James groaned, sounding knackered. "Come in if you want."

He'd been up until nearly midnight having a PlayStation competition with Kyle and a couple of Thornton kids. Kerry came through the door with Joshua in her arms and dumped him on James's bed.

"He wanted to wish you a happy birthday," she said.

James pulled his duvet over his face. Joshua tugged it back and giggled when James made a loud quacking noise.

"How come you didn't scream your head off when Kerry picked you up?" James asked.

"I think he's finally got used to me," Kerry smiled. "Can I leave him here while I get my books ready for school?"

Kerry went out. Joshua crawled up the bed and burrowed under a loose pillow near James's face. James moved in to blow a raspberry on Joshua's arm, but as he got close he recoiled from a powerful smell.

"Jeeeeeeesus," James shouted, covering his nose with his arm. "You smelly little . . ."

James jumped out of bed and picked up Joshua, holding him out at arm's length. He walked into the hallway, where Kerry and Nicole were wetting themselves laughing.

"I wondered when you'd smell it," Kerry said.

"You're evil," James grinned. "I'll get you two for this."

James carried Joshua downstairs to the kitchen. Zara was cooking a pan of sausages.

"Morning, teenager," Zara said. "There's presents and stuff on the table."

"This little monster filled his nappy," James said.

Zara grinned. "You know where the changing table is, James."

"Yes, I do, but you're not getting me anywhere near it."

"Think of it as a learning experience," Zara said. "An introduction to life as a young adult."

James knew Zara wasn't serious.

"Actually," he said, "a better introduction to young adulthood would be a crate of beer and some hot chicks."

Zara smiled. "I don't think so, somehow."

Ewart walked in behind James.

"You want to be careful," Ewart said, taking Joshua out of James's arms. "You start off with the hot chicks and before you know it you're leaning over a changing table with one of these little beasts peeing on you."

Ewart tickled his son's belly before taking him outside for a nappy change.

James sat at the table and started ripping into his cards. Because cherubs never have family, except brothers and sisters, they make a point of exchanging cards, even when they're away on missions. James had over thirty, including some with foreign postmarks redirected from campus. Gabrielle had sent one from South Africa. James's old training pals Callum and Connor had posted one from Texas, and Amy had sent a postcard with a picture of a giant pineapple on it from Australia. The tackiest-looking card was from Lauren.

"Here, Zara," James laughed. "Listen to what Lauren wrote. 'Dearest brother, you are an idiot. Sometimes you make me puke. I'll be in training by the time you read this and I wish you were doing it instead of me. P.S. Happy thirteenth birthday, I love U.' Then she's done a row of kisses."

James left opening his presents until Kyle and the girls had come down. The biggest box was from Ewart and Zara: a replacement for his stolen trainers. Nicole and Kerry had clubbed together and bought him a T-shirt he'd looked at the last time they went to the Reeve Center. He got a kiss from each of them when he said thanks. Kyle got him a pack of trendy men's toiletries. It included shampoo, conditioner, and a little bottle of aftershave. The label read, "Please use these regularly."

"This is all cool," James grinned. "Cheers."

He put his goodies aside and grabbed a sausage sandwich from the plate in the middle of the table. His mind wandered back a year to his twelfth birthday, just after his mum had died. He'd been living in a council home and wasn't allowed to see Lauren. It had been about the most desperate day of his life.

Then he thought about other birthdays, back when his mum was alive. Charging down the stairs to stacks of shoplifted toys and clothes, then racing to unwrap everything before school. When Lauren was tiny, she'd have to have a present as well, or she'd chuck a jealous fit.

Thinking back made James feel emotional and his eyes started glazing over. He didn't want to start bawling in front of everyone, so he scraped back his chair and bolted towards the stairs.

"Are you OK?" Zara shouted after him.

"Busting to pee," James lied.

He locked himself in the bathroom. He wasn't really miserable, it was just that thinking about his mum always made him feel empty. Even though there was loads of interesting stuff going on in his life, James often wished he could go back in time and spend a night in front of the TV with his mum.

After washing his eyes, James stared in the mirror at the same kid who'd been there the night before, only now he was a teenager. It didn't really make any difference, but it was a buzz all the same.

• • •

James, Junior, Nicole, and April arranged to meet at lunchtime, to bunk off and go to the cinema. They swapped uniform for casual clothes as soon as they got out of the school gate. James had loads of money, so he paid for tickets and popcorn and stuff.

It was a stupid thriller. Nicole started giggling every time this American actor spoke in a fake-sounding London accent. James and Junior started putting two fingers in their mouths and whistling noisily every time this fit actress came into shot.

The only other people in the cinema were a few pensioners. One bloke kept shushing them until Nicole turned back and waved her fist at him.

"Shut it, you old git."

The old man toddled off to make a complaint. The cinema manager came in and told them all to behave or else he'd chuck them out. James settled down to the film. He got a shock when he noticed Nicole and Junior had their arms around each other and an even bigger one a minute later when they started snogging.

They were all over each other. Nicole's leg was up in the air and James kept getting kicked. He got up and moved down two seats so he was sitting on the opposite side of April, away from any flailing limbs.

"They're getting on well," April grinned.

She grinned for a long time. James watched half a minute of the film and she was still grinning at him. He realized the girls had planned an ambush. Nicole already knew Junior fancied her because he'd asked her out before. James felt like he'd been hooked on a line and reeled in, but he checked April out and realized that as traps go, it wasn't a bad one.

April was decent-looking, with long brown hair and fit legs. James slid his hand under the armrest and put it on top of April's. She twisted in her seat, so she could rest her head on James's shoulder. James turned around, breathed April's smell and kissed her on the cheek while she grabbed a few of his Maltesers.

They stayed that way for a couple of minutes, until April moved away and blew chocolate breath over him.

"So," she whispered. "Are you gonna snog me or what?"

James figured, *"What the hell, it's my birthday."* They snogged for ten minutes, breaking up when the movie got near the end and turned into a big car chase and punch-up that was actually worth watching.

Nicole and Junior started messing around. They poured the dregs and melted ice from the Coke into one cup, then spat in chewed-up chocolate and bits of popcorn off the carpet. Nicole held the cup between James and April.

"Gob in that," Nicole said.

James and April obediently spat into the cup.

"That better not end up anywhere near me," James said.

Nicole grinned. "Don't you worry."

As soon as the titles came up, Nicole and Junior dashed over and caught up with the old man as he doddered up the aisle.

"Excuse me," Nicole said politely.

The old man turned suspiciously.

"What is it?"

"I just wanted to apologize for disturbing you," Nicole said. "I realize it was dreadfully inconsiderate of us."

The old man smiled. "That's OK, I suppose. Just don't do it again."

"Yeah," Junior said. "It's people like you that fought in hundreds of wars so that kids like us could be here today."

"We'd like you to have this as a token of our appreciation," Nicole giggled.

She chucked the contents of the cup at the old man, who wheezed in shock as the foul liquid drizzled inside his clothes. His jumper had massive stains and bits of popcorn stuck down the front.

"That'll teach you a lesson," Nicole shouted.

James looked stunned as Nicole and Junior broke into a run. He and April chased after them, knowing they'd get into trouble if they stuck around. When they got to the foyer, Junior launched himself into a rack of peanuts and snacks, spilling them over the floor. None of the cinema staff earned enough money to bother going after them.

They ran a few hundred meters from the cinema and cut into a side street. James was livid.

"Are you two retards or something?" he shouted. "What the hell did you do that for?"

"Who put a bug up your arse?" Nicole grinned.

Junior was laughing so hard he couldn't stand up straight.

"He was an old man," James stormed. "That was

totally out of order. You could have busted his hip or something."

April didn't say anything, but she stood beside James, showing she was on his side.

"I hope he *has* broken his hip," Nicole shouted bitterly. "I hope he drops dead."

"Nice," April said.

"I can't stand old people," Nicole said bluntly.

"You'll be old one day," James said.

"Nah," Nicole said. "Live fast, die young, that's my motto."

"Where are we going now?" Junior giggled. "Shall we get something to eat? I'm starving."

Being friends with Junior was part of James's mission, but sometimes your emotions take over no matter how hard you try.

"I'm going home," James said shortly. "I feel like a shower."

"You're not throwing a major strop, are you?" Junior asked. "You're still coming down the youth club tonight?"

"Sure," James said, half-heartedly. "Everyone's gonna be there."

"I'm smuggling some of my dad's beers in," Junior said. "Let's all get totally smashed."

Junior and Nicole wandered off towards a burger place with their arms around each other. James waited at the bus stop with April. When her bus came, he gave her a quick kiss.

"I'll see you at the youth club tonight," April said. "Don't let those two idiots spoil your birthday."

"I won't," James said.

But he couldn't help feeling it all the way home. There's a difference between mucking around and being nasty to someone. The thing with the old man had left a bad taste in his mouth.

CHAPTER 20

CELEBRATION

The incident with Crazy Joe was supposed to be kept quiet, but it was the kind of story that travels fast and gets wilder every time it's told. The story, combined with Keith Moore's seal of approval, had made James into a well-respected face.

He got a good vibe when he walked into the youth center alongside Kerry and Dinesh. Waves and smiles came from all directions. He sat at a table with Junior and Nicole, who looked like they'd already downed a few of the beers that were stashed under the table. Junior was in a good mood and James didn't want to make a big deal about what had happened at the cinema earlier.

"Beer?" Junior said, passing a can across the table.

Drinking was banned, but the youth club supervisor always just sat in the corner translating books into German. If there was a punch-up, he'd phone upstairs and get a couple of guys from the boxing club to sort it out; apart from that, you could get away with anything.

"Cheers," James said, cracking the can open.

April pulled up a chair next to James and they kissed. He felt awkward doing it with Kerry sitting a few meters away.

The next few hours passed in a blur. Kids came and went. Everyone was taking the mickey out of everyone else and drinking. Kerry and Dinesh only took sips, James and April had a couple of beers, while Nicole and Junior got completely trashed. One time, Nicole got the giggles so badly she fell off her chair.

The youth club closed at ten and James thought he'd better have a slash before they headed home. He was in a grand mood as he drifted downstairs to the foul-smelling basement toilets.

"You forgive me, don't you?"

James turned around and realized Junior was peeing beside him.

"For the old man?" Junior slurred. "Nicole's got a thing about old people. We got carried away."

"Course I forgive you," James said. "Don't sweat it."

"I've got something for you," Junior said. "Come outside."

They went into the space at the bottom of the stairs between the boys' and girls' toilets. Junior pulled a pillbox out of his jeans and popped off the lid. There was a stubby metal straw inside and a thin layer of white powder in the bottom.

"How long have you been snorting coke for?" James gasped.

"Since the cinema."

"No wonder you two have been acting like nutters," James said. He knew that coke gave you a high, but he'd never realized that it could make you act totally crazy.

"Give it a whirl," Junior said.

James had packets of cocaine in his locker at school and under his bed at home. He'd been tempted a couple of times, but it had never seemed quite this easy: a few centimeters from his face with a mate urging him to test it out.

"I'm not sure I want to get into that stuff," James said.

"You tart," Junior laughed. "What harm's one snort gonna do?"

Nicole came out of the girls' toilet and looked at James.

"The birthday boy doesn't want any," Junior giggled.

"Good," Nicole said. "More for me."

She shoved the metal straw up her nostril and vacuumed up half the coke left in the pot. Her head shot backwards and she wiped a tear off her cheek.

"You've *got* to, James," Nicole rasped, sounding like she was pinching her nose.

"It's not gonna blow your mind or nothing," Junior said. "It just makes the world seem a nicer place."

"Except inside your nose," Nicole giggled. "That goes like a chunk of rubber."

James looked into the dish. There was only a tiny bit left and he was curious to try it, just once. Nicole gave him the straw. James pushed it up his nose and leaned towards the white powder.

"Come on, you guys," Kelvin shouted. "I'm locking up."

He was at the top of the stairs. Junior pulled the coke out of sight before James had time to sniff. James spun around, hiding the metal straw in his hand.

"Give us a second," Junior shouted.

"*Now,*" Kelvin shouted. "Don't mess me about."

The three of them staggered upstairs, through the youth club and on to the pavement out front. The nights were starting to turn cold. Kerry, April, and a big bunch of other kids were standing around shivering. James found April.

"You want to come round to our house?" James asked. "It's only ten minutes' walk."

April shook her head. "Kelvin's giving me, Junior, and Dinesh a lift home. I'll have to smuggle Junior in round the back. If our dad sees him in that state, he'll go bonkers."

"OK," James said, leaning forward and giving April a kiss. "I'll speak to you tomorrow. Maybe we can go to the Reeve Center or something."

"Cool," April smiled. "It looks like you've got your own set of problems over there."

James turned around in time to see Nicole hurl up in the gutter.

Kerry went in first and checked the coast was clear. Ewart and Zara had gone up to bed early, which was a relief. James and Kyle dragged Nicole into the kitchen and draped her over a dining chair.

"I'm gonna die," Nicole sobbed, resting her elbows on the dining table. "I feel so ill."

Kerry ran her a glass of water. "Drink that," she said. "Alcohol dehydrates you. The water will stop you getting a hangover."

James hadn't drunk anywhere near as much as Nicole, but he decided a drop of water would do no harm and ran a glass for himself.

"I think I'm gonna be sick again," Nicole moaned.

Kyle got one of the buckets from under the sink and stood it on the table. Nicole leaned into it, her sobs echoing into the plastic.

"Get us a tissue," she groaned. "My nose is running."

James ripped off a square of kitchen towel and handed it over. When Nicole took the bucket away from her face, they all saw her nose bleeding.

"Oh, my God," Kerry gasped. "I think we should wake Zara up."

"No," Nicole begged. "I'll get into trouble. Take me to bed and I'll sleep it off."

Kerry grabbed the roll of kitchen towel and the bucket, and took them upstairs to the girls' bedroom. James and Kyle each wrapped one of Nicole's arms around their back, picked her off the chair, and helped her stumble along the hallway.

"Nicole," Kyle said firmly. "We're at the bottom of the stairs. Lift your legs."

Nicole's head slumped forward and her legs gave way. A fresh wave of blood began streaking out of her nose.

"*Oh, Jesus,*" Kyle said desperately. "Put her down."

Kerry was coming back down the stairs to help them. When she saw Nicole's limp body on the hallway carpet, she spun around and burst into Ewart and Zara's room. Ewart raced downstairs in his boxers. Kyle was taking Nicole's pulse.

"Her heartbeat's all over the place," Kyle said.

"Shall I call 999?" James asked.

"There's no point hanging around for an ambulance," Ewart said. "I'll drive her."

Zara was running downstairs in her dressing gown, carrying clothes and trainers for Ewart. Ewart stepped into the clothes before scooping Nicole off the floor. Out on the driveway, Kyle had opened up the people carrier.

"She's taken some cocaine," James blurted.

He didn't want to grass, but it might save her life if the doctors knew what was in her system.

"Christ almighty," Ewart shouted, as Kyle helped him lay Nicole across the back seat. "That's all we need."

Ewart climbed into the driver's seat and slammed the door so hard James thought the glass might break. When the car was out of sight, James closed the front door and turned around to face Kerry and Zara, who were both in tears.

"I hope she's OK," Kerry sniffed.

"You're absolutely sure she took cocaine?" Zara asked.

James nodded, feeling a lump forming in his throat. "I saw it."

"Why didn't you stop her?" Kerry asked angrily.

"I tried to," James lied. "She wouldn't listen to me."

"What about you, James?" Zara asked. "Did you take any?"

"No way," James said. "I'd never go near it."

"That's a relief," Zara said. "If they find traces of cocaine in Nicole's urine, they'll expel her from CHERUB."

"Is that for certain?" James asked.

"You both know the rules," Zara said. "There's zero tolerance for class A drugs. We even put the reminder at the bottom of the mission briefing when you guys signed your names, in case you considered anything silly."

"Are you two going up to bed?" Kerry asked anxiously.

"I suppose," Zara said. "Unless you want a drink or something first."

"I don't think I'll sleep," Kerry said. "I don't want to be on my own wondering what's happening with Nicole."

Zara pulled Kerry into her chest and gave her a hug. "I'll sit up with you for a while," she said. "Don't worry."

James thought about Nicole. Imagining her being wheeled into hospital and having tubes pushed down her throat and needles under her skin. He wondered what it would be like to go into a coma and realized he didn't feel like being on his own either.

James and Kerry got their duvets and sat together in the living room with their feet on the coffee table. It was a weird feeling; anxious for news, being exhausted but not able to sleep. The hands on the clock seemed to be frozen.

Zara had to go upstairs to sort out Joshua when he started bawling.

"Did you really snort any coke?" Kerry whispered.

"No," James said indignantly. "I already told you."

"In front of Zara," Kerry said. "What about just between you and me?"

"I saw them doing it and got offered a snort, but I said no."

"I'm glad," Kerry smiled. "I'd have bet my life savings that if something as dumb as that was going down on your birthday, you'd be into it."

"I'm not a complete moron, you know," James said.

Kerry's mobile started ringing. James had changed her ring tone to the national anthem for a joke while she was in the toilet at the youth center, but that didn't matter now.

"Dinesh," Kerry said, surprised. "Are you crying? Calm down . . . Tell me what the matter is. What the hell are you doing at the police station?"

CHAPTER 21

BRAINDEAD

Three hours earlier, Dinesh had hitched a lift home in Kelvin's car with April and Junior. He lived with his mum and dad in a flash house a few doors down from Keith Moore. Mr. Singh was in his study, working on his laptop. Dinesh wasn't surprised to find him there, even though it was past eleven.

"Good tme at the youth club?"

"Nothing very exciting," Dinesh said. "Did Mum ring up?"

"She asked me to make sure you washed behind your ears and changed your underpants."

"Very funny, Dad," Dinesh said, grinning. "I'm off to bed. Don't sit up working all night."

Dinesh had brushed his teeth and was getting into bed when he heard a saloon car pull on to the driveway. Sometimes cars used the drive to turn around, but this one stopped and Dinesh watched two doors open. Another car stopped behind. It was white, with blue lights and cop markings on the roof.

"Dad!" Dinesh shouted.

The two cops from the first car were in plain clothes. The three out of the second wore uniform and carried rifles. Two cops split off and jogged around the house, covering the back exit. Dinesh quickly slid on his tracksuit bottoms and ran on to the landing.

"Dad!" Dinesh shouted again, nervously. "The police are outside."

The front door exploded into the hallway. Police never ring the doorbell when it's a drug bust, because it gives the suspect a chance to destroy evidence. Dinesh had never seen a gun outside of a museum before. Now two were aimed at his head.

"On the floor," the cop barked. "Hands where I can see 'em."

They ran up the stairs towards Dinesh, who was trying to stop himself shaking.

"Don't be frightened, son," the cop said. "Where's your old man?"

Mr. Singh opened the door of his study. The guns swung towards him.

"Hands in the air."

One of the plain-clothes cops bounded up the stairs. He pushed Mr. Singh against the wall and locked the handcuffs.

"You have the right to remain silent. Anything you do say can be taken down and used in evidence against you. . . ."

The armed cop looked down at Dinesh.

"Who else is home?"

"Nobody," Dinesh said.

"Where's your mum?"

"Barcelona. She's back tomorrow."

"How old are you?"

"Twelve."

"We can't leave you here on your own," the cop said. "You'll have to come with us."

A police car pulled up on the driveway. Dinesh looked nervous when Zara opened the door.

"You don't mind me staying, do you?" Dinesh asked. "They asked me to think of somewhere I could go until Mum gets home. Kerry was the first person I thought of."

"Don't worry," Zara said, putting her hand on Dinesh's shoulder. "There are so many kids coming in and out of this house, one more won't make any difference."

The cop gave Zara a custody form to sign, while Dinesh wandered into the living room. Kerry stood up and gave him a hug.

"I'm so sorry about your dad," Kerry said.

"I told you he was a crook," Dinesh said angrily. "It was bound to happen sooner or later." He looked at the duvets and pillows scattered around the living room.

"We couldn't sleep," Kerry explained. "They had to take Nicole to the hospital."

"Is it serious?"

"Kyle called from the hospital. They gave her an adrenalin shot to bring her round. Then they pumped her stomach."

"I saw that on TV once," Dinesh said. "It's so nasty. They force a rubber tube down your throat and right down into your stomach."

"They'll keep her in under observation for a few hours," James said. "But they reckon she'll be OK."

Dinesh managed a smile. "I wouldn't want to be in her shoes when she gets home."

It was gone 3 a.m. when a cab dropped Kyle home from the hospital. Zara told them all to go upstairs and try to get some rest. Dinesh slept on Nicole's bed.

While the mission was going smoothly, Ewart had been acting calm, but when he shook James awake at eleven o'clock that Saturday morning, he looked rabid.

"In the bathroom, *now,*" Ewart barked.

"Uh?" James said, still half-asleep.

Ewart grabbed James by his wrist and practically dislocated his shoulder as he yanked him out of bed. He shoved James towards the bathroom, bolted the door, and pushed him up to the wall.

"We've got to keep the noise down while Dinesh is in the house," Ewart whispered. "But you better start giving me straight answers about last night, or I'm gonna make you sorry."

"I haven't done anything," James said.

"So what's *this* then?" Ewart asked, producing the metal straw that had come out of Junior's cocaine. There were still specks of white powder stuck on one end.

"It's not mine," James said.

"Liar," Ewart snarled. "I was checking inside the pockets before I put the washing on. It was in your jeans."

James realized he must have pocketed it when Kelvin had surprised them.

"I swear I never took coke," James said frantically. "That belongs to Junior. I must have picked it up by mistake."

Ewart opened the medicine cabinet and took out a plastic sample bottle.

"We'll see, won't we? I got three of these at the hospital last night," Ewart said. "Pee in that. I'm gonna have your, Kyle's, and Kerry's urine samples tested and if there's cocaine in there, you'll be out on your arse with Nicole."

James was pleased to see the sample bottle. The test would clear up any argument.

"Give it here," he said, smirking confidently. "How much do you want to bet that I'm clean? Fifty quid, a hundred?"

"Cut the smart mouth," Ewart said. "And piss."

James angrily snatched the bottle off Ewart, flipped up the plastic lid, and stood over the toilet. He was usually busting when he woke up, but he couldn't go with Ewart standing behind him.

"Can't you wait outside?" James asked.

"You might tamper with it," Ewart said. "Try thinking about waterfalls or something."

When he'd finished, James handed the bottle to Ewart.

"Any money you'd like," he said cockily.

His air of confidence had taken the edge off Ewart's anger. "Go back to your room and tell Kyle to get over here."

After Kyle had gone, James slumped on his bed feeling pleased with himself. Ewart would look like an idiot when the drug test came back. Then he had a horrible thought: if Kelvin had called down the stairs a couple of seconds later . . .

James relived the drunken instant when the dish of white powder was just centimeters from his face. He felt sick when he realized how close he'd come to snorting a dangerous drug—and getting himself booted out of CHERUB.

CHAPTER 22

NICOLE

Junior called James on his mobile.

"Dude."

"You sound happy," James said. "What's up?"

"It's pandemonium here," Junior said. "I've got a killer hangover and the pigs arrested over eighty KMG people last night. My dad thinks he's about to get busted. He keeps running up to the curtain every time a bird flies past the window."

"Mr. Singh got nabbed," James said. "Dinesh spent the night here. Ewart's taken him to the airport to meet his mum."

"They nicked Uncle George and Uncle Pete," Junior said. "They're not my real uncles, but they've been working for Dad since before I was born."

"So how come you're in a good mood?" James asked.

"Nicole, of course," Junior said. "I had my hands *everywhere*. No offense, James, I know she's your sister and everything."

"She's in hospital," James said. 'The coke did her in."

"No way," Junior gasped. "That explains why I couldn't get her mobile. Is she OK?"

"Yeah, but I wouldn't get your hopes up about seeing her any time soon. She overdosed once before," James said, repeating Zara's latest cover story. "Ewart and Zara are terrified that she's gonna end up killing herself. They've arranged for her to go back to a care home in London for a psychiatric assessment."

"Oh, my God," Junior blurted. "I'm really sorry, man. I'd never have offered her coke if I'd known she had a problem. How long will she be gone for?"

"Um," James said, scratching for an answer, "it all depends on the assessment, I suppose. . . . She might not be back at all . . . Anyway, I just heard Zara pulling up with a carload of shopping. She goes loopy if I don't help her unload."

"I'll see you then," Junior said. "April asked if you fancied coming round for Sunday lunch?"

"Maybe," James said. "I don't know what's going on at the moment, with Nicole and that. I'll ring you later."

James ended the call. There really was a car pulling up, but it was John Jones. Zara made tea while John Jones explained what had been going on over the last twenty-four hours.

"It all came out of the production facility you kids

found at Thunderfoods. KMG imports and distributes cocaine through lots of different channels, but you guys uncovered the weakest link in the chain. Almost every gram was being packaged in the automated plant at Thunderfoods.

"We wired the place with cameras and bugs and watched everybody who came and went through binoculars. I've been on drug investigations where you go months without finding a good lead. Once we had Thunderfoods under surveillance, we started getting so much information we had to bring in extra staff to handle it.

"You'd get a couple of guys coming in to mix and package a few kilos of coke. It's boring work, so they'd usually start gossiping. They were off guard and the quality of information was unbelievable. Names, dates, phone numbers, flight numbers. 'What are you doing next week? Where's your next shipment coming in? What deal is old so-and-so working on at the moment?'

"We've made a hundred arrests already, but we're not even scratching the surface. We're sending information to police stations all over the country and another two or three hundred guys are gonna get pulled over the next few days. By the time we're done, KMG will be lucky if it can sell a bag of sweets in a school playground."

"I just spoke to Junior," James said. "Keith Moore still hasn't been arrested."

"That's politics," John said. "Us MI5 guys wanted to keep the undercover work going until we had enough evidence to get Keith, but the police wouldn't hold out. They've got hundreds of people working on Operation Snout. Not just police officers, but the administration and back-up staff that go with them. It's costing over a million pounds a month and there was talk of shutting it down if they didn't start getting results."

"So Keith Moore might get off?" Kerry asked.

John smiled uneasily. "I hope not, Kerry. I'd say out of the top ten people in KMG, we've got enough evidence to put eight in prison. We're gonna try and flip a couple of those guys. We're offering total immunity from prosecution. Given a choice between twenty years in prison and walking home to your wife and kids, we reckon a few people might start tattling on Keith Moore."

"So is there anything special we should be looking out for?" Kyle asked.

"I'd be amazed if you kids make another breakthrough to match the one you've already made," John said. "Just keep in with the bad guys and we'll see if anything else turns up."

"Actually, kids," Zara said, "I had to phone Mac and explain what happened with Nicole. He seems to think we've achieved most of what we set out to do. He's not impressed by what happened to Nicole and he wants the rest of you out of harm's way. I expect we'll be heading back to campus in a few weeks, so you might want to start dropping hints to your friends. Suggest that Ewart has gone for a job interview and there's a chance you might be moving back to London."

John Jones did his routine of shaking everyone's hands before he left.

"Of course," he said, holding on to Kerry's hand after he'd shaken it, "this young lady is the biggest hero of the lot."

Kerry still had an ear-to-ear grin five minutes after John Jones had driven away. James got sick of looking at it and chucked Joshua's furry cement mixer at her head. Kerry chucked it back and they ended up chasing each other around the dining table, along the hallway, and into the living room.

"I'm a hero," Kerry sang as she ran. "Hero, hero, hero. Hero, hero, hero."

James chucked a couple of sofa cushions at her. Kerry pushed James on to the floor and pinned him down. She grabbed his ankle and started tickling the bottom of his foot. It was James's weakest spot. Within thirty seconds she'd reduced him to a drooling wreck.

"OK," James gasped. "You're a hero. You're a hero."

Kerry stood up sharply and straightened her expression. Ewart and Nicole stood in the doorway, stone-faced. James got off the floor and wiped his lips on his sleeve.

"They tested your samples at the hospital," Ewart said. "You two are both clean for drugs, though they found higher levels of alcohol than I'd like to have seen, especially you, James. I know you're allowed to drink if you're in a situation where the kids around you are drinking, but that's not a license to go crazy."

"So you're glad you didn't bet me fifty quid?" James grinned.

Ewart gave James a vicious look. He definitely wasn't in the mood for joking.

"Go help Nicole pack and say your good-byes," Ewart said. "I'm driving her back to campus in half an hour. Where's Kyle?"

"He's in the kitchen," Kerry said.

"Right," Ewart said angrily. "Let's go and sort him out."

Ewart stormed off and slammed the kitchen door.

"What's Kyle done?" Kerry asked, looking at Nicole.

"Don't know, don't care," Nicole said bitterly. "I suppose he failed his drug test."

"No way," James said.

"He wasn't doing coke with me and Junior," Nicole said. "But he's been going to loads of parties. Who knows what he gets up to?"

"Oh, my God," Kerry said, cupping her hands over her face. "This is so sad."

Nicole started up the stairs. Kerry and James followed her.

"How do you feel?" Kerry asked.

"Not bad, except my stomach's agony and I feel like I've got an elephant standing on my head."

"I'm really sorry what happened to you," James said, as they stepped into the girls' bedroom. "It could have been any one of us."

Nicole smiled. "By the skin of your teeth, James."

"How's that?" Kerry asked.

"He was ready to snort a line," Nicole explained. "But he got distracted."

"You moron," Kerry said, giving James a shove. "You told me you tried to stop Nicole."

"That's not what I said," James squirmed.

"That's *exactly* what you said, James."

"So, anyone who takes drugs is a moron?" Nicole asked. "Eh, Kerry?"

"Nicole," Kerry said angrily, "if you'd passed out when you were in bed instead of on the stairs, nobody would have realized until morning. You might have *died*."

"You're so sly, Kerry," Nicole stormed. "You and your prissy 'I'm a good girl' act."

"What do you want me to do?" Kerry asked. "Congratulate you on getting expelled?"

"I don't care about any of this CHERUB stuff," Nicole said defiantly. "It's just a bunch of dumb kids getting hot under the collar over who wears what color T-shirt and what stupid missions they've been on. Who cares about any of that anyway? They're gonna set me up with a foster family and a place in a nice public school. I can have a boyfriend, chill out, and lead a normal life."

"Don't you get it, dumbo?" Kerry said, tapping her head with her finger. "You nearly died last night."

"You don't know what you're talking about," Nicole said, shoving Kerry backwards.

"Don't dare touch me," Kerry said, rearing up on the balls of her feet. "I could kick your butt so easily, but you're such a worthless tramp I can't even be bothered."

Kerry spun around and stormed towards the door. James went to follow her, but Nicole called him back.

"Stay and help me pack, James."

There was a desperate touch in Nicole's voice that made him turn back.

"Go ahead, help her," Kerry said. "You can make sure she doesn't rip off my stuff."

Kerry banged the door and stomped downstairs to the living room. Nicole dragged a sports bag from under her bed and started filling it.

"You know, James," Nicole said, "you're a good laugh, you don't belong at CHERUB either."

"You've no idea how badly I need CHERUB," James said. "Sometimes all the work and training does my head in, but my life was a nightmare before I came here. I was in some crummy council home and I kept getting in trouble. If CHERUB hadn't picked me, I probably would have ended up in prison."

"I'm glad I'm out of it," Nicole said, zipping up her bag. "As long as my new foster parents don't turn out to be old farts."

"What is it you've got against old people?" James asked.

Nicole sat on the edge of her bed. "You know my family died in a car crash?"

"I'd heard."

"They were crossing a road in broad daylight. This stupid old fool sailed his car through a red light and smashed into them. They tested his eyes after the accident and it turned out he could barely see past the end of his nose."

"That's so bad," James said. "I'm sorry."

"If it had been a young guy, they would at least have locked him away. But no, because it was some old fart, they took pity and let him off. My mum, my dad, and my little brothers were killed and he totally got away with it. Then everyone goes around telling me I should have respect for old people. Well, they can shove that idea right up their arse."

Ewart leaned in the door and looked at Nicole.

"Are you packed?"

"Just finishing off," Nicole said.

"OK," Ewart said. "I'm going to the toilet. I'll see you at the bottom of the stairs in five minutes."

"Wish me luck?" Nicole asked, looking at James.

"Sure," James said, wrapping his arms around her and giving her a squeeze. She had a tear rolling down her cheek.

James carried one of Nicole's bags out to the people carrier. Kerry stood in the living room doorway with folded arms and a frosty expression. James thought it was a shame Kerry and Nicole had fallen out. They'd got on well up to now.

Zara came out from the kitchen, gave Nicole a hug, and wished her good luck with whatever life she chose to lead. When the car started pulling off the driveway, Kerry had a change of heart and ran on to the doorstep. She stood between James and Zara, and waved Nicole off.

"I hope she sorts herself out," Kerry said.

"We'll set her up with a good family," Zara said. "I think she'll be better off in the long run. Not everyone is cut out to be a cherub."

"Oh," James said, suddenly remembering, "what happened with Kyle?"

"It's his business," Zara said. "It's up to him whether he wants you guys to know or not."

James and Kerry found Kyle face down on his bunk, having a sulk.

"Why was Ewart having a go at you?" James asked.

"They found traces of cannabis in my urine sample," Kyle said. "Almost every drug you could name passes through your body in a day or so. Unfortunately for me, cannabis lingers in your system for up to three weeks."

"But you *did* take some?" Kerry said, sounding outraged.

"It's not some massive deal, Kerry," Kyle said defensively. "I had a few puffs of a joint that was going around at some kid's house two Saturdays ago."

"So how come you're not expelled?" Kerry asked.

"Cannabis is a class C drug," Kyle explained. "I would have been sent back to campus, but they could hardly send me and Nicole away on the same day without it looking suspicious."

"So you're gonna get your botty spanked when we go back to campus?" James grinned.

"That's how it looks," Kyle said. "Probably a few weeks scrubbing floors, followed by a few months suspended from missions."

CHAPTER 29

LUCK

Sunday morning, James was in the living room on his PlayStation. Ewart came in and pushed his feet off the coffee table.

"You just gonna sit around doing nothing all day?" he asked.

"That was plan A," James grinned. He'd missed a lot of sleep over the last couple of weeks. It was nice to bum around indoors for a change.

"What about deliveries?" Ewart asked.

"Kelvin called me," James said, reluctantly pausing his game. "The nice lady who calls me with my deliveries has been busted. Not that it matters, because there aren't any customers. Everyone's heard about the arrests and they're scared that if they ring up for a drug delivery, they'll have PC Plod turning up on their doorstep rather than the likes of me."

"Does Kelvin think KMG is ruined?"

"He says it'll take at least a month to get new supplies of coke and set up distribution. Even then, customers will be wary. Other gangs will move in and snatch a lot of the business, but Kelvin thinks KMG has the clout to get back on top of things, provided Keith Moore doesn't get nicked."

"What about Junior and April? Have you heard from them?"

"I've spoken to both of them. I got invited to lunch, but I can't be arsed."

Ewart sounded slightly annoyed. "Why aren't you going?"

"What's the point?" James shrugged. "The mission's as good as over. We'll all be back at campus in a week or two."

"James, the mission carries on either until Keith Moore is caught, or we officially get told to come home. You're our closest link to the Moore kids now Nicole is gone. I'd be interested to know what Keith is up to at the moment."

James reached forward and switched off the PlayStation, looking thoroughly put-out.

"Fine," he huffed. "I'll call Junior and reinvite myself."

Ewart left James at the Moore house, then drove on a few hundred meters to drop Kerry at Dinesh's.

James thought there might be a bad atmosphere, but

when Keith opened the door he was in swimming shorts with a big grin on his face. The house was huge and even though they had a cleaner, you could tell four kids lived there the second you walked through the door. There were trainers and cushions chucked everywhere, dirty cups and plates. James thought it was cool. He hated it when you go round some kid's house and the mother goes hysterical when you put your cup down in the wrong place.

"Come in," Keith said, dripping over the floor tiles. "April and Junior are swimming."

"I never realized you'd be in the pool."

"Don't worry. Go up to Junior's room. He's got about ten pairs of swimming shorts in his middle drawer."

"Cheers," James said.

Junior had a massive room with a big screen TV and video, a wardrobe full of decent clothes, and a gumball machine. It wasn't a bad spread for a kid who claimed to be hard done by.

James stripped off and came down in a pair of orange shorts with seahorses on them. The indoor pool was about fifteen meters long, with palms and flowerbeds along one side. Ringo and Keith were swimming laps. April and Junior were at the far end in a whirlpool tub. James stepped into the steaming water, gave April a kiss, and sat beside her. She looked fit in her swimming suit.

Once he was in the tub, James was glad Ewart had made him get out of the house. The warm jets of water made him feel relaxed and having April cuddled up close was a bonus. He took his hand off her back when Keith wandered up.

"I'm ordering take-away," Keith said, raising his voice

above the bubbling water. "What do you guys want?"

"Indian," April said.

"Pizza," Junior said.

Keith looked at James. "Deadlock. The guest gets the casting vote."

James didn't like Indian much, but April had a cute grin on her face and she started sliding her toes up his leg.

"Indian," he said.

"Traitor," Junior said, slicing his hand through the water and giving James a soaking.

James, Junior, and April had a splashing battle, then toweled off and put on robes before the food arrived. Ringo and Keith sat on the sofa while James, April, and Junior arranged themselves on cushions around the coffee table will all the boxes of food on it.

Keith found the remote between two sofa cushions and switched the TV hanging on the wall to News 24. They all concentrated on stuffing their faces until the TV cut to a policeman. The title up on screen said: "Superintendent Carlisle, Operation Snort." He started speaking to the camera.

"We've made over one hundred and fifty arrests in the last three days and believe we have taken a major step against illegal drugs in this country. . . ."

A lump of prawn vindaloo smacked Superintendent Carlisle in the forehead and began sliding down the screen.

". . . This represents a giant stride forward in our war against illegal drugs in the U.K. . . ."

"Try and catch me, Superintendent," Keith shouted, chucking another prawn.

Keith's kids joined in, hurling lumps of curry and

handfuls of rice until the screen was a blurry mess. Everyone laughed, but it had a hollow ring, like they were really scared by the arrests.

Junior turned and looked at his dad. "Did you ask James about Miami?"

"No," Keith said.

"Miami?" James asked.

"I usually take the boys to my place in Miami for half-term," Keith explained. "But Ringo says he's got a lot of homework and doesn't want to go this year."

"He's having a party," April explained. "I expect we'll come home and find this house razed to the ground."

"Who says I'm having a party?" Ringo said defensively.

"It'll be boring without Ringo," Junior said. "And the plane ticket's paid for, so Dad suggested I take a mate."

"Cool," James said, bursting into a grin. "I'll have to check with my parents, but it should be OK. Are you going, April?"

"No," April said. "Me and Erin are skiing with our mum."

"It's a family tradition," Keith explained. "We all used to go on holiday together, but I'd always be strangling my wife, Junior and April usually end up rolling around the floor if they're together for more than a few hours, and Erin . . ."

"We think the real Erin was abducted at birth and replaced by an alien from Neptune," Junior explained.

"I've been here about ten times and I've still never met Erin," James said.

Keith shook his head and smiled. "That girl may be

my daughter, but I haven't got a clue what goes on inside that little head of hers."

"You'll love Miami," Junior said. "It's boiling hot and our house is right on the beach. You can crawl out of bed, run down the beach, and be in the sea within thirty seconds."

"I'll ring Zara up right now," James said.

"Is Kyle home?" Ringo asked.

"Probably," James said. "Did you want a word with him?"

Ringo gave his dad a mischievous grin as he spoke. "Just tell Kyle there's a big party going down here, Friday after next."

Keith burst out laughing. James thought Keith was a really cool dad, especially considering the stress he was under.

"You can have your party," Keith said. "But Kelvin and a couple of other guys from the boxing club are gonna chaperone it, in case any of your pals decide to start peeing on the carpets or stubbing out ciggies on my Egyptian rug."

"What?" Ringo asked. "I don't want some crew of muscle heads bossing my mates around. I'll be totally embarrassed."

"Don't worry," Keith said. "I'll tell them to keep a low profile."

James gave Zara a call. She was surprised, but she said it was OK to travel.

It was already turning dark when James got home. He recognized John Jones's Toyota on the driveway. He was in the living room, with Zara, Ewart, Kerry, and Kyle.

"What's this in aid of?" James asked.

John Jones explained. "As soon as Zara heard about your little holiday, she contacted me and I rushed over here."

"Why is me going on holiday such a big deal?" James asked.

"Miami is the center of the world drug trade," John explained. "It's no coincidence that Keith Moore has a home there. The saying goes: 'If you want a gram of cocaine, stand on any street corner. If you want a ton of cocaine, stand on any street corner in Miami.'

"There are twenty smaller gangs snapping at the heels of KMG. Keith has to get his hands on fresh supplies of cocaine and get KMG working again. A lot of his top people have been arrested and he won't know who he can trust, so he'll be brokering the deal himself."

"So what can I do?" James asked.

"We know KMG has a long-standing relationship with a Peruvian drug cartel called Lambayeke," John explained. "To pay Lambayeke, Keith will have to transfer millions from his overseas bank accounts. If we can find out what bank and country Keith's money is coming from, we'll have a lead that could help us unravel the whole financial structure of KMG and maybe even Lambayeke as well.

"Keith can't keep every detail of his business in his head. He'll be going to Miami carrying some piece of information that links him to his money. It might be a bank account number, or the phone number of a bank, or a file on the hard drive of his laptop. Whatever it is, you're going to be in Keith Moore's house for seven days. You're never going to get a better opportunity to grab information than that."

James smiled. "So much for bumming around on the beach all day."

"As soon as this meeting is over, I'm driving you back to campus for two days' emergency training," Ewart said. "There's a lot you need to learn, but we don't want you away from the Moore family for more than a few days."

"What excuse will we use for me not being at school?"

"We'll tell everyone you were planning to visit your aunt and cousin Lauren during half-term, but we brought it forward because of your trip to Miami."

CHAPTER 24

FACTS

James slept better than he had for ages. His bed in Luton was cramped and had springs that jammed into your back; plus on campus there was no Kyle squirming in the top bunk and no 300-seater jets whizzing overhead. The plumbing worked better as well. James put on a Metallica CD and rocked out in his shower, without having to worry about getting scalded every time someone touched the tap in the kitchen.

When he was clean, he put on his CHERUB uniform. The rooms and corridors in the main building reminded James of a hotel. As he waited for the lift down to the dining room, he reflected that the only thing lacking was room service.

He loaded up a plate with bacon and hash brown and ate bits with his fingers while one of the staff cooked him a mushroom omelette. Most kids had gone off to first lesson, but Amy was sitting at a table dipping a finger of toast into a soft-boiled egg.

"You're wearing a white T-shirt," James said, taken aback.

You got the white shirt when you retired as a cherub.

"My undercover days are over," Amy said.

James looked sad. "But . . ."

"I'm seventeen, James," Amy said. "I took my A-levels in the summer. I'm working here as an assistant dogsbody to earn some cash, then I'm off to see the world before I start university in January."

"Where are you going?"

"Cairns, Australia. My big brother lives there."

"That's the other side of the world," James said miserably. "I'll probably never see you again."

"You've only got to hop on an airplane. My brother set up a diving school when he finished university. He took me up to the Great Barrier Reef a couple of weeks ago. It's so beautiful there."

"So you're training me up for my Miami trip?" James asked.

Amy nodded. "And you better behave. Now I'm staff, I'm allowed to dish out punishments."

"Cool," James grinned. "Who have you nailed?"

"Only one kid," Amy said. "I was covering for one of the judo instructors. This horrible little red-shirt boy kept giving me lip. He got a week cleaning up the changing room near the cross country trail."

"It always gets really muddy in there," James smiled. "How old was this kid?"

"Eight," Amy said. "He started bawling his eyes out, but I didn't back down. After that, all I got from the other kids in the class was, 'Yes Miss, No Miss, Of course Miss.'"

"So what have I got?" James asked.

Amy slid a heap of books across the table. They were all weighty. One was called *The Ultimate Hacker's Reference* and was over ten centimeters thick.

"It's gonna be a busy couple of days," Amy said. "I'll try and get you through techniques for hacking Keith's computer by this afternoon. Then we'll make a start on international banking."

"What's that in aid of?" James asked.

"Suppose Keith was on the telephone and he mentioned a euro CD and an order party. Unless you know about banking, you wouldn't be able to tell whether Keith is on the phone to a Russian money laundering syndicate, or organizing a disco."

"Sounds like this is gonna be a real riot," James said, flipping through one of the giant books as he tucked in a fork-load of bacon.

Amy ignored him. "MI5 are preparing a dossier on the Lambayeke cartel. They'll e-mail it here and we'll work on that tomorrow morning. Tomorrow afternoon we'll finish up by testing out your hacking skills on real computers."

James and Amy studied into the evening. You normally got at least two weeks on the background material for a mission, but everything had to be crammed into a couple of days. When it got to eight o'clock, Amy finally let him off.

"I feel like a swim," she said. "Coming?"

CHERUB had four pools. The learners' pool was the smallest and least attractive, but Amy had taught James to swim there before and they both wanted to go back for old times' sake. There was nobody else around. Most kids preferred using the main pool, which had diving boards and water slides.

They had a ten-lap race. James kept up with Amy until they made the last turn, when she blasted off into the distance. They got out and sat on the edge. James felt like his lungs were about to burst.

"You're getting stronger," Amy grinned, not even short of breath. "You might be able to give me a real race when you grow a bit bigger and shed the puppy fat."

James's heart sank when he realized Amy had been toying with him.

"I'll definitely come and visit you in Australia when I'm older," he said, circling his big toe through the water. "If that's all right."

Amy smiled. "Of course it's all right. My brother has mates from his CHERUB years turning up all the time."

"It's weird," James said. "I never even think about the kids I knew before I came to CHERUB, but I feel really close to the kids I know here."

"It's a defined psychological phenomenon," Amy said.

James looked mystified. "You what?"

"All humans have a basic need to share their lives

with someone," Amy explained. "Children with their parents, adults with their wives, husbands, or whoever. Because the kids at CHERUB have no parents, they make very strong bonds with each other. There's a big reunion on campus every couple of years. You'd be amazed how many cherubs end up marrying each other."

"Sometimes it really gets on my nerves how smart-assed everyone at CHERUB is," James grinned. "I mean, how come you know stuff like that?"

"I'm doing psychology at university," Amy said. "They gave us a list of books to read before the course starts. Besides, James, you're not exactly dumb yourself. CHERUB wouldn't even sniff at a kid who wasn't way above average."

"When I'm at a normal school, I'm always one of the cleverest," James said. "But I'm just kind of ordinary here."

"So anyway," Amy said. "When you arrived at CHERUB a few months after your mum died, it was natural that you formed a strong attachment to any girl who played a big part in your life."

"Like you, because you were teaching me how to swim."

Amy nodded. "And Kerry, because she was your partner in basic training. Have you asked her out yet?"

"God! Don't you start," James moaned. "It's bad enough Kyle was always going on about it."

"But you and Kerry are always *so* sweet together. I love the way you two pick at one another like some old married couple."

James didn't want to hear it. He slipped off the side of the pool and began swimming towards the deep end.

The dossier that arrived from MI5 on the Lambayeke cartel ran to over three hundred pages, though a lot of it was photos and maps. James and Amy spent Tuesday morning in one of the mission preparation rooms, skimming through the chapters and marking the most relevant stuff with highlighter pens. James could take the books on computer-hacking back to Luton for study, but the Lambayeke dossier wasn't allowed off campus.

After they'd worked through the dossier, Amy got five laptop PCs out of a storage room and lined them up on a desk. She set an ancient wind-up timing clock to count down from fifteen minutes.

"Each of these PCs has a list of stolen credit card numbers hidden on the hard drive," Amy explained. "You've got to hack each one inside the time limit, without leaving any footprints behind."

"Which one first?" James asked.

"Doesn't matter," Amy said, leaning over and starting the timer. "Go."

James had a mini heart attack before grabbing a laptop, flipping up the screen and tapping a couple of keys.

"What do I do?" he said to himself, drumming his hands on the desk in front of him.

"Turning it on would be a good start," Amy smirked. "Don't forget to read the BIOS screen before Windows starts."

James read the figures aloud. "Two-fifty-six meg of memory. Windows ME. The hard drive isn't partitioned.

If it's ME it uses a FAT32 file system, so if I press F8 and enter DOS, I'll be able to open any file, even if it's password protected."

James hunted around the desk for a floppy disk. He waved it at Amy.

"This is the disk with the utility on that lists every file on the PC, isn't it?"

Amy nodded. "I'm not supposed to be helping you."

James looked around the side of the PC for somewhere to slot the floppy disk.

"Oh . . . This bloody thing doesn't have a floppy drive. Is there an external drive for this somewhere?"

Amy shook her head.

"Well, what do I do?"

Amy shrugged and looked at the timer. "You've got twelve minutes left to figure it out."

James fiddled hopelessly with the laptop for another three minutes. He could have happily chucked the clicking timer out the window.

"Nine minutes left."

"Tell us, Amy," James begged. "I'm totally stuck. How can I get this floppy running?"

"The computer has a network interface on the back," Amy said. "You could wire it up to one of the other laptops that has a floppy drive. Then you could go into the network properties on the second laptop and change it to a networkable floppy drive. Then the floppy drive on the second PC will work as if it's attached to the first one."

"I'm never gonna get all that done in nine minutes," James gasped.

"You might if you hurried. But why not try something much simpler?"

"Like what?" James asked.

"What's the first thing I taught you about computer hacking? The first golden rule?"

"'The weakest link is the human link,'" James said.

Amy nodded. "You're trying to find a back door into the operating system before you've tried the front door. Never assume the information you're looking for is encrypted or hidden. For all you know, you can open the document you want just by clicking on it."

"You're telling me I've just wasted six minutes?"

"Nearer to seven now," Amy said, smirking.

James switched off the computer and started from scratch. The computer only had a few programs installed and the documents were all in one folder. James opened up the list and spotted one called "Card Numbers." He double-clicked the mouse to open the file. A single line of text popped up on the screen: YOU DIDN'T THINK IT WAS GOING TO BE THAT EASY, DID YOU?

James was in too much of a state to see the funny side. He looked at the long list of documents on the screen in front of him. There wasn't time to open every one, but James realized he was looking for a list of numbers, which meant the file would be fairly small. He changed the view, so the computer showed him the size and format of each file. He skipped down the list, opening any text file that looked likely to be the list of numbers.

"Three minutes left," Amy said. "Better get your skates on, cowboy."

James started opening up files as fast as he could.

A few demanded a password before they'd open. James dragged these into a separate folder. When he ran out of documents that didn't need a password, he decided to try and guess the password of the encrypted ones.

A password can be any combination of letter and numbers, but James knew the golden rule of computer hacking: OVER 75% OF PASSWORDS ARE EASILY GUESSED. He started working down the list of most commonly used passwords that Amy had made him memorize the day before. Things like "password" "open," and "security."

After these failed, James tried to find personal details about the man who owned the laptop. He remembered that one of the documents he'd opened had been a letter to a school. He clicked on the file and skimmed through it. It was signed off by a man called Julian Stipe and mentioned the names of his three children. James tried the name "Julian" in the password box, then "Stipe." Then "Julian Stipe" with and without a space in between.

"Ninety seconds," Amy said.

He started trying the names of Mr. Stipe's kids and hit the jackpot when he typed "Jennifer." The document opened, only it wasn't the credit card numbers. The other protected documents opened with the same password and James got a massive rush when a sheet of sixteen-digit credit card numbers popped up on a screen.

"Bingo," James shouted.

"Fifteen seconds," Amy said.

"I've got them," James said. "What are you on about?"

"Time's up," Amy said. "Better luck next time."

"But I got them," James said tetchily.

"I know," Amy said. "But you weren't supposed to leave any traces behind. It was a good idea to move the password-protected documents, but you should have put them all back where they belonged and deleted the new folder you created. . . . Ready for the next one?"

"My head's spinning," James said. "Can't I have five minutes' break?"

Amy gave him an evil grin. "You don't deserve a break after that sorry performance."

She tapped the reset button on top of the clock, then flipped up the lever to set it ticking.

CHAPTER 25

DIGGING

James made such a hash of the laptop-hacking test, Amy kept him upstairs in the mission preparation room until gone nine o'clock for extra tuition. He got ratty with her as his brain stubbornly refused to accept any more information.

When they got downstairs to the dining hall, the kitchen had finished serving. There was a fridge stocked up with sandwiches and microwave meals, but James had been looking forward to a proper dinner before his return to Luton and Zara's dodgy cooking.

James slammed the door of his bedroom. He was in a stinking mood. He packed his hacking textbooks and some odd bits in a backpack, then stripped to his boxers and went to take a pee before getting in bed. There was a muggy smell as he got near his bathroom, like the smell trainers get after a couple of hours on a muddy football field. It spooked him a bit. His imagination toyed with dead rats and leaking sewage as he leaned in warily and flipped on the light.

"What the hell . . ."

It was Lauren, propped on the toilet lid in her filthy training clothes. Her hair was cropped, she had a nasty scab down her face, and all the cuts and bruises you'd expect after a month of basic training.

"What's going on?" James asked.

"I messed up," Lauren said miserably. "And I'm in so much trouble."

She did a massive sniff, followed by a howling noise. Then she broke into five minutes of the most desperate bawling James had ever heard. He tried to give her a hug, but she wouldn't let him anywhere near her.

"Lauren," James pleaded, "I want to help you, but I can't until you tell me what's happened."

"I . . . I . . . hit," she sniffled, unable to control herself.

She stood up and draped her filthy arms around James's back. Her clothes stank of mud and sweat.

He stepped backwards out of the bathroom, with Lauren flopped over him. It felt like dancing with a drunk. When he got near his bed, James peeled off Lauren's arms and she slumped on to the corner of his mattress.

"I hit him," Lauren sniffed.

"Who?" James asked.

"Mr. Large."

James sat down beside her. "I doubt he even felt it, Lauren. He's ten times your size."

"He felt it all right," Lauren said, salvaging a touch of composure.

James reached over to his beside table and got her a tissue.

"Bethany injured her back yesterday morning," Lauren explained. "We were on the assault course. I was helping her as much as I could, but she was still slow. We finished the course miles behind the other kids. Mr. Large started shouting his head off! 'You two are worthless. You're not even fit to be cherubs. You're not even fit to eat your own puke.' He got two spades and told us to start digging our own graves."

It was a standard torture from Mr. Large's repertoire. James and Kerry had got it a couple of times when they were in basic training. Large made you dig a massive hole, then fill it in. If he decided you weren't fast enough, he'd make you do it again.

"It's so tough," Lauren said. "I managed, but my back and shoulders were killing me. Bethany had a bad back to start with, so you can imagine how she was after two hours' digging. Large made me stand to attention at the edge of my grave until Bethany had finished. She kept slowing down, until she could barely drag her shovel. She begged Mr. Large for a drink, so he got that massive fire hose and drenched her with it. But the time he'd finished, the water was up to her knees. She was crying and sobbing, covered from head to toe in really thick mud. Then he started kicking the mud she'd already dug up back into the hole.

"It was hitting her in the face and he screamed at the top of his voice: 'You're too weak, little girl. You'll never make it. Why don't you quit?' It made me so angry. I was so sick of his stupid voice. I just got this urge to make him shut up. Then I realized I still had my spade on the ground, right in front of me."

"You didn't," James gasped.

"When Mr. Large turned around, I took this massive swing with it and whacked him behind the knees to knock him over. The first time only made him go wobbly. He started running towards me and I was *so* scared. I thought he was gonna kill me, so I whacked him again. As he went down, he caught his head on a rock and got knocked out."

James couldn't help smiling. "You knocked out Mr. Large! That's pure class."

"It's not funny, James," Lauren moped. "I'm probably gonna get expelled. I thought I'd killed him for a minute. There was all blood coming out of his head. I was so afraid, I ran out of the training compound and didn't stop. I wanted to speak to you before anyone else, so I went to my room and phoned you. Zara said you were on campus, but I'm not allowed upstairs to mission preparation, so I waited for you in here."

James pondered for a few moments.

"First things first," he said. "You better wash up, then we'll have to find Mac and sort this whole mess out."

"Do you think they'll boot me out?" Lauren asked.

"I hope not," James shrugged. "But laying out a teacher . . . Let's just say it's not gonna go down too well."

• • •

James found some of his smaller clothes for Lauren to wear after she got out of the shower. When they got down to the ground floor, Mac's office was locked. They asked the receptionist on the front desk.

"Mac usually heads home at about eight," he explained. "But one of the training instructors got injured and I think he's still over at the medical unit. I can ring his mobile if it's urgent."

"I think you'd better," James said.

The receptionist had a short conversation before putting down the receiver.

"Mac's coming over ASAP," the receptionist said. "I don't know what you two have done, but judging by the tone of his voice, I wouldn't want to switch shoes with you at the moment."

A few minutes later, Mac rolled up the gravel driveway outside in one of the golf buggies the staff used to move around campus.

"This way," he said stiffly, striding through reception.

He pulled a great bunch of keys out of his jacket and unlocked his door.

"Sit at the desk."

James nervously sank into one of the leather chairs at the big oak desk. Lauren looked ready to start crying again.

"So, young lady," Mac snapped. "Would you be so kind as to tell me why my senior training instructor is lying in the medical unit with a serious concussion and eight stitches in the side of his head?"

"I'm really, really sorry," Lauren groveled. "He made

me so mad. Poor Bethany could hardly stand up and Mr. Large wouldn't leave her alone."

"If Bethany was injured, she should have quit," Mac said. "It wasn't your business to interfere."

"So what are you gonna do to her?" James asked.

"I don't like expelling people," Mac said. "But if I don't expel a cherub for a serious assault on a member of staff, then what exactly *do* you get expelled for?"

"I know what Lauren did was wrong," James said. "But it's not like she walked into a classroom and belted a teacher for no reason. She was knackered and she was watching one of her friends get tortured by a raving lunatic. Everyone wants to take a swing at Mr. Large at some point during basic training. It's just unlucky Lauren happened to have a spade nearby when the thought crossed her mind."

"Hmm," Mac said, covering a tiny smile with his fingers. "I suppose there's an element of truth in that. If I did expel Lauren, though, we'd send her to a good school and set her up with a foster family near campus so that you could visit her at weekends."

"I don't care if she only lives across the street," James said. "If she goes, I'm going with her. We were separated after our mum died and I don't ever want that again."

"Recruiting cherubs is tricky," Mac said, "and I don't want to lose either of you two. But if I allow Lauren to stay, she'll have to accept a stiff punishment; otherwise, we'll have every kid on campus taking pot shots at the training staff."

"Please let me stay," Lauren begged. "I'll do whatever you want and I'll be so good, I swear."

"James," Mac said. "Do you have any thoughts on how we should make Lauren suffer?"

James looked uneasily at his sister.

"It's obviously got to be the worst punishment going," he said. "And it'll have to last the whole two and a bit months until she can restart basic training."

"Agreed," Mac nodded.

"What about cleaning toilets and changing rooms?" James said. "Everyone always says that's really horrible."

"Not hard enough," Mac said, sweeping the idea away with his hand. "Kids get toilets and changing rooms for swearing or skipping lessons. It's unpleasant, but all it boils down to is pushing a mop and squirting disinfectant."

"Worse than toilets, then," James said, trying to work out how Mac had twisted the situation around so that he was trying to think up some awful punishment for the person he was supposed to be helping out.

"Well," Mac grinned. "It just so happens, I did have an idea. There's a drainage problem in the wooded area on the far side of campus. The fields keep flooding because the ditches have gradually become blocked with silt. I reckon someone Lauren's size would take a couple of months to clean them all out. She'll have to work hard, every day before and after school, plus all days on Saturdays and Sundays. How do you like the sound of that, Lauren?"

"I've got to be punished," Lauren said, nodding meekly. "If that's what you want, I'll do it."

"Ditches it is," Mac said, clapping his hands together.

"And I'll be putting you on final warning, Lauren. That means if you do one more thing wrong, you'll get kicked out. And I mean *every* tiny thing. Run in the corridor, you're out. Miss a homework assignment, you're out. For the next three months, you're walking on eggshells. Your behavior must be immaculate. Is that understood?"

Lauren nodded.

"And there's one more condition," Mac said. "For you, James."

"For me?" James gasped.

Mac nodded. "You've talked me into giving Lauren a final chance. In return, I want something from you. If Lauren breaches her final warning, I want you to promise that you'll stay at CHERUB."

James thought for a couple of seconds. "But you'll put her with a family nearby so I can still see her when I'm not on missions?"

Mac nodded. "That seems reasonable."

"I suppose, then," James said.

It seemed pretty convenient, the way Mac had found the perfect punishment for Lauren. James suspected Mac had worked everything out in advance. The expulsion threat was a ploy to make him and Lauren squirm.

"And of course, Lauren," Mac grinned, "once you've cleaned out those ditches and start your second attempt at basic training, I'm sure Mr. Large will wreak his own special revenge."

Lauren slept in James's room. The bed was a double, but the two of them cuddled up in the middle. Lauren woke early and didn't seem too miserable, considering that the next five months of her life looked like being a living hell.

"Have you got a diary?" she asked.

"It's in my desk," James said, still buried under his duvet.

Lauren used the diary to work out that it was one hundred and seventy-four days until she finished her punishment and basic training. She took a sheet of paper and began writing the numbers from 174 down to zero in her neatest writing.

James poked his head out of his covers. "What are you doing, Lauren?"

"Making a countdown chart. For the next hundred and seventy-four days, I'm not gonna whinge or cry about anything. I'll take this piece of paper everywhere I go. However bad it gets, all I'm going to think about is how many hours it is until I can tick off the next number. In one hundred and seventy-four days I *will* pass basic training. I swear it, on our mum's grave."

James scrambled out of bed.

"No way," he said angrily. "You can't swear something like that on Mum's grave. Some things are out of your control. What if you get injured, or sick?"

"I won't," Lauren said sternly. "If something hurts, I'll close my eyes and think about the piece of paper in my pocket."

"It's a good idea to focus your mind," James said, sliding his legs into a pair of tracksuit bottoms. "But try and be realistic. There are quite a few kids who've taken three or more attempts to get through basic training. You could be setting yourself up for a big disappointment."

Lauren stood in front of James and barked an order. "Slap my face."

"Yeah, I'm really gonna hit you," James said, shaking his head with contempt.

"I'll show you I can take it," Lauren said. "As hard as you like."

"Give us a break, Lauren. You realize we could have lain in bed for at least another half hour?"

Lauren lunged forward, grabbed hold of James's nipple and gave it a savage twist. James rolled backwards on to his bed, howling in pain.

"What the *hell* did you do that for?" he shouted.

"Slap my damn face," Lauren shouted back.

"You really want to see you tough you are?" James raged. "Fine. Maybe I'll knock some sense into you."

There was a sharp *crack* as his hand hit her face. It was more painful than Lauren had expected, but she stifled her groan and toughed it out with a thin-lipped smile.

"One hundred and seventy-four days," Lauren said. "Believe it."

James grinned. "Will you be coming down to breakfast with me, or are you too tough for food as well?"

There were about sixty cherubs in the dining-hall when James and Lauren arrived. It took a couple of seconds for the room to go quiet, then chairs grated backwards and everyone stood up and started clapping and banging cutlery on the table. There were shouts of "Lauren" and whistles as well.

Shakeel was standing nearby; James looked over at him.

"What's this all about?"

"Your sister," he said, as if James was some kind of idiot. "She's the biggest hero in the history of CHERUB. Everyone dreams of getting revenge on Mr. Large, but I never imagined any kid would really have the guts to do it."

Kids piled in from all directions, until Lauren stood in an ocean of hugs and handshakes. A couple of stocky teenager boys hoisted Lauren off the ground, balanced her on their shoulders, and took her on a victory parade around the dining room. She had a mixture of emotions on her face; happy, freaked out, and afraid of getting her head smacked on a light fitting. As Lauren was galloped around the room, the kids at the dining tables were all pledging to help her dig.

"Dig what?" James asked.

"We heard Lauren's got to clean out the ditches at the back end of campus," Shakeel explained. "Everyone is putting on their wellies and going up there Saturday morning to help her out. We reckon with a hundred or more kids on the job, we'll get the whole lot cleared away in a day."

"Cool," James said. "That's really great of everyone."

"It's what she deserves," Shakeel said. "I wish I'd belted Mr. Large one. There's a collection going around as well. Everyone's putting money in and we're gonna get her something from that shop in town that does trophies."

Amy came up to James as Lauren was on her third circuit of the dining room.

"We had a whip round up on my floor," Amy said. "We got seventy quid. What's Lauren's favorite shop?"

"She gets a lot of stuff from Gap Kids," James said. "Why?"

"There's already more than enough for the engraved tankard," Amy explained. "We were thinking of getting her some gift vouchers, or maybe a humongous teddy bear. . . ."

CHAPTER 26

SOCKS

"You're such a jammy little git," Kerry said. "You realize me and Kyle are stuck here on Thornton until this mission is finished?"

It was Friday night. They were in the boys' bedroom and James was packing a hold-all for his flight to Miami in the morning.

"That's the wrong attitude," James said, grinning. "We're all equally important members of a team. It's just that my role is toasting on some beach in Florida, while you get to spend half-term here. If you're lucky, someone might start a fire and you can watch one of the derelict houses burn out."

"You're *such* a funny guy," Kerry sneered.

"How many socks do you reckon?" James asked.

"At least one pair for each day."

James looked in his underwear drawer and realized he only had two clean pairs. He started hunting around the floor and balling odd socks together.

"Aren't those dirty?" Kerry asked.

"A bit," James said. "But I've only worn most of them once. They don't smell that bad." He put one of them under Kerry's nose. "See."

"For *God's* sake," Kerry said angrily, pushing James's arm away. "They're appalling."

James gave them a sniff.

"*Phew,*" he gasped. "Those ones are a bit ripe. I think they're what I wore to boxing club last night. But most of these are OK."

Kerry shook her head. "You're an animal, James."

She slid off the bed and walked across the hallway to her own room. James's mobile rang.

"Hey, April," James said. "Where are you?"

"I'm at the airport with Erin and my mum," April said. "We're sitting here waiting to board the plane and I thought I'd say hi."

"I only saw you a few hours ago," James said.

"Don't you want to talk to me?" April said, with a hint of acid in her voice.

"Of course I want to talk to you," James lied. "It's just . . . I'm really busy, packing and stuff."

"I'm wearing your Nike watch," April giggled. "So I can think about you whenever I look at the time."

"Don't forget to give that back," James said. "It's my only good one."

"Blow me a kiss," April said.

James shook his head before doing a couple of quick smooches into his phone.

"I think Zara's calling me downstairs, April. I've got to hang up. Have a wonderful trip, bye."

"James. I—"

"Gotta go, April, sorry."

James ended the call and tutted. Kerry had walked back in behind him. She was holding four pairs of clean sports socks.

"Girl trouble?" she inquired.

"Don't ask," James said.

"Borrow these," Kerry said. "My feet aren't much smaller than yours. Just make sure you wash them before you give them back."

"Cheers," James said, tucking the socks into his holdall. "You know, April's driving me round the bend."

"Why?" Kerry asked. "She seems like a really nice girl."

"She is," James said. "But she's too intense. She phones me *all* the time. She follows me everywhere at school and starts putting her arm around me. If I'm talking to someone else, she pulls me away and whispers stuff in my ear."

"She's got a crush on you," Kerry said. "You should be flattered."

"It's more than a crush," James said. "I bet she's already picked out the wedding dress, and now she's working out the names of our kids."

"Typical man," Kerry said indignantly. "You like having a girl draped off your arm, but only so you can snog her and impress your stupid mates."

"Give over," James said. "It's just, April is a lot keener on me than I am on her. It's not my fault girls can't resist me."

"In your dreams," Kerry grinned. "I suppose you'll dump April and leave her in a state, like you did with Nicole."

"Nicole?" James said, looking mystified. "I only kissed her once, for about two seconds."

"Nicole asked if you liked her," Kerry said. "So you snogged her, then you dumped her."

"I just didn't snog her again," James said. "I don't know why you're turning it into some big deal."

"But you didn't have the decency to face her. You just skulked around the house avoiding her for the next couple of days. Nicole was really upset."

"Well . . ." James said. "I didn't mean to hurt her feelings."

"Yeah, right."

"Look, Kerry, I don't deliberately treat girls like that. To tell the truth, there's someone else I really like."

"You mean Amy?" Kerry said. "You can practically see the drool run out of your mouth every time she comes near you, but get over it, she's seventeen years old."

"That shows how much you know," James said tersely. "Every boy on campus fancies Amy, but it's not her I'm talking about."

"Who is it then?"

"None of your business."

"Huh," Kerry sneered. "You're making it up so I don't think you're a pig."

"No," James said.

"Do I know her?" Kerry asked.

"Yes."

"It's not Gabrielle, is it?"

James laughed. "No."

"You're such a plonker," Kerry said. "I don't know why I'm even bothering to talk to you."

James loved the way she reared up on the balls of her feet whenever she got ratty.

"You really want to know who I like?" James said.

"I don't care," Kerry said, folding her arms.

"Fine, I won't tell you then."

But James had piqued Kerry's curiosity and she quickly changed her tack. "Oh . . . go on then."

James toyed with the idea of making someone up, or saying something stupid, but he realized he was never going to have a better opportunity to tell Kerry how he really felt. He couldn't carry on bottling it for the rest of his life. He took a deep breath.

"I . . ."

His mouth dried up. He felt like his head was about to explode.

Kerry shook her head. "I knew you were lying."

"No, I like *you,*" James blurted.

He stared at Kerry for what felt like a trillion years, studying her face for some kind of reaction.

"Are you winding me up?" Kerry asked, suspiciously.

"Ever since basic training," James rambled. "Even when we were covered in mud doing combat practice and you were battering me, there was something about you that I really liked. I mean . . . We're always really good together, because you're kind of stuffy and do everything by the book and I'm kind of . . . Well . . . I suppose you could say I'm an idiot at times."

"You really like me?" Kerry grinned.

James felt like he wanted to die. "Yes."

"So you're serious?" Kerry asked. "Because if you're messing with me, I'll punch every single tooth out of your dumb head."

"I swear," James said. "So, you know . . . Am I wasting my time? . . . Or?"

Kerry smiled a bit. "Everyone we know has been going on about us having a thing for each other. I never thought you really liked me though. You're always going on about tits and I've hardly got any."

"Yeah, well," James said. "I'm not perfect either. But you do like me?"

Kerry nodded. "When you're not driving me insane, you're just about my favorite boy on campus."

James leaned forward to kiss her, but the hold-all was stuck in the middle of the tiny room and they had to shuffle around it. It was only a quick peck on the lips, but James got a massive rush.

"I wish you were coming to Miami with me," he said.

"It's only a week," Kerry smiled. "And there's one condition if I'm gonna be your girlfriend."

"What?" James asked.

"From now on, your underwear only gets worn once."

CHAPTER 27

MIAMI

James and Junior touched down in Miami on Saturday evening. Keith had changed his plans and flown out a couple of days earlier with his minder, George. The beefy ex-heavyweight met the boys at immigration and drove them to Keith's house in a Range Rover.

James spent the whole drive with his face stuck up against the window like a five-year-old. He loved the differences that make you know you're in a different country: traffic lights strung over the road on wires, billboards with prices marked in dollars, the huge double-trailer trucks that looked like they'd roll over your car without the man in the cab feeling so much as a jolt.

Automatic gates parted obediently when the car got

near Keith's house. The pastel blue building sprawled out behind a mass of palm trees. There were two stories, with balconies overlooking the ocean and lush terraces planted with palm trees and flowering cacti.

"Your dad is *so* loaded," James said as he stepped out of the car, shaking his head in disbelief.

"Come and check out his cars," Junior said.

There was a separate garage, the size of which reminded James of a fire station. The boys wandered in as George dealt with their bags. There was a row of everyday modern BMWs and Mercedes, but the exciting stuff was parked behind: the outlines of seven Porsches, clad in protective blankets. Junior pulled up a corner of one, revealing a headlamp.

"This ran in the Le Mans twenty-four-hour race," Junior said. "My dad had it taken up to Daytona for a track day. He got it up to three hundred kph on the straight."

"Class," James said.

"Like my motors, James?" Keith asked.

James turned around to see Keith standing in the doorway, wearing pool shoes and an unbuttoned Hawaiian shirt.

"You've got a different Porsche for every day of the week," James grinned.

"I'll take you for a cruise down South Beach in one of them tomorrow night," Keith said. "It's all lit up with neon signs after dark and there's heaps of great restaurants. Did you see anything else you wanted to do in that guidebook?"

"Is it too far to go up to Orlando?" James asked. "Junior said Universal Studios is cool."

"It's a few hundred kilometers," Keith said. "But it's no hassle driving out there. We can stay overnight and get a couple of theme parks in if you want. I've got some business to sort out, but that should be wrapped up in a day or two. Was there anywhere else?"

James shrugged. "I dunno, don't put yourself out or anything. Me and Junior can hang out on the beach, go shopping and stuff."

"The fan boats over the everglades are good fun," Keith said. "And how are you fixed for spending money?" He pulled a roll of dollars from the back of his shorts.

"I can't take money off you as well," James said. "You've already paid for my flight and everything."

Keith handed James three hundred-dollar bills and gave the same to Junior.

"Buy something for April at the mall," Keith said. "She's sweet on you."

"Cheers," James said. "Is it all right if I use the phone to tell Zara I've arrived?"

"Sure," Keith said, spreading his arms out wide. "With a house this size, the phone bill is the least of my worries."

After a quick call home, the two boys stripped to their boxers, jumped off the wooden decking at the back of the house and sprinted across the deserted white beach towards the ocean. James was feeling grotty after eight hours crammed on an airplane, but all that washed away as he curled his toes in the mushy sand and let the sea water spew over his chest.

"I'm so glad you came instead of Ringo," Junior said,

raising his voice above the waves. "This week is gonna be such a laugh."

James slept in one of the guest bedrooms. He had a four-poster bed, plus an en-suite bathroom with a giant marble tub. When he woke up, he slid on shorts and a T-shirt and opened up a set of glass doors that led on to a balcony overlooking the ocean. He took some lungfuls of sea air and leaned against the metal railing, letting the sun toast his skin.

The coastline was dotted with yachts and motor launches out for a Sunday morning cruise. An elderly Hispanic gardener was hosing the terraces below. The man nodded politely when their eyes met. It made James wonder where he'd end up in life. Would he have the $10 million oceanfront house, or would he be like the crinkled old guy who watered the flowers?

"Yo," Junior shouted.

He came strolling through James's bedroom and stepped on to the balcony.

"What you doing out here?" Junior asked.

James shrugged. "Just thinking."

"Dumb idea," Junior said. "Thinking wears out your brain. My dad wants us downstairs. We're going to IHOP for breakfast."

"You what?"

"It's a pancake place," Junior explained. "I'm getting a stack of strawberry whipped cream pancakes. They give you so many you can barely move when you finish. Dad and George are going into town for some business meeting, so they're dropping us at the mega-mall.

It's about twenty times the size of the Reeve Center. We can spill some dosh on shopping, then there's a sixteen-screen cinema and a rollercoaster if we get bored."

"Sounds good," James grinned.

James bought himself new jeans and swimming shorts and a couple of CDs, including one as a present for Kerry; then they caught a movie and waited around until George arrived to collect them. It was mid-afternoon when they got back to the house.

"How was the meeting?" James asked.

"Good," Keith grinned. "Very, very good."

"Does that mean I'll be able to go back to making money from deliveries?"

"I don't know about that," Keith said awkwardly. "Everything is gonna be different. Do you fancy going for a swim now the sun's lower?"

"Actually," James said, "do you mind if I use your laptop to e-mail my family?"

"No worries," Keith said.

George, Keith, and Junior put on swimming shorts and walked down to the sea. Once they were out of sight, James raced up to his room and got a couple of USB memory sticks and a hacker's toolkit CD-ROM out of the bottom of his bag. He climbed on to one of the metal stools at the breakfast bar in the kitchen, turned on Keith's laptop and connected to the Internet.

James clicked on Hotmail and checked the e-mails in an account he'd set up for his James Beckett alias. He had three messages from April, including one that contained a blurry photo of April and Erin in their ski suits with the message "Miss U already, April, XXX." James replied insincerely with "Miss U2," before writing a longer message to Kerry, gloating about the weather and the beautiful house he was staying in.

When he'd finished typing his e-mails, James stood up and peeked out the window, making sure Keith, George, and Junior were well clear of the house. As he flipped confidently through the files on the laptop, he realized that his marathon training sessions with Amy had been worth the brain-ache.

He clicked on Keith's documents folder. There were a couple of hundred files inside. Most had a little padlock symbol next to them, meaning they were encrypted. James decided it was too risky trying to read stuff with Keith just down on the beach. Instead, he plugged a memory card into the USB socket on the side of the laptop. The card was only the size of a pen top, but it held as much data as six CDs.

A gray box popped up on the screen: NEW USB DEVICE DETECTED. James checked the size of Keith's documents folder and realized there was enough space on the memory card to copy the whole lot over. He waited a couple of anxious minutes while the computer copied Keith's files. Then he switched off the laptop and walked back to his bedroom. He got his mobile out of his luggage and set it to search for an American network. When it found a connection, James speed-dialed the number of a local Drug Enforcement Agency office he'd been given before he left.

John Jones answered. "James?"

"Hi."

"Settled in OK?" John asked.

"Not bad," James said. "You?"

"My flight was fine, but the heat out here does me in. I'm more of a fish-and-chip-supper-on-a-cold-winter-night kind of guy."

"I can't talk for long," James said. "But I've been through Keith's laptop."

"Anything exciting?"

"Dunno," James said. "I checked for fancy stuff, like hidden partitions on the hard drive, but there's none of that. All Keith's documents are encrypted. I didn't want to fiddle about trying to open them. I've copied the whole lot on to a memory card for you guys to deal with."

"Good work," John said.

"The only thing is, how do I get the card to you?"

"We can schedule an unscheduled rubbish collection for this evening. Have you got something you want to throw out that you can hide the memory card inside?"

James looked around the room.

"There's a half-eaten box of Milk Duds I got at the cinema," he said. "I can stick the memory card inside that then throw it out."

"Perfect," John said. "Scrunch the box up, so the card doesn't fall out. Then make sure you put your rubbish in the main bins out by the road. We'll send a dustcart along to pick them up."

"Will you guys be able to break the encryption?" James asked.

"Depends on what software Keith's using," John said. "But probably. Is there anything else you'd like to report?"

"One thing Keith said struck me as odd," James said. "I asked him when I'd be able to go back to making deliveries. Keith goes, 'I don't know, everything's gonna be different.'"

"Hmm," John said. "I've no idea why he'd say that, but it's certainly interesting."

"I better go anyway," James said. "They'll be wondering what I'm doing."

"OK then," John said. "Keep up the good work and watch out for yourself."

CHAPTER 28

ORLANDO

James was having one of the best weeks of his life. Monday he went out on a fishing boat with Junior. He'd never fished out in the ocean, but the crew showed him the basics and helped him reel his first catch.

He called John Jones from the beach that evening with some snippets he'd picked up from Keith's telephone conversations. John told James that American drug enforcement agents had retrieved his Milk Duds box and MI5 specialists had managed to read most of the files. They contained details of several foreign bank accounts with transactions linking Keith to a money-laundering operation whose specialty was collecting your cash, bouncing it around the world banking system until it was untraceable, and finally depositing it in an anonymous foreign bank account—minus their 25 percent commission.

John didn't think it was enough information to get Keith convicted, but he reckoned it was a useful piece of the jigsaw.

The next day, James, Junior, and Keith set off early for the 350-kilometer drive up to Orlando. It was low season, so the boys had a great time at Islands of Adventure, scaring themselves witless on all the roller coasters and simulator rides, without wasting too much time queuing. James went nuts in the gift shop, buying T-shirts for Kyle and Kerry, and a little bib and shorts for Joshua. When he went to pay at the till, Keith put the whole lot on his credit card.

By mid-afternoon, they were all knackered and sunburnt, so they checked into a hotel and showered before heading down to the restaurant. They got an outdoor table at the edge of a man-made lake with ducks and fountains in the middle. Keith ordered tagliatelle, while James and Junior got half-pound burgers and fries. The waitress brought walnut bread and olive oil to the table while they waited for their food.

"I think I'm safe to talk here," Keith said. "Unless a bunch of cops follow me here and they're pointing a parabolic microphone at me from the other side of the lake."

James looked away from the ducks, which were scrapping over a handful of bread he'd thrown into the pond a second before he noticed the PLEASE DO NOT FEED THE DUCKS sign.

"Talk about what?" Junior asked.

"Anything," Keith said.

"Do you think the cops are listening to you most of the time?" James asked.

"The cops have microphones everywhere," Keith said. "The house in Luton, the house in Miami, my cars, my offices. I don't even know what people I can trust any more. I've even got the secret service after me."

"MI5?" James asked.

"They've been after me ever since the corruption allegations inside Operation Snort." Keith nodded. "One of my better sources told me George is working for the cops. I don't think it's true, but you can never be sure. He's a family man with a couple of kids. If the cops threatened him with a long stretch in prison, who knows what he'd be prepared to do?"

"Are you gonna have him whacked?" Junior asked.

Keith burst out laughing. "Son, if I had somebody killed every time I head a rumor about an informant, I'd be a mass murderer. The cops plant most of these rumors, hoping it will create friction inside KMG. We get our own back by dropping rumors that straight cops are taking bribes."

"Have you ever had anyone killed?" Junior asked.

"I get problems and I tell people to make them go away," Keith said. "It's not my business to know whether they tickle the guy's feet until he promises to be a good boy, or chuck him off a tenth-floor balcony."

"Cool," Junior said, grinning.

"You know that scene in the movies, where the car's heading for the edge of the cliff, and the cop cars are chasing?" Keith asked. "That's where everyone thinks I'm at, but the cops don't realize something."

"What?" Junior said.

"I've bailed out of the car," Keith said. "Everyone thinks I'm out here buying drugs, trying to get KMG up and running again. I've made a few noises in that direction, but all I'm really doing is settling debts and sorting out finances. I'll be staying in America for a few months, until things die down back home, then I'm gonna rest of my laurels. How many millions does a man need anyway?"

"That's cool, Dad," Junior smiled. "I don't ever want you going to prison."

"What will happen to KMG without you?" James asked.

"I expect it'll break up into a thousand pieces," Keith said. "Some people will go to prison. Some of the ones left on the outside will make contacts with my overseas suppliers and start importing cocaine themselves. In a year or two, nobody will even remember me. The same guys will be making deliveries and selling coke on the street; it'll just be new faces supplying them and stacking the big money into foreign bank accounts. Give it four or five years and you'll probably find one group has become dominant; a new KMG. The police will set up another Operation Snort type deal; they'll break it up. Then the whole cycle will start again."

"Stopping KMG must have some effect on the cocaine trade," James said.

"The police have budget cuts and efficiency targets, the drug dealers have got billions of pounds," Keith said. "It's like the weediest kid in Year Seven picking a fight with the entire Year Twelve rugby team. The police might land the odd punch, but they're always gonna get their arses kicked at the end of the day."

"Do you think you'll stay out of prison?" James asked.

"I'm shelling out enough in bribes and legal fees," Keith said. "So let's hope for the best, eh?"

The waitress came over with the three plates of food.

"Anyway," Keith said, shovelling down his first mouthful of pasta, "all this serious talk's gonna spoil my appetite. You boys want to go see a movie or something tonight?"

James waited until Junior was asleep before slipping out of the hotel room. He made his nightly call to John Jones from an alcove down the corridor that had an ice dispenser and a couple of Pepsi machines in it. James explained about Keith's retirement plans.

"We've tracked down more of Keith's money with the information you copied off the computer," John said. "I was starting to suspect Keith wasn't in Miami to do a drug deal and what you said confirms this. But I still don't think he's told you the whole truth."

"Why's that?" James asked.

"We traced a transaction from one of Keith's bank accounts in Trinidad. Keith just purchased half a million dollars' worth of U.S. treasury bonds in the name of Erin Moore. We contacted the bank and asked for details. Keith Moore has handed the bonds over to the bank, with instructions to sell them on Erin Moore's eighteenth birthday and pay her the money. Keith has made similar transactions for Junior, April, and Ringo. He's also set up a trust fund for his ex-wife. He's paid off the mortgages for the two houses in England and sold the house in Miami for a lot less than it's worth, to raise fast cash."

"But Keith told me he's planning to stay in Miami until the heat dies down back in England."

"There's a new owner moving into the Miami house in three weeks," John said. "And we can't find any trace of the eleven million dollars he got from the sale."

"Do you think he's using the money to buy drugs?" James asked.

"I don't think so."

"What then?"

"How many boats have you seen since you got to Miami?" John asked.

"Millions," James said. "They're everywhere."

"Once he's set up the arrangements to provide for his family, I think Keith is going to sneak out of the house, climb aboard one of those boats, and vanish like a puff of smoke."

"How come?" James asked.

"Keith can feel the net closing in. He has informants inside Operation Snort, so he knows we're close to having enough evidence to put him behind bars for a seriously long stretch."

"Where will he go?" James asked.

"Eleven million bucks will go a long way in South America. My money would be on Brazil. It's easy to disappear in a country with two hundred million people. He can buy a new identity off some corrupt government official, maybe even have a spot of plastic surgery to change his appearance."

"What about his kids and stuff?"

"They'll be set for life financially," John said. "Keith will have made double sure that the money set aside for his family can never be traced back to drug dealing."

"But he'll never be able to see them again."

"He won't see much of them from inside a jail cell, either," John said. "You keep telling me Keith is in a good mood, but that's all front. He's got to make decisions and none of his options are easy."

"So what are you doing to stop him disappearing?" James asked.

"We have a big problem. We've asked the Americans to put a twenty-four-hour watch on Keith, but they're only prepared to spare us one DEA agent. We've even offered to pay their costs, but they're short-staffed and they've got their own bad guys to catch. We're having more meetings with the Yanks to try and sort out a deal, but for at least the next few days, there's nothing to stop Keith Moore slipping off into the night."

"Except me," James said.

"Remember you're undercover," John said. "And you're supposed to be a regular kid, so don't interfere. All you can do is call me if you think he's about to leg it."

James heard someone coming along the corridor and quickly hung up his phone. It was Keith, wearing a hotel gown and carrying the ice bucket from his room. James was in a T-shirt and boxers, so he had nowhere to hide his phone.

"Trouble sleeping?" Keith asked. "Who are you ringing at this time of night?"

CHERUB training teaches you to always have an excuse ready.

"Zara," James said. "It's morning back home and Joshua always wakes her up early."

"Most mobiles don't work in America," Keith said. "You must have a tri-band."

James's mobile phone had been modified by the intelligence service so it worked on just about any network in the world, but he couldn't tell Keith that.

"I've got no idea," James said, shrugging. "I just turned the thing on and it worked. I stepped out here because I didn't want to wake Junior up."

"You know it's about four quid a minute using your mobile from America?" Keith said.

"Is it?" James gasped, acting like he was really worried. "Ewart will murder me when he gets the bill."

Keith filled his ice bucket from the dispenser and put quarters in the Pepsi machine.

"I must have got dehydrated walking about in the sun all day," he said. "I woke up with a raging thirst. Do you want one?"

James nodded. "Yeah, I wouldn't mind."

Keith fed in more quarters until a second can dropped out of the machine. He handed it to James and they both pulled back the tabs and swallowed a couple of gassy mouthfuls.

"I'm really grateful you brought me out here on holiday," James said. "Ewart and Zara could never afford to take me abroad."

"That's OK," Keith said, smiling. "When Ringo dropped out, it was me who suggested you came instead."

"Really?" James said. "Why?"

"You're the only one of Junior's mates I thought I

could rely on to look after him if something bad happens," Keith said.

"Bad like what?" James asked.

"They could arrest me at any time, James. I know Junior likes to think he's the big man, but he's led a pretty sheltered life and I'm a lot happier knowing there's a guy like you with him."

"You've got George back in Miami," James said.

"George is good for two things," Keith laughed. "Breaking heads and polishing cars. I've known the man since infant school and I love him, but frankly, it's a miracle he can tie his own shoe laces."

"Who knows?" James said. "Maybe you'll never get arrested."

"Life is certainly full of surprises," Keith said. "I'll tell you that for nothing."

He ripped off a monster belch that echoed down the corridor. James giggled and responded with a tiny burp.

"Pathetic," Keith said. "Check this out."

Keith tipped back his head to drain his can, then rolled out the longest, loudest belch James had ever heard. An elderly American was toddling along the corridor. She had giant rectangular sunglasses and the wrinkled face of somebody who'd spent too much of her life in the sun.

"Why don't you mind your damn manners?" she said furiously.

"Don't worry, ma'am," Keith said, giggling as he gently cuffed James around the back of the head. "I'm make sure the boy doesn't do it again."

"It wasn't me," James gasped, struggling to keep a straight face.

The woman shuffled a few more steps and stopped outside her room. As she rummaged through her handbag for the plastic card that unlocked her door, Keith stepped into the corridor and belched again. It wasn't as big as the first two, but it was still loud. James couldn't control himself and started howling with laughter. The woman scowled so hard, he half expected laser beams to shoot out of her eyes.

"This hotel used to attract decent people," she shouted. "Why don't you act your age?"

Her door slammed. James and Keith stood there laughing for about ten minutes. James got it so bad his sides started hurting.

Keith looked at his watch. "You better get back to bed, it's gone midnight and we're doing another theme part tomorrow."

James crept back into his room, being careful not to wake up Junior. He took a quick pee before sliding between his sheets. He was tired, but his brain kept churning over as he lay away, listening to Junior's gentle breathing.

James wondered if Keith really was planning to do a runner. It seemed sad that a guy who'd been showing him the time of his life was facing a choice between twenty years in prison and running off and never seeing his family again. James asked himself what he'd do if he saw Keith making a run for it. Would he grab his mobile the second he realized, or give Keith time to get away?

They left the hotel early next morning and went to DisneyWorld, then spent the afternoon cooling off at a water park. It was getting dark by the time they left Orlando for the five-hour drive back to Miami.

James woke up late Thursday morning on his four-poster bed in the Miami house. He was on top of his duvet, wearing the trainers and clothes he'd had on the day before. The last thing he could remember was falling asleep in the backseat of the car. He needed a shower and his mouth tasted like a sewer, but before any of that, he scrambled downstairs to see if Keith was still around.

George, Keith, and Junior sat at the breakfast bar in the kitchen, wearing swimming shorts and watching a daytime talk show.

"Here's sleeping beauty," Keith said.

Junior started to laugh.

"What?" James asked.

"I pinched your cheek and everything," Keith said, "but you didn't bat an eyelid. I had to get George to carry you upstairs and dump you on your bed."

"All red-faced and tired-out," Junior giggled. "You looked like a little angel."

"I can't remember a thing," James gasped. "God . . . That's so embarrassing."

"It's all those midnight phone calls," Keith said. "You're not getting enough sleep."

James had a mental jolt. He'd missed his nightly call and John Jones might be worried.

"I better go freshen up," James said.

As soon as he got to his room, he found the overnight bag he'd taken to Orlando and grabbed his mobile. He tried to switch it on, but the battery was dead. He hunted around the room until he found his charger and his American socket adapter. The phone bleeped to life as soon as it was plugged in.

"Rip Van Winkle," John Jones said. "How you feeling?"

"Don't you start," James said. "How did you know about that?"

"When it got to one in the morning and I still hadn't heard from you, I got worried. We got a track on your mobile phone signal and realized you were driving back from Orlando. Then your mobile stopped transmitting."

"It went flat," James explained. "I forgot to take my charger with me."

"Pretty basic operational mistake, James," John said, tutting. "But I guess we have to make allowances for the fact you're thirteen years old."

"I'm glad *you* make allowances at MI5," James laughed. "Nobody from CHERUB ever does."

"Anyway, I thought I'd better check you were OK, so I hid in the bushes out back and watched George carry you out of the car. You looked like you were six years old, all bundled up in his big fat arms."

"I'm never gonna live this down," James said. "So, apart from me making an idiot of myself, nothing much happened yesterday. What about your end?"

"The Yanks want to help us watch Keith, but they don't have the manpower. We think we've got enough evidence to convict Keith on tax evasion and money-laundering charges, but that's only worth a two- to five-year sentence. We wanted to wait until we could bust him on drug charges, but with no twenty-four-hour surveillance and the risk of Keith running off for good, we've decided to move now."

"Extradition?" James asked.

"That's right, James. Bedfordshire Police will be contacting the DEA later today, asking them to arrest Keith on money-laundering charges and send him back to Britain. We have to present evidence to an American judge before they issue an arrest warrant. It'll take a day or so to get the paperwork together and organize the hearing."

"So you're hoping Keith doesn't leg it in the meantime."

"Exactly," John said. "And one final thing. I got a message from Zara. Dr. McAfferty has decided to pull the CHERUB side of this operation whether or not Keith Moore is in jail. Tell Junior and Keith that Ewart's been offered a better job and you're all moving back to London."

CHAPTER 29

NIGHT

That night James ended up in Junior's room watching a horror film on DVD. James got up to go back to his room when it finished.

"That sofa pulls out," Junior said. "You can sleep in here if you want."

James smiled. "Scared of being on your own? Think that guy with the bloody ax might come bursting through your window?"

"No," Junior said defensively. "I just thought we could talk and stuff."

James fetched his duvet and pillows while Junior pulled out the sofa bed. They switched the light off and lay in the dark talking. "If you could have any car in the world, what would it be? What if you could live anywhere you wanted?"

"Would you stick your tongue up a dog's arse for a million pounds?" Junior asked.

James thought for a couple of seconds. "Yes."

Junior started rolling about laughing. "EUGHH, James. You filthy animal."

"It's OK for you," James said, laughing. "Your dad's loaded already. But a million pounds would change my life. I'd never have to go to work. I could have a decent house and a cool car and stuff."

"What if you had to do it on TV and everyone knew about it?"

"Doesn't make any difference," James said. "A million would set you up for life."

"OK," Junior said. "What's the *least* amount? Would you do it for ten thousand?"

"No way."

"What then?"

"I dunno," James said. "Half a million, maybe . . ."

An arc of light burst into the room and Keith's head appeared in the doorway.

"Come on, guys," Keith said. "Be sensible. It's one in the morning. We're going out early tomorrow and you two are gonna be wasted. Calm down and go to sleep."

Both boys struggled to stop laughing.

"Good night, Dad," Junior said.

"Get some sleep," Keith said firmly.

He closed the door. The boys waited until they were fairly sure Keith was in his bedroom.

Junior sounded sad. "You know," he whispered, "if

you're moving back to London, I'll probably never see you or Nicole again."

"I'll miss you as well," James said. "You're one of the best mates I've ever had."

"Maybe we could visit each other in the holidays," Junior said.

"Maybe," James said, although he knew it could never happen. "It's only half an hour on the train to London. You know what else?"

"What?" Junior asked.

"I was looking forward to boxing against you."

Junior thought for a second. "Do you want to fight right now?"

"Your dad will go psycho," James said.

"There's gloves that go with the punchbag downstairs in the gym. We can fight on the beach in the moonlight. You can't see from the house if you stay down near the sea."

"OK," James said, sitting up on the sofa bed and smiling. "Just don't start bawling to Daddy when I punch the snot out of you."

Junior sneered. "You talk pretty big for someone who's only ever done sparring."

Junior flicked on the lamp beside his bed and put on his watch. Both boys slipped on shorts and trainers. They sneaked downstairs and got the gloves. James was surprised when he saw how small they were.

"These are pro-weight," Junior whispered. "Much less padding than for amateur boxing. You really feel a sting if you get hit with one of these."

"Are there head guards?" James asked.

"We're fighting like men," Junior said. "No finger tape, no head guards, no gum shields, pro-gloves. Not chicken, are you?"

James was starting to wonder if fighting was a good idea. The CHERUB staff wouldn't be impressed if he got himself injured in an unnecessary midnight boxing match, but he was too proud to back down.

They walked through to the living room and got a fright when George let out a loud snore. He'd fallen asleep in front of the TV. Junior quietly slid one of the French doors open and they jumped off the decking onto the beach.

The tide was on its way out. The moon was bright and the wet sand near the sea squelched under their trainers. Junior used a stick to draw the outline of a lopsided boxing ring, before setting his watch to do a three-minute countdown.

"Three rounds, lasting three minutes each," Junior said. "If you go down three times you're out of the fight."

James felt nervous as he pulled his second glove on with his teeth.

"Go to your corner," Junior said.

When Junior's stopwatch bleeped, the two boys charged forward and started throwing punches. With amateur gloves, even a full-force punch barely hurts, but Junior's first barrage with the professional gloves connected hard. One punch knocked James off balance. He couldn't catch his breath as he stumbled backwards. Junior sunk a blow below the elastic of James's shorts, doubling him over. Junior's next punch caught James in the side of the head. He splattered helplessly into the damp sand.

"Low blow," James wheezed, clutching his abdomen.

The fight had only been going a few seconds, but it was a warm night and both boys were pouring sweat.

"It wasn't low," Junior said. "That counts as my first knockdown."

James clambered to his feet. He usually loved the rush you got during a fight, but Junior was fast and strong. James had a nasty feeling he'd bitten off more than he could chew.

"So we're fighting dirty, are we?" he said, holding back a burst of anger. "That's fine by me."

He threw a fast punch. Junior wasn't ready and the thinly padded glove smashed into his nose. James's next shot was an uppercut that snapped back Junior's head.

"Stop," Junior shouted, groaning in pain as he wrapped his arms over his face. "Jesus Christ . . . You idiot."

"What?" James asked.

"You've got sand in your gloves. It's gone in my eye."

Junior tore off a glove and started rubbing his eye.

"Sorry," James said. "I never realized. Are you OK?"

Junior broke into an uneasy smile as he blinked out the sand.

"You know what?" he said. "I blame the idiot who thought up this stupid idea in the first place."

James laughed. "That would be you."

"Call it a draw, eh, James?"

"Fair enough," James said. "Now we know why they don't have beach boxing."

"I'm going for a swim," Junior said, kicking off his trainers. "I need to wash all this sweat off."

James thought he heard a banging sound as he pulled off his gloves.

"Did you hear that?"

"What?" Junior asked.

"I thought I heard something up in the house."

Junior smiled. "Maybe George woke up and fell off the sofa."

"Yeah," James laughed. "Either that or they've set loose the ax-wielding maniac from that movie."

Junior waded into the sea and dived forward, turning a somersault underwater. James pushed off backwards and let a wave wash him back towards the beach.

"You ever had a nightmare after watching a scary movie?" Junior asked.

"You know the film *Seven*?" James asked as he bobbed in the surf.

"I love that movie," Junior said. "It's totally sick."

"When my mum was alive, I showed off until she let me watch the video. I woke up in a state and climbed in her bed. My sister, Lauren, heard about it and didn't stop ribbing me for about a week."

"Your sister?" Junior said, surprised.

"I mean cousin," James said, nervously covering his mistake. "It was the summer holidays and Lauren was staying at our house."

"Ringo used to tease me when I was little," Junior said. "I'd ask him to put on my *Pingu* video and he'd stick on *The Terminator* to scare me."

"We better go to bed," James said, as he picked his

boxing gloves off the sand and slid his wet feet inside his trainers. "I'm looking forward to the air-boat ride tomorrow."

"We never usually do half the cool stuff we've done this week," Junior said. "My dad really likes you for some reason."

James thought Keith was spoiling them because he was planning to disappear in a few days and would most likely never see Junior again. As they walked towards the house in their dripping shorts, Junior turned around and started walking backwards, staring at the moonlit sea.

"Just think," he said, spreading his arms out wide. "If you count the time difference between here and London, in less than three days' time we'll be getting up for another miserable Monday at Gray Park School."

"Cheer us up, why don't you?" James said. "Is your eye OK now?"

"Stings a bit," Junior said. "I wish we could have had a proper fight."

James clambered onto the wooden decking at the back door of the house and put his foot inside the sliding door. His trainer slipped in something wet. He rested his palm on the wall to steady himself. The light was on in the kitchen and George's body had rolled off the sofa on the floor.

"Something's going on," James said edgily.

Junior grinned. "What is it, the ax murderer?"

"I'm serious," James said, lifting his trainer out of the sticky liquid.

He felt like his head was going to explode when he realized it was blood.

"Give over, James," Junior said. "You're not scaring me."

Junior stepped through the door and noticed George on the floor.

"He really did fall off the sofa," Junior laughed.

James crouched down and clicked on a table lamp. Junior saw George was dead, realized his trainers were planted in a puddle of blood, and let out a massive scream.

CHAPTER 90

BODY

James was still haunted by the cold touch of his mother's fingers the night he found her dead in front of the TV. George's body didn't affect him the same way, though the sight was more horrible. There was blood seeping from a bullet wound under his shirt. It was draining down a hanging arm and along the joins in the floor tiles, creating a grid of red lines leading to the pool of blood by the sliding doors.

James felt like everything was happening in slow motion. He could feel every vibration in Junior's screams and watch the droplets of saliva spraying out of his mouth.

James had a theory: Keith had shot George for betraying

him, then disappeared. But the theory sprang apart as he crept across the room and stared down the hallway through the half-open kitchen door. Three armed men had Keith Moore pinned on a stool at the breakfast bar. It looked like they'd roughed him up.

"Leave the boys," Keith shouted when he heard Junior scream. "I'll tell you everything."

James knew he had only milliseconds before one of the men beating up Keith came out of the kitchen pointing a gun at him and Junior. He turned back to Junior, who stood rigid in the doorway, staring at George's body.

"Run!" James shouted. "Get help."

Junior snapped out of his panic long enough to hear the order. He jumped off the wooden decking and began sprinting down the beach. James hoped he'd have the sense to run to one of the neighboring houses and call the police.

James planned to follow Junior, but a thuggish-looking guy emerged from the kitchen before he got the chance. James could see tattoos through the sweat-drenched vest clinging to his skin.

"Get here, kid!" he shouted, sliding out the pistol tucked into his jeans.

James burst through the nearest door, into the front living room where Keith kept his hi-fi and record collection.

"Hey!" the man shouted furiously. "You wanna mess with me? I'll kill you before you reach the door."

He sounded Mexican or something. James didn't know what the men wanted from Keith, but they'd shown they were prepared to kill and he didn't fancy being their next victim. He thought about climbing out of the window, but the room only had a long narrow window up near the ceiling. He'd never get through before the man shot him.

There was a key inside the door. Turning the lock bought James a few seconds. He pushed an armchair against the door as the gunman rattled the handle on the outside. James desperately needed some kind of weapon.

"Unlock this or I'll shoot you to pieces," the man shouted, as he pounded the door with his fist.

James slid one of Keith's LPs off its rack. He'd learned in weapons training that you can make a dagger by shattering any object made out of hard plastic. He leaned the record sleeve against the wall and stamped on it with his bloody trainer.

The gunman shoulder-charged the door.

One of his colleagues shouted after him from the kitchen. "You need a hand?"

The gunman didn't sound worried. "It's just some smartass kid who's gonna be feeling a lot of pain real soon."

Three deafening shots fired into the door, blasting away the lock. James tipped the pieces of the album out of its sleeve and grabbed the longest shard of what, until a few moments earlier, had been a valuable purple vinyl edition of Led Zeppelin IV.

The gunman kicked the door twice, barging the armchair out of the way. James backed up to the wall beside the door, with the shard of purple vinyl clutched tightly in his hand. His heart drummed like it was set to burst.

If he got this wrong, he'd end up with a bullet through his head.

The second he saw the pistol coming through his door, James grabbed the muzzle with one hand while plunging the sharp piece of plastic into the gunman's wrist. The man screamed out. His fingers sprang apart and James snatched the gun, before backing up to the opposite wall and turning it around so that his finger was on the trigger.

The man tugged the plastic out of his arm as he stumbled over the armchair. He faced James off with a self-assured grin.

"Big gun for a little boy, eh?" he said, showing off a rack of yellow teeth. "Are you really going to shoot me?"

Some sort of commotion broke out in the kitchen. Keith Moore screamed in pain.

"Get on your knees and put your hands behind your head," James stuttered.

The man edged closer. James remembered his firearms training: from a safe position you can shoot to wound, but if you're in mortal danger you can't risk missing. You have to aim for the biggest target: the chest.

"Don't make me shoot you," James said desperately.

The gun weighed a billion tons in his trembling hands. The man ignored the threat and kept moving closer. James didn't want to shoot, but what choice was there? He held his breath to steady the gun.

"You ain't gonna kill *noooooo*body," the man sneered, as he lifted his shoe off the carpet, preparing to take a step that would bring James into reach.

A shockwave ripped through the room. The bullet

slammed into the gunman's chest from less than two meters. His feet lifted off the floor as his body crashed backwards into the upturned armchair. Stunned by the fact that he'd just fired a bullet into a real human being, James felt sick as he scrambled over his bleeding victim and out into the hallway.

James ran into the front living room, planning to escape via the beach, but another gunman was frog-marching Junior across the sand towards the house. He ducked back into the hallway, hoping the man walking up the beach hadn't spotted him. It could only be a matter of seconds before the men in the kitchen came out to investigate the gunshot. The only way out of the front of the house was by walking past the kitchen door, which would be suicidal. That only left one option.

Still holding the pistol, James ran upstairs. He went into his room, grabbed his mobile phone off the bedside table, and called John Jones. A woman answered.

"Is John Jones there?"

"I'm Beverly Shapiro," the woman said. "Is that James Beckett?"

"Yeah," James said. "Where's John?"

"He's in the restroom. You sound worried, James. You can talk to me. I'm the Drug Enforcement Agency officer working with John."

James gasped with relief. "Thank God. Listen, I'm at Keith Moore's house. There's a whole bunch of gunmen downstairs. They're beating up Keith, trying to get some kind of information out of him."

"I'll call the local cops out," Beverly said. "Can you make it out of the house?"

"They caught Junior running down the beach. I think they've got guys watching the outside."

"I'm calling the cops right now," Beverly said. "You find yourself a good place to hide and keep this line open."

James thought about hiding, but he didn't think he'd be safe for more than a few minutes. The cops would take longer than that to arrive and even when they did, they'd be unlikely to come charging straight into the house and risk getting shot. James considered hiding out at the top of the stairs and shooting at anyone who tried to come up. It might have worked in a house with one staircase, but Keith's Miami home had three. Four if you counted the metal walkway that led across to the garage.

The garage.

James realized that was his best chance. He leaned out into the corridor as Beverly said something into the phone.

"What?" James asked.

"I said, the police are on their way. Have you found a safe place to hide?"

"I don't think it's safe up here," James said. "Someone's gonna come up looking for me any second."

"I *told* you to hide," Beverly said stiffly. "Keep calm and wait for the police."

"No way," James said. "I've got to bust out."

He tucked the phone into the waistband of his soggy shorts, without ending the call. He sprinted down the hallway to the master bedroom and found Keith's trousers on the floor. He grabbed a bunch of keys from the pocket and rapidly flipped through them. There were keys to a couple of the Porsches and Mercedes, but James thought the huge four-wheel-drive Range Rover would give him his best chance of escape.

When he got back into the hallway, he heard footsteps on the staircase. He fired a shot towards the stairs, knowing it would make the men stay back for a minute or two.

James cautiously opened the door at the end of the hallway. He checked no one was around outside, before stepping on to the metal steps that linked the house to the garage. He opened the door into the garage and walked down a set of spiral stairs to ground level, before unlocking the Range Rover and sliding on to the driver's seat.

He put the key in the steering column and started the engine. Clipping on his seatbelt to cut off the annoying bing-bong noise, he pressed the button on the dashboard that opened the garage doors and the iron gates at the front of the house.

The wooden doors, less than a meter from the front of the car, began parting slowly. James knew someone would hear them if he just sat waiting. He put the car in drive, floored the accelerator pedal, and ploughed through. He had to slam on the brake to avoid a brick wall as chunks of wood sprayed in all directions around the car.

As he put on full steering lock and turned towards the gate, James's heart sank. The front gates were still closed. The button on the dashboard hadn't worked. James realized the gunmen must have short-circuited the automatic gate when they broke into the house. The

Range Rover might have been able to break them open, but the gunmen had their two cars parked in front of the gates, ready for a quick getaway.

As James looked around, frantically trying to work out an alternative escape, a bullet came out of the first-floor window, ripping through the roof of the car, and punching a neat hole through the front passenger seat. James floored the accelerator and spun the car around. He pointed the Range Rover at the thickly planted terraces around the house, hoping the car was powerful enough to punch through a hundred meters of plants and trees. If it was, he'd be able to escape onto the beach at the back of the house.

The chunky front tires reared onto a set of narrow steps. The car crawled up a gentle slope, rocking from side to side as it trampled bushes and tore a couple of small trees out of the ground. Chunks of stone and wood clattered against the underside of the car, then it hit a massive palm tree and ground to a halt.

The car slipped backwards as a second bullet ripped through the tailgate. The noise made James's eardrums pop. He thought he might have to bail out and run for it, but the car's automatic gearbox slipped into its lowest ratio. The rear tires dug into the soft ground. James dabbed the accelerator. After a touch of wheelspin, the car toppled the palm tree and bounced over its thick trunk.

At the top of the slope, the ground leveled off onto a tiled patio. James swerved around Keith's brick barbecue and picked up speed as he rolled downhill. It was much easier navigating through the low bushes and flowerbeds on the windswept ocean side of the house. At the bottom, James swerved to avoid Keith's fishpond, then floored the accelerator. He needed speed to break through the fence at the back of the house.

A thin concrete post shattered as the front of the car ripped a hole through a tangle of plastic mesh and barbed wire. The car nose-dived off a meter-high wall. The back wheels spun in free air until the front wheels burrowed into the soft sand and pulled the front of the car forward. Once all four wheels were firmly planted on level ground, James hit the accelerator and began tearing along the sand, dragging a ten-meter section of chain-link fence behind him. He nudged the steering wheel left to right until the wire disentangled itself from the rear bumper.

Once the wire was gone, everything seemed eerily calm; just the gentle whoosh of the air-conditioning and a few hundred meters of level sand lit up by the headlamps. James looked back in the mirror. Nobody seemed to be coming after him. He reached into his shorts and grabbed his mobile.

"Beverly, are you still there?"

"What the hell was that noise?" John Jones asked, sounding like he was in a bit of a state. "Did I hear gunshots? Are you OK?"

"I'm OK, but I might have just killed some maniac and now they've got hold of Junior. I'm driving along the beach in Keith's Range Rover. When I see a gap between the houses, I'm gonna pull up on to the road."

"OK," John said. "You're sure nobody's following?"

"Not so far as I can tell."

"Do you know how to drive to the IHOP from where you are at the moment?"

"Sure," James said. "It's only a couple of kilometers."

"I'll meet you there in fifteen minutes. Beverly will be with me. She knows you're my informant, but she doesn't know anything about CHERUB, so watch what you say."

"No worries," James said.

"Get off the beach as quickly as you can and drive sensibly. You don't want to get picked up by the cops."

The pancake place was closed, so they ended up in a twenty-four-hour McDonald's across the street. John sat across the table from James, while Beverly got apple pies and coffees at the counter. James looked between his legs at his blood-stained trainers.

"A hundred and nineteen ninety-nine," James said bitterly. "The first lot got stolen, now this lot are ruined."

John Jones laughed. "Maybe it's God's way of telling you that a hundred and twenty pounds is an obscene amount of money to pay for a pair of plimsolls."

Beverly put the tray of coffee on the table and squeezed up next to James on the plastic bench. She was small, about twenty-five, with long chestnut hair and freckles. She didn't look hard enough to be a drug enforcement agent.

"I spoke to the local units," Beverly said. "The bad guys got rattled when you escaped. They tried to take Keith Moore away in their car. The police spotted them and there was a shoot-out. Keith Moore took a bullet through his shoulder. It's early days, but they think he'll be OK."

"What about Junior?" James asked.

"The guys knocked him around quite badly. He's been taken to hospital, but it's too early to say what kind of state he's in."

"I hope he's OK," James said anxiously. He took a sip from his steaming polystyrene cup. "So who were those guys? What did they want with Keith?"

"They're probably linked to the Lambayeke cartel," John said. "I'd bet my last dollar bill that they were after the numbers of Keith's secret bank accounts."

"I thought Keith dealt with the Lambayeke," James said. "Weren't they friendly?"

"Keith dealt with the Lambayeke cartel for twenty years," John said. "But they're not the kind of people you invite round to your house for a dinner party. As long as Keith was buying drugs from Lambayeke and making them money, they left him alone. Then KMG collapsed around Keith's ears. He's not going to buy any more drugs, he doesn't know who he can trust, and he's sitting on a big pile of money."

"So they decided to rob him?" James said.

"That's right," John nodded. "Keith Moore has millions stashed away in illegal bank accounts. So they send some thugs in to take Keith hostage and smack him around until he gives them all the bank account details and transfers all his money over to them."

"Keith would have had no comeback," Beverly added. "You can hardly go to your local precinct and complain that the money you made selling drugs that's stashed away in illegal overseas bank accounts has been stolen."

"It's almost the perfect crime," John said. "Except

the guys they sent in were so incompetent they forgot to check upstairs and get you and Junior out of bed."

"Actually," James said, "we weren't in bed. Me and Junior sneaked out and went down the beach for a midnight swim."

He thought it was best not to mention the boxing match.

"Well, it's a good job you did," John said, breaking into a smile. "Otherwise you'd have woken up with a gun pointing at your head."

CHAPTER 61

CATCH

James grabbed a few hours' sleep in Beverly Shapiro's office at the DEA's Miami headquarters. She woke him up at ten the following morning and dumped clean clothes and trainers on the desk in front of him.

"We got those from the house," Beverly said. "There are showers down the hall if you want to clean up. We're going to speak to Keith Moore in about forty minutes. John said you can sit in the observation room and watch if you want to."

"I thought Keith had been shot," James said.

"Only in the shoulder. It'll heal up."

"How's Junior?" James asked.

Beverly sighed. "The bad guys didn't think Keith was

telling them everything about his bank accounts, so they stopped hurting Keith and started on Junior. He's got a broken nose, broken collar bone, and some serious internal injuries."

James felt sick when he tried to imagine what Junior must have gone through. "I should have done something to help him," he said.

"What could you have done against eight armed men?" Beverly asked, smiling sympathetically.

"So is Junior going to be OK?"

"He won't be able to fly home for a while. He's asked to see you, but you don't exist anymore."

"What do you mean?" James asked.

"The United States has no immigration record for James Beckett. You're booked on a flight to London this evening. We want you to disappear before people start asking questions about you and the guy you shot in the chest."

"Oh," James said. "I kept having these creepy dreams about the gun going off and the room where it happened. Is he dead?"

"Yes."

"He wouldn't stop coming closer," James said, feeling tense as he replayed the scene in his mind. "I tried getting him to back down. I thought about shooting him in the leg, but I was taught to go straight for the chest."

"I would have done the same," Beverly said. "You can't take chances, especially when it's not your own weapon. You didn't know how many bullets you had, or if the gun was some rusty piece of junk that'd jam up the second the barrel gets hot."

"I just can't believe I killed someone."

• • •

James showered in the men's locker room. There was paraphernalia everywhere—police radios, holsters, body armor. James stared at his hands while the water rushed over his body, studying the finger that had killed someone a few hours earlier. He didn't exactly feel guilty about killing a man who was going to kill him, but it did make him a bit sad. The guy probably had a mother, or a kid, or something.

"Hey, boy, what you doing?"

James looked up to see a couple of muscular cops stripping off their clothes.

"Beverly Shapiro said it was OK to clean up in here."

"You sound English."

James nodded. "I'm from London."

"Cool," the cop said. "You ever met one of the royal family?"

"Sure," James said, laughing. "I hang out with them all the time."

James stepped out of the shower and started toweling off. He looked at the cops' guns lying on the slatted wooden bench and wondered if they'd ever been used to kill anyone. Then he wondered what it would be like to die. He hadn't given it a thought while he was trying to escape, but there were the two bullet holes in the Range Rover, less than a meter from where he'd sat.

Beverly took James to the canteen. She told him to put his bacon and scrambled eggs in a polystyrene box so he could eat it in the observation suite. It was a narrow room, with a row of plastic chairs and black and white monitors. There was a giant one-way mirror in one wall that looked into an interrogation room. Keith Moore was in there. He stared into space, nervously drumming his fingers on the table in front of him. His T-shirt was bulked out by the dressing wrapped around his shoulder.

"You'll have to keep quiet in here," Beverly said. "It's quite a thin partition."

She walked out, leaving James with the eerie sound of Keith's breathing, amplified through the tinny loudspeakers in the ceiling.

Seconds later, Beverly walked into the interrogation room behind John Jones.

"Good morning," John said, pulling out a chair opposite Keith and sitting down. "My name is John Jones. I'm here to help you out."

"I want a lawyer," Keith said. "I've been shot. I've no sleep. You can't question me like this."

"I'm with British Intelligence," John smiled. "I have no authority here in the United States. All we're doing is having an informal chat."

"I don't care if you're the grand wizard of the Ku Klux Klan," Keith said. "I'm not saying one word until I see a lawyer."

"The local cops found a deceased member of the Lambayeke cartel and a bunch of unlicensed firearms in your house," John said. "Somebody killed him, and unless the bad guys decided to start shooting one another, you're the main suspect."

"I want a lawyer," Keith said sourly.

John turned and looked at Beverly. "What's the standard sentence for a drug-related murder in Florida?" he asked.

"Life without parole, on a good day," Beverly said, smiling. "Though if the judge doesn't like the look of you, he might bump that up to death by lethal injection."

"What if Keith claims self-defense and puts in a guilty plea to a charge of manslaughter?" John asked.

"Between twenty and fifty years in prison," Beverly said.

"Man," John Jones laughed. "They're certainly tough down here in Florida. Keith Moore, I believe you're in a big heap of trouble."

"I've got money," Keith said, trying to sound confident. "I can afford a very smart lawyer."

"You reckon this case will ever make it anywhere near a courtroom?" John asked.

"Why shouldn't it?" Keith asked.

"You'll be charged with murdering a member of the Lambayeke cartel," John said. "You're a foreign citizen on a murder charge, so there's not a hope in hell you'll get bail. You'll be banged up on remand, awaiting trial, in a Florida prison stuffed with members of the Lambayeke cartel. How long do you think you'll last before one of them sticks a knife in your back?"

Keith looked a lot less sure of himself when he thought about this. John theatrically slammed his mobile phone on the desk.

"There's my phone, Keith. Go ahead, call your big-shot lawyer if you want to. The Florida legal system will take you under its wing and you'll be a dead man by Christmas."

"So what's my alternative?" Keith asked.

"You'll have to sign a deal," John explained. "The DEA will grant you immunity from prosecution in the United States, if you give a full and accurate account of your dealings with the Lambayeke cartel over the last twenty-whatever years. And you'll have to agree never to set foot in the United States again.

"The DEA will pass all the information you give to the British police. I'm sure you'll have given them enough to prosecute you. You'll face the full weight of British justice, which will probably be a twenty to twenty-five year prison sentence. With remission for good behavior, you could be a free man inside fifteen years."

"Why not leave me out here to rot?" Keith asked.

"This deal makes everyone happy," John said. "The Americans get lots of valuable information on the Lambayeke cartel, rather than a big bill for prosecuting you and trying to keep you alive in prison. Back in Britain, the home secretary gets to stand up in parliament and mouth off about the success of Operation Snort and his big crackdown on drugs. And most importantly, you'll still be alive this time next year."

"What if the Lambayeke cartel comes after me in Britain?" Keith asked.

"They might try to get at you," John said, shrugging. "But Lambayeke members are thin on the ground in British prisons, whereas you'll be on home turf. I expect a man with your resources will be able to find plenty of friends to protect you."

"You've got it all worked out," Keith said, shifting uneasily in his chair.

"This is a once in a lifetime deal," John said. "There

won't be any negotiation. You've got one hour to make a decision."

Keith leaned back in his chair and ran a hand through his sweaty hair. "You know what?" he said. "I reckon I've been in business long enough to know when someone's got you by the balls."

He reached his arm across the table to shake John Jones by the hand.

"I think you've got yourself a deal, Mr. Jones."

When the interview was over, James went back to Beverly's office and called the house in Luton.

"Kyle?" James asked. "Is that you?"

"James, what's happening?"

"John Jones just nailed Keith Moore," James said. "They arrested him last night and he's cut a deal to save his butt."

"Excellent," Kyle said. "We're just packing up here. We've had to tell everyone we're moving back to London."

"How was half-term?"

"Ringo's party was nuts. Kids were smashing up furniture, puking on the stairs. I met this cool kid called Dave, he's really cute and—"

"Stop, stop, *stop,*" James said sharply. "I can just about get my head around you being gay, Kyle. That doesn't mean I want graphic details . . . What about Kelvin and that? I thought they were supposed to be looking after Keith's house."

"Didn't you hear?" Kyle said. "The police raided the boxing club on Tuesday night. They arrested Kelvin, Marcus, Ken, and that tall kid in your class."

"Del?"

"Yeah, Del, and loads of other guys. The cops found the contact diary of the woman who used to organize the deliveries. They nabbed all the young couriers. You probably would have got busted if you'd been there."

"So is Kerry in?" James asked. "Can I have a quick word?"

"She's with Max Power."

"Who?" James gasped.

"This new kid turned up in her class on Monday. They're all over each other, snogging morning, noon and night."

James realized it was a wind-up. "Yeah, right, Kyle."

"I had you going for a second." Kyle giggled. "Kerry . . . it's your new beau. He wants to talk to you."

Kerry came to the phone.

"We busted Keith," James said. "He's looking at twenty-five years."

Kerry let out a big shriek. James had to move the phone away from his ear.

"Brilliant," she said. "We're heading back to campus tomorrow morning. When will you be home?"

"I'm flying out of here this evening," James said. "I'll probably get to campus about the same time as you guys."

"You *were* serious about the boyfriend-girlfriend thing, weren't you?" Kerry asked.

James smiled. "Oh, yeah. I can't wait to see you."

CHAPTER 32

LAST

James walked into Meryl Spencer's office, which overlooked the athletic track on CHERUB campus. Even though the window was open, you still got a hint of the damp smell from the changing room across the hallway.

"Ewart is impressed," Meryl said. "Zara's impressed and even Mr. Jones from MI5 is impressed. I have to say it, James, *I'm* impressed."

James smiled at his handler as he placed a blank bin liner on the desk and sat down opposite her. Meryl tipped out the contents. There were clothes, trainers, CDs, an envelope with over five hundred pounds in cash, and the five PlayStation games he'd stolen from the Reeve Center.

"I trust there's nothing else hidden up in your room?" Meryl asked.

"No," James said. "That's everything I either stole, or earned from selling drugs. Except for money I spent on food and going out, some presents I got for Joshua, and Lauren's birthday money."

"Which charity do you want me to give it to?"

"Me and Kerry looked on the Internet. She found this hostel near Luton that helps young people with drug problems. Gets them off drugs, finds them jobs, and gets them places at college and stuff."

"That sounds excellent," Meryl said. "You're due over thirty pounds' pocket money for the time you were away, and the clothes won't go for much in charity shops. If you want, I'll put the pocket money in the envelope and you can keep the clothes and trainers."

"Cool," James said. "I'll go for that."

"You know, James," Meryl said. "It must be Kerry's influence, I could almost mistake you for a reformed character."

James couldn't help smiling at the compliment. "I've been at CHERUB for exactly a year," he said. "I reckon I've spend too much of that time scrubbing corridors, peeling vegetables, and running punishment laps to mess you around any more."

Meryl burst out laughing. "That's what I like to hear," she giggled, "total obedience . . . But seriously, James, your performance on this mission shows that the training and hard work have paid off. When Keith Moore was being held hostage a few nights ago, you kept your head in a very nasty situation and thought your way out of it. If you'd found yourself in that position before you came here, I'm sure your reaction would have been very different."

James nodded. "I probably would have freaked out, like Junior did."

"And the bond you made with Keith Moore was tremendous."

"Keith's really nice guy," James said. "I know he's a drug dealer, but I almost feel sad that he's gonna go to prison."

"Well, *don't,*" Meryl said sharply. "Keith had enough money and power to keep his distance from the nasty side of the drug business. He might have spent his days swanning around his pool acting like a cool guy, but he knew what was going on. KMG was a ruthless organization that didn't hesitate to use violence and intimidation to get what it wanted. For every person KMG made rich, there's probably a thousand more who messed up their lives with drugs. Either by taking them, or getting caught selling them."

"Keith said breaking up KMG wouldn't even make a difference to the amount of cocaine being sold on the streets."

"Maybe there's some truth in that," Meryl said. "But you can't stop fighting against something just because it's difficult. That's like saying there's no point having doctors and hospitals because everyone eventually dies."

"So when's my next mission?" James asked.

"Ah," Meryl said, "bad news on that score, I'm afraid. You've been on two long missions already this year and you've missed a lot of school. We're not looking to send you off campus again until the new year."

"That's not so bad, actually," James said. "Missions are hard work. It'll be nice to go a few months without waking up every morning wondering what my name is and if I'm gonna get shot at."

"I heard about the man you killed. We do all we can to keep our agents out of situations like this, but it's an unfortunate fact that drug dealers and guns are inextricably linked. Have you thought about it at all since you got back?"

"A bit," James said. "But I get more freaked-out wondering what would have happened if me and Junior hadn't decided to go down the beach for a boxing—erm . . . For a swim, that night."

"Have you had trouble sleeping, or nightmares?"

"I was lying awake thinking about the car chase on the plane home," James said. "The woman sitting next to me said I looked pale. She got me a little tub of mineral water."

"I'll arrange some sessions with a counselor," Meryl said. "You've been through a traumatic experience and it's important that you talk about your feelings with someone."

Kerry was sitting on a bench for the athletics track waiting for James when he got out of Meryl's office. He gave her a quick kiss and sat next to her.

"How many punishment laps did Meryl give you?" Kerry asked.

"None," James said.

"That's got to be a first."

"I didn't do anything bad."

Kerry started giggling. "Another first."

"They don't want to send me on another mission until the new year. It'll be cool if we can just chill out on campus together. Watch movies, do homework and stuff."

"That's OK for you to say, James. You've already fluked into the lead role on two major missions and earned your navy T-shirt. I'm still a nobody."

"It's not such a big deal," James said casually. "It's just a T-shirt."

Kerry huffed. "If there's one thing I really hate, it's people who have something and say that it doesn't matter. It's like those rock stars on MTV who go on about how their millions and supermodel girlfriends haven't made them any happier. But you never see them giving it all away and going back to live in Mummy's trailer home, do you?"

James thought it was best to change the subject before Kerry got into one of her moods. "Do you fancy taking a stroll over to the back of campus?"

"That would be nice," Kerry said, breaking into a smile. "The leaves are pretty colors at this time of year. I never thought you had a romantic side, James."

"Actually, Kyle and Lauren are up there cleaning out ditches. I thought we could go over and wind them up a bit."

Kerry gave James a gentle shove. "I might have known you *didn't* have a romantic side. . . . What happened about Lauren, anyway? The last I heard, everyone was gonna go up there and help her out."

"Mac said Lauren had to be punished and that anyone caught helping her dig would have to run thirty laps every day for a month. Everyone's making her life easier in other ways though: doing her laundry, letting her jump the queue in the canteen, copying homework, that kind of stuff.

"It was so funny when Kyle got back from ditch-clearing last night," James continued. "You know how he's always immaculate? His uniform was plastered in mud and it smelled *so* bad. A lot of the water in those ditches runs off the farms around here. It's all full of cow and pig manure, and God knows what else."

"Serves him right for taking drugs," Kerry said.

"Give over, Kerry, all he did was take a puff on a joint. He would never have got caught if Nicole hadn't collapsed."

"I don't care," Kerry said. "If something's against the law, you shouldn't do it. Especially drugs."

James started to laugh.

"What's so funny?"

"You," James said. "You're always *such* a Goody Two-shoes."

Kerry jabbed a finger in James's ribs.

"What was that for?"

"I'm not a Goody Two-shoes."

James grinned. "Little Miss Perfect."

"Take that back or I'll make you sorry."

James mocked her voice. "Take that back or I'll make you sorry."

"Don't start repeating what I say."

"Don't start repeating what I say."

"That's *it,* James," Kerry said angrily.

"That's *it,* James." James leaned forward and planted

a cheeky kiss on Kerry's face. She broke into a smile.

"I knew you weren't really mad at me," James giggled. "I'm too delightful."

He stopped giggling when he realized it wasn't Kerry's nice smile. It was her evil smile. She jabbed James in the ribs again, then used the moment while he was in spasm to wrap her arm around the back of his neck and wedge him into a headlock under her arm.

"Still Goody Two-shoes, am I?" Kerry grinned as she tightened her grip.

"No," James croaked.

"Quite sure?"

"You're not a Goody, Kerry," James squirmed. "Just . . . Please . . . Let me go."

Kerry let James loose. As he straightened up, James couldn't but help see the funny side of being effortlessly humiliated by a twelve-year-old girl wearing pink and white striped socks with penguins embroidered over the ankle.

Kerry got off the bench.

"Where are you going?" James asked.

"Romantic stroll," she explained, as she marched towards the trees. "Are you coming or not?"

After their walk, James, Kerry, and a big bunch of other kids spent Sunday evening at the bowling alley in the nearest town. They got beaten three games to two by the identical twins Callum and Connor. James and Kerry had a total laugh. James had never felt so relaxed with a girl before. Now he'd asked Kerry out, it seemed dumb that he'd spent so long finding excuses not to.

James lay awake until gone midnight. His body was still running on Miami time and it was early evening over there. He tucked his hands under his head and stared at the shadows on the ceiling.

He wondered how Junior was doing in hospital and got pissed off when he remembered that April still had his Nike watch. But the KMG mission already seemed distant, like part of some other kid's life. James Beckett was no more. James Adams felt warm and comfortable under his duvet. He realized he was the happiest he'd been since his mum died.

James thought about life on campus. He knew the quickest routes around every building. He knew everyone's names. Which kids not to start a conversation with in the lift because they'd bore you to tears. Which teachers would have a laugh with you and which ones would hammer you for the tiniest little thing.

James knew there would always be mornings when he woke up and didn't want to get out of bed for two hours' combat training, or a brain-numbing double history lesson. But when he pulled on his uniform and walked down to breakfast, he knew most other kids looked at him with respect. Whenever James got to the dining room and looked around for a seat, there were always a few tables where he could sit amongst friends, spreading the latest gossip and winding each other up.

A year earlier, CHERUB campus had been a bunch of strange faces, winding corridors, and scary teachers. Now it felt like home.

EPILOGUE

KELVIN HOLMES was sentenced to three years' youth custody for conspiracy to supply drugs. Most of the younger boys who worked as delivery riders for KMG got off with police cautions and supervision orders. A few who had previous drug convictions received 3–6 months in youth custody.

Without funding from Keith Moore, the JT Martin youth center and boxing club closed its doors for the final time after the 2004 Christmas party. No charges were brought against KEN FOWLER, who died of a heart attack a few months later.

MADELINE BURROWS, the nice lady who called James with his deliveries, got a five-year prison sentence, as did her younger brother JOSEPH BURROWS (Crazy Joe). Over 130 other members of KMG received prison sentences as a direct result of the MI5 surveillance operation on Thunderfoods.

Dinesh's dad, PARVINDER SINGH, received a twelve-year prison sentence. DINESH SINGH and his mother moved away, to live near relatives in south London.

KEITH MOORE spent over a week being interviewed by DEA officials at their headquarters in Washington, D.C. Keith was bitter about the Lambayeke cartel's brutal attempt to steal his money and provided a mass of information that led to the immediate seizure of $130 million in drug money and the arrest of several senior figures within the Lambayeke organization.

Keith was later flown back to Britain, where he pleaded guilty to numerous charges relating to money-laundering and drug-trafficking. The judge sentenced Keith to eighteen years in prison and recommended that he should not be considered for early release until he had served at least ten.

The police have uncovered £12 million of Keith's personal fortune, but he is still believed to have at least another £40 million in secret bank accounts.

JUNIOR MOORE fully recovered from his injuries and flew back to Britain. Shortly afterwards, he was expelled from Gray Park school for persistent truancy. His mother said she was "sick of his behavior" and didn't want him ending up like his father. She found him a place at a tough boarding school that specializes in dealing with difficult boys.

APRIL MOORE quickly grew tired of James Beckett not responding to her text messages and e-mails. She returned James's best watch to the address where the Beckett family had supposedly moved and it was eventually forwarded to CHERUB campus. When James opened the envelope, he found his watch had been hammered into a dozen pieces. It was accompanied by a note reading: "You could at least have had the decency to dump me to my face. Hope you die slowly, April."

JOHN JONES announced he was leaving MI5 after nineteen years' service. He has accepted a new job as a CHERUB mission controller.

EWART & ZARA ASKER are expecting their second child in April 2005.

NICOLE EDDISON now lives with two retired cherubs on a farm in Shropshire. She has two young stepbrothers whom she adores and a boyfriend called James. She attends twice-weekly counseling sessions and is slowly coming to terms with the loss of her family.

Dr. McAfferty's beloved mission preparation building is on schedule to be completed in February 2005. He conducted a review of Nicole's recruitment to CHERUB, to see if any mistakes had been made. His report reached the following conclusion:

"If anything, the tests Nicole Eddison completed before

being asked to join CHERUB show that she had an above average chance of becoming a successful agent. Unfortunately, no recruitment test yet devised can account for all the complexities of human nature. It seems likely that a small number of unsuitable candidates will be recruited into CHERUB for as long as the organization exists. All we can do is remain vigilant and try to keep this number at a minimum."

A few weeks after James returned from Miami, AMY COLLINS left campus to live with her brother in Australia. James was part of the crowd that waved her through the departure gate at Heathrow airport.

It took KYLE BLUEMAN and LAUREN ADAMS two months to clean out all the ditches at the back of campus. Kyle was suspended from missions for another four months. Lauren re-entered basic training, with her daily countdown paper in her pocket and a grim determination to make it through no matter how tough Mr. Large tried to make it.

After a few weeks back on campus, KERRY CHANG was sent to Hong Kong on a mission that looked set to last several months. James and Kerry are exchanging daily e-mails and occasionally speak to each other on the phone.

JAMES ADAMS used his time on campus to catch up on schoolwork. He has recently started studying for GCSE exams in three of his strongest subjects, has begun regular weight training, and narrowly failed a second-dan black belt grading in karate class. He expects to be assigned to another undercover mission in early 2005.

CHERUB: A HISTORY (1941–1996)

1941 In the middle of the Second World War, Charles Henderson, a British agent working in occupied France, sent a report to his headquarters in London. It was full of praise for the way the French Resistance used children to sneak past Nazi checkpoints and wangle information out of German soldiers.

1942 Henderson formed a small undercover detachment of children, under the command of British Military Intelligence. Henderson's Boys were all thirteen or fourteen years old, mostly French refugees. They were given basic espionage training before being parachuted into occupied France. The boys gathered vital intelligence in the run-up to the D-Day invasions of 1944.

1946 Henderson's Boys disbanded at the end of the war. Most of them returned to France. Their existence has never been officially acknowledged.

Charles Henderson believed that children would make effective intelligence agents during peacetime. In May 1946, he was given permission to create CHERUB in a disused village school. The first twenty CHERUB recruits, all boys, lived in wooden huts at the back of the playground.

1951 For its first five years, CHERUB struggled along with limited resources. Its fortunes changed following its first major success: Two agents uncovered a ring of Russian spies who were stealing information on the British nuclear weapons program.

The government of the day was delighted. CHERUB was given funding to expand. Better facilities were built and the number of agents was increased from twenty to sixty.

1954 Two CHERUB agents, Jason Lennox and Johan Urminski, were killed while operating undercover in East Germany. Nobody knows how the boys died. The government considered shutting CHERUB down, but there were now over seventy active CHERUB agents performing vital missions around the world.

An inquiry into the boys' deaths led to the introduction of new safeguards:

(1) The creation of the ethics panel. From now on, every mission had to be approved by a three-person committee.

(2) Jason Lennox was only nine years old. A minimum mission age of ten years and four months was introduced.

(3) A more rigorous approach to training was brought in. A version of the 100-day basic training program began.

1956 Although many believed that girls would be unsuitable for intelligence work, CHERUB admitted five girls as an experiment. They were a huge success. The number of girls in CHERUB was upped to twenty the following year. Within ten years, the number of girls and boys was equal.

1957 CHERUB introduced its system of colored T-shirts.

1960 Following several successes, CHERUB was allowed to expand again, this time to 130 students. The farmland surrounding headquarters was purchased and fenced off, about a third of the area that is now known as CHERUB campus.

1967 Katherine Field became the third CHERUB agent to die on an operation. She was bitten by a snake on a mission in India. She reached hospital within half an hour, but tragically the snake species was wrongly identified and Katherine was given the wrong antivenom.

1973 Over the years, CHERUB had become a hotchpotch of small buildings. Construction began on a new nine-story headquarters.

1977 All CHERUBs are either orphans, or children who have been abandoned by their family. Max Weaver was one of the first CHERUB agents. He made a fortune building office blocks in London and New York. When he died in 1977, aged just forty-one, without a wife or children, Max Weaver left his fortune for the benefit of the children at CHERUB.

The Max Weaver Trust Fund has paid for many of the buildings on CHERUB campus. These include the indoor athletics facilities and library. The trust fund now holds assets worth over £1 billion.

1982 Thomas Webb was killed by a landmine on the Falkland Islands, becoming the fourth CHERUB to die on a mission. He was one of nine agents used in various roles during the Falklands conflict.

1986 The government gave CHERUB permission to expand up to four hundred pupils. Despite this, numbers have stalled some way below this. CHERUB requires intelligent, physically robust agents who have no family ties. Children who meet all these admission criteria are extremely hard to find.

1990 CHERUB purchased additional land, expanding both the size and security of campus. Campus is marked on all British maps as an army firing range. Surrounding roads are routed so that there is only one road onto campus. The perimeter walls cannot be seen from nearby roads. Helicopters are banned from the area and airplanes must stay above ten thousand meters. Anyone breaching the CHERUB perimeter faces life imprisonment under the State Secrets Act.

1996 CHERUB celebrated its fiftieth anniversary with the opening of a diving pool and an indoor shooting range.

Every retired member of CHERUB was invited to the celebration. No guests were allowed. Over nine hundred people made it, flying from all over the world. Among the retired agents were a former prime minister and a rock guitarist who had sold 80 million albums.

After a firework display, the guests pitched tents and slept on campus. Before leaving the following morning, everyone gathered outside the chapel and remembered the four children who had given CHERUB their lives.

Don't miss Mission 3:

MAXIMUM SECURITY

Before you entered basic training, you probably heard stories from qualified CHERUB agents about the nature of this one-hundred-day course. Although every basic training course is designed to teach the same core abilities of physical fitness and extreme mental endurance, you can expect your training to differ from that of your predecessors in order to retain the element of surprise.

(Excerpt from the CHERUB Basic Training Manual)

It looked the same in every direction. The sunlight blazing off the field of snow made it impossible for the two ten-year-old girls to see more than twenty meters into the distance, despite the heavily tinted snow goggles over their eyes.

"How far to the checkpoint?" Lauren Adams shouted, breaking her stride to stare at the global positioning unit strapped around her best friend's wrist.

"Only two and a half kilometers," Bethany Parker shouted back. "If the ground stays flat, we should be at the shelter in forty minutes."

The girls had to shout for their voices to override the howling wind and the three layers of clothing protecting their ears.

"That's cutting it close to sundown," Lauren yelled. "We'd better get a move on."

They'd set off at dawn, dragging lightweight sleds that could be hooked over their shoulders and carried as backpacks on difficult terrain. The good news was, the two CHERUB trainees had the whole day to trek fifteen kilometers across the Alaskan snowfield to their next checkpoint. The bad news was that at this time in April, the daylight lasted just four hours and wading through half a meter of powdery snow put enormous strain on their thighs and ankles. Every step was painful.

Lauren heard a howling noise rising up in the distance. "It's gonna to be another big one," she shouted.

The girls crouched down, pulled their sleds in close and wrapped their arms tightly around each other's waists. Just as you can hear waves approaching a beach, out here in the Alaskan snowfields you could hear a strong gust stirring up in the distance.

They were both dressed for extreme cold. Lauren's normal underwear was covered with a long-sleeved thermal vest and long johns. The next layer was a zip-up suit made from polar fleece that covered her whole body, except for a slit around the eyes. The second fleece was designed to trap body heat. It looked like a baggy Easter bunny suit, minus the pom-pom tail and sticking up ears. Then came more gloves, another balaclava, snow goggles, and waterproof outer gloves that went all the way up to Lauren's elbows, ending in a tightly fitting elastic cuff. Finally, on the outside was a thickly padded snowsuit and snow boots with spiked bottoms.

The clothing was enough to keep them comfortable as

they walked, despite the temperature being minus eighteen centigrade, but this dropped another fifteen degrees whenever a strong gust hit. The wind pushed the insulating layers of warm air between the girls' clothes into all the places where it wasn't needed, leaving nothing but a couple of centimeters of synthetic fiber between their skin and the ferociously cold air. Each blast ripped into their bodies, delivering searing pain to any exposed area.

Lauren and Bethany used their sleds as windbreaks when the gust hit. A spike of cold air punched through the tightly fitting rim of Lauren's goggles. She pushed her face against Bethany's suit and squeezed her eyes shut, as snow and ice pounded deafeningly against her hood.

When the gust passed and the snow had settled, Lauren brushed the dusting of powder off her suit and stumbled back to her feet.

"Everything OK?" Bethany shouted.

Lauren stuck up her thumbs. "Ninety-nine days down, one to go," she shouted.

Lauren and Bethany's home for the night was a metal container painted in a high visibility shade of orange. It was the kind of container you'd normally expect to pass on the motorway, mounted on the back of an articulated truck. There was a radio mast and a shattered flagpole lashed to the roof.

The girls had beaten the darkness. The sun's distant face was already touching the horizon and the light it sent through the mist of falling snow gave the whole landscape a powdery yellow hue. The girls were too exhausted to appreciate its beauty; all they cared about was getting warm.

It took a few minutes to dig out the snow from around the two metal doors that formed one end of the container. Once they were open, Lauren dragged the two sleds inside, while Bethany searched along a wooden shelf until she found a gas lamp. Lauren closed the metal doors, creating a boom that would have been deafening if the girls' ears hadn't been shielded by their outdoor clothes.

"We've got even less fuel tonight," Lauren shouted, as the lamp erupted in an unsteady blue glow. She looked at the single bottle of gas as she peeled off her goggles and outermost set of gloves. Her hands were freezing, but it was impossible to manipulate anything with three sets of gloves on.

On the first night of their week in the Alaskan wilderness, the girls had found two large bottles of gas in their shelter. They'd heated the room until it was toasty, cooked lavishly, and warmed up water to wash with. The fun ended abruptly when the gas ran out in the middle of the night and the indoor temperature rapidly dropped back below freezing. After this harsh lesson, the girls took pains to ration their energy supply.

Bethany fixed a hose from the gas bottle to a small heater and lit just one of its three chambers. This would slowly bring the temperature inside their container above freezing. Until it did, the girls would keep as many of their outdoor clothes on as the task at hand allowed.

They spent the next few minutes rummaging through the supplies that had been left for them. There were plenty of high-energy foods, such as tinned meats, flapjacks, instant noodles, chocolate bars, and glucose powder. They also found their mission briefings, clean underwear, fresh boot liners, and floor mats. Combined with the pots, utensils, and sleeping bags packed in their sleds, it would be enough to make the nineteen hours until the sun returned reasonably comfortable.

Once the girls had ensured that they had all the basics, Lauren couldn't help wondering what was under the tarpaulin at the back of the container.

"That's got to be something to do with our mission for tomorrow," Bethany said.

They stepped across and dragged the tarp off a giant cardboard box. It was over two meters long and almost up to Lauren's shoulders. Scraping at the layer of frost over the cardboard revealed a Yamaha logo and an outline drawing of a snowmobile.

"Cool," Bethany said. "I don't think my legs could handle another day trudging through that snow."

"Have you ever driven one?" Lauren asked.

"Nah," Bethany said, shaking her head excitedly. "But it can't be much different from the quad bikes we drove last summer at the hostel. . . . Let's open our briefings and work out what we've got to do tomorrow."

"We'd better take our temperatures and radio base camp first," Lauren said.

There was a radio set already linked up to the aerial on the roof. Its battery was cold and it took several seconds for the orange frequency display on the front panel to light up. While they waited, the girls took turns measuring their body temperatures with a small plastic strip that you tucked under your armpit.

The indicator lit up between the thirty-five and thirty-six degree marks on both of them. It meant the girls were running slightly below normal body temperature, which is exactly what you'd expect for two people who'd just spent several hours in extreme cold. Another hour would have been enough for them to develop early symptoms of hypothermia.

Lauren grabbed the microphone and keyed up. "This is unit three calling Instructor Large. Over."

"Instructor Large receiving . . . Greetings, my little sugar plums."

It was reassuring hearing a human voice other than Bethany's for the first time in twenty-four hours, even if it was that of Mr. Large, CHERUB's head training instructor. Large was a nasty piece of work. Pushing kids through tough training courses wasn't just part of his job; he actually enjoyed making them suffer.

"Just reporting in to say that everything is fine with me and unit four," Lauren said. "Over."

"Why aren't you using the coded frequency? Over," Mr. Large asked angrily.

Lauren realized her instructor was right and hurriedly flipped the scramble switch on the front of the receiver.

"Oh . . . Sorry. Over."

"You will be tomorrow morning when I get my hands on you," Large snapped. "Minus ten house points for Hufflepuff. Over and out."

"Over and out," Lauren said bitterly. She put down the microphone and kicked out at the side of the metal container. "God, I *really* hate that man's guts."

Bethany laughed a little. "Not as much as he hates you for knocking him head first into that muddy hole with a spade."

"True," Lauren said, allowing herself a grin as she

recalled the event that had brought her first attempt at basic training to an abrupt end. "I suppose we'd better get cracking. You start translating the briefing. I'll go outside and bring in some snow to melt for drinking water."

Lauren found a bucket and grabbed the torch out of her sled. She pushed the metal door of the container and squeezed herself and the bucket through a small gap, so as not to let out too much heat.

The sun was gone and only the tiny shaft of light from inside the container enabled Lauren to notice the giant white outline in the snow. Half convinced that she was overtired and imagining things, Lauren flicked on her torch.

What Lauren saw left her in no doubt. She screamed as she scrambled back inside the container and swiftly pulled up the metal door.

"What's the matter?" Bethany asked, turning sharply from her mission briefing.

"Polar bear!" Lauren gasped. "Lying in the snow right outside the door. Luckily it seemed to be resting; another few steps and I would have trodden on it."

"It *can't* be," Bethany said.

Lauren waved the torch in her training partner's face. "Here, take this. Stick your head out and look for yourself."

It only took the briefest of glances to confirm it. The mat of white fur, with plumes of hot breath steaming out of its nostrils, lay less than five meters from the entrance to the container.

Once Lauren recovered from her near-death experience, the girls thought things through and decided that the situation wasn't too serious.

They could get all the drinking water they needed by leaning out of the metal doors and scooping up the snow around the entrance. Once they'd got enough snow, they decided to leave the giant bear in peace. It seemed unlikely the animal would leave itself exposed to the cold all night. Surely it would move away to find shelter before the sun came back up.

The inside of the container had now warmed up enough for the girls not to be able to see their breath curling in front of their faces. After their day in the cold, it seemed toasty. They stepped out of their boots and outer suits, hanging them on a line in the warm air above the gas heater, so that the moisture in them would evaporate overnight.

The metal floor of the container was cold to touch, so they put on trainers and laid out insulating foam mats retrieved from their sleds. They turned the heater up and lined icy tins of corned beef and fruit in front of it, as Bethany melted a saucepan of snow over a portable stove.

It took an hour to read the briefings for the final twenty-four hours of their course, under the flickering light of two gas lamps. The briefings only ran to five pages, but were written in languages with non-European alphabets that the girls had only started learning at the beginning of the course: Russian for Bethany and Greek for Lauren.

The gist of the briefings was simple. The girls had to unpack the snowmobile from its shipping crate and prepare it for first use: a task that involved screwing various bits together, lubricating the drive track and engine, and filling the tank with petrol. From sunup, they'd have two hours to make a thirty-five-kilometer journey by snowmobile to a checkpoint where they would liaise with the four other trainees for something the briefing ominously described as the "*Ultimate test of physical courage in an extreme weather environment*."

"Well," Lauren said, as she dug her spoon into a can of corned beef that was warm and greasy on the outside but rock hard in the centre, "at least the instructions for the snowmobile are in English."

ABOUT THE AUTHOR

Robert Muchamore was born in London in 1972 and used to work as a private investigator. CHERUB is his first series and is published in more than twenty countries.

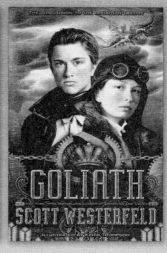

CHERUB

MISSION 1
THE RECRUIT

ROBERT MUCHAMORE

Simon Pulse
New York London Toronto Sydney

This book is a work of fiction. Any references to historical events, real people, or real locales are used fictitiously. Other names, characters, places, and incidents are the product of the author's imagination, and any resemblance to actual events or locales or persons, living or dead, is entirely coincidental.

SIMON PULSE
An imprint of Simon & Schuster Children's Publishing Division
1230 Avenue of the Americas, New York, NY 10020
This Simon Pulse paperback edition December 2010

Originally published in Great Britain in 2004 by Hodder Children's Books
Published by arrangement with Hodder and Stoughton Limited

Also available in a Simon Pulse hardcover edition.
For information about special discounts for bulk purchases, please contact
Simon & Schuster Special Sales at 1-866-506-1949 or business@simonandschuster.com.
The Simon & Schuster Speakers Bureau can bring authors to your live event.
For more information or to book an event contact the Simon & Schuster Speakers Bureau at
1-866-248-3049 or visit our website at www.simonspeakers.com.
The text of this book was set in Apollo MT.
Manufactured in the United States of America
8 10 9 7
Library of Congress Control Number 2004118121
ISBN 978-1-4169-9940-9 (hc)
ISBN 978-1-4424-1360-3 (pbk)

WHAT IS CHERUB?

During World War Two, French civilians set up a resistance movement to fight against the German forces occupying their country. Many of their most useful operatives were children and teenagers. Some worked as scouts and messengers. Others befriended homesick German soldiers, gathering information that enabled the resistance to sabotage German military operations.

A British spy named Charles Henderson worked among these French children for nearly three years. After returning to Britain, he used what he'd learned in France to train twenty British boys for work on undercover operations. The codename for his unit was CHERUB.

Henderson died in 1946, but the organization he created has thrived. CHERUB now has more than two hundred and fifty agents, all aged seventeen or under. Although there have been many technical advances in intelligence operations since CHERUB was founded, the reason for its existence remains the same: Adults never suspect that children are spying on them.

CHAPTER 1

SCIENCE

James Choke hated Combined Science. It should have been test tubes, jets of gas, and sparks flying all over the place, like he'd imagined when he was still at primary school. What he got was an hour propped on a stool watching Miss Voolt write on a blackboard. You had to write everything down even though the photocopier got invented forty years earlier.

It was his second to last class, raining outside and turning dark. James was sleepy because the lab was hot and he'd been up late playing Grand Theft Auto the night before.

Samantha Jennings sat next to him. Teachers thought Samantha was fantastic: always volunteering for stuff, neat uniform, glossed nails. She did all her diagrams with three different colored pens and covered her textbooks in wrapping paper so they looked extra smart. But when the teachers weren't looking, Samantha was a total cow. James hated her. She was always winding him up about his mum being fat:

"James's mum is so fat, they have to grease the bath tub or she gets stuck in it."

Samantha's cronies laughed, same as always.

James's mum *was* huge. She had to order her clothes out of a special catalog for fat people. It was a nightmare being seen with her. People pointed, stared. Little kids mimicked the way she walked. James loved his mum, but he tried to find excuses when she wanted to go somewhere with him.

"I went for a five-mile jog yesterday," Samantha said. "Two laps around James's mum."

James looked up from his textbook.

"That's so funny, Samantha. Even funnier than the first three times you said it."

James was one of the toughest kids in Year Seven. Any boy cussing his mum would get a punch. But what could you do when it was a girl? Next lesson he'd sit as far from Samantha as he could.

"Your mum is so fat—"

James was sick of it. He jumped up. His stool tipped over backwards.

"What is it with you, Samantha?" James shouted.

The lab went quiet. Every eye turned to the action.

"What's the matter, James?" Samantha grinned. "Can't take a joke?"

"Mr. Choke, pick up your seat and get on with your work!" Miss Voolt shouted.

"You say one more word, Samantha, I'll . . ."

James was never any good at comebacks.

"I'll bloody . . ."

Samantha giggled. "What will you do, James? Go home and cuddle big fat Mommy?"

James wanted to see something other than a stupid grin on Samantha's face. He grabbed Samantha off her stool, pushed her up against the wall, then spun her around to face him. He froze in shock. Blood was running down Samantha's face. Her cheek had a long cut where it had caught on a nail sticking out of the wall.

James backed away, scared. Samantha cupped her hands over the blood and started bawling her head off.

"James Choke, you are in extremely serious trouble!" Miss Voolt shouted.

Everyone in James's class was making some sort of noise. James couldn't face up to what he'd done. No one would believe it was an accident. He made a run for the door.

Miss Voolt grabbed James's blazer.

"Where do you think you're going?"

"Get out of my way!" James shouted.

He gave Miss Voolt a shove. She toppled backwards, limbs flipping helplessly in the air like a beetle turned upside down.

He slammed the classroom door and ran down the corridor. The school gates were locked, but he escaped over the barrier in the teachers' car park.

James stormed away from school, muttering to himself, getting less angry and more scared as it dawned that he was in the deepest trouble of his life.

He was twelve in a few weeks' time. He started wondering if he'd live that long. His mum was going to kill him. He'd definitely get suspended. It was probably bad enough to get expelled.

By the time James got to the little playground near his flats he felt sick. He looked at his watch. If he went home this early his mum would know something was up. He didn't have change for a cup of tea in the chip shop. The only thing to do was go into the playground and shelter from the drizzle in the concrete tunnel.

The tunnel seemed smaller than James remembered. There was graffiti sprayed all over and it smelled like a dog had peed inside. James didn't mind. He felt he deserved to be somewhere cold that smelled of dog. He rubbed his hands to get them warm and remembered when he was little.

His mum was nowhere near as fat in those days. Her face would appear in the end of the tunnel with a daft grin. She'd speak in a deep voice, "I'm coming to eat you up, James." It was cool, because the tunnel had a killer echo when you were sitting inside. James tried the echo:

"I'm a total idiot."

The echo agreed with him. He pulled his coat hood up and did the zip to the top so it covered half his face.

After half an hour sulking, James knew he had two options: stay in the tunnel for the rest of his life, or go home and get killed.

James stepped in the hallway of his flat and checked the mobile phone on the table under the coatrack:

12 MISSED CALLS
UNIDENTIFIED NUMBER

It looked like school had been trying to get hold of his mum pretty bad, but she hadn't answered. James thanked God, but wondered why she hadn't picked up. Then he noticed Uncle Ron's jacket hanging up.

Uncle Ron had turned up when James was a toddler. It was like having a loud, smelly rug in the flat. Ron smoked, drank, and only went out to go to the pub. He got a job once, but it only lasted a fortnight.

James had always thought Ron was an idiot and his mum had eventually agreed and kicked him out. But only after she'd married him and given birth to his daughter. Even now James's mum had a soft spot for Ron. They'd never got divorced. Ron turned up every few weeks, supposedly to see his daughter, Lauren. But mostly he came when Lauren was at school and he was short of a few quid.

James walked into the living room. His mum, Gwen, was spread out on a sofa. Her feet were up on a stool and her left leg was bandaged. Ron was in an armchair, feet on the coffee table, toes poking out of his socks. They were both drunk.

"Mum, you're not supposed to drink with your pills," James said, so annoyed he forgot his problems.

Ron straightened up and took a drag of his cigarette.

"Hey Jamie boy, Daddy's home," Ron said, grinning.

James and Ron eyed each other up.

"You're not my father, Ron," James said.

"No," Ron replied. "Your dad legged it the day he saw your ugly face."

James didn't want to say about school in front of Ron, but the truth was eating at him.

"Mum, something happened at school. It was an accident."

"Wet your pants again, did you?" Ron giggled.

James didn't want to take the bait.

"Listen, James, me darlin'," Gwen said, slurring her words. "Whatever trouble you're in this time, we'll talk later. Go and get your sister from school. I've had a few too many drinkies and I'd better not drive."

"I'm sorry, Mum, it's really serious. I have to tell you. . . ."

"Just get your sister, James," his mum said sternly. "My head is pounding."

"Lauren's big enough to come home on her own," James said.

"She isn't," Ron interrupted. "Do what you're told. He needs my boot up his backside if you ask me."

"How much money does he want this time?" James asked sarcastically.

Gwen waved her hand in front of her face. She was fed up with both of them.

"Can't you two stay in the same room for two minutes without fighting? James, go to my purse, buy something for tea on the way home. I'm not cooking tonight."

"But . . ."

"Get out, James, before I lose my temper."

James couldn't wait until he was old enough to batter Uncle Ron. His mum was OK when Ron wasn't around.

James found his mum's purse in the kitchen. A tenner was enough for his dinner, but he took two twenties. Ron would steal everything in the purse before he left, so James wouldn't get blamed. It felt nice stuffing forty quid into his school trousers. Gwen never left anything lying around that she didn't expect James or Ron to steal. She kept the big money upstairs in a safe.

CHAPTER 2

SISTER

Some kids were happy to have one games console. James Choke had every console, game, and accessory going. He had a PC, an MP3 player, Nokia mobile, widescreen TV, and DVD recorder in his room. He never looked after any of it. If something broke he got another one. He had eight pairs of Nike trainers. A top-line skateboard. A £600 racing bike. When his bedroom was in a mess it looked like a bomb had gone off in Toys "R" Us.

James had all this because Gwen Choke was a thief. She ran a shoplifting empire from her armchair while she watched daytime soaps and stuffed chocolates and pizza. She didn't steal, herself. Gwen took orders and passed them down to thieves who worked for her. She covered her tracks, never going near stolen goods herself and switching mobiles every few days so the police couldn't trace her calls.

It was the first time James had been back to primary school since his last day as a pupil before the summer holidays. A few mums stood at the gate nattering.

"Where's your mum, James?" someone asked.

"Off her face," James said sourly.

There was no way James was covering for her after she'd kicked him out of the flat. He saw the other mums exchange glances.

"I want Medal of Honor for PlayStation," one of them asked. "Can she get it?"

James shrugged. "Course, half price, cash only."

"Will you remember, James?"

"No. Give us a bit of paper with your name and phone number and I'll pass it on."

The gaggle of mums started jotting things down. Trainers, jewelry, radio-controlled car. James stuffed the papers into his school blazer.

"If you want to tell my mum something, write it down. I won't remember."

The kids all started coming out. Nine-year-old Lauren was last out of her class. She had her hands tucked in her bomber jacket and mud on her jeans from playing football with the boys at lunchtime. Lauren had blond hair, same as James, but she kept asking her mum to let her dye it black.

Lauren was on another planet to most girls her age. She didn't own a single dress or skirt. She'd microwaved her Barbies when she was five and hadn't touched one since. Gwen Choke said if there were two ways of doing something, Lauren would always pick the third one.

"I hate that old bat," Lauren said, when she got near James.

"Who?" James asked.

"Mrs. Reed. She gave us sums. I did them in about two minutes, and she made me sit still for the rest of the lesson waiting for all the dumb kids to finish. She wouldn't even let me go to the cloakroom and get my book."

James remembered Mrs. Reed had done the same thing when she was his teacher three years earlier. It was like getting punished for being clever.

"Why are you here, anyway?" Lauren asked.

"Mum's drunk."

"She's not supposed to drink until after the operation."

"Don't tell me," James said. "What can I do about it?"

"How come you got home early enough to pick me up?"

"Got in a fight. They sent me home."

Lauren shook her head, but she couldn't help smiling.

"Another fight. That's three this term, isn't it?"

James didn't want to talk about it.

"What do you want first?" he asked. "Good news or bad news?"

Lauren shrugged. "Just tell us."

"Your dad's indoors. The good news is Mum gave us money to get take-away. He should be gone by the time we get home."

They ended up in a burger place. James got a double cheeseburger meal. Lauren only wanted onion rings and a Coke.

She wasn't hungry, so she got handfuls of little milks and sugar packets and made a mess on the table while James ate. She tipped out loads of sugar, soaked it with milk, then shredded the paper wrappers and stirred it all up.

"What are you doing that for?" James asked.

"As a matter of fact," Lauren said acidly, "the entire future of Western civilization depends upon me making a smiley face with this ketchup."

"You realize some poor sod has to clean all that up?" James said.

"Not my problem," Lauren shrugged.

James tucked in the last mouthful of his burger and realized he was still starving. Lauren had hardly touched her onion rings.

"You eating those?" James asked.

"Have them if you want. They're stone cold."

"This is all we've got for dinner. You better eat something."

"I'm not hungry," Lauren said. "I'll make toasted sandwiches later."

James loved Lauren's toasted sandwiches. They were mad: She got Nutella, honey, icing sugar, golden syrup, chocolate chips. Whatever sweet stuff was around, all poured on thick. The outside was crispy and the hot gloop was about three centimeters deep in the middle. You couldn't eat one without burning your fingers.

"You better clean up afterwards," James said. "Mum blew her stack last time you made them."

When James turned into his road it was nearly dark. Two guys came out from behind a hedge. One of them grabbed

James and knocked him against a wall, pulling his arm tight behind his back.

"Hello, James," he said, his mouth up against James's ear. "We've been waiting for you."

The other guy grabbed Lauren and stuck his hand over her mouth to stop her screaming.

James's opinion of his own intelligence hit an all-time low. While he'd been worrying about getting in trouble with Mum, school, and maybe even with the police, he'd forgotten something: Samantha Jennings had a sixteen-year-old brother.

Greg Jennings hung out with a gang of crazies. They were kings of the neighborhood where James lived: smashing up cars, mugging people, getting into fights. If another kid saw them he'd look down at his shoes, cross his fingers, and be happy if all he came away with was a slapped face and his money taxed. A good way to upset the gang was to beat up one of their little sisters.

Greg Jennings grazed James's face along the bricks.

"It's your turn now, James."

He let go of James's arm. James could feel blood dribbling down his nose and cheek. There was no point struggling: Greg could snap him like a twig.

"Scared?" Greg asked. "You ought to be."

James tried to speak, only his voice didn't work and the way he was trembling seemed to answer anyway.

"Got money?" Greg asked.

James took out the rest of the forty pounds.

"Nice one," Greg said.

"Please don't hurt my sister," James begged.

"My sister has eight stitches in her face," Greg said,

pulling a knife out of his pocket. "Lucky I don't go round hurting little girls, or your sister might have ended up with eighty."

Greg sliced off James's school tie. Then he cut the chest buttons off his shirt and slashed up his trousers.

"This is just the start, James," Greg said. "We're gonna be seeing a lot of each other."

A fist smashed into James's stomach. Ron had hit James a few times, but never that hard. Greg and his henchman walked off. James crumpled up on the ground.

Lauren walked over to James. She didn't have much sympathy for him.

"You got in a row with Samantha Jennings?"

James looked up at his sister. He was in a lot of pain and ashamed of himself.

"She got cut by accident. I only meant to scare her."

Lauren started walking away.

"Help me up, Lauren. I can't walk."

"Crawl then."

Lauren went a few more paces before she realized she couldn't abandon her brother, even if he *was* an idiot. James stumbled towards home with his arm around Lauren's back. It took all her strength to hold him up.

CHAPTER 9

WORSE

James stumbled into the hallway, one hand clasped over his stomach. He glanced at the display on his mum's mobile:

48 MISSED CALLS
4 TEXTS

He turned the phone off and stuck his head in the living room. The light was off, TV on. His mum was asleep in her chair and there was no sign of Ron.

"He's gone," James said.

"Thank God for that," Lauren said. "He always kisses me and his breath's revolting."

Lauren pushed the front door shut and picked a handwritten note off the doormat.

"It's from your school."

Lauren read aloud, struggling with the messy handwriting:

"'Dear Mrs. Choke, Please contact either the school secretary or myself urgently on one of the numbers below, con . . .' *Con* something?"

"Concerning," James guessed.

"'Concerning James's behavior at school today,'" Lauren continued. "'Michael Rook, Deputy Head Teacher.'"

Lauren followed James into the kitchen. James ran a glass of tap water and slumped at the table. Lauren sat opposite and kicked off her trainers.

"Mum will absolutely massacre you," Lauren grinned. She was looking forward to seeing James suffer.

"Can't you shut up? I'm trying not to think about it."

James locked himself in the bathroom. He was shocked by what the mirror showed him. The left side of his face and the ends of his cropped blond hair were bloodred. He emptied his pockets and stuffed his wrecked clothes in a bin-liner. He'd hide them under the other rubbish later so his mum didn't find them.

Ending up in this mess made James start asking questions about himself. He knew he wasn't a very good person. He was always getting in fights. He was clever, but he never did any work so he got bad marks. James remembered all the times his teachers had told him he was wasting his potential and that he'd end up in a bad way. He'd sat through billions of lectures with his brain turned off. Now he was beginning to think they were mostly right and that made him hate them even more.

James unscrewed the cap on a tube of antiseptic, but realized it was pointless without washing off the blood first. The hot shower soothed his face and stomach as a red puddle whirled around his feet.

James wasn't sure if God existed, but he couldn't see how everything just got here without something making it. If there was ever a time to pray, this was it. He wondered if you were supposed to pray while naked in the shower, but figured what the hell and pressed his wet hands together.

"Hello, God . . . I'm not always good. Not ever, really. Just help me be good and stuff. Help me be a better person. Cheers . . . Amen. And please don't let Greg Jennings kill me."

James looked awkwardly at his hands, not convinced about the power of prayer.

After the shower, James put on his favorite clothes: an Arsenal shirt and a pair of tatty Nike tracksuit bottoms. He'd had to hide them from his mum. She chucked out anything that didn't look as if it had been shoplifted the previous week. She never understood that it was cooler if some of your clothes were a bit on the shabby side.

After milk, two of Lauren's toasted sandwiches, and half an hour playing GT4 with his duvet over him, James felt a bit better. Except his stomach killed him if he moved suddenly and he wasn't looking forward to telling his mum what he'd done when she woke up. Not that she looked like she was waking up soon. She must have had loads to drink.

James crashed his car into the barrier and six cars whizzed past, leaving him in last place. He hurled the joypad. He always got that corner wrong. The computer-controlled cars went round like they were on rails, which made it seem like the game was rubbing it in. It was boring playing alone, but there was no point asking Lauren. She hated computer games. She only ever wanted to play football or draw.

James grabbed his mobile and called his friend Sam. Sam lived down the balcony and was in James's class.

"Hello, Mr. Smith. It's James Choke. Is Sam there?"

Sam picked up the phone in his bedroom, sounding excited.

"Hey there, psycho," Sam said, laughing. "You are in *soooo* much trouble."

That wasn't how James wanted the conversation to start.

"What happened after I left?"

"Man, it was the sickest thing ever. Samantha had blood gushing out of her face. Down her arms, everywhere. They took her in an ambulance. Miss Voolt hurt her back, she was crying and going: 'This is the last straw. I'm taking early retirement.' Both the deputy heads and the headmaster came in. The headmaster saw Miles laughing and gave him a three-day suspension."

James couldn't believe it. "Three days' suspension for *laughing*?"

"He was livid. You're totally expelled, James."

"No way."

"Yes way, psycho. You never even made it to your first half-term. That's got to be a record for getting expelled. Did your mum give you beats?"

"She doesn't know yet. She's asleep."

Sam burst out laughing again. "Asleep! Don't you think she might want you to wake her up to tell her you've been expelled?"

"She won't care," James lied, trying to sound cool. "So you wanna come over and play PlayStation?"

Sam's voice got more serious. "No, man, I've got homework."

James laughed. "You *never* do homework."

"I started. The folks are pressuring me. Birthday presents hang in the balance."

James knew Sam was lying but couldn't figure out why. Normally, Sam asked his mum if he could come and she always said yes.

"What? What have I done to upset you?"

"It's not that, James, but . . ."

"But what, Sam?"

"Isn't it obvious?"

"No."

"You're a mate, James, but we can't hang out until this dies down."

"Why the hell not?"

"Because Greg Jennings is going to totally mash you and if I'm seen with you I'll be dead as well."

"You could help me stand up to him," James said.

Sam thought this was the funniest thing yet.

"My skinny arse is not gonna make any difference against those guys. I really like you, James. You're a good friend, but at the moment being your friend is a suicide mission."

"Thanks for your help, Sam."

"Should have switched your brain on before you decided to stab the hardest kid in school's little sister on a rusty nail."

"I never meant to hurt her. It was an accident."

"Ring me back when you get Greg Jennings to believe that."

"I can't believe you're doing this to me, Sam."

"You'd do the same if it was me. And you know it."

"So that's it. I'm a leper."

"It's a toughie, James. Sorry."

"Yeah."

"We can talk on the phone. I still like you."

"Thanks, Sam."

"I better go. Bye, James. I'm really sorry."

"Enjoy your homework."

James ended the call and wondered about praying again.

James watched rubbish TV until he fell asleep. He had a dream where Greg Jennings stood on his guts, and woke with a jolt.

He needed to pee bad. The pain in his guts was fifty times worse than earlier. The first drop of his piss hitting the toilet was red. James did a double-take. Bright red. He was peeing blood. After he'd been to the toilet the pain was mostly gone, but he was scared. He had to tell his mum.

The TV in the living room was still turned up loud. James flicked it off.

"Mum," James said.

James felt weird. His mum was too quiet. He touched her hand. Cold. He put his hand in front of her face. She wasn't breathing. No pulse. Nothing.

James hugged Lauren in the back of the ambulance. Their mum's corpse was two feet away with a blanket on top. Lauren's hands clawed into James's back. James was freaking, but he tried to keep a lid on himself to stop Lauren from getting worse.

When the ambulance arrived at emergency, James watched his mum get wheeled off on a trolley. He realized this was going to be his final memory of her: a bulging blanket lit by flashing blue bulbs.

James had to step off the ambulance with Lauren holding on. There was no way she was letting go. She'd stopped crying and was panting like an animal.

Lauren walked like a zombie. The driver led them through the waiting room to a cubicle. A doctor was waiting. She knew what had happened.

"I'm Dr. May. You must be Lauren and James."

James rubbed Lauren's shoulder to try and calm her down.

"Lauren, can you let go of your brother so we can talk?"

Lauren acted deaf.

"It's like she's dead," James said.

"She's in shock. I'll have to give her something to calm down or she'll pass out."

Dr. May picked a syringe off a trolley and pulled up the sleeve of Lauren's T-shirt.

"Hold her still."

As soon as the needle went in, Lauren went limp. James leaned her down on the bed. Dr. May picked up Lauren's legs and covered her with a blanket.

"Thank you," James said.

"You told that ambulance driver that you had some blood in your urine," Dr. May said.

"Yeah."

"Did something hit you in the stomach?"

"Some*one,*" James said. "I got in a fight. It is bad?"

"When you were hit, your insides started to bleed. It's the same as a cut on the outside. It should heal itself. Come back here if it hasn't stopped by tomorrow night."

"So what happens to us now?" James asked.

"There's a social worker coming to see you. She'll contact your relatives."

"I don't have relatives. My nan died last year and I don't know who my dad is."

CHAPTER 4

CARE

James woke up the next morning in a strange bed with sheets that smelled of disinfectant. He had no idea where he was. The last thing he remembered was a nurse giving him a sleeping pill and walking towards a car with his head weighing a million tons.

He had his clothes on, but his trainers were on the floor. He took his head out of the covers and saw another bed with Lauren poking out of it. She was sleeping with her thumb in her mouth. James hadn't seen her do that since she was little. Whatever dreams Lauren was having, the thumb wasn't a good sign.

He got out of bed. The pill had made him dull, his jaw felt stiff and there was a weird ache in his forehead. The room was bright, even though the curtains were drawn. James slid a door and found the shower and toilet. He was relieved to see that his pee came out the normal color. James splashed water on his face. He knew he ought to be upset about his mum dying, but he felt dead inside. Everything felt so unreal; it was like sitting in an armchair watching himself on television.

James peeked out of the window. Tons of kids were running around. He remembered that one of his mum's favorite threats was to stick him in a home if he didn't behave.

A buzzer sounded when James went out of the room. A care worker came out of an office and offered him her hand. James shook it, a bit stunned by her purple hair and the metalwork hanging off each ear.

"Hello, James, I'm Rachel. Welcome to Nebraska House. How are you?"

James shrugged.

"I'm really sorry about what happened to your mum."

"Thank you, Miss."

Rachel laughed.

"You're not at school here, James. They call me all sorts of rude things, but never Miss."

"Sorry."

"I'll give you the tour, then you can have some breakfast. You hungry?"

"A bit," James said.

"Listen, James," Rachel said, as she walked. "This place is a dump and I know your life seems horrible now, but there are lots of good people here to help you."

"Right," James said.

"Our luxury spa," said Rachel.

She pointed out of the window at a paddling pool filled with rainwater and cigarette ends. James smiled a bit. Rachel seemed nice, even though she probably used the same lines on every freak that ended up here.

"State-of-the-art sports complex. Strictly out of bounds until homework is finished."

They walked through a room with a dartboard and two pool tables. The green felt was stuck down with carpet tape and there was an umbrella stand filled with tipless and split cues.

"All the rooms are upstairs. Boys first floor, girls second. The baths and showers are down here," Rachel continued. "We usually have trouble getting you lads into them."

"My room has a shower in it," James said.

"That room's the reception for new arrivals. You only get one night in there."

They reached the dining room. There were a couple of dozen kids, mostly in school uniform. Rachel pointed everything out.

"Cutlery there, hot food at the bar, cereal and fruit juice. Make your own toast if you want it."

"Cool," James said.

He didn't feel cool. The room full of strange, noisy kids was intimidating.

"When you've eaten, see me in my office."

"What about my sister?" James asked.

"If she wakes up, I'll bring her to you."

James got some Frosties and sat on his own. The other kids ignored him. New arrivals were obviously nothing unusual.

• • •

Rachel was on the phone. Her desk was stacked with papers and folders. A cigarette burned in an ashtray. Rachel put the phone down and took a puff. She saw James glance at the NO SMOKING sign.

"If they sack me, they'll be six staff short," she said. "Do you want a cigarette?"

James was shocked to be offered a cigarette by an adult.

"I don't smoke."

"Good," Rachel said. "They give you cancer, but we'd rather give them to you than have you stealing them from shops. Shift my junk, make yourself comfortable."

James moved a pile from the chair with the least stuff on it and sat down.

"How do you feel, James?"

"I think the sleeping pill they gave me is making me groggy."

"That'll wear off. I really mean how do you feel about what happened to your mum?"

James shrugged. "Bad, I guess."

"The important thing is not to keep it to yourself. We'll schedule some time with a counselor, but you can chat to any of us house parents in the meantime. Even if it's three in the morning."

"Does anyone know why she died?" James asked.

"As far as I understand, your mum was taking painkillers for an ulcer on her leg."

"She wasn't supposed to drink," James said. "It's something to do with that, isn't it?"

"The painkillers and the alcohol mixed up put your

mum into a deep sleep. Her heart stopped beating. If it's any comfort, your mother wouldn't have suffered."

"What happens to us?" James asked.

"I don't believe you have any relatives."

"Only my stepdad. I call him Uncle Ron."

"The police found him last night."

"They probably had him in a cell," James said.

Rachel smiled. "I sensed that the two of you don't get on when I spoke to him last night."

"You spoke to Ron?"

"Yes . . . Do you get on well with Lauren?"

"Mostly," James said. "We row ten times a day, but we always have a laugh."

"Ron was still married to your mum when she died, even though they lived apart. Ron is Lauren's father, so he gets automatic custody of her if he wants it."

"We can't live with Ron. He's a bum."

"James, Ron has very strong feelings that Lauren shouldn't be taken into care. He's her father. There's nothing we can do to stop him unless there is a history of abuse. The thing is, James . . ."

James fitted the pieces together for himself.

"He doesn't want me, does he?"

"I'm sorry."

James looked down at the floor, trying not to get upset.

Being in care was bad. But Lauren getting stuck with Ron was worse.

Rachel walked around her desk. She put her arm round him. "I'm *so* sorry, James."

James wondered why Ron even wanted Lauren. "How long can we stay together?"

"Ron said he'd come in later this morning."

"Can't we stay together for a few days?"

"This might seem hard to understand now, James, but delaying the separation will make things worse. You'll still be able to visit each other."

"He won't look after her properly. Mum does all the washing and stuff. Lauren's scared of the dark. She can't go to school on her own. Ron won't help her. He's useless."

"Try not to worry, James. We'll make regular visits to see that Lauren settles into her new home. If she's not properly looked after, something will be done."

"So what happens to me? Am I stuck here?"

"Until we find you a foster home. That means you go and live with a family that takes in children like you for a few months at a time. There's also a chance that you'll be adopted, which means another couple will look after you permanently, exactly as if they were your real parents."

"How long does all that take?" James asked.

"We're short of foster families at the moment. A few months at least. Perhaps you should spend some time with your sister before Ron comes."

James went back to the bedroom. He gently nudged Lauren awake. She came round slowly, sitting up and picking sleep out of the corners of her eyes.

"What's this?" Lauren asked. "Hospital?"

"Children's home."

"My head aches," Lauren said slowly. "I feel all queasy."

"You remember last night?"

"I remember you telling me Mum died, and waiting for the ambulance to come. I must have fallen asleep."

"They had to give you an injection to calm you down. The nurse said you'd feel weird when you woke up."

"Are we staying here?"

"Ron's coming to pick you up later."

"Just me?"

"Yeah."

"I think I'm gonna spew," Lauren said.

She covered her mouth. James sprang back, not wanting to get sprayed. "There's a toilet in there," he said, pointing.

Lauren dashed into the bathroom. James heard her throwing up. She coughed for a bit, then flushed the toilet. It went quiet for a minute. James knocked.

"You OK? Can I come in?"

Lauren didn't answer. James stuck his head round the door. Lauren was crying.

"What's my life gonna be like living with Dad?" she sobbed.

James wrapped his arms round his sister. Her breath smelled like puke, but James didn't care. Lauren had always just been there. James had never realized how much he'd miss her if she was gone.

Lauren calmed down a bit and had a shower. She couldn't face breakfast, so they sat in the games room. All the other kids had gone to school.

The time until Uncle Ron arrived was painful. James wanted to say something amazing to cheer her up and make things right. Lauren looked down at the floor, banging her Reeboks on the chair leg.

Ron arrived with ice cream. Lauren said she didn't want it, but took it anyway. She wasn't in any state to argue. James tried not to cry in front of Ron. Lauren was so choked up she couldn't talk.

"If you want to see Lauren, here's the number," Ron said.

He handed James a scrap of paper.

"I'm having the flat cleared," Ron said. "I spoke to the social worker outside, they're taking you round later. Any of your crap still there on Friday goes in the rubbish."

James couldn't believe Ron was acting nasty on a day like this.

"You killed her," James said. "You brought all that drink to the flat."

"I didn't force it down her throat," Ron said. "And don't get your hopes up about seeing Lauren very often."

James felt like he was about to explode. "When I'm big enough I'll kill you," he said. "I swear to God."

Ron laughed. "I'm quaking in my boots. Hopefully some of the bigger lads here will knock some manners into you. It's about time somebody did."

Ron grabbed Lauren's hand and took her away.

CHAPTER 5

SAFE

James racked up the pool balls and blasted the white into them. It didn't matter where the balls went. He only wanted a distraction from the awful stuff going around his head. He'd been playing for hours when a jug-eared twenty-something introduced himself.

"Kevin McHugh. Dogsbody, former inmate." He laughed. "I mean resident, of course."

"Hey," James said, not in the mood for jokes.

"Let's get your stuff."

They walked outside to a minibus.

"I heard about your mum, James. That's tough." Kevin craned his neck, looking for a gap to pull out into the traffic.

"Thanks, Kevin. You lived here once?"

"For three years. Dad went down for armed robbery. Mum had a breakdown. I got on all right with the staff here, so they gave me this job when I turned seventeen."

"Is it OK?" James asked.

"It's not a bad place. Look after your stuff though, everything gets nicked. First chance you get, buy a decent padlock and stick it on your locker. Sleep with the key tied around your neck. Don't even take it off in the bath. If you've got cash we'll get you a lock on the way back."

"Is it rough?" James asked.

"You'll be OK. You look like you can stand up for yourself. There's a few hard cases same as anywhere, just don't wind them up is all."

The flat was a tip. A lot of valuable stuff had disappeared. The TV, video, and hi-fi were gone from the living room. The telephone was gone in the hall and the microwave from the kitchen.

"What happened?" Kevin asked. "Was it like this last night?"

"I half-expected this," James said. "Ron's been here and stripped the place. I hope he's left my stuff alone."

James ran upstairs to his room. His TV, video, and computer were gone.

"I'll stab him," he screamed.

James kicked his wardrobe door. At least Ron had left the PlayStation 2, and most other stuff. Kevin came in.

"You're not going to be able to take all this," Kevin said, looking at the piles of stuff. "Your mum must have been loaded."

"We'd better take as much as we can. Ron says the house is being cleared Friday."

James had a thought. He asked Kevin to start packing his clothes in bin-liners and went to his mum's room. Ron had taken the portable TV and the jewelry box from the dressing table, but that was no biggie because Ron had stolen all the good jewelry years ago.

James opened his mum's wardrobe and looked at her safe. There were thousands inside. Gwen Choke was a criminal; she couldn't keep money in the bank without people wanting to know where it came from. Judging by the tools on the carpet and the scratches around the safe door, Ron had made a fairly pathetic attempt to get in. He'd be back with better equipment.

James knew he'd never break open the safe. When it was delivered it took three guys to carry it up the stairs. There was no key; you dialed a combination of numbers with the big knob on the front. The only clue that James had was that one time he'd walked in and surprised his mum while she was unlocking it. She'd been holding a Danielle Steele novel and it made sense that she would hide the combination inside the kind of book he and Ron wouldn't touch with a ten-foot pole. But what if she'd changed the combination since then? It was James's only chance to beat Ron to the money, so he was at least going to try.

Gwen had a handful of novels on a shelf over her bed. James found the Danielle Steele and flicked through the pages.

"Are you all right in there, James?" Kevin shouted from the other bedroom.

James was so tense that he flew about a meter up in the air and dropped the book.

"Fine," James shouted.

He picked the open book off the floor. There was a set of numbers written in the margin on the page in front of him. The book must have been opened to the same page hundreds of times. It sprung to the right place as soon as he let it go. James felt luck was on his side for the first time in days. He scooted across the carpet and dialed in the numbers: 262, 118, 320, 145, 077. He grabbed the handle. Nothing happened. It wasn't going to work. The thought of Uncle Ron getting his hands on the money made James gag.

Then he noticed a sticker under the dial with instructions on how to use the safe. He read the first instruction:

> *(1) Dial the first number of the combination by turning the dial in an anticlockwise direction.*

James hadn't realized that the direction you turned the dial made any difference. He dialed in the first number and carried on reading:

> *(2) Dial the subsequent four numbers by turning the dial as follows: clockwise, anticlockwise, anticlockwise, and clockwise. Failure to observe this procedure will result in non-operation of the mechanism.*

He dialed the first four numbers.

"What are you playing at?" Kevin asked.

James spun around. Kevin was standing in the doorway.

Luckily the open wardrobe door stopped him from seeing the safe. Kevin seemed nice, but James was sure any adult who found out about the safe would make him give the contents either to the police or to Uncle Ron.

"Looking for stuff," James said, convinced he sounded suspicious.

"Come and help me pack, James. I don't know what you want."

"I'll be out in a minute," James said. "I'm just looking for photo albums."

"Do you want me to help you look for them?"

"No," James said, practically squealing.

"We've got fifteen minutes," Kevin said. "I've got to do a school run in an hour."

Kevin finally went back to the other room. James dialed in the fifth number. The safe made a satisfying click. He read the third instruction before he pulled on the handle and couldn't help smiling.

(3) For security purposes, this sticker should be removed once you are familiar with the unit.

James swung the heavy door open. The inside of the safe was surprisingly small because the metal lining was so thick. There were four tall piles of cash inside and a tiny envelope. James took a bin-liner and shoved the money in. He tucked the envelope into his pocket.

James imagined Ron's face when he walked in and saw the safe open. Then he thought of something even better. He peeled the instruction sticker from the safe door and put it and the Danielle Steele novel inside. As a final touch, to make Ron extra mad, James took a framed picture of himself from his mum's bedside and stood it inside the safe so it would be the first thing Ron saw when he eventually broke it open. James shut the door, gave the dial a spin, and replaced the tools exactly how Ron had left them.

James was in a slightly better mood when he walked back to his bedroom holding the cash. The room looked bare. Kevin had bagged up all the clothes and bedding that was usually strewn over the floor.

"I found the photo albums," James said.

"Good. But I'm afraid you're gonna have to make some sacrifices, James. All you've got in Nebraska House is one wardrobe, a chest of drawers, and a locker."

James started hunting through the toys and junk on the floor. He was surprised how little he cared about most of his stuff. He wanted his PlayStation 2, mobile phone, and portable CD player, but that was about it. Everything else was toys and stuff he'd grown out of. The annoying thing was, Ron had taken his TV so he had nothing to use the PlayStation on.

Kevin crouched down looking at a Sega Dreamcast and a Nintendo GameCube.

"Don't you want these?" Kevin asked.

"I only use PlayStation 2," James said. "Take them if you want them."

"I can't take gifts from residents."

James kicked the consoles into the middle of the floor.

"I don't want my stepdad to get the money from selling them. I'm not taking them with me. If you don't take them, I'll trash 'em."

Kevin didn't know what to say. James slammed the heel of his trainer into the Sega. Surprisingly little happened, so he picked it up and threw it at the wall. The case smashed. It slid down the wall and dropped behind the bed. Kevin quickly bent down and rescued the GameCube.

"OK, James, I tell you what. I'll take your GameCube and the games and in return I'll buy your padlock for you on the drive back. Is that a deal?"

"Fair enough," James said.

When they'd packed up the last few things and carried the bin-liners out to the minibus, James had a quick last look into every room of the flat he'd lived in since he was born. By the time he reached the front door he had tears on his face.

Kevin tapped the horn of the minibus. He'd already started the engine. James ignored him and went back one last time. He couldn't leave the flat without a memento of his mum. He rushed upstairs to her room and looked around.

James remembered that when he was a toddler he used to sit at his mum's dressing table after they'd shared a bath. She'd pull a pajama top over his head, then stand over him and brush his hair. It was before Lauren was born. Just the two of them, feeling tired and smelling of shampoo. James felt warm and sad. He found the battered wooden hairbrush and tucked it into the waistband of his tracksuit bottoms. Once he had the brush it felt easier to leave.

CHAPTER 6

HOME

James realized he was stupid. He should have left a bit of cash in the safe. That way Ron would never know he'd been in there. Leaving the photo was a nice gag, but Ron would realize James had taken the money when he saw it. He might try and steal the money back. And if Ron was angry he'd make it ten times harder for James to visit Lauren.

Kevin found James a room and showed him the ropes. Like where the washing machines were and where he could get toiletries and stuff, then left him to unpack. The room had a bed, a chest of drawers, a wardrobe with a locker on each side, and two writing desks under the window. The kid who lived on the other side had decorated his wall with Korn and Slipknot posters. There was a skateboard on the floor and boarder clothes hung neatly in the wardrobe: baggy cargos, a hooded top, and T-shirts with Pornstar and Gravis logos on them. Whoever James's roommate was, he looked pretty cool. The other good thing was that the kid had a portable TV on his desk, meaning they could use the PlayStation.

James looked at his watch. He reckoned there was about an hour until his roommate got out of school. James got the cash out of the bin-liner. It was all £50 and £20 notes, separated into bundles by elastic bands. He counted a couple and realized each bundle was £1,000. There were forty-three bundles.

James thought of a way to hide the money in case Ron came after it. He had a portable cassette radio from the flat. It was wrecked; half the buttons had broken and the tape player didn't rewind. James had only taken it because Ron had stolen the good one with a CD player on it.

James rummaged through his bags of stuff until he found his Swiss Army knife. He picked out the screw-driver and undid the back of his cassette player. The inside was all circuit boards and wires. James worked fast, taking the guts out of the player, unscrewing and snapping plastic, leaving only the bits you could see from the front, like the speaker and the slot where the tape went in. He stuffed all but £4,000 of the cash inside the hole, packing the money tight so it didn't rattle. He screwed the back on again, and slid the radio cassette into his locker.

James took the four odd £1,000 bundles and hid them in obvious places: the back pocket of a pair of jeans, inside a shoe, inside a book. He peeled a hundred off the last bundle to use as walking-around money and taped the rest to the inside of his locker.

The idea was, if Ron tried to break into James's room he'd find £4,000 easily, and never realize there was £39,000 more stuffed inside a cassette radio so crummy-looking even Ron wouldn't steal it.

James filled the locker with the rest of his valuables. He banged it shut and put the padlock key on a cord around his neck. He couldn't be bothered unpacking anything else. He threw as many bags as he could in the wardrobe and kicked what was left under his bed.

Then he slumped on his bare mattress, staring at the wall. There were hundreds of pin holes and blobs of Blu-tack where previous kids had decorated the walls. He wondered what Lauren was doing.

Just after four, James's roommate, Kyle, came running in. He was a skinny kid, a bit taller than James, wearing school uniform. Kyle slammed the door and tried to get his key in the hole to lock it. James wondered what the hell was going on.

Kyle couldn't lock the door before another kid rammed it. This kid looked older. Same height as Kyle but twice the width. Kyle jumped on to his bed. The big kid bundled Kyle over and pulled him to the floor. He sat astride him and punched him a couple of times in the arm.

"You think you're so smart," the thug said.

"Take it," Kyle said.

Kyle took a couple of slaps in the face. The thug slid a diary out of Kyle's blazer and cracked him on top of the head with it.

"Touch my stuff again, doughnut, I'll smash your face in."

He got off Kyle, kicked him in the thigh and walked out.

James sat up on his bed. Kyle tried to act like it was nothing but couldn't hide the pain as he raised himself on to his bed.

"I'm Kyle," Kyle said.

"I'm James. How'd you upset him?"

"His diary fell out of his pocket this morning. I found it. Most of it's bogus, but he'd written this poem about a girl."

James laughed. "That big moose writes poetry?"

"Yep," Kyle said. "I read a couple of lines out in front of his mates. He took it badly." Kyle was holding his face.

"You OK?" James asked. "You took some serious beats."

"I thought he'd grab the diary back, not try to kill me. . . . One bit of the poem was great. 'You give me a buzz that's like a bee. Even when I feel melancholy.' Isn't that cute. . . . Man, is that what it looks like?"

"What?" James asked.

"That skateboard under your bed must have cost over a hundred quid."

"You reckon?" James asked. "I only used it about twice."

Kyle started laughing. "That board is a legend, James. Kids die to get their hands on them and you've used it twice. Can I see it?"

James shrugged. "Whatever."

Kyle seemed to forget his pain as he reached under James's bed and wheeled out the board. He sat back on his bed twisting it in his hands.

"Nice. Hard wheels, must be fast. Can I try it?" Kyle asked.

"Sure. I never use it. As long as I can use my PlayStation 2 on your telly."

"PlayStation 2! We have PlayStation 2 in this room? James, you're a little beauty. What games have you got?"

"I don't know. About sixty different ones," James said.

Kyle rocked back on his bed and started kicking his feet in the air.

"Sixty games! I don't believe you, James. You must be the most spoiled kid in the world and you don't even realize it."

"What?" James asked. "Don't kids in here have games consoles?"

"We get three pounds a week for pocket money. You see that Gravis shirt on the floor? Twenty-five quid. I had to save up two pounds for twelve weeks to get that. I had to steal my Stussy shorts from a shop at Camden Lock. Would have ended up with a security guard standing on my head if I didn't know a few moves."

"You want to try the PlayStation now?" James asked.

"After my homework," Kyle said. "I always do homework first."

James laid back on his bed, wondering if Kyle was a swot. Someone knocked.

"Yeah?" James said.

It was one of the house parents, a bearded hippy type. He looked at James.

"I've sorted you a place at West Road School. You can start there in the morning. You'll have to come back at lunchtime. The counselor wants to see you."

James was miffed. He thought that his mum dying, and getting expelled, would get him off school for at least a couple of weeks.

"OK," James said. "Where's West Road?"

"Kyle," the care worker said, "can you find James a school uniform and show him to school tomorrow?"

"No worries," Kyle said.

Kyle and James spent the whole evening together. After his homework Kyle took James down to dinner. The food wasn't the best but it was better than James got at home. Afterwards they set up the PlayStation. While they played they told stories about stuff, like fights at school and how they ended up here. James was surprised that Kyle was thirteen and already in Year Nine. Kyle said he was good at everything except sports. He had a hard time because the rest of his class were bigger than him. James said the only things he was any good at were sports and maths.

Before they went to bed, Kyle took James to the laundry and found a box of school uniforms. James already had school shirts and trousers, but he needed a blazer with the West Road badge and a school tie. There wasn't much choice and everything was trashed. They found a blazer that fitted James OK and a school tie that was in threads.

• • •

Kyle fell asleep. James's head was too busy. Tomorrow was going to be the first day of a new routine: eating meals with all the other kids, going to a new school, coming home, and spending time with Kyle. It wasn't the end of the world, but he wished Lauren was here.

James remembered the little brown envelope in the safe. He'd forgotten until now. He scrambled out of bed and slipped his tracksuit bottoms on. He rummaged in his pockets. His heart skipped when he didn't find it straight away. He had to go somewhere light where he could look without anyone seeing. The toilet was the obvious place.

James locked himself in a cubicle and opened the envelope gently so he'd be able to reseal it. There was a key and a business card:

REX DEPOSITARY
Deposit Your Valuables with Total Discretion and Security
Individual Boxes in Eight Different Sizes

James flicked the card over. The address was on the back. It looked like his mum had another hidden stash. He put the key on the cord around his neck.

CHAPTER 7

SHRINK

James had always been in mixed schools, but West Road was all boys. The lack of girls gave the place an air of menace. It was noisier and everybody in the corridor pushed harder than at his old school. It felt like something could go off any second.

A Year Seven got a hard shove from a Year Ten and knocked into James. The kid went down and yelped as the Year Ten stamped on his hand. The kids were all heading somewhere. James had a map which made no sense whichever way he turned it.

"Nice tie, girlie," somebody said.

James thought it was aimed at him. The tie was a wreck. He decided to steal one from some weed the first chance he got. The bodies were all disappearing into classrooms and within a couple of minutes James only had a few late arrivals for company.

A couple of nasty-looking Year Ten kids blocked James's way. One of them had spiked hair and a Metallica T-shirt under his blazer. Both were wearing menacing-looking steel-toe-capped boots with fat laces dragging behind.

"Where are you going, squirt?"

James looked up at them, thinking he was going to die before he even made it to his first class.

"Registration," he said.

The Metallica kid snatched the map out of James's hand.

"Well, you're not going to make it," Metallica said.

James braced himself for a boot or fist.

"Try using the side of the map that says main building, not annex. It's over there."

Metallica turned the map over and handed it back to James. He pointed at a yellow door up a corridor on the left.

"Thanks," James said.

He hurried off. Metallica shouted after him, "Take that tie off!"

James looked down at the tie. He could see it was tatty but why all the fuss?

James handed his form teacher a note. All the kids in his new class were staring at him as he looked for a seat. He sat at the end of a row, next to a black kid called Lloyd.

"You one of the little orphans from the council home?" Lloyd asked.

The kids sitting around James laughed. James knew first impressions counted. If he said nothing he'd look soft. His reply had to be sharp, but not so nasty it started a fight.

"How'd you know?" James said. "I suppose your mum saw me when she cleaned our toilets."

The group of kids laughed. Lloyd looked angry for a second, then he laughed too. "Like your tie, sister," he said.

James had had enough with the tie. He pulled it off and looked. Then he looked at Lloyd's tie. It wasn't the same color. Nor was anyone else's.

"What *is* this tie?" James asked.

"The good news, orphan," Lloyd said, "is that you have a West Road tie. The bad news, it's from West Road *Girls* School."

James laughed with the others. These kids seemed OK. He was angry Kyle had tricked him, though.

James left at lunchtime to see the counselor. Her office was on the second floor of Nebraska. It had spider plants branching off everywhere. The counselor, Jennifer Mitchum, was a rake, barely taller than James. She had veins poking out of her hands that James didn't want to look at and she sounded really posh.

"Would you feel more comfortable in the chair or on the couch?"

James had seen all the psychiatrist scenes on TV and felt he had to lie on the couch to get the full effect.

"Cool," he said, settling himself down. "I could sleep all night on this."

Jennifer walked slowly around the room, lowering the blinds so it was almost dark. She sat down.

"I want you to be relaxed around me, James. Everything you say stays between us. When you talk, don't try and say the correct thing; say what you really think, and remember I'm here to help you."

"OK," James said.

"You said you could fall asleep on the couch. Have you been sleeping properly at night?"

"Not really. I have too much to think about."

"What do you think about most?"

"I wonder if my little sister is OK."

"It says in the file you're concerned about Ron's ability to look after Lauren."

"He's a retard," James said. "He couldn't look after a hamster. I don't even understand why he wanted her."

"Perhaps he loves Lauren, but found it difficult to express that while your mother was alive."

James laughed. "That's total rubbish. You'd have to meet him to understand."

"If you see Lauren regularly, that should help both of you feel better."

"Yeah, but it won't happen."

"I'll talk to Ron and see if we can set up a schedule of meetings. Perhaps you and Lauren can spend every Saturday together."

"You can try, but Ron hates my guts. I don't think he'll let me see her."

"What about your mother? How do you feel about her?"

James shrugged. "She's gone. What can I do? I wish I'd been better when she was alive."

"In what way?"

"I was always in trouble. Getting in fights and stuff."

"What made you get in trouble?"

James had to think hard.

"I don't know. I always do stupid stuff without meaning it. I'm a bad person, I guess."

"The first question I asked you was what you thought about most. You said you were worried about your sister. Wouldn't a bad person always think about himself first?"

"I love Lauren. . . . Can I tell you something I did?"

"Of course, James."

"Last year at school. I got in this row with a teacher, so I stormed out to the toilets. This kid in the year below me was in there. I just laid into him. He didn't say one word. I just started beating him."

"Did you know that what you were doing was bad at the time you were doing it?"

"Of course I knew beating someone up was bad."

"So why did you do it?"

"Because . . ." James couldn't bring himself to be honest.

"When you were hitting that boy, how did you feel?"

James blurted it out. "It was the best feeling. He was crying his eyes out and I felt fantastic."

James looked at Jennifer to see if she was shocked, but her face was calm.

"Why do you think you enjoyed it?"

"I told you already. I'm sick in the head. Someone rubs me the wrong way and I go psycho."

"Try and describe how you felt about the person you were hurting."

"I owned him. There was nothing he could do, no matter how much I hurt him."

"You went from a situation with your teacher, where you were powerless and had to do what you were told, into the toilet where you saw someone weaker than yourself and exercised your power over him. That must have been satisfying."

"You could put it like that," James said.

"It's a frustrating situation at your age, James. You know what you want but you have to do what you're told. You go to school when you're told, go to bed when you're told, live where you're told. Everything is controlled by other people. It's common for boys your age to enjoy sudden outbursts where they have control over someone else."

"But I'll end up in loads of trouble if I keep getting in fights," James said.

"I'll teach you some techniques to manage your anger over the coming weeks. Until then try and remember that you're only eleven years old and nobody expects you to be perfect. Don't think of yourself as being a bad person or that you're sick in the head. In fact, I want to do something we call Positive Reinforcement. I want you to repeat what I just told you."

"Repeat what?" James asked.

"Say 'I'm not a bad person.'"

"I'm not a bad person," James said.

"Say 'I'm not sick in the head.'"

"I'm not sick in the head." James smiled. "I feel like an idiot."

"I don't care if you feel like an idiot, James. Take a

deep breath, say the words and think about what they mean."

James had thought that seeing the counselor would be a waste of time, but he did feel better.

"I'm a good person and I'm not sick in the head," he said.

"Excellent, James. I think that would be a positive note on which to end the session. I'll see you again on Monday."

James slid off the couch.

"Before we finish, there is one detail on the notes from your school that made me curious. What's one hundred and eighty-seven multiplied by sixteen?"

James thought for about three seconds.

"Two thousand, nine hundred and ninety-two."

"Very impressive," Jennifer said. "Where did you learn to do that?"

"I just can," James shrugged. "Right from when they first started teaching me numbers. I hate it when people ask me to do it; it makes me feel like a freak."

"It's a gift," Jennifer said. "You should be proud of it."

James went down to his room. He started doing some geography homework but his heart wasn't in it. He switched on the PlayStation. Kyle came in from school.

"How was your first day?" Kyle asked.

"Pretty good, no thanks to you."

"That was a good gag with the tie," Kyle said.

James jumped up off his seat and grabbed Kyle by his shirt. Kyle shoved James away, sending him crashing into a desk. He was stronger than James had expected.

"Jesus, James. I thought you were cool."

"Pretty nice thing to do. First day at a new school and you make me look like a tit."

Kyle threw his schoolbag down.

"I'm sorry, James. If I knew you were gonna have a tantrum I wouldn't have done it."

James wanted to start a major row, but Kyle was the only kid in Nebraska he could even put a name to. He didn't want to fall out with him.

"Just stay out of my face," James said.

James sat on his bed sulking while Kyle did his homework. After a bit he got fed up and went for a walk. He saw the kid in the Metallica T-shirt he'd met at school. He was in a corner with a gang who all looked pretty rough. James walked over to them.

"Thanks for helping earlier," James said.

Metallica looked him over. "No worries, man. Name's Rob. This is the gang. Vince, Big Paul, and Little Paul."

"I'm James."

There was an awkward silence.

"You want something else, squirt?" Big Paul asked.

"No," James said.

"Piss off then."

James felt his face turn red. He started to walk away but Rob called him back.

"Hey, James, we're going out tonight. Wanna come?"

"Cool," James said.

After dinner James went back to his room to change out of school uniform. Kyle had finished his homework and was lying on his bed reading a skateboarding magazine.

"You want to play PlayStation?" Kyle asked. "I'm sorry about earlier, James. It was mean to trick you on your first day."

"You play it," James said. "I'm going out."

"Who with?"

"Some guy called Rob."

"You mean Robert Vaughn? The guy who wears a heavy metal shirt under his blazer?"

"Yeah, him and some mates."

"Seriously," Kyle said, "don't hang out with those guys. They're mental. They go out stealing cars and shop-lifting and stuff."

"I'm not sitting in here watching you doing your homework every night. Get a life, man."

James put his trainers on and walked to the door. Kyle looked offended. "Hey, I warned you, James. Don't whinge to me when you land in deep shit."

"Use the PlayStation whenever you want," James said.

James sat on a brick wall at the back of an industrial park. The gang were all older. Rob and Big Paul were fifteen. Vince was fourteen. He was the meanest looking, with bleached hair and a busted-up nose. Little Paul was twelve, Vince's younger brother.

They passed cigarettes around. James told them he didn't smoke. This didn't look cool but he thought it was better than pretending he smoked and coughing his guts up.

"I'm bored," Little Paul said. "Let's do something."

They walked to a car park full of Fiesta vans and climbed

through a gap in the fence. Vince and Rob walked along the row of vans trying the back doors to see if any were unlocked.

"Bingo," Rob said.

A door swung open in his hand. Rob leaned in and took out a bag of tools. He put the bag down and unzipped it.

"Feel like causing damage, James?" Rob asked.

James reached in the bag and pulled out a hammer. The others all grabbed something.

James was nervous, but it was cool walking down the street in a gang carrying hammers and wrenches. A woman nearly got herself run over crossing the street to avoid them. James didn't know what they were looking for. Vince stopped when they found a flash Mercedes. The two Pauls walked into the road.

"Go," Rob shouted.

Rob smashed his hammer through the back window of the Merc. The alarm started screeching. The others all joined in. James hesitated, then took out a side window, knocked off the wing mirror, and made two big dents in the door with his hammer. In twenty seconds every panel was dented, the lights and windows all smashed. Vince led off, running up the road and taking a couple more car windows out along the way.

They ran on to another neighborhood, down a narrow alley, and into a concrete square surrounded by flats. James was out of breath but fear kept him moving. A few more turns, over a fence, and they were in a playing field. James's trainers slid in the mud. They all stopped, plumes of breath rising into the freezing air. James started laughing, even though he had a stitch burning down his side. Rob put his hand on James's shoulder.

"You're OK, James," Rob said.

"That was *so* cool." James laughed. The mix of fear, tiredness, and excitement made his head spin. He couldn't believe what they'd just done.

CHAPTER 8

BIRTHDAY

James felt like he was floating through his life. Every day was the same. Get up, go to school, come back, play football, or hang out with Rob Vaughn and his gang. James never got into bed before midnight: He knew if he was exhausted he wouldn't lie awake feeling miserable about Lauren and his mum.

The only time he'd seen Lauren in the three weeks since his mum died had been at the funeral. The telephone number on the bit of paper Ron had given him didn't work. Ron had told Jennifer Mitchum that James was a bad influence. He didn't want him near his daughter.

• • •

"You stink," Kyle said.

James sat on the edge of his bed rubbing his eyes. He didn't need to get dressed because all he'd done the night before was kick off his trainers and climb into bed wearing his football shirt and tracksuit bottoms.

"You've had the same socks on for days," Kyle said.

"You're not my mum, Kyle."

"Your mum never had to sleep in a room that stinks of your BO."

James looked down at the blackened bottoms of his socks. They reeked, but he'd got used to the smell.

"I'll have a shower," James said.

Kyle tossed a packet of Twix bars on to James's bed.

"Happy twelfth birthday," Kyle said. "Should have got you deodorant."

James was pleased that Kyle remembered. It wasn't much of a gift, but five Twix was quite expensive for someone on three quid a week.

"You'd better clean yourself up, anyway. You've got to go to the police station today."

James looked at Kyle. His hair was gelled down and his school uniform immaculate, with the shirt tucked in and the tie done at the proper length, instead of ten centimeters long like most kids did it. James looked at the black under his nails, ran his hand through his gluey tangle of hair and couldn't help laughing about the mess his life was in.

Rachel was in a mood. Her car was overheating, the traffic was awful, and there was no space in the police station car park.

"I can't park, you'll have to go in by yourself. Have you got the bus fare to come back?"

"Yeah," James said.

He got out of the car and walked up the steps of the police station. He'd dressed in chinos and his best fleece, even combed his hair back after the shower. Everyone said getting a police caution was no big deal, but it didn't feel that way as James walked up to the desk and said his name.

"Sit," the policewoman said, pointing at a row of chairs.

James waited for an hour. People came in and filled forms, mostly reporting stolen cars or mobiles.

"James Choke."

James stood up. A fit-looking cop reached out and gave him a crunching handshake.

"I'm Sergeant Peter Davies, juvenile liaison officer."

They went upstairs to an interview room. The sergeant got an inkpad and a piece of card out of a filing cabinet.

"Relax your hand, James. Let me do all the work."

He dabbed the tips of James's fingers in the ink, then rolled each tip firmly against the card. James wished they'd given him a copy because the fingerprints would look cool pinned on his bedroom wall.

"OK, James, this is the caution. Any questions?"

James shrugged. Sergeant Davies began reading from a piece of paper:

"'The Metropolitan Police have received information that on October 9th, while attending Holloway Dale School, you seriously assaulted one of your classmates, Samantha Jennings. During the assault Miss Jennings received a severe cut to her cheek, resulting in the need for eight stitches. During the same incident you also assaulted the class teacher Cassandra Voolt, who received injuries to her back.

"'As this is the first criminal charge you have faced, the Metropolitan Police have decided to give you a formal caution if you admit to what you have done. Do you admit to the offenses detailed above?'"

"Yes," James said.

"'If you are found guilty of another criminal act before you reach the age of eighteen years, details of this offense will be given to the Magistrate or Judge and it is likely to increase the severity of the sentence you receive.'"

Sergeant Davis put the piece of paper down and tried to sound friendly. "You look like a decent kid, James."

"I never meant to cut her face. I just wanted to make her shut up."

"James, don't kid yourself into thinking it's not your fault Samantha got hurt. You can never predict what will happen in a fight. If you're stupid enough to start one, you're to blame for what happens whether you mean it or not."

James nodded. "That's true, I suppose."

"I don't want to see you here again, James. Will I?"

"I hope not," James said.

"You don't sound too sure. Do you know what sentence you would have got for what you did if you were an adult?"

"No," James said.

"A young girl with stitches in her face, you'd be looking at two years in prison. That's not funny, is it?"

"No," James said.

• • •

James was pleased the caution was out of the way. Everyone was right; it was no worse than getting told off at school. He'd taken some money out of his locker and thought he'd buy himself a birthday present. He got a new game for the PlayStation and a Nike tracksuit. Then he stuffed himself at the buffet in Pizza Hut. He made sure he didn't get back to Nebraska House until it was too late to go to afternoon lessons.

James put his new game on and lost track of time. Kyle came in and sat on the edge of his bed, the same as he did every day. Kyle felt something under the covers. He pulled them back and found James's Arsenal shirt.

"Why's your stinking football shirt in my bed?"

James knew he'd be furious. Kyle was a total girl when it came to cleanliness. When Kyle moved the shirt a new CD Walkman slid out on to the bed.

"James man, did you steal it?"

"I knew you'd say that," James replied. "Receipt's in the box."

"This is mine?" Kyle asked.

"You've been whining about your old one since I got here."

"Where'd you get the money, James?"

James liked Kyle, but he didn't trust him enough to say about the cash in his locker.

"Tied an old lady to a tree, beat her mercilessly, and stole her pension," James said.

"Yeah right, James. Seriously, where did you get sixty quid?"

"Do you want it? Or do you want to ask me stupid questions about it?" James said.

"This is sweet. I hope you didn't get yourself in any trouble. When I get my pocket money on Friday I'll buy you that deodorant you need."

"Thanks, I think," James said.

"So you want to do something tonight for your birthday? We could go to the cinema or something?"

"No," James said. "I said I'd go out with Rob and the gang tonight."

"I wish you'd stop hanging around with those freaks."

James sounded annoyed. "You give me the same lecture every time."

It was freezing cold sitting on the wall at the back of the industrial park. After the first night all they'd done was hang around smoking. Big Paul had punched a public schoolboy's tooth out and taken his mobile and wallet, but James hadn't been with them.

The gang congratulated James on his first criminal offense. Vince said he'd been arrested fifteen times. He had half a dozen court cases coming up and was facing a year in a young offenders' prison.

"I don't care," Vince said. "Brother's in young offenders. Dad's in prison. Granddad's in prison."

"Nice family," James said.

Rob and Big Paul laughed. The look James got from Vince was scary.

"You say anything about my family again, James, you're dead."

"Sorry," James said. "I was out of order."

"Kiss the floor," Vince said.

"What?" James said. "Come on, I said sorry."

"He said sorry," Rob said. "It was only a joke."

"Kiss the floor, James," Vince repeated. "I'm not saying it a third time."

Fighting Vince would be suicide. James slid off the wall. He was worried Vince would jump on his back or kick him in the head when he crouched down. But what choice was there? James put his palms on the pavement and kissed the cold stone. He wiped his lips on his sleeve and stood up, hoping Vince was satisfied.

"You know what keeps out the cold?" Rob said. "Beer."

"Nobody will serve us round here," Little Paul said. "Got no cash either."

"That liquor store up the road keeps the trays of twenty-four cans stacked up in the middle of the shop," Rob said. "You could run in, grab one and be halfway up the street before the tub of lard got out from behind the counter."

"Who's gonna do it?" Little Paul asked.

"The birthday boy," Vince said, laughing.

James realized he should have taken a beating; at least that way Vince would still respect him. Showing weakness to a guy like Vince was inviting him to tear you apart.

"Come on, man. I just got a caution this morning," James said.

"I've never seen you do anything," Vince said. "If you want to hang out with us, you'd better be prepared for some action."

"Fine, I'll go home. This is boring anyway," James said.

Vince grabbed James and shoved him into the wall.

"You'll do it," Vince said.

"Leave him, Vince," Rob said.

Vince let go. James gave Rob a nod of thanks.

"You better do it though," Rob said. "I don't like being called boring."

James wished he'd listened to Kyle.

"OK," he said, now he had no choice. "I can handle it."

The gang walked to the liquor store. Big Paul gripped James's shoulder, making sure he didn't run.

"Be really quick," Rob said. "In and out, they'll never get you."

James walked inside the shop, nervous as hell. The warm air was beautiful. He rubbed his freezing hands together and looked for courage.

"Can I help you, son?" the guy behind the counter asked.

James had no reason to be in a liquor store. The clerk knew something was up. James made a quick grab at the cans of beer. They were heavy and his frozen fingers didn't have much grip.

"Put those down, you little . . ."

James spun around and tore towards the door. He crashed into the glass. Vince and Big Paul were holding the door shut from outside.

"Let me out!" James shouted, hammering the glass.

The assistant lumbered around the counter.

"Please, Vince," James begged.

Vince gave James an evil smile and flicked him off. James knew he was done for.

Little Paul was jumping for joy. "You're busted, you're busted."

The clerk grabbed James's hands and dragged him backwards. Vince and Big Paul let go of the door and walked off casually.

"Nice night in the cells, faggot!" Vince shouted.

James stopped wriggling. There was no point, the clerk was five times his size. He dragged James behind the counter and shoved him into a chair. Then he called the police.

They'd taken James's shoes and everything out of his pockets. He'd been sitting here three hours. Back to the wall, arms around his knees. James had expected the hard rubber mattress and graffiti but he'd never realized how bad a cell smelled. It was a mixture of disinfectant and everything nasty a body could pump out.

Sergeant Davies came in. James had hoped it wouldn't be him. He looked up nervously, expecting an explosion of rage, but the sergeant seemed to find it funny.

"Hello, James. Did you have a problem grasping the meaning of our little chat this morning? Fancied a few beers to celebrate getting off easy?"

The sergeant took James to an interrogation room. Rachel was there, she looked angry. The sergeant was still smiling as he put a cassette into a recorder and spoke his and James's names into the microphone.

"James," the sergeant asked, "bearing in mind that

the liquor store you were arrested in has three video cameras inside, do you admit trying to steal twenty-four cans of beer?"

"Yes," James said.

"On the video you can make out a couple of monkeys holding the door and not letting you out of the shop. Would you care to tell me who they were?"

"No idea," James said. He knew he'd be dead if he grassed on four of the hardest kids in Nebraska House.

"Why not tell me, James? You wouldn't be here if it wasn't for them."

"Never seen them before in my life," James insisted.

"They look like Vincent St. John and Paul Puffin to me. Do those names ring a bell?"

"Never heard of them."

"OK, James. I'm ending the interview."

Sergeant Davies turned off the cassette recorder.

"Play with fire and you get burned, James. Hanging out with those two is more like playing with dynamite."

"I messed up," James said. "Whatever punishment I get I deserve it."

"Don't worry about this one, James. You'll go to juvenile court. The magistrate will probably give you a twenty quid fine. It's the bigger picture you want to look at."

"What do you mean?" James asked.

"I've seen hundreds of kids like you, James. They all start where you are now. Cheeky little kids. They get a bit older. Spottier and hairier. Always in trouble, but still nothing serious. Then they do something really stupid. Stab someone, get caught selling drugs, armed robbery, something like that. Half the time they're crying. Or so shocked they can hardly speak. They're sixteen or seventeen and looking at seven years banged up. You might get off easy at your age, but if you don't start making better choices you'll be spending most of your life in a cell."

CHAPTER 9

STRANGE

This room was flashier than the one at Nebraska House. It was a single for starters. TV, kettle, telephone, and miniature fridge. It was like the hotel when his mum took him and Lauren to Disney World. James didn't have a clue where he was or how he'd got there. The last thing he remembered was Jennifer Mitchum asking him up to her office after he got back to Nebraska House.

James burrowed around under the duvet and realized he was naked. That was freaky. He sat up and looked out of the window. The room was high up overlooking an athletics track. There were kids in running spikes doing stretches. Some others were getting tennis coaching on clay courts off to the side. This was clearly a children's home, and miles nicer than Nebraska House.

There was a set of clean clothes on the floor: white socks and boxers, pressed orange T-shirt, green military-style trousers with zipped pockets, and a pair of boots. James picked the boots up and inspected them: rubbery smell and shiny black soles. They were new.

The military-style clothes made James wonder if this was where kids ended up if they kept getting into trouble. He put on the underwear and studied the logo embroidered on the T-shirt. It was a crosshair with a set of initials: CHERUB. James spun the initials in his head, but they didn't make any sense.

Out in the corridor the kids had the same boots and trousers as James, but their T-shirts were either black or gray, all with the CHERUB logo on them.

James spoke to a boy coming towards him.

"I don't know what to do," James said.

"Can't talk to orange," the boy said, without stopping.

James looked both ways. It was a row of doors in either direction. There were a couple of teenage girls down one end. Even they were wearing boots and green trousers.

"Hey," James said. "Can you tell me where to go?"

"Can't talk to orange," one girl said.

The other one smiled, saying, "Can't talk," but she pointed towards a lift and then made a downward motion with her hand.

"Cheers," James said.

James waited for the lift. There were a few others

inside including an adult who wore the regulation trousers and boots but with a white CHERUB T-shirt. James spoke to him.

"Can't talk to orange," the adult said before raising one finger.

Up to now James had assumed this was a prank being played on the new kid, but an adult joining in was weird. James realized the finger was telling him to get out at the first floor. It was a reception area. He could see out the main entrance into plush gardens where a fountain spouted water five meters into the air. James stepped up to an elderly lady behind a desk.

"Please don't say 'Can't talk to orange,' I just—"

He didn't get to finish.

"Good morning, James. Doctor McAfferty would like to see you in his office."

She led James down a short corridor and knocked on a door.

"Enter," a soft Scottish accent said from inside.

James stepped into an office with full height windows and a crackling fireplace. The walls were lined with leather-bound books. Dr. McAfferty stood up from behind his desk and crushed James's hand as he shook it.

"Welcome to CHERUB campus, James. I'm Doctor Terrence McAfferty, the chairman. Everybody calls me Mac. Have a seat."

James pulled out a chair from under Mac's desk.

"Not there, by the fire," Mac said. "We need to talk."

The pair settled into armchairs in front of the fireplace. James half-expected Mac to put a blanket over his lap and start toasting something on a long fork.

"I know this sounds dumb," James said. "But I can't remember how I got here."

Mac smiled. "The person who brought you here popped a needle in your arm to help you sleep. It was quite mild. No ill effects, I hope?"

James shrugged. "I feel fine. But why make me go to sleep?"

"I'll explain about CHERUB first. You can ask questions afterwards. OK?"

"I guess."

"So what are your first impressions of us?"

"I think some children's homes are much better funded than others," James said. "This place is awesome."

Doctor McAfferty roared with laughter. "I'm glad you like it. We have two hundred and eighty pupils. Four swimming pools, six indoor tennis courts, an all-weather football field, a gymnasium and a shooting range, to name but a few. We have a school on-site. Classes have ten pupils or fewer. Everyone learns at least two foreign languages. We have a higher proportion of students going on to top universities than any of the leading public schools. How would you feel about living here?"

James shrugged. "It's beautiful, all the gardens and that. I'm not exactly brilliant at school though."

"What is the square root of four hundred and forty-one?"

James thought for a few seconds.

"Twenty-one."

"I know some very smart people who wouldn't be able to pull off that little party trick." Mac smiled. "Myself included."

"I'm good at maths." James smiled, embarrassed. "But I never get good marks in my other lessons."

"Is that because you're not clever or because you don't work hard?"

"I always get bored and end up messing around."

"James, we have a couple of criteria for new residents here. The first is passing our entrance exam. The second, slightly more unusual requirement, is that you agree to be an agent for British Intelligence."

"You what?" James asked, thinking he hadn't heard right.

"A spy, James. CHERUB is part of the British Intelligence Service."

"But why do you want children to be spies?"

"Because children can do things adults cannot. Criminals use children all the time. I'll use a house burglar as an example:

"Imagine a grown man knocking on an old lady's door in the middle of the night. Most people would be suspicious. If he asked to come in the old lady would say no. If the man said he was sick she'd probably call an ambulance for him, but she still wouldn't let him in the door.

"Now imagine the same lady comes to her door and there's a young boy crying on the doorstep. 'My daddy's crashed up the street. He's not moving. Please help me.' The lady opens the door instantly. The boy's dad jumps out of hiding, clobbers the old dear over the head and legs it with all the cash under the bed. People are always less suspicious of youngsters. Criminals have used this for years. At CHERUB, we turn the tables and use children to help catch them."

"Why pick me?"

"Because you're intelligent, physically fit, and you have an appetite for trouble."

"Isn't that bad?" James asked.

"We need kids who have a thirst for a bit of excitement. The things that get you into trouble in the outside world are the sort of qualities we look for here."

"Sounds pretty cool," James said. "Is it dangerous?"

"Most missions are fairly safe. CHERUB has been in operation for over fifty years. In that time four youngsters have been killed, a few others badly injured. It's about the same as the number of children who would have died in road accidents in a typical inner-city school, but it's still four more than we would have liked. I've been chairman for ten years. Luckily, all we've had in that time is one bad case of malaria and someone getting shot in the leg.

"We never send you on a mission that could be done by an adult. All missions go to an ethics committee for approval. Everything is explained to you, and you have an absolute right to refuse to do a mission or to give it up at any point."

"What's to stop me telling about you if I decide not to come here?"

Mac sat back in his chair and looked slightly uncomfortable.

"Nothing stays secret forever, James, but what would you say?"

"What do you mean?"

"Imagine you've found the telephone number of a national newspaper. You're speaking to the news desk. What do you say?"

"Um . . . There's this place where kids are spies and I've been there."

"Where is it?"

"I don't know. . . . That's why you drugged me up, isn't it? So I didn't know where I was."

Mac nodded. "Exactly, James. Next question from the news desk: Did you bring something back as evidence?"

"Well . . ."

"We search you before you leave, James."

"No then, I guess."

"Do you know anyone connected with this organization?"

"No."

"Do you have any evidence at all?"

"No."

"Do you think the newspaper would print your story, James?"

"No."

"If you told your closest friend what has happened this morning, would he believe you?"

"OK, I get the point. Nobody will believe a word I say so I might as well shut my trap."

Mac smiled.

"James, I couldn't have put it better. Do you have any more questions?"

"I was wondering what CHERUB stood for?"

"Interesting one, that. Our first chairman made up the initials. He had a batch of stationery printed. Unfortunately he had a stormy relationship with his wife. She shot him before he told anyone what the initials meant. It was wartime, and you couldn't waste six thousand sheets of headed notepaper, so CHERUB stuck. If you ever think of anything the initials might stand for, please tell me. It gets quite embarrassing sometimes."

"I'm not sure I believe you," James said.

"Maybe you shouldn't," Mac said. "But why would I lie?"

"Perhaps knowing the initials would give me a clue about where this place is, or somebody's name or something."

"And you're trying to convince me you wouldn't make a good spy."

James couldn't help smiling.

"Anyway, James, you can take the entrance exam if you wish. If you do well enough I'll offer you a place and you can go back to Nebraska House for a couple of days to make up your mind. The exam is split into five parts and will last the rest of the day. Are you up for it?"

"I guess," James said.

CHAPTER 10

TESTS

Mac drove James across the CHERUB campus in a golf buggy. They stopped outside a traditional Japanese-style building with a single-span roof made of giant sequoia logs. The surrounding area had a combed gravel garden and a pond stuffed with orange fish.

"This building is new," Mac said. "One of our pupils uncovered a fraud involving fake medicine. She saved hundreds of lives and billions of yen for a Japanese drug company. The Japanese thanked us by paying for the new dojo."

"What's a dojo?" James asked.

"A training hall for martial arts. It's a Japanese word."

James and Mac stepped inside. Thirty kids wearing

white pajamas tied with black or brown belts were sparring, twisting one another into painful positions, or getting flipped over and springing effortlessly back up. A stern Japanese lady paced among them, stopping occasionally to scream criticism in a mix of Japanese and English that James couldn't understand.

Mac led James to a smaller room. Its floor was covered with springy blue matting. A wiry kid was standing at the back doing stretches. He was about four inches shorter than James, in a karate suit with a black belt.

"Take your shoes and socks off, James," Mac said. "Have you done martial arts before?"

"I went a couple of times when I was eight," James said. "I got bored. It was nothing like what's going on out there. Everyone was rubbish."

"This is Bruce," Mac said. "He's going to spar with you."

Bruce walked over, bowed and shook James's hand. James felt confident as he squashed Bruce's bony little fingers. Bruce might know a few fancy moves but James reckoned his size and weight advantage would counter them.

"Rules," Mac said. "The first to win five submissions is the winner. An opponent can submit by speaking or by tapping his hand on the mat. Either opponent can withdraw from the bout at any time. You can do anything to get a submission except hitting the testicles or eye gouging. Do you both understand?"

Both boys nodded. Mac handed James a gum shield.

"Stand two meters apart and prepare for the first bout."

The boys walked to the center of the mat.

"I'll bust your nose," Bruce said.

James smiled. "You can try, shorty."

"Fight," Mac said.

Bruce moved so fast James didn't see the palm of his hand until it had smashed into his nose. A fine mist of blood sprayed as James stumbled backwards. Bruce swept James's feet away, tipping him on to the mat. Bruce turned James on to his chest and twisted his wrist into a painful lock. He used his other hand to smear James's face in the blood dripping from his nose.

James yelled through his gum shield, "I submit!"

Bruce got off. James couldn't believe Bruce had half killed him in five seconds. He wiped his bloody face on the arm of his T-shirt.

"Ready?" Mac asked.

James's nose was clogged with blood. He gasped for air.

"Hang on, Mac," Bruce said. "What hand does he write with?"

James was grateful for a few seconds' rest but wondered why Bruce had asked such a weird question.

"What hand do you write with, James?" Mac asked.

"My left," James said.

"OK, fight."

There was no way Bruce was getting the early hit in this time. James lunged forward. Trouble was, Bruce had gone by the time James got there. James felt himself being lifted from behind. Bruce threw James on to his back then sat astride him with his thighs crushing the wind out of him. James tried to escape but he couldn't even breathe. Bruce grabbed James's right hand and twisted his thumb until it made a loud *crack*.

James cried out. Bruce clenched his fist and spat out his gum shield. "I'm gonna smash the nose again if you don't submit."

The hand looked a lot scarier than when James had shaken it a couple of minutes earlier.

"I submit," James said.

James held his thumb as he stumbled to his feet. A drip of blood from his nose ran over his top lip into his mouth. The mat was covered in red smudges.

"You want to carry on?" Mac asked.

James nodded. They squared up for a third time. James knew he had no chance with blood running down his face and his right hand so painful he couldn't even move it. But he had so much anger he was determined to get one good punch in, even if it got him killed.

"Please give up," Bruce said. "I don't want to hurt you badly."

James charged forward without waiting for the start signal. He missed again. Bruce's heel hit James in the stomach. James doubled over. All he could see was green and yellow blurs. Still standing, James felt his arm being twisted.

"I'm breaking your arm this time," Bruce said. "I don't want to."

James knew he couldn't take a broken arm.

"I give up!" he shouted. "I withdraw."

Bruce stepped back and held his hand out for James to shake it. "Good fight, James," he said, smiling.

James limply shook Bruce's hand. "I think you broke my thumb," he said.

"It's only dislocated. Show me."

James held out his hand.

"This is going to hurt," Bruce said.

He pressed James's thumb at the joint. The pain made James buckle at the knees as the bone crunched back into place.

Bruce laughed. "You think that's painful, one time someone broke my leg in nine places."

James sank to the floor. The pain in his nose felt like his head was splitting in two between his eyes. It was only pride that stopped him crying.

"So," Mac said. "Ready for the next test?"

James realized now why Bruce had asked which hand he wrote with. His right hand was painful beyond use. James sat in a hall surrounded by wooden desks. He was the only one taking the test. He had bits of bloody tissue stuffed up each nostril and his clothes were a mess.

"Simple intelligence test, James," Mac explained. "Mixture of verbal and mathematical skills. You have forty-five minutes, starting now."

The questions got harder as the paper went on. Normally it wouldn't have been bad but James hurt in about five different places, his nose was still bleeding, and every time he shut his eyes he felt like he was drifting backwards. He still had three pages left when time ran out.

James's nose had finally stopped bleeding and he could move his right hand again, but he still wasn't happy. He didn't think he'd done well on the first two tests.

The crowded canteen was weird. Everybody stopped

talking when James got near them. He got "Can't talk to orange" three times before somebody pointed out cutlery. James took a block of lasagne with garlic bread and a fancy-looking orange mousse with chocolate shreds on top. When he got to the table he realized he hadn't eaten since the previous night and was starving. It was loads better than the frozen stuff at Nebraska House.

"Do you like eating chicken?" Mac asked.

"Sure," James said.

They were sitting in a tiny office with a desk between them. The only thing on the desk was a metal cage with a live chicken in it.

"Would you like to eat this chicken?"

"It's alive."

"I can see that, James. Would you like to kill it?"

"No way."

"Why not?"

"It's cruel."

"James, are you saying you want to become a vegetarian?"

"No."

"If you think it's cruel to kill the chicken, why are you happy to eat it?"

"I don't know," James said. "I'm twelve years old, I eat what gets stuck in front of me."

"James, I want you to kill the chicken."

"This is a dumb test. What does this prove?" James asked.

"I'm not discussing what the tests are for until they're

all over. Kill the chicken. If you don't, somebody else has to. Why should they do it instead of you?"

"They get paid," James said.

Mac took his wallet out of his jacket and put a five-pound note on top of the cage.

"Now you're getting paid, James. Kill the chicken."

"I . . ."

James couldn't think of any more arguments and felt that at least if he killed the chicken he would have passed one test.

"OK. How do I kill it?"

Mac handed James a biro.

"Stab the chicken with the tip of the pen just below the head. A good stab should sever the main artery down the neck and cut through the windpipe to stop the bird breathing. It should be dead in about thirty seconds."

"This is sick," James said.

"Point the chicken's bum away from yourself. The shock makes it empty its bowels quite violently."

James picked up the pen and reached into the cage.

James stopped worrying about the warm chicken blood and crap on his clothes as soon as he saw the wooden obstacle. It started with a long climb up a rope ladder. Then you slid across a pole, up another ladder, and over narrow planks with jumps between them. James couldn't see where you went from there because the obstacle disappeared behind trees. All he could tell was that it got even higher and there were no safety nets.

Mac introduced James to his guides, a couple of fit-looking sixteen-year-olds in navy CHERUB T-shirts called

Paul and Arif. They clambered up the ladder, the two older boys sandwiching James.

"Never look down," Arif said. "That's the trick."

James slid across the pole going hand over hand, fighting the pain in his right thumb. The first jump between planks was only about a meter. James went over after a bit of encouragement. They climbed another ladder and walked along more planks. This set were twenty meters above ground. James placed his feet carefully, keeping his eyes straight ahead. The wood creaked in the breeze.

There was a one and a half meter gap between the next set of planks. Not a difficult jump at ground level but between two wet planks twenty meters up, James was ruffled. Arif took a little run up and hopped over easily.

"It's simple, James," Arif said. "Come on, this is the last bit."

A bird squawked. James's eyes followed it down. Now he saw how high he was and started to panic. The clouds moving made him feel like he was falling.

"I can't stand it up here," James said. "I'm gonna puke."

Paul grabbed his hand.

"I can't do it," James said.

"Of course you can," Paul said. "If it was on the ground you wouldn't break your stride."

"But it's not on the bloody ground!" James shouted.

James wondered why he was standing twenty meters up, with a headache, an aching thumb, plus dried blood and chicken crap all over him. He thought about how rubbish Nebraska House was and what Sergeant Davies had said about his knack of getting into trouble landing him in prison. The jump was worth the risk. It could change his whole life.

He took a run up. The plank shuddered as he landed. Arif steadied him. They walked to a balcony with a hand rail on either side.

"Brilliant," Arif said. "Now there's only one more bit to go."

"What?" James said. "You just said that was the last bit. Now we just go down the ladder."

James looked. There were two hooks for attaching a rope ladder. But the ladder wasn't there.

"We've got to go all the way back?" James asked.

"No," Arif said. "We've got to jump."

James couldn't believe it.

"It's easy, James. Push off as you jump and you'll hit the crash mat at the bottom."

James looked at the muddy blue square on the ground below.

"What about all the branches in the way?" James asked.

"They're only thin ones," Arif said. "Sting like hell if you hit them though."

Arif dived first.

"Clear," a miniature Arif shouted from the bottom.

James stood on the end of the plank. Paul shoved him before he could decide for himself. The flight down was amazing. The branches were so close they blurred. He hit the crash mat with a dull *thump*. The only damage was a cut on his arm where a branch had whipped him.

• • •

James could only swim a couple of strokes before he got scared. He'd had no dad to take him swimming. His mum had avoided the pool because she was fat and everyone laughed at her in a swimming suit. The only time James had been swimming was with his school. Two kids James had bullied on dry land had pulled him out of his depth and abandoned him. He'd got dragged out and the instructor had had to pump water out of his lungs. After that James refused to get changed and spent swimming lessons reading a magazine in the changing rooms.

James stood at the edge of the pool, fully dressed.

"Dive in, get the brick out of the bottom, and swim to the other end," Mac said.

James thought about giving it a go. He looked at the shimmering brick and imagined his mouth filled with chlorinated water. He backed away from the pool, queasy with fear.

"I can't do this one," James said. "I can't even swim one width."

James was back where he'd started, in front of the fire in Doctor McAfferty's office.

"So, after the tests, should we offer you a place here?" Mac asked.

"Probably not, I guess," James said.

"You did well on the first test."

"But I didn't get a single hit in," James said.

"Bruce is a superb martial artist. You would have passed the test if you'd won, of course, but that was unlikely. You retired when you knew you couldn't win and Bruce threatened you with a serious injury. That was important. There's nothing heroic about getting seriously injured in the name of pride. Best of all, you didn't ask to recover before you did the next test and you didn't complain once about your injuries. That shows you have strength of character and a genuine desire to be a part of CHERUB."

"Bruce was toying with me, there was no point carrying on," James said.

"That's right, James. In a real fight Bruce could have used a choke-hold that would have left you unconscious or dead if he'd wanted to.

"You also scored decently on the intelligence test. Exceptional on mathematical questions, about average on the verbal. How do you think you did on the third test?"

"I killed the chicken," James said.

"But does that mean you passed the test?"

"I thought you asked me to kill it."

"The chicken is a test of your moral courage. You pass well if you grab the chicken and kill it straight away, or if you say you're opposed to killing and eating animals and refuse to kill it. I thought you performed poorly. You clearly didn't want to kill the chicken but you allowed me to bully you into doing it. I'm giving you a low pass because you eventually reached a decision and carried it through. You would have failed if you'd dithered or got upset."

James was pleased he'd passed the first three tests.

"The fourth test was excellent. You were timid in places but you got your courage together and made it through the obstacle. Then the final test."

"I must have failed that," James said.

"We knew you couldn't swim. If you'd battled through and rescued the brick, we would have given you top marks. If you'd jumped in and had to be rescued, that would have shown poor judgment and you would have failed. But you decided the task was beyond your abilities and didn't attempt it. That's what we hoped you would do.

"To conclude, James, you've done good. I'm happy to offer you a place at CHERUB. You'll be driven back to Nebraska House and I'll expect your final decision within two days."

CHAPTER 11

GO

James was shut in the back of a van for the first part of the drive back to Nebraska House. Even though he was knackered and the driver wasn't allowed to talk, he couldn't sleep. After a couple of hours the driver stopped at Motorway Services. They both drank nasty tea and used the toilet. James was allowed in the cab for the rest of the journey. He read the first road sign he saw; they were near Birmingham, heading towards London. It wasn't much of a clue about where CHERUB was. James reckoned they'd already gone more than a hundred kilometers.

It was three in the morning when James arrived back at Nebraska. The entrance was locked. James rang the doorbell and waited ages. A house parent shone a torch in James's face before unbolting the door.

"Where on earth have you been?"

It hadn't occurred to James that CHERUB had taken him without telling anyone. He scrambled for an excuse.

"I went for a walk," James said.

"For *twenty-six hours*?"

"Well . . ."

"Get to bed, James. We'll deal with you in the morning."

Nebraska looked even dingier after CHERUB. James crept into his room, but Kyle woke up anyway.

"Hey, Einstein," Kyle said. "Where've you been?"

"Go back to sleep," James said.

"I heard about your adventure in the liquor store. Ten out of ten for being a dumbass."

James gave his nose a blast of some pain relief spray CHERUB had given him and started undressing.

"Can't say you didn't warn me," James said.

"Vince is crapping himself," Kyle said. "He reckons you grassed him up and they've moved you to another home for protection."

"I never grassed," James said. "I've got to get him back though."

"Don't mess, James. He'll cut you up if you give him an excuse."

Rachel shook James awake.

"What are you still doing here, James? It's ten-thirty. You should be in school."

James sat up and rubbed his face. His nose was tender. At least the headache was gone.

"I didn't get in until gone three in the morning."

"Bit young to be out clubbing, aren't you?"

"I just um . . ."

James still couldn't think of a decent excuse for turning up at 3 a.m.

"I want you in school uniform and out of the door in twenty minutes."

"I'm tired."

"Whose fault is that?"

"I'm sick," James said, pointing at his nose.

"Fighting, I suppose?"

"No."

"How then?"

"I think I must have slept in a funny position."

Rachel started laughing.

"James, I've heard some excuses in my time, but a swollen nose and a black eye from sleeping in a funny position is the worst ever."

"I've got a black eye?"

"A shiner."

James explored the tender area under his eye with his fingers. He'd always wanted a black eye; they looked cool.

"Can I see the nurse?" James asked hopefully.

"We don't have a nurse here. There's one over at West Road School, though."

"Please let me off school, Rachel. I'm dying."

"You've been here for three weeks, James. You've been cautioned by the police, arrested for stealing beer, we've had a complaint from school about your behavior in class, and now you disappear for a day and a half.

We're pretty lax here, but we have to draw a line somewhere. Get your uniform on. If you want to complain, go and see the superintendent."

James was putting his schoolbooks in his backpack when Jennifer Mitchum came in.

"Aren't you too tired for school, James?"

"Rachel's making me go."

Jennifer locked the door and sat on Kyle's bed.

"Those tests are exhausting, aren't they?"

"What?"

"I know where you were, James. I was one of the people who recommended you."

"The last thing I remember is being in your office upstairs. Was it you that gave me the injection to make me sleep?"

Jennifer smiled. "Guilty as charged . . . So have you thought about joining CHERUB?"

"It's so much better than here. I can't see any reason not to go."

"It is a fantastic opportunity. I thoroughly enjoyed my time there."

"You were in CHERUB?" James asked.

"Back in the Stone Age. My mother and father died in a gas explosion. I was recruited from a children's home, just like you."

"You went spying and everything?"

"Twenty-four missions. Enough to earn my black shirt."

"What's that?" James asked.

"Did you notice everyone at CHERUB was wearing different color T-shirts?"

"Yeah. Nobody would talk to me because I was wearing orange."

"An orange shirt is for guests. You need clearance from Mac to talk to a guest. The red shirt is for younger kids being educated on the CHERUB campus. When they reach ten years old they can do basic training and become agents if they choose to. The pale blue shirt is for trainees. When you qualify you get the gray shirt. After that, you can 'go dark,' which means you get awarded the navy T-shirt after an outstanding performance on a mission or missions. The real high flyers get awarded the black shirt, which is for outstanding performance over a large number of missions."

"How many?"

"It could be three or four really outstanding missions; it might take ten. The chairman decides. The last shirt is the white one; that's for staff and old girls like me."

"So you still work for CHERUB?" James asked.

"No, I work for Camden Council, but when I see someone like you I make a recommendation. I'd like to give one warning before you decide, though."

"What?"

"Life on the campus will be hard to begin with. You have to learn a lot of skills and CHERUB needs you to learn them before you're too old to use them. Everyone will seem better than you at everything. How do you think you'll cope with that?"

"I want to try," James said. "When I got arrested the other night the policeman said kids like me get out of their depth and end up in prison. It freaked me out when he said it because that's *exactly* what always happens. I never try to get in trouble, but somehow I always do."

"So would you like longer to think, or shall I ring CHERUB and tell them you're coming?"

"I've got nothing to think about," James said.

James was being picked up at three, leaving tons of time to get packed. He felt a bit sorry for Kyle. He was a nice kid who deserved more from life than a crummy room at Nebraska House and three-quid-a-week pocket money. James peeled two £50 notes out of his wad and stuck them under Kyle's bedcovers. He scribbled a quick note.

KYLE,
YOU'VE BEEN A MATE. MOVING TO ANOTHER HOME.
JAMES

Kyle came in the door. James panicked; he was crap at making excuses.

"What time's our pick-up?" Kyle asked.

"What?" James asked.

"You heard. When's the bus to CHERUB?"

"They recruited you as well?"

"When I was eight."

"I don't understand," James said.

Kyle started pulling everything out of his wardrobe.

"Four months ago I was on a mission for CHERUB in the Caribbean. I put something I shouldn't have been touching back in the wrong place. The bad guys noticed, got suspicious, and disappeared. Nobody knows where.

Two years' work for a dozen MI5* agents down the toilet. All thanks to me."

"What's that got to do with you living here?" James asked.

"I wasn't exactly the golden boy when I got back to CHERUB, so they sent me on a recruitment mission."

"Here?"

"Bingo, James. Stuck in this dump trying to find another kid to join CHERUB. Jennifer thought you looked the type when she saw your school record. She made sure you got this room so I could evaluate you."

"So what you told me about your parents and stuff was lies?"

Kyle smiled. "Hundred percent fiction, sorry . . . You wanted to get Vince back. Did you have a plan?"

"You said stay away from him."

"I hate him," Kyle said. "He was in a foster home and picked a fight with a seven-year-old. Threw him off a roof and broke his back. The kid's in a wheelchair for the rest of his life."

"Jesus."

"You know where they keep the spare sand for the kiddies' pit?" Kyle asked.

"Under the stairs."

"Get two bags. I'll meet you outside Vince's room."

"It'll be locked," James said.

"I can deal with that."

James struggled upstairs with the sand. Kyle had picked Vince's lock and was already in his room.

---

*MI5 is the adult branch of British Intelligence.

"I thought *you* were a slob until I saw this," Kyle said.

Vince and his little brother Paul weren't big on housekeeping. There were dirty clothes, magazines, and CDs everywhere.

"It's a normal boys' bedroom," James said.

"It's not going to be for long. Start tipping the sand everywhere; I'll find some liquid."

James put sand in the beds, drawers, and desks. Kyle smuggled catering-size bottles of Pepsi out of the kitchen. They shook each bottle up so it exploded when the lid came off. When they finished, everything was soaked in gritty brown sludge.

James laughed. "I'd love to see his face."

"We'll be long gone. Want to see what's in his locker?"

Kyle pulled a metal object out of his pocket.

"What's that?" James asked.

"It's a lock gun. Does most locks. You'll learn to use it in basic training."

"Cool," James said.

Kyle slid the gun into Vince's padlock and wriggled it until the metal door sprung open.

"Girlie mags," Kyle said.

Kyle tipped the magazines on to the floor.

"Hang on."

"What?" James asked.

"Look at these."

There was a row of savage-looking knives in the bottom of the locker.

"I'll be confiscating these," Kyle said. "Get me something to wrap them in."

"Everything's soaked."

"I don't care," Kyle said. "I can hardly walk down the corridor with that lot in my hand."

James found a sweatshirt under Paul's bed that only had a bit of sand on it. Kyle bundled up the knives.

"OK, James, how long to pick-up?"

"Twenty minutes."

"Twenty minutes too long," Kyle said. "I hate this dump."

CHAPTER 12

NAME

James sat in Meryl Spencer's office wearing a CHERUB uniform with the pale blue trainee T-shirt. Meryl was James's handler at CHERUB. She'd won a sprint medal for Kenya at the Atlanta Olympics and taught athletics on campus. Her legs looked like they could break rocks.

Meryl held James's safety deposit key in the air over the desk between them.

"Not many kids come in with one of these," Meryl said.

"I got it when my mum died," James said. "I don't know what's inside the box."

"I see," Meryl said suspiciously. "We'll keep the key safe for you. What about the cash Kyle found in your room?"

James was prepared for questions about his cash. He'd realized Kyle had been through all his stuff when he saw him crack Vince's locker.

"It was my mum's," James said.

"How much is there?" Meryl asked.

"There was four thousand. But I've spent a couple of hundred."

"Just four thousand?"

Meryl reached into her desk drawer and pulled out a green circuit board and a tangle of electrical wires. James recognized them from when he'd ripped them out of his cassette player.

"Oh," James said. "You know about that?"

Meryl nodded.

"Kyle found the insides of the tape player in the bin the day he met you. He found the hidden cash and we worked out that it was from your mother's safe. You even left some lying around in obvious places to deceive Ron if he came after it. Everyone here was impressed when they realized what you'd done. It's one of the reasons you were invited to join CHERUB."

"I can't believe you found all that out about me," James said.

Meryl burst out laughing.

"James, we struggle to find stuff out about the international drug-smuggling cartels and terrorist groups. Twelve-year-old boys are less tricky."

James smiled uneasily. "Sorry I lied. I should have realized."

"You see that track outside my window?" Meryl asked.

"Yeah," James said.

"Next time you lie to me, you'll be running laps around it until you're dizzy. Play it straight with me, OK?"

James nodded.

"So what happens to my money? Will you hand it in to the police?"

"Lord no," Meryl said. "The last thing we want is the police asking questions about you. Mac and I discussed it before you arrived. I think you'll find we've come up with a reasonable solution."

Meryl got two little red books out of her desk.

"Savings accounts," she explained. "Half for you. Half for your sister when she turns eighteen. You can withdraw thirty pounds a month if you want to, plus a hundred on your birthday and at Christmas. Does that sound fair?"

James nodded.

"What's your sister's name?"

"Lauren Zoe Onions."

"And your name?"

"James Robert Choke."

"No, your new name," Meryl said.

"What new name?" James asked.

"Didn't Mac ask you to think about a new name?"

"No."

"You can keep your first name if you want, but you have to take a new surname."

"Anything I like?"

"Within reason, James. Nothing too unusual and it has to match your ethnicity."

"What's ethnicity?" James asked.

"Your racial origin. It means you can't call yourself James Patel or James bin Laden."

"Can I think about it for a while?"

"Sorry, James. There are forms to fill out. I need a name."

James thought having a new name was cool, but his mind was blank.

"Well, who's your favorite pop star? Or your favorite footballer?" Meryl asked.

"Avril Lavigne is OK."

"James Lavigne then."

"No, I've got it," James said. "Tony Adams, the old Arsenal player. I want to be James Adams."

"OK. James Adams it is. Do you want to keep Robert as a middle name?"

"Yeah. But can I be James Robert Tony Adams?"

"Tony is an abbreviation of Anthony. How about James Robert Anthony Adams?"

"Sure," James said.

James Robert Anthony Adams thought his new name sounded classy.

"I'll get Kyle to show you your room. Basic training starts in three weeks if you pass your medical and learn to swim."

"Learn to swim?" James asked.

"You can't start basic training until you can swim fifty meters. I've put you down for two lessons a day."

Kyle took James upstairs to the living quarters.

"Bruce Norris said he wants to see you."

Kyle knocked on a door.

"It's open," Bruce shouted from inside.

James followed Kyle into Bruce's room. One wall had shelves stacked with trophies. The other was a mass of gory martial arts posters.

"Mental posters," James said.

"Thanks," Bruce said, getting off his bed and putting out his hand for James to shake.

"I wanted to make sure you're not holding a grudge against me after the test."

"No worries," James said.

"You want a drink or something?" Bruce asked, pointing towards his fridge.

"He's not seen his own room yet," Kyle said.

"Is he on this floor?" Bruce asked.

"Yes," Kyle said. "Across from me."

"Cool," Bruce said. "I'll see you at dinner."

James and Kyle went outside.

"He's a bit scary," James said. "It's weird being in a room with someone who could kill you with their bare hands."

"Most kids here could kill you in two seconds flat, me included. Bruce is hilarious. He acts all macho, but he's a total baby sometimes. After he finished basic training and got his grey shirt he heard all the little red-shirt kids were going on an Easter egg hunt. They wouldn't let him go so he burst into tears. He laid in his room and cried for like, three hours. And you'll never guess what else."

"What?"

"He sleeps with teddy."

"No way."

"I swear to God, James. Bruce forgot to push his door

shut one night and everyone saw it. Little blue bear in the bed with him."

Kyle stopped at a room with a key in the door.

"There you go," Kyle said. "Home."

James's stuff was in bags on the floor. Everything in the room looked new. A decent-size TV and VCR. A computer, kettle, microwave, and minifridge. The double bed had a thick duvet and a pile of pressed CHERUB uniforms on top of it.

"I'll leave you to turn it in to a tip," Kyle said. "I'll call you when it's time for dinner."

James swished open his curtains and saw kids playing football on Astroturf. All ages, boys and girls. Nobody was taking it seriously. Little kids got carried on bigger kids' shoulders.

James fancied joining in, but he was more interested in his new room. There was a telephone beside the bed. He picked up, wondering who he could call, but he got a recorded message: "Dial out privileges are currently suspended."

The computer looked new and had a flat LCD monitor and Internet access. James realized the best thing of all: For the first time in his life he had his own bathroom. There was a thick dressing gown hanging on the door, piles of different size towels and flannels. The bath was big enough for James to lie flat in. For some reason, he decided to stand in it fully clothed and try out the shower, soaking himself.

He stepped out of the tub and looked at all the unopened bottles and packets: soap, shampoo, electric toothbrush, deodorant, even a box of chocolate bath bombs.

James lay on his bed and sank into his duvet. He rocked the mattress gently, smiling uncontrollably to himself. It was hard to imagine the room being any cooler.

Dinner should have been good. The food was top: choice of steak, fish, Chinese, or Indian and wicked desserts. James sat with Bruce and Kyle and a whole group of other kids. They all seemed nice and James thought the girls looked cute in their CHERUB uniforms. The downer was, as soon as they saw James's pale blue trainee shirt everyone started telling horror stories about basic training: being cold and muddy, not getting enough to eat, smashed bones, stitched-up cuts, being forced to exercise until you either puked or fainted. It sounded bad.

James stood in the food store. There were snacks and soft drinks piled on the shelves.

"Take whatever you want for your fridge," Kyle said. "It's all free."

James looked miserably at the goodies and didn't say anything.

"They shitted you up, didn't they?" Kyle said.

James nodded. "Is it as bad as they all said?"

"I can't sugarcoat it," Kyle said. "Basic training is the worst hundred days of your life. That's the point. Once you've been through it you're not scared of much else. . . . At least it doesn't start for three weeks."

James walked to his room. A timetable had been slid under the door while he was at dinner. Tomorrow he had a medical, a dentist appointment, and two swimming lessons.

CHAPTER 19

NEEDLE

His alarm went off at 6 a.m. James noticed that a set of swimming shorts and a map had been put on his desk while he was asleep. Nobody else was about this early. James walked to the canteen where a couple of teachers were eating breakfast. He found a newspaper and looked through the sport pages while eating cereal. The map was easy to follow, but James hesitated when he read the sign on the pool door: LEARNING POOL. CHILDREN UNDER TEN ONLY.

James stuck his head round the door. The pool was empty, except for a girl of about fifteen who was swimming laps. When she saw James she swam to the side and propped her elbows on the edge.

"Are you James?" she asked.

"Yeah."

"I'm Amy Collins. I'll be teaching you how to swim. Go in the back and get changed."

James undressed. He noticed Amy's black CHERUB T-shirt on the bench and her bra and knickers on a hook. James had worried his instructor would be some tough guy shouting and bawling at him. Seeing Amy's undies made James realize that making a fool of himself in front of a girl was even worse. He stepped out of the changing room and stood by the steps at the shallow end of the pool.

"Come up to this end!" Amy shouted.

James walked along the twenty-five-meter pool, nervously reading the depth markings. The deep end leveled off at three and a half meters.

"Stand with your toes curled over the edge," Amy said.

James shuffled up to the edge. The bottom looked like a long way off and the chlorine smelled like the time he nearly drowned.

"Take a deep breath. Jump in and hold the air until you come back up to the surface."

"Won't I sink?" James asked.

"People float in water, James. Especially if their lungs are full of air."

James crouched down to jump. He could almost feel the water blocking his mouth.

"I can't," James said.

"I'm right here to catch you. Don't be scared."

James didn't want to look soft in front of a girl. He raised his courage and leapt in. The quiet when his head went under was eerie. James's feet touched the bottom of the pool and he pushed himself upwards. As his face broke the surface he let out a gasp and thrashed his arms. He couldn't see Amy. He felt the same terror as when his classmates had nearly drowned him.

Amy grabbed James and with a few powerful kicks she pushed him to the edge of the pool. James clambered out and doubled over, coughing.

"Well done, James. You've learned the most important lesson: You float back to the surface when you jump in the water."

"You said you'd catch me," James said.

He tried to sound angry, but he let out a big sob in the middle of the sentence.

"Why are you upset? You did really well."

"I'm never gonna learn to swim," James said. "I know it's stupid, but I'm scared of water. My nine-year-old sister can swim, but I'm too scared."

"Calm down, James. It's my fault. I wouldn't have asked you to do that if I'd known you were so frightened."

Amy took James back to the shallow end. They sat with their feet dangling in the water while Amy tried to calm James down.

"You must think I'm a wimp," James said.

"Everyone is scared of something," Amy said. "I've taught loads of kids to swim. You may take longer to learn than someone more confident, but we'll get through it."

"I should have stayed where I was," James said. "I'm not good enough for a place like this."

Amy put her arm around James. James was uncomfortable at first. He felt too old for a cuddle, but Amy was nice.

"Get down off the treadmill," the doctor said. His German accent made him sound like an extra from a World War Two film.

James wore shorts and trainers. Sweat dripped out of his hair and streaked down his face. A nurse started peeling off the sticky patches on his chest. They were all wired up to a machine. The doctor touched the machine and a half-meter-long strip of paper shot out. He stared at the paper and shook his head.

"Do you watch a lot of TV, James?"

"I suppose," James said.

"You just ran one kilometer and you're exhausted. Do you play any sport?"

"Not much," James said.

The doctor pinched a roll of fat on James's stomach.

"Look at that flab. You're like a middle-aged man."

The doctor untucked his shirt and slapped a six-pack stomach.

"Like steel," he said. "And I'm sixty years old."

James had never thought of himself as fat before. But now that he looked, he *was* a bit soggy around the middle.

"When does your basic training start?" the doctor asked.

"Three weeks. If I learn to swim."

"You can't swim either? Pathetic! No need to swim in front of the television, I suppose, James? I'll send you down to the athletics department. Get you to do some running. No puddings, no chocolates. The good news is, apart from too much puppy fat, you seem fine. Now, injections."

The nurse pulled a plastic tray with hundreds of syringes lined up on it out of a fridge.

"What are all these?" James asked, alarmed.

"CHERUB can send you anywhere in the world at a moment's notice. You have to be vaccinated. Influenza, cholera, typhoid, hepatitis A, hepatitis C, rubella, yellow fever, Lassa fever, tetanus, Japanese encephalitis, tuberculosis, meningitis."

"I'm having all those now?" James asked.

"No, that would overload your immune system and make you sick. Only seven injections today. Then five in two days' time and another four in a week."

"I've got to have sixteen injections?"

"Twenty-three actually. You'll need some booster jabs in six months."

Before James could comprehend the full horror of this, the nurse wiped his arm with a sterile swab. The doctor tore the packaging off a syringe and jabbed it into James's arm. It didn't hurt.

"Influenza," the doctor said. "Thought I'd start you off with an easy one. This next one goes into the muscle and you may feel a teensy little pinch."

The doctor pulled the cap off a five-centimeter needle.

"OOOOOOOOOWWWWWWWWWW."

James was sitting in the changing room in his swimming shorts waiting for his afternoon lesson. Amy rushed in. She threw a bag of school books on the floor and started unlacing her boots.

"Sorry I'm late, James. Got talking and lost track of time. How's your day been?"

"Awful," James said.

"What's wrong with your voice?"

"Four fillings at the dentist. I still can't feel my tongue."

"Does it hurt?" Amy asked, taking off her boots.

"Not as bad as my arse where the doctor stuck two needles in it. Plus he says I'm fat and unfit. I've got to run fifteen laps five times a week and I'm not allowed to eat desserts."

Amy smiled. "Not a good day, then."

CHAPTER 14

SWEAT

Fifteen laps of a 400-meter track is six kilometers. James had no time limit; he could walk it in about an hour but that was boring. He wanted to go fast. The first day he raced off and died after three laps. He staggered the rest of the way with his legs aching and it took nearly an hour and a quarter. Next morning James's ankles were puffed up and even walking was agony.

Meryl Spencer showed James warm-up and cool-down stretches and told him only to run every third lap, then gradually to move up; running a lap and a half out of every three, then two out of three, and so on until he could run the six kilometers without a rest.

The third day it rained so hard James could hardly

see through the wet hair stuck to his face. Meryl and the other athletics coach hid in the dry. James figured nobody was watching and after thirteen laps went into the changing room where the other drowned-rat kids were diving under the shower.

"Was that fifteen laps?" Meryl asked.

James knew he was busted from her voice.

"Come on, it's belting down, Miss."

"You cheat, James, you start again. Fifteen laps. Get going."

"What?"

"You heard me, James. One smart word and I'll make it thirty laps."

By the end, James's lungs felt like they were going to explode. Kyle and Bruce thought it was superb when James told them what had happened. Amy said it was good to learn early that discipline at CHERUB was stricter than James was used to.

A fortnight later James was getting fitter. He could run two laps out of every three fast and jog the other one. It was Friday, lap fifteen. The pulse in his neck felt like it was about to burst. His body was begging him to quit, but James wanted to do his laps in under half an hour for the first time and he wasn't giving in so close to the end.

James overtook a set of identical twins on the final bend and sprinted to the line. He glanced at his stop-watch: 29:47. Twenty seconds inside his previous best. As James looked at the watch he put a foot down awk-wardly and overbalanced. The track slashed the skin off his knee, ripped his T-shirt and grazed his shoulder.

The pain from the cuts wasn't as bad as the pain in his lungs, but James didn't care because he'd broken half an hour.

James clamped his hand over his knee. The twins stopped to help.

"You OK?" one of them asked.

"Fine," James lied.

James hadn't seen them before. He noticed they were wearing pale blue shirts.

"You two starting basic training week after next?"

"Yeah. We arrived last night. I'm Callum, this is Connor. You want us to help you back to the changing room?"

"I'll manage," James said.

"It's my birthday today," Amy said.

They were in the pool together. James's cuts were stinging from the chlorine.

"How old?" James asked.

"Sixteen."

"I would have got you a card or something," James said. "You never said."

"I'm having a little gathering. Just a few friends in my room this evening. Want to come?"

"Sure," James said.

James was more excited about going to Amy's party than he would admit. He liked her a lot. She was funny and beautiful. He was sure Amy liked him, but like a little brother, not a mate.

"You have to do something first though."

"How far?" James asked.

"From the steps in the middle of the pool on that side, to the opposite corner."

"That's almost a length."

"Almost. You can do it, James. Your stroke is getting stronger. Basic training starts in nine days and if you don't make it, it's three months until the next course starts."

"I'll have three months to learn to swim. That's not bad."

"They'll put you in a red T-shirt," Amy said.

"I'm twelve. Red is for little kids."

"No, James. Red shirts are for kids who are not qualified for training. Mostly that's because they're too young. But in your case it will be because you can't swim."

"I'll be two years older than anyone else in a red shirt. I'll be slaughtered."

"James, I'm not trying to pressure you, but if you have to spend three months in a red shirt, your life won't be a lot of fun."

"You *are* trying to pressure me," James said.

"On the bright side, James, red-shirt kids are allowed to keep a gerbil or a hamster in their rooms."

"Well funny, Amy." James laughed, but he knew this was serious. Kyle, Bruce, and everyone else would wet themselves laughing if they put him in a red T-shirt. James started walking through the water towards the steps, determined to swim further than before.

He managed. Amy gave him a hug.

"You'll be OK, James."

James wasn't so confident.

• • •

Amy's door was wedged open and you could hear her stereo as you stepped out of the lift. The room was crammed with people and more lined the corridor outside. Everyone was dressed in normal clothes. After two weeks on campus seeing people in olive trousers and boots, James had almost forgotten skirts existed.

Amy had on bright pink lipstick that matched her miniskirt. James felt self-conscious because everyone was older and he didn't know anyone. Amy spun around when she saw James. She had a cigarette in one hand and a can of beer in the other. She gave James a kiss on the cheek, leaving a blur of lipstick.

"Hey James," Amy said. "I don't think I'll be in any state for a swimming lesson tomorrow morning."

"Is this the kid who can't swim?" a guy sitting on the floor asked loudly.

Everyone heard. James thought people were looking at him thinking he was a wimp.

"You want a beer, kid?" a guy sitting by Amy's fridge asked.

James didn't know what to say. If he said yes everyone might laugh because they thought he was too young. If he said no he'd look soft. James picked yes. Nobody laughed at him. James caught the can and pulled the tab. Amy grabbed it out of his hand.

"Don't give him beer, Charles. He's only twelve."

"Come on, Amy," Charles said. "Let's get the little kid drunk. It's always a laugh."

Amy smiled and handed James the can.

"One can, James," Amy said. "No more. And don't tell anyone we let you have it."

• • •

Once James had sneaked two of Uncle Ron's beers and got a bit drunk, but this was way beyond that. Amy's girlfriends all loved James. They kept giving him more beer. James blushed when one of them kissed him. So they all kissed him until his face was a mass of lipstick smears. As they got drunker one of the girls decided it would be funny to give him a love bite. They tickled James until he gave in. He knew he wasn't much more than their drunken pet, but it was fun being the center of attention.

Some of the kids on Amy's floor complained about the racket, so the party had to move outside. It was midnight now and pitch dark. James followed the noise from Amy's portable CD player.

"Wait for me!" James shouted. "Busting to piss."

James wandered into a bunch of trees. Suddenly there wasn't any ground under his trainers. His heart shot into his mouth as he lost his balance. He slid two meters down an embankment and crashed into a muddy ditch.

James dragged himself up, spitting nasty-tasting water out of his mouth. His sweatshirt was ripped. He shouted for help, but the others couldn't hear over Amy's music. By the time James scrambled back up the embankment there was no sign of anyone.

Campus was bigger than James realized. He got totally lost trying to find the main building. He felt sick from all the beer and started to panic. When he finally sighted the changing room at the edge of the athletics track he was thrilled.

James peered in the window. The lights were off. He

tried the door; it wasn't locked. James crept in. The heating was off but it was still warmer than outside. James rubbed his hands together to try and get some feeling back. He found a bank of switches and flipped on the light in the boys' changing room. He left the others off. Any light shining through the frosted windows might have caught someone's attention.

James looked at himself now he could see and was gutted. He'd put his best clothes on for the party. An almost new pair of Nike Air trainers and some Diesel jeans. The bottom of the jeans had mud soaked through them and the trainers were a wet mess, coated with mud. James knew the route back to his room from here, but there could be awkward questions if he got seen like this. He had to tidy himself up.

James kicked his trainers off to avoid marking the floor. He went into the boys' changing room. Fear of getting caught had sobered him up a bit. The changing room was a mess. There was sweat in the air and quite a few bits of clothing tossed about. James found a grey CHERUB T-shirt scrunched up under a bench. It smelled nasty, but it was less suspicious than walking into the main building in a torn sweatshirt. James pulled it on. There were no clean tracksuit bottoms to replace the muddy jeans, so James pushed his jeans down his waist and turned the bottoms up so the muddiest area looked smaller. All he needed now was some trainers that wouldn't spread mud everywhere. There were a few running spikes laying around, but they'd be no good indoors.

James stepped across the hallway into the girls' changing room. He hadn't been in here before, of course. The difference from the boys' room was amazing. It smelled fresh. There was a counter stocked up with toiletries and perfumes. Best of all, there were two pairs of trainers on top of the lockers. One pair was James's size but pink. The other pair was smaller, but James could easily hobble a couple of hundred meters through the main building in them. He squeezed them on.

He caught himself in the mirror and realized his face was filthy. He wished Kyle could see all the lipstick marks. James damped a towel, scrubbed his face and hands, gave the smelly T-shirt a blast with deodorant, and gargled mouthwash to mask the smell of beer.

He did a final inspection: not bad. If anyone asked why he was out so late, James decided to say he couldn't sleep, went for a walk, and got lost. The only thing that might be tricky was explaining why he was wearing the wrong color T-shirt.

James stepped into the corridor. A hand clamped his ankle. James shot about a meter in the air with fright.

"Caught you in the girls' changing room, pervert."

James didn't recognize the voice. Torch beams lit up his face. Amy and the girl who'd given him the love bite burst out laughing. They had changed out of party clothes into uniform.

"Why are you hanging around the girls' changing room, James?" Amy asked.

James panicked. It was so embarrassing.

"I couldn't go back to the main building all muddy, so I came in here to clean up."

"We're pulling your leg," Amy said. "I saw the light was on. We've been watching you for about five minutes. When I realized you didn't make it back we came out looking."

James smiled with relief. "I really thought you were going to tell everyone I was a pervert."

"We still might," the love bite girl giggled.

"Next time you say only have one drink, Amy, I will. I swear."

"What makes you think I'll invite you next time? I know a back way into the main building. Let's not hang around here."

"You saved my life, Amy. Thanks."

Amy laughed. "If you turned up drunk after half the school saw you at my party I'd be in as much trouble as you."

CHAPTER 15

TOWN

James swore he'd never drink again. It was a rough night. Throwing up, head floating, dry mouth, and a throat like sandpaper. Lucky it was only three steps to the bathroom. It was 3 a.m. before James settled into an uneasy sleep. He kept jerking awake from weird dreams where everything was spinning.

"James!" Kyle shouted.

It was 7 a.m., Saturday morning.

"Wake up, man."

James sat up in bed rubbing his eyes.

"You got drunk, didn't you?" Kyle said.

"Ugh."

"This room stinks of beer."

"I feel like I'm dying," James groaned. "How did you get in here?"

"Picked the lock. I did knock first but you didn't answer."

"Can't you leave me to die?"

"James, shut up and listen. There's a mission in London tonight. Nine of us are spending the day up there hanging out. You're not supposed to come, but it's all been thrown together at the last minute and it's a Dennis King production so we can smuggle you on to the train."

"What's a Dennis King production?"

"He's one of the mission controllers," Kyle explained. "He's a sweet old guy, but he's a bit doddery and he'll never notice an extra kid tagging along."

"I've got a hangover," James said. "And I'm sick of always getting in trouble."

"Don't you want to visit your sister then?"

"How will we do that?" James asked, excitedly kicking off his duvet and swinging out of bed. "Ron won't let me in the flat."

"If Lauren's home, we'll find a way. I wanted to help you visit her when we were at Nebraska House, but I couldn't without breaking my cover. This is your only chance. Once you start basic training, you're cut off from everything for three months."

"When are we leaving?" James asked.

"Twenty minutes. Have a quick shower, put on civilian clothes, and get your butt downstairs."

It was weird being back. London seemed dirty and noisy, even though James had lived here until a few weeks before. The kids all split up when they arrived at King's Cross station. A bunch of girls were going shopping in Oxford Street. Most boys in the group were going to Namco Station, a big amusement arcade opposite Big Ben. They all had to meet outside Edgware Underground at 6 p.m. for the mission. Bruce wanted to go to Namco, but decided to stay with Kyle and James once he heard what they were doing.

"You'll get bored," Kyle said. "We're just going to James's old neighborhood to visit his little sister."

"You might need me for protection," Bruce said.

Kyle laughed. "Protection from what, Bruce? Come if you want. Just don't whine all day if you get bored."

Bruce had never been on the Underground before. He looked at the map and counted how many stops like a five-year-old. Ron lived behind Kentish Town station, a couple of streets from where James used to live with his mum.

"What do we do?" James asked when they reached the flat.

"Ring the doorbell," Bruce said.

"Ron won't let me in, dummy," James said. "I wouldn't need you guys if I could just ring the doorbell and get in."

"Oh," Bruce said. "I could kick the door down."

"Like his stepdad isn't going to notice somebody kicking his front door down," Kyle said sarcastically. "What's your sister likely to be doing if she's inside?"

"Either drawing in her room or watching TV," James said.

"And Ron?"

"He'll have been out drinking last night. Probably won't be out of bed for another hour."

Kyle stuck his lock gun in the keyhole. He turned the lock but the door wouldn't budge.

"Bolt on the inside," Kyle explained.

"Ring the doorbell," Bruce said again.

"We can't. I just told you," James said.

"You and Kyle hide. I'll ring the doorbell," Bruce said. "You said your stepdad is probably asleep, so I bet your sister answers. If she answers, I'll say what's going on. If Ron answers I'll tell him I've made a mistake."

Kyle and James walked away. Bruce rang the bell. A few seconds later Lauren's eyes appeared in the letterbox.

"How many packets do you want?" Lauren asked.

"I'm a friend of your brother James. Is your dad awake?"

"You don't want cigarettes?" Lauren asked.

Bruce waved for James to come to the door. James crouched at the letterbox.

"Let us in," James said.

"James," Lauren grinned. "You better not let Dad see you. Every time I mention your name he looks like his head's gonna explode."

Lauren undid a bolt on the bottom of the door.

"Is Ron asleep?" James asked.

"Won't get up until the horse racing starts," Lauren said, opening the door.

"Hide us in your room," James said.

Lauren led the boys into her bedroom. The room was divided by a curved wall built out of thousands of cigarette cartons.

"What's all this?" James asked. "You started smoking?"

"Dad buys them cheap in France," Lauren said. "He smuggles them in and sells them. He's making loads of money."

Bruce studied the wall of cartons. "Did you build this?"

"Yeah," Lauren said. "I was bored so I started messing about with the cartons."

Bruce laughed. "It's brilliant."

"She always messes with stuff," James said. "When she had chicken pox she got every CD and video case in our flat and used it to make a pyramid."

Lauren sat down on her bed.

"So what are you up to?" James asked.

"I go round with the kids down the balcony a lot. Ron gives their mum money and she gets me from school and makes my dinner."

"So you're doing OK?"

"Could be worse," Lauren said. "You been in any more trouble?"

"No," James said.

Kyle and Bruce both grinned.

"Pants on fire," Kyle muttered under his breath.

"So you want to go out or something?" James asked. "Can you sneak out?"

"Easy," Lauren said. "Dad doesn't like me waking him up. I'll do a note to say I'm round a mate's house."

James took Lauren shopping and got her some jeans she wanted in Gap Kids. They ate pizza and went ten pin bowling. James and Lauren versus Bruce and Kyle. It started getting dark, but they still had an hour to kill before they headed up to Edgware for the mission.

They ended up in the little swing park near James's flat. James hadn't been back there since he'd hidden in the tunnel the afternoon before his mum died. Kyle and Bruce mucked about trying to make each other dizzy on a roundabout. Lauren and James sat next to each other on the swings, swaying gently and dragging their trainers in the gravel. They both felt a bit sad, knowing that their day together was running out.

"Mum used to take us here when we were little," James said.

Lauren nodded. "She was good fun when she wasn't in a mood."

"Remember when you used to climb up the slide, but you could never work out how to sit your bum down and push yourself off the top. I always had to climb up and rescue you."

"No," Lauren said. "How old was I?"

"Only two or three," James said. "You know, I can't come back to London till after Christmas."

"Oh," Lauren said.

They tried not to make eye contact in case they made each other upset.

"That doesn't get you out of buying me a present," Lauren said.

James smiled. "Are you getting me one?"

"You can have a box of cigarettes if you want."

"Well, well, well," someone said. "Haven't seen you around much lately, James. Been hiding from me?"

It was Greg Jennings and two of his mates.

"I've been looking everywhere for you," Greg said. "I knew you couldn't hide that nasty little face forever."

The three boys squared up to James, all of them about twice his size. Greg put the toe of his trainer on the swing between James's legs.

"My sister has a scar on her face, thanks to you. The only thing that cheered her up was finding out that your pig mother dropped dead."

"Leave her out of this," James said angrily, bunching up his fist.

"Oh no," Greg said, putting on a high-pitched voice. "The little faggot's gonna hit me. I'm so scared!"

A small rock bounced off Greg's head.

"Hey turd!" Bruce shouted. "Why don't you pick on someone your own size, like me?"

Greg turned around and couldn't believe such a skinny little kid was being so brave.

"Get out of here," Greg said, pointing at Bruce. "Unless you want your legs smashed."

Bruce tossed another rock at Greg's head. James laughed. Greg gave James a slap, then spoke to his two sidekicks.

"Snap that little idiot in half."

James knew Bruce was a good fighter, but he was only eleven and the two guys sizing up to him were massive. Kyle was nowhere to be seen.

Bruce backed into the roundabout, holding his hands out meekly, acting scared. He grabbed the rails on the roundabout and sprung his whole body behind a two-footed kick. One of the thugs crumpled up. Kyle jumped out from behind the roundabout and barged the thug over, then smashed him with an elbow that burst his nose and left him unconscious.

Meanwhile, Bruce had taken on the other one. The kid plucked Bruce off the ground. Bruce kicked him in the balls, then put a sharp pinch on his neck. He'd been trained to target the main vein running up the side of the neck. It caused an instant build-up of blood in the thug's head. He passed out and hit the ground like a falling tree, with Bruce holding on. Bruce clambered out from under his victim and ran toward Greg Jennings.

Greg still had his trainer pressed in James's crotch. There was a weird look on Greg's face; like his brain wasn't believing what his eyes were seeing. Greg reached inside his coat. James realized he was going for a knife. He dived backwards off the swing and grabbed Lauren.

Greg pulled the knife. Bruce faced him off.

"I'll stick that knife in you if you don't put it down," Bruce said.

Greg lunged forward with the blade. Bruce stepped backwards. Greg lunged again. Bruce sidestepped. Bruce reached into his pocket and pulled out a coin. The next time Greg moved, Bruce threw the coin in Greg's face. Greg didn't know what was coming towards him and blocked the coin with his free hand. Bruce used the distraction to grab Greg's wrist, twist his thumb into a lock, and slide out the knife. Now they were back facing each other, only Bruce was holding the knife.

"I'll stick this knife in you if you don't start running," Bruce said.

Greg was too proud to run, but he walked off fast. Lauren ran over to Bruce.

"That was like something out of Jackie Chan," she said. "You're the best fighter ever."

"I like to think so," Bruce said casually, tucking his coin back in his pocket. "At least for my age."

James was amazed. First Kyle had set the whole day up for him. Now Bruce had saved him from a beating.

"You guys are great," James said. "I owe both of you."

"I'll settle for cash," Kyle said, looking at the dirt on his trousers. "These are Billabong trousers. Sixty quid they cost me and they're filthy."

"You know what I really want?" Bruce said. "Some business cards with 'Bruce Norris Kicked Your Arse' printed on them. I can stick them in people's mouths when I knock them unconscious, just in case they don't remember me when they come round."

"Bruce, what you *need*," Kyle said, "is some serious time with a psychiatrist."

The kids were gathered in a quiet corner of the car park outside Edgware station. Dennis King passed out copies of the mission briefing.

"You all know the deal," he said. "Read the mission and sign your name at the bottom if you want to come along."

"Don't sign it, James," Kyle whispered. "Remember, you're not supposed to be here."

CLASSIFIED MISSION BRIEFING

TARGET:
Bishops Avenue, London. Home of Solomon Gold, owner of Armaments Exchange plc. Gold is suspected of illegally selling American-made tank-buster missiles to terrorist groups in Palestine and Angola.

OBJECTIVES:
Solomon Gold has gone away for the weekend. His home is protected by a two-man security post. Gas will be released inside the post. The gas will make the guards sleep for about three hours. This task will be undertaken by an MI5 agent, posing as the security guard's supervisor.

Mr. Gold is highly suspicious. The area around his house is monitored by thirty-six video cameras. Adult intruders will be suspected of being MI5 agents or undercover police. A decision has been taken to use CHERUB operatives, who must behave like vandals to minimize suspicion.

CHERUB operatives will enter the house through the main gate. Three operatives will search the office on the first floor for documents and make copies using handheld photocopiers. Six operatives will be issued with spray paint, bats, and hammers. Their objective is to damage fixtures and fittings, creating the impression that the only intention was mindless vandalism.

Afterwards all CHERUB operatives should leave the scene and meet at an agreed point two kilometers from the break-in.

Local police have no knowledge of this operation. If an operative is arrested, they should give false identification details and await release.

Bishops Avenue was locally known as Millionaire's Row, though billionaires was more like it. The houses were all massive. Most were set back behind six-meter-high walls. Video cameras stared in every direction.

A bus dropped the ten kids a few streets away. Solomon Gold's house was fifteen minutes' walk. James, Bruce, and Kyle were at the back of the group, walking fast. It was dark and raining hard.

"You excited?" Kyle asked.

"Nervous," James said. "It said in the briefing about getting arrested. If I get arrested they'll know I'm on the mission."

"Try not to get arrested, then," Kyle said. "Bruce will look after you."

"What about you?" James asked.

"I'm upstairs photocopying documents."

"Boring," Bruce said. "We get to smash stuff up. It's gonna rock."

Ever since the fight, Bruce had been in the best mood.

"I thought missions would be all sneaking around and stuff," James said. "Not bursting in the front door and trashing the joint."

"What?" Kyle said. "A bunch of twelve-year-olds creeping around in balaclavas and gloves, disabling burglar alarms, and cutting holes in windows? Can you think of anything more likely to attract attention? The first thing you'll learn in basic training is that a CHERUB has to act like a normal kid."

Bruce laughed. "CHERUB has a fifty-year tradition of mayhem and destruction."

"I never realized," James said. "Cool."

The girl leading them stopped by an open metal gate. She was called Jennie. Fifteen years old, she was mission leader.

"Everyone inside," Jennie said.

James stepped through the gate last. He noticed the security guards asleep in their glass booth. A couple of kids were already in there grabbing the house keys.

"We've got twenty minutes," Jennie whispered. "Keep the noise down and pull the curtains or blinds before you turn any lights on. The only exit is back the way we came, so if the police turn up we're all spending the night in a cell."

It was a hundred meters along a path lined with sculptured hedges to the house. The hallway was huge. Kyle took a miniphotocopier out of his backpack and ran upstairs to find the office. James and Bruce found the kitchen. Bruce opened the fridge, which was empty except for a packet of cream cakes and some milk.

"Thank you," Bruce said, stuffing a whole cake in his gob and glugging the milk. "I'm starving."

James had popped the top off his aerosol paint and started spraying ARSENAL in meter-high letters on the kitchen units. Bruce found the crockery cupboard and tipped it all on to the floor. James stomped the few plates and cups that weren't already broken. A girl came in.

"Bruce, James, come and help us out."

They ran after the girl to the swimming pool. A few plastic chairs had already been thrown in. Two kids were trying to move a grand piano.

"Come on, help us."

Five kids, including Bruce and James, lined up behind the piano and pushed it into the pool. A great wave of water sprayed up. The piano hit the bottom of the pool, making a crack in the tiles, before floating back to the surface. Bruce leapt on to the floating piano, pulled down the front of his tracksuit bottoms, and started pissing in the pool. Before he finished, a huge air bubble burst out from under the piano lid and capsized it. Bruce fell in and swam to the side. James and the others were cracking up.

They all ran to the living room. James tucked some DVDs in his jacket, then picked up a little coffee table, and used it to destroy the plasma TV hanging on the wall. The room stank from all the aerosol paint that was being sprayed. James was smashing ornaments and really getting into the swing of mindless destruction when a deafening alarm sounded and the room started filling with purple smoke.

Jennie was shouting from the hallway, "Everybody get the hell out of here!"

"Stay with me, James!" Bruce shouted.

They ran through the hallway. Jennie counted them out of the main gate. "Run away!" she shouted. "Split up!"

James and Bruce sprinted up Bishops Avenue. Two police vans were heading towards them.

"Walk," Bruce said. "It looks less suspicious."

The vans sped past. James's skin and clothes were stained purple from the smoke.

"What's this stuff?" James asked.

"Never seen it before. Probably harmless. Food dye or something," Bruce said. "Whoever did the security survey on that house messed up big time."

"There's none on you," James said.

"I suppose it didn't stick to me because I'm still wet from the pool."

"What about Kyle? Did you see him?"

"He was upstairs. He wouldn't have got out before us. Probably been nabbed. Better start running again. Those cops saw us. It won't take them long to work out what's going on and come back for us."

CHAPTER 16

PENALTY

"This is beyond stupid. . . . This is beyond a shambles. And you three . . . I'm lost for words. . . . You're the biggest idiots of the lot, aren't you?"

Mac was pacing up and down in his office. Not happy. Kyle, Bruce, and James kept sinking lower in their chairs.

Kyle had a black eye and his arm in a sling. He'd punched a policewoman trying to escape. Her three colleagues got revenge when he was handcuffed in the back of the police van.

"We never messed up the security survey," Kyle blurted. "That was MI5's fault."

"The security survey was fine," Mac said. "The alarm

was deactivated. Unfortunately some idiots cracked the bottom of the swimming pool with a grand piano and the leaking water caused the security system to short circuit. That's what set off the alarm and smoke."

James and Bruce sank lower still.

"So, your punishments. What's it to be? Kyle, you messed up in the Caribbean. You messed up at Nebraska House, now you mess up here," Mac said.

"You told me I did a good job when I got back from Nebraska House," Kyle whined.

"When you first got back, Kyle. Then two days later I hear from Jennifer Mitchum that the social workers want you punished. Something about filling someone's room up with sand and spraying Coke everywhere?"

"Oh, that," Kyle said. "The guy was a dick."

"You and James were supposed to disappear *quietly*. No questions asked. I don't like answering questions about where you've gone. I'm sending you on another recruitment mission, Kyle."

"No," Kyle said.

"A delightful children's home in a run-down area of Glasgow. I understand kids with English accents are particularly unpopular there."

"I won't do it," Kyle said.

"Do it, or I'll put you in a foster home."

Kyle looked shocked.

"You can't kick me out," he said.

"I can and I will, Kyle. Pack your stuff and get on the train to Glasgow tomorrow morning or you're out of CHERUB for good. So, Bruce."

Bruce sat up in his chair.

"Why did you go along with Kyle's idea to take James on the mission?"

"Because I'm a total idiot," Bruce said.

Mac laughed. "Good answer. You spend a lot of time in the dojo, don't you?"

"Yeah," Bruce said.

"For the next three months you're suspended from missions. I want you in the dojo at the end of every day. Wash the floors, polish the mirrors, tidy the changing rooms, and load all the towels and stinking clothes into the washing machines. Then in the morning, unload all the clothes, put it in the driers, and fold it ready for use. Should take three hours a day if you work fast."

"Fine," Bruce said.

But he didn't look fine.

"Now, James."

James was nervous. He didn't know where to look.

"You're new here. Keen to make friends. Two qualified agents put you up to something. Basic training starts in a few days and should straighten you out. You get away with this one. But next time I'll come down like a hammer. Understood?"

"Yes, Mac."

"I'm Mac on a good day, James. Today you call me Doctor McAfferty or Doctor. Got that?"

"Yes, Doctor."

James couldn't stop a little smile. Then he saw how upset Kyle and Bruce looked and straightened his face.

"Bruce, Kyle, you can go," Mac said.

They walked out.

"I understand you went to London to see your sister," Mac said.

"Yes," James said. "I know I shouldn't have. But I wanted to see her before Christmas."

"I wasn't aware you had difficulty getting access. I'll try and sort something out."

"My stepdad doesn't want me near her."

"I can be very persuasive," Mac said. "I can't make any promises, but I'll do my best."

"Thanks," James said. "I know it's not my place, but I think you're being too hard on Kyle. He only wanted to help me see Lauren."

"He's nearly fourteen. Kyle should be in a navy shirt doing the most difficult missions; instead he keeps making silly errors of judgment. If you'd come and asked me, I would have let you go and see your sister. You could have waited at the station while the others went on the mission. Have you swum your fifty meters yet?"

"No," James said.

"Only five days to go, James. I won't be happy if you fail."

CHAPTER 17

WATER

Amy and James walked towards another swimming lesson.

"I spoke to the head swimming instructor," Amy said. "He suggested we try something different. It's a bit drastic, but there are only two days left. Your stroke is good enough to swim fifty meters. What's holding you back is your fear of the water."

They reached the learners' pool. James stopped.

"We're not going in there this morning." Amy led James to another set of doors. There was a red warning notice: DANGER. DIVING POOL: NO ADMITTANCE WITHOUT A QUALIFIED DIVING INSTRUCTOR.

James stepped through the doors. The pool was fifty

meters long. At one end diving suits and oxygen tanks hung from hooks. The water was clear, cleaned with salt instead of chlorine. James read the depth markings: six meters at the shallow end, fifteen meters at the deep end.

"No way am I swimming in that," James said, scared out of his mind.

"I'm sorry, James," Amy said. "There's no more time for the gentle approach."

Paul and Arif were walking towards James wearing swimming shorts and bright red T-shirts with DIVE INSTRUCTOR printed on them. James had seen Paul and Arif around, but hadn't spoken to them since they'd helped him through the obstacle course.

"Come here, James!" Paul shouted. "Now!"

James started walking. He looked back at Amy. She looked worried. Paul and Arif walked James to the deep end of the pool.

"These are the rules," Arif explained. "You either dive in or we throw you in. If you swim fifty meters that's the end. If you climb out before you swim fifty meters, you get a one-minute rest before you jump back in or we throw you back in. After thirty minutes you get a ten-minute rest, then we go for another thirty minutes. If you still don't swim fifty meters we'll do more lessons with the same rules. Don't try to run off, don't fight, don't cry. We're bigger and stronger than you. It won't get you anywhere and it will make you tired. Do you understand?"

"I can't do this," James said.

"You haven't got a choice."

They were at the end of the pool.

"Dive in," Arif ordered.

James stood at the edge and hesitated. Arif and Paul each took an arm and a leg and flung him into the water. It was freezing. Salt burned James's eyes. James tipped his body forward to start swimming. His head went under and he breathed a mouthful of salty water. He started panicking. The side of the pool was only a few meters away. He struggled to the side, pulled himself up, and took a long gasp of air.

"One minute," Arif said, looking at his divers' watch.

James could hardly see.

"Please don't make me."

"Thirty seconds," Arif said.

"Please, I can't do this," James begged.

Paul took James by the arm and marched him to the end of the pool.

"If you dive in you get an easier start than if we throw you," Paul said.

"Time," Arif said.

James tried not to think of the fifteen meters of freezing water below him. If he could just get his stroke going and not drink any water it wouldn't be so bad. James managed to swim ten meters, but the salt was blinding him and he had to give up.

By the fourth attempt James was used to the salt and cold. He made it nearly halfway along the pool, as far as he'd ever gone without stopping.

"Brilliant!" Amy shouted. "You can do this, James!"

James was tired but Arif and Paul showed no mercy, giving him one minute and making him dive back in. James only got a few meters before his aching arms got the better of him.

"Not good enough," Arif said. "You don't deserve a rest."

James could hardly hear above his pounding heart and gasps for air. They marched him up the pool and James jumped rather than suffer the humiliation of being thrown. He was so tired he'd forgotten to be scared. He swam a few meters, but his stroke was weak and he swallowed some water. Paul had to lift him out of the pool. James started coughing up water and snot on the poolside. Arif found a cloth and threw it at James.

"Wipe it up, fast."

James meekly bent over and wiped the tiles. He was in a state, but he didn't want Paul and Arif to see. Paul grabbed him to march him back to the top of the pool. He broke free and swung a wild punch.

"Leave me alone!" James shouted.

Paul grabbed his arm and twisted it tight behind his back. James sobbed in pain.

"You think you can beat us up, James?" Paul asked. "I'm twenty kilos heavier than you and I've got black belts in judo and karate. The only way you can beat us is to swim that pool."

Paul let go of James's arm and shoved him into the water.

"Twenty meters this time, James!" Paul shouted. "You want to punch me? Twenty meters or you're eating my fist."

James started to swim. He was shattered, but he was scared of what Paul would do when he got out of the pool. James managed twenty meters and a couple more. He swam back to the side. Paul reached to lift James out of the water. James grasped his hand nervously.

"Not bad," Paul said. "That's thirty minutes. You've got a ten-minute rest."

James slumped at the side of the pool. Amy rushed up and handed him a carton of orange juice. Arif and Paul sat down a few meters away.

"You OK?" Amy asked.

"Never better," James muttered, gulping back a sob.

"Don't cry, James," Amy said. "This is tough, but so are you."

"I'm not crying," James said. "It's the salt in the water."

James sucked his juice and worked something out. If he was able to swim fifty meters, his best chance would be when he was refreshed after the break. If he couldn't do it straight away, he was in for another half hour of humiliation. The prospect of being dragged about and forced back in the water seemed worse than drowning. If he passed out, so what? Anything was better than this.

"Time," Arif said.

James walked to the end of the pool. It sounded fine in his head, but the pool still looked terrifying when his toes were curled over the edge. He started swimming strongly. He got some water in his mouth and spat it out. For the first time ever it didn't freak him out. Twenty-five meters. It didn't feel too bad. It was a personal best anyway.

James managed another ten meters. His pace was slowing. It was hard to keep his head up long enough to breathe. By forty meters his shoulders were agony. Amy was screaming her head off; James couldn't understand a word. The more effort he put in, the slower he seemed to get.

"Nearly there, James!" Amy screamed. "Come on!"

The last few meters were just mad thrashing about. He'd lost his breathing pattern, swallowed gallons, and was holding his breath. But he made it. James lifted his face out of the water and took in the most beautiful air of his life.

Amy lifted him out and gave him a hug. She was crying, which made James start crying again. He walked over to Paul and Arif.

"I can't believe I'm saying this," James said, "but thank you."

"Your fear of us has to be greater than your fear of the water," Paul said. "It's not fun, but it works."

CHAPTER 18

BASIC

James was due at the basic training compound at 5 a.m. He set an alarm and left it on his bedside table. Worrying about training kept him awake for ages. When he woke it was light. It's never light at 5 a.m. in November. This was bad.

The alarm clock was gone. Not set wrong. Not tipped on the floor and the battery dropped out. Someone had crept in while he was asleep and taken it. Kyle warned him they'd play tricks, but James hadn't expected them to start before he'd even arrived.

Clothes and a backpack had been dumped on the floor. There were two differences from standard CHERUB uniform. The T-shirt and trousers had white number sevens on them. Second, instead of being fabric-conditioned and pressed, everything was wrecked. Big stains, rips in the trousers. The underwear was disgusting and the boots had done hard time on somebody else's feet. James moved the backpack. There was tons of equipment in it. He probably should have got up early and looked at everything.

James had to wear the wrecked T-shirt and trousers because they had numbers. But he had his own pristine underwear, and boots that were broken in and only smelled of his own feet. Would he get punished for not wearing the clothes on the floor? Or would he get laughed at for being the only one dumb enough to put on secondhand underwear? The state of the boxer shorts made his mind up. He was wearing his own stuff.

There was no time for teeth, comb, or shower. He ran out with the backpack. The lift took ages, like it always does when you're in a rush. There were two older kids in the lift. They knew where James was going from the numbers on his uniform.

One of the kids looked at his watch.

"You starting basic training this morning?" the kid asked.

"Yeah," James said.

"It's half past seven," the kid said.

"I know," James said. "I'm late."

The kids burst out laughing.

"You're not late. You're dead."

"*So* dead," the other kid said, shaking his head.

• • •

The training building was a concrete box in the middle of a huge muddy enclosure, with no windows and no heating. Five-meter-high fences separated it from the rest of campus. Just the look of the place scared James.

He ran inside, puffing from running. The room had ten rusty beds with wretched-looking mattresses. Three girls and four boys were in front of the beds, crouching on the balls of their feet with hands on heads. After about ten minutes in that position the bottom of your legs goes dead. Six of the seven had been that way for two and a half hours, waiting for James. The odd one out had done an hour.

The head instructor, Mr. Large, and his two assistants stood up and walked toward James. Large's white CHERUB T-shirt was the biggest size you could get, but it still looked like all the muscles inside wanted to burst out. He had buzz-cut hair and a bushy mustache.

James flinched when Large reached out and delicately shook his hand.

"Good morning, James," Large said in a soft voice. "Smashing of you to pop in. Nice breakfast, was it? Put your feet up, did you? Good read of the papers? No need to worry, James. I didn't want to start without you, so I made all your new friends wait in a highly uncomfortable position until you arrived. Should I let them stand up now?"

"Yes," James said weakly.

"OK, kiddies," Large said. "Up you get. James, why don't you shake all of their hands as a little thank-you for waiting?"

The kids stood up, groaning in agony and trying to

wriggle cramp out of the backs of their legs. James went along the line, shaking everyone's hand and getting killer looks.

"Stand at bed seven, James," Large said. "Nice clean boots, I see."

Large lifted up the leg of James's trousers and peered at his sock. Large's wrist was bigger than James's neck.

"Clean socks too," Large noted. "Anyone else wearing their own boots and clean socks?"

James was relieved that a few hands went up.

"Very sensible," Large said. "Sorry about putting those filthy rags and boots out. Must have been some kind of terrible mix-up. Still, you've only got to wear them for a hundred days."

James smiled and got daggers from the red-headed girl standing on his right in filthy boots.

"Now, before I make my welcome speech," Large continued, "let me introduce my two wonderful friends who'll be helping me to look after the eight of you. Mr. Speaks and Miss Smoke."

If you wanted two people to make your life a misery, Speaks and Smoke looked ideal. They were both in their twenties and almost as muscular as Mr. Large. Speaks was black, shaved bald, sunglasses. Total hard case. Smoke had blue eyes, long blonde hair, and was about as feminine as a dustcart.

"Miss Smoke," Large said, "would you kindly fetch me a bucket? And James, would you be sweet enough to stand on one leg?"

James stood on one leg, trying to keep his balance. Smoke handed Large a metal bucket.

"Hopefully this will teach you to be more punctual from now on."

Large stuck the bucket over James's head. James's world turned black and the smell of disinfectant blasted his nose. He could hear the other kids laughing. Large pulled a baton out of his belt and rapped it over the top of the bucket. Inside the noise was deafening.

"Can you hear me speak, number seven?" Large asked.

"Yes sir," James said.

"Good. I wouldn't want you to miss my speech. The rule is, every time your foot touches the floor you get another crack with the baton, like this."

The baton whacked the bucket again. James was learning that standing on one leg is harder when you're blind.

"So kiddies, you're mine for the next hundred days," Large said. "Every day will be equally joyous. There are no holidays. No weekends. You will rise at 0545. Cold shower, get dressed, run the assault course. 0700 breakfast, followed by physical training until school starts at 0900. Lessons include espionage, language, weaponry, and survival skills. At 1400 you run the assault course again. Lunch at 1500. At 1600 two more hours of physical training. At 1800 you return here."

James's foot touched the floor. Large smashed the baton into the bucket. The noise inside was incredible.

"Keep that foot up. Where was I? At 1800 you return here. Another shower, warm water if I'm feeling kind. Wash your clothes in the sinks and hang them up so they're dry for morning. Then clean and polish your boots. At 1900 you get your evening meal. 1930 to 2030 homework. Brush your teeth, lights out at 2045. There will also be trips off campus for survival training, the last of which will take us to sunny Malaysia.

"If anyone is accusing me of cruelty, I remind you that the fences that surround us are not to keep you in, but to keep your little chums from slipping in and giving you a helping hand or a tasty snack. You are free to leave the training facility at any time, but if you wish to be a CHERUB agent you will have to resume basic training from day one. If you get an injury that stops you training for more than three days, you start again from day one. James, put your foot down and take off the bucket."

James lifted the bucket off his head. It took his eyes a few seconds to readjust to the light.

"You were very late this morning, James, weren't you?" Large said.

"Yes sir," James said.

"Well everyone, because James is still so full after his lie-in and his cooked breakfast, I think you can all skip lunch. Not to worry though. It's only eleven and a half hours until dinner."

The eight kids in training were split into pairs. The first pair, numbers one and two, was Shakeel and Mo. Shakeel was as big as James but only ten years old. Born in Egypt, he'd been at CHERUB for three years and in that time he'd learned a lot that would help in basic training. James realized he was going to be at a big disadvantage to trainees who had spent years in a red shirt.

Mo was another veteran, three days past his tenth

birthday. A policeman had found him abandoned at Heathrow Airport when he was four. Mo's parents were never found. Mo always jiggled his bony arms like he was trying to swat flies off himself.

Three and four were Connor and Callum, the twins James had met on the running track a few days earlier. James had had a few conversations with them and they seemed OK.

Five and six were Gabrielle and Nicole. Gabrielle was from the Caribbean; her parents had died a few months earlier in a car wreck. Eleven years old, she looked tough as boots. Nicole was smaller. Twelve, red-haired, and overweight.

Number eight, James's partner, was Kerry. She was eleven years old, small, and boyish with a flat face and dark eyes. Her black hair was shaved down to a number one. James had seen her in a red shirt with shoulder-length hair a few days ago. Now she looked totally different. She didn't look as nervous as the others.

Large led them out to the assault course at a jog.

"Do exactly what I do," Kerry said as their feet squished in the mud.

"Who made you the boss?" James asked.

"I've been at CHERUB since I was six," Kerry said. "I did sixty-four days of this course last year before I broke my kneecap and got chucked off. You've been here what? Two weeks?"

"About three," James said. "Why did you cut off your hair?"

"Quicker to wash, quicker to dry, doesn't get in

your face all day. If you do things quickly and get a few minutes' extra rest, it makes a difference. I'll do everything I can to make life easy for you, James, if you do one thing for me."

"Protect my knee," Kerry said. "There are titanium pins holding the bits together. When we do karate, please don't kick me on that part of my leg. If we have to run with heavy packs, take some of my weight for me. Will you help me, James, if I help you?"

"Whatever I can do," James said. "We're partners anyway. How come they're letting you take this course if your knee isn't better?"

"I lied. I said the pain was gone. All the kids I grew up with are living in the main building and going on missions. I spend my evenings watching six-year-olds cut up sticky paper. I'm getting through basic this time or I'll die trying."

Kerry knew all the cheats on the assault course. One side of the muddy tunnel was drier than the other. There was a knack to how you caught the rope to swing across the lake. She pointed out one of the hidden video cameras. The instructors dragged you out of bed at 3 a.m. and made you rerun the whole course if they caught you cheating on videotape. Best of all, Kerry knew there was a raised bar under the water, which cut ten meters out of the swim across the lake.

"You swim like a five-year-old," Kerry said.

After fifty minutes, James was muddy and freezing cold, but they'd finished tons ahead of anyone else. erry found a standpipe, turned on the water, and pulled off her T-shirt. She started washing out the mud.

"James, always wash out your T-shirt. Use it to wipe yourself off, then wash it again. It will be freezing when you put it back on, but we do the assault course first thing every morning and have to wear the same clothes for the rest of the day. If you leave the mud on, it dries out and itches like crazy."

"What about the trousers?" James asked.

"Won't get time to wash them. But first chance you get, pull off your boots and wring the water out of your socks. You hungry?" Kerry asked.

"I never had breakfast despite what Large said. I'll be starving by this evening."

Kerry unzipped a pocket on her trousers and pulled out a king-size Mars bar.

"Cool," James said. "I'm sorry it's my fault we're not getting any food till this evening."

Kerry laughed. "It's not you, James. There's always some excuse why you don't get lunch. Or why everyone has to do an extra run of the assault course. Or why everyone has to drag their beds outside and sleep in the open air with no covers on. They try and find ways to make you hate everyone else. Don't let it get to you. Everyone will get their turn."

Kerry bent the Mars bar in half.

"You want this, James? Make the promise first," Kerry said.

"I promise I'll help protect your knee," James said.

"Open wide."

Kerry crammed half a Mars bar into James's mouth.

Shakeel and Mo were heading across the last obstacle,

with Callum and Connor a few meters behind. James could hear Large shouting at Nicole in the distance:

"Move that bum before I stick my boot up it!"

James felt a bit sorry for her; but on the other hand, as long as they were shouting at Nicole, they weren't shouting at him.

Everyone had to do physical training in the mud. Crunches, squats, push-ups, star jumps. After an hour James was numb all over from cold and muscle pain. His uniform was a heavy sheet of mud.

Nicole was on the ground, too tired to move. Miss Smoke put her boot on Nicole's head, dunking her face in the mud.

"Get up, tubby!" Smoke screamed.

Nicole got up and stormed toward the gate.

"You can't come back!" Smoke shouted. "One step outside and that's it!"

Nicole didn't care. She went out the gate. Fifteen minutes later she was back. Bawling her eyes out and begging for another chance.

"Come back in three months, sweetheart!" Large shouted. "Get rid of that wobbly arse or you'll never make it!"

It was a bit of a sensation being down to seven kids on day one. All the trainees talked about it. Nicole seemed soft giving up so early. On the other hand they were all envious, imagining her back in her room watching TV after soaking in the bath.

James had warmed up as much as he could in the shower and now sat at the table with the other six trainees, waiting for dinner. Having Kerry for a partner was great. Especially watching the other kids make all the mistakes Kerry warned him about.

The dinners got wheeled up from the main building in a heated trolley. Smoke handed out the dishes. James ripped off the metal lid. The stir-fry rice was a bit dry from being kept warm, but it tasted OK and everyone was starving. Kerry got her plate last. James could tell something was wrong from the noise when it hit the table.

Kerry lifted up the lid. She had no food, just an empty Mars bar wrapper in the middle of her plate. She looked gutted. Large rested his massive hands on Kerry's shoulders.

"Kerry, poppet," Large said, "you're not the first kid to come back here. You may think you know all the tricks, but so do we."

Large walked away. Kerry stared at her empty plate. James couldn't let her starve after all the help she'd given him. He made a line down the middle of his plate and gave half to Kerry.

"Thanks, partner," Kerry said.

CHAPTER 19

MERRY

Imagine you are on an early level of a video game. It seems hard. Everything happens too fast, but you eventually make it through. You progress through the game to much higher levels. One day you try the early level again. What was once fast and difficult now appears easy.

This is the principle behind basic training. You will be asked to perform difficult tasks while under physical and mental strain. You will achieve things far beyond what you dreamed possible. When basic training is over, your mind and body will be able to perform at a higher level.

(From the introductory page of the* CHERUB Basic Training Manual*)

Callum dropped out on day twenty-six. He fractured a wrist on the assault course. The course wasn't that hard, but it was easy to have an accident when you'd already done three hours' physical training and hadn't slept the night before because Large blasted everyone in their beds with a fire hose.

Connor got partnered up with Gabrielle, but he'd never spent more than a few hours without his identical twin before. He was thinking about giving up and restarting with his brother in a few months' time.

The physical training was the hardest thing James had ever done. The first time he threw up from exhaustion he froze in shock. Kerry told him to keep running but James didn't listen. Speaks shoved James in the back, then crushed James's hand under his boot.

"If you stop training, you'd better be dead or unconscious!" Speaks shouted.

That was the closest James had come to quitting.

James was getting used to life in hell. He counted twelve scabs and twenty-six bruises on his body. That didn't include places he couldn't see. He showered twice a day, but he never had time to scrub the filth from difficult spots like nails or ears. His hair felt like straw, and grit sprayed out if he ran his hand through it, even if he'd just washed. If he got a chance for a haircut he was having the lot chopped off.

The worst part about training wasn't exhaustion; it was always being cold. James slept under a wafer-thin blanket in an unheated room. In the morning the floor was like ice on your soles. The instructors forced everyone under a freezing shower. Breakfast was always cereal and cold juice. Clothes never dried; they were damp and stiff as soon as you put them on. Not that it mattered for long. After five minutes on the assault course you were drenched in icy water and mud that crept down your trousers and kept you soggy for the rest of the day.

The trainees only felt tiny hints of warmth and each was bliss. Hot drinks at lunchtime, the warm evening shower and meal. If you were lucky you got an injury serious enough for a visit to the medical center but not so bad you were thrown off course. Then you got to wait for the nurse in a room kept at 22° C with a coffee machine and chocolate digestives, which you could dunk in your coffee and eat soggy and warm. Shakeel and Connor got these golden injuries; James could only dream.

The five hours of lessons sandwiched between physical training were the easiest part of the day. Weaponry was coolest. Shooting was only part of it. James now knew how to strip and clean a gun, how to defuse a bullet so it doesn't go off, how to put a gun back together wrong so it jams. Even how to take a bullet apart so that it explodes inside the chamber and blows away the finger on the trigger. They were starting knives in the next lesson.

Espionage was all about gadgets. Electronic listening devices, computer hacking, lock picking, cameras, photocopiers. Nothing as fancy as you see in the movies. Mrs. Flagg, the ex-KGB espionage teacher, always stood in the unheated classroom wearing fur-lined boots, a fur coat, hat, and scarf while the trainees shivered in damp T-shirts. Occasionally she would bang her gloved hands together and moan about the cold not doing her varicose veins any good.

The best espionage lessons were about explosives. They were taught by Mr. Large. He dropped his usual psycho persona and took childlike pleasure in showing off the finer details of dynamite sticks and plastic explosive putty. He blew stuff up at every opportunity, even sticking a directional charge on James's head. The charge leapt up and blew a golf ball–size hole in the ceiling.

"Of course, little James would have been killed if I had placed the charge upside down. Or if the charge had misfired."

James hoped he was joking, but judging by the size of the hole in the ceiling, he wasn't.

Survival skills was taught by the three instructors and took place outdoors. It was interesting, building shelters, learning what parts of animals and plants were safe to eat. The best lessons were on fire-building and cooking because you got a chance to get warm and eat extra food, even if it was squirrel or pigeon.

There were two lessons James hated. The first was language. Kids like Kerry who had been at CHERUB for a few years already had good language skills. Kerry was fluent in Spanish and decent at French and Arabic. For basic training everyone started a new language from scratch and had to master a thousand-word vocabulary by the end of the course. CHERUB picked a language from a country that matched your ethnicity. Mo and Shakeel got Arabic, Kerry got Japanese, Gabrielle got Swahili, James and Connor got Russian. The languages were extra hard because none of them use a Latin alphabet, so you had to learn to read and pronounce weird-looking letters before you could try saying the words.

For two hours each day James and Connor sat next to each other while the Russian teacher barked orders and insults. He smacked pens out of their hands, whacked them with his wooden ruler, and showered them in spit as he spoke. By the end of a lesson Mr. Grwgoski left the two boys with sore hands and blurred minds. James wasn't sure he was learning anything except that learning Russian made his head hurt. On his exit, Grwgoski often shouted to one of the instructors that James and Connor were bad pupils and deserved to be punished. This usually cost the pair an hour of precious sleep while they were made to stand in the cold wearing shorts. If Large was bored he might give them a good blast with the fire hose too.

The other lesson James hated was karate.

"Day twenty-nine," Large said.

Large had a green baseball cap on his head. His two sidekicks weren't beside him, for the first time ever. It was 0550. The six remaining trainees stood rigid at the foot of their beds.

"Can anybody tell me what is special about day twenty-nine?"

They all knew the answer. They wondered if it was the answer Large wanted. Your answer to Large's questions could have nasty consequences. Best to cross your fingers and hope somebody else took the bullet.

"Number seven, can you tell me why today is special?"

James cursed his luck.

"It's Christmas Day," he said.

"That's right, my little pumpkins. Christmas Day. Two thousand and three years since the birth of our Lord, Jesus Christ. What should we do to celebrate, James?"

This was the trickiest kind of question because it didn't have an obvious answer.

"Get the day off," James said optimistically.

"Well that would be nice," Large said. "Miss Smoke and Mr. Speaks have the day off. All your teachers have the day off. It's just you six little muffins and my good self. I think we'll have a little celebration of Christmas. Then we'll devote the rest of the day to karate and physical training without any of those pesky lessons that usually get in the way."

Large pushed a button on his baseball cap. Red lights illuminated in the shape of a Christmas tree and it played a tinny rendition of "Jingle Bells."

"That was so beautiful it brought a tear to my eye," Large said, throwing away the cap. "Now that celebrations are behind us, shall we get on with the training?"

The trainees didn't get to use the springy floors of the dojo. They learned karate in the fields surrounding the training building, freezing mud smothering bare feet. All the lessons were the same. You learned a move or two, then drilled until it was perfect. Then you drilled on other moves you'd learned before. Each lesson ended with full contact sparring.

James liked the idea he was learning karate. He'd always wanted to do it but had been too lazy to stick at it. He was doing five lessons a week now which meant he was learning fast, but he couldn't stand being partners with Kerry. She was already a black belt. While James was falling over and getting out of breath, Kerry did every move effortlessly. She helped James and saved him from getting punished by the instructors at least once every lesson, but James hated the smug look on her face when she pointed out his mistakes and she always killed him in the sparring at the end.

You were supposed to anticipate attacks and dodge or block most of them. But Kerry was fast and knew moves James hadn't even tried. He always ended up on the ground in pain, while Kerry hardly took a hit. James was too proud to admit he was getting hurt. Kerry was smaller, younger, and a girl. How could he whimper that she was beating him up?

Without the usual lessons, Christmas morning turned into six hours of merciless physical training. The trainees could barely walk. Large didn't let them have breakfast. James's vision was blurry from the water running into his eyes, but his hands were so numb from the cold he couldn't do anything to wipe it away. On top of all his usual aches and pains, Kerry gave him a painful kick in the side during sparring.

At 1300 Large walked the six trainees out of the training compound. They buzzed with excitement. They hadn't been out since day one. Maybe they were getting a Christmas treat. But they'd all played enough of Large's mind games not to get their hopes up.

Large told the trainees to stop walking when they

were close enough to see through the windows of the dining hall in the main building. The room had a four-meter tree in the center, decorated with thousands of twinkling lights. The tables had been put together to make four long bars, covered with gold tablecloths. Each place was set with fancy cutlery and crackers. All James could think about was how warm it must be.

"If you quit right now," Large said, "you could run up to your room, have a shower, and be down in time for Christmas dinner."

James knew Connor was thinking about quitting and was sure this would push him over the edge. Large made them run on the spot and do squats and star jumps. Inside kids were taking up places at the dinner table. Some waved to the trainees outside. James looked for Kyle, Bruce, and Amy, but couldn't see any of them.

"You might as well give up now!" Large shouted. "None of you will make it. Go inside. Have a nice dinner. Chat to all your friends. You know you want to. . . . No? Are you sure, cupcakes? How about thinking the idea over while you do twenty push-ups?"

When they stood up after the push-ups Callum and Bruce were by the windows inside. Callum had a cast over his hand. He opened a window.

"Don't give up, Connor!" Callum shouted. "The next time I see you, you'd better be wearing a gray T-shirt!"

Connor nodded to his brother. "I'll do what I can. Happy Christmas!" Bruce shoved Callum away from the window.

"Don't worry about Mr. Large!" Bruce shouted. "He's just a sad old creep who likes pushing little kids around!"

James smiled a bit, but not enough that Large might see it. Large ran up to the window.

"Shut that window, now!" Large shouted.

"OK, saddo," Bruce said.

Bruce shut the window. When Large turned around his face was burning. "Right, all of you, run back to the assault course."

Kerry and James led on the assault course. They still managed it a bit faster than the others. Large had gone. Kerry and James reckoned he was sitting in his heated office stuffing Christmas lunch while watching their suffering on a TV screen.

Near the end of the assault course was a two-hundred-meter stretch where you ran over jagged rocks. As long as you didn't trip it was nothing, but when you were exhausted you made mistakes. Kerry lost her footing. James saw her hand on the rock in front of him and thought about all the times she'd hurt him in karate class. He felt a surge of anger and crunched his boot over her hand. Kerry screamed out.

"What did you do that for, arse-wipe?"

"It was an accident," James said.

"I saw you look at my hand! You practically had to turn round to step on it!"

"You're nuts, Kerry."

Kerry shoved James backwards.

"We're supposed to be a team, James. Why did you hurt me?"

"You always hurt *me* in karate class!" James screamed back.

"You only get hurt because you suck."

"You could go easy on me, Kerry. You don't have to batter me every single time."

"I *do* go easy on you."

James lifted up his T-shirt to show Kerry a massive bruise across his ribs.

"You call that going easy?"

Kerry launched a kick at James. She always hit him in the ribs, but this was a few centimeters lower, slamming his kidneys. James doubled up in the most unbelievable pain.

"*That's* how I can kick you if I want to!" Kerry shouted. "If I go too easy the instructors will know I'm not trying and punish both of us."

James could see Kerry was right. He'd been a total idiot, but he was past logic. James lunged at Kerry. She stumbled back on the rocks. James started throwing crazy punches. Kerry got him back with a powerful fist on the nose. James felt himself being pulled up.

"Break it up!" Gabrielle shouted.

Connor and Gabrielle struggled to pull James off Kerry.

"Care to tell me what's going on here?" Large said, running towards the scene.

Nobody knew what to say.

"Connor, Gabrielle, scram! Kerry, show me your hand."

Large looked at the cut.

"Go to the medical center."

Large crouched in front of James and looked at his nose.

"You'd better go with her. When you get back, you're *both* in a lot of trouble."

James sat in the warm room waiting for the nurse. Hot coffee wrapped in his hand, downing one mushy chocolate digestive after another. Kerry sat opposite doing the same. They wouldn't even look at each other.

CHAPTER 20

COLD

"Welcome back, my two little bunny rabbits," Large said. "Nice warm afternoon, was it? Lovely choccy biscuits? Nursey made you all better? Well I have another special treat for you two love birds. Take off your boots and everything but your underwear, then go outside and, in the unlikely event you make it through the night, I'll let you come back in the morning. Remember, it's nice and warm in the main building if you want to quit."

James and Kerry stripped off and stepped into the dark.

"Merry Christmas!" Large shouted after them.

The door shut, closing off the last tiny arc of light. The wind was bitter. Frost burned their feet. Kerry was only a few meters from James, but he could barely see her. James heard her sob.

"I'm sorry, Kerry," James said. "This is all my fault."

Kerry didn't answer.

"Please talk to me, Kerry. I know I was stupid. Seeing everyone sitting in the warm and it being Christmas made me crazy. You know?"

Kerry started crying quite noisily. James touched her shoulder. She backed off.

"Don't touch me, James."

This was the first thing Kerry had said to James since the fight.

"We can get through this together," James said. "I'm so sorry. You want me to beg? I'll go down on the ground and kiss your feet if you just start talking to me."

"James," Kerry sobbed, "we're done for. You can say you're sorry a thousand times, but you've still got us both thrown out."

"We can get through this, Kerry. Find somewhere warm and go to sleep."

Kerry laughed a little.

"Find somewhere warm! James, there is *nowhere* warm. There's a big muddy field and an assault course. Nothing else. It's already close to freezing. An hour out here and we'll start getting frostbite in our toes and fingers. It's fourteen hours until morning. If we fall asleep we'll die of cold."

"You don't deserve this, Kerry. I'll bang on the door and ask to speak to Large. I'll say it's all my fault and that I'll quit if he lets you back inside."

"He won't bargain with you, James. He'll laugh in your face."

"We could start a fire," James said.

"It's raining. It's pitch dark. We'd need something dry to start a fire and somewhere out of the wind to start it. Any suggestions?"

"The bridge over the lake on the assault course," James said. "There's a gap under there before the water starts. We could put branches and stuff along the sides to keep out the wind."

"I suppose," Kerry said. "We've got to try. There might be stuff in the rubbish."

"What?"

"There are two rubbish bins at the back of the building," Kerry said. "We could go through them. There might be stuff inside we could use."

Kerry led James to the back of the training building. They each pulled the lid off a bin. Both were full of rubbish tied up in bags.

"Reeks," James said.

"I don't care *what* it smells like," Kerry said. "Here's what I'm thinking. We take the bins with all the stuff in to the bridge. Then we go through all the bags. Hopefully there's something to start a fire with. The bags will help us keep warm if we wear them."

It was hard finding the bridge in the moonlight. It was too dark to make out any more than the outline of the ground. There was a risk of hitting something sharp with each step. James and Kerry took a bin each. They weighed a ton. James tried rolling his instead of carrying it, but the bin kept jamming in the mud. Kerry was having an even tougher time because her hand was bandaged. They walked the path at the side of the assault course. James's feet were numb already. He thought about the gruesome photos of black frostbitten toes in the training manual and shuddered.

The wooden bridge spanned twenty meters over the river in the middle of the assault course, and was about two meters wide. When they reached it, Kerry started untying and rummaging around the stinking rubbish bags. James clambered into the low space under the bridge.

"It's pretty dry under here," James said. "It's concrete, no mud."

"OK," Kerry said. "I'm trying to get stuff to start a fire."

James ran back and forth, stripping off branches and wedging them against the side of the bridge. Kerry dunked her hand in a bag and hit a mix of food slops and muddy rags used for boot cleaning. She sniffed her hand and couldn't believe she was touching all this nasty stuff. She threw anything that was dry and would burn into an empty bin.

Kerry tore the bags up, covered her feet in the boot-cleaning rags, and then wrapped them with plastic. She tore holes in the bin bags to make a plastic smock and skirt for herself and James. They looked like muddy scarecrows, but the important thing was it kept out the cold. James finished turning the bridge into a shelter and they clambered under, rubbing their hands together.

"Here," Kerry said.

She handed James two small boxes. It was too dark to see what they were. James felt the familiar shape of a straw on the side of a carton.

"Breakfast," James said. "This was in the rubbish?"

"God must be on our side," Kerry said. "Six cartons of orange juice, six minipackets of cereal, all unopened. Large must have thrown them out this morning when he didn't give us breakfast."

James punched the straw into the orange juice carton and sucked the contents in two long gulps. Then he ripped open the cereal and scoffed dry flakes.

"We've got clothes, food, and shelter," James said. "We should last till morning."

"Maybe," Kerry said. "I'd be happier if I could get the fire going."

"There's tons of stuff there that will burn," James said.

"But the only way I know to start a fire is with two dry pieces of timber. We've got zero."

They sat there for a few minutes, huddled close, jiggling arms and legs to keep warm.

"I think I know a way to start a fire," James said. "You know the security cameras all over the assault course?"

"What about them?" Kerry asked.

"They must be powered by electricity."

"So what?"

"So if we find one and pull the power cord out the back then we can use it to make a spark."

"It's pitch dark," Kerry said.

"I know roughly where a few of the cameras are."

"James, you're talking about messing with electricity. You could end up getting killed."

James stood up.

"Where are you going?"

"Have faith, Kerry. I'm going to start a fire."

"You're a total idiot, James. You'll get zapped."

James clambered out of the shelter. The foot coverings Kerry made kept his feet warm but slid everywhere. He found the bin Kerry had filled with flammable stuff. He tucked bits of tissue and cardboard inside his plastic suit, then grabbed a dustbin lid and started his search. James found a camera only a few meters from the shelter. The tiny red lamp below the lens made it easier to spot the cameras in the dark than in daylight.

James felt behind the camera and tugged the wires out of the back. One looked like the picture output, so he threw it away. The other wire had a two-pronged rubber plug on the end. James figured this was the power supply. He twisted the plug until it snapped off, leaving two bare wires at the end of the lead.

It had seemed a good idea in theory. But now he was on the spot, with his little store of fuel standing on the dustbin lid, water all around, and a live electric cable in his hand, James's confidence plummeted.

He crouched over the bin lid. He split the cable, pulling the two bare ends of wire further apart, then lined them up over a piece of tissue. He slowly moved the two ends closer together. A blue spark lit up James's face. The corner of the tissue ignited. A couple of embers flew off and the fire snuffed out. James's heart stopped. He doubted he'd get another chance because the spark had probably fused the circuit. Then a second burst of flame rose from the center of the tissue. James dipped a scrap of cardboard in the flame. The fire caught hold.

He had to move back to the bridge before the fuel burned out. His feet slid everywhere and the wind was doing its best to kill the flames.

"Kerry!" James shouted. "Get some of the fuel!"

Kerry dashed out and put more bits of cardboard on the fire. The metal lid was getting hot in James's hands and the last part of the journey was trickiest, down the muddy river bank and into the shelter. Kerry helped keep the lid steady. James pushed the lid into the shelter, careful not to set light to the branches lining the sides. Kerry got the rest of the fuel and they cuddled up to each other as the shelter filled with flickering orange light. The smoke made their eyes sting, but all they cared about was being warm. Kerry rested her head on James's arm.

"I still can't believe you stomped my hand," Kerry said, looking at her bandage. "I thought we were a good team."

"I know sorry doesn't make it all better, but I really am. If there's anything I can do to make it up, I will. Just name it."

"You know what," Kerry said, "I'll forgive you now. But after training finishes I'll fight you in the dojo. I'll beat you until you scream for mercy. Then I'll beat you some more."

"Deal," James said, hoping she was joking. "It's what I deserve for getting us into this mess."

Mr. Speaks stuck his head inside the shelter. It was starting to get light. The fire was burned out. James and Kerry were asleep with their arms around each other.

"Wake up," Speaks said.

James and Kerry rustled to life in their plastic suits. Kerry had said it was best not to go to sleep; better to stay alert and not get frostbite. But the shelter was warm and they'd both drifted off.

"I love you two with all my heart," Speaks said.

Speaks reached into his trouser pocket and pulled out a couple of bars of Fruit and Nut. James couldn't understand why Speaks was being nice to them.

"I am so impressed with the way you two got through this. Mr. Large was convinced you would quit. He couldn't find you. All the video cameras have stopped working for some reason."

"What time is it?" Kerry asked, cheeks stuffed with chocolate.

"Six-thirty. You two better run back to the main building and get dressed. Mr. Large is going to be furious when he sees you."

"Doesn't he like us?" James asked. "I mean, I know he hates everyone, but why is he so keen to get rid of us?"

"You don't understand," Speaks said. "We had a bet. Fifty pounds that Mr. Large could make a trainee quit on Christmas Day. He thought making Connor watch his brother eat Christmas dinner would work, but Callum told him to stick it out. Then you two started fighting, which gave him the excuse to punish you. He was sure he'd broken you. I can't wait to see the look on his face."

"After this he's gonna make our lives even more miserable," Kerry sighed.

CHAPTER 21

AIR

The six trainees and three instructors were heading to Malaysia for the final days of basic training. James's only previous flight was an eight-hour holiday trip to Orlando, crammed with hundreds of wriggling kids and bawling parents. This time it was business class.

James's toes couldn't reach the seat in front. The puffy leather chairs had pull-up screens for Nintendo and movies and a button that tipped the seat back so it was like a bed. Before takeoff the stewardess came round serving sandwiches and fruit juice. It would have been good any time. After thirteen hard weeks, he was in heaven.

The jumbo finished its climb out of Heathrow and the seatbelt sign beeped out. James slouched with his headphones on, flipping through the different music channels until he came across Elton John's song "Rocket Man." His mum had loved Elton John. James felt guilty that he'd hardly thought about her since he got to CHERUB.

Kerry's sock flew over the screen between the seats and landed in James's lap. He sat up as Kerry lowered the screen and yanked off his headphones.

"What was that for?" James asked.

"You wanted to know how long the flight was. Turn your TV to channel fifty."

James flicked his remote. The screen changed to a blue map with London on the left and Kuala Lumpur on the right. Every few seconds the screen switched to a bank of figures, which included distance traveled, air speed, external temperature, and time to destination.

"Thirteen hours, eight minutes," James said. "Cool. I think I could sleep about that long."

Kerry looked disappointed.

"Don't you want to play Mario Kart?" she asked.

"A couple of games, I guess. I'll sleep after they serve dinner."

The sign over the automatic door of the airport terminal said ENJOY YOUR STAY IN MALAYSIA. The doors split apart. James slung his backpack over his shoulder and took his first outdoor breath. The screen on the plane said it was 40° C when they landed. James knew that was hot, but the baking air was beyond anything he'd imagined.

"Imagine running in this heat," Kerry said.

Connor and Gabrielle walked behind.

"I bet we won't need to imagine for long," Gabrielle said.

Large, wearing shorts and a Hawaiian shirt, wound the group through lanes of jammed traffic to a shuttle van. Speaks peeled notes out of a bundle of currency and handed them to the driver while everyone else climbed in with their luggage.

They pulled into the flow and drove for half an hour along wide empty roads, heading against the evening rush hour. The trainees watched out of the windows. It could have been a modern city anywhere. Only the wide storm drains and the odd palm tree amongst the concrete told them they were in the tropics.

The other trainees had been James's only human contact for three months. They hadn't spoken much. If you got a spare half hour, you didn't waste it talking; you used it to sleep. The few conversations they'd had were mostly bitching about training over the dinner table.

The instructors punished everyone for an individual mistake, so the trainees developed a sixth sense for covering each others' weaknesses. James knew before a long swim that Kerry and Shakeel would stick close and grab him if he lost his nerve. Everyone took Kerry's stuff when her knee was painful. Mo was weedy and needed help climbing and lifting. They all needed each other for something.

James wasn't worried about the four-day tropical survival course. He knew it would be tough, but everything had been tough since day one. Training had succeeded: exhaustion and danger didn't scare James any more. He'd been pushed to the limit so often it felt routine. It was something you didn't enjoy but always got through, like a trip to the dentist or a science lesson.

The hotel was plush. James and Kerry shared a room with two queen beds and a balcony that overlooked the pool. It was nine at night, but they'd all slept on the plane and felt lively. The instructors were going to the hotel bar and didn't want to be bothered. The trainees were given the run of the hotel and told to order whatever they wanted from room service, but not to stay up late because there was an early start in the morning.

The six kids met by the outdoor pool, the first chance they'd had to relax as a group. It was dark now. There was a breeze but the temperature was still in the thirties. Millions of insects chirped and smacked into the mosquito nets that wrapped the pool area. An attendant in a bow tie handed out robes and cotton slippers.

It was the first time in weeks that James had felt well-fed and relaxed. He also felt awkward. All the others were dive-bombing the pool and swimming confidently. James was ashamed that all he could manage was a clumsy front crawl and sat with his ankles in the water sucking Coke through a straw.

"Come on, James," Kerry shouted. "Chill out!"

"I think I'll go back to the room," James said.

"Misery," Kerry said.

James walked up to his room. He took a leak, then caught himself in a mirror for the first time since training started. It was weird seeing his own body but not quite recognizing it. The belly that rolled over the elastic of his shorts was gone. His chest muscles and biceps were bigger, and he thought the razor-cut hair and all the scabs and bruises made him look hard. James couldn't help smiling. He was totally in love with himself.

He lay on his bed and watched TV. Only a few channels were in English. He found BBC World and realized half the planet could have been rubbed out in a war for all he knew. He hadn't seen a newspaper or TV for the three months he'd been isolated in the training compound. It didn't look like much had changed. People still killed each other for no good reason, politicians wore dull suits and gave five-minute answers that had nothing to do with the question. At least they showed Arsenal winning in the sports roundup. After the sports, James flipped through channels and wished he'd stayed downstairs with the others.

Suddenly, the door of the hotel room opened and the light went out.

"Shut your eyes!" Kerry shouted.

"Why?" James asked.

"We've got a surprise."

James could hear the other trainees outside in the corridor.

"No way, what are you gonna do?"

"If you don't shut your eyes, you'll never know."

It was unlikely to be anything good if they were asking him to shut his eyes, but James didn't want to seem boring.

"OK, they're shut."

James heard them all file in. Kerry emptied an ice bucket over his chest. The cubes slid down inside his robe and down his back. Connor, Mo, Gabrielle, and Shakeel followed with more ice buckets. James jumped off his bed and trod on an ice cube.

"Scumbags!" James yelped, shaking the cubes out of his robe and laughing.

The others were cracking up. Kerry put the light back on.

"Thought we'd all order room service in here," Kerry said. "If you're not still sulking."

"Whatever, cool," James said.

They sat on the balcony talking about training and picking bits of each other's food. Afterwards the four boys decided to impress the girls by standing in line and pissing on to the plants two floors down. Kerry and Gabrielle slipped inside and locked the French doors.

"Let us in!" Connor shouted.

"Tell us how beautiful we are!" Kerry said.

"Ugly pigs!" Shakeel shouted. "Let us in!"

"Sounds like you're staying out there for a long time," Kerry said.

James looked down. They were too high to jump. He walked to the glass and spoke.

"I think you're both beautiful."

"Arse kisser," Connor said.

James looked at Connor. "You want to stay out here all night?"

"Very beautiful," Connor agreed.

"Supermodels," Mo added.

The girls looked at Shakeel.

"Well?"

Shakeel shrugged. "You're two radiant beams of sunshine! Come on, let us in!"

"Shall we?" Kerry asked Gabrielle, enjoying her sense of power.

Gabrielle put a finger on her mouth and acted puzzled.

"If they kiss the glass to show us how much they love us," she decided.

Kerry laughed. "You heard her, boys. Nice big smooch on the glass."

The four boys looked at each other.

"Oh, for God's sake," Connor muttered.

Connor kissed the glass first. The other three did the same.

Someone knocked at the door. Kerry answered. It was Large and Smoke. Gabrielle unlocked the French doors. The boys rushed inside, hoping they hadn't been spotted peeing on the plants.

Large sounded drunk. "It's gone eleven. I want you all in bed in five minutes."

The others filed out. James and Kerry got into bed.

CHAPTER 22

BEACH

A military helicopter picked them up from the hotel roof before dawn. The trainees sat on their packs in the dusty cargo area behind the pilots. The tropical uniform had lightweight trousers, long-sleeved blue tops without numbers or CHERUB logos, and hats with pull-down flaps to protect their necks and ears from the sun.

Large crawled around fitting each trainee with an electronic wristband. The plastic strap locked on so it could only be cut off with a knife.

"Don't remove the bracelet under any circumstances!" Large shouted over the noise of the rotor. "In an emergency, unscrew the button on the side, and press it down firmly. The helicopter is on standby and will reach you within fifteen minutes. If you get bitten by a snake, press it right away.

"We'll be at the first drop point soon. Everything you could possibly need is in the backpacks. It's now 1000 hours. Each team has four checkpoints to reach within the next seventy-two hours. If you don't reach all the checkpoints before the target time, you have failed training and you'll have to start again at day one. Remember, this is not a training area. Mistakes down there will not get you punished, but they might get you killed. There are about a thousand things in the jungle that will kill you or make you so sick you'll wish you were dead."

The helicopter stopped moving about ten meters off the ground. The side door slipped open, filling the cargo area with sunlight.

"One and two, get out there!" Large shouted.

Mo and Shakeel dangled their feet over the side of the helicopter. Large threw out their backpacks. James saw the boys disappear, but couldn't see if they'd landed OK because of the dust blown up by the rotor. Large gave the pilot a thumbs-up and the helicopter moved on to the next drop. Kerry looked unhappy. Jumps put a strain on her weak knee. Gabrielle and Connor dropped. Then they moved to the final position.

James looked down. There was wet sand covered with a few centimeters of seawater beneath him. He watched his pack splash down, summoned his courage and slid off the platform. They'd been trained how to jump safely. The trick was to collapse on to your side so the impact was absorbed by the whole body. If you landed too straight, you risked smashing your hips or ankles. Too flat and your body smacked down hard, often breaking an arm or shoulder. James got the landing spot on. He scrambled up, splattered in wet sand but unhurt.

Kerry screamed as she hit the ground. James rushed over.

"You OK?" he asked.

Kerry got up slowly and took a few nervous steps on her weak knee.

"No worse than usual," she said.

The helicopter flew off. James shielded his eyes from the swirls of sand. They dragged their backpacks out of the wash and up the beach. The sun made the white sand dazzle.

"Let's get into the shade," James said.

They settled under a palm. James rubbed wet sand off his hands on to his trousers. Kerry found the mission briefing in her pack.

"Oh crap," Kerry said.

"What?"

Kerry showed James a page of her briefing. It was in Japanese. James quickly found his own copy. His heart sank.

"Great, all in Russian," James said. "If I'd known my life would depend on it, I probably would have paid more attention in class."

They realized the two briefings were identical. James could understand half the Russian. Kerry was a bit better with the Japanese. By comparing the two versions and making a few assumptions, they worked out almost everything.

There were a couple of sketchy maps, marked with

the position of the first checkpoint, but no indication of where they had been dropped or where they had to go after that. They had to reach the first checkpoint by 1800 and sleep there overnight.

"I suppose there'll be another briefing when we get there," Kerry said.

James went through his backpack. There were tons more than they could carry. What was worth taking? Some stuff was obvious: machete, compass, plastic pool for collecting rainwater, emergency rations, empty water canteen, first-aid kit and medicine, water purification tablets, sunscreen, mosquito nets, matches, Swiss Army knife. A roll of plastic bin-liners weighed next to nothing and had a dozen potential uses. There was also a tent with poles.

"Leave it," Kerry said. "It weighs a ton and we can make a shelter out of palms."

They threw out a lot of heavy items: spare boots, umbrellas, cutlery, thick jackets. Some items were bizarre. They couldn't think of any use for a rugby ball or a table tennis bat. The paperback edition of *The Complete Works of William Shakespeare* might have helped start a fire, but they decided it was too bulky. The packs were manageable once they were stripped out. James kicked through the stuff in the sand, hoping they hadn't left anything that would turn out to be useful.

"What now?" James asked.

Kerry held out the map and pointed to a mountain in the distance.

"The checkpoint is on the bank of the river," Kerry said. "That mountain over there is marked on the far side of the river so we walk towards it."

"How far?"

"Impossible to tell. There's no scale on the map. We'd better move fast though. We'll never find the checkpoint once it gets dark."

The plan was to follow the coastline until they hit the river mouth, then walk upstream to the checkpoint. Walking inland was more direct, but there would be no way to tell which direction to turn when they reached the river.

Walking on the beach was impossible because of the bright sun and heat. Instead they stuck to the jungle a hundred meters or so inland. The trees here formed a shady canopy filled with screeching birds. The only plants beneath the canopy were a few mosses and fungi. Apart from giant tree roots and the odd detour around a fallen trunk, the terrain was level and they made a steady pace.

It was a battle keeping insects off. Kerry had a screaming fit when a ten-centimeter-long millipede tickled up her leg. Its bite swelled into a red lump. Kerry reckoned it hurt worse than a wasp sting. After that they tucked their trousers into their socks.

Once an hour James and Kerry moved on to the beach. Trees nearer the beach were smaller and more spread out. They knocked down coconuts and, once they got the knack of opening them, gorged on the sweet milk. There were fruit trees everywhere, but they only ate fruits they recognized in case any were poisonous. After drinking, they would put down their packs, kick off their boots, and run fully clothed into the sea.

The biggest risk in the jungle doesn't come from

predators, but mosquitoes. The tiny flying insects stick their proboscis under the skin to drink your blood. The bite only leaves an itchy red mark, but the microscopic malaria parasites they spread from one victim to the next can make you sick or even kill you. The kids hadn't been given malaria tablets, so all they could do was cover up their skin, try to keep dry, and wear insect repellent.

Mosquitoes are attracted to the smell of sweat, so after each dip James and Kerry put on dry clothes. They wrung out the sea-drenched clothes and draped them over their backpacks, knowing the heat would dry them before the next stop. After changing, they smeared on mosquito repellent and sunscreen before heading back into the shade under the dense trees.

The coconuts and fruit juice were too rich to keep drinking in large quantities. The fruit acid gave James a sickly burn in the back of his dry mouth. By early afternoon thirst was slowing them down.

Seawater is too salty to drink and all they could find in the jungle were stagnant pools, swarming with mosquitoes and probably contaminated by animal urine. There was no chance of finding a spring unless they diverted towards higher ground inland. They wouldn't get fresh water until it rained. A storm was a certainty. The tropical heat evaporated so much water that by afternoon the skies were bursting with clouds. James and Kerry watched the sky gradually darken. When the first lightning cracked, they ran to the nearest stretch of beach, inflated a plastic paddling pool, and waited.

The rain was like nothing they'd ever seen. The first spots were the size of Ping-Pong balls. James tipped his head back to drink. When the sky opened properly, it was like being under Large's fire hose. The water blasted holes in the smooth sand. James wrapped one arm over his face and struggled to hold the pool as it filled up.

Kerry sheltered their packs under a tree. They stuck their faces in the pool and gulped. When the shower finished, there was enough in the pool to fill both canteens. Rather than risk going thirsty again, they tipped the rest into a plastic sack and took it with them.

Once they reached the river mouth, the going was easier. The river mouth was bordered by an unmade path, chewed up with tire tracks. Kerry counted the bends in the river to find the checkpoint. They arrived an hour inside the deadline, feet killing them after walking for nearly seven hours.

The checkpoint was marked by a flag. A three-meter-long wooden boat with an outboard motor stood at the edge of the river under a tarpaulin. James lifted back the cover and was pleased to discover junk food, cooking pots, and cans of fuel inside the hull. Then something moved. At first James thought it was just a trick of the light, but it moved again and hissed. James dropped and scrambled backwards.

"Snake!" he screamed.

Kerry rushed across from the riverbank.

"What?"

"There's a bloody enormous snake in that boat."

"Are you sure?" Kerry asked. "The manual says snakes are very rare out here."

"The instructors must have put it there," James said. "I suppose if we pull the cover, it will slide away."

"How big did you say it was?" Kerry asked.

"Huge," James said, making a twenty-centimeter circle with his hands.

"There's no snake in Malaysia that big," Kerry said, puzzled.

"You're welcome to stick your head in there if you don't believe me."

"I believe you, James. But I don't think we should let it go. I think it was put there for our dinner."

"What? That thing could be poisonous. How are we going to kill it?"

"James, were you listening during survival training? The only snakes that size are constrictors: snakes that crush you by wrapping themselves around you. It's not poisonous, but if we let it go, what's to stop it coming into our shelter and squishing us in the night?"

"OK," James said. "You want snake for dinner. How do you plan to kill it?"

"Pull back the cover, poke it till it sticks its head out, then hack it off with the machete."

"Sounds like fun," James said. "This is your idea, so I'm poking it and you're doing the hacking."

"Fine," Kerry said. "But if I kill it, *you're* cutting all the guts out and cooking it."

There was loads to do before dark. Kerry made a clearing near the river. James built a fire and butchered the snake, throwing the remains into the river to keep scavengers away.

Kerry put the finishing touches to a shelter made with giant palms as the sky blacked out. She protected the floor with the tarpaulin and lined the inside with mosquito nets.

They ate the snake meat with coconut and instant noodles. James made wire traps baited with leftover meat and pressed them into the river bed by torchlight, hoping they would have fish in them by morning. Well-fed but exhausted, they climbed into the shelter. They tried to translate the briefing while pricking the blisters on their feet with a sterile needle.

Reaching the second checkpoint involved a twenty-five-kilometer cruise upstream, navigating a complicated network of channels and tributaries, until they reached a giant lake. The checkpoint was located aboard an abandoned fishing trawler on a mud bank near the far side of the lake. They had to get there by 1400. It would be an early start.

The temperature hardly dropped in the night. It was boiling in the shelter, hard to sleep. The wailing birds were harmless, but served as an eerie reminder that civilization was a long way off. They kept a small fire burning to deter animals and insects.

James was awake to see dawn. Sun burst over the river and in minutes the dry ground was too hot to touch. James checked inside his boots for nasties before slipping them on his painful feet and walking to the river to check the traps. Two of the four traps had caught fish, but one fish had been ripped apart by a predator. James grabbed his catch and held it in the air until it stopped struggling. It was enough to make breakfast for the two of them.

Kerry built up the fire and began purifying river water. She boiled it for ten minutes, then dropped in chlorine tablets. James cooked the fish and picked a heap of mangoes. He saved one each for breakfast and loaded the rest into the boat.

The fish cooked quickly. He sliced one of the mangoes in half and called Kerry. "Breakfast's ready."

James couldn't see Kerry either near the camp or at the riverside.

"Kerry?" he called, slightly worried.

He pulled the steaming fish off its skewer and split it on to two plastic plates. Kerry emerged from behind some trees.

"I had to crap," Kerry said. "All that fruit I ate yesterday cleaned me right out."

"Thanks for the detail, Kerry. I'm just about to eat."

"Something occurred to me," she said.

"What?"

"Remember we left *The Complete Works of Shakespeare* on the beach?"

"Yeah."

"I think we were supposed to use it as toilet paper."

CHAPTER 29

CRUISE

James and Kerry stood on either side of the outboard motor with their palms pressed against the back of the boat. It had taken a succession of almighty shoves to nudge the bow over the edge of the riverbank.

"We should have emptied everything out first," Kerry said, wiping a gallon of sweat off her face.

"Not worth it now," James puffed. "I think the next one will do the trick. Ready?"

They pushed the hull past its center of gravity. It tipped forward and began sliding. A backwash ran up the shallow embankment, the muddy water swirling over the toes of their boots.

Water surged over the bow as the boat punched the

water. For a second, they both thought it was going under. When the craft stopped rocking, the rum of the hull was only a few centimeters above the waterline. Each swell in the river splashed a drop more water over the side. The river wasn't deep enough to put the boat beyond rescue if it sunk, but the engine and half their equipment would be wrecked, along with any chance they had of making the next checkpoint.

Kerry waded in up to her waist and grabbed a can of fuel out of the boat, being careful not to lean on the hull. James positioned himself nearer to shore, took the can off Kerry, and hurled it towards dry ground.

Once they'd pulled out their sodden packs, fresh water and fuel cans, the boat sat higher in the water.

"Phew," James gasped. "That was too close."

"Brilliant time-saving idea," Kerry said furiously. "I told you we should have taken the stuff out."

"You didn't," James said.

James was nearly right. Leaving the stuff in the boat was his idea, but Kerry's objection had been on the basis that they wouldn't have the strength to push it, not that the extra weight might make the boat sink when it hit the water.

James grabbed a couple of cooking pots from the shore and they bailed out all the water. When the bottom of the boat was dry, they turned to the fuel and equipment scattered along the embankment.

"I suppose it's the same as yesterday," Kerry said. "What do we need? What can we leave behind?"

It made James queasy when he thought about how close they'd come to failing on the ninety-eighth day out of a hundred. Failing this close to the end of training would completely do your head in. The boat was now trundling upstream, against the current. Their sodden packs and equipment were spread over the deck, drying in the morning sun.

The river varied in size. Some places, shallow water stretched over thirty meters wide. They had to go slowly, with James leaning over the bow, shouting directions so that Kerry didn't ground the hull. When things got desperate, James used a wooden oar to nudge them away from disaster. In the narrow sections, the river was deeper and the currents stronger. Trees and bushes loomed over the water and they had to duck under low branches.

When it was plain sailing, Kerry would open up the throttle and the gentle put-put of the engine turned into a whine, accompanied by thick blue exhaust fumes. She stayed on the wooden bench near the outboard motor, making gentle adjustments to their course and marking off progress on her chart. James's job was more physically demanding; but even though the sun was fierce and working with the oar strained his shoulders, he preferred it to taking responsibility for navigating them safely through the dead ends and tributaries leading toward the lake.

It was the hottest part of the day when they broke on to open water. The lake ran further than you could see through the glaring sun. James abandoned his oar and sat on a fuel can in the middle of the boat, occasionally bailing out the water sloshing around the hull.

"Can you see the trawler anywhere?" Kerry asked. "If

I've read the Japanese in my briefing right, it's on a mud bank at the north end of the lake, marked by three red warning buoys."

James stood up, squinting in a vain attempt to cut out the glare off the water. It was a pity they didn't have sunglasses. "I can't see squat," James said. "We'll just have to keep cruising around the edge until we spot it."

Kerry looked at her watch.

"We've got two hours until the deadline, but the sooner we get to this checkpoint, the longer we have to reach the next one."

There was no other traffic on the lake. The fishing wharves, shacks, and warehouses along the shoreline were desolate. There were well-maintained roads and even a couple of telephone boxes, but no people anywhere. Red warning posts were hammered into the mud every few hundred meters. The writing was in Sarawak, so James couldn't read the words, but the yellow and black stripes and the bolts of lightning sent out a message that was clear in any language: stay the hell out of here.

"This is freaky," James said. "What's going on?"

"According to this map, they're building a giant dam upriver," Kerry said. "I guess this whole area is going to be flooded. Everyone's had to leave, which makes this the ideal spot for us to train without any locals sticking their noses in."

James toppled backwards as Kerry put on full rudder and opened up the throttle. For a couple of nervous seconds, he thought he was going over the side.

"For God's sake!" James shouted furiously. "Tell me before you do that next time!"

The boat bounced over tiny waves towards the silhouette Kerry had spotted in the distance. The rusting trawler was about fifteen meters long, leaning on its side in the mud. Another boat, identical to their own, was tied to the metal deck rail.

Kerry bumped the boat into the mud bank. James hopped over the bow and tied it off.

"Anybody in there?" James shouted.

Connor stuck his head through a window.

"What took you so long?" Connor asked.

The exterior of the boat was crusted in bird crap. They tried not to touch it as they crawled through a lopsided doorway into the bridge. There were masses of holes and hanging wires. Everything of value had been stripped for salvage, including the navigational equipment, the glass in the windows, and even the seat cushion off the captain's chair. Connor and Gabrielle looked muddy and tired. They had maps and briefing papers spread out over the floor.

"How long have you been here?" Kerry asked.

"Twenty minutes or so," Gabrielle said.

"Any sign of Shakeel and Mo?"

"They'd been and gone before us," Gabrielle said. "They left the envelope from their dossier on the floor. Yours is over there as well."

Kerry grabbed the padded envelope, tore it open and handed James the half written in Russian.

"So we're running last," James said.

"We've already worked out most of ours," Connor said. "Maybe we can help you two catch up."

James thought it was a kind offer, but Kerry took it the wrong way.

"We're quite capable of working it out for ourselves," she said indignantly. "We've all come from different camps and we're all going to different places. Maybe we had a longer first stint and a shorter second stint. I don't see how anyone could have done the journey much faster than we did."

"We wasted a good half hour when we nearly sank the boat," James said.

Connor laughed. "How did you manage that?"

"It was loaded up when we pushed it off the embankment."

"God," Gabrielle gasped. "You never would have got up the river if you'd flooded the engine."

"I know you guys are on a different route to the final checkpoint," Connor said. "But if your briefing is the same as ours, it tells you to take a different route back towards the sea and get to the third checkpoint, less than fifteen kilometers away, by 2200."

Kerry had done a quick skim through her briefing and nodded. "Different route . . . Fifteen kilometers by 2200 . . . That's more or less what it says here."

James broke into a grin. "Fifteen kilometers in nine hours. That's easy."

Connor, Gabrielle, and Kerry all stared at him like he was a total idiot.

"Oh," James said, when it clicked into place how dumb he was being. "There's going to be some kind of catch, isn't there?"

CHAPTER 24

FLASH

"We could play I Spy," James grinned, trying to break the tension as they headed downstream.

Kerry didn't appreciate his stab at humor.

"Shut your face, and keep your eyes open."

"It'd better not be rapids," James said anxiously. "I couldn't handle that."

"For the hundredth time, James, they won't send us down rapids. This is the wrong type of boat. We'd disintegrate in two seconds."

James could cope with swimming in a pool, or a fairly still section of river, but the idea of getting thrown into raging water without a life jacket scared him like mad.

Things were easier for Kerry. She had the map spread

over her lap and the boat to steer. All James had was twitchy fingers and a brain packed with unpleasant thoughts about whatever awaited them.

"Maybe nothing will happen," James said. "Maybe the trick is to make us think something horrible is going to happen when nothing really is."

"A few seconds' warning could make all the difference," Kerry said sharply. "Be quiet and concentrate."

When the skies darkened for the afternoon rains, James stretched the tarp over their stuff and lashed the paddling pool on top, to capture a fresh supply of drinking water. The violent rain made it impossible to navigate safely. As soon as it started, Kerry pulled into the embankment. James tied the boat to a branch and they snuggled under the tarp until it stopped.

Before setting off again, they quickly changed into dry clothes and put on more insect repellent. James's body was a mass of angry red bites.

"This is getting out of hand," James said. "Even my bites have got bites on them. Do you think we could get malaria?"

"Maybe," Kerry shrugged. "But there's nothing we can do, so what's the point dwelling on it?"

An hour after the rain, they spotted a light pulsing in the trees up ahead.

"Did someone just take our photo?" James asked.

Before Kerry could answer, an electronic squeal broke out under the top of the outboard motor. She cut the throttle and reached into her pocket for her utility knife.

"Is that some kind of warning buzzer?" James asked.

Kerry shrugged. "I'll have a look under the engine cover, but I'm no mechanic."

She undid the two plastic catches with the blade of her knife and lifted off the plastic faring.

"Jesus," Kerry gasped. "I think we've got a bomb on board."

Not quite believing his ears, James scrambled down the boat and looked at the metal cylinder duct-taped to the engine block. James recognized the timing switch from Mr. Large's weapons and explosives class. Unlike the ones you see in movies, it didn't have a clock saying how long you had until the bomb exploded.

A wire ran from the timer and out of the engine, alongside the rubber hose linking the outboard motor to the auxiliary fuel tank. James had noticed the wire before, but he'd never given it a thought.

"Did the flashing light set off the timer?" James asked.

"It must have a photo trigger," Kerry said. "Remember when Mr. Large showed us how you could set up a motion detector and a photographic flashgun to set off a bomb? It's ideal if you want something to explode when it reaches a certain position."

"We could die," James said.

"Don't be dopey," Kerry said. "They're not gonna kill us. It's probably just a tiny bit of explosive that will blow a hole somewhere in the—"

The center of the boat suddenly ruptured upwards. James got the first whiff of burning as the shockwave threw him into the water.

He blacked out for a few seconds. The next thing he knew, he was floating in the river, surrounded by smoke and chunks of wood. His ears were ringing and petrol in the water was stinging his eyes so badly that he couldn't open them.

"Kerry!" James shouted desperately as he thrashed about. "Please . . . Kerry!"

The petrol was burning his throat and he felt like he was choking.

"Kerry, I can't see!"

"Stand up!" she shouted.

James could barely hear her voice over the ringing in his ears. Her hands slid under his armpits.

"Put your feet down."

James felt a surge of relief as his boot touched the sandy river bottom, just over a meter below the surface.

"I thought I was going to drown," James gasped, as Kerry steadied him. "I thought it was deep."

Kerry led James by the hand towards a boulder sticking out of the water. His eyes felt like they were on fire. All he could see were blurs of light.

"Sit there a minute," Kerry said. "Keep blinking as much as you can."

"Are your eyes OK?" James asked.

"Fine," Kerry said. "I jumped off the back of the boat and swam away from the debris."

Kerry had spotted her backpack tangled in a bush on the riverbank and waded to its rescue. By the time she got back, the stinging had died down enough for James to keep his eyes open for a couple of seconds at a time.

"Give us some drinking water," James said.

Kerry looked inside her sodden pack.

"There isn't any," Kerry said. "My canteen was out on the deck."

"How far do you reckon it is to camp?"

"Three kilometers," Kerry said. "We'll have to swim it."

"I've never gone more than a hundred meters," James said warily.

"I'll make you a float out of the backpack."

"It's a long way," James said. "Couldn't we walk along the bank?"

Kerry pointed at the tangle of branches and leaves hanging over the edge of the river.

"You'll never crawl three kilometers through that lot in a million years."

"I suppose," James said.

"You'll swim better without boots. Give them to me and I'll tie them around my waist."

"Seriously, Kerry, I don't think I'm up to this."

As James pulled off his soggy boots, Kerry found the roll of plastic bin-liners in her pack. She stripped out everything but absolute essentials: knife, map, insect repellent, and compass. Then she got one of the bin-liners and blew it up until it was big enough to fill the backpack.

"We'll both hold on to the straps and float downstream," Kerry said. "Just kick gently. The current will do most of the work for us."

Training was supposed to push you to the limit. They could starve you, humiliate you, and work you until you were begging to quit; but at the end of the day, they didn't want to kill you. The route downriver had been carefully selected by the instructors so that the danger to anyone who could swim was minimal. The water was never more than a few meters deep, the currents were moderate, and the banks were rarely more than twenty meters apart.

That still left water snakes and sharks to worry about. The sharks were only little, but they looked perfectly capable of nipping off fingers and toes, and it wasn't a nice feeling when one swam up close, showing off rows of teeth. James panicked a couple of times when he lost sight of Kerry and grazed his thigh on a jagged rock, but they reached the checkpoint as it was turning dark, with three spare hours before the 2200 deadline.

They were desperate for water and James had a couple of leeches stuck on his back, but apart from that, they felt OK as they staggered out of the water. The checkpoint was on an open stretch of land that had been cleared out by a logging company. There was a tin shed that had once served as sleeping quarters to half a dozen loggers. Ever wary of traps, James nervously poked his head inside the metal door and was surprised to find Mr. Speaks sitting in a hammock doing a crossword.

"Good trip?" he asked, pushing his ever-present sunglasses down his nose and giving them the once-over.

"Not bad," Kerry gasped.

Their eyes fixed on a giant bottle of mineral water glinting on the window ledge.

"Help yourself," Mr. Speaks said. "There are fresh packs and equipment for both of you, plenty of food in the ice box, and there's a tank of rainwater on the roof that links up to the shower head if you want to use that.

After that, I suggest you read your briefings and try to grab some sleep before the helicopter picks you up. It's the only rest you'll get in the next thirty-eight hours."

"Aren't we sleeping here tonight?" James asked.

"If you want to reach the fourth checkpoint, you're not sleeping anywhere, either tonight or tomorrow night. The chopper picks you up here at 2200 and drops you on a footpath 188 kilometers from your final checkpoint. That's the exact distance from London to Birmingham and you've got until 1000 hours on the final day to get there. If you fall asleep, you'll never make it."

CHAPTER 25

JOLLY

Going 188 kilometers in thirty-six hours works out at slightly over five kilometers an hour. That's about normal walking pace, but you had to stop to eat and drink, to check you weren't veering off an overgrown footpath in the middle of the night, and when the pain got so bad that you couldn't take another step. It wasn't just James's and Kerry's legs that hurt from the walking; their whole bodies ached with tiredness.

Precautions went out the window. Sweaty and covered in insect bites, there wasn't any time to put on dry clothes or insect repellent. Their canteens were empty. They didn't have time to stop and collect rainwater, so they had to drink water trapped on giant palms and leaves. James and Kerry dumped most stuff and carried one light pack between them, with nothing in it but a torch, compass, and maps.

They reached the final checkpoint in less than half an hour before the deadline. As they staggered towards a wooden building, Gabrielle and Shakeel ran out and gave them fresh water.

"We were getting worried about you two," Shakeel said. "You cut it pretty close."

The building was locked, but there was a tap on the outside. Kerry filled a rusty bucket, threw half at James, and poured the rest over her head.

The trainees were too tired to do anything but crash out on the shady side of the building, waiting for the instructors to turn up.

"I hope we don't get malaria," James said, scratching the bites on his neck.

"It's not a malaria zone," Gabrielle said matter-of-factly.

"What makes you say that?" Kerry asked.

"I knew we were going to the jungle and they didn't give us malaria tablets before we left," Gabrielle said. "That made me think. The night we were in the hotel I sweet-talked the guy behind the front desk and he let me use the Internet. No malaria in this part of Malaysia."

"Smart thinking," Kerry said. "You could have told us."

"I told James in the helicopter before the drop," Gabrielle said. "Same time I told Shakeel."

"You didn't," James said defensively.

"She told both of us. I saw you nod," Shakeel said.

"Oh," James said. "It was noisy. I thought you were saying good luck, so I nodded."

Kerry punched James on the arm.

"Dumbo," Kerry said. "You know how much time we could have saved not changing clothes so often? And I was worried to death we were going to get sick."

"I'm *sorry,*" James said. "There's no need to start hitting me."

"Idiot," Kerry laughed. "I can't wait to get you in that dojo."

"What?" James asked.

"Remember our deal after you stomped on my hand? The day after training stops, I get to fight you in the dojo."

"I thought you were joking," James said.

Kerry shook her head. The others were all laughing.

"She'll mash you," Connor said. "Can we watch?"

"Who says you're both gonna make it through training?" Mo asked. "It's a four-day course and it's only the morning of the fourth day. I bet the instructors will have something else up their sleeves."

The instructors led them inside. The trainees each had a chair with two buckets in front of it. Speaks covered their eyes with a mask. Smoke tied their ankles to the frame of the chair.

"Welcome to the ultimate test," Large said. "Before we can make you six tired little bunnies into operatives, we need to be sure you can cope with the worst thing that could ever happen to you. Number eight, what do you think is the worst thing that can happen on a mission?"

"We could be killed," Kerry said.

"Death would be easy by comparison," Large said.

"I was thinking about torture. What happens if you're captured on a mission? You know something, and some people will do anything to get that information from you. Don't expect mercy because you're children. They'll still slice your toes off. Rip out your fingernails or teeth. Wire you up and blast those sweet little bodies with a thousand volts of electricity. We hope it never happens to any of you, but we have to know you can take the pain if it does.

"This test will show us if you've got guts. It will last one hour. You each have two buckets in front of you. Miss Smoke is placing a jellyfish in the buckets to your left. Its tentacles have hundreds of microscopic spikes; each one packs a dose of poison. A few minutes after contact, your skin will start to burn. Within ten minutes the pain is extreme. A few years ago an operative jumped a fence, misjudged the jump, and ended up with a metal railing stuck in her back. Afterwards she said it was less painful than this test.

"The bucket on your right contains an antidote to the poison. Within a few seconds of touching the antidote, the pain will begin to decrease. After two minutes the pain will be almost gone."

James felt his head being grabbed.

"Open wide," Smoke said.

Smoke shoved a rubber plug into James's mouth. It was held in with an elastic strap that wrapped around the back of his head.

"You are being given mouth guards," Large continued, "because it is not unknown for people in extreme pain to bite off their own tongues. You will each place your hands in the bucket, knuckles touching the bottom, for thirty seconds. The jellyfish will grab you. You will feel nothing at first. You will have to tolerate the pain for one hour. Anyone placing their hands in the antidote before one hour has elapsed has failed the entire course. Due to the toxicity of the poison, you may not retake the test. Any questions?"

None of the trainees could talk with the plugs in their mouths.

"OK then. Put your hands in the bucket."

James leaned forward, feeling blindly for the bucket. He'd thought he had the measure of training but this was scary. What if the pain was so bad he couldn't help sticking his hands in the antidote? Ninety-nine days of training for nothing.

The water was tepid. He felt something light and rubbery wrap itself around his wrists.

"Take them out," Large said. "If the jellyfish sticks, slide it off gently."

James lifted his hands and pushed off the gripping tentacles. He sat up straight and waited for the pain to start.

"Two minutes," Large said. "It should start hurting soon."

James's hands began to feel hot. Sweat was running down his forehead, building up along the rim of the eye mask. He didn't wipe it off in case it spread the poison to his face.

"Five minutes," Large said.

The heat in James's hands was gone. He wondered if he'd imagined it. Kerry sounded like she was struggling with her mouth guard. It looked like the pain had got to her sooner.

"Ten minutes. You all seem to be holding up quite well. But I can see some twisted faces," Large said.

Kerry shouted out:

"What would be the point of an animal stinging you if it didn't hurt straight away?"

Large ran over to Kerry.

"Get that guard back in now!"

James could hear Kerry squealing as they shoved the plug back in her mouth.

"The next person who spits out their guard has to go two hours without touching the antidote!" Large shouted.

Kerry had made James think. There still wasn't any pain from the jellyfish and what Kerry said made sense. What good would an animal sting do if it only hurt its enemy *after* it had been eaten or attacked?

"Fifteen minutes," Large said.

"Two hours without the antidote?" Gabrielle shouted. "Why not make it ten? Tell you what, I'll stick my head in the bucket."

James couldn't see the commotion, but heard water running and a plastic bucket rolling across the floor.

"This is totally bogus," Kerry said calmly.

James was sure it was a trick now. He pulled down his eye mask. Kerry had plucked a harmless white squid out of her bucket and was holding it up for inspection. James took off his mouth guard.

"OK, people," Large said. "Glad you all enjoyed my little joke. Don't forget to untie your ankles before you stand up."

Kerry was looking at James with a massive grin.

"Were you scared?" James asked.

"I thought it was a trick," Kerry said. "Why put the eye masks on us unless it was fake?"

"That never occurred to me," James said. "I was too scared to think straight."

"Look under your seat," Kerry said.

Something had been put under everyone's chair while they were blindfolded. James undid his ankles and picked up the present. It was gray. He unfurled it and looked at the winged baby sitting on the globe and the letters: CHERUB.

"Beauty!" James shouted.

Kerry was already putting her T-shirt on. James pulled off his blue shirt for the last time. When his smiling head popped through the neck hole, Large was standing in front of him holding out his hand. James shook it.

"Congratulations, James," Mr. Large said. "You two worked well together."

It was the first nice thing James had heard him say.

CHAPTER 26

BACK

You weren't supposed to wear the CHERUB uniform off campus for security reasons, but James wore his gray shirt all the way home hidden under his tracksuit. He woke up on the plane and peeked down his chest to make sure it wasn't a dream. Kerry was asleep in the next seat. James could see the gray tail of her CHERUB shirt hanging out the back of her jeans.

Everyone was in a good mood. Even the instructors, who got a three-week holiday before the next batch started training. Kerry stopped acting tough and surprised James by turning into a normal eleven-year-old girl. She told James she couldn't wait until her nails and hair grew back. She even bought a pen and card in the airport gift shop and got everyone to sign it for the instructors. James told her he thought it was dumb. He remembered that Large had been happy to get them thrown off the course to win a bet. It might be Large's job to make trainees suffer, but he seemed to enjoy it as well.

The van from the airport left them at the training building. The new operatives picked a few things up from their lockers and changed out of their casual travel clothes into uniform. James kept one of the filthy blue shirts with the number seven on it as a memento. Kerry was holding out a key.

"Help me move my stuff?" Kerry asked.

"Where to?" James asked.

"The main building. Red shirts live in the junior block."

The instructors wanted them all out of the training area fast so they could get home.

Callum was waiting for his twin outside the training compound. His arm was out of the sling. James felt sorry for Callum having to start training again. James gave him a friendly shove.

"You'll get there," James said. "No worries."

Connor put his arm round his brother.

Kerry was running ahead, excited. "Come on, James."

James went after her to the junior block. He hadn't been there before. It was the middle of the morning so everyone was in class. Kerry's room had kiddie furniture: a plastic desk, bunk beds, and a big wooden trunk with MY TOYS painted on the side. The wardrobe had a green teddy on the doors.

"What a divine room," James said, trying not to laugh.

"Shut your pie hole," Kerry said, "and carry."

She had packed everything before training started.

"You must have been confident," James said.

"If I failed this time, I was going to leave CHERUB. You don't have to become an agent if you don't want to."

"Where do you go if you leave?" James asked.

"They send you to a boarding school. In the holidays you stay with a foster family."

"You really would have left?"

"I promised myself," Kerry said. "That's why I got so upset on Christmas Day when you got us in trouble."

James stayed quiet. He didn't want the conversation straying towards their agreement to fight in the dojo. They packed Kerry's stuff on to one of the electric buggies that staff used around campus.

"Where's your new room?" James asked.

Kerry showed him the number of her key ring.

"Sixth floor," James said. "Same as me. We're practically neighbors."

They walked back to Kerry's old room and did a final check to make sure nothing was left behind. Kerry had tears streaking down her face.

"What?" James asked.

"This had been my room since I was seven," Kerry sobbed. "I'll miss it."

James didn't know where to look.

"Kerry, the rooms in the main building are about fifty times cooler. You've got your own bathroom and computer and everything."

"I know, but still . . ." Kerry sobbed.

"Give over," James said. "Can I drive the buggy? I've never done it before."

• • •

The buggy was overloaded with Kerry's stuff and felt like it might tip over on a bump. The bell had gone for a lesson change. Kids were going between the buildings. A few of Kerry's friends stopped the buggy and congratulated them on passing basic.

Amy burst out of a door.

"Hey!" she shouted.

James hit the brake.

"Congratulations," Amy said, leaning into the buggy and hugging both of them.

"You taught James to swim, didn't you, Amy?" Kerry asked.

"Yes," Amy said.

"What's with all this?" Kerry asked, flapping her arms about in a wobbly front crawl.

"I don't swim like that," James said peevishly.

Amy and Kerry both laughed.

"I only had three weeks to teach him," Amy said. "He's getting more lessons."

Amy copied Kerry's impression of James's swimming and they both laughed even harder. James would happily have thumped them, only they could both easily batter him.

"Anyway, James," Amy said. "I've been looking for you everywhere. I've got something to show you."

"What?" James sulked.

"James, I'm sorry," Amy said. "I'm your teacher so I shouldn't laugh at you. I promise I'll cheer you up if you come with me."

James climbed out of the buggy.

"Where to?"

"You look really fit, James," Amy said.

James wasn't sure if she was saying it to make him feel better.

"Are you OK to move that stuff on your own?" Amy asked Kerry.

Kerry nodded. "Someone will help."

Amy led James back towards the junior building.

"What is this?" James asked.

"I wasn't sure you'd make it through training the first time," Amy said. "I'm impressed."

James smiled. "Another three of four compliments and I'll forgive you for what you said about my swimming."

They walked into the education block in the junior building. It looked like any ordinary primary school, with little kids' paintings on the walls and Plasticine models on the window ledges. Amy stopped by a classroom door.

"There," Amy said.

"What is this?" James said. "Can't you just tell me?"

Amy pointed at the door. "Have a look."

James stuck his face up to the glass. Inside, ten kids sat on the floor chanting phrases in Spanish. The red shirts wore the same uniform as everyone else, only with trainers instead of boots.

"See it?" Amy asked.

"No," he said impatiently. "I don't even know what I'm looking for."

Then it hid James like a bomb.

"Shit," he said, grinning.

He knocked on the classroom door and walked in.

"Shit," James said loudly, in front of the teacher and all the kids.

The Spanish teacher looked furious.

"My sister," James said.

He couldn't think of anything else to say and stood there with his mouth open.

"Excuse our interruption, Miss," Amy said calmly. "This is Lauren's brother, James. He's just finished basic training and was wondering if you could excuse her."

The teacher flicked her hand at Lauren. "Go on, just this once."

Lauren scrambled up from the carpet and jumped into James's arms. She was heavy. James stumbled back a couple of paces before he got his balance.

"Hola hermano grande," Lauren said, grinning.

"What?" James asked.

"It's Spanish," Lauren said. "It means 'Hello, big brother.'"

Amy had a lesson to go to. Lauren walked James to her room.

"I can't believe this," James said, grinning uncontrollably.

The best he'd hoped for was being able to see Lauren a couple of times a month. Having her walking along in front of him in a CHERUB uniform was too much to take in.

Lauren's room was like Kerry's old one, except everything was newer.

"Can't believe this," James said again, slumping on to a beanbag. "I just cannot believe this."

Lauren laughed. "So you're pleased to see me?"

She got Cokes out of her fridge and threw one at James.

"I mean how . . . I mean . . ." James giggled. "Why are you here?"

"Because Ron punched me in the face," Lauren said.

"He did *what*?" James said, shocked.

"Punched me. I had massive black eyes."

"That arsehole!" James shouted, kicking out at the wall. "They never should have let him look after you. I knew something like that would happen!"

Lauren squeezed up next to James on the beanbag.

"I hate Ron's guts," Lauren said. "Mrs. Reed asked what happened to my eyes when I went to school the next day."

"You told her the truth?" James asked.

"Yeah. She got the police. They saw all the smuggled cigarettes when they went round to arrest him, so they busted him for that as well."

James laughed. "Serves him right."

"I got taken to Nebraska House," Lauren said. "Nobody could find where you'd gone. I got really upset. I thought I was never gonna see you again."

"So how long did it take them to find me?" James asked.

"I was at Nebraska House three days. Fourth day I woke up here."

James laughed. "Freaks you out, doesn't it?"

"They wouldn't let me speak to you. Mac took me to see you, though. I watched you and that Chinese girl doing karate. She was killing you. It was so funny."

"Did you have to do the tests to get in?"

"No," Lauren said. "They're only if you're older and you're going straight into training."

"That's so jammy," James said. "Those tests half killed me."

Lauren whacked him across the arm. "Leave my hair alone."

James was winding it around his fingertips. She hated him doing that.

"Sorry," he said. "Never even realized I was doing it."

"I'm on a special program," Lauren said. "Loads of running, swimming, karate, and stuff, so I'm really fit when I start basic training."

"You're ten this year, aren't you?" James said.

Lauren nodded. "September. I'm trying not to think about basic training."

"But you think it's cool here, don't you?" James asked. "You're happy?"

"It's superb," Lauren said. "There's always loads to do. Did I tell you, they took us skiing? I got this bruise on my arse the size of a CD."

James laughed. "I can't imagine you on skis."

"And you want the best news?"

"What?"

"They found drugs and tons of stolen stuff in Ron's flat. Guess how long they put him in prison for?"

James shrugged. "Five years?"

Lauren pointed a finger at the ceiling.

James grinned. "Seven years?"

"Nine," Lauren said.

James punched the air.

CHAPTER 27

ROUTINE

They had a week off after training finished. James went to check out Kerry's room now that she'd unpacked. He wasn't happy.

"My new timetable is mental," James said. "Six hours of lessons every day. Two hours' homework a night and two hours of lessons on *Saturday* morning. That's forty-four hours a week of schoolwork."

"So?" Kerry said. "What did you do at your old school?"

"Twenty-five hours at school and a few hours' homework, which I never did. There's no way I'm doing all that homework."

"Better get used to scrubbing floors, then," Kerry said.

"For not doing homework?"

"Yep. Or cleaning out the kitchen, mowing lawns, wiping windows. Repeat offenders get toilets and changing rooms. The reason you do all those lessons is you miss loads when you're on missions and you have to catch up. They're not all lessons anyway; some are sports and teaching and stuff."

"That's the other thing," James said. "I've got to teach maths to little kids."

"All gray and dark shirt kids have to teach. It gives you a sense of responsibility. Amy teaches swimming. Bruce teaches martial arts. I've got to do Spanish with the five- and six-year-olds. I'm really looking forward to it."

James slumped on Kerry's bed.

"You sound exactly like Meryl Spencer, my handler. I can't believe you're happy about all this work."

"It's not much more than I had as a red shirt."

"I wish I'd never come here."

"Stop being a drama queen," Kerry said. "CHERUB gives you a great education and a cool place to live. When you leave here, you'll speak two languages, have qualifications coming out of your ears, and be set for life. Think where you'd be now if you hadn't come here."

"OK," James said. "My life was down the toilet. But I hate school. It's so boring I want to smash my head up against the wall half the time."

"You're lazy, James. You want to sit in your room with your stupid PlayStation going blip, blip, all day. You said yourself you were gonna end up in prison the way you were carrying on. If you get bored in a classroom, how would you like eighteen hours a day in a cell?

And take those filthy boots off my bed before I bust your head open."

James put his feet down.

"PlayStation is not a waste of time," he said.

"You want the best reason why you should work hard?"

"What?"

"Lauren. She loves you. If you do good, she'll do good. If you muck up and get thrown out, she'll have to make a choice between staying with you and staying at CHERUB."

"Stop being right," James said. "Everyone in this place is clever, level-headed, and I'm always wrong. I hate all of you."

Kerry started laughing.

"It's not funny," James said, starting to smile.

Kerry sat beside him on the bed.

"You'll get used to it here, James."

"You're right about Lauren," James said. "I have to think about her."

Kerry moved a bit closer and rested her head on James's shoulder.

"Beneath that dumb exterior you're a good person," Kerry said.

"Thanks," James said. "So are you."

James put his arm round Kerry's shoulders. It felt like the natural thing to do, but two seconds after he did it, his brain was spinning. What did this mean? Did he want Kerry to be his girlfriend, or was it just that they'd been through so much together in training? He'd showered with her and slept next to her, but until training ended James had barely noticed that Kerry was a girl. Not a dream girl like Amy, but not bad either. He thought about kissing her cheek, but chickened out.

"The room looks nice," James said, scratching for something to say. "All your pictures and stuff. I'll have to get some. My walls are white."

"I was thinking," Kerry said. "We should renegotiate our deal."

James had avoided Kerry for two days, hoping she'd forget.

"How?" he asked.

"Friday night," Kerry said. "Take me to the cinema. I pick the movie. You pay the bus fare, the cinema tickets, hot dogs, popcorn, Pepsi, and whatever else I want."

"That's gonna be easily twenty quid for the two of us," James said.

"That kid you're friendly with. Bruce."

"What about him?"

"He broke his leg once," Kerry said. "When we were eight."

"He said it broke in nine places."

"He exaggerates. I only broke it in seven places."

"You?" James said.

"Snapped it like a twig. Kicked him in the head for luck."

"OK," James said. "Cinema, my treat."

Kyle arrived back from a mission Friday morning with sunburn and a sack-load of fake designer gear. James followed Kyle into his room. It was freakishly neat. Even inside the wardrobe Kyle's clothes were all in dry cleaner's bags, above a row of boots and trainers with shoe trees in them.

"Philippines," Kyle said. "I'm back in Mac's good books."

"What happened?" James asked.

"Confidential. Here, these were supposed to make you feel better when you got kicked out of training."

Kyle tossed over a pair of fake Ray-Ban sunglasses. James slipped them on and posed in the mirror.

"These are cool, cheers," James said. "Everyone thought I'd fail."

"You would have," Kyle said. "If you hadn't got Kerry as a partner, Large would have chewed you up in a week."

"You know Kerry?" James asked.

"Bruce does. He said you had a chance once he found out Kerry was your partner. She cost me ten quid."

"You bet against me getting through training?"

"No offense, James, but you're a spoiled brat and a total whiner. I thought I'd make an easy tenner."

"Thanks," James said. "Good to know who your friends are."

"You want to buy a fake Rolex watch?" Kyle asked. "Same as the real thing, four quid each."

The whole crowd went to the cinema Friday night. Bruce, Kyle, Kerry, Callum, Connor, James, Lauren, and a few other kids. James was happy being part of a big group, all messing about and slagging each other off. The film was a twelve. The rest of them could pass for twelve, but they had to smuggle Lauren through the emergency exit.

James worried about what would happen with him and Kerry, especially with everyone else watching. He sat down. Kerry sat with one of her girlfriends a few seats away. James was relieved, but disappointed as well. The more he thought about it, the more he realized how much he liked her.

Four days into the timetable James realized he could live with it. In his old life he'd always got up late, sat in class mucking about all day, then came home and either played PlayStation, watched TV, or hung out in the neighborhood with his friends. Most of the time he was bored. The routine at CHERUB was hard, but it never got dull.

You weren't allowed to slack off in lessons. Every class had ten kids or fewer, which meant as soon as you stopped working, the teacher was on your back asking what the problem was. Pupils were picked by ability, not age. Some classes, like James's advanced maths group, had kids who were fifteen and sixteen. His Spanish, Russian, and self-defense classes were with six- to nine-year-olds.

Punishments were psycho if you got out of line. James swore in history and got a ten-hour shift repainting the lines in the staff car park. Next day his palms and knees were blistered from crawling around on tarmac.

Most days had a PE session. After training, James was really fit. Two hours' running felt like a warm-up. They started with circuit training inside the gym. The second half was always a game of football or rugby. James liked it best when they played girls versus boys, which usually went a bit mad, with insane tackles and punch-ups breaking out everywhere. What the girls lacked in strength, they made up for with cunning and gang tactics. Boys always scored most goals; the girls edged the carnage.

After lessons James got an hour's rest before dinner. Then it was a scramble to do homework before rushing off to extra martial arts training. James volunteered because he was ashamed that half the nine-year-olds at CHERUB could beat him in a fight. On the nights he didn't have martial arts he'd go to the junior building and hang out with Lauren.

At the end of each day James was worn out. He'd sit in his bath and watch whatever was on TV through the doorway before drying off and collapsing into bed.

CHAPTER 28

DETAIL

It was two months since training. Kerry had done a mission, come back, and gone on another. She was so superior about it, James could have thumped her. Gabrielle was in Jamaica. Connor had disappeared with Shakeel. Bruce was away for days at a time. Kyle went off one morning promising that this mission was going to earn him his navy shirt. James was still at CHERUB and felt like a lemon.

Amy was the only one who hadn't been away. She spent hours on the eighth floor in one of the mission preparation rooms. James still got to swim with her four times a week. He was good now. Four hundred meters front crawl, keeping his body under the water and tipping his face to the side to breathe without lifting his head out of the water. He never got scared and Amy said his stroke was almost perfect.

James and Amy were putting their uniforms back on. All they'd done was swim lengths together, then sit on the poolside and talk for a bit.

"That was our last lesson," Amy said.

James had known it was coming for ages, but that didn't stop him from feeling bad. He liked hanging around with Amy. She was funny and always gave good advice on stuff.

"Is your mission starting?" James asked, sitting down to lace up his boots.

"In a couple of weeks," Amy said. "I need to devote all my time to it."

"I'll miss having lessons with you. You're a brilliant teacher."

"Thanks, James, you're sweet. You should go swimming with Kerry when she gets back. You swim as well as she does now, probably better."

"She'll be too busy rubbing my nose in it about her mission experience. I saw Meryl Spencer again yesterday. She still says there's no mission for me."

"I can confess now," Amy said. "I had you suspended from mission activity."

"Because of swimming?" James asked.

Amy went in her swimming bag and got out a plastic card. James had seen people swipe them in the lift to get up to the secure part of the main building where missions were planned.

"This is yours," Amy said, handing it across.

James broke out smiling. "I've got a mission with you?"

"Yes," Amy said. "I put in some work on this job before you even came here. When you arrived, I realized we looked alike. Same color hair, similar build. I knew you could pass as my little brother. We set you up with Kerry so you had the best chance of passing training. I wasn't happy when I heard you started a fight with her and nearly got thrown out."

"Don't remind me," James said. "I was so dumb."

"You're lucky Kerry didn't retaliate. All she had to do was flip you up and break your arm and you would have been out of training. Nobody would have blamed her either."

"I was on top of her," James said. "She couldn't get up."

Amy laughed, "If you got on top of Kerry, it's because she let you. She could squash you like an egg under her boot if she wanted."

"Is she that good?" James asked.

Amy nodded. "She must like you a lot to let you off like that."

The eighth floor was exactly like the accommodations floors below: a long corridor with rooms off either side. Entering the mission preparation room meant swiping your security card and staring into a red light while the blood vessels in your retina were scanned for identification.

After the hi-tech entry, James expected something

flash inside: a map of the world with a bank of computer screens above it or something. It was actually a bit of a dump. Old computers, chairs with sponge bursting out of cushions, and metal cabinets covered with stacks of files and papers. The only good feature was the view over campus.

Ewart Asker stuck his hand out for James to shake and introduced himself as the mission controller. He was in his twenties, CHERUB uniform, bleached hair with black roots, and a stud through his tongue.

"First mission, James," Ewart said. "Worried?"

James shrugged. "Should I be?"

Ewart laughed. "I'm nervous, James. This baby is complicated. You wouldn't normally get something like this until you'd done a few easy missions, but we needed a twelve-year-old boy who could pass for Amy's brother, and you're the best we've got.

"There's a ton of stuff to learn. I've cut your school schedule back. Amy has written a mission dossier for you. Don't be afraid to ask questions. The mission starts in about ten days."

James pulled up a chair and opened the briefing:

*****CLASSIFIED*****
MISSION BRIEFING FOR JAMES ADAMS
DO NOT REMOVE FROM ROOM 812
DO NOT COPY OR MAKE NOTES

(1) Fort Harmony
In 1612 King James made a fifty square kilometer area near the Welsh village of Craddogh into common land. The charter allowed

people to graze animals and build a small shelter on the land. By the 1870s everyone who lived on Craddogh Common had moved to the village to work in the coal mine. Nobody lived on the land for the next ninety-seven years.

In 1950 Craddogh Common was made part of West Monmouthshire National Park. In 1967 a small group of hippies led by a woman called Gladys Dunn settled on Craddogh Common. Gladys named the settlement Fort Harmony. They kept chickens and built wooden shelters, claiming they could do so under the 1612 charter.

At first the National Park tolerated the settlers, but numbers grew, and within three years about 270 hippies lived in a hundred or so ramshackle buildings. The National Park Authority began legal action to evict the hippies. After two years the High Court decided that the king's charter ended when Craddogh Common was made part of the National Park. The court gave the hippies one week to pack up and leave.

The hippies would not go. Police began destroying huts and arresting the hippies in the winter of 1972. The size of the community soon dropped to less than fifty, but this hard core was determined to stay.

(2) The Battle

The Fort Harmony residents fled every day, allowing police to demolish the shelters. They returned and made new shelters every night. The hippies dug underground tunnels. They also dug traps for the police to fall into.

In one incident a series of nets were hidden under leaves. When police moved in to demolish huts, the trap was sprung. Three policemen were left swinging in nets twenty meters above the ground. The hippies tied off the nets and ran away. A fire engine came to the rescue, but got bogged down in thick mud. It was seven hours before firemen found a way to cut down the nets without their cargo crashing to earth. Pictures of the policemen in the nets made most newspapers the following day.

Newspaper coverage of the battle attracted dozens of new residents to Fort Harmony.

On 26 August 1973, police launched an all-out effort to destroy Fort Harmony. Three hundred police were drafted from across Britain. Television and newspaper journalists watched. Roads were blocked to stop supporters reaching Fort Harmony. Police destroyed the camp and arrested anyone who resisted.

By late morning only twenty hippies remained, all barricaded in underground tunnels. Police decided entering the tunnels was too dangerous and waited for the hippies to come out for food and water.

At 5 p.m. a section of tunnel collapsed under a passing police car. Police rushed to grab a pair of legs sticking out of the earth. Joshua Dunn, aged nine, son of the founder of Fort Harmony, was pulled out of the mud. While two officers held the wriggling boy by his ankles, a third officer hit him over the head with a truncheon. A photographer captured the brutality. Pictures of the boy being stretchered into an ambulance made the television news. This incident caused a surge of public support for the hippies.

The crowd trying to break through blockades and reach Fort Harmony grew to more than a thousand. By midnight the police were exhausted. There were no reinforcements. By 3 a.m. the following morning police lines were broken. At sunrise on 27 August, over 700 supporters were camping in the mud around Fort Harmony. A stream of cars and vans brought wood and supplies to build new shelters. The hippies left the tunnels and began rebuilding their homes.

Next morning the photograph of police beating nine-year-old Joshua Dunn made the front page of every newspaper in Britain. The police announced they would withdraw and destroy the camp at a later date. The police made a plan. A thousand officers would be needed to destroy Fort Harmony while successfully blockading the surrounding countryside. The police and National Park Authority didn't have enough money to pay for such a massive operation, so nothing further was done.

(3) Fort Harmony Today

Thirty years later Fort Harmony still exists. The residents live a harsh life, without running water or electricity in their homes. Camp founder, Gladys Dunn, is now seventy-six. She wrote a bestselling autobiography in 1979. Her three sons—including Joshua, who suffered brain damage from the police assault—still live on site, as do many of her ten grandchildren and twenty-eight great-grandchildren. The camp has about sixty permanent residents. In warmer months Fort Harmony swells to as many as two hundred, mostly students and backpackers who think Gladys Dunn is a hero.

(4) Green Brooke

By 1996 the nearby village of Craddogh was in crisis. The coal mine was closed. Over half the population was unemployed and the village population had fallen from 2,000 residents in 1970 to less than 300. Run-down houses and mountains of black coal waste meant tourists didn't stop at Craddogh on their way to Fort Harmony or the National Parks.

Because of the high local unemployment, the National Park allowed Green Brooke Conference Center to be built on part of Craddogh Common. Green Brooke opened in 2002. It is enclosed by a five-meter-high fence with video cameras and electrified razorwire along the top. The Center hosts conferences and training courses. Facilities include a 765-room hotel, 1,200-seat auditorium, gym, spa, and two golf courses. There is parking for 1,000 cars and thirty helicopters.

Many residents of Craddogh and Fort Harmony work in Green Brooke as receptionists, cooks, and cleaners.

(5) Petrocon 2004

In late 2003 Green Brooke announced the most prestigious event in its brief history. Petrocon takes place in May 2004. It is a secretive three-day meeting of two hundred oil executives and politicians. The media is kept out. Among the guests will be oil ministers from Nigeria and Saudi Arabia and the chief executives of every major oil company. The two most important guests will be the United States secretary of energy and the deputy prime minister of Great Britain.

Security will be handled by the diplomatic protection branch of the police, with MI5 and a small unit from CHERUB.

(6) Help Earth
At the end of 2003 a series of bombs were posted to United States congressmen and members of the British Parliament who support the oil industry. Four workers in the U.S. Congress building suffered injuries. Help Earth claimed responsibility. A month later a French oil company executive working in Venezuela was killed by a car bomb. Help Earth again claimed responsibility.

Shortly before its first attacks, Help Earth sent letters to the editors of several international newspapers, stating its aim to "Bring an end to the environmental carnage wreaked on our planet by the international oil companies and the politicians who support them." It then added,

"Help Earth is the desperate cry of our dying planet. Time is running out. We are prepared to use violent means in the battle to save our environment."

Peaceful environmental groups are at pains to distance themselves from Help Earth and have helped investigators compile a list of likely terrorist suspects. Despite this, nobody involved with Help Earth has been identified, although several environmental campaigners with a violent history are under suspicion. Four of these suspects are current residents of Fort Harmony.

The limited information on Help Earth suggests an attack on Petrocon 2004 is likely. The size and nature of the attack is unknown. It could range from a small bomb destroying a car or helicopter, to a device capable of killing hundreds.

Any Help Earth members planning terrorist action at Petrocon 2004 will probably attempt to make links with Fort Harmony residents for the following reasons:

a) Many Fort Harmony residents are veteran environmental campaigners.

b) All Fort Harmony residents have a good knowledge of the local area.

c) Many Fort Harmony residents

have worked inside Green Brooke and can provide terrorists with information on operations and security.

(7) The Role of CHERUB
MI5 already has informers and undercover agents within the environmental movement. However, MI5 wants extra agents at Fort Harmony in the buildup to Petrocon 2004.

Any new adult residents arriving at Fort Harmony before Petrocon will be suspected of being undercover police or MI5 operatives. The chances of them getting useful information are small. Therefore, it has been decided that two CHERUB operatives posing as relatives of Cathy Dunn, a long-standing member of the Fort Harmony community, will have the best chance of a successful undercover mission. Children will not be suspected of being intelligence agents, and they should mix easily with other members of the community.

CHAPTER 29

AUNTIE

James reckoned he now knew more about Fort Harmony than anyone, including the people who lived there. He'd read Gladys Dunn's autobiography and three other books, as well as seeing tons of press cuttings, videos, and police files. He'd memorized the names and faces of every current Fort Harmony resident and loads of regular visitors. James also read the criminal records and MI5 files on anyone likely to be involved in the terrorist group Help Earth.

James's undercover name was Ross Leigh. His job was to hang out with kids at Fort Harmony, picking up gossip, sticking his nose where it didn't belong, and reporting anything suspicious to CHERUB.

James had a mobile to call Ewart Asker. Ewart was staying at Green Brooke for the duration of the mission. James's other equipment included a digital camera, his lock gun, and a can of pepper spray that was only for an emergency.

Amy was his sister, Courtney Leigh. Her job was to befriend Scargill Dunn, the seventeen-year-old grandson of Fort Harmony founder Gladys Dunn. Scargill was a loner who had dropped out of school and washed dishes in the kitchen at Green Brooke.

Scargill's twenty-two-year-old twin brothers, Fire and World, had both served short prison sentences for attacking the chairman of a fast-food chain. MI5 believed Fire, World, and a couple called Bungle and Eleanor Evans were the residents of Fort Harmony most likely to be part of Help Earth.

Cathy Dunn had briefly been married to Fire, World, and Scargill's dad, some years before they were born. Since then, Cathy had lived alone at Fort Harmony. Like most residents, she grew food and kept a few chickens, but it wasn't enough to survive. She did odd jobs when they cropped up: cleaning, fruit picking. Sometimes Cathy sold information to the police.

There were always a few dodgy people at Fort Harmony. If a drug dealer or a runaway kid turned up, Cathy would walk to Craddogh and call from the village phone box. Half the time the police weren't interested in what Cathy had to tell them. If they were, they only paid ten or twenty quid. Maybe fifty if it was a drug dealer and they caught him with a lot of stuff.

Cathy wasn't comfortable being a snitch, but sometimes it made the difference between having enough to buy a bottle of gas for the heater and freezing in her hut.

After Petrocon was announced, the police got more interested in what Cathy had to say. The value of information went up. Cathy got at least thirty pounds every time, and they wanted to know everything that was going on at Fort Harmony. Who came, who went, if anyone did anything suspicious, if there was an argument. Cathy got a taste for the money. She soon had a roll of notes stashed in a baked-bean tin.

MI5 made Cathy an offer: £2,000 to let a couple of undercover agents stay with her at Fort Harmony in the weeks before Petrocon. Cathy didn't like the idea much; she'd lived alone for thirty years. MI5 offered more money until Cathy gave in.

James, Amy, and Ewart walked into the Bristol Travelhouse. It was a basic hotel attached to a motorway service station. Cathy Dunn was waiting in her room in a cloud of cigarette smoke.

"My name is Ewart, these two are Ross and Courtney."

Cathy sat up on her bed. She looked half drunk and tons older than in all the pictures James had seen of her.

"Who the hell are you?" Cathy asked.

"We spoke on the phone," Ewart said. "You're going to be looking after Ross and Courtney until the conference."

"You've had me stuck in this hole for three days," Cathy said. "Now you turn up with two kids. If this is your idea of a joke, I'm not laughing."

"You made a deal with us," Ewart said. "This is the deal."

"I agreed to let two undercover agents stay with me. Not look after two kids."

"Ross and Courtney are agents. Make their breakfast and send them to school for a few weeks. It's not brain surgery."

"The government uses *children* to do its dirty work?" Cathy asked.

"Yes," Ewart said.

Cathy laughed. "That's absolutely appalling. I won't do it."

"You already took our money," Ewart said. "Can you afford to pay us back?"

"I went to Greece, and I spent some money tidying up my hut."

"Looks like you're stuck with us then."

"What if I refuse to take them?" Cathy asked. "What if I went to the press and told everyone you're using kids to spy on people?"

"If you go to the press, they'll just think you're some flaky old hippy," Ewart said. "Nobody will believe a word out of your hole. Even if you get someone to believe you, you signed the Official Secrets Act before you took the money. You'd be looking at ten years in prison for releasing classified information."

Cathy looked upset. "I've always helped the police, now you treat me like dirt."

Ewart grabbed Cathy's jumper. He lifted her up and knocked her against the wall.

"You don't break deals with us!" Ewart shouted.

"There's six months' work gone into this operation. You're getting eight grand to look after these kids for a few weeks. If that's being treated like dirt, you can treat me like dirt whenever you like."

James was shocked at seeing Ewart flip out. Until now the mission had felt like part of a competition to do better than Kyle, Bruce, and Kerry. Now it felt real. People could get blown apart by bombs or end up in prison for the rest of their lives. James suddenly didn't feel up to the job. He was a twelve-year-old kid who should be going to school and messing around with his mates.

Amy noticed the scared look on James's face. She put a hand on his shoulder.

"Stand outside if you want to," Amy whispered.

"I'm fine," James lied.

Amy gave Ewart a shove.

"Calm down! Leave her alone!" Amy said.

Ewart backed off, giving Amy a filthy look. Cathy sat on the bed. Amy passed Cathy a cigarette. Amy had to light it because Cathy's hands were shaking.

"Sorry about Ewart," Amy said. "Bit of a short fuse. You OK?"

Cathy nodded.

"Listen, Cathy," Amy said gently. "We get up, go to school, hang out at Fort Harmony. Then we go away again. It's the easiest money you'll ever make."

Cathy shook her head. "It's all a bit of a shock, that's all."

Amy smiled. "It always is. Nobody gets told we're kids until the last minute."

"How can I explain that I've got you two living with me?" Cathy asked, taking a deep puff on her cigarette.

"Niece and nephew," Amy said. "Remember your sister?"

"I haven't seen her in twenty years," Cathy said. "She wrote a few times."

"Remember what your sister called her kids?" Ewart asked, voice back to normal.

Cathy worked it out.

"Ross and Courtney," she said.

"We tracked down your sister," Ewart said. "She lives in Scotland. Still married. The real Ross and Courtney are fine. But here's your story:

"A week ago, you got a letter. Your sister is going through a nasty divorce. You rushed to London to meet her. She couldn't cope with her kids, especially Ross who's been expelled from school. You got on well with the kids, so you offered to look after them at Fort Harmony until your sister gets her life back on track."

Ewart handed Cathy a set of car keys.

"Land Cruiser," Ewart said. "Big four-wheel drive. It's a couple of years old. Worth about ten grand. Tell everyone it's your sister's car. If you look after the kids and the mission works out, we won't be asking for it back."

The four of them made their way down to the hotel lobby.

"You better go in the toilet with me," Ewart said. "It's a long drive down to Wales."

"I just went," James said.

Ewart gave James a look. James realized Ewart wanted to speak to him. The toilet was deserted.

"You OK, James?" Ewart asked, unzipping his jeans. "You looked a bit off-color when I grabbed Cathy."

"Why'd you go psycho on her?"

Ewart smiled. "Ever hear of Good Cop, Bad Cop?"

"They do it on TV," James said. "Is that what you and Amy just did?"

"If Cathy's not sure whose side she's on, you and Amy wouldn't be safe. Once I realized Cathy was getting stroppy, I had to be the bad cop and scare her. Amy's job was to be the good cop. Amy defended Cathy when I threatened her, then calmed her down."

James smiled. "So Cathy's afraid of what might happen if she doesn't do what we want her to do, but at the same time she thinks Amy is her friend."

"Exactly, James."

"You could have told me when you arranged to do it."

"We didn't arrange it. Amy knew what to do when I started getting rough with Cathy. Amy's brilliant at picking up stuff like that."

"What if Cathy caused any more problems? Would you really hurt her?"

"Only if the mission depended on it and I had no other choice. Sometimes we have to do bad things to make missions work. Remember when you sneaked to London before training?"

"Sure," James said. "Smashing up that big house."

"The security guards on the gate got gassed by MI5. What do you think happened to them after they woke up?"

"How should I know?"

"They got sacked for sleeping at work. They won't get another security job with that on their records."

"So what happened to them?"

"We ruined their lives," Ewart said. "Hopefully they got jobs doing something different."

"We didn't help them or nothing?"

"No. We couldn't without risking the secrecy of the mission."

"That's terrible," James said. "How can we do that to people?"

"We were trying to get info about a man selling weapons to terrorists. The weapons could kill hundreds of people, so we decided it was OK if two people lost their jobs."

"And it's the same thing with scaring Cathy," James said. "People could get killed."

"Like they say, James: You can't make an omelette without breaking eggs."

Cathy enjoyed driving James and Amy in the Land Cruiser; blasting down the M4, testing all the buttons and gadgets. Amy was up front. James lay flat across the back seat. Cathy and Amy chatted like old pals.

When they stopped for petrol, Cathy bought a Jefferson Airplane CD with some housekeeping money Ewart had given her. She put it on full blast. Amy and Cathy puffed one cigarette after another. James stuck his coat over his head to escape the noise and the smoke.

James sat up when they got off the motorway. He was impressed with the green fields and hills with sheep dotted over them. They stopped in Craddogh for cigarettes and groceries and reached Fort Harmony soon after 3 p.m. Half a dozen grimy kids ran toward the four-wheel drive as it climbed uphill to Cathy's hut. James knew the name and age of every kid.

Cathy's ex-husband, Michael Dunn, and his brother, Joshua, walked toward the car. Michael thumped the bonnet.

"Nice wheels, Cathy," Michael said. "You win the lottery or something?"

James got out. His trainer was swallowed by mud. The camp looked a mess, flaking paint and windows stuck up with tape. James decided he was going to hate living here. Amy squelched to the back of the car and grabbed two pairs of wellies.

"My niece and nephew," Cathy said.

James sat in the car and pulled on his wellies. Joshua Dunn held out a gloved hand. James shook it.

"Come soup," Joshua stuttered.

Amy and Cathy were heading towards a big hut. James and Joshua followed. About fifteen people were inside. Chickens and a huge pot of vegetable soup cooked over an open fire.

"Vegetarian?" Joshua asked.

James shook his head.

Joshua fetched James a bowl of soup and some chicken. There were cushions and beanbags along the walls, but the kids all sat cross-legged near the fire. James sat with them. He ate a couple of spoonfuls of soup. It tasted pretty good. Then he looked at his hands. They were filthy, but the other kids, who were all ten times dirtier, scoffed the chicken with bare fingers.

A hand rested on James's shoulder. It was Gladys Dunn.

"A bit of dirt won't harm you, boy," she laughed.

Gladys looked her seventy-six years, but the outdoor lifestyle kept her lean and she moved well for her age.

A five-year-old girl sitting beside James ran her tongue up her filthy palm and held it out for James to see. James grabbed a bit of chicken and stuffed it in his mouth. The girl smiled.

A group led by Michael Dunn built an extension on Cathy's hut for James and Amy to sleep in. It was impressive watching the community work as a team.

First they laid out paving slabs to raise the floor off the ground. The floor was chipboard wrapped in plastic. The framework was timber. Michael Dunn had obviously built a lot of huts. He sawed each piece without measuring and never made a mistake. Others took the wood as soon as it was cut and knew where each piece fit.

Thick corner posts were bashed into the ground. Trusses were nailed between them. Hardboard was nailed to either side of the frame, with shredded paper packed in the cavity for insulation. A hole was made in one side and a recycled window was fixed in. When it got dark, Cathy turned on the Land Cruiser headlamps. Once the roof was on, two boys were lifted up. They crawled around, nailing down a layer of waterproof felt. Inside James helped seal the gap between the floor and the walls with gray putty.

After it was finished, Amy got a rug from the Land Cruiser and set out sleeping bags and pillows. Cathy found a small paraffin heater. Michael Dunn said he would paint the outside in the morning. Finally, James and Amy were left alone.

CHAPTER 60

CAMP

The new shelter was quite cozy once you got used to the wind blasting the outside. James's sleeping bag rested on a foam camping mattress. He couldn't get comfortable. Amy snored. James shouted at her twice. The third time, Amy said she'd punch him if he woke her up again. James stuck a pillow over his head.

James woke at 3 a.m., busting for a pee. He was used to walking two steps to his bathroom at CHERUB. It was tougher here. He couldn't find his torch, so he had to put on jeans in the dark, then make his way blindly through the main part of the hut, stepping around Cathy who was sprawled over a futon. James felt for the door, where all the wellies were lined up. He wasn't sure which pair was his, so he stuck on the first pair he found and stepped into the blackness.

There were portable toilets on site, but James couldn't find them in the dark so he wandered into the nearest group of trees. He wiped mud off his hands on to his trousers, undid his jeans, and started to piss. Something shrieked and brushed against his leg. James jolted. He was peeing on one of the chickens that roamed around camp.

He turned away, but that was into the wind, so his urine got blown all over his jeans. James stumbled back, tripped over the hysterical chicken, and hit the mud. There was no way to get clean. He wondered why this type of thing never happened to spies in films.

Amy was up, and she'd slept fine. She stuck her foot over James's face to wake him up.

"Shower day, Ross," Amy said.

James burst to life.

"Get that stink off my face," James said, pushing Amy's foot away. "Who's Ross?"

"You are, stupid," Amy whispered.

"Sorry," James gasped, realizing where he was. "I *must* remember that."

"There's a rota for hot water," Amy said. "You get one shower a week. Friday is boys."

"One shower a week?" James said. "With all this mud?"

"How do you think I feel? I've got to wait four days and I don't exactly smell great now."

Cathy showed him where the wash hut was. It was narrow, with a reservoir of rainwater on the roof. Every morning a gas boiler heated enough water to run the showers for ten minutes. If you missed out, you stank for another week. James dashed to the shower hut and stripped. There were eight boys under the water, sharing bars of soggy white soap and messing about. Mums stood outside, telling the little ones to get a move on. The water was barely warm. James rubbed soap in his hair as the hot ran out. The others knew better and scrambled off. James had to rinse with a bucket of freezing rainwater. He sprinted back to Cathy's hut wearing wellies and a big towel.

Cathy was cooking bacon and eggs on a portable gas stove. It smelled good and there was plenty of it.

"Do you kids drink coffee?" Cathy asked. "It's all I've got."

James didn't care what it was as long as it was warm. He drank two cups and stuffed down four rashers of bacon and two runny fried eggs, mopping the yolk off his plate with white bread.

"I've got to go enroll Ross in school," Cathy said. "Then I'll go to Tesco. Anything you two want?"

"Mars bars," James said. "What about enrolling Courtney?"

"After you went to bed, I met this guy Scargill," Amy said. "He said he'd try and fix me a job at Green Brooke."

James was impressed Amy had made such a fast attachment to Scargill. He was also miffed that she'd got out of school.

"I guess you'll start school on Monday, Ross," Cathy

said. "Friday night here is usually a laugh. Everyone turns up after dark. We build a bonfire and play music and stuff."

Amy stayed in the hut making phone calls to Ewart Asker, telling him the change in her plans and getting him to sort out the paperwork she needed to get a job. James spent the morning exploring.

There were about fifty buildings at Fort Harmony. They varied—from the main hut, with space for thirty and its own supply of electricity, down to rat holes fit only for storing junk. Between huts were chicken coops, vegetable patches, strings of washing, and a range of battered cars. There were rusty vans everywhere, though most had no wheels and rested on bricks.

Everyone James met had grubby clothes and long tangled hair. The older men had beards; most of the younger ones had daft goatees and piercings everywhere. They all acted friendly and everyone asked James the same questions about how he ended up here and how long he was staying. By the time he'd met five people, James was sick of repeating himself.

Before long James realized he had a tail: three-year-old Gregory Evans. He was the son of Brian "Bungle" Evans and his partner Eleanor. MI5 thought they might have links to Help Earth.

Gregory followed James at a distance. When James looked around, Gregory would crouch down and cover his face with his hands. It turned into a game. James stopped walking and looked around every few steps. Gregory was giggling. After a bit Gregory got up his courage and started walking beside James. James remembered he had a couple of Maltesers in his pocket and gave them to the toddler. After stuffing them, Gregory ran off. He stopped, turned, and shouted at James.

"Come to my house!"

James felt odd being bossed around by a three-year-old. They ran about a hundred meters, Gregory leading James by the hand.

Gregory sat down on the doorstep of a smartly painted hut and pulled off his wellies.

"Come in," Gregory said.

James put his head in the door. The hut had room for six to sleep. The floor was painted bright orange, with shocking green walls and a purple ceiling. Plastic dolls hung everywhere. James noticed they were mutants, with blood painted on their faces and freaky punk hairstyles.

"Who's that?" Bungle asked, with an American twang.

James was embarrassed, standing in a strange doorway on the orders of a three-year-old.

"Sorry, Gregory brought me here," James explained.

"What you sorry for, boy?" Bungle said. "We're a community. Come in, get your boots off. Gregory's always dragging kids in here. You want hot milk?"

James pulled his wellies off and stepped inside. It was wonderfully warm, but smelled like farts and sweat. Eleanor lay on a mattress. She had nothing on but knickers and a Nirvana T-shirt stretched over a pregnant belly.

Gregory gave his mum a cuddle. Bungle made introductions, asked James the same questions as everyone else, then handed him a mug of hot milk.

"Unzip your tracksuit top, Ross," Bungle said.

James was mystified but did what he was told.

"Reebok," Bungle said triumphantly.

"What?" James asked, confused.

"He hates people who wear clothes with trademarks on," Eleanor explained.

"What's wrong with what I'm wearing?" James asked.

"I don't hate the people," Bungle said. "I hate the clothes. Look at yourself, Ross. Puma jacket, Nike tracksuit, Reebok T-shirt. Even his socks have logo on them."

"Just ignore Bungle," Eleanor said. "He thinks people wearing labels on their clothes is a sign that they can't think for themselves."

Bungle rushed over to a bookshelf and passed James a book called *No Logo*.

"Give your brain a bit of exercise," Bungle said. "Read it. If you want, we can discuss it when you bring it back."

James took the book.

"I'll look at it," James said. "All my stuff is Nike and that. At my old school you got your head stuck down the toilet if you wore unfashionable clothes."

"For God's sake, Bungle," Eleanor said. "He's a kid. He's not interested in that stuff."

James didn't care what some hippy thought about his clothes, but the book gave James an excuse to come back and hang around a prime suspect, so he put it in his pocket and said thanks.

"Ross, ask him about the dolls before he bores you to death talking about the evils of world capitalism," Eleanor said.

Bungle sounded annoyed. "You handed out leaflets with us, Eleanor."

Eleanor laughed. "Ross, in principle, I support fair wages for people in poor countries. I want to help save the environment. I want Bungle and his pals to save the world. But I'm eight months pregnant. The baby presses on my insides, so every half hour I waddle through two hundred meters of filth to go sit on a stinking portable toilet. Gregory is driving me crazy. My ankles are swollen like beach balls and I'm half terrified the car we borrowed is going to break down on the way to the hospital when I go into labor. I'd happily surrender all my principles for a comfy bed in a private hospital."

James sat on the floor and sipped his hot milk.

"The dolls are excellent," he said. "Did you make them?"

"That's my living," Bungle said.

Bungle pulled one of the dolls off the ceiling and dropped it into James's lap. It was the torso and head of an Action Man, but it wore a tutu and had skinny ballerina legs glued on. The hair was spiky purple. One hand was cut off and the stump was painted with fake blood.

"Cool," James said.

"I buy the dolls at jumble sales and boot fairs. Then I mix all the bits up and make weird costumes and stuff out of scraps."

"How much?" James asked.

"Depends where," Bungle said. "Cardiff market, they're all poor, nobody will pay more than ten pounds. If I get a stall at Camden in London, you can sell them for eighteen a throw. When it's packed out in the summer, you can shift sixty dolls a day. One time I sold eighty-four."

"One thousand, five hundred and twelve quid in a day," James said. "You must be loaded."

"You some sort of human adding machine?" Bungle asked.

James laughed. "Kind of."

"Takes over an hour to make each one. Painting all the fiddly bits does your eyes in. You want a doll, Ross?"

"They're cool," James said. "I haven't got any money though."

"Take one," Bungle said. "Maybe you can do us a favor. Look after Gregory for a couple of hours one day or something."

It was an unwritten Fort Harmony rule that there was a free evening meal in the main hut for anyone who wanted it. Gladys Dunn bought vegetables from local farmers with the money she earned from her book. Joshua spent his afternoons preparing the vegetables and making either stew or a curry. Everyone eating together was what made Fort Harmony a community, rather than a bunch of separate families.

James ate with the kids when they got out of school. Michael Dunn collected a vanload of scrap from a local dump. All the kids helped pile up old doors and bits of furniture to make a bonfire for the evening festivities. James tried to make friends with Sebastian and Clark Dunn. They were ten- and eleven-year-old brothers, cousins of Fire, World, and Scargill. The Dunns were a close family, and Sebastian and Clark were James's best chance to pick up all the gossip.

CHAPTER 91

NIGHT

James found Amy and Scargill sitting on Amy's bed smoking. Scargill looked like a geek: spindly arms and legs, greasy black hair tied back in a ponytail. He wore a kitchen uniform from his job at Green Brooke.

"It stinks in here," James said, stepping in through the hole between the old and new parts of Cathy's hut.

"This is my little brother, Ross," Amy said. "He's a whiny little shit."

"You're *harsh,* Courtney," Scargill said, laughing.

James was hurt. They had to act like brother and sister, but he didn't see why she had to be nasty. He was also jealous: Scargill was getting to spend all his time with Amy.

"Why are you here, Ross?" Amy asked.

"This *is* my room as well," James said.

"Scargill and me want privacy, so get what you came in for and sod off."

"Did you get a job?" James asked.

"I'm an attendant at Green Brooke spa," Amy said. "Four days a week."

James started rummaging through his stuff.

"What do you want, Ross?" Amy asked.

"My mobile," James said. "I was gonna see how Mum is."

"Take mine, it's charging up in the car."

"Thanks, Courtney," James said.

James sat in the front seat of the Land Cruiser and made a call to Ewart Asker.

"Hey, James, how's it going?" Ewart asked.

"Not bad. Amy's pissing me off."

"She with Scargill?"

"Permanently," James said.

"That's her job, James. She's got to get as close to him as she can."

"She told him I was a whiny little shit."

Ewart cracked up. "That gives Scargill a sign that she prefers him to her kid brother. She doesn't mean it."

"Scargill must be in heaven," James said. "Scrawny little nerd and he's got Amy all over him."

"You've got a soft spot for Amy, don't you?" Ewart asked.

James's instinct was to deny it.

"A bit," he admitted. "If I was older, I'd ask her out. How did you know?"

Ewart laughed. "You get this glazed look in your eyes when she's in the room."

James panicked. "What? Is it that obvious?"

"I'm joking, James," Ewart said. "So how's Cathy?"

"Seems OK now," James said.

"How did you get on with Sebastian and Clark Dunn?"

"Bad," James said. "They're weird kids. Tough-looking and smelly. They talk to each other as if you're not even there. None of the other kids hang out with them much either."

"Keep trying, but don't force it. Any other news?"

"I got one good break," James said. "I made friends with Gregory Evans, Bungle's son. I spent nearly an hour with them. Bungle gave me a book called *No Logo* to read."

"Good book," Ewart said. "Read it. Go and see him, pretend you don't understand something, and use it as an excuse to hang around."

"There's not much about Bungle on file, is there?" James asked.

"No. He's been seen with all the bad guys, but he's never been arrested. There are over a thousand people called Brian Evans in Britain; we don't know which one he is. We don't even know exactly how old he is or where he comes from."

"He sounds American," James said. "He's got that twangy sound in his voice. I think they call them rubber-necks."

"What's a rubberneck?"

"Like in the movies. Cowboy types, kind of stupid, he sounds like one of those."

Ewart laughed. "You mean a *redneck*?"

"That's it," James said. "He sounds like a redneck."

"That's useful to know. I'll get the Yanks to see if they have anything on him. What we need is for you to get in Bungle's hut, take some pictures, and have a rummage through any paperwork you can find. But don't take any risks to make it happen. If you're seen taking pictures for no good reason, it will blow your cover."

"Bungle said they might ask me to keep an eye on their little boy when they go out."

"That would be an ideal opportunity, especially if the kid falls asleep. Are you sure they'd trust someone your age to look after him?"

"Bungle suggested it," James said.

"Don't sound too eager; they might think it's odd. Anything else?"

"That's all I can think of," James said.

"Keep in touch, James," Ewart said. "It sounds like you're doing a grand job."

"Thanks. Bye, Ewart."

It was past eleven and people were still arriving. They came in groups of four and five, pulling booze, food, and firewood out of cars. Portable CD players competed with didgeridoos, tom-toms, and guitars. The crowd was mostly teenagers and twenty-somethings: students from Cardiff and kids from the local villages, with a few old hippies who had turned up every Friday since the year dot.

James wandered. He felt awkward. Younger kids rushed around chasing and fighting, older ones drank beer and snogged. James didn't fit in well with either group. He moved away from the party into the forest. He could hear bangs from a clearing in the distance. As James got closer, he worked out it was the sound of an air pistol. The kids were Sebastian and Clark Dunn. They were freaks. If James wasn't on a mission, he would have steered clear, but it was his job to make friends. He decided to have another go.

Sebastian and Clark vanished before James reached the clearing. There was a bird on the ground, cooing loudly and struggling in the mud. It was hard to see what was wrong in the dark, but the bird was in a bad way. James crouched down. He wondered if he should bash the bird with a rock to put it out of its misery.

Sebastian bolted out from the trees. He landed on top of James and tried to pin him, but James was too strong. James elbowed Sebastian in the stomach. Clark came out to help with the ambush. He was almost as tall as James and probably heavier. Clark bashed James over the head with a heavy torch. The brothers managed to get James under control.

Clark pressed the torch head into James's eye and clicked the bulb on. Squeezing his eyelid tight didn't stop the light from burning his eye. James was worried. Hopefully they would just rough him up, but who knew how crazy these kids were? If James yelled, nobody would hear over all the noise from the party.

"Why are you following us, scum?" Clark asked.

"I wasn't," James said. "I just came this way."

Clark grabbed a chunk of James's hair and tugged his head out of the mud. James felt Sebastian, who was sitting on his legs, shift his weight slightly. James kicked up both legs, hitting Sebastian in his back. Sebastian yelled out and tumbled off. Now his legs were free, James thrashed about and tried to release his arms, which were pinned to his sides by Clark's thighs.

"I'll knock you out," Clark said.

Clark punched James in the head. James put all his strength into lifting his stomach off the ground, making space under himself to slide out his hands. He scrambled from under Clark and stood up. Clark ran at James. James realized that months of getting hammered by black belts at CHERUB was about to pay off. Without the element of surprise, Sebastian and Clark didn't have a chance.

James waited till Clark got close. He sidestepped, kicked Clark full force in the stomach, punched him in the mouth, and finished off stamping him behind the knee so he smacked into the ground. Sebastian looked angry but didn't fancy joining in. Clark looked pleadingly at James from his knees, hoping his beating was finished.

"I don't want to hurt you," James said. "Just say you quit."

Clark scrambled up, gasping for air. He was hurt, but a smile came on to his face.

"I've battered kids heaps bigger than you," Clark said. "Where'd you learn to fight?"

James found a tissue in his pocket. He gave it to Clark to wipe the blood off his split lip.

"Self-defense classes," James said. "Back in London."

Clark turned to his brother.

"They were serious punches, Sebastian."

"You have to put your whole body into it," James

said. "Starts at the hips. If you get the technique right, it's eight times harder than a normal punch."

"Let him hit you in the guts, Sebastian," Clark said. "I bet you double over."

"I don't want to hit him," James said.

"We hit each other to keep tough," Clark said. "If I hit him in the guts, he doesn't even flinch."

Sebastian stood with his hands behind his back ready to take a hit.

"I'll hit his shoulder," James said.

"You can hit my guts," Sebastian said. "I can take it."

"In the arm first," James said. "Then I'll do it in your guts if you still want me to."

Sebastian turned so his side was facing James. James didn't want to have to hit him in the stomach; he knew it could do serious damage, so he gave Sebastian his hardest shot in the arm. Sebastian stumbled sideways and screamed out in pain, clenching his upper arm with his hand. Clark was wetting himself laughing.

"I told you it was hard," Clark said.

Sebastian tried not to show the pain. James felt bad for hitting him so hard.

All this time the pigeon was still thrashing about in the mud. James looked at it.

"What happened to it?"

"Shot it with the air pistol," Clark said.

"Wasn't dead," Sebastian said. "So I cut one of its wings off with my pen knife."

"You guys are lunatics," James said, grimacing.

"Better hope the shot kills you," Clark grinned. "If it doesn't, it's torture time."

"Can't you put the poor thing out of its misery?" James said.

"If you want me to," Sebastian said.

Sebastian walked toward the bird. It didn't have much life in it. Sebastian pressed his heel into the bird. It let out a final desperate noise as its bones were crushed. Sebastian had a big smile on his face.

James realized he'd made friends with a couple of seriously twisted kids.

CHAPTER 32

GIRL

Sebastian, Clark, and James went to the main hut to feed. Guests had brought meat to barbecue, as well as the cold dishes laid out on a long table. Joshua Dunn was serving vegetable curry. James wasn't mad on curry, but it was good stuff after being out in the cold. They took the food outside to the bonfire. A few dozen people sat on waterproof sheets around the fire. Sebastian and Clark found Fire and World and sat beside them.

"Hey, little psychos," Fire said.

"Hey, jailbirds," Clark said, referring to his cousins' spell in prison.

Fire and World were non-identical twins, with plaited hair and pierced eyebrows.

World looked at James. He sounded drunk. "Care to tell me what your sexy sister sees in our baby brother?"

James shrugged. "She's not fussy. Snogs anything with a pulse."

"What was that?" Amy said.

James hadn't noticed her sitting a few meters away. All the Dunns laughed. Amy faced James off with her hands on her hips. James couldn't decide if she was angry or just messing.

"Nothing," James squirmed. "I was just saying what a nice couple you and Scargill make."

Amy crushed James with a hug that took his feet off the ground.

"That's really sweet of you, Ross," Amy said. "Because after what I thought you said, I was going to kick all your teeth out."

James finished his curry and wandered off on his own. He noticed a girl leaning against a tree smoking. Long hair, baggy jeans. She was about James's age, nice looking. He didn't remember her from any of the intelligence files.

"Hey, can I have a drag?" James said, trying to sound cool.

"Sure," the girl said.

She passed James the cigarette. James had never tried one before and hoped he wasn't about to make an idiot of himself. He gave it a little suck. It burned his throat, but he managed not to cough.

"Not seen you here before," the girl said.

"I'm Ross," James said. "Staying here with my aunt for a bit."

"Joanna," the girl said. "I live in Craddogh."

"Haven't been there yet," James said.

"It's a dump, two shops and a post office. Where you from?"

"London."

"I wish I was," Joanna said. "You like it here?"

"I'm always covered in mud. I want to go to bed, but there's a guy playing guitar three meters from where I sleep. I wish I could go home, have a warm shower, and see my mates."

Joanna smiled.

"So why are you staying with your aunt?"

"Long story: Parents are getting divorced. Mum freaking out. Got expelled from school."

"So you're good-looking *and* you're a rebel," Joanna said.

James was glad it was quite dark because he felt himself blush.

"You want the last puff, Ross?"

"No, I'm cool," James said.

Joanna flicked the cigarette butt into the night.

"So, I paid you a compliment," Joanna said.

"Yeah."

Joanna laughed. "So do I get one back?" she asked.

"Oh, sure," James said. "You're really like . . . nice."

"Can't I get any better than nice?"

"Beautiful," James said. "You're beautiful."

"That's more like it," Joanna said. "Want to kiss me?"

"Um, OK," James said.

James was nervous. He'd never had the courage to ask a girl out. Now he was about to kiss someone he'd known for three minutes. He pecked her on the cheek. Joanna shoved James against the tree and started kissing his face and neck. Her hand went in the back pocket of James's jeans, then she jumped backwards.

"What did I do?" James asked. He'd just started enjoying himself.

"Police car," Joanna said. "Hide me somewhere."

James saw a flashing blue light and a couple of cops getting out of a car a few hundred meters down the hill.

"Are you a runaway or something?" James asked.

"Hide me first, questions later."

James led Joanna up the hill. The policemen were heading in the same direction. They seemed friendly and stopped to chat with a couple of people. James undid the padlock on Cathy's hut and clambered inside. Joanna slammed the door behind her.

"What's going on?" James asked.

"Peek outside," Joanna said. "Tell me what the police are doing."

James stepped up to the window. "I can only see one of them," he said. "He's talking to some guy."

"What's he saying?"

"He's standing twenty meters away and it's dark. You expect me to read his lips? . . . Wait . . . The guy he's talking to is pointing at this hut."

Joanna sounded hysterical. "I'm in so much trouble!"

"Why?"

"I'm supposed to be sleeping over at my friend's house, but we came up here instead."

"Where's your friend?" James asked.

"She met up with her boyfriend and abandoned me."

"But why are the police out searching for *you*?"

The door of the hut came open and a policeman shone his torch in Joanna's face.

"Hello, Daddy," Joanna said.

"You'd better get out here, young lady. I'm driving you home. And as for you . . ."

The policeman moved the beam of his torch so James's face lit up.

". . . I don't know what you and my daughter have been up to, but you'll stay away from her if you know what's good for you."

James watched Joanna's dad take her to the police car. He didn't feel like going back outside. He lit the gas lamp, found his packet of Mars bars, and poured a glass of unrefrigerated milk.

"I hear you tried to jump Sergeant Ribble's daughter," Cathy said.

She looked smashed.

"I met her five minutes before her dad turned up," James said. "We had one little kiss."

"So you claim, stud," Cathy said.

She pinched James's cheek and laughed. Nobody had done that to James since he was about five.

"It's nice having you kids here," Cathy said. "Livens the place up."

"I thought you didn't want us," James said.

"It was a shock. But it gets dull here after thirty years."

"Why don't you move on?"

"I might after you two go," Cathy said. "Cash in that

monster car, travel for a bit. Don't know what after that. Maybe I'll try getting a flat and a job. I'm getting too old to keep scratching for a living round here."

"What kind of job?" James asked.

Cathy laughed. "God knows. I don't suppose there's anyone queuing up to employ fifty-year-old women who last had a job in 1971."

"What doing?" James asked.

"I worked in the Student Union shop at my university. Met Michael Dunn there. Married him a few years later. Came here. Had a little boy. Got divorced."

"You have a son?" James asked.

"Had a son," Cathy said. "He died when he was three months old."

"I'm sorry," James said.

Cathy looked upset. She dragged out a wicker hamper and found a photo album. She flicked to a picture of a newborn in a white crochet hat.

"Harmony Dunn," Cathy said. "That's my only picture of him. Michael took it the day he was born."

Seeing Cathy upset about her baby made James think about his mum. He felt a tear well up. He wanted to tell Cathy about his mum dying, but it would be breaking the rules of the mission. Cathy noticed James looked upset and put her arm around him.

"There's no need to get upset, Ross. It happened a long time ago."

"Your whole life might have been different if he'd lived," James said.

"Maybe," Cathy said. "You're a nice boy, Ross, or whatever your real name is."

"Thanks," James said.

"I don't think it's right the government using kids. You two could get hurt."

"It's our choice," James said. "Nobody forces us to do it."

"Courtney is using Scargill to get to Fire and World, isn't she?"

James was impressed Cathy had worked it out. It seemed pointless to deny it.

"Yeah," he said.

"All the Dunn family have been good to me, even after I divorced Michael," Cathy said. "But those two have always been different. They're definitely up to something."

"What makes you sure?" James asked.

"I've known Fire and World since they were born. There's something not right about them. A shiver goes up me when they walk into a room."

CHAPTER 33

FREAK

7 a.m. Monday, James's travel alarm went off to wake him for school. Amy threw a pillow at him when he didn't turn it off. He stumbled out of bed, rubbing his face, and unpinned a corner of the sheet over the window to let in some light.

"Can't you leave it dark?" Amy moaned from under her covers.

"I've got to go to school."

James started putting on a sweatshirt and tracksuit bottoms.

"It's freezing," James said.

"It's warm under here," Amy said smugly. "I don't have to get up for three hours."

"I can't believe you got out of school; it's not bloody fair."

Amy giggled under her covers. "It's toasty at Green Brooke. The water in the Jacuzzi is beautiful, and I get a hot shower before and after my shift."

"I'm filthy," James said. "I'm gonna get so much stick from the other kids going to school looking like this."

"Put clean clothes on and use some of my deodorant."

"I'm wearing clean stuff. I'll still be covered in mud three steps out the door. Where's your deodorant?"

"Down at the end of my bed."

Amy's deodorant was in a pink can with pictures of butterflies on it. James figured it was better smelling girly than stinking of BO so he gave himself a good blast.

"I'm glad I don't have to get up," Amy giggled. "This bed is really comfortable."

James noticed Amy's leg poking out and tickled the sole of her foot. She pulled her leg in and squealed.

"Serves you right for teasing," James said.

Amy flew out of bed, grabbed James around the waist, and started tickling under his ribs.

"No, please," James giggled.

James's legs buckled from laughing. His face was red and spit dribbled down his chin.

"Beg for mercy, weakling," Amy said.

"No way," James spluttered.

James couldn't wriggle free. Amy unleashed another wave of tickles.

"Oh no. Please . . . OK mercy. Stop . . . Mercy. I SAID MERCY."

Amy stopped. Cathy's head poked in from her part of the hut. Her hair was all tangled.

"What's going on?" Cathy asked.

"Tickling," James said, gasping for air.

"I thought you were dying or something. I was trying to sleep."

"I've got to go to school," James said.

"Do it quietly, Ross," Cathy said. "I'm laying in all morning."

"Nice life for some," James said. "Is there anything for my breakfast?"

Cathy thought for a second.

"There's cold curry, or you could have the last one of your Mars bars."

"Great," James said.

Amy had snuggled back into bed and was laughing under her sheets.

It was a two-kilometer walk to the school bus stop in Craddogh. A few older Fort Harmony kids showed James the way. Joanna was at the stop with some friends. James said hello but she ignored him. The village kids wore smart casual clothes. Fort Harmony kids were tramps in comparison.

It was a half-hour ride to school, stopping a few times to pick up more kids. James rested his face against the window and watched the sun rise over the passing countryside.

Gwen Morgan School looked better than James's old school in London. The modern classrooms were in single-story clusters with covered walkways between them. The areas between buildings had flower beds and neatly trimmed grass with KEEP OFF signs. When the bell rang kids walked to registration. No shoving or fights breaking out. Even the boys' toilets were clean. James washed as much filth as he could off his face and hands before finding his class. He handed a note to his form teacher and found a desk.

"This is Ross," the teacher announced. "Please make him feel welcome here at Gwen Morgan and help him find his way around."

The kids all looked polite and well behaved. Nobody spoke to James.

First lesson was science. James asked a kid if it was OK to sit next to him. The kid shrugged.

The lesson was dull. They were halfway through a topic, but James was bright enough to pick up what had gone on before and was soon bored. It felt really different to CHERUB where all the kids were clever and the teachers kept you on your toes. He wrote neatly in his new exercise book and homework diary, but it seemed like a waste of time. He would only be here a few weeks.

Between first and second lesson a couple of kids in James's class called Stuart and Gareth gave him a shove.

"Wait till break time, hippy boy," one of them said.

James wasn't worried. He'd be able to fight them off if they tried anything.

He got another shove and a punch in the back at the start of morning break. James knew he'd become a target if he looked soft, but he didn't want to end up rolling around the floor fighting on his first day, so he punched Gareth in the face and ran off. He spent the rest of morning break wandering on his own, paranoid that everyone was staring at him like a freak.

Gareth had a tissue plugged up his nose to stop it bleeding for the whole of third period. After lunch James wanted to join the kids playing football on the all-weather pitches, but Gareth, Stuart, and a couple of their pals were playing. James thought it best to steer clear. He found a quiet spot at the back of the school, sat against the outside wall of a classroom, and started doing his homework.

James noticed a shadow over his science book and looked up. Gareth and Stuart were standing over him with six friends for backup. James was furious with himself for letting them get so close without noticing.

"You killed my nose, Harmony boy," Gareth said.

"I didn't ask for trouble," James said. "Leave me alone."

Gareth laughed. "In your dreams."

"We hate all you Fort Harmony filth," Stuart said. "They should send the police up there and set dogs on you."

James reckoned he could have beaten any two of them, managed to get a few hits in and escape against three or four, but eight against one . . . No chance.

"Stand up, hippy," Gareth said.

If he stayed on the ground, he could roll in a ball to protect himself. Standing would only mean getting knocked back down.

"Get your arse *up*," Gareth repeated.

"Piss off," James said. "Haven't got the guts to fight me on your own, have you?"

Gareth kicked James in the knee. A few of the others moved closer so there were ten legs circling. James braced himself for pain. Kicks came fast; luckily there were so many legs flying they used a lot of energy hitting each other. James tried to tuck his knees into his chest, but a trainer clamped his stomach to the floor. He kept his legs together to protect his balls and wrapped his arms over his face.

The main beating lasted about a minute. A couple of the kids who weren't in the surrounding group gave some brutal kicks in the side to finish off.

"Better learn some respect, hippy," Gareth said.

The gang walked off, mocking the way James was groaning in pain on the floor. James couldn't stop the tears forming, but he was determined not to cry out. His arms and legs were dead from the beating.

James got his books into his backpack and stumbled a couple of meters holding on to the wall before his knee gave out. He sat there until a teacher came to unlock his classroom. He tried to pretend he'd slipped and twisted his ankle, but the teacher could see James was hurting all over. The teacher put his arm around James and helped him hobble to the first-aid room.

Mr. Crow, the deputy headmaster, came into the first-aid room. James was sitting on the edge of a bed in his boxers, holding a cup of orange squash. He had plasters on his legs and arms.

"Who did this to you, Ross?" Crow asked.

He was a small, friendly-sounding man with a Welsh accent.

"I don't know," James said.

"Were any of them in your class?"

"No," James said.

James thought it was best not to grass. The school wouldn't expel eight kids. They would only get suspended for a few days. Then all their mates and older brothers would be after James for grassing. His life would be hell. If he didn't grass and managed to make a few friends to back him up, things might be OK.

"Ross, I understand it's your instinct not to tell on your classmates. But this is your first day here and you've been seriously assaulted. That is not acceptable. We want to help you."

"I'll be OK," James said. "It's no big deal."

By home time, James could walk again, sort of. He was let out of the first-aid room before the bell, giving him a chance to get on the bus without being caught up with everyone else. Joanna climbed on and sat next to him. It was the first good thing that had happened to him all day.

"What happened to you?" Joanna asked.

"What does it look like?" James said angrily. "I got the crap beaten out of me."

"Gareth Granger and Stuart Parkwood," Joanna said.

"How did you know?" James asked.

"It's always them. They're not even tough; it's just they hang out in a big group and stick up for each other."

"I just hope they don't make it a regular thing," James said.

"You need a bath," Joanna said.

"No chance of that at Fort Harmony."

"Have one at my house if you want."

"What about your dad?"

"Working till six. Then he usually goes for a drink."

"Your mum?"

"Lives in Cardiff with my big brothers."

"Are they divorced?" James asked.

"A few months ago."

"What happened after your dad caught you on Friday?"

"Lost my pocket money, grounded for a fortnight."

"Rough," James said.

Joanna smiled. "It's so stupid. My dad grounds me, but he's never home to stop me going out."

Joanna's house was a little cottage on the edge of Craddogh with frilly net curtains and ornaments everywhere. Joanna flicked on MTV. They ate cheese on toast and drank tea while James's bath ran.

The soap made his cuts sting, but the hot water soothed his pains and it was nice feeling clean again. Joanna opened the bathroom door and tossed in a clean T-shirt and an old set of her brother's boxers. She cracked up when she saw James in the huge pair of shorts and a Puma T-shirt almost down to his knees.

Joanna took him into her room.

"Lie on my bed."

She peeled off all James's soggy plasters, wiped his cuts with disinfectant, and stuck on new ones. James stared at Joanna's long hair and the curve of her back as she leant over him. She looked beautiful.

James wanted to kiss her again, but Joanna was a year older and she'd mentioned a couple of previous boyfriends. He felt like he was in way over his head.

CHAPTER 34

SICKIE

It was cold, spitting with rain. Every step back to Fort Harmony was agony for James's battered legs. He was facing an evening sitting around in a cold hut with no TV. Then he had to spend the night on a crappy mattress listening to Amy snore. Tomorrow he'd probably get beaten up at school.

But James was in the best mood: ninety minutes lying on Joanna's bed kissing and moaning about their lives. She put on a Red Hot Chili Peppers CD and they sang all the words out loud. Every time James thought about Joanna, he got such a rush nothing else mattered. When he got back to the hut, Cathy and Amy were out. He was too excited to eat. James crashed on to his bed and daydreamed about Joanna.

• • •

"Are you deaf?" Sebastian shouted, a few centimeters from the end of James's bed. "I knocked four times. Fire's got our radio-controlled cars running. Want to try them?"

James turned over. He didn't want to get up, but it was part of his mission.

James had had a radio-controlled car before his mum died. It was good fun, but it wasn't safe using it around his flats. Someone would have stolen or smashed it in five minutes. Sebastian's and Clark's cars were superb. They were beach buggies with big rear tires that sprayed up mud. Instead of batteries there were tiny petrol engines between the rear wheels. Clark stopped his car in front of James and handed him the radio control.

"Gently," Clark said.

"I've driven a car before," James said, as if Clark was stupid.

James put the car full on forward. The engine buzzed noisily and a blue plume shot out of the exhaust. It didn't move a millimeter. The wheels dug into the mud.

"Gently, dingus," Clark said.

Sebastian lifted the car. James lightly nudged the stick and the car blasted off at about fifty kilometers an hour.

James laughed out, "Cool."

He drove a big circle, nearly crashing into some trees, running under the Land Cruiser, and almost rolling the car on its side as he did a sharp turn to bring the car back near to his feet.

"That was excellent," James said. "So fast. Where did you get them?"

"Fire and World made them when they were teenagers," Clark said. "Only thing is they're always going wrong and Fire never wants to fix them for us. He's got about six more cars in his workshop."

"Can I see them?"

"Won't let us in there any more."

The workshop sounded interesting, but James didn't want to seem pushy about finding more out.

"What do they do there?" he asked.

"Dunno," Sebastian said. "Trying to take over the universe, knowing those two."

"Anyway, I heard you got battered at school today," Clark said.

"Yeah," James said.

"Didn't grass, did you?"

"No way."

"Me and Sebastian used to get beaten up all the time because we're from Fort Harmony. It's not so bad now; we're two of the biggest in our school."

"We're the kings," Sebastian said. "There's a guy in my class so scared of us we click our fingers and he licks our trainers. Don't have to hit him or nothing."

"You start at Gwen Morgan in September?" James asked.

"Both of us do," Clark said. "There's only a ten-month age gap between us."

"At least you can back each other up."

"We've been suspended for fighting three times," Clark said. "Next time we get expelled, but I'd rather be expelled than let people dump on us."

"What do your mum and dad say?"

"Never met our dad. Our mum knows the score. All the boys who live at Fort Harmony get bullied by the normal kids."

"What did you think of us at first?" Sebastian asked.

James laughed. "Not much. You weren't exactly friendly."

"If you got treated like you were today, every single day since you were five years old, you wouldn't be friendly either."

"What should I do?" James asked.

"You were right not to grass," Clark said. "If you're a snitch, the whole school will be against you. Never give in. Never grovel or beg; it only encourages them. For a tough kid like you, Ross, best thing to do is get one of the leaders on his own and massacre him."

"They'll kill me if I do that," James said.

"There's a big choice of targets," Clark said. "A gang will think twice before picking on a kid who can get them back when they're on their own."

"I don't want to get into trouble," James said. "I got expelled from my last school."

Sebastian laughed. "Better get used to having someone standing on your nuts then."

After eating in the main hut, James lay on his bed again. Amy was furious when she got out of work and saw the state he was in.

"I'll go down to that school and kick their butts myself!" Amy screamed. "Nobody does that to my baby brother!"

"I can handle it," James said.

"You *can't* handle it. Why didn't you tell the school who did it?"

"I'm not a grass," James said. "Grasses are lower than kids who wet their pants."

"I think you should go to a hospital; you might have concussion," Amy said.

"I can't have concussion. I didn't get kicked in the head," James lied. "Can we talk about something more important?"

"What's more important than you coming home looking like a bus ran over you?"

"Have you seen Fire and World's workshop?" James asked.

"I've seen their hut. You certainly couldn't call it a workshop."

"Sebastian said they've got a workshop. Him and Clark aren't allowed in it any more. Sounds like the sort of place we should be checking out."

"Did you ask where it was?"

"No, I'll try and find out."

"I'll see if I can wangle something out of Scargill," Amy said. "I bet it's one of those huts that looks like it's been abandoned."

James sat in the Land Cruiser and phoned his daily report to Ewart. He left out how much of a crush he had on Joanna.

"Does it matter if I get in trouble at school?" James asked.

"Like how?" Ewart asked.

"If I get suspended. I figured it might even be good for the mission because I'd get to spend more time snooping around here."

Ewart laughed. "And by lucky coincidence you get out of school for a few days."

"That hadn't even crossed my mind," James said, but gave himself away by laughing.

"I suppose it wouldn't be much of a problem. But you're not above the law just because you're on a mission, so don't go burning down the school or anything."

7 a.m. Tuesday, James's travel alarm went off for school. He turned it off and pulled the covers over his head.

"You'll miss the bus if you don't get a move on," Amy said.

"Not going," James said. "My back's stiff. I can hardly move."

"You were shooting stuff with Sebastian and Clark until nearly midnight. You seemed all right then."

"Must have tightened up in the night," James said.

Amy laughed. "Pull the other one. It's got bells on."

James lay in until ten, deliberately staying under the covers until after Amy got up for work. Cathy was in a good mood. She sent James out to collect eggs from the chicken coop and made omelettes with mushrooms and bacon.

James read the first few chapters of *No Logo,* in case Bungle asked him any questions about it, then went for a walk. Joshua Dunn was in the main hut preparing a mountain of vegetables. Gladys Dunn was there as well, reading the morning paper.

"Can I look at the sports?" James asked.

She handed him the paper.

"Rough time at school, I hear," Gladys said.

"Yeah."

"Not a good place for young boys here," Gladys said. "All my grandsons are a funny lot. Get bullied at school. Take it out on the local wildlife or hide inside books."

James smiled. "They're not so bad."

"You've brought it home to me, Ross. One day and you're beaten up. You don't even look or dress like the other kids here. Boys are so cruel."

"What can you do?" James asked.

"We had a school here once. Parents took it in turns to teach the kids. All turned into squabbling about who taught the lessons."

"Everyone here has been really nice to me," James said. "But I don't understand why people want to live here."

Gladys wagged her finger. "You put your finger on a question I've been asking myself lately. At first Fort Harmony was about freedom and some young people having fun. When the police tried to destroy us, we sent out a signal that a bunch of nobodies could stand up against the government and win. But what are we now? A trendy campsite for backpackers. Half the people who live here clean and cook for rich businessmen in that bloody conference center."

James was a bit stunned. "So why stay?"

"Can you keep a secret, Ross?" Gladys asked.

"I guess."

"My second book comes out in September. It should earn me enough to buy a house somewhere warm. I'll take Joshua. The others can fight over Fort Harmony."

"I read your first book," James said. "It was interesting."

Gladys looked surprised. "I didn't have you pegged for a bookworm, Ross."

James kicked himself for revealing that he'd read the book. Twenty-year-old memoirs of life on a commune aren't exactly standard reading for twelve-year-old boys.

"Cathy had a copy," James stuttered, wondering if she actually did. "And there's no TV here."

"Thank goodness," Gladys smiled.

"I liked the bit where you were all hiding from police in the tunnels and you were trying to keep the kids quiet. Must have been scary."

"I should never have taken my boys underground. Joshua was the brightest one. Now he's happy spending four hours a day peeling vegetables."

"I suppose the tunnels are all gone," James said.

"There's bits and pieces left. I wouldn't try playing in them, Ross, not very safe."

"Don't worry, I wouldn't go into them. It's just that I've not seen any sign of them."

"That's because the camp has moved. We started off at the bottom of the hill down by the road. The main hut was under a meter of water sometimes, so we moved up here where the water drains away."

James stuck his head round the door of Bungle's hut. He was sitting around drinking coffee with Fire, World, and Scargill. Gregory was racing Matchbox cars over his parents' bed.

"I just came to say hello," James said. "I'll go away if you're busy."

Bungle laughed. "You're too polite, Ross. Sit down. You want coffee or tea?"

"Tea," James said.

James sat on the floor. He assumed Bungle and the Dunns would be having some deep political conversation, but they were debating who was sexier out of Julia Roberts and Jennifer Lopez. Gregory got a picture book and sat on James's leg.

"Trains," Gregory said.

James opened the book on Gregory's lap. Gregory told him what color all the trains in the book were and James pretended to be impressed. Bungle passed out jam rings and Gregory thought it was great dipping his biscuit in James's mug, especially when the end dropped off into the tea.

"I'm taking these guys into town and picking up Eleanor from the village," Bungle said. "Can you keep an eye on Gregory for an hour?"

"No worries," James said.

"If you have any probs, there's a mobile phone on the table, and there are plenty of adults around. I'm on the speed dial."

James was well pleased. Now he could get photos of Bungle's hut and have a rummage around. It made his decision not to go to school look like a masterstroke.

CHAPTER 95

PAST

James left Fort Harmony after lunch. He ran a couple of kilometers, checked nobody was around, and waited for Ewart. Ewart drove up in a BMW. He'd taken all his earrings out and was dressed like a businessman in a pin-striped suit and tie.

"Nice threads," James laughed.

"Got to blend in at Green Brooke."

Ewart drove a few kilometers and parked in a farm access road.

"So, what did you get?" Ewart asked.

James handed over the memory card from his digital camera and some screwed-up pieces of notepaper.

"Plenty of pictures there," James said. "Everything in

Bungle's room, on the bookshelves, close-ups of stuff like his address book. I've written a list of all the numbers stored in his mobile, plus there's his bank account and passport details."

"Good job, James. Look at this."

Ewart handed James a folder with an FBI crest on the front. James opened it and saw a black-and-white picture of Bungle, looking about ten years younger with long hair.

"That's him," James said.

James flipped to the next page. It was a standard FBI record. James had seen a few when he was preparing for the mission. Bungle's rap sheet only had three typed lines:

Student at Stamford, M.A. Roommate of known felon Jake Gladwell.
Questioned. Released. 6.18.1994
Traffic violation Austin, TX 12.23.1998

"Not very exciting," James said.

"That's what I thought," Ewart said. "Then I had a little look into Jake Gladwell. He's doing eighty years in San Antonio Prison, Texas."

"What for?"

"Trying to blow up the governor at a charity fund-raiser. The bomb was found before the event and defused. Police caught Gladwell on the night of the fund-raiser. He was outside the hotel with a radio control under his jacket. Know what the former governor of Texas is up to these days?"

"What?" James asked.

"George Walker Bush. President. And you know what else? There were eight big cheeses from the Texas oil industry sitting around Bushy when that bomb was supposed to go off."

"Bungle was hanging around with Fire and World today," James said.

"I found the connection between Fire, World, and Bungle. Fire and World did two years at York University before they went to prison. York has a teacher exchange program with Stamford University in America. Bungle was a guest professor at York. He taught Fire and World microbiology for two terms before he quit his job and moved to Fort Harmony."

"So we're sure they're part of Help Earth?" James asked.

"We can't prove squat. We always thought Bungle, Fire, and World were involved. Now we've found out Bungle's background, I'd bet my life savings, but there's still no hard evidence. All we can do is keep working and hope you or Amy get a lead before a bomb goes off."

Ewart reached around to the back seat and handed James a small box of fancy chocolates.

"Give them to Joanna, they're her favorites."

James was freaked out.

"What are you on about? I only went round to her house for a bath."

Ewart laughed. "That's not what I heard. What about all the smoochies?"

"Are you having me watched?" James asked.

"No."

"So how do you know we kissed?"

"MI5 is monitoring all the Internet use around here. They send me a briefing if anything interesting crops up. About eight o'clock last night Joanna logged into a chatroom. Spoke about a new boyfriend called Ross. Says he's a total hunk. Got really cute blond hair. Can't wait to see him at the bus stop in the morning."

"I wish I'd gone to school now," James said. "What about the chocolates?"

"I hacked her user profile on the Web site. She likes Thornton's handmade chocolates, rock music, blond-haired boys, and her ambition is to ride a Harley Davidson across America."

"Can you drop me near the village so I can give them to her when she gets off the bus?"

Joanna hugged him when he gave her the chocolates. They went back to the cottage, drank cocoa, slagged off all the bands on MTV Hits, and chased around tickling and throwing sofa cushions at each other. James stayed until her dad got in from work, then sneaked out the back door and walked to Fort Harmony with an ear-to-ear grin.

James was starting to understand all those terrible romantic films his mum used to watch where the leading man ends up in a state over some woman. He lay awake half the night thinking about Joanna. He realized when the mission ended he'd have to go back to CHERUB and never see her again.

He got up extra early and waited for her at the bus stop.

• • •

Everyone looked at James when he got to class. Stuart and Gareth dropped snide comments all morning.

"After school it's round two," Stuart said, as James stood in the line to get lunch.

The last thing James wanted was to miss the bus and lose time with Joanna.

"What about right here, right now?" James said. "Without all your pals backing you up?"

"If you want to start it, hippy boy, we'll finish it."

The kids standing around them in the queue were excited about a punch-up. Normally James wouldn't start a fight where everyone could see, but he was trying to get suspended so it didn't matter. James waited while the queue shuffled forward.

"Chickened out, did you?" Gareth asked.

James flicked Gareth off. He was waiting until they were level with the baked beans. When they got there, he hit Gareth in the stomach, grabbed him behind the neck, and dipped his face in the beans. Gareth screamed, hot orange sauce burning his face. Stuart whacked James over the head with his lunch tray. James doubled Stuart up with an elbow and followed with some punches that took him down. Gareth was blind, screaming, and wiping his face with his sweatshirt. James battered Stuart until he got dragged off by a couple of teachers. Two hundred sets of eyes were on James as the teachers dragged him off, kicking and shouting.

Joanna thought James getting suspended was superb. James was lying face down on her bed after a bath. Joanna rubbed his wet hair with a towel.

"You're so bad," Joanna purred. "And you don't even care."

She threw the towel on the floor and kissed the back of James's neck.

"We'll run away to Scotland and get married when we're sixteen," Joanna said. "Then we'll go all over the country robbing banks. We'll live big with all the money we steal. Flash restaurants, big sports cars."

"You've put a lot of thought into this," James said, grinning. "I've only known you for a week."

"Then you'll get shot by the police in a robbery."

"You're so full of shit." James giggled.

"Don't worry, Ross. You'll recover, but you'll have to do five hard years in prison. You'll kiss my photo every day. I'll go to America and ride a Harley Davidson across the country. When you get out, you'll be all beefy from lifting weights, and have tattoos all over you. When the prison gates open, I'll be waiting on my Harley. We'll kiss. You'll climb on the back and we'll ride off into the sunset."

"I'm not so sure about getting shot and going to prison," James said. "Why can't *you* get shot and I'll ride the Harley across America?"

"You want me to be all muscled and covered with tattoos?" Joanna asked.

James rolled over and kissed Joanna on the cheek.

CHAPTER 96

mess

"Ring Ewart," Amy said when James got back to the hut. "He's pissed at you."

James went out to the Land Cruiser and made the call.

"Hello, James, nice time with your girlfriend?" Ewart asked bitterly.

"What did I do?" James asked.

"Your headmistress blew her stack over your antics in the canteen. She rang one of your supposed old schools; luckily she got the number from the fake file and the call went through to CHERUB, but if she'd got the school's real number and they'd told her they'd never heard of you, it would have made a right mess."

"Is the headmistress really mad?" James asked.

"I called her back pretending to be one of your old teachers and I think I smoothed things over. I said you were mischievous but basically harmless."

"You said I was allowed to get suspended."

"Yes," Ewart said. "But I didn't expect you to dunk a kid's head in a vat of baked beans. He's apparently got a nasty burn on his nose."

"Sorry," James said, trying not to laugh.

"Sorry solves nothing!" Ewart shouted. "What time did you get back to Fort Harmony?"

"Just now. About half seven."

"Have you seen Clark and Sebastian today?"

"No."

"Why not?"

"You know why. I was with Joanna."

"The mission is about Sebastian and Clark, not your little girlfriend. I've told Cathy to ground you for getting suspended from school. You can't leave Fort Harmony for a week."

"But what about Joanna?" James asked.

"Tough," Ewart said. "Focus on your mission. You mess up like this again and I'll have you back at CHERUB scrubbing toilets on your hands and knees."

"I've got to see Joanna, please," James begged.

"Don't wind me up, James, I'm in no mood. There's two things for you to keep an eye out for. In your photos of Bungle's shack there's a white folder with an RKM logo on the side. It's on the bottom of the bookshelf under the window. Try and get a look at it. It looks like a computer manual, but Bungle doesn't have a computer. It might give us a clue what they're up to. Second, look out for a red van. Amy spotted Fire and World getting out of it, but couldn't get the whole number plate. Got all that?"

"Yes, Ewart," James said miserably.

"Start using your brain, James."

James heard the line go dead. He punched the dashboard, ran back to his bed, and yelled into his pillow.

"What happened?" Amy asked.

"Leave me alone," James said.

"It can't be so bad, Ross. You got out of school."

"He said I can't go down to the village and see Joanna."

"You know we'll only be here for a few weeks," Amy said. "I wouldn't get too fond of her."

James got off his bed, put his boots on, and walked out into the dark.

He lay in the long grass down the bottom of the hill and didn't care that his clothes got soaked. He thought about sneaking down to the village to see Joanna, but he wasn't brave enough to mess with Ewart. If Ewart sent him back to campus in disgrace, he'd never get another decent mission.

James wanted to go back to the hut, but Amy would be there with a lecture waiting. He thought about finding Sebastian and Clark, but he didn't want to spend all night shooting the local wildlife. So he stayed where he was, sulking.

James heard an animal or something running through the grass around him. He looked up and saw it was two radio-controlled cars. Electric ones. The only noise was rustling as they brushed the grass. He spotted the chrome radio control aerials reflecting moonlight. World and Scargill had them. After a couple of quick circuits they picked the cars up, pulled up their sweatshirt hoods, and jogged away.

James decided it was too risky to follow. He crawled through the mud towards where Scargill and World had been standing and almost fell into a hole. It was one of the old tunnels. James grabbed his mobile and called Amy.

"Where are you?" Amy asked.

"Down near the road. Something weird is going on."

James explained everything.

"The tunnel has a door with a padlock on it," James said. "I don't have my lock gun."

"I'll be five minutes," Amy said. "Do nothing. If they come back, say you were just exploring."

Amy ran down to James, keeping herself low to the ground. She shone a torch into the hole and quickly shut it off again.

"They could be back any minute," Amy said. "You any good with the lock gun?"

"OK," James said.

"Got your camera?"

"Yes."

"Go have a look," Amy said. "Take as many pictures as you can and get out fast."

"Will you keep lookout?" James asked.

"No. If they catch you, say the lock was left off and you just walked inside. Me sitting out here looks suspicious. I'll keep back unless something starts getting heavy."

James took Amy's torch and lock gun and dropped into the hole. There was a deep puddle in the bottom.

The padlock was easy. Inside was three meters of wood-lined tunnel with a low room at the end. James crawled down and started taking pictures. There wasn't much to see. Shelves of radio-controlled cars and spares, and a workbench with an orange plastic tub underneath. James opened every drawer and took pictures inside.

James turned to leave, half convinced someone would be behind him. Nobody was. He scrambled back down the tunnel, shut the padlock, and ran uphill to Amy.

"Sweet," Amy said. "See anything?"

"Toy cars and junk. Hard to see with the torch."

"The flash on the camera will pick up more than you saw in the dark," Amy said. "Maybe something will turn up on the photos."

"There must be stuff worth hiding in there," James said. "Otherwise they wouldn't bother keeping it secret."

"I'm gonna stick around and see if they come back," Amy said. "You go up to the hut and ring Ewart. Arrange to meet him somewhere. He'll want to look at the pictures straight away."

After he'd met Ewart, James went back to the hut and fell asleep. He got the best sleep he'd had in ages, without Amy there snoring.

Amy shook James awake at 2 a.m. She looked happy.

"It's all going down, James. Fire came to the workshop. You were nearly caught, only missed him by about three minutes. He took a big backpack of stuff out and walked off. I followed him up the hill to Green Brooke. You'll never guess what the radio-controlled cars are for."

"What?" James asked.

"They have a storage tray. They load them up with stuff and push them through a tiny gap in the security fence around Green Brooke. They drive the cars inside the fence and drop the cargo at the back of the conference hall. The cars are too small and fast to get detected by the security cameras and alarms."

"Couldn't they book a room and bring the stuff into the hotel?" James asked.

"Every guest brings luggage into Green Brooke hotel," Amy said. "But the conference hall is under police guard until Petrocon starts. Everyone gets searched on the way in. There's X-ray machines. All your bags get turned out, they pat you down, and go in your pockets."

"So," James said, "they're smuggling a bomb into the conference hall, bit by bit, on the back of radio-controlled cars. There must be someone working on the inside screwing all the pieces together."

"Must be. I spoke to Ewart. They're sending people down to look at the stuff the cars dropped, but they won't take it away. They want to see who comes and picks it up."

James laughed. "They're gonna lock those guys up and throw away the key."

"Poor Scargill," Amy said.

"You don't actually *like* that freak, do you?" James asked.

Amy shrugged. "I feel sorry for him. He's just a lonely kid trying to impress his big brothers. The tough guys in prison will eat him for breakfast."

"You *do* like him," James laughed. "He's the world's biggest nerd."

"You're such a twelve-year-old sometimes, James," Amy said. "You've never even had a conversation with Scargill. There's more to a guy than looking good and having big muscles."

"Marry him and get it over with," James said. "So what happens next?"

"Nothing changes. We keep our ears to the ground and see what comes up. Ewart wants you to concentrate on Bungle and Eleanor. We know they're involved, but there's still no proof."

CHAPTER 97

BUG

Amy shook James awake. It was still dark.

"Get dressed now," Amy snapped. "I just had Ewart on the phone. He's coming to get us."

James rubbed his eyes. Amy was on one leg, stepping into a pair of ripped jeans.

"What's going on?"

"I have no idea," Amy said. "Ewart said our lives are in danger if we don't get out fast."

James put on jeans and trainers. He grabbed his jacket and dashed after Amy. Cathy woke up and asked what was going on. She didn't get an answer. They ran to the bottom of the hill where the BMW was waiting.

"Both of you in the back," Ewart said.

The tires squealed. Ewart was in a major hurry about something. He threw some medical supplies at Amy.

"Give James four tablets and two shots in the arm. You OK with injections, Amy?"

"In theory," Amy said.

Branches lashed the side of the car as it sped down an unlit country lane.

"What's wrong with me?" James asked nervously.

"Get your coat off," Amy said.

She squeezed four pills out of their blisters and handed them to James. James looked at the box. It was an antibiotic called Ciprofloxacin.

"I need water to swallow them," James said.

"None here," Ewart said. "Forgot. Ball up some spit. The faster they're in your system the better."

James's mouth was dry from running. It took a while to get the tablets down.

"I can't hold the needle still while the car's moving," Amy said.

Ewart stamped the brakes and pulled into the side of the lane. Amy roughly stabbed James with the first needle. It hurt like hell.

"Have you ever done that before?" James asked.

Amy didn't answer and punched him with the second jab. Ewart hit the accelerator.

"Will you tell me what the hell is going on?" James shouted.

"It wasn't a bomb they were building," Ewart said. "It was a bioweapon. The radio-controlled cars were carrying cylinders of bacteria."

"Oh, God," Amy said. "It's obvious now you say it.

Bungle was a microbiology professor. Fire and World studied biology at university. They'd know all about that stuff."

"It all fell into place at once," Ewart said. "The best way to spread a disease through a large building is the air-conditioning. I checked out the van Amy saw. It belongs to a man who services the air-conditioning at Green Brooke. Then there was the folder with the RKM logo in Bungle's hut. I thought it was a computer manual, but RKM also makes air conditioners."

"What is it?" Amy asked.

"The police haven't analyzed the cylinders," Ewart said. "But anthrax is most likely."

"Jesus," Amy said.

"I don't understand half what you two are on about," James said. "Can one of you speak to me in English?"

"Do you know what anthrax is, James?" Ewart asked.

"No idea, but I'm guessing it's not good and you think I've got it."

"Anthrax is a unique disease. Most diseases can only survive outside your body for about eight minutes," Ewart explained. "Anthrax can survive in almost any temperature for up to sixty years. That makes it easy to store and use as a weapon. A cupful of anthrax spores in the air could kill hundreds of people."

"How did I get it?" James asked.

"You might not have it," Ewart said. "The antibiotics are a precaution. Remember the bright orange box under the bench in the underground workshop?"

"Yeah," James said.

"It's a sealed disposal unit for toxic waste. You're

supposed to incinerate it in a two-thousand-degree furnace."

"I pulled the lid off and stuck my hand inside," James said.

"Unfortunately you did," Ewart said. "I've got a picture you took of the contents. Gave me a heart attack when I saw it. Looks like the gloves and face masks they used when they were handling the anthrax bacteria ended up in there."

"Could I die?" James asked.

"I've got to be honest, James. If you breathed the bacteria, you're in trouble. Even with the antibiotics we've given you, there's a fifty percent death rate."

"Could I have given it to Amy or anyone?" James asked.

"It's possible some bacteria stuck on your fingers, but the disease is only serious if you breathe thousands of spores. They'll check out Amy at the hospital to be safe."

"If I die," James asked, "how long will it take?"

"It starts off like the flu about a day after the infection. Most people die within nine days."

"What hospital are we driving to?" Amy asked.

"There's a military hospital near Bristol, about seventy kilometers away," Ewart said. "They've got a doctor flying in from Manchester. He knows as much about anthrax as anyone on the planet."

Four nurses in army uniform grabbed James out of the car and stuck him on a trolley, even though he could walk. They burst through doors. Lights on the ceiling whizzed by. James spotted Meryl Spencer and Mac running behind the trolley. They had flown from CHERUB by helicopter.

The nurses wheeled James into a huge ward. There were thirty beds in three rows, all empty. A male nurse pulled James's trainers and socks off, then grabbed his jeans and boxers down in one. James was embarrassed because Amy, Ewart, Meryl, and everyone were standing around watching. Once James was naked, they lifted him on to a bed.

"Hello, James. I'm Doctor Coen."

The doctor looked like he'd been dragged out of bed. He wore Nikes, jogging bottoms, and a shirt with the buttons done up in the wrong holes.

"Has the disease been explained to you?" the doctor asked.

"Mostly," James said. "Do I need thirty people standing around looking at me naked?"

Dr. Coen smiled. "You heard the patient."

Everyone but three nurses and a couple of doctors headed out. Dr. Coen continued:

"First we need to take blood samples and see if you've been infected with anthrax. However, if you have the disease, your chances of survival decrease with every minute treatment is delayed, so we're going to assume the worst and begin treatment now. A nurse will fix a tube into your arm. We're going to pump you with a mixture of strong antibiotics and other drugs. Some of the drugs are toxic. Your body will react violently. You can expect vomiting and fever."

Amy and Meryl stayed by James's bed. He started feeling weak and shaky a couple of hours after treatment started.

His face went pale and he asked for something to throw up in.

Amy went outside looking upset. Meryl gripped his hand.

It got worse in the hours that followed. James's stomach and rib cage felt like they were tearing apart. The tiniest movement, even a deep breath or a cough, made his vision blur and a wave of nausea shoot up from his stomach. The two army nurses wiped up every time he got sick. When he got really bad, they injected him with anti-vomiting drugs.

The wait for test results was unbearable. James wanted to pass out or fall asleep. He watched the door, silently praying for Dr. Coen to come back with good news. James wondered if this room might be the last thing he ever saw.

Doctor Coen didn't come back until 8 a.m. on Thursday.

"It's bad," Dr. Coen said. "We just got the results from your tests. We'll keep giving you the drugs."

CHAPTER 86

DEATH

James woke up. He'd been in the hospital thirty hours. A drip ran up his nose and down into his stomach. Meryl had stayed the whole time.

"How do you feel?" Meryl asked.

"Weak," James croaked; the tube down his throat made it hard to speak.

"The doctor says the level of bacteria in your system is going down. The antibiotics are working."

"What are my chances?" James asked.

"Dr. Coen said over eighty percent because the treatment started so early."

"I feel so rough I wish I was dead."

"Lauren's here," Meryl said.

"Is she OK?"

Meryl shrugged. "Pretty shook up. She waited all day for you to come around. She's sleeping upstairs."

"Me dying, after Mum and that," James said. "She'll be in a right state."

Meryl stroked the back of James's hand.

"You won't die," she said. "Fort Harmony has been in all the papers. Headline news."

Meryl handed James a *Daily Mirror*. He could see the giant headline, but his vision was too blurry to read the text.

"Read it to me," James said.

FORT TERROR
Britain's oldest hippy commune, Fort Harmony near Cardiff, was rocked in a stunning raid by anti-terrorist police yesterday.

Three grandsons of the cult writer Gladys Dunn were arrested after anthrax bacteria was found at the nearby Green Brooke Conference Center.

Twins, Fire and World Dunn, 22, and their brother, Scargill Dunn, 17, were arrested early yesterday morning.

Also in custody are Kieran Pym, an air-conditioning engineer, and Eleanor Evans.

Police are seeking a sixth suspect, Brian "Bungle" Evans. Police believe he is the ring-leader and a founder member of the terrorist group Help Earth.

Police also discovered an underground bunker where the deadly cargo was stored before being smuggled into a secure area at Green Brooke. The bunker was not equipped to manufacture the bacteria.

A nationwide search has been launched for the hi-tech laboratory where the killer bug was bred.

It is believed the terrorists were targeting the upcoming Petrocon conference at Green Brooke. If anthrax had been successfully used during the conference, most of the 200 oil industry delegates would have been killed, alongside more than fifty Green Brooke staff and bodyguards.

MORE ON PAGES 2, 3, 4 & 11
LOTTERY PAGE 6

"It's the main story on TV," Meryl said. "Bungle's picture was on the cover of every paper. There's all kinds of rumors about where he's gone."

"I feel sorry for their little boy," James said. "He's only three."

Mac came into the ward an hour later. Lauren was with him, dressed in pajamas. She jumped on the bed and gave James a hug. She looked like she'd just heard the funniest joke ever.

"There's nothing wrong with you," Lauren squealed. "Thanks for scaring me."

"What are you on about?" James asked.

"James," Mac said. "Have you spoken to Doctor Coen yet?"

James shook his head. "No."

"We just found out that the bacteria in your system is harmless," Mac said. "Scargill Dunn claimed they were using a weak strain of anthrax. They were only going to use the bad stuff on the day of the conference. A laboratory in London rechecked your blood sample and the anthrax inside you couldn't kill a flea."

James let out a big smile.

"I don't understand," he said. "What's the point of harmless anthrax?"

"Bungle only wanted to kill the Petrocon delegates," Mac said. "He made the first batch of anthrax with what's called an 'attentuated strain.' It's used in the anthrax vaccine. It makes you immune to the nasty variety. It's been in the air-conditioning at Green Brooke conference hall for weeks.

"Security guards, cleaners, catering staff, and anyone else who works regularly in the conference hall would be vaccinated by the time Petrocon started. On the first day of the conference a lethal strain of anthrax was going to be put in the air-conditioning, but only the conference guests would get the disease."

Dr. Coen stopped James's antibiotics. By Friday evening he felt much better. The drip was taken out and James managed to eat without feeling sick. By Saturday morning he was almost back to normal. Ewart drove up from Wales.

"Is Amy with you?" James asked.

"No, she's back at Fort Harmony, keeping her ear to the ground to see if any information comes through about Bungle. It's not very likely with all that's going on: There are about fifty cops camped out at the bottom of the hill and loads of huts have got police on the doorstep guarding evidence."

"How did Amy explain me disappearing?"

"You got into a fight with Amy in the night. Ran off. Stormed down the road and got run over by some lunatic driving a BMW. Amy lifted you into the car and the driver rushed you to hospital. You lost some blood and you've got a broken arm, but otherwise you're OK. They're keeping you in for observation."

"Good story," James said. "I should be allowed out today."

"After all you've been through this week, I'll understand if you want to go back to CHERUB and rest," Ewart said. "But I'd appreciate it if you could show your face at Fort Harmony for a few days. A week at most."

"Will I be allowed to see Joanna?" James asked.

"Why not?" Ewart grinned. "Keep hanging out with Sebastian and Clark. Some little tidbit of information might pop out, but mostly it's to cover Cathy. It would look suspicious if you disappeared on the morning before the arrests never to be seen again."

A nurse fitted James with a plaster cast on his fake broken arm. On the drive back to Wales James read all the latest stuff in the papers about the anthrax terrorists and the continuing hunt for the laboratory and Bungle. It was odd seeing the newspapers filled with stuff he knew about.

The stories made Bungle sound like a supervillain, but James could only remember a big friendly American who cared about workers' rights and the environment.

Cathy was waiting in the Land Cruiser fifteen kilometers outside Craddogh. James ran between the two cars and waved to Ewart as he drove off.

"Hello, Ross," Cathy said. "Fake broken arm?"

James nodded. "It itches exactly like a real broken arm."

As they got near the camp, a policewoman pulled the Land Cruiser over and asked Cathy where she was going. Cathy got waved on. She had to drive across country because the bottom of the hill near the underground workshop was sealed off by police.

The main hut was packed when James and Cathy arrived. The residents seemed edgy about all the police and media people hanging around. A few journalists and photographers were scrounging free stew. Amy hugged James when she saw him. James wanted to go down to the village and see Joanna, but it was already late and he didn't know if her dad was home.

Sebastian tapped James on the back.

"Hey, cripple," Clark said. "Feeling OK?"

"Not bad, a bit weak."

"You're lucky that driver didn't splatter you," Clark said.

"Would have been wicked getting up and seeing you mashed into the road," Sebastian laughed. "Got any scars?"

James pulled up the sleeve of his T-shirt and showed the mass of bruises and cuts where the antibiotics had been injected.

"Is that where the car hit you?" Clark asked.

James nodded.

"We were gonna ask you something the night you got run over," Clark said. "But we couldn't find you."

"Ask what?"

"If you wanted to sleep over in our hut."

"Cool," James said.

CHAPTER 90

FUNERAL

James couldn't decide if he liked Sebastian and Clark. They had a dark side, but that made them interesting to be around. They slept in a rusty panel van next to their mum's hut.

James thumped the metal. Clark slid the side door open.

"Get your butt in here!" Clark yelled.

James bent over to slip off his boots. It had become habit after a few days at Fort Harmony.

"Leave them on," Clark said. "The filth is what gives our van character."

James stepped inside. Two gas lamps pushed out gloomy orange light. His hair brushed the roof. Clark's mattress was below the cracked windscreen where the seats used to be. Sebastian lay at the other end, toying with a big hunting knife. The metal floor was wet and had grass poking up through rust holes. Everything was thrown about: dirty clothes, air guns, knives, shredded school books.

"Duck!" Sebastian shouted.

Sebastian flung his boot across the van. It skimmed past Clark and clanged on the side, leaving a muddy splat on the wall. The second boot hit James in the back.

James looked at the muck on his sweatshirt and smiled.

"You're so dead," he said.

He hurled the boot back, then dived on to Sebastian and squashed him under the cast on his arm.

"Bundle!" Clark shouted and jumped on the pair of them.

The three boys rumbled until they were all red-faced and out of breath. James was almost as dirty as Sebastian and Clark by the time they'd finished. Clark passed a bottle of water. James took a few gulps and tipped some over his head to cool off.

"Want to go out and do something?" Clark asked.

James shrugged. "Long as it doesn't involve killing stuff."

"You're such a girl," Clark said. "I want to go down the hill and shoot one of the cops up the arse with my air pistol."

Sebastian laughed. "That would be so cool. You haven't got the guts."

Clark picked his air pistol up off the floor, pumped it, and loaded a pellet.

"Want a bet?"

"Five quid," Sebastian said, holding out his hand for Clark to shake.

Clark thought about taking the bet, then started laughing.

"I knew you wouldn't," Sebastian said.

"I hate the cops," Clark said. "Fire and World were the best guys around here."

"I hope Mum lets us see them in prison this time," Sebastian said.

"It would have been superb if they'd pulled it off," Clark said. "We would have been related to two of the biggest murderers in British history, and by the time people started getting sick, Fire and World would have been gone. Nobody could have touched them."

"Two hundred dead though," James said. "They all would have had families and stuff."

"They were rich scum," Clark said. "With fat, ugly wives and spoiled kids. The world would have done fine without them."

"Ross, you should have heard some of the stuff Fire told us about all the evil shit the big oil companies do," Sebastian said. "This farmer in South America had an oil pipe burst over his land. His whole farm was trashed. So he goes to the oil company and asks them to clean up the mess. They beat him up. He complained to the police, but the police were getting bribes from the oil company. They stuck the farmer in a cell and didn't give him anything to drink until he signed a confession saying he blew up the pipe himself. Once he'd signed the confession, he got fifty years in prison. They only let him out when loads of environmentalists complained."

"That sounds fake," James said.

"Next time you go on the Internet look it up for yourself," Clark said. "There are tons of stories like that on there."

"Fire told us loads of babies in poor countries die because their drinking water gets poisoned by spilled oil," Sebastian said.

"Still, you can't go round killing people," James said.

"You say we're sick," Clark said. "So how sick are those guys going to Petrocon? They've all got millions, but they won't spend any of it to stop babies getting poisoned."

They decided it wasn't worth going out; you couldn't do much with all the police and journalists around. Clark rigged up a target box at one end of the van and they had a shooting competition with air guns. James had shot real guns in basic training and wasn't bad, even though he could only hold the gun with one hand. Sebastian and Clark were brilliant. Every pellet passed through the center of their paper targets. Afterwards the brothers showed off tricks. Clark managed to shoot between the eyes of the grinning kids on the cover of his maths textbook while holding the gun behind his back.

At midnight Clark and Sebastian's mum stuck her head in and told them to go to sleep. They rearranged the mess so there was room for James to lay out his sleeping bag and turned out the gas lamps. The boys talked in the dark, mostly about Fire and World. Sebastian and Clark knew tons of funny stories about things Fire and World did at school and in prison. They sounded cool. James almost felt bad about being one of the people who'd got them caught.

• • •

Somehow they ended up fighting again. Battering each other with pillows and throwing stuff around. The darkness made it more exciting because everyone could launch sneak attacks. James's sleeping bag got ripped open in a tug-of-war and the stuffing flew everywhere.

Clark fired his air pistol. Sebastian and James dived for cover. They couldn't tell if they were being shot at, or if Clark was only trying to scare them. Sebastian and Clark's mum came back. All three boys dived under their covers, giggling.

"It's one in the morning!" she shouted. "If I hear any more noise, I'm coming in there and you'll be sorry!"

Their mum must have been tough because after she threatened them, Sebastian and Clark straightened up their beds and said good night. James was sweaty, filthy, and his burst sleeping bag was on a metal floor, but he was so knackered after the last few days that he closed his eyes and was instantly asleep.

James first thought the banging was some prank by Sebastian and Clark. Clark lit his torch.

"What is that?" James asked.

Someone was thumping on the outside of the van.

"Open up in there. Police."

Clark shone the torch on the back of Sebastian's head.

Clark laughed. "Nothing wakes him up. I set a firework off next to his ear once and he didn't even budge."

Clark got out of bed wearing shorts and a T-shirt and unlocked the door. Two powerful torches pointed in his face. A policeman grabbed Clark out of the van and turned his torch on James.

"Boy," the policeman shouted to James, "get out of there now!"

James put his bottoms and boots on with his free arm and stepped out. Fort Harmony was ablaze with flashing blue lights and torch beams. Police in riot gear were dragging everyone out of their huts. Kids were crying. Residents and police shouted at each other.

The policemen knocked James against the van beside Clark.

"Anyone else in there?" one policeman shouted.

"My little brother," Clark said. "I'll go and wake him up."

"No you don't, I'll do it," the policeman said.

One policeman stepped into the van. James spoke to the other one.

"What's going on?"

"Court order," the policeman said. He pulled a piece of paper out of his pocket and read from it. "'By order of the High Court all residents of the community known as Fort Harmony shall leave within seven days. Dated Sixteenth September 1972.'"

"That's over thirty years ago," James said.

The policeman shrugged. "It took us a bit longer than expected."

The policeman inside the van screamed. He staggered out, holding his thigh. James spotted the glint of Sebastian's hunting knife sticking out of his leg. The other policeman shouted into his radio.

"Code one! Code one! Officer down. Serious injury."

About ten cops came swarming over. Two grabbed the cop with the knife in his leg and carried him off. Two slammed James and Clark hard into the side of the van and started searching them for weapons.

"Not those two, there's a kid in the van," a policeman said.

Clark shouted out, "I said I'd wake him up for you! He's scared of the dark so he sleeps with the knife beside him."

"Shut your hole before I shut it for you," a policeman said.

Six policemen surrounded the door of the van. Three of them had guns drawn.

"Get out here, now!" a sergeant shouted.

Sebastian shouted from inside, "Don't shoot me! Put the guns away."

"Put them down, he's only a kid," the sergeant said. "What's your name, son?"

"Sebastian."

"Sebastian, I want you to come slowly out of the van with your hands in the air. We know it was an accident. We won't hurt you."

Sebastian stepped into the torchlight. When he got near the door, the police grabbed him and slammed him into the mud. One cop put his boot on Sebastian's back and locked on handcuffs. He looked tiny compared to the policemen all bulked out by riot gear. They dragged Sebastian off to a police car.

"Let me go with him," Clark said.

A policeman slammed Clark against the van again.

"You don't learn, do you?" the policeman said.

Sebastian's mum was dragged out of her hut and put in the police car with her son.

"What about us?" James asked.

"We're taking everyone to the church hall in the village. There's a coach at the bottom of the hill," the sergeant said.

"I need to get my tracksuit and boots," Clark said.

"You can't go in there, it's a crime scene."

"I'm barefoot," Clark said. "It's freezing."

"I don't care if you've got to walk across broken glass!" the policeman shouted. "Get down to that coach or you'll have more than cold feet to worry about."

James and Clark walked off.

"I've got to find my sister and Auntie Cathy," James said.

Police were everywhere, over a hundred. A chain of residents was heading down the hill. Anyone who put up a fight found the riot cops weren't shy about pulling batons. James and Clark dodged into some trees and reemerged beside Cathy's hut. There was no sign of Amy, Cathy, or the Land Cruiser. They went into the hut. Amy and Cathy had taken most stuff with them.

"What you looking for?" Clark asked.

"My mobile," James said. "Looks like my sister took it with her. What shoe size are you?"

"Two."

James kicked a pair of his Nikes into the middle of the floor.

"Those are a three. You'll grow into them. Take whatever clothes you want."

"Cheers," Clark said.

Clark put on tracksuit bottoms and trainers. James found him a warm top with a hood.

"My sister's probably down at the village," James said. "Might as well get on the coach."

James and Clark sat next to each other on the coach. It gradually filled up with residents, all of them carrying what they could. Clark was trying to hide how upset he was from James, but couldn't hold himself together.

"He's only ten. They'll realize it was an accident," James said.

"Don't bet on it, Ross. The cops will switch their stories around so he gets done. Whose story are they going to believe? A couple of kids who are always in trouble, or the police?"

"I'll be a witness," James said.

"If Sebastian gets sent away, I'll stab a cop myself so I can stay with him."

CHAPTER 40

HALL

Craddogh Church Hall was a madhouse. Eighty people with no air to breathe. Kids ran around screaming. Journalists kept asking Gladys Dunn for quotes and pictures, but the old lady needed rest. Michael Dunn threw a punch and got dragged away by police in a blaze of camera flashes.

The residents wanted to go back to Fort Harmony to get their stuff, but police blocked the road and nobody got through. The police said everything was being collected and would arrive in a few hours.

Clark had turned into a basket case. Sobbing for his brother and mum and screaming to any nearby cop that he was going to kill him first chance he got. James tried to calm him down, without much success.

"You're the first kid who's ever been nice to us," Clark said to James.

James felt bad. Clark wasn't his real friend. He'd used him to help with the mission.

On TV you knew who the baddies were and they got what they deserved at the end of the show. Now James realized baddies were ordinary people. They told jokes, made you cups of coffee, went to the toilet, and had families who loved them.

James totted everyone up: Fire, World, and Bungle were obviously bad guys for trying to kill everyone with anthrax. The oil company people were also bad for trashing the environment and abusing people in poor countries. The police were bad guys; they had a tricky job to do, but they seemed to enjoy throwing their weight around more than they should. The only good guys were the Fort Harmony residents and they'd all got chucked out of their homes.

James couldn't figure out what he was himself. As far as he could tell, he'd stopped one small bunch of bad guys killing a big bunch of bad guys, and as a result the good guys got chucked out of their homes by another bunch of bad guys. Did that make him good or bad? James only knew that thinking about it gave him a headache.

James left Clark with his family and went outside. There was no sign of Amy or Cathy. James didn't have his mobile and the village phone box had about twenty people queuing up, trying to find somewhere to stay now

Fort Harmony was shut off. James realized he might be able to phone Amy or Ewart from Joanna's house. He was sure Joanna's dad would be on duty with all that was going on.

Joanna and her dad stood by their garden gate in night clothes, watching the arguments and blue lights in the center of the village.

"Hey," James said.

Joanna gave James a smile that made him feel better. James was still wary of Sergeant Ribble after he'd caught them in Cathy's hut, but he sounded OK.

"What's going on up there?" Sergeant Ribble asked.

"Everyone's been chucked out of Fort Harmony," James said. "How come you're not involved? You're a policeman."

"That lot don't give me the time of day. I'm just the local bobby," Sergeant Ribble said. "As soon as they found the anthrax, the anti-terrorist squad turned up and took everything off my hands."

"Can I use your phone?" James asked. "I've lost my aunt and my sister."

"Of course you can, son. Jojo will show you where the phone is."

James took off his boots and stepped into the house with Joanna. She was wearing slippers and a Daffy Duck nightie.

"Hi Jojo," James said, laughing.

"Shut up, Ross. Only my dad and big brothers call me that."

"I'll probably have to go back to London now," James said.

"Oh," Joanna said.

James was glad she sounded upset. It meant Joanna liked him as much as he liked Joanna. She showed him the phone. It took him a minute to remember Amy's mobile number.

"Courtney," James said. "Where are you?"

"Cathy went nuts," Amy said. "She thinks what happened tonight is her fault for letting us into Fort Harmony. She dumped me a few kilometers outside Craddogh with most of our stuff. Ewart's coming to fetch me. He should be here any minute."

"I'm at Joanna's house in the village," James said. "What should I do?"

"Stay where you are," Amy said. "I'll get Ewart to pick you up after me. If anyone asks questions, say Ewart's a minicab driver and Cathy has arranged for us to get the first train to London from Cardiff in the morning. We should be with you in half an hour."

"Are we going home?" James asked.

"Mission's over, James. With no Fort Harmony, there's no reason to stay."

James put the phone down and looked at Joanna.

"Minicab is on its way. I'm going back to my mum in London."

"Let's go to my room," Joanna said. "Good-bye kiss."

Joanna's dad was too busy watching outside to notice his daughter sneaking James into her bedroom. She didn't care that James was all muddy. She leaned against her bedroom door to stop her dad bursting in and they started kissing. Joanna was soft and hot to touch, her hair smelled like shampoo and her breath like toothpaste. It felt great, but James ached knowing they only had a few minutes and then he'd never see her again.

The door hit Joanna in the back.

"What are you two doing in there?" Sergeant Ribble said.

James and Joanna moved away from the door. Her dad came in. They probably could have made some excuse, if Joanna's nightdress hadn't been covered in James's muddy handprints.

"Joanna, you're thirteen years old!" her dad yelled.

"But Daddy we were just . . ."

"Put something clean on and go to bed. And you . . ."

Joanna's dad grabbed James by the back of his neck.

"Did you make your phone call?"

"Yes," James said, "There's a minicab coming for me."

"You can wait for it outside."

Joanna's dad shoved James out of the house and made him sit on the garden wall facing the road. James felt totally miserable. He was worried what would happen to Sebastian, he felt guilty that he and Amy finding out about the anthrax had led to Fort Harmony being destroyed, and worst of all the best girl he'd ever met was trapped in a house a few meters away and he'd never see her again.

James heard a window open behind him. He watched Joanna throw out a paper airplane. Her dad charged back into the house.

"I ordered you to bed, young lady."

James jumped into the garden and picked up the airplane. He realized there was something written on the paper and unraveled it.

Ross,
Please phone me. You're so cute.
Joanna
XXX

James folded up the paper, put it in his pocket and felt even sadder.

Ewart drove Amy and James back to Fort Harmony in the BMW.

"Why are they smashing it up?" James asked.

"I spoke to someone at the anti-terrorist squad," Ewart said. "They say Fort Harmony is a security risk. They wanted it wiped out before Petrocon started, and the law was on their side."

"I wish I'd never come here," James said. "It's our fault this has happened."

"I thought you hated Fort Harmony," Amy said.

"I didn't say I wanted to live there," James said. "Just, it's not fair kicking everyone out."

"Fort Harmony was doomed either way," Ewart said. "If Fire, World, and Bungle had killed all those people, they would have wiped the camp out after the conference instead of before. All you would have done is delayed the end by a month."

"Did you know it was going to happen, Ewart?" James asked.

"I wouldn't have sent you back for one night if I had."

"Where's Cathy gone?" James asked.

"She was upset," Amy said. "She said something about staying with friends in London."

"Cathy broke the deal," Ewart said. "She wasn't supposed to abandon Amy in the middle of nowhere. I want that money back when I catch up to her."

"Leave her alone," Amy said. "She's lived at Fort Harmony for thirty years and got in a bit of a state when all those cops showed up. She did a perfect job looking after us until tonight."

"A sixteen-year-old girl dumped in the middle of the countryside at night, with four bags of luggage," Ewart said. "Lucky your mobile had reception. You could have been picked up by some nutter and murdered."

"But I *wasn't*," Amy said sharply. "So leave Cathy alone. We got everything we wanted from her."

Ewart banged the steering wheel. "OK, Amy, if you say so. Cathy's come out of this with eight thousand quid and a car. It's better than she deserves after treating you like that."

Ewart slowed down at a police checkpoint. He showed an ID and they waved him through. The sun was coming up. Riot police were working their way across Fort Harmony. One crew emptied out the shelters, bagging up the contents and loading them into a truck. A follow-up team worked with chainsaws and sledgehammers, knocking the huts down and smashing the timber into small pieces so there was no way anything could be rebuilt.

Ewart, James, and Amy got out of the BMW. Ewart was wearing scruffy jeans and looked too young to be anyone important. A couple of policemen walked towards them.

"Get back in the car and drive on!" a policeman shouted.

Ewart ignored him and headed for Cathy's hut. James and Amy followed.

"You're asking for a day in the cells," the policeman said cockily.

The cop made a grab for Ewart. Ewart dodged him and pulled out his ID. The policeman looked a bit stunned.

"Um, what are you here for?"

"Sir," Ewart said.

"What?" the policeman said.

"Don't you call a senior officer 'sir'?"

"What can I do for you, *sir*?"

"Get me some plastic bags," Ewart said.

They walked across to Cathy's hut and started packing up. A chief inspector rushed over. She sounded apologetic.

"Sorry about the mix-up. We got a message not to touch this hut. Can I double-check your ID?"

Ewart handed it to her.

"I've never seen one of these before," she gushed. "Level-one clearance. The commissioner of the anti-terrorist unit only has level two. What are you doing here?"

Ewart snatched it back out of her hand.

"You should know better than to ask questions," Ewart said. "Take this down to my car."

Ewart dumped a bin-liner stuffed with clothes in the chief inspector's arms. James thought it was funny watching a senior policewoman carrying a bag of his dirty clothes down a muddy hill.

"I thought only Mac had level-one security clearance," Amy said.

Ewart shrugged. "That's right."

"So what did you show her?" Amy asked.

"A very good fake."

James laughed. "That's so cool."

They loaded all their stuff in the back of the car. James turned back for a last glance at Fort Harmony and took a couple of pictures of a tree with his digital camera.

"What's with the tree?" Amy asked, after they'd driven off.

"Not telling," James said. "You'll take the piss."

Amy wriggled her fingers in the air. "I'll tickle it out of you."

"OK," James said. "But promise not to laugh."

"I promise," Amy said.

"It's where I first kissed Joanna."

Amy smiled. "That is *so* sweet."

Ewart put his fingers in his mouth and pretended he was being sick.

"You promised," James said.

Ewart laughed. "Amy promised. I never said a word."

"I can't wait to tell Kerry all about your smooching with Joanna," Amy said.

"Oh God, don't . . . Please," James said.

"Why would you care what I told Kerry about you, unless you like her more than you're willing to admit?" Amy teased.

James wanted to storm off, but that was difficult in a car doing eighty kilometers an hour. He folded his arms and stared out the window, trying to hide how upset he was about not being able to see Joanna again.

CHAPTER 57

DARK

When they got back to CHERUB, Amy took James to the woodwork shop. She found an electric drill and fixed on a circular cutter. James gave the silver teeth a grim look.

"You're not cutting it off with that," James said. "You'll kill me."

"Stop being such a pansy. Put these on."

Amy threw James a set of protective goggles and fixed a pair on herself.

"Put your arm on the bench," Amy said.

"Have you ever done this before?"

Amy smiled. "No."

James rested his cast on the workbench. Amy gave the drill a couple of test spins, then set to work. Plaster shards pelted James's face and the white dust dried his mouth. James thought he felt the blade tickling the hairs on his arm, but hoped he was just imagining it.

Amy stopped the drill and cracked off most of the cast, leaving the part around the elbow.

"OK, last bit," Amy said.

Amy cut in at a different angle. When she was done, James pulled the last bit of plaster down his arm and went into a scratching frenzy.

"That feels so much better," James said. "OHHHHHH."

"Leave it alone, you'll tear all your skin off," Amy said.

"Don't care."

James took off the goggles and flicked white dust out of his hair.

"Go have a shower and take your clothes to the laundry," Amy said. "Mac will want to see you in his office when you're ready."

"Just me?" James asked.

"It's a standard thing," Amy said. "He does it with everyone after their first mission."

Mac was dressed in shorts and a T-shirt when James got to his office.

"Come in, James. How are you feeling?"

"Fine now," James said. "Bit tired."

"Ewart seemed to think you had some doubts about the value of your mission."

"It's confusing," James said.

"He said you didn't seem sure that we'd done the right thing," Mac said.

"I heard some stuff about the people going to Petrocon,"

James said. "They poison people and beat people up and stuff. I'm not even sure it's true."

"It's mostly true," Mac said. "Oil companies have a terrible environmental and human rights record. Without oil and gas, the world stops working. No airplanes, no ships, no cars, very little electricity. Because oil is so important, companies and governments bend rules to get it. Help Earth and a lot of other people, including me, think they go too far."

"So you support Help Earth?" James said.

"I want to stop people getting exploited and poisoned by oil companies. I don't agree that terrorism is the way to do it."

"I understand," James said. "Killing people never solves anything."

"Think about what would have happened if all those people got killed at Petrocon," Mac said. "Would Help Earth have attacked somewhere else? What if the anthrax got into the hands of another terrorist group? You'll never know for certain what would have happened if Fire and World Dunn weren't caught. The next attack could have been in the middle of a city. Stick some anthrax in a London Underground station and you'd be looking at five thousand dead people. That's how many lives you and Amy might have saved."

"Bungle's still on the loose though," James said.

"Can I trust you with some information?" Mac asked.

"What?" James said.

"You're the only person who knows besides Ewart and myself, so if this gets out, I'll know you leaked it."

"I swear," James said.

"MI5 knows where Bungle is," Mac said.

"So why don't you get him?"

"They're tracking him," Mac said. "Bungle won't tell us anything if we arrest him, but by letting him wander he might lead us to other members of Help Earth."

"What if you lose him?" James asked.

Mac laughed. "You always ask me the question I don't want to answer."

"Have they lost anyone before?" James asked.

"Yes," Mac said. "It won't happen this time. Bungle can't stick a finger up his nose without ten people knowing about it."

"It makes more sense now you've explained it," James said. "I still feel sorry for all the people who got chucked out of Fort Harmony. They're a weird lot, but basically they're OK."

"It's a shame," Mac said. "But a few families losing their homes is better than thousands of people getting killed.

"So I want to thank you for doing a brilliant job, James. You made friends with the right people, didn't break your cover, and polished off the mission in half the time we expected."

"Thanks," James said.

"I also owe you a massive apology," Mac said. "You nearly died. We had no idea Help Earth was planning an anthrax attack. If we'd known, we never would have sent someone as inexperienced as you on this mission."

"It's not your fault."

"You must have been frightened, but you handled yourself tremendously. You kept a level head and even agreed to return to the mission. I've decided to classify your overall performance as outstanding."

Mac pulled a navy CHERUB T-shirt out of his desk and threw it to James.

"Wow," James said, grinning. "When Kerry sees this, she's gonna be so pissed off."

"I'll pretend I didn't hear that," Mac said. "But if you use that sort of language in my office again, I'll make you a very unhappy boy."

"Sorry," James said. "Can I put it on?"

"Don't be modest on my account," Mac said.

James ripped off his Arsenal shirt and pulled the navy CHERUB T-shirt over his head.

The kids at CHERUB were allowed to sleep late and wear normal clothes on Sundays. It was still early and nobody was around. James ate breakfast alone in the dining room, with one eye on the television. There was a story about Fort Harmony being destroyed on News 24. They cut to a clip of Michael Dunn waving his fists in the air and vowing he would spend the rest of his life rebuilding Fort Harmony if that was what it took.

Kerry came down in shorts and a denim jacket. She gave James a hug.

"I was so happy you *finally* got a mission," Kerry said. "I got back from my third mission on Thursday."

James loved the way she couldn't resist mentioning it was her third mission. He wondered how long it would be before she noticed his navy shirt. Bruce came down and joined Kerry at the breakfast buffet.

"Good mission?" Bruce asked, as he put his tray on the table next to James.

James acted casual. "Mac seemed to think I did OK."

Kerry sat opposite James. She only had a bran muffin and a couple of bits of fruit.

"On a diet?" James asked.

"I'm trying to eat less greasy stuff," Kerry said.

"Good," James said. "You're starting to look a bit fat."

Bruce burst out laughing and spat half his bacon across the table. Kerry kicked James in the shin.

"Pig," Kerry said.

"That kick hurt," James said. "I was only joking."

"Did you see me laughing?" Kerry asked.

James got a punch in the back. "Stop being rude to Kerry," Lauren said. "You should ask her out now you're back. It is so obvious you two fancy each other."

James and Kerry blushed. Lauren got her breakfast and sat next to Kerry.

Callum and Connor sat at the next table a few minutes later. James hadn't seen them together since Callum restarted basic training.

"Which one of you is Callum?" James asked.

Callum raised a finger.

"You passed basic training now?" James asked.

"Got back from Malaysia on Tuesday," Callum said. "Slept for twenty hours solid."

"Bet you're glad that's out of the way," James said.

"You know that navy T-shirt you're wearing is a CHERUB shirt?" Callum said.

James was pleased someone had finally noticed.

"Yes," he said casually.

"You'd better take it off, James," Bruce said. "Kids work really hard to earn them. They'll kill you if they catch you wearing it."

"It's my shirt," James said. "I did earn it."

Kerry laughed. "Yeah, James, and I'm the queen of China."

"Don't believe me then," James said.

Bruce sounded a bit desperate. "I'm serious, James. People get angry when you wear a shirt without earning it. Take it off. They'll stuff your head down the toilet or something."

"I'd pay money to see him bog-washed," Lauren giggled. "Leave it on."

"I'm not taking it off," James said. "It's mine."

"You're such an idiot," Kerry said. "Don't say we didn't warn you when we're scraping you off the floor."

Amy came in. She had Arif and Paul with her. The three of them rushed over to James.

"Too late now," Bruce said. "You're dead."

James was worried. He wasn't sure if Amy knew Mac had awarded him the navy shirt. He stood up from the table and turned to face Amy. Paul and Arif looked intimidating, muscles everywhere.

Amy wrapped James in her arms.

"Congratulations," Amy said. "You really deserve that shirt. You were brilliant."

Amy let go. Paul and Arif shook James's hand.

"I can't believe you're that wimp we had to keep throwing in the diving pool," Arif said.

James looked back at his friends sitting around the table. They all looked amazed. Lauren jumped up and hugged her brother. Kerry's mouth was open so wide you could have shoved a tennis ball in without touching a tooth. James couldn't help smiling.

It was beautiful.

EPILOGUE

RONALD ONIONS (UNCLE RON) had had difficulty adjusting to life behind bars. He received two broken arms during a fight with a fellow inmate. He is scheduled to be released in 2012.

GLADYS DUNN used the money from her second book to buy a farm in Spain. She lives on the land with her son JOSHUA DUNN, who makes curry, stew, or paella every day for the thirty former Fort Harmony residents who joined them. Gladys jokingly refers to her farm as "Fort Harmony 2, but warmer and without the mud."

CATHY DUNN sold the Land Cruiser, purchased a round-the-world air ticket, and went backpacking in Australia.

SEBASTIAN DUNN was released from police custody without charge. The stabbing of the policeman was classified as an accident. The policeman returned to duty a few months later.

Sebastian now lives in a cottage in Craddogh with his mother and brother CLARK DUNN. Sebastian and Clark have denied links to a number of cats that have disappeared since their arrival in the village.

FIRE AND WORLD DUNN were tried and convicted at the Old Bailey in London. They were each sentenced to life in prison. The judge recommended they serve a minimum of twenty-five years.

As SCARGILL DUNN was only seventeen and had no previous criminal convictions, he was sentenced to only four years in a young offenders' prison. With early release for good behavior he could be out within two years. He has begun studying for A-level exams and hopes to go to university after he is released.

Police suspect ELEANOR EVANS is a member of Help Earth who helped to plan the anthrax attacks on Petrocon 2004. No evidence was found and she was released from custody without charge. She now lives in Brighton with her mother, her son GREGORY EVANS, and her newly born daughter, Tiffany.

BRIAN "BUNGLE" EVANS slipped MI5 surveillance after a few weeks. He is now one of the world's most wanted men. Police in Britain, the United States, France, and Venezuela all wish to question him about terrorist activity.

JOANNA RIBBLE was disappointed that Ross Leigh didn't write or call. She now has a new boyfriend. James kept her paper airplane and the photograph of the tree where they first kissed.

KYLE BLUEMAN returned from his eighteenth mission and finally got his navy CHERUB shirt. He was reportedly "upset" that James got his navy shirt before him. Kyle reckons James only got the navy shirt because Mac felt sorry for him when he got anthrax.

BRUCE NORRIS AND KERRY CHANG frequently remind James that although he earned a navy shirt, they have both done more missions than him and can easily kick his butt any time he starts to get cocky.

AMY COLLINS hopes to complete a couple more missions before she leaves CHERUB and goes to university.

LAUREN ADAMS (formerly LAUREN ONIONS) is enjoying life at CHERUB. She starts basic training shortly after her tenth birthday in September 2004.

JAMES ADAMS (formerly JAMES CHOKE) got his karate black belt shortly after returning from his mission. His exuberant celebrations ended badly and his punishment was one month cleaning up in the CHERUB kitchen every night after dinner.

He is currently preparing for his second mission.

CHERUB: A HISTORY (1941–1996)

1941 In the middle of the Second World War, Charles Henderson, a British agent working in occupied France, sent a report to his headquarters in London. It was full of praise for the way the French Resistance used children to sneak past Nazi checkpoints and wangle information out of German soldiers.

1942 Henderson formed a small undercover detachment of children, under the command of British Military Intelligence. Henderson's Boys were all thirteen or fourteen years old, mostly French refugees. They were given basic espionage training before being parachuted into occupied France. The boys gathered vital intelligence in the run-up to the D-Day invasions of 1944.

1946 Henderson's Boys disbanded at the end of the war. Most of them returned to France. Their existence has never been officially acknowledged.

Charles Henderson believed that children would make effective intelligence agents during peacetime. In May 1946, he was given permission to create CHERUB in a disused village school. The first twenty CHERUB recruits, all boys, lived in wooden huts at the back of the playground.

1951 For its first five years, CHERUB struggled along with limited resources. Its fortunes changed following its first major success: Two agents uncovered a ring of Russian spies who were stealing information on the British nuclear weapons program.

The government of the day was delighted. CHERUB was given funding to expand. Better facilities were built and the number of agents was increased from twenty to sixty.

1954 Two CHERUB agents, Jason Lennox and Johan Urminski, were killed while operating undercover in East Germany. Nobody knows how the boys died. The government considered shutting CHERUB down, but there were now over seventy active CHERUB agents performing vital missions around the world.

An inquiry into the boys' deaths led to the introduction of new safeguards:

(1) The creation of the ethics panel. From now on, every mission had to be approved by a three-person committee.

(2) Jason Lennox was only nine years old. A minimum mission age of ten years and four months was introduced.

(3) A more rigorous approach to training was brought in. A version of the 100-day basic training program began.

1956 Although many believed that girls would be unsuitable for intelligence work, CHERUB admitted five girls as an experiment. They were a huge success. The number of girls in CHERUB was upped to twenty the following year. Within ten years, the number of girls and boys was equal.

1957 CHERUB introduced its system of colored T-shirts.

1960 Following several successes, CHERUB was allowed to expand again, this time to 130 students. The farmland surrounding headquarters was purchased and fenced off, about a third of the area that is now known as CHERUB campus.

1967 Katherine Field became the third CHERUB agent to die on an operation. She was bitten by a snake on a mission in India. She reached hospital within half an hour, but tragically the snake species was wrongly identified and Katherine was given the wrong antivenom.

1973 Over the years, CHERUB had become a hotchpotch of small buildings. Construction began on a new nine-story headquarters.

1977 All CHERUBs are either orphans, or children who have been abandoned by their family. Max Weaver was one of the first CHERUB agents. He made a fortune building office blocks in London and New York. When he died in 1977, aged just forty-one, without a wife or children, Max Weaver left his fortune for the benefit of the children at CHERUB.

The Max Weaver Trust Fund has paid for many of the buildings on CHERUB campus. These include the indoor athletics facilities and library. The trust fund now holds assets worth over £1 billion.

1982 Thomas Webb was killed by a landmine on the Falkland Islands, becoming the fourth CHERUB to die on a mission. He was one of nine agents used in various roles during the Falklands conflict.

1986 The government gave CHERUB permission to expand up to four hundred pupils. Despite this, numbers have stalled some way below this. CHERUB requires intelligent, physically robust agents who have no family ties. Children who meet all these admission criteria are extremely hard to find.

1990 CHERUB purchased additional land, expanding both the size and security of campus. Campus is marked on all British maps as an army firing range. Surrounding roads are routed so that there is only one road onto campus. The perimeter walls cannot be seen from nearby roads. Helicopters are banned from the area and airplanes must stay above ten thousand meters. Anyone breaching the CHERUB perimeter faces life imprisonment under the State Secrets Act.

1996 CHERUB celebrated its fiftieth anniversary with the opening of a diving pool and an indoor shooting range.

Every retired member of CHERUB was invited to the celebration. No guests were allowed. Over nine hundred people made it, flying from all over the world. Among the retired agents were a former prime minister and a rock guitarist who had sold 80 million albums.

After a firework display, the guests pitched tents and slept on campus. Before leaving the following morning, everyone gathered outside the chapel and remembered the four children who had given CHERUB their lives.

Don't miss Mission 2:

THE DEALER

WOOF.

The boys snapped their necks around. The mother of all rottweilers stood five meters away. The huge beast had muscles swelling through its shiny black coat and strings of drool hanging off its jaw.

"Nice doggy," Bruce said, trying to keep calm.

The growling dog moved closer, its black eyes staring them down.

"Who's a nice doggy-woggy?" Bruce asked.

"Bruce, I don't think it's gonna roll over and let you tickle its tummy."

"Well, what's your plan?"

"Don't show it any fear," James quaked. "We'll stare it down. It's probably as scared of us as we are of it."

"Yeah," Bruce said. "You can tell. The poor thing's cacking itself."

James began creeping backwards. The dog let out more volcanic barks. A metal hose reel clattered as James backed into it. He considered the reel for a second, before leaning over and unrolling a few meters of plastic hose. The dog was only a couple of steps away.

"Bruce, you run off and try to open a door," James gasped. "I'll try fending it off with this pipe."

James half hoped the dog would go after Bruce, but it kept its eyes fixed, pacing closer to James until he could feel its damp breath on his legs.

"Nice doggy," James said.

The rottweiler reared up on its back legs, trying to knock James over. James spun away and the paws squealed down the glass door. James lashed out with the hosepipe. It cracked against the dog's rib cage. The beast made a high-pitched yelp and backed up slightly. James cracked the pipe against the patio tiles, hoping the noise would scare the dog away, but if anything the whipping seemed to have made it crazier.

James felt like his guts were going to drop out, imagining how easily the huge animal could rip into his flesh. James had nearly drowned once. He'd thought nothing could ever be scarier, but this had the edge.

A bolt clicked behind James's head and the French door glided open.

"Would Sir care to step inside?" Bruce asked.

James threw down the hose and leapt through the opening. Bruce rammed the door shut before the rottweiler made a move.

"What took you so long?" James said anxiously, trying to stop his hands from shaking. "Where is everyone?"

"No sign," Bruce said. "Which is definitely weird. They'd have to be deaf not to hear that psycho mutt barking at us."

James grabbed one of the curtains and used it to wipe the dog crap off his leg.

"That's so gross," Bruce said. "At least it's not on your clothes."

"Have you checked all the rooms out?"

Bruce shook his head. "I thought I'd make sure you weren't being eaten first, even if it meant we got caught."

"Fair play," James said.

They worked their way across the ground floor, creeping up to each door and checking out the rooms. The villa looked lived-in. There were cigarette butts in ashtrays and dirty mugs. There was a Mercedes in the garage. Bruce pocketed the keys.

"There's our getaway vehicle," he said.

There was no sign of life on the ground floor, which made the staircase likely to be some sort of trap. They stepped up gingerly, expecting someone to burst onto the landing pointing a gun at them.

There were three bedrooms and a bathroom on the second floor. The two hostages were in the master bedroom. The eight-year-olds, Jake and Laura, were tied to a bedpost, with gags over their mouths. They wore grubby T-shirts and shorts.

James and Bruce pulled the hunting knives off their belts and cut the kids loose. There was no time for greetings.

"Laura," James barked. "When did you last see the bad guys? Have you got any idea where they might be?"

Laura was red-faced and seemed listless.

"I dunno," she shrugged. "But I'm busting to pee."

Laura and Jake knew nothing about anything. Bruce and James had been expecting a battle to get at them. This was far too easy.

"We're taking you to the car," James said.

Laura started limping towards the bathroom. Her ankle was strapped up.

"We don't have time for toilet breaks," James gasped. "They've got guns and we haven't."

"I'm gonna wet my knickers in a minute," Laura said, bolting herself inside the en-suite bathroom.

James was furious. "Well, make it snappy."

"I need to go too," Jake said.

Bruce shook his head. "I don't want you disappearing. You can pee in the corner of the garage while I start the car."

He led Jake downstairs. James waited half a minute before thumping on the bathroom door.

"Laura, come on. What the hell is taking you so long?"

"I'm washing my hands," Laura said. "I couldn't find any soap."

James couldn't believe it.

"For the love of God," he shouted, hammering his fist on the bolted door. "We've got to get out of here."

Laura eventually hobbled out of the bathroom. James scooped her over his shoulder and sprinted downstairs to the garage. Bruce sat at the steering wheel inside the car. Laura slid onto the backseat next to Jake.

"It's kaput," Bruce shouted, getting out of the car and kicking the front wing. "The key goes in but it won't turn. It's showing a full tank of petrol. I don't know what's wrong with it."

"It's been sabotaged," James yelled back. "I bet you any money this is a trap."

Bruce looked awkward as the realization dawned.

"You're right. Let's get out of here."

James leaned inside the Mercedes.

"Sorry you two," he said, looking at Jake and Laura. "Looks like we've got to make a run for it."

But it was too late. James heard the noise, but only turned around in time to see the gun pointing at him. Bruce screamed out, as James felt two rounds smash into his chest. The pain knocked the air out of his lungs. He stumbled backwards, watching bright red streaks dribbling down his T-shirt.

ABOUT THE AUTHOR

Robert Muchamore was born in London in 1972 and used to work as a private investigator. CHERUB is his first series and is published in more than twenty countries. For more on the series, check out CherubCampus.com/usa.

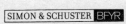